Orders to Kill

Orders to Kill

EDWARD MARSTON

Allison & Busby Limited
11 Wardour Mews
London W1F 8AN
allisonandbusby.com

First published in Great Britain by Allison & Busby in 2021.
This paperback edition published by Allison & Busby in 2022.

A CIP catalogue record for this book is available from
the British Library.

10 9 8 7 6 5 4 3 2 1

ISBN 978-0-7490-2781-0

Typeset in 11/16 pt Adobe Garamond Pro by
Allison & Busby Ltd.

Printed and bound by
CPI Group (UK) Ltd, Croydon, CR0 4YY

To my wonderful son, Conrad

CHAPTER ONE

December, 1917

Days began early for Ada Hobbes. It was just past four o'clock in the morning when she let herself out of her house and felt the first blast of an icy wind. Head down and teeth clenched, she began the long walk over frost-covered pavements that did their best to bring her crashing down on the stone slabs. But she was far too watchful and sure-footed to slip and fall. Now in her fifties, Ada was a short, skinny woman, wrapped up in a moth-eaten fur coat that had been through three generations before it had reached her. The scarf around her neck also covered her mouth and her hat was pulled down over her face. Though she looked frail and defenceless, she was quite the opposite.

Scarred by loss and tested by recurring misfortune, she had survived both. Ada was a fighter.

To reach the offices where her working day started, she had to walk the best part of two miles, leaving the drab, cheerless, overcrowded district where she lived before arriving in a more affluent area. Her destination was an imposing Victorian residence converted into offices by an insurance company. Those who worked there expected three things on their arrival. They wanted their waste-paper baskets to be empty, their desks to be polished and fires to have been laid in their respective grates. Ada never let them down.

She was quick yet thorough, cleaning each office in turn and leaving it spotless. After putting everything away, Ada went on a final tour of the building to make sure that nothing had been missed. Then she picked up the envelope on the hall table and slipped it into her handbag. There was no need to count the money. Her employers trusted her enough to give her keys to the property and she trusted them. Ada was soon letting herself into a house less than a hundred yards away and tackling another set of offices. Tireless and methodical, she went through the same routine. A second envelope was dropped into her handbag.

Her third assignment that morning was her favourite. It was in a detached house that stood in a tree-lined avenue. Ada only had to satisfy the needs of one person this time instead of whole groups of them. Her employer was specific. When she entered the house, she found his instructions awaiting her. After making a mental note of them, she bustled along the passageway, went into the kitchen and through into the room beyond it. Expecting to find all that she needed, she reached for a sweeping brush. Then she realised that there was an unexpected visitor in the room.

Opening her mouth in horror, she staggered back against the wall, then slid down it until she hit the floor and passed out.

CHAPTER TWO

No sooner had they arrived at Scotland Yard that morning than they were sent out again. Inspector Harvey Marmion climbed into the rear of the police car with Joe Keedy. It sped away from the kerb and dodged through traffic.

'Where are we going?' asked the sergeant.

'Edmonton.'

'Why?'

'We'll find out when we get there.'

'Didn't Chat tell you anything?'

'It's a gruesome murder, Joe. That's all we need to be told.'

'We always get the messy cases,' complained Keedy.

'That's because we usually solve them.'

'There's more to it than that. Chat has been throwing his weight around ever since he got promoted and we are his main targets. Other detectives get nice, easy, open-and-shut cases involving batty old women who commit suicide with an overdose of pills. The moment a severed head or a mutilated body is involved, we get lumbered with the investigation.'

'I don't see that as a punishment,' said Marmion, easily. 'In his own peculiar way, Superintendent Chatfield is paying us a compliment. And you must never sneer at batty old women. When people are driven to kill themselves, they deserve our sympathy. It may seem small beer to you, but it involves motives far more complex than those that make someone commit murder.'

'That's a fair point,' conceded Keedy.

'Remember it.'

'What's the name of the murder victim?'

'George Tindall.'

'What did Chat say about him?'

'Very little.'

'He must have given you some details.'

'He told me the one thing that was important.'

'What was that?'

'Tindall was a doctor.'

Keedy was shocked. 'Somebody murdered a doctor?'

'So it seems.'

'That's terrible. At a time like this, we desperately need people like him.'

'He worked at the Edmonton Military Hospital.'

13

'Then he was doing a vital job. Wounded soldiers sent there have the most appalling injuries. The wonder is any of them survive – yet they do, somehow.'

'That's because of the medical team.'

'They're real heroes in my book.'

'I agree, Joe.'

'I take my hat off to them.'

He was speaking metaphorically. In fact, he kept his hat on at its usual jaunty angle. Even though wrapped up in his winter wear, Keedy contrived to look smart. Marmion, by contrast, was as untidy as ever in crumpled clothing that never seemed to fit him properly. After a couple of minutes staring out of the car window, he turned to Keedy.

'As for batty old women, there's something you should remember.'

'Is there?'

'When you finally marry our daughter,' said Marmion with a grin, 'you'll become part of the family.'

'So?'

'For a start, Ellen and I will be happy.'

'And?'

'Imagine what may happen in due course.'

'I don't follow.'

'You may one day have a batty old woman as your mother-in-law.'

War had changed Ellen Marmion's life completely. It had imprisoned her in a routine that she did not even notice at first. Her day began with making an early breakfast for her husband

and herself. After waving him off, she washed the plates and cutlery in the sink and left everything to dry on the draining board. She then did a sequence of chores that never varied. When she had finished, she took down the framed photograph of her son from the mantelpiece and began to rub it with a duster even though it was gleaming. Ellen then had her long, daily, ruminative stare at Paul.

Mixed emotions stirred inside her. Pride was uppermost. Dressed in army uniform, Paul was smiling at the camera, glad that he had joined up in a moment of patriotic fervour. He was the wonderful, confident, happy-go-lucky son his mother had adored. But unfortunately he no longer existed. Paul had been one of thousands injured at the Battle of the Somme and shipped back to a hospital in England. Temporarily blinded, he also had afflictions that seemed worryingly permanent. The cheerful extrovert of the Marmion family had become morose and confused. He could not understand why so many of his close friends had been killed in action while he had crawled away alive from the battlefield. Paul felt guilty and bereaved in equal measure.

The family was warned that it might take him a long time to adjust to home life, but he showed no inclination even to try. Ellen made allowances for him but even her patience was tested. Instead of getting better, her son got steadily worse, revealing a nasty streak she had never seen before and behaving in ways that shocked her. Her husband was away from the house for much of the day and her daughter, Alice, no longer lived at home. For the most part, therefore, Ellen was left alone to cope with Paul and his increasingly dangerous moods.

Then, suddenly, he disappeared without a word of explanation. They had no idea where he was or what his intentions were. Marmion organised a search for their son, but it was fruitless. When they did finally discover where he might be, Paul had vanished before they got there. Looking now at the dutiful son she had once loved, she felt the photograph was like a ton weight in her hands.

When they arrived at the scene of the crime, the detectives were relieved to see that they would not be hampered by a large and intrusive crowd. That would certainly have been the case if they were somewhere in central London with people swarming about. Instead, they were in a quiet avenue of detached properties. Standing outside the one owned by George Tindall was a burly uniformed police officer. When he saw them approach, he raised a hand.

'There's no need to introduce yourselves, Inspector,' he said. 'I've seen photos of you and the sergeant in the newspapers many times.'

'Our fame is spreading,' said Keedy with a smile. 'What's your name?'

'Constable Fanning, sir.'

'Are you on your own?'

'No, sir, I'm with a colleague, Constable Rivers.'

'Where is he?' asked Marmion.

'He's in the house next door,' said the other, indicating it. 'When we got here, Mrs Hobbes was in quite a state.'

'Who is she?'

'The cleaner.'

'Why did Dr Tindall need a cleaner? A house this size would surely run to a servant or two.'

'That puzzled me as well.'

'Who raised the alarm?'

'Mrs Hobbes did – when she recovered, that is. She was so upset by what she saw, she fainted. When she came to, she remembered that there was a telephone in the house.'

'Yes, that would be essential for a doctor. The hospital might have needed to summon him at short notice.' Marmion flicked a hand. 'Go on with your story, Constable. Tell us why you took her next door.'

'We needed to get her out of there, sir. She was shaking like a leaf and who could blame her? I've seen gory sights in my time, but nothing to touch this. I'd warn you to be prepared.'

'I'm grateful for your warning,' said Marmion, 'but it doesn't apply to the sergeant. He used to work in the family undertaking business and often saw dead bodies in a deplorable condition. He learnt to take everything in his stride. Nothing unsettles him.'

'Well, it unsettled me, sir,' admitted Fanning.

'Then you'd better stay out in the fresh air.'

'Where is the victim?' asked Keedy.

'He's in the room at the back,' said Fanning. 'Go through the kitchen.'

'Thank you.'

Marmion led the way into the house, pushing open the unlocked front door. He went along the passageway to the kitchen, then stopped in front of the door to the room off it. He studied it warily.

'Perhaps you should open it, Joe,' he suggested.

'Is that a challenge?'

'No – but you've got a stronger stomach than I have.'

17

'You're not going to faint, are you?' teased Keedy.

'Get on with it.'

Grabbing the handle, Keedy opened the door and looked inside the room. George Tindall lay sprawled on the floor in the remains of his pyjamas amid a jumble of brushes, mops, buckets and other cleaning paraphernalia. Blood was everywhere. The victim had been tied up and gagged before being hacked to death. Marmion forced himself to look and wrinkled his nose in disgust. Keedy ran his eye over the multiple injuries.

'Someone enjoyed doing this,' he said.

Thanks to a cup of tea and the kindness of the neighbours, Ada Hobbes was feeling much better. She was sitting in the lounge next door with Stanley and Enid Crowe, an elderly couple who had been shaken by news of the murder. Standing by the door was Constable Rivers, a tall, thin, willowy man who kept shifting from one leg to another. Ada kept apologising to all three of them for causing so much trouble.

'I'm ashamed of myself for passing out like that,' she said. 'I always prided myself on being able to cope with any problem.'

'You shouldn't blame yourself,' said Enid Crowe. 'It must have been a terrible shock for you. Simply hearing about it has frightened the wits out of me.'

'That goes for me as well,' confessed her husband.

'Besides,' said Rivers, taking a step forward, 'you deserve praise for what you did. As soon as you recovered, you had the presence of mind to pick up the phone and call the police.'

'You did the right thing bringing Mrs Hobbes here, Constable,' said Crowe.

'Thank you, sir.'

'You're welcome to stay as long as possible, Mrs Hobbes,' said Enid.

Ada gave her a smile of thanks. She had only been cleaning Dr Tindall's house for a month or so. Like her, the neighbours could not understand why anyone would want to kill such a decent and dedicated man. Ada looked up at Rivers.

'You will catch whoever did this, won't you?' she asked.

'Yes,' he replied, confidently. 'We'll catch him, Mrs Hobbes, and when we do, he'll pay for this crime with his life.'

While they waited for the Home Office pathologist to arrive, Marmion and Keedy searched the house for information about its owner. Even in the study there was little of real use. Drawers in the desk had been left open, showing that someone had been there before them to remove items such as a diary and an address book. All that they could find was correspondence relating to patients at the hospital. It was when they went into the master bedroom that they had some insight into what had happened. As they opened the wardrobe, Keedy gasped in admiration at the suits hanging up inside.

'These are top quality,' he said, opening a jacket to read the label.

'Why did he have so many?' asked Marmion. 'Two is enough for anyone.'

'He lived in a different world from us.'

'Yes – and on a far better income.'

Breaking away, he walked slowly around the room and looked carefully at everything. Marmion stopped beside a landscape painting on the wall. He scrutinised it for over a minute.

'What do you think of this, Joe?' he asked.

'I hate it.'

'Why?'

'It's so dull and uninteresting.'

'It's also completely the wrong colour for the room. It doesn't match anything. You can see from what is in his wardrobe that he was a man with taste, yet he puts this unsuitable painting in here. There must be a reason for that.'

'What is it?'

'Who knows?' said Marmion. 'Perhaps it's hiding something.'

Lifting the heavy frame carefully off its hook, he revealed a safe set in the wall. Keedy stepped forward to grab the handle and discovered that it turned easily.

'It's not locked,' he said, opening the door and peering inside. 'And the safe is empty.' He snapped his fingers. 'That could be the motive behind the murder. Dr Tindall was burgled. Perhaps he made the mistake of catching the man in the act.'

'There wasn't only one man,' explained Marmion, lowering the painting to the floor. 'It would have taken two of them to overpower him and truss him up like that. In any case, he was not killed here because there's no sign of a struggle. The butchery took place downstairs. Why did they choose there?'

Keedy shrugged. 'Search me.'

'And there's another thing that puzzles me.'

'What is it?'

'When we examined the body, I noticed that Dr Tindall was wearing a wedding ring. What happened to his wife? Why aren't her clothes in the wardrobe?'

'Perhaps she died.'

'Then why aren't there any photos of her on display? If she died before her time, he would surely want to preserve her memory. Yet there's not a single photo of Mrs Tindall anywhere. I find that weird.'

'Maybe the burglars took all the photos away.'

'Why?' asked Marmion. 'What possible interest would photos hold for them? They came to kill him and helped themselves to the contents of the safe while they were here. That is how it looks to me, anyway.' He rubbed his chin. 'All of a sudden, this case has become a lot more interesting.'

CHAPTER THREE

Before the conversation could continue, they heard a car pulling up outside the house. They crossed to the window and saw a short, stubby man coming up the drive.

'It's the pathologist,' said Marmion. 'I'll handle him, Joe. You go next door and take a statement from Mrs Hobbes. With luck, she's had time to recover and may be more coherent.'

'Right,' said Keedy, following him out of the bedroom and down the stairs. 'Will you want to speak to her yourself?'

'There's no need. Just remember to be gentle with her.'

'I will.'

As they reached the hall, the pathologist was coming through the front door.

'Good morning, Harvey,' he said, cheerily, 'and the same to you, Sergeant.'

'Good morning,' said Keedy, going past him. 'You'll have to excuse me.'

'Joe has gone to interview the poor woman who found the body,' explained Marmion. 'We're surprised that she didn't have a heart attack.'

'Is the victim in that bad a state?'

'You need to brace yourself, Tom.'

'Nothing will shock me,' said the other with a chuckle. 'I've just come from examining three people who were killed when a German bomb landed on their house. It's frightening to see what tons of rubble can do to the human body.'

Thomas Harrison was a middle-aged man with a puffy face and a habit of lowering his head so that he could look over the top of his glasses. He and Marmion knew each other well. They went through to the kitchen. When the pathologist put his bag down, Marmion opened the door of the room where the body lay. Harrison remained calm.

'That's what I'd call a comprehensive murder,' he said, quietly. 'The killer certainly went to extremes.'

'We believe that two people might have been involved.'

'Your guesses are usually right.'

'They're based on instinct.'

'That comes with experience,' said the other, studying the corpse with a practised eye. 'It's about the only virtue of getting older. Ah, well,' he went on, taking off his coat. 'I'd better get busy, I suppose.' Marmion was about to reply when he heard the telephone ring.

'Do what you have to do, Tom,' he said. 'I'll have to answer that.'

Going quickly back to the hall, he picked up the receiver.

'Hello . . .'

'Can I speak to Dr Tindall?' asked a crisp, male voice.

'I'm afraid not.'

'I'm ringing from the hospital. He was expected here over an hour ago.'

'Yes,' said Marmion, heaving a sigh, 'I daresay that he was. I have bad news, I fear. It's my sad duty to tell you that he won't be able to come today – or on any other day, for that matter.'

'What do you mean?'

'I am Detective Inspector Marmion of the Metropolitan Police Force. I'm investigating the doctor's unexplained death.'

Keedy was pleased to meet Stanley and Enid Crowe and grateful for the way that they had looked after Ada Hobbes. The cleaner seemed to have recovered well from her grim discovery and was eager to answer any questions. She explained what had happened when she entered the house, scolding herself for passing out.

'I should have been more careful,' she admitted.

'What do you mean?' asked Keedy.

'Well, whenever I've finished cleaning the house, I collect an envelope from the hall table. My money was in it. I should have noticed that the envelope wasn't there today. If I'd done that, I'd have been warned something strange had happened.

Dr Tindall was very particular, you see. He'd never have left the house without putting my money on the table.'

'How often did you go there?'

'Twice a week.'

'Didn't he have a servant who could have done what you did?'

'Dr Tindall was a very private man. He preferred to live alone.'

'It's true,' said Crowe, intervening. 'He moved in next door almost three years ago. His wife died and he wanted to get away from the house where they lived. Yet, strangely enough, that is not what he did. He brought her with him. There were photographs of his wife everywhere.'

'She was beautiful,' said Ada. 'I should know. I had to polish the frames every time I came. That was always on his list of instructions. There was a photo of him and Mrs Tindall on his desk in the study.'

'Well, it's not there now,' said Keedy.

'Really?' She was scandalised. 'Do you mean that it's been stolen?'

'Probably.'

'That's dreadful!' exclaimed Ada.

'Let's go back to your job there. Who cleaned the house before you?'

'It was Kathy Paget, who is my sister. She had arthritis but kept going until the pain was too much to bear. Kathy knew I clean offices not far away. She asked me if I'd like some extra work. I told her I did so she spoke to Dr Tindall, and he took me on.'

'We remember Mrs Paget,' said Enid. 'We used to see her hobbling up the drive. I'm surprised Dr Tindall didn't recommend something for her arthritis.'

'He wasn't that kind of doctor,' Crowe reminded her. 'He was an orthopaedic surgeon.'

'I'm still trying to understand how he managed without a servant or two,' said Keedy. 'Who did his shopping? Who laid the fire? Who prepared his meals?'

'He was quite capable of making his own breakfast, Sergeant. That seemed the only meal he ever had at home. The hospital made great demands on his time. I know that he often ate there. Sometimes he even stayed the night at the hospital.'

'In all the time we've known him,' added Enid, 'he only once accepted an invitation to come here for dinner.'

'Yes, it was a rather awkward occasion.'

'Why was that?' asked Keedy.

'There was the age gap, for one thing,' said Crowe. 'We were at least thirty years older than him. I am a retired bank manager and he was a highly qualified doctor. We didn't talk the same language.'

'He just sat there in silence most of the time,' recalled Enid. 'The only thing he really talked about was his late wife.'

'That's another thing I should have spotted,' said Ada, slapping her knee. 'Her photo was missing from the hall table. It had pride of place there and was the first thing he saw when he came into the house. It should have been the first thing I saw as well when I let myself in, but I didn't. Dr Tindall would never have moved that photo from the table.'

* * *

When Alice Marmion and Iris Goodliffe set off on their beat, a steady drizzle was falling. It was one of the few times when they were grateful to be wearing their uniforms. One of the setbacks of joining the Women's Police Force was that their dark blue jackets and ankle-length skirts were very unbecoming. It was something that Iris complained about regularly, fearing that no man would look at her twice because of the way she was dressed. Proud of her hair, she hated wearing a hat that all but obscured it completely. She was glad of it now. As the drizzle turned to rain, they stepped into a shop doorway for shelter.

'Do you think this will turn to snow?' asked Iris.

'I'm not sure,' replied Alice.

'When I was a little girl, I prayed for a white Christmas. Now, I'd hate it.'

'Why?'

'We'd be sitting targets for snowballs.'

'The city has to be policed, Iris.'

Alice was an attractive young woman with an air of vitality about her. Though she sorely missed the children she taught before the war, she felt that she was doing a more important job now. It meant that she, her father and her fiancé were all in the same profession. Iris envied her. Big, chubby, and decidedly plain, she wished that she had some of Alice's good looks and assurance.

'Have you had many Christmas cards?' she asked.

'Yes,' said Alice. 'Quite a few.'

'I don't suppose . . . ?'

'No, we haven't had one from Paul, but we never expected to. We had no birthday cards from him either. We don't even know if he's still alive.'

'He must be. You said that he was very fit.'

'He used to be, Iris. He joined up with the rest of his football team for which he played. He loved exercise of every kind. One of the sad things was that the war squeezed most of the energy out of him.'

'At least he didn't come back with hideous injuries,' said her friend, 'or with a limb missing. On my way home last night, I saw that soldier who lost both of his legs. He was sitting in his wheelchair, trying to play the accordion. I put sixpence in his hat.'

'Paul hasn't reached the stage of begging yet – I hope not, anyway.'

'It must feel odd, not having him home for Christmas. How do you cope?'

'We pretend he's there.'

Alice was fond of her colleague but, as a rule, she kept her very much at arm's length. Aware how desperate Iris was for a closer friendship, she usually refused any invitations to go out together in the evening. Today was different. Alice suddenly felt a pang of guilt at the way she treated Iris and she felt a need to atone for her behaviour.

'We have a day off tomorrow,' she said.

Iris laughed, 'You don't need to tell me that.'

'Do you have any plans?'

'No, Alice. I'll probably end up working for my father.'

'You can't waste a day off by serving in a chemist's shop.'

'It's better than sitting at home and moping.'

'I've got an idea,' said Alice. 'I still have presents to buy. Why don't we go to the West End for the morning?'

'Yes, please!'

'We can go around the department stores. You are always saying you'd like to cheer yourself up by buying a new dress. Get one tomorrow.'

'I will,' said the other. 'Thank you so much, Alice.'

'It's not often we have a day of freedom. Let's make the most of it.'

'We will.' Iris hugged her. 'You've just given me the most wonderful Christmas present.'

During his career, Marmion had attended many murder scenes. The majority had been in isolated locations where contact with Scotland Yard was impossible. This time it was different. He had access to a telephone. When the initial phases of the investigation were over, therefore, he felt able to ring Claude Chatfield. Predictably, the superintendent was critical.

'Why didn't you get in touch with me earlier?' he demanded.

'There was a lot to do, sir.'

'I need to release information to the press.'

'I'm aware of that,' said Marmion, 'and I've taken the trouble of drafting a statement for you. Do you have pen and paper at hand?'

'Of course, I do. I'm sitting at my desk.'

'Then here it is.'

Reading from his notebook, Marmion dictated the statement slowly so that the superintendent could write it down. He could hear grunts of approval from the other end of the line. When he had finished, he closed his notebook.

'You've got the salient facts there, sir,' he said, 'but we're not giving too much away. I do not want newspapers speculating wildly about this case. It's far more complicated than they'll imagine.'

'Who discovered the body?'

'It was a cleaner by the name of Mrs Hobbes.'

'I suppose she was a gibbering wreck.'

'Then you are quite wrong, sir. The lady is very resilient, according to Sergeant Keedy. Mrs Hobbes was able to give him a clear account of what she discovered and provided useful details about the victim.'

'How will she bear up under pressure from reporters?'

'I'd rather keep her name out of it altogether. After taking her statement, the sergeant got our driver to take her home. It was the least we could do for her. Mrs Hobbes was helpful – and so were the next-door neighbours, a Mr and Mrs Crowe. We can hide the cleaner from the howling mob from Fleet Street, but it will be impossible to do that for the neighbours. They will be fair game. Sergeant Keedy warned them to say nothing whatsoever about Mrs Hobbes.'

'That was a wise move.'

'Yes, sir.'

'It's time for details, Inspector,' said Chatfield, fussily. 'What have you found and what have you and the sergeant deduced?'

After clearing his throat, Marmion gave a fuller account of what had happened since they had been there, telling him what the pathologist had said and how the body had now been removed. Chatfield got a clear, concise, measured synopsis. What he was not given were a few things that Marmion preferred to keep to himself.

'Where's the sergeant now?' asked the superintendent.

'He's making door-to-door enquiries, sir, to see if anyone heard anything unusual during the night.'

'What time did the murder take place?'

'Tom Harrison couldn't give a precise time. His guess would be somewhere between midnight and four o'clock.'

'Did the doctor have any known enemies?'

'That's what I'm hoping to find out.'

'He sounds like a strange fellow. Why live in a house entirely on his own? It is a rather spartan notion of life, isn't it? You'd expect him to have servants, surely.'

'Dr Tindall lived for his work, sir.'

'I live for mine but that doesn't mean I punish myself. My wife and I could not manage without a maid. One is entitled to some luxuries.'

Marmion said nothing. Unlike the superintendent's wife, his own would have been insulted at the idea that she could not cope without help. Ellen made light of the drudgery involved. She did what most mothers in London did and accepted her lot.

'What's your next move?' asked the superintendent.

'I'm going to the hospital where he worked,' said Marmion. 'His colleagues deserve to know more than I've told them over the phone and I want to find out exactly what sort of man Dr Tindall really was.'

'In a word, how would you describe him?'

'Mysterious.'

When she was offered a lift home, Ada Hobbes at first turned it down but Keedy had insisted. He knew that people who had witnessed horrific sights could not simply shrug off the memory. Though she seemed calm enough, the cleaner would be haunted

31

by the event on the long walk home. As she sat beside the driver, Ada realised that it was the first time she had been inside a car since her husband's funeral. An untimely death had once again earned her the bonus of a lift.

Keedy had warned her to say nothing to her friends and neighbours about her experience that morning. If she spoke freely about it, he said, she would make herself a target for press interrogation. Ada took his advice. When she arrived home in a car, she was bound to arouse curiosity. She therefore rehearsed the explanation she would give to everyone. Inside the vehicle, she felt safe and comfortable. When she was dropped outside her home, however, she felt her legs give way slightly.

Reality had caught up with her.

Keedy worked his way along one side of the avenue, knocking on each door in turn and explaining why he had done so. Ordinarily, a couple of detective constables would be doing the repetitive chore, but manpower was limited at Scotland Yard. Keedy was not dismayed. He felt that he could do the job quickly yet thoroughly. When he reached the house on a corner, he used the knocker firmly. Moments later the front door opened and an elderly, white-haired woman gave him a hostile glare.

'We don't buy anything at the door,' she said.

'I'm not selling anything, I promise you.'

'Then why are you bothering us?'

'I'm Detective Sergeant Keedy of the Metropolitan Police,' he said. 'There's been a serious incident in a house further up the avenue and we're anxious to see if anyone can help us.'

'Which house was it?'

'Number twenty-three.'

'That's Dr Tindall's house,' she said in alarm.

'Do you know the gentleman?'

'We know of him. He works at the Military Hospital. My husband and I look up to him.'

'Well,' sighed Keedy, 'I'm afraid you won't be able to do that again.'

'Why not?' Seeing the look in his eye, she gasped. 'Has something happened to him?'

'His body was taken away almost an hour ago.'

'Do you mean that he . . . ?'

'Yes, I do. You'll now understand why I'm keen to find out if anyone heard anything unusual in the middle of the night.'

'Dr Tindall?' she said. 'I can't believe it.'

'Did you hear my question?'

'Yes, I did, young man, but I'm not the person to answer it. I sleep like a log, but my husband doesn't. You need to speak to him.' She raised her voice. 'Ronald!' she yelled. 'Come here at once, Ronald! It's the police.' She whispered to Keedy. 'You'll have to speak up. He's deaf in one ear.'

Deafness was clearly the least of his afflictions. When he finally appeared, the old man was shuffling along with his spine so bent that his head was almost level with his stomach. One blue-veined hand was holding a walking stick. His other arm was in a sling. He peered up at the visitor through watery eyes.

'Who are you?' he asked.

'I'll explain later,' said his wife. 'Tell him what you told me.'

'I told you lots of things, Mary.'

33

'Tell him what you heard last night.'

'I hear all sorts of things,' he said to Keedy. 'I have strange noises in my ears. There is nothing they can do. I have to live with them.'

'But you heard a particular noise, Ronald,' prompted his wife. 'You went to the bathroom and heard it very clearly.'

'Oh, yes, I remember it now.'

'What exactly did you hear, sir?' asked Keedy, leaning closer to him. 'You were in the bathroom, you say. Which side of the house is that?'

'It's around the corner,' replied the woman.

'And what was this sound your husband heard?'

'It was a loud, nasty, rasping sound.'

'Yes,' said the man, taking up the story. 'I'm not completely deaf. I heard it clearly. I mean, they should not have been out there at that time of night. It was against the law. They had no respect for other people.'

'Who didn't?' said Keedy.

'The two of them.'

'What my husband heard,' explained the woman, 'was the noise of two motorbikes. I do not think Ronald imagined it. When he opened the bathroom window, the sound was just beneath him. Then it suddenly stopped. If he says there were two motorbikes just around the corner, then there were.'

Keedy smiled. He had learnt something useful at last.

CHAPTER FOUR

The Edmonton Military Hospital had begun life as an infirmary for the adjacent workhouse. An iron fence stood between them. The outbreak of war in 1914 had brought huge numbers of casualties in its wake. Edmonton was one of many districts in London that soon acquired a military hospital into which an endless stream of wounded soldiers were taken. Built in Silver Street, it comprised a cluster of sizeable buildings supplemented by a series of large huts, hastily constructed in the grounds to house additional patients. When he was driven through the entrance, Marmion noticed the two red crosses painted on the gates.

The police car pulled up outside the main building and the inspector got out.

He turned to see an ambulance coming in through the gates. It was moving slowly, as if the driver was anxious not to shake up the wounded soldiers he was carrying. Marmion wondered from which battleground they had come. He felt a pang as he thought about the time when his son had been ferried back from France to a military hospital. He hurried into the building and was soon being conducted into the office occupied by the person in charge of the hospital.

Major Howard Palmer-Loach was a square-jawed, straight-backed man of medium height with a neat moustache decorating an impassive face. When Marmion introduced himself, the major shook his hand and motioned him to a chair.

'This is terrible news,' he said. 'Dr Tindall was a brilliant man. More to the point, he was indefatigable and worked more hours than anybody else on my staff. As a result of his death, we've had to cancel a number of crucial operations.'

'I'm sorry to hear that.'

'He's irreplaceable. There'll be a lot of tears when the word spreads.'

'What sort of man was he?' asked Marmion.

'The best kind for an emergency – committed and eager. When the war first broke out, he spent six months working in a field hospital in France, getting to grips with the scale of the horrors of war. I was lucky enough to get him shortly after we converted this place into a military hospital.'

'How many patients do you have here?'

'Our total bed complement is one thousand. Soldiers are sent here in pieces. We try to put them together again. Many manage to survive but we have our losses as well. It is not only physical wounds that need treatment, of course. Our patients usually come with mental scars.'

Marmion said nothing but an image of Paul had popped into his mind again.

'On the telephone,' recalled the major, 'you talked of an unexplained death.'

'Dr Tindall was murdered.'

The major gulped. 'How?'

'Unnecessary violence was used.'

Choosing his words with care, Marmion told him what they had found and how the safe had been emptied. He was careful not to release too much information. Palmer-Loach shook his head in disbelief.

'Why pick on George Tindall, of all people?'

'I intend to find out.'

'It makes no sense. He didn't have an enemy in the world.'

'That's what we've been told.'

'Can I help in any way?'

'Yes,' said Marmion. 'I'd be grateful if you could tell me more about him and what sort of work he did here at the hospital. The more information we have, the more able will we be to understand him. We know that he was still grieving over the loss of his wife, and it appears that he had almost no social life. Is that true?'

'I'm afraid so, Inspector. It was strange, really. He was a handsome, intelligent man with great gifts. Most of the nurses here adored him yet he hardly noticed them. As for what he did here,' said the major, rising to his feet, 'I suggest that you come and see for yourself. Dr Tindall was the heart and soul of this place.'

* * *

The prospect of going to the West End next day had lifted Iris Goodliffe's spirits. She could not stop thinking about it. Even when a ragged old man made a filthy gesture at her before scuttling away with a cackle of delight, she was neither upset nor annoyed. Iris walked on happily with her friend at her side.

'The rain has stopped,' said Alice.

'I didn't notice.'

'You didn't notice when you stepped in that puddle either.'

'Who cares about that?' said Iris with a giggle. 'I was too busy thinking about the dress I'm going to buy tomorrow. What colour should it be?'

'What colour would you like?'

'My mother always said that I looked best in blue but I'm not sure. Besides, I'm wearing navy blue all day long. I want a change.'

'Then I'd suggest a shade of green.'

'Really? That's a bit . . . daring for me.'

'Why?' asked Alice. 'You could carry it off easily. Green is a colour that would cheer you up whenever you looked at yourself in the mirror.'

'What about red?'

'That might be going too far.'

'I'll try on every colour of the rainbow,' said Iris with another giggle, 'then choose the one I fancy.'

'Yes, that's the right attitude.'

'What about you, Alice?'

'Oh, I'll be looking for a new dress as well.'

'You could get away with any colour.'

'Joe doesn't think so. He hates it if I wear anything with beige in it.'

'Why?'

'He says that it makes me look like my mother.'

'What a cheek!'

'Joe claims that it's the kind of colour you wear to hide behind.'

'That shows how much he knows about dresses,' said Iris.

'I told him that the best colour is the one we feel most comfortable in. We dress for ourselves – not for someone else's benefit.'

'What did he say to that?'

It was Alice's turn to giggle. 'I'm not telling.'

'What will you be looking for tomorrow?'

'I simply want something to catch my eye.'

'Will it be a dress for a particular occasion?'

'Not really,' said Alice, shaking her head.

'Then we're going to the West End for different reasons.'

'Are we?'

'Yes, I'm on the lookout for something special,' confided Iris, 'because it will be for a special occasion.'

'And what occasion will that be?'

Iris clicked her tongue. 'As if you need to ask me, Alice Marmion. It's for your wedding to Joe Keedy.' There was an awkward pause. 'I am invited, aren't I?'

Having recorded the old man's testimony in his notebook, Keedy soon found people who could corroborate the evidence. Once he turned the corner into the next road, he spoke to other witnesses roused from their sleep by the sound of two motorbikes. None could give him an exact time, but the general feeling was that it was somewhere between midnight and three o'clock in the morning. That was good enough for Keedy. It fitted in with the timescale given by the pathologist.

Marmion had been right, he accepted. There were two people involved. They had driven at low speed as far as the corner of the road, switched off their engines and parked their motorbikes. The pair had then turned into the avenue and walked along until they reached Tindall's house. Keedy had no idea how they had got into it, but he believed he knew why the killers had not driven up to the victim's doorstep. The sound of two noisy engines might have awakened the neighbours and even Tindall himself. Once they had done what they had planned to do, he decided, the couple had walked back to the place where they had left their motorbikes and roared away at full speed.

There were lots of questions still to be answered but Keedy nevertheless allowed himself to feel optimistic. He felt that he had picked up a trail.

As he led the way out of his office, Major Palmer-Loach turned to his companion.

'Have you ever been to a military hospital before, Inspector?' he asked.

'As a matter of fact,' replied Marmion, 'I've been inside two. The first was Royal Victoria in Netley, when we went to visit my son.'

'Where was the other?'

'Endell Street.'

The major's face darkened. 'The Suffragettes' Hospital,' he said with a note of disapproval. 'I don't think I could put my trust in a place run entirely by women.'

'Its doctors have a good reputation and I've never been anywhere that was so spotless. What I liked was the way they'd introduced a lot of colour to brighten the hospital up.'

'I don't question their medical expertise,' said the other. 'It's their political opinions that I can't stomach.'

'If a female doctor has the skill to save my life, I wouldn't care two hoots about any political opinions she held. You should have this conversation with my daughter,' added Marmion, smiling. 'Alice would enjoy locking horns with you.'

'Does she work at Endell Street?'

'No, she's in the Women's Police Force. But she has a friend who works as a doctor there and who took us both around the hospital. I was impressed.'

'I hope that you're equally impressed with what you see here.'

The major took him down a main corridor, acknowledging staff and patients alike with a curt nod. Marmion was struck by how many people were about. Legless soldiers were propelling themselves in wheelchairs and those with one leg used crutches to manoeuvre themselves along. A blind man was being led by a nurse as he took his first tentative steps. Some of the soldiers wore pyjamas and dressing gowns but a few were in saxe blue suits made of a lightweight flannel material. Marmion noticed their bright red ties.

'We try to get them outside whenever we can,' explained Palmer-Loach, 'but this weather is far too cold. Many of those who are convalescing will soon move on and make way for a new batch. They keep coming and coming.'

'They must be so relieved to be on British soil again.'

'Most of them are, Inspector, but there are some who wish they'd died in action. A Blighty Wound is not always a form of escape. When you are paralysed from the waist down and blind into the bargain, your future is going to be bleak. We have had more than one patient begging to be put out of his misery. It was another important aspect of Dr Tindall's work here.'

'What was?'

'He knew how to talk to men who felt they had nothing to live for,' said the major. 'It was extraordinary. He somehow gave them hope. It took time in some cases, but he usually succeeded in the end.'

They paused outside a ward and Marmion was able to glance inside. Rows of beds ran down both sides of the ward and all were occupied by patients with what appeared to be serious injuries. Some were almost invisible beneath heavy bandaging. A doctor was making his rounds with a nurse at his elbow. There was a sense of order about the scene. A faint smell of disinfectant lingered.

'Dr Tindall operated on some of these men,' explained the major. 'They're going to be horrified when they discover they'll never see him again.'

'He was obviously popular here.'

'That's an understatement, Inspector. He was revered.'

'We need to get in touch with his next of kin,' said Marmion. 'His neighbours told us that he had no children. What about his parents? Are they still alive?'

'Yes, they live in the north of Scotland somewhere.'

'Do you have an address for them?'

The major nodded. 'It's in my office.'

'Did he ever speak of relatives – brothers, sisters, cousins?'

'No, he didn't. If they exist, he saw them as irrelevant. As soon as he came into the hospital, he only talked about one thing and that was the care of his patients.'

'You make him sound as if he was a paragon.'

'In some ways, I suppose that that's exactly what George Tindall was.'

Marmion looked him in the eye. 'Then why did someone want to kill him?'

If Ellen Marmion wished to hear the latest news, she did not need to buy a newspaper. All she had to do was to visit the grocer's shop. Geoffrey Biddle, the grocer, kept abreast of current affairs. He seemed to pick up information that nobody else had access to and enjoyed passing it on to his customers. Biddle was a tall, skinny, red-faced man in his fifties with a bald head that looked as if it had just been polished. He had a quiet, confiding manner and a habit of tapping the side of his nose.

'Is there anything else you need, Mrs Marmion?' he asked.

'I don't think so.'

'How about sugar?'

'We've got enough to last until next week.'

'It might be safer to get more while you can,' he warned. 'German submarines are causing havoc with our food imports. They seem to be sinking our ships at will. Everything is going to be rationed soon. Sugar will be on the list.'

'But we can't do without it, Mr Biddle.'

'Coal has already been rationed. Sugar may be next, then meat, then butter, then something else we need. The Germans are trying to starve us to death, Mrs Marmion.'

'I thought our convoys were getting through.'

'Then where are our food supplies? Whenever I try to restock my shelves, I buy smaller amounts than usual. Lots of items are just not available. If things don't improve, everything will be rationed. We will have long queues of people getting more and more impatient. I dread it.'

'Perhaps I'd better have some more sugar, then,' she decided.

'Good thinking.' He took a packet from the shelf and put it on the counter. 'Is that the lot, then?'

'I think so. How much do I owe you?'

'Let me see.' He added up the figures and showed her the bill. 'Check it, if you like.'

She smiled. 'I know you well enough to trust you, Mr Biddle.'

After putting the bag of sugar into her basket, she paid the grocer and left the shop. Ellen did not get far before she recognised someone coming towards her. It was Patricia Redwood, a fleshy, middle-aged woman who belonged to the same sewing circle as Ellen. The two women had been friends until Paul Marmion had insulted Patricia's daughter, Sally, then gone on to pester her. It had destroyed the friendship between the two older women.

'Good morning,' said Ellen, politely. 'How are you?'

'I'm fine, thank you, and I've got some good news to pass on.'

'Oh?'

'Sally has met a young man,' said Patricia, proudly. 'That's an achievement when so many lads have gone off to war. Norman would have done the same, of course, only he damaged a hand in an accident. He's just what Sally needs. Norman works for that printer in the high street.'

'I know the one.'

'Then you'll know that it's almost opposite the jewellery shop where Sally works. He waved to her through the window one day. She was too shy to wave back at first. Sally's always been a bit of a shrinking violet,' she went on, releasing a sudden laugh. 'She takes after me in that respect.'

Ellen had to repress a laugh of her own. Nobody was less like a shrinking violet than Patricia Redwood. Whenever she came to the sewing circle, she dominated the conversation in a braying voice.

'I'm so pleased for Sally,' said Ellen.

'She and Norman make a lovely couple.'

'That's good to hear.'

'Meeting him has helped her to get over . . . well, you know what.'

Ellen winced at the mention of her son's involvement with the girl. Paul had treated her very badly and refused to apologise. His mother had suffered a fierce confrontation with the woman she was now facing.

'Is there any word of Paul?' asked Patricia.

'I'm afraid not.'

'Can he still be alive after all this time?'

'We don't know.'

'Most sons would at least let his mother know where he was,' said the other, pointedly. 'It's cruel to keep you in the dark – but then, he always did have a cruel streak, didn't he?'

'That's not true at all.'

'Look at the way he treated Sally.'

'I've apologised for that.'

'The memory of it still upsets my daughter. In fact—'

'You'll have to excuse me,' said Ellen, interrupting. 'I have more important things to do than stand gossiping here with you.'

Turning on her heel, she walked quickly away.

When he got back to the house, Keedy saw that Constable Fanning was on duty alone outside the front door.

'Is Rivers still in with the neighbours?' he asked.

'No, sir,' said Fanning. 'He's gone back to the station. It doesn't need two of us to keep people at bay. Inspector Marmion said it would be all right.'

'Then I've no complaint. How have you got on while I was away?'

'I've been busy. I don't know what you told people when you knocked on their doors, but it flushed them out good and proper. Dozens of them came to gawp at the house. One man dared to ask if he could peep inside so I gave him a flea in his ear. Then a woman strolled past, pretending not to look in this direction but she was just as nosey as the others.'

'That's the effect a murder has on a community,' said Keedy.

'I know, Sergeant. It becomes a sideshow.'

'I'm going back inside to conduct a more thorough search. When the inspector comes back, tell him where I am.'

'I suppose there's no chance of a cup of tea, is there?'

Keedy chuckled. 'You'll have to wait until I get thirsty.'

He let himself into the house and began a systematic search, going from room to room and opening every drawer and cupboard as he did so. What was clearly lacking was a woman's touch. Keedy imagined what Alice would say if she saw the curtains in the lounge. Dark green in colour, they clashed with the furniture and with the carpet. There was also a glaring absence of ornaments. Had she lived there, Tindall's late wife would surely have wanted some on the mantelpiece and the window sill. They would have been of personal significance to the couple. Looking around, Keedy concluded that Dr Tindall was determined to live in a bachelor domain. He might have kept photographs of his wife everywhere but there was nothing else to remind him of what he claimed had been a happy marriage. It was almost as if he had deliberately suppressed memories of her.

Keedy was upstairs when he heard a car pulling up outside. He assumed that it would be Marmion, returning from the hospital, but, when he glanced through the window, he saw two men climbing out of the vehicle. One was carrying a camera to take photographs of the crime scene and the other had a small case. His task, Keedy knew, was to collect fingerprints. It had been Sir Edward Henry, the Metropolitan Police Commissioner, who had founded the Fingerprint Bureau. During his time as Inspector General of the Bengal Police, he had seen the value of fingerprinting. It was now an important tool for Scotland Yard and Keedy had seen how effective it could be. He knew that there would certainly be fingerprints on the safe in the main bedroom and in the storeroom where the murder had occurred. If the intruders had a police record, their fingerprints would be on file.

He went quickly downstairs to welcome his colleagues and give them their instructions. When he opened the front door, he saw Fanning's face light up.

'Are you feeling thirsty yet, sir?' asked the constable.

Claude Chatfield was seated behind his desk when there was a tap on the door and the tall, elegant figure of Sir Edward Henry came in. The superintendent rose to his feet out of deference and the two men exchanged greetings. Ordinarily, the commissioner did not take a specific interest in most of the crimes with which Scotland Yard dealt. The latest case was an exception to the rule.

'I've just had a call from the War Office,' said Sir Edward. 'I gather that a surgeon at one of the military hospitals has been murdered.'

'That's true,' Chatfield told him. 'The hospital is in Edmonton.'

'The victim, apparently, was a man with rare skills.'

'So I was given to understand, Sir Edward.'

'I hope that you've assigned the best detectives to the investigation.'

'Inspector Marmion and Sergeant Keedy were despatched as soon as they arrived here. I've already had a telephone call from the inspector, giving me a statement to release to the press.'

'That's typical of him. Marmion always thinks ahead.'

Chatfield winced. He hated to hear praise of the inspector, especially when it came from the commissioner. While he recognised Marmion's efficiency, he always found ways to criticise him. The enmity between the two men went back years.

Chatfield never let Marmion forget that he had been promoted to a higher rank in preference to his rival.

'I'd like to see the press statement, if I may,' said Sir Edward.

'Yes, of course,' replied Chatfield.

He picked up a sheet of paper from his desk and held it out to his visitor. The commissioner took it from him and read it carefully.

'Excellent!' he cried.

Clenching his teeth, Chatfield glowered.

'I'm glad that you picked the right man for the task, Superintendent. I'll ring the War Office and read this statement out to them. It may calm their jitters a little. They monitor activities at their military hospitals,' he went on, 'and quite rightly. If we ask young men to face appalling conditions in the trenches, we owe them the best medical treatment when they get wounded. Dr Tindall, I gather, was a leader in his field.'

'That's what I've been led to believe, Sir Edward.'

'When will you get a fuller report?'

'I'll have to wait until Marmion and Keedy return here.'

'Let me know what they've discovered.'

'I will.'

'A case like this will feature in all the newspapers,' said the commissioner. 'We must be careful to control the amount of information we give. Reporters always have voracious appetites. Feed them carefully. In fact,' said the commissioner as an idea came into his mind, 'it might be better if Inspector Marmion was responsible for the press conferences.'

'I disagree, Sir Edward,' said Chatfield, insulted at the suggestion.

'But he knows the situation in detail.'

'When it comes to detail, I have a gift for selecting how much to reveal. Besides, we both know that Marmion is at his best when he's out there in pursuit of the person or persons who committed a foul murder.' He thrust out his chin. 'That's where I intend to keep him.'

When they started out on the return journey, Keedy reflected that some of the most important conversations he had ever had with Harvey Marmion had been in the rear of a police car. They had always been close, but their friendship had been put under severe pressure when Marmion realised that his daughter was the latest in a long list of young women in whom Keedy had taken an interest. He did not wish Alice to be courted then discarded like her predecessors. It was a time when there were a lot of strained silences during lifts together in the car. When he saw that Keedy's commitment was sincere, however, Marmion eventually warmed to the idea of becoming his father-in-law. The ritual jibes that the sergeant received from the other detectives gradually died away. Joe Keedy had reformed.

He listened patiently to Marmion's account of his visit to the hospital.

'It was both depressing and inspiring, Joe,' said the inspector. 'My heart sank when I saw the state of some of those men. They were clinging on to life by their fingertips but what future could they have when they'd be severely disabled? Then I saw the way that the doctors and nurses were giving them hope and helping them to adapt. They treated every individual as a war hero and that raised morale. It really lifted my spirits.'

'Who was in charge?'

'Major Palmer-Loach.'

'I hate people with double-barrelled names.'

'He's doing a good job. The place is run with military precision. Thanks to the major, the hospital now has an X-ray department, and it also has a sausage-machine that can turn out the best part of a thousand bangers a day.'

Keedy laughed. 'We could do with one of those at Scotland Yard.'

'There's even a potato-peeling machine there.'

'What did this Major Thingumajig say about Dr Tindall?'

'He had nothing but praise for him, Joe,' said Marmion. 'As a surgeon, he was outstanding. Every doctor I spoke to told me the same. I was shown the operating theatre where Tindall should have been this morning. You should see the equipment there, streets ahead of anything you'd find in a field hospital in France or Belgium.'

'What about Tindall's family?'

'It seems to have been rather small. His parents were the only ones for whom they had an address. Mr and Mrs Tindall live in Scotland, apparently. They have no other children. I will have to ask Chat to ring the nearest police station so that someone can break the news to them. It's going to shake them to their roots,' said Marmion. 'They must idolise him.'

'Doctors are like policemen. They run in families. Maybe the father is also a doctor.'

'Judging by the address,' said Marmion, 'he's more likely to be a farmer or a fisherman. They live somewhere near Aberdeen. It seems as if Tindall preferred a career this side of the border.'

He looked at Keedy. 'Anyway, tell me what you've been up to while I was away.'

'I was following your orders.'

Keedy described what he had learnt by knocking on doors, then talked about his search of the house. His impression was that the dining room and two of the bedrooms were never used.

'I think he spent most of his time in his study,' he decided. 'The shelves were stacked with medical books of one sort or another. There was nothing there you could read for pleasure. No wonder Mrs Hobbes enjoyed working at the house. She hardly needed to touch some of the rooms. They were always clean and tidy.'

'How strange!'

'Why did the doctor live like a hermit?'

'The Scots are a funny people, Joe.'

'I disagree. The ones I know love company, especially if there's plenty of booze at hand. They know how to enjoy themselves to the full. I reckon that Tindall was the odd man out.'

'The wonder is that he married.'

'Yes, it is.'

'My guess is that his wife might have been a nurse. They look so fetching in those starched uniforms.'

'Now, now,' warned Keedy. 'Calm down or I'll tell Ellen what you said.'

'Funnily enough, she thought about becoming a nurse once.'

'What stopped her?'

'We had children,' said Marmion. 'Right, let's put our thinking caps on and work out what we can tell Chat.'

'We believe the doctor was killed by two men who drove motorbikes.'

52

'What else?'

'Tindall spoke fondly about his late wife.'

'Most widowers do that, Joe. It's not a reason to murder him.'

'Well, those men obviously had a strong motive,' said Keedy, thinking it through. 'If he'd confronted them, they could have killed him with one thrust of a knife. Instead of that, they carved him up like a Christmas turkey then stole the most precious things he had – photographs of his wife.'

'That's where we start,' declared Marmion. 'We must find out who the woman was and how she died. Hopefully, his parents may be able to give us that information and there must be other members of the family we can track down.'

'If anyone has to go up to Scotland, I'll volunteer.'

'I need you here – and so does my daughter, for that matter.'

'I'd arranged to see Alice tomorrow evening.'

'Well, you'll have to cancel that,' said Marmion. 'We're going to be under great pressure from now on. Until we find the killers, your social life does not exist.'

Keedy's face fell.

CHAPTER FIVE

Ada Hobbes was in a quandary. She had been warned to speak to nobody about the way that she had stumbled upon a murder victim. At the time, she had agreed willingly, glad to block the experience out of her mind instead of having to relive it in front of a group of reporters. But it was not as easy to forget it as she had hoped. No matter what she did to distract herself, the image kept flashing before her eyes. She was terrified of going to bed in case the mutilated body of Dr Tindall reappeared in a nightmare. Ada wished that she had never worked for the man.

As she sat beside the kitchen table, the cup of tea she had made earlier stood untouched beside her. She had neither the urge nor the appetite to reach for it. Since she had come home, Ada had made no effort to take off her fur coat, hat, scarf and gloves. She just sat there, wishing that her husband was still alive to help, advise and simply hug her. Bert Hobbes, a sweep by trade, had been a chirpy, kind, hard-working man until his lungs became so silted by soot and cigarettes that he had coughed his way to an early grave. She had never felt his absence quite so keenly. Tears welled up in her eyes.

His death was not the only loss she had had to bear. Ada had somehow coped with recurring tragedies, adapting to a life on her own and learning to be proud of her independence. She could draw no strength from it now. Depressed, anxious and aching with fatigue, she felt utterly lost. At a time when she most needed the person who could offer love and support, she had been warned by the police to keep away from her. They had promised that Kathy Paget, her sister, would be informed of what they had described as an unforeseen development at Dr Tindall's house.

All that Ada could do was to stay alone at home and suffer.

They were in the superintendent's office. After reading the report that Marmion had typed out laboriously with his index fingers, Claude Chatfield looked up at the inspector and sniffed.

'I was hoping for more detail,' he complained.

'You know everything that we found out, sir,' said Marmion.

'There are too many gaps.'

'We'll do our best to fill them in.'

'You seem to have discovered so little about the victim himself.'

'Dr Tindall is to blame for that. He kept himself to himself. Even his closest colleagues said that they never really knew him. They described him as driven.'

'Yes,' said Chatfield, 'I know the feeling. I am driven as well. I am driven by the desire to solve this murder as swiftly as possible. The commissioner has taken a personal interest in this case. It seems that the War Office have been on to him.' He glanced at the report. 'He'll have hoped for more information than this.'

Chatfield was a tall, thin, pallid man with a meticulous centre parting in his hair. Beside the chunky figure of Marmion, he looked undernourished. They had never liked each other but had somehow managed to work well together. Chatfield put the report aside.

'What is your next move, Inspector?' he asked.

'You have his parents' address. They need to be contacted immediately and informed that their son is dead. We are certain that the victim is Dr Tindall but identification by a family member is always important.'

'I agree.'

'All I can tell you is that Dyce is north of Aberdeen.'

'Then let us see if we can find its exact location.' He reached for a map book on the shelf beside his desk and leafed through the pages until he came to the index. When he found what he wanted, he turned to the appropriate page. Marmion stood behind him so that he could see the map of north-east Scotland as well.

'There it is, sir,' he said, jabbing a finger.

'All right, all right,' said Chatfield, testily, 'I can see it.'

'Dyce is close to Aberdeen. It might even be a suburb.'

'I'll find the number of the Aberdeen City Police and give them a ring.'

'Advise them to pass on the news gently,' suggested Marmion. 'They may be quite elderly and—'

'Don't tell me how to do my job. I know exactly what to tell them.'

'Yes, of course, sir.'

'What are you going to do?'

'Firstly, we're off to Edmonton again to speak to a woman named Mrs Paget. She was the cleaner at the house for years and knew Dr Tindall far better than Mrs Hobbes. The two women are sisters, by the way,' explained Marmion. 'I was anxious that we told Mrs Paget what had happened instead of letting her sister do so. Given the circumstances, Mrs Hobbes has been remarkably composed, but she is bound to feel the full impact of the tragedy when she's alone. I didn't want her rushing around to her sister's house.'

Chatfield frowned. 'I'm not entirely happy about this, you know.'

'About what, sir?'

'Relying on the word of two cleaners. I mean, neither of them is going to tell you anything of real import. They just came to do a menial task and went on their way. From what you have told me, they hardly ever saw Dr Tindall.' He curled a lip. 'Their evidence will be of little use. We need hard facts and I expected you to get far more of them at the hospital.'

'So did I, sir, but it was not to be. As for the cleaners,' said Marmion, 'it's unfair to sneer at them. They have both seen inside that house, which is far more than any of the neighbours have done. When he was not on duty, Dr Tindall appears to have been something of a recluse.'

'With luck, his parents will be more sociable.'

'I'll leave you to get in touch with the police in Aberdeen, sir.'

'Remember what I said,' warned Chatfield. 'The commissioner will be watching this investigation closely. If you fail to make visible progress, you'll have Sir Edward barking at your heels.'

'That makes two of you,' said Marmion. 'You'll be able to bark in unison.'

Pounding the streets had become much easier for them with no rain beating down. Alice Marmion and Iris Goodliffe kept their eyes peeled for incidents that might require some intervention on their part. Iris kept pressing for details of her friend's wedding plans but Alice tried to steer the conversation in another direction. She and Keedy had not finalised the list of those who would attend their wedding. Eager to keep the numbers down, they had yet to include Iris's name on the list.

They were coming around a corner when they saw a woman approaching them. The newcomer stared at Alice before letting out a cry of pleasure.

'Alice!' she exclaimed. 'It is you, isn't it?'

'Yes, Gwenda, it is,' said the other, recognising her.

'I'd heard that you were a policewoman.'

'Somebody has to be,' said Alice.

She introduced Iris to Gwenda Powell and explained that they had worked together as teachers. Her friend was a stout, middle-aged woman with a warm smile and a pleasant manner.

'Why aren't you at school this afternoon?' asked Alice.

'We have a half-day off,' explained the other.

'We have a whole day off tomorrow,' Iris told her, 'and we're going shopping in the West End.'

'I wish that I could have done that, Iris, but I had to visit my parents instead. They're in their seventies now and both are in poor health. They keep wondering if this war will ever be over.'

'We all ask that question,' sighed Alice. 'But how are things at school?'

'There have been some changes since you left. The big one, I suppose, is that Mrs Latimer has finally retired.'

'Ah, so you've got a new headmistress.'

'Actually,' said the other, 'I've replaced her.'

'Congratulations, Gwenda!' said Alice, embracing her. 'You should have been promoted years ago.'

'Thank you. I got there in the end. How are you enjoying your new life?'

'I love it – don't I, Iris?'

'We both enjoy it,' agreed Iris, 'most of the time, anyway.'

'That's a pity,' said Gwenda. 'It means that I can't lure Alice back to teaching. We could really do with you. The children are a handful at times, and you always had the knack of controlling them.'

'I'll stay where I am,' said Alice.

'You obviously enjoy your new job but it's only voluntary. If you policed children instead, you'd get paid as well.'

'We can't spare her,' said Iris, laughing as she put a possessive arm around Alice. 'She belongs to us now.'

'But she always loved teaching,' said Gwenda, 'and the children loved her. They still ask after Miss Marmion.'

'I'm sure they do. It's nice to be wanted like that, Alice.'

'Yes, it is,' agreed her colleague.

'Think about it,' urged Gwenda. 'We'd love to have Miss Marmion back.'

'That will soon be impossible,' said Iris with a grin. 'Miss Marmion is going to become Mrs Keedy in the new year. Alice is marrying a detective sergeant, so she'll be handcuffed to the police for life.'

When they reached the house, they saw that it was a small, neglected, end-of-terrace dwelling with faded paintwork and missing slates. The detectives knocked on the door and waited. They could hear a distant door opening and the sound of a walking stick tapping on the tiled passageway. The front door finally opened to reveal Kathleen Paget, a heavy woman in her late fifties with thick lenses in her spectacles that enlarged her eyes dramatically. She regarded the visitors with suspicion.

'Mrs Paget?' asked Marmion.

'Yes,' she replied. 'That's me.'

'I'm Detective Inspector Marmion from the Metropolitan Police Force and this is Detective Sergeant Keedy.'

'We've done nothing wrong, have we?' she asked, fearfully.

'No, Mrs Paget. We've come to talk to you about a gentleman whose house you used to clean.'

'Which one? There were lots over the years.'

'Dr Tindall.'

'Why? Has something happened?'

'Perhaps we'd better come in,' suggested Marmion.

'Well, yes, if you must, but you'll have to excuse the mess. I can't look after the place the way I used to, and Alf is in no position to help. He's my husband.'

She stood back so that they could step inside, then she closed the door behind them. Moving with difficulty, she led them down the passageway and into the living room. It was cold, gloomy and noisome, smelling of a compound of stale food, pipe tobacco and the dog sprawled on the mat in front of the tiny fire. After giving them a welcoming yap, the animal went back to sleep.

'It's all right,' said Kathleen. 'He doesn't bite.'

'That's good to hear,' said Keedy.

'Sit down.'

She moved her knitting off a mottled sofa and they lowered themselves onto it. As they glanced around, they noticed for the first time that there was someone else there. Alfred Paget was sunk deep in an armchair in the corner, sucking a pipe that no longer housed any tobacco. He gazed at them with a mixture of resentment and apprehension.

'These gentlemen are from the police,' said his wife, raising her voice and talking very slowly. 'You just sit there and be quiet, Alf. I can handle them.' She looked at the visitors. 'My husband doesn't remember things any more. And he has other problems. Take no notice of him.'

Marmion and Keedy found themselves unable to obey her. Looking at Paget, they saw that he was a skeletal man in a collarless grey shirt, baggy trousers and gravy-stained waistcoat. His head kept nodding and his body made involuntary lurches from side to side.

'Now, then,' she continued, 'what's this all about?'

'We have sad news, Mrs Paget,' said Marmion, quietly.

61

'Oh?'

'I'm afraid that Dr Tindall . . . died earlier today.'

'Are you sure?' she asked, eyes widening in alarm. 'This can't be true. I mean Dr Tindall was in good health. People like him don't die.'

'Someone killed him.'

'Never!' she exclaimed, hand to her heart. 'Not our dear Dr Tindall, surely.'

'Some time in the night, intruders got in.'

'Your sister, Mrs Hobbes, discovered him,' said Keedy. 'There was a telephone in the house, so she called the police.'

'Yes, I know there's a telephone. In fact, I showed Ada how it worked before she took over the cleaning. She'd never held one before, you see.' She suddenly buried her face in her hands for a couple of minutes before making a partial recovery and staring at them through misted spectacles. 'I'm so sorry but . . . it was a pleasure to work for Dr Tindall. He was kind to me, and Ada told me he treated her just the same.' She removed the spectacles to dab at her eyes with a handkerchief. 'I kept that house gleaming,' she said, proudly, 'and I kept my own home the same until my arthritis got the better of me. It turns my hands into claws some days.'

'We're sorry to hear that,' said Marmion, 'and we're sorry about your husband's problems.' He cleared his throat. 'Before we discuss what happened last night, we must warn you not to talk to any reporters about the murder. We want to protect you from them.'

'I won't tell them a thing, Inspector.'

'With luck, they may not even find you.'

'What about Ada?'

'We've given her the same advice.'

'How is she?'

'Mrs Hobbes is bearing up,' said Keedy. 'I had her taken home in a car. She's had a very nasty experience, as you can imagine.'

'I must go to her. She needs me.'

'Before you do that, there are some questions we'd like to ask.'

'Yes,' said Marmion, taking over. 'Without realising it, you may have information that could be helpful to us.'

'I'll tell you whatever you want,' she said, handkerchief still at the ready.

Marmion nodded to Keedy who took out his notebook and pencil.

'How long did you work for Dr Tindall?' asked the inspector.

'It must be . . . oh, almost two years,' she replied. 'With Alf being like he is, I was ready to take on all the work I could get. Well, we had to survive somehow. I don't often have any luck, but I got it that time. I couldn't have found a better person to work for. Dr Tindall was wonderful . . .'

Patricia Redwood had left the sewing circle so Ellen felt able to go there that afternoon. She was still jangled by her earlier confrontation with the other woman but, the moment she stepped into the room, her discomfort vanished. She was among friends, dedicated women who got together on a regular basis to make gloves, socks, scarves and anything that soldiers might need at the front in the freezing days of December. Ellen loved to work with such a companionable group and enjoy a gossip while she did so. Since they all knew about the disappearance of her son, none of the others ever mentioned Paul. In any case, many of them had their own sorrows to bear. Some had lost sons in the mud of France and Belgium. Others had seen them invalided out of the army and trying to adjust to a new life after their ordeal. Their individual tragedies had helped the women to bond.

Fear of rationing was the main topic of conversation. Ellen was able to pass on what Geoffrey Biddle had told her. They envied her for being able to buy extra sugar.

'I couldn't do that,' admitted one of them. 'My husband wouldn't let me. He checks the order before I leave the house. Money is scarce and every penny counts. That's what he keeps saying. If I'd bought anything extra like Ellen did, he'd make me pay for it myself.'

'Them German submarines are going to win this war,' said another, gloomily. 'Most of the food from abroad is at the bottom of the sea.'

'We'll manage somehow,' said Ellen.

'How do you do it?' asked the woman.

'Do what?'

'Well, you always keep your spirits up somehow. Even when things go wrong, you never complain whereas the rest of us would be screaming our heads off. What's your secret?'

Ellen shrugged. 'I don't know that I have one, Marge.'

'Something keeps you afloat.'

'Yes, it's a cup of tea whenever I want and a good old gossip with friends.'

'There's more to it than that, Ellen.'

'I suppose there is,' said the other, thoughtfully. 'Whenever I have bad things in my life, I try to think of the good things as well. They take my attention off something nasty and give me a boost. Today, for example,' Ellen went on, 'I had a row with a woman who likes to bait me. I couldn't get away quick enough. It troubled me. Then I stepped in here and forgot all about her – because I was among friends. Something good drove out something bad.'

'I wish that worked for me,' said Margery.

'You should try it.'

'In my case, the bad always drives out the good.'

'Then try to fix your mind on something special,' advised Ellen. 'It's what I've been doing for days. My daughter is going to spend tonight at home for a change. Ever since Alice moved into that flat of hers, I've missed her dreadfully – but not tonight. We're going to spend the whole evening catching up on each other's news and just enjoying each other's company.' She beamed. 'Just thinking about that has put a smile on my face for days.'

Listening to Kathleen Paget had been a revelation. In the twenty minutes or so that they were there, the detectives learnt far more about George Tindall than they had from any other source. In view of her arthritis, it was amazing that she had kept cleaning the house until she did. Other women would have given up earlier, but she hated the idea of letting her employer down.

'Dr Tindall was special,' she said. 'That's why I struggled on until he was the only person I used to work for.'

'You speak of him as if he was a friend,' observed Marmion.

'That's exactly what he was, Inspector. He didn't look down his nose the way that most of the others did. He treated me with respect. When I told him about Alf, he gave me some advice about how to make life a little easier for him. It's what the nurses do at the hospital, see. They think of special ways to help each of their patients. They really care. So do I.' She glanced across at her husband. 'Alf knows that. I'm nursing him. I'm doing what Dr Tindall suggested.'

'Why do you think he lived alone?'

'But he didn't, Inspector. He shared it with the ghost of his wife.'

'What was Mrs Tindall's first name?'

'Eleanor.'

'Was she from Scotland as well?'

'Oh, no, Inspector. She was from somewhere in Devon. He told me that he was born near Aberdeen, but the funny thing was that he didn't sound Scottish. He was . . . well, posh.'

'He probably had an expensive education,' said Keedy. 'If you go to the right school, they train you to speak with that toffee-nosed accent.'

'Did he ever have guests to stay at the house?' asked Marmion.

'None that I knew of,' she said. 'I'd have seen the signs. Mind you,' she added with a smile, 'I did fancy that he might have had a lady staying there one night. There was this smell of perfume in the bathroom. When I mentioned it to him, the doctor said that it was his wife's favourite. Every so often, he liked to sprinkle a little of it in memory of her.'

'That's an odd thing to do.'

She was philosophical. 'People remember loved ones in different ways. For the doctor, it was Mrs Tindall's perfume. When Alf goes,' she said, 'I'll always remember the smell of his pipe.'

'Why were some of the rooms never used?'

'I've no idea, Inspector.'

'What about his wife's clothes?' asked Keedy. 'We know she never lived there but we expected to find some of her things hanging in the wardrobe.'

'He got rid of them for some reason.'

'Do you have any idea what that reason might be?'

'No,' said Kathleen. 'I was there to clean, not to ask questions.' She gave a shudder. 'Oh, I do feel so sorry for Ada. She always has such bad luck. Finding him like that must have frightened her to death. Wish it had been me. I don't scare so easy.'

'What do you mean?' asked Marmion.

'It's the other job I had, see. We have a lot of old people around here. When one of them passes away, I'm often called in to lay them out proper. They need to be cleaned and made decent, like. I enjoyed the work. It never upset me.'

'You provided a valuable service,' said Keedy. 'I used to work for the family undertaking business and we sometimes found cadavers in a shocking condition. I wish that everyone had someone like you to call upon.'

'Let's go back to Mrs Hobbes,' said Marmion. 'You told us that she always had bad luck.'

'It was more like a curse, Inspector,' she explained. 'Her first baby was stillborn, then her second died of diphtheria before he reached his fourth birthday. They never had another child. Then Bert died when he was only thirty-nine. He was a sweep, you see, and he'd always had a weak chest. If my husband had gone at that age,' she admitted, 'I'd have been grieving for years. Do you know what Ada did?'

'Please tell us.'

'She took over his round. Yes,' she went on as they both looked surprised, 'she carried on where Bert left off and came home filthy at the end of the day. She's not the only woman who's become a sweep, you know. The work did get too much for her in the end, so she let someone pay her to take over her customers. After that, she went cleaning full time. Ada's a fighter,' she told them, 'but I don't think she'll have much fight left in her just now.'

Ada Hobbes had volunteered to clean the local church once a week. Although she had been there two days earlier, she went back and gave it a supplementary clean, working away with her usual vigour. Anybody coming into the church would have assumed that she was simply there to do a job but that was not the case at all. As she got on her knees to brush under a pew, she was praying for the image of Dr Tindall's corpse to be taken out of her mind, but the plea evoked no response from above.

Chatting with her beat partner made Iris Goodliffe's job much easier. She was therefore surprised and disappointed when Alice fell silent for five minutes and failed to hear her companion's voice. Iris resorted to a nudge.

'Oh,' said Alice, coming out of her reverie. 'What's happened?'

'Nothing has happened and that's the point. You went off into a daydream and didn't hear what I said.'

'I'm sorry, Iris.'

'You're entitled to think about Joe. I would, in your place.'

'I wasn't thinking about him. It was what Gwenda told me about the school.'

'You don't want to go back there, do you?' asked Iris, worriedly.

'In a way, I do.'

'You can't leave the Women's Police Force. You were made for it.'

'I used to be made for teaching,' recalled Alice. 'But don't worry. I'm not thinking of resigning. I just wondered if I might go back to give the children a talk about something.'

'Such as?'

'Well, the importance of obeying the law and why we now have women in police uniform as well as men. I'd never have considered offering to do that if Mrs Latimer was still headmistress.'

'Why not?'

'She was a real dragon. When I went to the school as a child, I was terrified of her and it was no different when I taught there. Mrs Latimer never let any of us forget that she was in charge.'

'What about the friend we met earlier?'

'Oh, Gwenda Powell was the opposite. She was warm, kind and ready to help me in any way. I missed her when I left the school. I'm so glad that she's the headmistress now. Mrs Latimer was a tyrant.'

'I can't even remember the teachers at my infant school,' confessed Iris, 'and I'd never dream of going back to give a talk there. I'm hopeless at speaking in public. I get so flustered. How would you remember what to say?'

'I'd write it down beforehand, then learn it.'

'You must have a good memory then. Mine is like a sieve.'

'Public speaking is easy when you've had some practice.'

'It's all right for you, Alice. Being a teacher gave you confidence. All I ever did before I joined the WPF was to serve behind the counter in a pharmacy.'

'You must've talked to dozens of different people every day and I've seen how good you are with complete strangers who ask us for help.'

'That's not the same as giving a talk.'

'I've got an idea,' said Alice, turning to her. 'Why don't you come with me? We could give the talk together. Before the war, there was no Women's Police Force. If we explain how and why it came into being, we might give some of the girls the ambition to do what we did.'

'But there may not be a WPF after the war.'

'Oh, yes, there will be.'

'How do you know?'

'We've proved that we can do a valuable job during a crisis,' said Alice, proudly. 'There's no turning back now. We're here to stay.'

As they got back into their car, the detectives were able to discuss their visit.

'What did you make of her, Joe?' asked Marmion.

'She's different from her sister. Mrs Paget looks as if she eats too much, and Mrs Hobbes looks as if she eats too little. The other thing is that Mrs Paget has much more to say for herself than her sister. When the two of them get together, I bet that only one of them does the talking.'

'How many pages of your notebook did you fill?'

'Too many.'

They shared a laugh. 'I'm glad we met her,' said Marmion. 'Her version of Dr Tindall differs a lot from the one that I got from Major Palmer-Loach. He talked about him as a surgeon. Mrs Paget talked about him as a human being.'

'According to her, he spoke as if he had a plum in his mouth.'

'Yes, that was a surprise. Scots tend to keep their native accent.'

'Maybe he had a good reason to change it.'

'What did you make of Mrs Paget's story about the perfume?'

'It made me think how weird Dr Tindall must have been. What sort of man sprays perfume to remind him of his late wife?'

'I think he's the sort who tells barefaced lies to his cleaner.'

Keedy was surprised. 'Didn't you believe what he told her?'

'Frankly, I didn't.'

'Why not?'

'It's because I reckon that Mrs Paget made the right assumption. A woman had stayed at the house one night. That could be an important discovery. We've found a human weakness in him, after all,' said Marmion with a smile. 'Dr Tindall may not be as spotless as we've been led to believe that he was.'

CHAPTER SIX

Superintendent Claude Chatfield was accustomed to using the telephone to issue orders or to demand information. His rank ensured that officers obeyed him at once. That, at least, was what happened in England and – to a lesser extent, perhaps – in Wales. Both countries seemed to play by the same rules. Scotland, he had now learnt, was a foreign country that operated on a system he could neither understand nor admire. Ringing the Aberdeen City Police was an essay in frustration. It took him an age to make what he thought was a simple request. He wanted someone to track down Mr and Mrs Bruce Tindall of Kilbride Avenue, Dyce and give them some distressing news about their son. The parents would be asked to get in touch with Scotland Yard for more detail. By the time he lowered the receiver, Chatfield's arm was aching, and his temper frayed.

It was over an hour when he finally got news about his request. Someone spoke to him in an impenetrable accent that meant he only understood one in ten of the words that were fired at him like so many bullets. When he asked the caller to talk in English, he got an indignant reply. The man went on to speak to him as if he were a child, putting great emphasis on each word. Chatfield eventually understood much of what he was being told.

'Thank you, Inspector,' he said, mastering his irritation.

'It's nae trouble.'

'You've been . . . helpful.'

'Aye, I know.'

Replacing the receiver, Chatfield sat back in his chair and breathed a sigh of relief. Next time he rang anyone in Aberdeen, he promised himself, he would have an interpreter standing beside him.

It was only when she left the church that Ada Hobbes remembered how early she had had to get up. Every bone in her body seemed to be crying out in protest. On the walk back home, she acknowledged greetings from some of her neighbours but made sure that she did not stop to talk to them. She simply wanted to get back to the safety of her own four walls. When the house came into view, however, she was dismayed to see someone standing outside the front door. Her first instinct was to dodge down a side street and hide there until her visitor had left. Then she realised who the woman was. Breaking into a trot, she waved her arms in greeting.

'Kathy!' she cried. 'Thank goodness you've come.'

'I felt that I had to, Ada. Oh, come here,' she said, spreading her arms to embrace her sister and plant a kiss on her cheek. 'Let's go inside and have a cup of tea. Then we can talk.'

'But we can't, I'm afraid.'

'Why not?'

'The police told me I was to speak to nobody. I gave them my word. They'll be very cross with me if I break my promise.'

'It's different now, Ada.'

'Is it?'

'Yes. When I told them I'd come here, they didn't try to stop me. I think they wanted me to comfort you.'

Ada was taken aback. 'You've seen them?'

'I've seen them and had a long talk with them. They asked me all sorts of questions about Dr Tindall. As soon as they left, I came straight here. Now, get your key out and let us in.'

'Oh, I'm so relieved to see you, Kathy.'

'Hurry up, woman. I want my blooming tea.'

Ada smiled and hugged her.

Before they went back to Scotland Yard, they returned to the hospital. Marmion was keen to make a second visit because Major Palmer-Loach had promised to search for as many photographs of George Tindall as he could find.

'It will make a big difference if we can release a photo of him to the press,' said Marmion. 'It's bound to jog memories.'

74

'Why were there no photos of him at his home?' asked Keedy.

'I suspect that they were deliberately stolen, Joe. The killers removed lots of things that might have been of use to us.'

'That's worrying.'

'It's annoying, I grant you that.'

'It tells us something about those two men. They were cold, brutal and well-organised. They've obviously gone out of their way to make our job more difficult. We're up against professionals, Harv.'

'Then we must rise to the challenge.'

When the car stopped outside the main building at the hospital, Marmion got out and went inside. Keedy decided to take a walk around the complex. He had read a great deal about military hospitals but had never been inside one before. As he strolled off, another building soon came into view and he was able to identify it at once as the nurses' home. He stopped to admire the nurses going into or coming out of the building. Marmion had been right. There was something about their crisp, white uniforms that gave the women a special lustre. Even the older ones looked attractive. He stood there gazing at the nurses as they flitted to and fro.

His surveillance was interrupted by a firm tap on the shoulder.

'Excuse me, sir,' said a voice.

Keedy turned to see a uniformed soldier glaring at him.

'Do you have a legitimate reason to be on the premises,' continued the man, 'or did you just come here to ogle the nurses?'

75

'I resent that question,' said Keedy, taking out his warrant card. 'I'm Detective Sergeant Keedy of the Metropolitan Police Force and I'm investigating the murder of one your surgeons.' He showed his card. 'Are you satisfied now?'

'Yes, sir. I'm sorry. I was only doing my job.'

'Do it better next time.'

'We don't allow intruders on the site.'

'Do I really look like an intruder?'

'To be honest – yes, you do.'

Keedy grinned. 'Fair enough,' he said, putting his card away. 'Which surgeon was it?'

'Dr Tindall – George Tindall.'

The soldier recoiled. 'No – I don't believe it.'

'I'm afraid that it's true.'

'Someone killed him? Why ever would they do that? I don't know the names of all the surgeons here, but I know his. Dr Tindall stood out from the others. He was so popular.'

'That's what we've been told. His patients will be shocked.'

'Not only his patients,' said the soldier with a sly wink. 'Think of those nurses. Some of them worshipped him – lucky devil. If he'd wanted to, he could have had his pick of them.'

During the time that Marmion had been away, the major had been busy. By raiding his files and scouring the hospital, he had gathered a whole dossier of photographs. Most of them were taken of groups of patients and staff, carefully arranged by the photographer. Everyone looked happy in front of the camera. Once the doctor had been pointed out to him, Marmion found it easy to pick out George Tindall in every group. He was a tall, slim man in his early forties with a dignified air.

'The patients in this one,' said Palmer-Loach, handing him a photograph with over fifty people on display, 'were all due to be released. It's a farewell photo. That's why they've got those broad grins. They were the lucky ones,' he added. 'Many of their friends left in a hearse.'

'They must have arrived here in a bad state,' observed Marmion.

'Some came straight from the battlefield with their mud-covered uniforms still clinging to them. They had to be cut off.'

'These photos are fascinating, Major, but they're not really suitable for our purposes, I'm afraid.'

'That's why I brought some others.'

The major showed him some photographs taken of three surgeons, holding their masks as they stood outside the operating theatre. Tindall was among them. Of the new batch, the best photograph showed him standing beside a colleague in the open air. He looked weary but managed a smile.

'This is the one for me,' said Marmion, 'but, if I may, I'll borrow a couple of the others as well.'

'We would like them back, Inspector. They're a precious record of how this hospital works. Take great care of them. I'm only sorry that we don't have one with Dr Tindall entirely on his own.'

'Don't worry. We have a man at Scotland Yard who is a genius at cropping photographs. And if we still fail to get a satisfactory result,' said Marmion, 'we have an artist who can produce a good likeness of Dr Tindall.'

The major put the selected photographs in a large brown envelope and handed it over to his visitor. Marmion thanked him once again.

'You've made a significant contribution to the investigation, sir,' he said.

Since they had started their shift early, Alice and Iris had finished by mid afternoon. When they returned to their headquarters, the redoubtable Inspector Thelma Gale was waiting for them. Even though relatively short, she had an imposing presence. She ran a critical eye over their respective uniforms to see that they were clean and being worn properly.

'Anything to report?' she asked.

'Not really,' said Alice. 'All in all, it was a rather quiet day.'

'It's true,' added Iris. 'The most exciting thing that happened was the chat that Alice had with an old friend.'

The inspector bristled. 'You are there to keep the peace,' she snarled, 'not to talk to a passing acquaintance.'

'Oh, she was more than an acquaintance, Inspector. Alice used to work at the same school with her. Mrs Powell was rather naughty,' she went on with a giggle. 'She tried to poach Alice from the WPF.'

'I don't like the sound of that.'

'It was not serious, Inspector,' explained Alice. 'Gwenda – Mrs Powell – is now the headmistress at the school. They have some unruly children there now, apparently. She remembered that I was good at keeping discipline.'

'You're far more use to us than you'd be in a classroom,' said the other with a peremptory snort. 'Put the idea out of your head.'

'Yes, Inspector.'

'You hold a responsible position. Never forget that. Women are making an important difference in the war effort. We've proved ourselves in every way.'

'Alice knows that,' said Iris, unguardedly. 'She'd never desert us. But there's no reason why she shouldn't help the school when she's off duty, is there?'

'There's every reason,' hissed the inspector, turning to glare at Alice. 'Have you made this friend of yours some sort of promise?'

'Not really,' said Alice. 'I was just thinking, that's all.'

'Thinking about what, may I ask?'

Iris blurted it out. 'She thought it might be a good idea to give a talk to the pupils. Alice was a born teacher. They'd listen to her.'

'And what sort of talk did you have in mind?' demanded the inspector.

'It was just an idea,' said Alice, wishing that the subject had never come up. 'I can see now that it was a mistake. For a start, I simply don't have the time.'

'You could make time,' suggested Iris.

'I'd rather forget the whole thing.'

'But the children keep asking after you. In fact—'

'That's enough,' said Alice, cutting her off. 'The matter's closed.'

'It certainly is,' agreed the inspector. 'When you joined the WPF, you made certain commitments. I expect you to honour them and not get distracted by the prospect of working in a school again. You operate in the adult world now.' She drew herself up to her full height. 'Do you understand what I'm saying?'

'Yes, Inspector.'

'Don't forget it.' She turned on Iris. 'The same goes for you.'

'Yes, Inspector,' said Iris, meekly.

'The Women's Police Force must always come first!'

Having delivered her final warning, Inspector Gale gave each of them a withering look before stalking off to her office. Alice was dazed by the confrontation and angry with Iris for mentioning the conversation about the school. There were times when her beat partner's loose tongue maddened her, and this was one of them. Iris sensed that she had done the wrong thing.

'We're still going to the West End tomorrow, aren't we?' she whispered.

The first pot of tea steadied them and gave them the strength to cope with the shock they had both had. By the time that Ada Hobbes had brewed a second pot, they felt restored. Kathleen Paget rolled her eyes.

'Dr Tindall was my best client,' she said. 'I'd do anything for him.'

'So would I, Kathy,' said her sister.

'Apart from anything else, he paid me more than the others.'

'I didn't do his cleaning for the money. It was just a pleasure to be on my own in such a lovely, big house. I was able to set my pace without having someone standing over me. I just wish Bert had still been alive for me to tell him all about Dr Tindall.' She became reflective. 'He was funny, though.'

'Who – Bert or the doctor?'

'The doctor, of course,' said Ada. 'When I first saw all those photos of his wife, I thought it was wonderful of him to remember her that way. I'm not so sure now. I mean, it's not something I did when my husband died. If I put a photo of Bert in every room, it would unsettle me. Wherever I went, he'd be watching me.'

'I'd feel the same about Alf.'

'Does that mean we're bad people?'

'It means that we grieve in our own ways, Ada.'

They drank their tea and lapsed into a companionable silence. It was minutes before Ada remembered something.

'Thank you, Kathy.'

'I should be thanking you. It's a lovely cup of tea.'

'I'm so grateful that you recommended me to Dr Tindall.'

'What's the point of family if we can't help each other?'

'That's true.'

'And you deserved something good for once. You've had so many blows in your life, Ada, and you never felt sorry for yourself.'

'Yes, I did,' recalled her sister. 'When I took over Bert's round, I felt very sorry for myself. Sweeping chimneys almost crippled me. The soot got everywhere. And I hated being laughed at by children in the street.'

'Those days have gone now.' Kathy sipped her tea. 'I've got to do some thinking,' she said, putting the cup back in the saucer. 'The police told me that, if I remembered anything about Dr Tindall I thought might be useful, I was to get in touch with them at once. But my brain just won't work properly.'

'Mine's the same, Kathy. It's the shock.'

'That'll wear off, I hope. When it does, I'll remember things he said or did. Think of that, Ada. What I tell them about the doctor might help them to catch whoever killed him.' She tapped her head. 'I might have some important information locked away inside here.'

On the drive back to Scotland Yard, they studied the photographs. Keedy was fascinated by the way that Tindall caught the eye immediately.

'Even when he's wearing a white coat,' he said, 'he somehow manages to look smart. The two doctors with him in this photo just disappear.'

'Think of those suits in his wardrobe, Joe.'

'I'm still green with envy.'

'He really cared about his appearance.'

'Yes, and he was a good-looking devil. No wonder he made so many hearts flutter in the nurses' home. It makes you wonder, doesn't it?'

'What do you mean?'

'Well,' said Keedy, 'both the neighbours and those two cleaners told us that Dr Tindall was obsessed with his late wife. Yet that smile on his face and those expensive suits of his suggest he might – just might – be a ladies' man.'

'Then there was the smell of perfume in his bathroom.'

'I hadn't forgotten that.'

'Let's not jump to conclusions,' warned Marmion. 'Mr and Mrs Crowe knew him much better than us and so did Mrs Hobbes and Mrs Paget. Then there was Major Palmer-Loach, of course. He gave me the impression that Dr Tindall was on duty at the hospital almost every single day. In fact, he stayed the night there sometimes. That's real devotion to duty.'

Keedy studied the last of the photographs, then handed it back. Marmion slipped it into the envelope. He remembered something.

'The major has been extremely helpful,' he said, 'but, on my first visit there, we did have a difference of opinion.'

'What about?'

'Endell Street Hospital.'

'Ah, yes,' recalled Keedy. 'You went there with Alice, didn't you?'

'I was intrigued to find out if a hospital with an entirely female staff could function properly. Endell Street gave me the answer. It could match any other military hospital. I thought it was remarkable.'

'What was the major's opinion?'

'He called it "the Suffragettes Hospital" as if that were something obscene. I told him how impressed I was, but he'll never change his mind. He prefers hospitals where men make all the decisions.'

'You'll have to set Alice on to him.'

'It would be a waste of time. The major has a closed mind.' Marmion patted the envelope. 'We got what we came for, that's the main thing. A photo is better than a thousand words. If we can get Dr Tindall's face in tomorrow's papers, we're going to reach people nationwide.'

'My guess is that we'll have a big response,' said Keedy.

'It's what I'm hoping for, Joe. Before we can solve this murder, we need to find out a hell of a lot more about the victim.'

It was weeks since Ellen Marmion had seen her daughter and she was filled with nervous excitement. She had baked some cakes for the occasion and cleaned Alice's room in readiness. Uncertain of what time she would arrive, Ellen was torn between going to meet the bus and waiting at the house. In the event, the decision was taken for her. Before she could put on her coat to go out, she heard a key being inserted in the front door. When her daughter suddenly appeared, her mother flung her arms around her.

'You're earlier than I expected,' said Ellen.

'Is that a complaint, Mummy?'

'Of course not. This is a wonderful surprise.'

After an exchange of greetings, Alice took off her coat and hat and followed her mother into the kitchen. She saw the plate of cakes on the table.

'Oh, that's just what I need!'

'You look exhausted. Have you had a tiring day?'

'Not really,' said Alice. 'It was just . . . irritating.'

'Sit down and tell me all about it. I'll put the kettle on.'

'Can I have one of those cakes first?'

Ellen laughed. 'Have as many as you like.'

The two of them were soon sitting opposite each other at the table. Alice was able to relax for the first time that day. Being back home was a tonic for her.

'Now, then,' said her mother. 'What made the day so irritating?'

'Iris.'

'I thought the pair of you got on so well together.'

'We do as a rule,' said Alice. 'In fact, I was enjoying her company so much, I suggested that the pair of us should go to the West End tomorrow on our day off.'

'She'd have been thrilled at that.'

'Iris couldn't stop talking about it. Then we bumped into a friend of mine . . .'

Alice told her about the chat with Gwenda Powell and about the latter's attempt to get her back to school again. Ellen was interested to hear that Gwenda was now headmistress.

'I thought that Mrs Latimer would never retire,' she said. 'You used to be so frightened of that woman.'

'I still am.'

'But she's left the school altogether.'

'Yes,' said Alice, 'and she's turned up under another name. Inspector Gale is Mrs Latimer in disguise – just as strict and twice as nasty. And what does Iris do?'

'Tell me.'

'When we get to the end of our shift, Gale Force is waiting for us. Iris tells her that Gwenda Powell was trying to lure me back into teaching, so I get told off good and proper. Oh,' she cried through gritted teeth, 'I could kill Iris sometimes. The worst of it is that I've got to spend most of the day with her tomorrow.' She held up an apologetic hand. 'I'm sorry, Mummy. I shouldn't go on about it. And I have got something lined up for tomorrow. It will wipe away all memory of Iris Goodliffe. Joe is taking me out.'

'Ah,' said Ellen, 'I'm glad you mentioned Joe.'

'We haven't spent time together for weeks.'

'You may have to wait a little longer, I'm afraid.'

'Why?'

'Joe rang me from Scotland Yard about an hour ago. He sends his love and says how sorry he is, but something has come up – a murder in Edmonton. He and your father will be working on it around the clock.'

Alice sagged. The next day began to look bleak.

They were still examining the body when Marmion came into the morgue. Harrison broke away and took him into his office where the smell was less pungent.

'There's still a long way to go, Harvey,' explained the pathologist. 'I tell you the same thing every time. You can't rush a post-mortem.'

'Just bring me up to date, Tom.'

'Time of death is what I told you earlier.'

'It fits in with what Joe discovered.'

'Oh?'

'He did a stint at door-knocking. At a house on the corner, he found an old man who was in his bathroom when he heard two motorbikes drawing up and stopping. We think that whoever had been riding them walked up to Dr Tindall's house and somehow got in. The result is out there on your table.'

'How do you know that the motorcyclists committed the murder?'

'They came as quietly as possible,' said Marmion, 'and left as fast as they could. Everybody in the next street heard them roar away.'

'I see.'

'What can you tell me about the nature of the injuries?'

'Do you really want to know?' Marmion nodded. 'They made sure he died slowly and in great pain. He was tortured. They cut lumps off him as they went along. His stomach was cut open and his testicles sliced off. I could go on and on.'

'That's enough, Tom. I'd prefer to see it all in a report.'

'There's one thing you might care to know.'

'Is there?'

'Something bigger than a knife was used to inflict some of those wounds. If you asked me for a guess, I'd say it was a bayonet.'

Marmion gulped. 'A bayonet?'

'Now where would they get hold of that?'

As soon as they had reached Scotland Yard, Keedy had gone off to pursue a line of enquiry on his own. He kept thinking about the suits hanging in the wardrobe in Dr Tindall's house. A surgeon would be paid far more than a detective sergeant but not enough, he believed, to be a regular client in Savile Row. A large amount of money had been lavished on the suits and other items of menswear they'd found. There had also been three pairs of gold cufflinks. The array of hats alone would have been well beyond the reach of Keedy's modest income.

When he was dropped off by the police car in Savile Row, he remembered a case that had taken him and Marmion to nearby Jermyn Street. It had concerned the murder of a Jewish tailor, the rape of his daughter and the burning down of his premises. Keedy hoped that the current investigation would be less complex and bewildering. Before he went into the shop, he looked in the window of Boyle and Stoddard, Bespoke Tailors. To someone as interested in the latest styles as he was, the suits on display were minor works of art. He enjoyed a momentary fantasy of wearing one of them as he took Alice to dinner at The Ritz.

Keedy entered the shop to be given a practised smile by an immaculately dressed man in his thirties with carefully barbered hair and moustache.

'Good afternoon, sir,' he said. 'How may we help you?'

'I've come in search of information about a client of yours.'

'I'm sorry, sir, but such information is strictly confidential.' Keedy produced his warrant card and held it in front of his face. 'Ah,' said the man, reading the name and changing his tone, 'that's different.'

'Good.'

'In which of our clients are you interested?'

'Dr Tindall.'

'May I ask why?'

'We are investigating his murder.'

After his visit to the pathologist, Marmion went off to report to Claude Chatfield. The superintendent was as peppery as ever and was only partly mollified by the sight of the photographs from the hospital. He sifted through them before picking out the one with only two figures in it. 'Let's see what we can do with this,' he said. 'Now, what else have you found out? Were he here – as he was, a mere twenty minutes ago – the commissioner would be asking you the same question.'

'Then my answer is this, sir . . .'

Marmion gave him an abbreviated account of the visits to Kathleen Paget and the hospital, then mentioned that Keedy had gone off to Savile Row. The superintendent was not encouraged by the news.

'What the devil is he doing there?' he howled.

'Well, he hasn't gone to be measured for a new suit,' said Marmion, drily. 'The sergeant felt that he might get another piece of the jigsaw named George Tindall. Slowly and surely, we'll build up a complete picture of the man.'

'You won't do that if you rely on the word of two cleaners and a tailor.'

'You missed out Major Palmer-Loach.'

'He at least seems to have been helpful to us.'

'You also overlooked the people living next door to Dr Tindall.'

'They admitted quite frankly that they never really got to know him. And please don't tell me that a tailor is going to supply us with a fund of insights.'

'Be patient, sir. In the past, tailors have provided vital information and I am not simply referring to the case that took us to Jermyn Street. Tailor and client have a close relationship. They get to know each other well.'

'Does that mean Sergeant Keedy will come back here with the doctor's chest measurement?' said Chatfield, scornfully. 'Or has he gone there in search of details regarding his inside leg?'

'You may be pleasantly surprised, Superintendent.'

'I doubt it.'

'Let's wait and see,' said Marmion. 'Meanwhile, I'm dying to ask if you got anywhere with your call to Aberdeen. If you sent them off to speak to the doctor's parents, we may soon get several new pieces of the jigsaw.'

'That's a forlorn hope, Inspector.'

'Why?'

'I'll draw a veil over my protracted attempts to get the Aberdeen City Police to speak in a language compatible with English,' said Chatfield. 'Eventually, they managed to understand my request and were, to be fair to them, quite efficient. They went in search of Dr Tindall's parents in Kilbride Road.'

'And?'

'It does not exist.'

'Are they sure?'

'Yes, Inspector. They also went through a list of residents in Dyce. Bruce Tindall and his wife were not among them – nor were they living anywhere else in the area. The police were thorough. We've been misled.'

'Major Palmer-Loach gave me that address in good faith.'

'I'm not blaming him. The finger points at Tindall himself. He deliberately gave false information.' Picking up a photograph, he studied the doctor's face. 'He looks so honest and trustworthy, doesn't he?'

'The major vouched for his reliability.'

'Then he was mistaken,' said Chatfield. 'Dr Tindall lied about his parents' whereabouts. How many more lies has he told? I'm sorry, Inspector,' he went on. 'You've just lost most of the pieces in your jigsaw. I suggest that you start this investigation all over again.'

CHAPTER SEVEN

Though she was bitterly disappointed, Alice Marmion adapted quickly to the news that she would not, after all, be spending the following evening with her fiancé. When Keedy was involved in a major investigation, it took precedence over everything and she accepted that. Besides, there was something that she did not tell her mother. Even if he were forced to cancel an arrangement with her, Keedy often went out of his way to make amends. On the last occasion when it happened, he had turned up at the house where she lived and woken her up by throwing pebbles at her window. Instead of the meal she had been promised, Alice had enjoyed a romantic walk with him in the moonlight.

'It's something I had to get used to,' said her mother.

'I know. Marry a policeman and you must take the rough with the smooth.'

'Work always comes first.'

'I've no quarrel with that, Mummy,' said Alice. 'Having been involved in police work myself, I know how the job can take over your life.'

'Perhaps you should have stayed in teaching.'

'I've wondered about that. Maybe I'll go back to it after the war.'

'If it ever ends, that is.'

They were seated together on the sofa in the living room. Darkness was falling so the curtains had been drawn. Alice felt warm, cosy and relaxed.

'It's strange, isn't it?' she said. 'I'm less upset about Joe's phone call than I am about the prospect of a day out with Iris. It's an awful thing to admit, but I find myself wishing that she was the person who rang to say that she had to pull out.'

'You'll enjoy it once you get there, Alice.'

'I'd enjoy it even more if you were with me.'

Ellen was interested. 'Would you like me to come along as well?'

'I'd love you to come, Mummy, but that would be unfair on Iris. I sort of promised that it would just be the two of us, off duty and on the loose. It means so much to her.'

'Then you'll be doing her a favour.'

'It's embarrassing sometimes. I'm fond of Iris but I do wish that she'd stop trying to be like me. She has to make her own decisions, not get me to make them for her.'

'Tell her that she has to find her own Joe Keedy.'

Alice laughed. 'There's only one and he's mine,' she said. 'I'm counting the days until I can walk down the aisle on his arm.'

'It won't be all that long now.'

'Iris reminds me of it every day.'

'What will you be looking for tomorrow in the West End?'

'The moment when I can say goodbye to her and go back to my flat. 'No,' she went on, apologetically, 'that sounds spiteful and I don't mean it in that way. It's just that I can only cope with so much of Iris's enthusiasm.'

'Is she looking for anything in particular?'

'That's my job, Mummy. What she wants is a new dress, but she won't actually choose it herself. I'll have to choose it for her – after she's tried on just about everything in her size.'

Ellen rolled her eyes. 'I'm relieved that I'm not coming with you.'

'Iris is Iris, I'm afraid.'

'Have you and Joe decided if she'll be invited to the wedding?'

'He's against the idea,' said Alice. 'I'm in favour.'

'Who is going to win that argument?'

'You'll have to wait and see.'

After making the call, Marmion lowered the receiver. He had just spoken to Major Palmer-Loach at the hospital, telling him that Dr Tindall had told a deliberate lie about the whereabouts of his family. There were no parents living near Aberdeen or anywhere else in the region. The major had been angry and embarrassed, furious at Tindall and red-faced at having been so easily deceived. Left on his own, Marmion looked through his notebook to see how much of the information he had gathered about Tindall must be considered as suspect. Identifying the killers was going to be difficult enough as it was. Before he and Keedy could do that, however, they now had the problem of finding out much more about the murder victim.

Marmion was still reviewing the case when the sergeant knocked and came into the office. He was beaming.

'You won't believe this,' he began.

Marmion silenced him with a raised hand. 'Let me have my turn first, Joe.'

'But this is interesting.'

'Everything has to be revalued in the light of what Chat has discovered. We've all been led up the garden path, Joe.'

Keedy blinked. 'Have we?'

'Yes – you, me, the superintendent, Mrs Hobbes, Mrs Paget, Mr and Mrs Crowe and, most of all, Major Palmer-Loach.'

'You've lost me, I'm afraid.'

'We've all been assuming that Dr Tindall has been telling the truth. He told the major that his family home was in Scotland. I passed on the parents' address to Chat. When he contacted the police in Aberdeen, he asked them to track down Mr and Mrs Tindall. They tried and failed.'

'Why?'

'It was a false address, Joe. If they're still alive – and I'm beginning to doubt even that now – they're not in Scotland.'

'Then where exactly are they?'

'God knows!'

'But I thought the major got the details from his official records.'

'They'll have to be amended.'

'How did Chat take the news?'

'He said that it was like being slapped in the face by a wet cod. I suppose that's appropriate for a fishing port like Aberdeen.'

'Wow!' said Keedy, dazed. 'You've taken the wind out of my sails.'

'Have I?'

'Yes, I thought I had big news to pass on, but it feels small now. If Tindall lied about his parents, he's obviously told a string of other lies as well.'

'What's your big news?'

'It's hardly worth telling.'

'You were grinning from ear to ear when you came in.'

'I can't even manage a smile now,' admitted Keedy. 'For what it's worth, here's what I found out. I went to Boyle and Stoddard, looked at the suits on display and realised I was in the wrong profession. Even as a superintendent, I could never afford the prices they charge.'

'Go on.'

'I went into the shop and was greeted by a man named Hugh Lucifer.'

Marmion gaped. 'Who?'

'Hugh Lucifer. Believe it or not, that was his name, and, in a strange way, it suited him. When I asked about Dr Tindall, he told me what a nice man he was and how he was regarded as a privileged customer.'

'That means he's spent a lot of money there.'

'When war broke out, Tindall stopped coming. Lucifer picked up a rumour that he'd gone to France to work in a

95

hospital there. Then one day last year, he walked in out of the blue and bought a new hat.'

'As news goes, Joe, this doesn't really qualify as "big".'

'I'm coming to the best bit.'

'Then let me hear it before I go to sleep out of boredom.'

'Tindall was living in that house in Edmonton, yet he gave an address on the south coast. Hugh Lucifer told me that that had been his permanent address for years. He assumed that Tindall was still based there.'

'Forgive my cynicism,' said Marmion. 'You did well to find that out. I believe that it could be significant news. The major told me that Tindall used to work at a hospital in Brighton.'

'He can't have two houses, can he?'

'I'm learning that anything is possible with him.'

'I've got the address but, unfortunately, not the telephone number. Tindall refused to give that.' Taking out his notebook, he flipped to a page, then showed it to Marmion. 'Hipwell Manor – sounds grand, doesn't it?'

'We'll have to find out,' said the other, getting to his feet.

Keedy was surprised. 'We're going there now?'

'Why not?'

'Don't you have to speak to Chat first?'

'No, he'll be too busy holding a press conference. He's hoping to give out copies of Dr Tindall's photograph so that it can appear in tomorrow's newspapers. It's time for us to show initiative.' He reached for his coat and hat. 'Come on, Joe. Let's be on our way,'

'But it's evening.'

Marmion grinned. 'Since when were you afraid of the dark?'

* * *

96

Ada Hobbes was in her kitchen, trying to cook herself a frugal meal. She felt rather queasy but told herself that she needed food inside her. While her sister's visit had cheered her up, Kathleen's departure had the opposite effect. Ada felt lonely and troubled. Though she had only known Dr Tindall for a short time, she had warmed to him. He had been so kind and considerate. To find his dead body in such a terrible state that morning had rocked her. As she recalled the horror, she closed her eyes tight. When she opened them again, she realised that the gas had gone out. Turning off the stove, she went across to the cupboard where she kept a supply of small change. After taking a shilling from the pot, she went into the front room and crouched down to put the coin into the meter. Gas began to flow again.

Ada then remembered something.

'That was a such a nasty thing to say,' protested Alice. 'She used to be a friend.'

'Paul put a stop to that friendship,' said Ellen.

'Mrs Redwood had no right to gloat.'

'It was upsetting, I must admit.'

'If I'd been there, I'd have given her a piece of my mind.'

Ellen gave a hollow laugh. 'Then I'm glad you weren't,' she said, 'or she'd have two reasons to get back at me – you and your brother.'

'Why did you bother to talk to her?'

'I had no choice. She just descended on me.'

Ellen had told her daughter about the bruising encounter with Patricia Redwood. Enraged by the woman's behaviour,

Alice had leapt to her mother's defence. She had an urge to go in search of Mrs Redwood.

'There's nothing you can do,' said Ellen. 'Besides, I can fight my own battles.'

'I felt sorry for Sally Redwood when we were at school together. She was so shy. The other girls teased her about her freckles and the boys called her rude names.'

'But none of them went to the lengths that Paul did. He not only drew a disgusting picture of her, he pinned it up on his dartboard and threw darts at it. I was ashamed of him.'

'Blame the war,' said Alice. 'It warped his mind.'

'It gave him a vicious streak, I know that. Sally was a nice enough girl and she had never done Paul any harm. Yet when she got that job at the jeweller's shop in the high street, he leered at her through the window. It gave her a real fright,' said Ellen. 'Her mother told me that Sally had difficulty sleeping.'

'It was wrong of Paul to stalk her. I accept that, Mummy. But it was also wrong of Sally's mother to crow over you.'

'Forget it. I have.'

'Then why did you mention it?' asked Alice. 'It's obviously preying on your mind. Mrs Redwood intended to hurt you and she did. I'm glad that Sally has found herself a boyfriend at last, but that doesn't give her mother the right to goad you about Paul. It's cruel.'

'It's also understandable.'

Alice was incensed. 'Whose side are you on – hers or Paul's?'

'Don't shout.'

'Then don't give me a reason,' said Alice. She took a few deep breaths before speaking. 'Let's get off the subject, shall we? As soon as I hear Mrs Redwood's name, I just want to—'

'That's enough,' said Ellen, interrupting firmly. 'I was hoping to enjoy some time alone with you. I've got so much more to tell you and I'm sure there are things you want to tell me. Promise me that you won't even mention Patricia Redwood again.' Alice glared mutinously. 'That's settled then.'

They burst out laughing and hugged each other.

Because they were anxious to get to Brighton, they got on the first train about to leave even though it was reserved for troops. Their status as detectives earned them a place in the middle of a mass of khaki uniforms. Marmion spoke to the soldiers packed into their compartment.

'Where are you going, lads?' he asked.

'We're orff to Paris to 'ave some fun,' replied a soldier with a cigarette in the corner of his mouth. 'Stand by, girls – we're on our way!'

'Don't listen to him,' said another. 'We're sailin' to Boulogne.'

'Where do you go from there?' said Keedy.

'They 'aven't told us but it'll be somewhere crawlin' with bleedin' Huns.'

'Watch out for mustard gas. That's what they're using now.'

'We know. We been practisin' with gas masks.'

'Where are you from?'

'Lambeth.'

'You don't look old enough to join the army,' said Marmion.

'Eighteen's old enough for anythin',' boasted the soldier. 'This time next year, I'll be sittin' back in Blighty, polishin' my medals. Before that, next summer, I'm gettin' married.'

'Don't bank on it, lad,' advised Marmion.

'I give Lil my word. Come 'ell or 'igh water, it'll 'appen some'ow.'

'I hope it does.'

Marmion spoke with more confidence than he felt. British casualties were still dauntingly high. Many of the soldiers on the train might add to the numbers of dead and wounded. Someone told a joke and there was ribald laughter. In the short time they had spent together in the army, they had obviously developed a sense of camaraderie. Marmion was reminded of Paul, going off with the same spirit and determination as the young men all round him.

For his part, Keedy had felt a pang at the mention of marriage. His own wedding would certainly go ahead in the new year, but he doubted very much if the youth seated opposite him would marry in the following summer. He was more likely to be killed, maimed or simply brutalised by the experience of warfare. Whatever happened, the cheeky grin would be wiped off his face.

'Why are you two goin' to Brighton, then?' asked someone.

'We plan to walk down to the beach,' replied Keedy, 'and dip our toes into the water. Then we split up and search for mermaids.'

The soldiers roared with laughter.

After addressing the press conference, Claude Chatfield went back to his office with a spring in his step. He felt that he had handled the various questions adroitly. The important thing was that he had been able to issue a copy of Tindall's photograph to each of the reporters. Before he could wallow in self-congratulation, he was joined by the commissioner.

'Good evening, Sir Edward,' he said.

'I just wanted a word, Superintendent.'

'Have as many as you wish.'

'I'm told that the press conference went well.'

'Did you have someone watching?'

'Yes,' said the other. 'I like to keep abreast of the latest developments. I'm glad that you were able to issue a photograph of the victim.'

'We need to thank our photographers for that, Sir Edward. They worked wonders. Because I impressed upon them how urgent it was, they managed to provide copies just in time. When I went to see how they were getting on, they also showed me the photos taken at the scene of the crime.'

'I made a point of looking at them myself. They were horrific. I also went out of my way to talk to the fingerprint expert who went to that house in Edmonton.'

'I thought you might, Sir Edward,' said Chatfield with a knowing smile. 'Fingerprints are your speciality.'

'They've proved their value time and again – but not in this case, I fear.'

'Why is that?'

'The killers were careful not to leave any. That means they had the sense to wear gloves. The fingerprints there belonged almost exclusively to Dr Tindall. They were able to take a set from him before he was cut open in the path lab.'

'I'm still waiting for the post-mortem report, Sir Edward.'

'The cause of death is all too apparent, alas,' said the other. 'Have you made any headway regarding the parents?'

Chatfield heaved a sigh. 'I'm afraid not.'

'Is there a problem?'

'Yes, there is – and it's a big one.'

He told the commissioner about his telephone call to the Aberdeen City Police and how they had established that Tindall's parents had not lived at the address given by their son. Indeed, they had no link whatsoever with the area.

Sir Edward was shocked. 'Can this be true?'

'The Aberdeen police were thorough.'

'But that means Dr Tindall deliberately misled everyone. What was the purpose of doing that?'

'The honest answer is that we don't know.'

'I have to say that the doctor's behaviour beggars belief. What was he hiding?'

'Whatever it is, Sir Edward, we'll find out.'

'Does the inspector have any theories?'

'He's usually prone to have too many of them,' said Chatfield, grimacing. 'In this instance, he's stumped.'

'Oh dear!'

'Wait until that photograph appears in the newspapers tomorrow. It is bound to be seen by one or more of Tindall's relatives.'

'Let's hope so,' said the commissioner. 'What is Marmion doing meanwhile?'

'I was just about to find out, Sir Edward, but you came into my office before I could do so.' He crossed to his desk. 'If he leaves Scotland Yard, he always tells me exactly where he's going. Here we are,' he said, picking up an envelope. 'I recognise his handwriting.'

Opening the envelope, Chatfield took out a sheet of paper. When he read the short message, he blenched.

'What's the trouble?' asked the commissioner.

'Inspector Marmion and Sergeant Keedy have gone to Brighton.'

'Did you authorise that?'

'I most certainly did not.'

'They must have a good reason for doing so.'

'It's a pity they didn't tell me what it was,' said Chatfield, ruefully.

'Let me know what they find, Superintendent. The inspector always comes back with some new evidence. He has an uncanny gift for sniffing it out.'

Since they could not discuss the case in a crowded compartment, the detectives sat back and listened to the soldiers who, at one point, broke into a toneless rendition of 'It's a Long Way to Tipperary'. What it lacked in harmony, however, it made up for in sheer gusto. Marmion had heard it sung by Irish soldiers who had brought out the full pathos in the lyrics. It had a defiant note here, sung by young men to keep up their spirits and conceal their fears. Listening to their companions helped the detectives to defeat time. They seemed to reach their destination far sooner than they expected.

When they arrived at Brighton railway station, they let the soldiers get out first and line up with the other members of their regiment. Only then did Marmion and Keedy step out onto the platform.

'We came too late, Joe,' said the inspector.

'I thought we were too early,' said Keedy. 'I've never known a train journey go so quick.'

'I was not talking about that. I was thinking about the early days of the war when a train or a convoy of lorries brought soldiers to Brighton. They would have been given a rousing welcome by a big crowd. The chief constable would have been here with the mayor and the local worthies. There might even have been a brass band. They were greeted as heroes.'

'They weren't greeted as heroes on the battlefield,' said Keedy, pursing his lips. 'I remember what Paul told me. It was a living hell over there.'

'We need a taxi.'

'Where do we go first – hospital or Hipwell Manor?'

'We'll go to the house first. That's where Dr Tindall used to live.'

'Do you want to bet on that?' teased Keedy.

Marmion grinned. 'I'm not that stupid, Joe.'

After picking their way past the soldiers, they found the taxi rank and climbed into a waiting car. The driver told them that their destination was over ten miles away. On their way there, he felt obliged to give them a potted history of life in Brighton since the war had begun. Keedy pulled a face and stopped listening to him, but Marmion was fascinated by what the man was saying.

Situated on the south coast, Brighton was not a regular target from the air or from the sea. If the Germans did try to invade, it was felt, they were more likely to approach the east of the country. Along with London, that was the major target for bombing raids. Since it had a marked degree of safety, Brighton was still a popular seaside resort during warmer months. Thousands of people, the driver boasted, poured in for

Easter and summer holidays. While it was certainly not a case of life as usual, the town was still able to operate as a magnet for pleasure-seekers.

'Our beach is the best in Britain,' claimed the man. 'You can go bathing, fishing or boating there. There's tennis for the younger visitors and bowls for the older ones. Our shops are as good as any in Oxford Street, and we have theatres and such like what do a roaring trade. This is the place to be, gents.'

His monologue took them all the way to Hipwell Manor. Marmion asked the taxi driver to wait for them. It was dark now and there was no light showing from the house because of the blackout. All they could see was a fuzzy outline of a Tudor farmhouse.

'Are you sure we've got the right place?' asked Keedy, doubtfully.

'Let's find out.'

Marmion went to the front door and pulled the bell rope. A curtain was tugged back, allowing a shaft of light to cut across them. It disappeared almost immediately. Moments later, the door opened to reveal a manservant. In the subdued light, they could hardly see his face, but his voice suggested age and gravitas.

'Yes?' he asked.

Marmion introduced them and asked if a George Tindall had lived there.

'I'm afraid not, Inspector.'

'He's an orthopaedic surgeon.'

'The house is owned by Captain Langford. He's away at sea at the moment but his wife and daughter are here. Would you like to speak to Mrs Langford?'

'We certainly would.'

The servant stood back so that they could enter the dimly lit hall. They were able to see that he was a short, round-shouldered man in his sixties with a quiet dignity about him. As he closed the front door, the one to the lounge opened and a woman popped her head out.

'Who is it, Pearson?' she asked.

'These gentlemen are detectives from London, Mrs Langford,' he told her.

She was irritated. 'Why have they come here? We're scrupulously careful about maintaining a blackout.'

Marmion introduced himself and Keedy, then asked if they could have a private word with her. She conducted them into the lounge, a large, characterful, half-timbered room with a low ceiling that warned them to duck under the beams. A log fire was crackling in the grate. There was a piano in one corner. After sizing them up, she waved them to a seat. Hats in hands, they sat together on the sofa.

'What is this all about?' she asked, taking an armchair opposite.

Caroline Langford was a tall, shapely woman in her late thirties with a sense of breeding about her. While Marmion admired her cheekbones, Keedy was struck by the quality of the jewellery she was wearing. She was patently annoyed at the intrusion and spoke with a slight edge to her voice.

'Well?' she prompted.

'The sergeant and I are leading a murder investigation,' explained Marmion.

She was taken aback. 'Really?'

'The victim was a George Tindall – Doctor George Tindall.'

'What has that got to do with me, may I ask?'

'We understood that he had some connection with this house.'

'Then I'm sorry but you've been misinformed. Who gave you this address?'

'It was a tailor in Savile Row,' replied Keedy. 'Dr Tindall had his suits made there. We knew that he once worked at a hospital in Brighton and wondered if he'd perhaps kept this house and rented it out.'

'I beg your pardon!' she said, clearly offended. 'Hipwell Manor has belonged to my family for generations. We would never rent it out to strangers, Sergeant.'

'I understand that your husband is in the navy,' said Marmion.

'That is correct. Michael is in command of a destroyer.'

'Where exactly is he at this moment, Mrs Langford?'

'Really, Inspector,' she replied. 'Shame on you for asking such a question. For obvious reasons, deployment of our navy is a matter of secrecy. I have no idea where my husband is and, even if I did, I would never tell you.'

'How long have you and Captain Langford been married?'

'What relevance can that possibly have to your investigation?'

'None at all,' he conceded.

'Then I need detain you no longer,' she said, rising to her feet. 'You have clearly made a ghastly mistake in coming here.'

'I blame Hugh Lucifer for that,' said Keedy under his breath.

'We are sorry to have disturbed you unnecessarily,' said Marmion, getting up from the sofa. 'Before we go, however, might I ask a favour?'

'What is it?' she asked, warily.

'Might we see a photograph of your husband?'

She bridled. 'Why on earth should you want to do that?'

'I'd be interested, that's all.'

'So would I,' added Keedy, standing up.

'Well,' she said, haughtily, 'I take exception to that request. Are you in the habit of invading people's privacy and asking to see family photographs? This really is intolerable. May I ask the name of your superior?'

'It's Superintendent Chatfield,' said Marmion.

'I'll need the address,' she said, crossing to a bureau and taking a notepad and pencil out of the top drawer. 'I'm ready, Inspector.'

Feeling chastened, Marmion gave her the full address. If she complained about their behaviour, there would be repercussions at Scotland Yard. He was already fearing the superintendent's reaction to the fact that they had returned empty-handed from Brighton. A letter from Mrs Langford would give Chatfield even more reason to berate them.

Once she had the details she requested, her manner softened slightly.

'I refuse to show you any photographs of myself and my husband,' she said, 'because they are private. But, if you must see what he looks like, I'll show you this one.' She took a framed photograph from the top of the piano. 'This appeared in one of the local newspapers.' She handed it to Marmion. 'My husband is the one in the captain's uniform.'

They looked at the photograph. It showed a group of men on the deck of a ship. Marmion picked out Captain Langford at once. He was a big, broad-shouldered man with a full beard. His upright stance gave him an air of authority.

'Are you satisfied now?' she asked, extending a hand.

'Yes, we are, Mrs Langford,' said Marmion, returning the photograph. 'I apologise for our mistake in coming here. We'll trespass on you no longer.'

After mumbling their goodbyes, he and Keedy left the house. As they got into the back of the waiting taxi, Marmion held up repentant hands.

'Yes, I know,' he said. 'It was my idea to come here.'

'Does that mean you'll take all the punishment from Chat?'

'No, it doesn't because I'm hoping we'll have more luck at the hospital. We know for certain that Tindall lived and worked down here in Sussex. He's bound to have left large footprints. Let's find them.'

CHAPTER EIGHT

Evenings were short for Ada Hobbes. Instead of being able to linger beside the fire and do some more knitting, she had to be in bed early so that she had a decent night's sleep before leaving the house at four the next morning. Her sister, Kathleen, had advised her to take a day off but Ada felt duty-bound to keep to her routine. In any case, if she failed to turn up, offices would not be cleaned and those who worked there would be justifiably livid. She winced at the thought that her name would be taken in vain. Her job was at stake and, since she relied on the money, she simply had to abide by her contract. Finding similar work elsewhere would be difficult for her. There was a great deal of competition, especially from younger women who would have more appeal to employers because they appeared stronger.

The fire had dwindled to a few glowing ashes, but she nevertheless put the fireguard in place. Ada slowly got herself ready for bed, shivering in the cold as she took off her clothes and put on her nightdress. Climbing into bed, she huddled under the sheets. At the end of a tiring day, she usually fell asleep quickly but there was no hope of her doing that now. The memory of what she had seen in Dr Tindall's house was still too fresh and painful. Ada believed that it would stay at the forefront of her mind until the police caught whoever was responsible for the crime.

She recalled the moment when she had fed a shilling in the gas meter. It had triggered a memory of something that might – just might, she prayed – be of some use to the police. Did she dare pass it on? Ada was unsure if she had the courage to do so. It was such a trivial incident that it should perhaps be best forgotten. The last thing she wanted to do was to invite Sergeant Keedy's scorn. He had been good to her, treating her gently and sending her home in the police car. If she bothered him with useless information, he might be less tolerant. The impulse she had felt beside the gas stove had to be suppressed and forgotten. Ada decided that she would need all her strength to fight off her demons in the night.

The reporters who swooped on Edmonton Military Hospital found little to fill their columns. Major Palmer-Loach gave them short shrift. He treated them with brisk politeness but refused to speculate on the possible motives behind the murder of one of his surgeons. When they tried to apply pressure on him, he strolled across to the door and held it open.

'A war is on,' he told them. 'Look in any of my wards and you'll see the results of it. Those wounded soldiers out there are my primary concern. If you have any more questions about Dr Tindall, please address them to Inspector Marmion.' He raised his voice. 'Good day to you, gentlemen.'

They trooped out resentfully. Neil Irvine watched them go. When the door had been closed behind them, he turned to Palmer-Loach.

'That was masterly, Howard.'

'Thank you.'

'You gave absolutely nothing away.'

'Inspector Marmion warned me to be economical with the facts.'

'You followed his advice to the letter.'

Irvine was a senior doctor in the hospital's medical team. He was a thin, dark, gangly man in his forties with a Scots accent. He was also Palmer-Loach's best friend. When alone together, they were completely at ease with each other.

'Out with it,' said Irvine, jocularly.

'Out with what?'

'Come on, Howard. I've known you long enough to be able to read the expression on your face. You hid something important from those reporters. Are you proposing to hide it from me as well?'

'No, of course not – I can trust you.'

'I'm all ears.'

The major told him about Marmion's telephone call regarding the futile search for Tindall's parents. They were not, after all, living at the address provided and they had never done so. Palmer-Loach was fuming.

'He had the gall to mislead us,' he said.

'Perhaps he had a good reason to do so,' suggested the other. 'Some of us are ashamed of our parents or have fallen out with them. I was guilty of both. When I decided to live and work in England, they accused me of betraying my country. In fact, I just wanted to put distance between me and them.'

'The inspector wonders if Tindall was a true Scot.'

'Oh, there's no doubt about that.'

'Why do you say that?'

'Because we once had a row about football,' said Irvine. 'I'm a Glaswegian and my loyalty is to Rangers. Tindall was a diehard Celtic fan. He was born within a mile of their ground.'

'If you're both from the same city, why don't you have the same accent?'

'I fancy that snobbery comes into it somehow, Howard. When I moved to England, I emphasised my accent – George did his best to lose his. He wanted to fit in. I chose a Scots wife, and he married an Englishwoman.' His eyes twinkled. 'That's when the rot set in.'

'I'll ignore that jibe,' said the major, good-naturedly. 'I'm just annoyed with myself for trusting the man.'

'What you trusted were his surgical skills and they were real. It's why you took him on in the first place, Howard.'

'True. He was exactly what we needed at the time.'

'Remember that,' said Irvine. 'Let these detectives explore his private life. You have other priorities.'

'I do, Neil,' said the other, seriously. 'To start with, I've got the job of replacing him with someone of equivalent ability. That's one heck of a challenge.'

* * *

When he was told which hospital they wanted, the taxi driver seized the opportunity to acquaint them with the various options available to them.

'Are you sure it's the Royal Sussex?' he asked.

'Yes,' said Marmion.

'The Kitchener Indian Hospital is more interesting. They have over two thousand beds in there. When the first load of wounded soldiers from the Indian regiments were shipped back to Brighton, there were big crowds at the dock to give them a welcome. Sir William Gentle was there in person.'

'Who is he?'

'He's the chief constable.'

'Do we need to be told all this?' complained Keedy.

'You're detectives, aren't you?' retorted the driver. 'Gathering facts is what you do, sir. It's the reason I'm giving them to you. Brighton is a town of hospitals, you see. The Royal Pavilion, the Dome and the Corn Exchange have all been turned into hospitals and so have other places. Then, of course, there's the French Convalescent Home. Don't forget that.'

The driver rambled on, unaware of the fact that neither of his passengers was listening. When they reached their hospital of choice, Marmion paid the fare and the two of them got out of the vehicle. The Royal Sussex County Hospital had been founded almost ninety years earlier and grown steadily ever since, becoming an accretion of buildings of varying shapes and sizes. Seen in silhouette against a dark sky, it looked rather forbidding. Marmion and Keedy headed for the main entrance.

'I'm beginning to wish we hadn't come here,' said Keedy.

'Don't be such a pessimist, Joe.'

'Why did Tindall give everyone a fake address in Brighton?'

'It wasn't fake,' said Marmion. 'It was all too real. Unfortunately, Dr Tindall never actually lived there. So why pretend that he had? It's near the top of the list of questions for which I want answers.'

'We're groping in the dark.'

'No, we're not.' When they reached the main door, Marmion opened it and light flooded out. 'There you are,' he said with a chuckle. 'Things are starting to brighten up already.'

Ellen Marmion had been relishing her daughter's visit so much that she had allowed something important to slip her mind. When she finally remembered what it was, she sat up guiltily on the sofa.

'Oh,' she said, 'I forgot something. Mrs Halliday is ready for you.'

'There's no great hurry, Mummy. We have weeks and weeks yet.'

'Making a wedding dress takes time, Alice. She must take measurements. Then you must choose the material. After that, there'll be a series of fittings.'

'I'll see Mrs Halliday next time I'm here.'

'And when will that be?'

'I don't know,' said Alice.

'You can't muck Minnie Halliday about,' warned her mother. 'You're not the only one on her list, remember. There will be quite a few weddings coming up in the new year. You need to see her soon. On the other hand,' she added with a grin, 'perhaps you want to order your dress from somewhere in the West End.'

Alice spluttered. 'How on earth would I pay for it?'

'You wouldn't. That's why we asked Minnie Halliday to make it.'

'Don't keep on at me. I know that I've been dragging my feet and I'm sorry. What about one day next week?' she said, mentally consulting her diary. 'I finish early on Thursday.'

Ellen was content. 'Let's settle for that, then. I'll tell her.' Her face clouded. 'There's still the thorny problem of Paul to consider.'

'He won't turn up, Mummy.'

'He might.'

'But he has no idea of the date of the wedding,' said Alice, 'and even if he did, he'd never dream of coming.'

'Just in case he does . . .'

'No, I won't even think about it.'

'I'm simply looking ahead, Alice.'

'Well, please don't bother.'

'It was your father's idea. He wants to cover every possibility.'

'Paul ignored our birthdays and didn't even bother to send a Christmas card. What else does he have to do to prove that he's left for good?'

Ellen bit her lip. 'You never know . . .'

'I do know, Mummy, and so do you in your heart. We should accept the truth. You no longer have a son, and I don't have a brother. In fact, I'm doing my best to pretend that he never existed.'

Wells was a cathedral city in the heart of Somerset. Reputedly the smallest city in England, it had a plethora of historic buildings, a bewitching charm and an air of tranquillity. During the day, it functioned in the same unhurried way it had done for centuries. Once engulfed by evening shadows, however, it obeyed the rules, dousing its lights and closing its curtains. Most people stayed in their houses or cottages, but a group of regulars could always be found at the City Arms in the high street. Seated around a blazing log fire, the men would talk endlessly about the progress of the war, breaking off from time to time to complain once more that their beer and cider had been watered by government decree.

That evening, it was different. There was a stranger in the bar. He was a stocky young man with a face half-hidden behind a ragged beard. Arriving in Wells on foot, he had come into the pub, dropped his haversack on to a settle and ordered a pint of cider. He had ignored the muttered welcomes of the regulars and sat down with his tankard held firm. In less than ten minutes, he had emptied it and put it on the table with a thud. Shortly after that, he had fallen asleep. Complaints soon surfaced. The newcomer had brought a stink into the pub. Dressed in tattered clothes, he looked like a tramp who had only come in to get warm. Worst of all, he was an interloper, disturbing the usual flow of conversation.

At length, the landlord was forced to act. He shook the young man's shoulder.

'Wake up, sir,' he said.

'Eh?' grunted the other, stirring. 'What's up?'

'If you've finished drinking, sir, it's time to go.'

'Piss off!'

'I'm asking you nicely,' said the landlord, injecting a note of warning. 'If you want to sleep, you'll have to pay for a room.'

But the words went unheard. The stranger had nodded off again. There was a barrage of protests from the regulars. The landlord waved them into silence.

'Leave him be,' he said. 'This is a job for the police.'

Their visit to the Royal Sussex County Hospital was productive. Its administrator was Cecil Wetherbridge, a stringy man of middle years with a straight back and close-cropped fair hair. His voice had a military authority to it. When he heard why the detectives had come, he was anxious to help. He pulled a file out of the cabinet and handed it over. As a result, Marmion and Keedy discovered that George Douglas Tindall had been born in Glasgow then educated privately in Edinburgh before going on to study medicine at St Thomas's Hospital in London. He had then moved on to a hospital in Kent and, when he had gained enough experience as a doctor, had set his sights on becoming a surgeon.

'His progress was quick and well deserved,' said Wetherbridge. 'By the time he came here, he'd worked at three other hospitals. Before the war broke out, he had become an orthopaedic surgeon but, as soon as wounded soldiers poured in here in large numbers, he had to turn his hand to anything.'

'How well did you know him?' asked Marmion.

'Not very well at all,' replied the other. 'I came here early in 1915 and he left a few months after that.' He grinned. 'I like to think that the two events were unrelated. In fact, we got on extremely well and I was sorry to lose him. But he had this urge to work in a hospital at the front and deal with casualties in need of immediate surgery.'

'He came back after six months or so, didn't he?'

'Yes, Inspector.'

'Why was that?'

'Personal reasons,' said Wetherbridge. 'His wife had been ailing for some time and began to go downhill rather fast. Dr Tindall took time off to nurse her.'

'Did you ever meet her?' asked Keedy.

'No, I didn't. When you work flat out during a crisis, you have little time for a social life. I have enough trouble meeting my own wife, let alone someone else's.'

'When he did work here, where did he live?'

'Didn't you see an address in the file?'

'Yes, but it's a flat here in the town.'

'We thought that he had a house closer to Worthing,' said Marmion.

'That's news to me, Inspector,' said Wetherbridge.

'When we called there earlier, we were told that they had never heard of Dr Tindall. Why should he provide false information like that?'

'It's uncharacteristic of him.'

'What about the flat?' asked Keedy. 'Are you sure that he lived there?'

'Oh, yes. I went there once. It was not all that far away and very comfortable. Dr Tindall had high standards.'

'We know. We saw his house in Edmonton.'

'It's odd,' said Marmion, leafing through the file. 'There's no mention of a house in this area. Where was his wife living at that time?'

'He mentioned a property in Kent on one occasion,' recalled Wetherbridge, 'but I fancy that it might have belonged to his wife's parents. They looked after her while he was away.'

'It would be useful to have that address. There are far too many loose ends in this case,' Marmion told him, handing back the file.

'We need to speak to a family member of some description,' added Keedy. 'At the moment, it seems, we're chasing shadows.'

Though she had seen it many times, Alice was always pleased to study the wedding photographs in the family album. Her parents looked impossibly young as they stood in the church porch. The bridegroom wore his best suit while the bride was in her wedding dress. Seated beside her mother, Alice picked out a detail.

'Your hair was much darker then, Mummy.'

'It was the same colour as yours.'

'I just wish that Daddy could have looked a bit smarter.'

'He wasn't your father at that point,' Ellen pointed out, 'and I loved him for his kindness and his crinkly eyes, not for the way he wore his clothes. Whenever he puts on a suit, it always manages to look crumpled somehow.'

'Why were there so few people at the service?'

'It was all we could afford, Alice. Times were hard for people like us. My father had scrimped and saved to pay for everything.'

'Well, that's not something Daddy will have to do on his own. Joe and I are insisting on making our contribution, whatever he may say.'

'You may have a job getting your father to accept it.'

'We've made up our minds.'

'So has he.'

Alice flipped over the pages until she came to a sequence of photographs of herself and her brother as toddlers. She stopped to scrutinise a snap of the two of them, standing on a sandy beach and wearing sun hats.

'Did we really look like that?' she wondered.

'Yes, you were angelic at that age.'

Alice laughed. 'Nobody would say that about me now.'

'You were such a biddable child.'

'What about Paul?'

'He behaved himself most of the time. In fact, he could be quite placid. He's a picture of innocence in this photo,' said Ellen, studying it. 'You'd never think that he'd turn out the way that he did.'

It took three of them to overpower him. In response to the landlord's summons, Constable Pellew, a brawny man in his thirties, was sent to the City Arms. Grabbing the shoulder of the sleeping customer, he shook him rudely awake.

'Wake up, sir,' he shouted. 'Time to go.'

'Get off me!' yelled the other, rising to his feet and pushing him away. 'I'm not going anywhere.'

'Oh, yes, you are,' said Pellew, grabbing him by the collar.

'Let go!'

'You're coming with me. sir.'

'Take your hands off me, you fat bastard!'

'I'm placing you under arrest.'

The young man picked up the glass tankard and swung it at him. Pellew moved his head quickly out of the way, but he still had to take a glancing blow on his cheek that ripped the skin away. It made him release his hold immediately.

'Who's next?' challenged the stranger, brandishing the tankard.

'Put it down,' ordered the landlord, waving a fist.

'Make me.'

Blood was trickling down the side of Pellew's cheek, but he did not back off. Instead, he got behind the young man and put an arm around his neck. It was the signal for the landlord to move in, grab the tankard and twist it out of the customer's hand. In return, he was given a sharp kick in the leg. The young man went berserk, pummelling the policeman with his elbows to get free, then swinging punches at random. There was uproar. Pellew and the landlord got hold of him again, then a third man joined in. Their quarry was held but by no means subdued. The moment that the policeman tried to reach for his handcuffs, the stranger fought like mad, kicking over a table and sending half-full tankards crashing to the floor. He was cursing at the top of his voice and spitting at anyone who came within range.

Constable Pellew had had enough. Taking out his truncheon, he felled him with one blow to the head. As the troublemaker slumped to the ground, the policeman turned to the landlord.

'When I've locked this maniac up,' he said, 'I'll be back for a free pint.'

Neither Marmion nor Keedy could stop yawning. The train to London stopped at almost every station on the way. The one benefit was that they had an empty compartment in which to discuss what they would tell the superintendent.

'He'll crucify us,' said Keedy.

'Chat is not that vindictive.'

'We've wasted time and money on a jaunt to the seaside.'

'I see it differently,' said Marmion, trying to raise his own spirits as well as those of his companion. 'It was a valuable fact-finding mission. We learnt things about Dr Tindall that we'd never have got from anywhere else.'

'All we learnt is that he was a compulsive liar who gave people the addresses of houses where he didn't actually live.'

'He lived in the flat in Brighton. We verified that. When we called there, the people who now own it said they bought it from him. Tindall was capable of honesty sometimes.'

'What did you think of it?'

'I was rather envious, Joe.'

'So was I,' said Keedy. 'It's the sort of place Alice and I would love to move into. There was so much space. Why did Tindall need a place of that size?'

'I can't answer that.'

'What puzzles me is the information in that file. Why didn't you get the same details at the hospital in Edmonton?'

'When the major searched for an orthopaedic surgeon, he got an application from Tindall, complete with wonderful references from two hospitals. The major took him on trust and never regretted it.'

'He's regretting it now.'

'Like us, he's learning about Tindall's defects.'

'He didn't just tell lies, he told whoppers.'

'Somehow he got away with it.'

'And what made him claim he owned Hipwell Manor?'

'It's too late to ask him.'

The train slowed, then came to a sudden halt, jerking them both forward.

'We should have come by car,' said Keedy.

'We'd have missed the fun of being with those soldiers on the way there. They were brave lads.'

'Yes, but only because they don't know what they'll find over there.'

'It'll change their lives for ever.'

'That's what it did for Paul.'

'Keep him out of this, Joe,' said Marmion, seriously. 'There are times when I can't bear thinking about him. Concentrate on the pleasure of our return to Scotland Yard. I bet that Chat is pacing up and down his office right now, wondering where his favourite detectives have gone.'

Badgered by the commissioner, Claude Chatfield was, in fact, standing behind his desk, trying to persuade his superior that headway had been made. Sir Edward Henry was not convinced. He needed hard evidence to appease the War Office. Dr Tindall had been an asset to the army. He had saved many lives and made many others more bearable thanks to his surgical expertise. Whoever had killed him had to be called to account.

'What did they find out in Brighton?' asked the commissioner.

'They have yet to return, Sir Edward.'

'They might have telephoned you.'

'They might indeed,' said Chatfield with a low growl. 'I intend to ask them why it never crossed their minds.'

'I'll be here until late.'

'So will I.'

'Then I expect to hear from you in due course.'

'Once I have their report, I'll come straight to your office.'

The commissioner took his leave and Chatfield was alone at last. He hated being put under pressure. Though he felt unfairly criticised, he had things to do. Instead of fretting about the murder investigation, he addressed his mind to the mass of paperwork on his desk. Since he had responsibility for other cases, there was a great deal to process. He was soon beavering away.

Constable Pellew did not stand on ceremony. With the help of the landlord, he dragged the semi-conscious stranger to the police station. Still in handcuffs, the prisoner was thrown into a cell. Sergeant Dear, the duty officer, looked at his colleague.

'You've got a bruise on your cheek,' he noted, 'and a spot of blood.'

'He caught me with a beer tankard,' said Pellew.

'It was my fault,' volunteered the landlord. 'I should have refused to serve him. I could see that he might cause trouble.'

'He fought like a demon. I had to use my staff in the end. When he wakes up, he'll have a lovely big lump on the back of his head.'

'Who is he?' asked Dear.

'You'll have to look in here, Sarge.'

Pellew handed over the prisoner's haversack and Dear began to take out the meagre belongings inside it. Among a motley collection of items was a long knife.

'You were lucky, Dave,' he said. 'He might have pulled this on you.'

'We'll have a lot to charge him with,' said Pellew. 'And if he turns out to be a deserter from the army, he'll be sentenced to death.'

The landlord nodded. 'It's no more than he deserves.'

'He was arrested in the right place,' observed Dear. 'The City Arms used to be the gaol in the old days. Pity you don't still have cells there.'

When he listened to their report, the superintendent's expression changed from one of exasperation to one of sheer incredulity. By the time that Marmion had finished his account, Chatfield was agog.

'Is that all you achieved?' he asked.

'We believe that we uncovered new and valuable intelligence, sir.'

'I agree,' said Keedy. 'Going to Brighton was a wise decision.'

'Let me deal with your mistake first, Sergeant' said Chatfield. 'You charged off – without asking my permission – simply because you'd picked up some bogus information from a tailor in Savile Row.'

'It didn't sound bogus, sir.'

'Let me finish, Sergeant.'

'That was the address Dr Tindall had given them.'

'Did it never occur to you that there was a much easier means of finding out the correct address? All you had to do was to ask the tailor for the name of the doctor's bank. It would have been simple for him to tell you from which bank the cheques were drawn. Even someone as slippery as Tindall,' he argued, 'would have to be honest with his bank manager.'

'I did ask for his bank details,' said Keedy, 'but he always paid in cash.'

Chatfield looked glum. 'Oh, I see.'

'The sergeant did well,' said Marmion, 'and our visit to Brighton did yield results. The background information we found about the murder victim was far more comprehensive than anything the Edmonton Military Hospital could supply. In fact,' he went on, 'we learnt something that may prove to be highly relevant.'

'What was it, Inspector?'

'He had private wealth, sir. He could indulge his taste in expensive clothing and in other things. That confirms what Major Palmer-Loach told me about him. Tindall was fully committed as a doctor. Most people as well off as him would be tempted to seek a more pampered and independent life.'

'We're dealing with a very unusual man,' said Keedy.

'I had the commissioner in here earlier,' Chatfield told them. 'He thinks you should spend less time on the doctor and much more on the people who killed him. So far you have yet to uncover a motive for his murder.'

'The inspector just gave you one, sir. Dr Tindall was a wealthy man.'

'That's right,' said Marmion. 'His safe had been emptied.'

'You told me earlier in the day that the theft was incidental,' Chatfield reminded him. 'Their primary purpose was a vicious murder.'

'I was only speculating.'

'Then perhaps you'd omit any further speculation and concentrate on the search for those villains. Thieves would have watched and waited, choosing a time to break into the house when it was unoccupied. These men came for blood.'

'We had reached the same conclusion,' said Marmion.

'Then let us forget about wasteful visits to Brighton, shall we?' said Chatfield. 'Or to any other addresses that may lead you astray.' He checked his watch. 'It's almost midnight. That means the pair of you have been involved in this investigation for somewhere in the region of sixteen hours.'

'Don't worry,' said Keedy. 'We'll apply for overtime.'

'Spare me your flippancy, Sergeant.'

'What I meant was that time is immaterial on a case like this. The inspector and I will work until the cows come home.'

'I'd prefer you to work until you get positive results.'

'We will, Inspector,' said Marmion. 'This case intrigues us.'

'Well, it's proving to be a flaming nuisance to me,' said Chatfield. 'I've got the combined weight of the commissioner and the War Office on my back – and I don't like it! Get them off!'

CHAPTER NINE

Though Alice Marmion woke early the next day, she was too late to catch sight of her father. He had been up over an hour before her and left the house the moment he had finished his breakfast. Marmion had asked Ellen to pass on his apologies to his daughter for not being able to spend time with her.

'When did Daddy come home?' asked Alice.

'It was past midnight. That's all I know.'

'Joe was right. It's a case that will take up all their time.'

'It pushes everything else aside,' said Ellen.

'Did you never have qualms about marrying a policeman?'

'Yes, but they were never about him working long hours.

I was afraid that he might get seriously hurt. His own father was killed while on duty, remember. Anyone who tries to police a city like this is putting himself in danger. When he was in uniform, I was terrified that your father would be injured.'

'Daddy can look after himself. Besides, he was never on patrol alone.'

'That didn't stop me worrying, Alice.'

'The irony is that the streets are much safer now. Thanks to the war, many of the worst criminals in London joined the army and went abroad. Unfortunately,' she added, 'so did a lot of young police officers. I'm glad Joe was not among them.'

'He and your father went to Brighton yesterday.'

'Why?'

'He didn't have time to tell me. Anyway,' said Ellen, 'let's forget about them and think about your trip to the West End.'

Alice shuddered. 'I'm dreading it.'

'Once you're there, I'm sure you'll enjoy it.'

'Oh, I'll enjoy being part of a crowd and looking in shop windows. I always love that part. But I'd love it even more if I was not saddled with Iris.'

'It was your idea, Alice.'

'Yes, I know and I'm still glad that the invitation gave her so much pleasure. It's just that she will be expecting to get far too much out of today.'

'And you're expecting to get too little.'

'I'm afraid so.' Alice looked at the clock on the mantelpiece. 'Oh, I must be off,' she said, rising from her chair.

'I'll come with you to the bus stop,' said Ellen, getting up.

'In that case, we can take the long way there.'

'Why should we do that?'

'Because we'll go right past Mrs Redwood's house,' said Alice, thrusting out her chin. 'If we bump into her, I'll have a few choice words to say.'

'Don't be ridiculous.'

'I'm not having her upsetting you, Mummy.'

'It was nothing.'

'Oh, yes it was. I know when you've been wounded.'

'I've got over it now.'

'Mrs Redwood needled you about Paul.'

'So what?'

'It must have hurt you, Mummy.'

'It did – and it didn't.'

'I don't understand.'

'Then you've obviously forgotten what you told me yesterday,' said Ellen. 'You don't have a brother named Paul any more, and I don't have a son of the same name. He vanished into thin air. No matter what Mrs Redwood says about him, it will not hurt me. Come on,' she said, giving Alice a hug. 'We'll go the shorter way to the bus stop.'

When he arrived at the police station in Wells, Constable Pellew found that Sergeant Dear was already there. The latter looked up from the pile of papers on his desk and they exchanged greetings. The sergeant noticed the purple bruise on the newcomer's face and the sticking plaster over part of it. Pellew nodded towards the cells.

'How did he behave last night?'

'He didn't. I'm told that he yelled his head off.'

'Who was on duty?'

'Constable Myler.'

'Frank Myler wouldn't stand for any nonsense.'

'You're right,' said Dear. 'He tried being reasonable but that didn't work so he threatened him. The prisoner gave him a real mouthful. Frank was not standing for that. He gave him another tap and knocked him out. That shut his gob.'

'What's the prisoner doing now?'

'He's fast asleep on his bed. I'm just checking through these lists,' said the sergeant, indicating the papers in front of him. 'I'm starting with army deserters. If he's not on any of these – and my guess is that he will be – then I'll have a go at the list of missing persons.'

'Why bother, Sarge?'

'It's my job.'

'You've seen the way he behaves,' said Pellew. 'He's wild and dangerous. Who would want someone like him back in their family? They'd be glad that the maniac had left home.'

After reporting to the superintendent, Marmion and Keedy were driven to the house once more. They were pleased to see a uniformed policeman on duty outside the front door. Letting themselves in with the key, they went slowly from room to room, searching for clues they might have missed on the previous day.

'Someone ought to clear up that mess in the room off the kitchen,' said Keedy. 'It will never sell if it's left in that state.'

'Does that mean you're interested in buying it, Joe?'

Keedy laughed mirthlessly. 'Oh, yes, I'll put in an offer tomorrow.'

'Then you must be on a better rate of pay than me.'

'What me and Alice want is a terraced house with a small garden at the back. The trouble is that we never have a chance to search for it together.'

'Look in the windows of estate agents.'

'They only shove the prices up so that they can get a good commission. We'd prefer a private sale. That means looking at adverts in the paper. That way we'd be dealing with the owner of a property and not a pushy estate agent.'

'Take Alice with you. She's good at haggling.'

'Chance would be a fine thing, Harv.'

'Then let's try to put this case to bed as quickly as we can,' said Marmion. 'The pair of you can then go house-hunting properly.'

They went upstairs and into the master bedroom. Keedy was thoughtful.

'He must have been asleep in here when they got into the house,' he said.

'How? The doors were securely locked.'

'Your guess is as good as mine.'

'Then let me try this idea,' suggested Marmion. 'Suppose that they didn't break in at all.'

'How else could they have got in?'

'There's one obvious way.'

'What is it?'

'Dr Tindall may have invited them in.'

'That's a barmy idea,' said Keedy.

'Is it? The major told me that Tindall sometimes worked at night. Suppose that there was an emergency and they needed him. What would they do?'

'Well, I daresay that they'd ring him up.'

'How would he get to the hospital?'

'How did he get there when he was still alive?'

'They must have sent transport.'

'A taxi, do you mean?'

'Well, they'd hardly send an ambulance, would they?' said Marmion. 'You must have noticed the motorbikes at the hospital. They came in and out all the time.'

'Yes,' said Keedy, 'but they were driven by soldiers.'

'All you need is a khaki uniform, and you'd look just like a soldier.'

'I suppose that's true.'

'A motorbike can carry two people. Perhaps that was how Tindall expected to get to the hospital.'

'Wait a moment,' said Keedy. 'Neither of the motorbikes came into this avenue. They were parked around the corner.'

'The killers didn't want to rouse the neighbours.'

'Wouldn't the doctor have been listening out for the sound?'

'All he knew – if I'm right – was that someone was coming to pick him up. When he heard a knock on the door, he opened it. Before he could protest, he was overpowered.'

Keedy pondered. Unlikely as the theory had seemed at first, it now had the ring of possibility. He was about to accept it when he spotted a problem.

'Are you saying that they rang the house first to alert him?'

'Yes, Joe. That's what they must have done.'

'How did they get hold of his number?'

'Ah,' said Marmion, sobered. 'I didn't think of that.'

Attending to the fire was an effort for Kathleen Paget. As she struggled to get up off her knees, she winced at the pain.

'My arthritis is worse than ever this morning, Alf.'

Her husband gave a grunt and shifted his pipe to the other side of his mouth. As soon as she moved out of the way, the dog resumed its position on the hearth. She headed for the kitchen.

'I'll put the kettle on.'

She was getting the cups off their hooks when there was a knock on the door.

'That sounds like the milkman,' she muttered to herself.

Kathleen went slowly along the passageway and opened the door. She was surprised to find her sister standing outside, looking anxious.

'I didn't expect to see you today, Ada,' she said.

'I felt I had to come.'

'Did you go to work?'

'Yes,' said Ada, 'I've not long finished. It's been preying on my mind.'

'What has?'

'I had to tell someone, Kathy.'

Her sister stood aside. They went into the kitchen where the kettle was beginning to sing. Kathleen was concerned.

'You don't look well, Ada. I told you to take a day off for once.'

'I couldn't do that. I had to keep my mind occupied.'

'Why?'

'It was something that happened at the doctor's house, you see.'

Forgetting about the tea, Kathleen sat opposite her at the table. Her sister had weathered many setbacks in her life and shown remarkable courage. Yet she was now pale and dithering. Something was amiss.

'Take a deep breath,' advised Kathleen, 'then tell me what's happened.'

'I put a shilling in the gas meter yesterday.'

'That's never upset you before, Ada.'

'Listen to me,' pleaded her sister. 'I need your help. It made me think of something that happened earlier in the week – only it wasn't my gas meter then.'

'You've lost me.'

'It was in the doctor's house. I was cleaning the kitchen when a man came to read the gas meter. He was dressed like the one who comes to read mine, so I let him in and thought no more of it.'

'The doctor's meter is under the stairs, isn't it?'

'Yes, it is.'

'What did you do while he was there?'

'I got on with my work.'

'Then what happened?'

'After a couple of minutes – maybe more – he called to say he was leaving. I heard the front door open and shut.'

'And that's it?'

'Yes, it is. Did I do the right thing, Kathy?'

'I'd have done the same as you,' said the other, 'except that I'd have stayed to keep an eye on him. It doesn't take long to read a meter, does it? When someone comes to read ours, he's in and out in less than a minute.'

'I hardly slept last night, thinking about it.'

'You must tell the police.'

'I'm afraid that I might be wasting their time.'

'Think what might happen if you don't mention it. It could be evidence, Ada.' She got up from the table. 'Let's forget about the tea.'

'Why?'

'Because we're going to the police station. Let me put my coat on.'

'I'll be too nervous to say a word.'

'No, you won't,' said her sister. 'You were the one who rang the police yesterday and they were glad that you did. That man who read the meter could be quite innocent, of course, but I have my suspicions. Let's go, Ada.'

Because they wanted to make an early start, the two friends had arranged to meet outside Swan and Edgar at ten o'clock. Alice Marmion was late but there was no complaint from Iris Goodliffe. Standing on the corner, she was enjoying the sight of a busy Piccadilly Circus and Regent Street. More to the point, she was wearing her best clothes and had no duties to perform in the policewoman's uniform she hated.

'Alice!' she cried, waving to her friend. 'Over here!'

Fighting her way through the crowd, Alice arrived and greeted her with a hug.

When she saw the beatific smile on Iris's face, she forgot her reservations about the outing. She was simply pleased to be able to give her friend so much joy.

'How long have you been here, Iris?' she asked.

'Oh, I don't know – twenty minutes, maybe?'

'I'm sorry to have kept you.'

'I don't mind. Watching people go past has been fascinating. Three soldiers came earlier,' said Iris, beaming. 'One of them whistled at me.'

'Were they British or American?'

'British, of course. I'd have looked the other way if they'd been American.'

'They're our allies, Iris.'

'I know, but they act as if London belongs to them.'

'It belongs to us today,' said Alice.

'Then we must savour every single moment of it,' said Iris, giggling. 'Now then, where do we start?'

'Right here in Swan and Edgar, I think. We can have endless fun looking at things we could never afford. After that, we'll work our way up Regent Street then visit all the big stores in Oxford Street.'

'I must buy something as a souvenir – and a new dress, of course.'

'I'm in search of Christmas presents.'

'What have you got in mind for Joe?'

Alice grinned. 'That's between me and him.'

When Pellew took him his breakfast, he thought that the prisoner was asleep. The latter was curled up under a blanket on the wooden board that acted as his bed. After unlocking the door, Pellew went into the cell with a tray in his hands.

'Wake up,' he called. 'I've brought you some grub.'

The prisoner suddenly came to life, throwing off the blanket and leaping up to knock the tray out of the constable's arms. Pushing him aside, he ran through the open door and along a short corridor until he reached another door. He flung that open and found his escape route blocked. Sergeant Dear stood there with his arms folded and an eyebrow arched.

'Where d'you think you're going, lad?' he asked.

Before the prisoner could work out what to do, he was seized from behind, lifted off his feet and hurled back to his cell. The door was locked behind him. On the floor, now empty, lay the tin teacup. Beside it was the sandwich that Pellew had deliberately stamped on. He glared at the prisoner.

'That's the last food you'll get all day,' he warned.

He ignored the howls of rage that came through the bars at him.

Moments after he had answered the telephone in Tindall's house, Marmion's face lit up. He was soon writing something down. Keedy wondered why the inspector had become so animated. Eventually, Marmion put the receiver down.

'Let me guess,' said Keedy. 'It was Chat, offering us a pay rise.'

'You're wide of the mark, Joe.'

'Who was on the other end of the line?'

'It was someone from the local constabulary,' said Marmion. 'Mrs Hobbes told them she might have some useful information to give us. They, in turn, contacted Chat who gave them this number.'

'What is this useful information?'

'That's what you're going to find out. She's over at her sister's. Get the driver to take you to Mrs Paget's house and bring Mrs Hobbes back here as quickly as you can.'

'You sound optimistic.'

'Let's just say that I'm . . . more than hopeful.'

Keedy let himself out and gave orders to the driver. The car pulled away. In little over ten minutes, it was back again. Marmion watched the sergeant helping Ada Hobbes out of the vehicle. The inspector held the door open for them to walk straight into the house. The three of them adjourned to the lounge. While the detectives sank into the sofa, Ada was perched on the edge of an armchair, looking around as if she feared being caught trespassing.

'What is it that you want to tell us, Mrs Hobbes?' asked Marmion.

'I could be mistaken,' she said, nervously.

'We're grateful to you for coming forward.'

'It was Kathy's doing.'

'I don't know the full details,' said Keedy. 'I thought we should hear them together. Right, Mrs Hobbes,' he continued. 'Tell your story.'

'Well,' she said, 'it was when I put a shilling in my gas meter . . .'

They listened patiently as she recounted the visit to the house of a man claiming that he had come to read the gas meter. Nothing about him aroused any suspicion at the time. In retrospect, however, she wondered if she should have been more watchful. While she spoke, Keedy took notes.

The moment she had finished, Marmion took over.

'Did you mention this man to Dr Tindall?'

'Yes, I did, Inspector. He said that I did the right thing.'

'We can soon find out if he was an employee of the Gas Board.'

'How?' she asked in surprise.

'If he was on his rounds,' said Marmion, 'he'd have called at each house in turn.' He looked at Keedy. 'Sergeant, will you please speak to Mr and Mrs Crowe next door to see if they had a visit from him that day?'

Keedy was on his feet at once. 'Just to make sure,' he said, 'I'll check the neighbours on the other side of the house as well.'

'Good idea.'

As soon as the sergeant had gone, Marmion tried to bolster Ada's confidence.

'Thank you so much for getting in touch with us, Mrs Hobbes.'

'It was my sister's idea, really.'

'You were the one who remembered the incident and had the sense to tell Mrs Paget about it. I wanted to speak to you here because you can show us exactly what you were doing while this man was on the premises.'

'Kathy thinks he was here far too long.'

'If that's the case, he came with an ulterior motive.'

Her face went blank. 'What's that?'

'He wanted to see the house from the inside.'

'Oh, I do feel guilty, Inspector,' she said. 'I shouldn't have let him in.'

'Can you describe him?'

'Well, let me think. He was a nice, good-looking man with a beard.'

'How old was he?'

'Oh, in his fifties, I'd say.'

'What else can you tell me about him, Mrs Hobbes?'

Ada struggled hard to chisel a few details out of her memory.

When he returned, Keedy came back into the house with a quiet smile.

'Well?' said Marmion.

'Nobody called to read the meter at the houses on either side. According to Mr Crowe, the man usually calls near the end of the month. Well done, Mrs Hobbes,' he said, turning to her. 'You've given us an important clue.'

'Have I?' she said.

'Yes,' said Marmion. 'Earlier on, the sergeant and I were wondering how the killers might have got hold of the telephone number here. Now we know. One of them tricked his way into the house. Thanks to you, we know the disguise he used. How long was he here? Earlier on, you said that it must have been almost a few minutes.'

'I couldn't be sure, Inspector. I was busy cleaning the kitchen. It could have been much longer, I suppose.'

Marmion got to his feet. 'If you'll excuse us,' he said, 'the sergeant and I will conduct a little experiment.'

They went into the hall and compared the time on their watches. Marmion then pretended to let Keedy into the house before opening the door under the stairs and switching on the light for him. While Keedy knelt beside the meter, Marmion walked to the kitchen and closed the door behind him. The sergeant came out at once and examined the rooms on the ground floor at speed. He then dashed upstairs to continue his

142

search, starting with the master bedroom and looking in the wardrobe. He pretended to search and find the safe. That left three more bedrooms and a bathroom to inspect. By the time he had finished his reconnaissance, he still had time in hand. While he waited, he made a note of the telephone number. A minute later, Marmion emerged from the kitchen.

'How did you get on, Joe?'

'I cased the whole house.'

'Well, I didn't hear a thing,' said Marmion, 'and neither did Mrs Hobbes when that man was here. I no longer believe they needed to wake the doctor up that night by claiming there was an emergency at the hospital. The man Mrs Hobbes let in here came in search of a means of getting into the house when it was locked.'

Claude Chatfield was disappointed. Seated behind his desk, he pored over a collection of the morning's newspapers. Only one of them had managed to put a photograph of Dr Tindall on the front page. As ever, the latest news about the war edged out events on the Home Front. The capture of Jerusalem took pride of place and General Allenby was lauded for his stunning achievement. The fall of the iconic city marked the climax of a brilliant offensive against the Turks that had begun over a year earlier. Understandably, most editors had wanted to trumpet good news about the war on their front pages. The fate of an orthopaedic surgeon at a military hospital could not compete with that. Reports of the murder were consigned to the inside pages and, in one case, reduced to a mere six lines. What irked Chatfield most was that his original statement to the press had been either truncated or mangled. He threw aside the last of the newspapers with something close to despair.

When he looked up, he saw that Sir Edward Henry was standing in front of his desk. The commissioner personified disappointment.

'You've obviously seen the papers, Sir Edward,' said Chatfield.

'Unfortunately, I have.'

'Don't they understand the importance of the murder?'

'The capture of Jerusalem has elbowed out everything else.'

'Why couldn't they print what I told them,' wailed the superintendent. 'I answered questions from reporters for almost an hour, yet little of what I said has been given any prominence.'

'Well,' said the other, philosophically, 'give Allenby his due. His success is a real shot in the arm for the British Army. I hope that it will serve to deflect the War Office away from us. What we really need is news of some startling progress in the murder investigation, but it's far too early to expect that. One thing is crystal clear,' he added, striking a pose. 'Letting your detectives slope off to Brighton was a bad mistake.'

'Inspector Marmion was responsible for making it.'

'You should have stopped him.'

'How could I? He sneaked off when my back was turned.'

'You failed to impose your authority, Superintendent. That's unlike you.'

Without another word, the commissioner turned on his heel and left the office. Chatfield was left yet again with the feeling that he was being blamed unjustly. He was blazing with suppressed fury.

'Damn you, Marmion!' he cursed. 'Do your job properly for once.'

* * *

The surge of pleasure that Alice experienced when she first met up with Iris Goodliffe had been steadily eroded. As she had feared, her friend's indecision was a huge problem. Even when trying to buy something as simple as a scarf, Iris kept changing her mind time and again. Constantly seeking Alice's advice, she would accept it, question it, reject it, accept it again, then decide she might be able to get more of a bargain at another store. By the time they stopped to have a cup of tea, Alice's patience was in tatters.

'I have an idea,' she said.

'So have I,' decided Iris. 'You were right about that scarf. I bought the wrong one. It's not my colour at all.'

'It's too late to worry about that now, Iris.'

'No, it isn't. We can go back and change it.'

'That would mean walking hundreds of yards. In any case, when you try on that red scarf again, you will probably want a second look at all the others as well. We've only got limited time.'

Iris was hurt. 'I thought we were here all day.'

'I promised my mother that I'd be back by mid-afternoon.'

'What a shame! I'm having such a wonderful time.'

'There's no reason why you can't stay here until the shops shut.'

'Yes, there is. I won't have you to advise me.'

Alice was sorry that she had invented an excuse to curtail the shopping spree, but it had turned out to be worse than she had feared. She felt less like a friend of Iris than a substitute mother, advising, cossetting, humouring and being at the mercy of her whims. Her irritation had evanesced into a sense of mild panic. Alice sought a means of escape.

'I have an idea, Iris.'

'What is it?'

'When we get to John Lewis's,' said Alice, 'why don't we split up?'

Her friend was shocked. 'I thought we were together.'

'We are. It's just that you were talking about a pair of slippers and I need to go to the menswear department to buy Joe a tie. We can arrange to meet somewhere in the store, then go our separate ways.'

'But I'd need your opinion about the slippers.'

'Buy the pair that feel most comfortable.'

'I could tell you which tie I think would suit Joe.'

'Oh, no,' said Alice, firmly. 'When it comes to my presents, I don't need a second opinion, thank you. Joe is very particular about every item he wears. That's why he always looks so smart.'

'What about that scarf I should have bought?'

'If it's that important,' said Alice, 'go back and change the one you bought by mistake. We can meet in the restaurant in John Lewis's. Will that suit you?'

'No,' replied Iris. 'I'll stay with you while I can. I feel safer that way.'

After hours with a colleague on their usual beat, Constable Pellew came back to the police station. Sergeant Dear looked up from his desk.

'Trouble?'

'It's as calm as a duck pond out there, Sarge,' said the other, 'but that wasn't the case last night. Before he got to the City Arms, our favourite prisoner was making enemies left, right and centre.'

'I'm not surprised.'

'He was turned away from the first pub he tried to get into, so he broke a window in the outhouse just to get even. Other landlords turned him away as well. They could see at a glance that he was bad news.'

Pellew went on to list other petty crimes that the young man had committed before going into the City Arms. Sergeant Dear made a note of each one, then looked up at the constable through doleful eyes.

'He's the last kind of visitor we need in Wells,' he said. 'His charge sheet gets longer and longer. Wherever he goes, he seems to enjoy causing havoc. Look what he did at the City Arms – assault, causing an affray, damage to property, possession of a dangerous weapon, foul language in a public place. Then there is his unruly behaviour since he got here and his attempted escape. Frank Myler said he was roaring like a bloody animal.'

'Has he calmed down a bit now?'

'Oh, no, he's complaining that we're trying to starve him.'

'He doesn't deserve food, Sarge.'

'What he really deserves is a good hiding. Unfortunately, I'm forbidden by law to give it to him. Why can't he be like everyone else?' asked Dear. 'If any of the local lads get drunk and start throwing punches, they go out like a light when we lock them up. Next morning, they have a pounding headache and are full of apologies. When the time comes, they pay the fine straight away. Not this one,' he continued, jerking a thumb towards the cells. 'He's been yelling his head off and stinking the place out. If we have any more of it, I'll turn a hose on him.'

'He won't be staying, Sarge. You found out he was a missing person.'

'Somebody had better reclaim him pretty soon,' threatened Dear, 'or off he goes. I'm not having that skunk polluting one of my cells.'

CHAPTER TEN

Using the telephone at Dr Tindall's house, Marmion rang the Gas Board. As soon as his suspicions were confirmed, he put down the receiver and turned to Ada Hobbes.

'You were right,' he told her. 'That man was an impostor.'

'But he looked so real, Inspector.'

'He chose a time when he knew you'd be here alone. He must have watched this house for some time to see who came and went.'

'That makes me shiver,' admitted Ada.

'Thank you again, anyway. There is no need for you to stay a moment longer. Since you've been so helpful, the least we can do is to send you home in a car again.'

'There's no need.'

'We can't let you walk all the way back home.'

'I'm not going to my house,' she said. 'It was my sister who made me get in touch with you. If I can have a lift, I'd like to be taken to Kathy's house, please. She'll want to know what happened.'

'Then you can tell her we think you're a real heroine.'

Ada tittered then let Marmion take her out to the police car and help her into it. After waving the vehicle off, he went back inside the house. Keedy was waiting for him with a triumphant grin on his face.

'I think I've found it,' he said.

'Found what?'

'The way they got in.'

Marmion's interest quickened. 'Show me.'

Keedy took him into the dining room, a large well-appointed room with an oval table that could accommodate six or more people if necessary. Marmion was envious. In his house, meals were eaten around the kitchen table. Once again, he wondered why Dr Tindall had bought a property full of rooms he never used. He thought of the flat where the surgeon had lived in Brighton. That, too, was an extravagance for someone living alone.

'Over here,' said Keedy, leading him to a window. 'What do you see?'

'The side of the house next door.'

'Look again, Harv.'

'I see a sash window, that's all.'

'You see a sash window with a dodgy catch.' He flicked a finger and the catch swung inwards. 'Hey, presto!'

'It wasn't locked properly.'

'Look at my finger,' said Keedy, holding it out. 'That's not moisture on the tip, it's oil. When he came to read the meter, that man made time to come in here, loosen the catch with a screwdriver, and oil it.'

'That would have taken no time at all.'

'My theory is that he left it almost in the closed position but . . .'

Using his knuckles, he tapped both sides of the frame at the same time and the catch slowly moved inwards until the window was unlocked. It would have been easy for someone to climb through it in the dark. Marmion was impressed.

'You should have been a detective, Joe,' he said.

'I've got the mentality of a crook – that's why I found it.'

They traded a laugh then moved to the table, sitting either side of it and luxuriating briefly in the fantasy that they were waiting for a maid to bring in a delicious meal prepared by their cook. Marmion opened his notebook.

'This is how Mrs Hobbes described the meter reader. He was clearly fit enough to get in through that window. His partner would have been equally lithe, I fancy. What else do we know about them?'

'They rode on motorbikes.'

'And?'

'They took no chances. Their preparation was meticulous.'

'How did they leave the house – window or front door?'

'Front door,' said Keedy, 'but only after they had pushed the window catch into its closed position. That's why we didn't spot the lubrication earlier.'

'Let's think about the safe,' suggested Marmion. 'There was no sign of it being jemmied open. How did they get hold of the key?'

'Intimidation, probably.'

'Tom Harrison told me they might have used a bayonet. If they had waved that in his face, I think Tindall would have given them the key. He probably hoped they would empty the safe and vanish.'

'Once they had the key,' said Keedy, 'I reckon they took him downstairs to kill him.'

'Why were they so considerate?'

Keedy was shocked. 'I don't call hacking a man to pieces an act of consideration. It was sadistic.'

'Yet it took place in the room off the kitchen. If they murdered him in his bedroom, imagine the unholy mess they would have made. That beautiful carpet would have been stained red. Until we found that open safe,' Marmion reminded him, 'the bedroom looked undisturbed.'

'That's true.'

'There's another possible reason why they chose the room downstairs.'

'Is there?'

'They knew that it would be the first place the cleaner would go to when she got here. If someone had kept watch, he would have seen Mrs Hobbes come and go. They wanted their crime discovered as soon as she arrived yesterday morning.'

'I don't agree,' said Keedy, 'and I can't see how they kept the house under surveillance. Neighbours would have noticed strangers hanging about all day.'

'They didn't need to do that, Joe. Their first task would have been to find out if anybody else was living in the house and that was easily done.'

'How?'

'By knocking on the front door during the day,' guessed Marmion. 'Once they knew that Dr Tindall had no servants, they established when the cleaner came and chose the night before one of her visits.'

'I find that baffling. Most killers would delay the discovery of what they had done. You claim that these two did the opposite.'

'Don't ask me why.'

'Someone must have seen a stranger lurking outside for long periods.'

'He didn't need to lurk, Joe. He went past in disguise.'

'Dressed as an employee of the Gas Board, you mean?'

'No,' said Marmion, 'he'd have been in army uniform, I fancy. And he would have driven past the house from time to time on his motorbike. Nobody would have given him a second glance. Soldiers on motorbikes are a common sight.'

'They're also trained to use a bayonet.'

'Neither of these men were real soldiers, Joe.'

'How do you know?'

'You've forgotten what their victim did for a living. He worked in a military hospital. Dr Tindall saved the lives of soldiers. He'd be revered by anyone in the army. One thing is certain,' Marmion concluded. 'The killers were not soldiers.'

In the living room of her sister's house, Ada Hobbes sipped her tea and looked at her brother-in-law with a mingled pity and curiosity.

'How is Alf?' she asked.

'Much the same,' said Kathleen.

'When I came in here the first time, he looked at me as if he'd never seen me before. The second time, I did at least get a nod from him.'

'His memory comes and goes. Mostly, it goes. He can still do some things, mind you. Alf lights the fire every morning and does odd jobs, but that's about all.' She gave a weary smile. 'He's not the man he used to be. If it wasn't so cold, I'd take him to the shops with me. Alf would like that.' She pursed her lips. 'We're in the same boat, Ada.'

'Are we?'

'Yes, we've both outlasted our husbands.'

'Alf is still alive.'

'Well – if you can call it that.'

'I miss Bert so much,' said Ada, sadly. 'I'd love to have seen his face if I'd come home in a police car like I did yesterday.'

'And you had a second ride in it today.'

'That was your doing. If you hadn't egged me on, I'd never have gone to the police. Inspector Marmion was so grateful to you.'

'Does that mean I get a lift in a police car as well?'

Their laughter brought Alf out of his reverie and he nodded his head.

'That was wrong of us, Ada,' said her sister, guiltily. 'A nice man like Dr Tindall gets murdered and we're laughing. We should be ashamed. We ought to be wondering if there's anything else we can remember that might help the police.'

'I still can't believe that he's dead, Kathy.'

'Why choose him of all people? Unless the killers made a mistake.'

'There was no mistake,' said Ada. 'The inspector was certain about that. He said it was all carefully planned. The doctor was the man they were after.'

Days were usually quiet at the police station in Wells, but their latest prisoner had changed all that. When he was not complaining, he was kicking the bars of his cell repeatedly or singing filthy songs as loud as he could. Pulsating with anger, Sergeant Dear went off to the cells.

'Shut up!' he yelled.

'Hello, Sarge,' said the prisoner. 'Any chance of some grub?'

'No, there isn't, but there's a good chance of a punch on the nose if you keep bellyaching. I know your game, lad. You're cold, hungry and your money's run out. You want to cause as much trouble as possible so that the magistrate will send you to prison for three or four months. That way, you have a roof over your head, regular meals and a warm cell.'

'That sounds good to me, Sarge.'

'Don't push me, lad. Your charge sheet is already long enough to get you a custodial sentence, so you can shut your trap. If you bother me again,' warned Dear, jabbing a finger by way of emphasis, 'we'll kick seven barrels of the smelly stuff out of you and leave you half-dead in the middle of it. Understand?'

The prisoner at last fell silent.

Iris Goodliffe was so afraid of losing sight of Alice that she clung to her like a limpet. Over lunch in John Lewis's, she apologised profusely.

'I know,' she admitted. 'It's all my fault. I just can't make up my mind. I can see how maddening that is from your point of view, Alice. I've been behaving like a child and not like a grown woman who's old enough to know what she likes.'

'We all like a second opinion about something we're about to buy.'

'You must have wanted to strangle me.'

'No, I haven't,' said Alice, trying to sound convincing. 'We're just not used to shopping when it's so crowded. It takes all the fun out of it.'

'But I was having great fun until I realised how unhappy you were.'

'I'd just like a little breathing space, Iris.'

'Yes, of course.'

'I don't blame you for getting overexcited.'

'Well, I blame myself,' said the other. 'From now on, we'll concentrate on buying your Christmas presents instead of mine. Agreed?'

'Agreed,' said Alice before dipping the spoon in her soup.

She was touched by Iris's apology and angry with herself for trying to get rid of her sooner than she had planned. When they had first walked the beat together, she had been the more experienced officer and acted as her friend's mentor. Iris had learnt quickly and no longer depended on Alice so much. Meeting up with her friend outside Swan and Edgar, however, the old Iris had been reborn – needy, indecisive, highly emotional and putting herself first. Now that she had recognised her faults, she would be a different person. Alice softened towards her.

'I tell you what,' she said. 'Let's look for your slippers together.'

'We're going up to the menswear department,' said Iris. 'It's time you took first place for once.'

'Thank you.'

'What sort of tie are you going to buy Joe?'

'Something I can actually afford,' said Alice. 'Most of the prices here are well beyond the scope of my purse.'

'I just love looking at all these Christmas decorations,' said Iris, gazing up at them. 'They lift my spirits.'

She grinned broadly and Alice's guilt stirred again. Because she had been so frustrated with her friend, she had cut hours out of their day together. Alice tried to offer something by way of compensation.

'I tell you what,' she said. 'I'll go an hour or so later than I planned. Mummy will understand. Is that okay?'

'It's wonderful!'

'That will give us plenty of time to buy your slippers and Joe's present.'

'There's something else we can fit in as well.'

'What is it?'

'We can go back to that shop and change my scarf.'

Alice sighed inwardly.

Claude Chatfield was in a less waspish mood than usual. Editors of two newspapers had rung him to apologise for being unable to give more prominence to the statement he had issued at the press conference the previous day. The report that Marmion had just given sweetened him even more. Signalling progress, it was useful ammunition to use against the commissioner.

'I think that all of your assumptions are sound,' he said.

'But they still are only assumptions, sir,' Marmion pointed out.

'Mrs Hobbes's account is based on fact. Someone pretending to be from the Gas Board did indeed come to the house and – as you found out – stayed long enough to find a means of getting into it at night.'

'Sergeant Keedy deserves credit for that discovery, sir.'

'Where is he, by the way?'

'He's using the telephone in my office. I asked him to ring all the places that advertise costume hire. We think that the killers acquired two army uniforms and one that seemed to have come from the Gas Board.'

'Good thinking.'

'We do get it right sometimes, Superintendent.'

'I always give praise where praise is due.'

Though the claim was far from the truth, Marmion did not challenge him. Chatfield went off into a brooding silence for a while, then blinked as if waking up.

'There's a cruel irony here,' he said.

'Is there, sir?'

'Yes. A man who spends most of his time slicing bodies open is himself the victim of surgery – albeit of a more grotesque kind. It is almost as if his death is a kind of parody. Do you get that impression?'

'I can't say that I do, sir,' said Marmion. 'You're introducing subtleties that don't exist, in my view. We believe the two men responsible were cold-hearted killers acting on orders from someone else.'

'Are you sure a third person was involved?'

'We're fairly certain.'

'Yet you're unable to provide a motive for him.'

'I can provide one now, sir.'

'What is it?'

'Punishment.'

'Why do you think that?'

'Look at the nature of the murder, Superintendent. Tom Harrison said that it must have been excruciating for Dr Tindall. It was almost medieval. They kept the victim alive to prolong the agony. I read the post-mortem report when I got back here earlier on and it was—'

'Yes, yes,' said Chatfield, cutting him short. 'I know. I read it myself. We're dealing with monsters here.'

'With two of them,' corrected Marmion.

'There may be no third person, Inspector.'

'Yes, there is, sir. I feel it in my bones.'

'Let's deal with the killers first,' suggested Chatfield. 'We know that they exist. Catch the pair. If we have clear evidence they were obeying orders from someone else, we can then go after him.'

'In my view,' said Marmion, 'we need to make three arrests. If we do that, newspaper editors will not be able to hide the murder behind the capture of Jerusalem. It will be front page news everywhere in this country.'

Keedy was unable to concentrate. Sitting in Marmion's office, he had been given an important job to do yet his mind kept straying to Alice. The promise of a whole evening alone with her had disappeared before his eyes. It was an all too frequent setback in their romance. Even when they were married, he knew, they would continue to be separated by the demands of Scotland Yard. But at least he would be able to go home at the end of the day to a loving wife in a warm bed. The thought revived him.

He dialled another number. Keedy was soon talking to a woman in charge of a costume hire shop. Like so many of the places he had contacted, she was unable to help him. He put the receiver down and crossed off the last name on his list. Marmion then came in.

'Any joy?' he asked.

'Yes and no,' said Keedy.

'What does that mean?'

'I'll explain in a moment. First, I need to pass on a message. I took a call from that Major Somebody at the Edmonton Military Hospital. He wants you to ring him.'

'Did he say why?'

'No, he didn't.'

'I'll get in touch with him after I've heard your news.'

'Most of the places I contacted had neither of the costumes I asked for, but there was one that's promising.'

'Where is it?'

'It's just off Shaftesbury Avenue and deals mainly with professional theatres. They've never been asked to supply a uniform like the one that employees of the Gas Board might wear.'

'What about army uniforms?'

'They had a fair number in stock,' said Keedy, 'because they are in demand. Companies have been putting on plays about the war to lift the morale of people on the Home Front.'

'We can all do with a boost to our morale, Joe.'

'There was an amateur company in Camden Town that hired two army uniforms from them. They were due to be returned but they never came back. Do you know why?'

'The company doesn't exist.'

'Oh, it exists but it denies hiring any army uniforms. For a start, they can't afford to do so. They always make their own costumes. I think I should get over to the place off Shaftesbury Avenue right away and ask for a description of the person who hired the uniforms.'

'When you've done that,' advised Marmion, 'track down this amateur theatre in Camden Town. Nobody would simply pluck their name out of the air. The man who hired those uniforms may have had some connection with the company in the past. Off you go, then.'

Keedy was on his feet at once. 'Where will you be?'

'I suspect that I may have to go to Edmonton again. Major Palmer-Loach would only want to speak to me if he had important news to pass on.'

Running a military hospital on such a large scale was a demanding assignment. It was not surprising therefore that Major Palmer-Loach rarely had time for chit-chat with members of his staff. They, too, were working hard. When he wanted a few words with Neil Irvine, he had to walk along a corridor beside him as Irvine was on his way to an operating theatre. Dressed in his surgeon's garb, he spoke to the major through his mask.

'You pick the weirdest times for a conversation, Howard,' he said.

'It's one we should have had years ago.'

'Why?'

'Well, I didn't know that you actually got any details out of George Tindall about his background. All he ever talked about with me were medical matters.'

'I had an advantage over you. Like George, I'm a fellow Scot.'

'Except that you're very unlike him in every way. While you are open and approachable, he was secretive. Inspector Marmion has discovered more about him in two days than I learnt in over two years.'

'I'd like to meet the inspector.'

'When the operation is over, you'll get your chance.'

Irvine was mystified. 'Will I?'

'Yes,' said the other. 'I've not long come off the telephone to Scotland Yard. He is anxious to question you. When I told him that you had to operate first, he said that he'd be waiting when you came out of theatre.'

'I can't shake hands with surgical gloves on, Howard.'

'He'll give you time to change, I'm sure.'

'It's not just a question of getting out of these clothes' said Irvine. 'Surgery demands total concentration. When I come out of theatre, I'll be locked in another world. The inspector will have to wait until my mind adjusts to reality again. I hope that he is a patient man.'

The major smiled. 'I got the feeling that patience is his watchword.'

It took Keedy some time to find the premises. He went down a street off Shaftesbury Avenue, turned into a lane and walked the length of it without seeing a sign for Pegasus Costumes Ltd. It was only after retracing his steps that he realised he had walked past a mews so narrow that he had never noticed it. The company was in a jumble of Victorian properties redolent of one of Dickens's darker novels. From the outside, the building looked too small to house a large collection but, once inside it, he saw that it opened out substantially at the rear. It also ran to four storeys.

A middle-aged woman was seated behind a desk, leafing through old theatre programmes. Plump, flame-haired and ostentatiously dressed, she reminded him of a madame he had once arrested in a brothel. She produced an open-mouthed smile for his benefit.

'Can I help you, sir?' she asked.

'My name is Sergeant Keedy,' he said. 'I rang earlier.'

'Ah, yes. You were asking about army uniforms.'

'That's right. Do you happen to remember who came to pick them up?'

'I remember him very well, Sergeant.'

'Did he give a name?'

'John Morris.'

'How would you describe him?'

'He was about your age,' she replied, 'but shorter than you and nowhere near as handsome. He was slim, dark and walked with a limp. Oh, and he had an ugly face. On the other hand,' she went on, 'he was offering me money and we never turn that away even if it is from a small amateur company.'

'Did he try on an army uniform?'

'He tried on two or three until he found one that fitted him. Then he picked out a second one that was bigger. To be fair to

162

him, he'd brought the measurements to make sure he got the right size.'

'What were the uniforms supposed to be for?'

'It was a play called *Soldiers of the Cross*,' she said. 'I'd never heard of it and, after thirty-eight years of working in the business, I've heard of most plays. This one sounded a bit too serious for my taste.'

'Was the theatre in Camden Town putting on a play of that name?'

'No, it wasn't. When I spoke to the man who runs the company, he'd never heard of it either.'

'Did he know anyone by the name of John Morris?'

She shook her head. 'I think it was a false name,' she admitted. 'He paid the fee and a deposit then walked off with two of our costumes. I was tricked, Sergeant, and that doesn't often happen. I can usually size up a man at a glance.'

'You said that he was ugly.'

'His face was but that didn't mean he was a wrong 'un. He had a Midland accent and a strange sort of charm. I liked him. That was before I realised what he'd done. Why are you trying to track him down, anyway?'

'This is a murder inquiry.'

'Goodness!' she cried. 'Do you mean that two of our costumes were involved? That's frightening. If they got covered in blood, they'd be ruined.'

'Let's just say that I don't think you'll be seeing the costumes again.'

'Thank goodness for that. We get all sorts in here, Sergeant, but, as far as I know, we've never had a killer before.'

'Did he tell you much about that play, *Soldiers of the Cross*?'

'All he said was that it was inspiring, and his eyes lit up. Do you know what I think?'

'What?'

'I fancy that he wrote it.'

Marmion did not complain about being kept waiting. He was able to update the major on the progress of the investigation, careful to release only some of the intelligence so far gathered.

'You and the sergeant have done splendid work,' said Palmer-Loach. 'I never thought that you'd find out so much so soon.'

'We're simply following routine, Major.'

'I'm impressed.'

They were eventually interrupted by Neil Irvine, who apologised for the delay. The major slipped out of the office so that the two men could talk alone.

'I suppose that we could have had this conversation over the telephone,' said Marmion, 'but it would not have been the same. How is it that you know so much about Dr Tindall while the major knows so little?'

'George and I were fellow surgeons, Inspector. We understand each other. Howard – Major Palmer-Loach, that is – is an administrator so he has different pressures to deal with. The honest answer to your question,' he continued, 'is that George Tindall was a closed book to me until he confided one day that it was his birthday. A true Scotsman like me could not let an event like that go uncelebrated. We were here overnight so we kept ourselves awake with a bottle of malt whisky that I happened to have hidden in my desk.'

'Did that open the closed book for you?'

'It allowed me a glimpse of a few chapters, that's all.'

Marmion took out his notebook. 'Carry on, please.'

He listened with fascination as Irvine recalled his conversation with Tindall. The murder victim slowly began to appear in a completely different light. In his younger days, he had been a fine all-round athlete and had won cups for his achievements as a tennis player. He had met his wife, Eleanor, at their tennis club and the first thing they did at the house they bought in Kent was to instal a lawn court in their garden.

'I'd never have dared to play tennis,' confessed Irvine.

'Why not?' asked Marmion.

'I was too afraid that I'd damage my hands or sprain my wrists. Surgeons live by the skill of their hands, Inspector. I took no chances. George was confident that he would never injure himself and he never did.'

Marmion remembered that Tindall's hands had been sliced off by his killers. It was a detail he kept from Irvine along with other grim discoveries contained in the post-mortem report.

'Why did Dr Tindall and his wife lead such a private life?' he asked.

'That was only the case when he worked in Brighton,' said Irvine.

'Oh?'

'In Kent, he told me, they had an active social life. Eleanor was a wonderful cook, apparently.'

'Did you never meet her?'

'No, she had died before I got to know George. However,' he went on, 'he did show me a photograph of her that he carried with him in his wallet. She was beautiful.'

Marmion knew that no wallet had been found in the house. The treasured photograph of Eleanor Tindall had vanished along with all the photographs of her. It was as if she had never existed.

'There's one thing I must ask you, Dr Irvine.'

'What is it?'

'I was told that Dr Tindall was a rich man.'

'It's true. He never boasted about it, but he was far wealthier than any surgeon can hope to be. It's the reason he was able to own a number of properties.'

'We know about the house in Edmonton and the flat in Brighton. And there was mention of a property in Kent.'

'There were at least two others. His favourite was the one in the south of France. He called it his escape hatch.'

'He won't have seen much of that during the war.'

'The closest he got to it was when he worked in a field hospital somewhere in north-east France. His command of the language came in useful there. He dealt with British casualties from the Battle of Loos.'

It was clear that Irvine had managed to get closer to Tindall than anybody else but there was a point beyond which even he was unable to get. Marmion asked him the question burrowing into his brain.

'Where did all his money come from?'

'Ah, well,' said Irvine, 'that's an interesting story. George's father was strict and a teetotaller into the bargain. Ironically, he inherited the family whisky distillery in Galashiels and promptly sold it. Instead of using the money to buy a bigger house, he left it in the bank. George hated having to live in such a modest house and be dragged to the kirk every Sunday. He promised himself that, if he ever got his hands on all that money, he would live in style. When his parents both died in a flu epidemic one winter, George became a rich man and spread his wings. He'd waited so long for that moment. Frankly,' added Irvine with a twinkle in his eye, 'I'd have preferred to keep the distillery.'

The latest developments in the case had pleased Sir Edward Henry. When he heard Superintendent Chatfield's account, he nodded in approval and congratulated him on having the sense to assign Marmion and Keedy to the case.

'They respond well to a challenge,' said the commissioner.

'As long as I keep cracking the whip, Sir Edward.'

'It's a complex investigation full of twists and turns. I daresay that there'll be a lot of surprises yet to come.'

'Incidentally,' said Chatfield, 'I had grovelling apologies from the editors of two national newspapers. They will give the murder of Dr Tindall better coverage tomorrow and be sure to include his photograph.'

'That's essential. A photograph of the victim may well jog memories.'

'Is it too early to think of offering a reward?'

'Let us see what happens in the next couple of days first.'

'I suppose that it's no use asking the War Office to provide the money?'

'No use at all,' said the commissioner. 'Every penny is already spoken for. The army's coffers have been drained to the limit and the same goes for the navy. War is ruinously expensive.'

'We have to pull out all the stops to win, Sir Edward.'

'I'm trying to remain optimistic but the news from Russia is ominous. Why the devil did they decide to have a revolution at a time like this?'

'It's an act of madness.'

'Because they made the insane decision to drop out of the war, we lost one of our major allies and are now struggling to survive. The Bolsheviks have a lot to answer for. However,' he continued, 'we must not be led astray. We are fighting our own war on the Home Front and it needs all the resources we can muster.'

'It's something I remind myself of every day.'

'Carry on the good work, Superintendent.'

'I will, Sir Edward.'

'And congratulate Marmion on the advances he's already made.'

'I'll be sure to do so,' said Chatfield, manufacturing a smile devoid of either warmth or sincerity. 'Encouragement from you is always heartening.'

'Then do something else to deserve it.'

The commissioner let himself out of the office and closed the door behind him. Chatfield sat down with a mixture of relief and envy, grateful to have survived a meeting with Sir Edward Henry without being criticised, yet wounded by the latter's appreciation of Marmion and Keedy. Not for the first time, the superintendent wondered what he had to do to receive the kind of praise that routinely went to detectives of a lower rank.

Before he could squirm at the injustice of it all, the telephone rang. He snatched it up as if he were trying to rescue it from a blazing fire.

'Superintendent Chatfield here,' he snapped.

As he listened to the voice at the other end of the line, he began to reel from the news he was given. It left him speechless. Reaching for a notepad, he wrote down all the details. When he put the receiver down, he tried to think of a way to conceal the information from the commissioner.

'Damnation!' he exclaimed. 'Why did that have to happen?'

CHAPTER ELEVEN

After a hectic day in the West End, Alice Marmion and Iris Goodliffe paused to compare their takings. While Alice had bought presents for Keedy and for her parents, her friend had bought a dress, gloves, scarf and slippers for herself. Before they parted, Iris embraced Alice and kissed her on both cheeks.

'What was that for, Iris?'

'It was my way of thanking you for putting up with me. This has been the best day of the year for me. I'm so grateful. It's been a struggle in the crowds but who cares about that?'

'We came through it,' said Alice.

'You'd better go. Your mother will be waiting.'

'Yes, she will, won't she?'

'Please give her my regards.'

'Of course.'

Iris gave her a long, affectionate stare. It was as if she had realised that Alice had been lying about her appointment and understood why her friend had deceived her. There was no malice in Iris's eyes. It was simply an unspoken acknowledgement that her behaviour had forced Alice to look for an early escape.

After taking their leave of each other, they headed off to their respective bus stops. The most she could hope for that evening was a chat with her fellow tenants or, at best, a game of cards with them. The prospect paled beside the pleasure of an evening with Joe Keedy.

Reviewing her day, Alice realised that everything she had done had been earmarked for somebody else. Though she had been tempted by many items on sale, she never yielded to it. At the time, it hadn't worried her. Buying for someone she loved was a treat. On the long bus ride to her digs, however, she began to feel lonely and neglected. The Christmas jollity in the West End had given way to boredom and resentment. One question dominated her mind.

'Where are you, Joe Keedy?'

The Camden Town Arts Theatre was in a backstreet, looking sad and down-at-heel. As soon as Keedy got there, the door opened and he was greeted by Roland Mandeville, a silver-haired man in his sixties with a full beard and a tendency to gesticulate. He was wearing a cloak and wide-brimmed hat.

'You must be Sergeant Keedy,' he said, offering his hand.

Keedy accepted the handshake. 'It's good of you to see me at short notice, Mr Mandeville. I got your telephone number from the lady at Pegasus Costumes.'

'Ah, Pegasus! They have an excellent stock of costumes, but they are far too expensive for us to hire. Anyway,' he went on, 'come on in, come on in. Enter the world of the Camden Town Arts Theatre.'

Keedy followed him into the foyer, then the auditorium, and saw that the inside of the building was a vast improvement on its shabby exterior. The place was clean and well appointed. Rows of chairs had been set out. Along the walls were framed photographs of former productions. The proscenium arch looked as if it had been recently painted and the drawn curtains were of good quality.

'This is my domain,' said Mandeville with a sweeping gesture. 'That's why I've invested so much of my hard-earned money in it.'

'How many people can you seat in here?'

'At a pinch, we can get a hundred and sixty patrons for each performance.'

'What sort of plays do you put on?'

'It's an eclectic mixture, Sergeant. We have staged everything from Ibsen to Music Hall. I shone in the title role of *The Master Builder* only last month.'

'Is that a play about a bricklayer?'

Mandeville laughed. 'I can see that you are no thespian,' he said. '*The Master Builder* is a dramatic gem by Henrik Ibsen. I think that Music Hall might be more to your liking – or even Shaw, perhaps. His plays are popular with our audiences. They usually have plenty of laughs in them.'

'The lady at Pegasus Costumes said you had never heard of a play called *Soldiers of the Cross*.'

'Even if I had, I'd never put in on here.'

'Why is that?'

'Because it sounds as if it's about the Crusades. Think of the cost of all that fake armour. It would be way beyond our budget.'

'I don't think it's anything to do with the Crusades,' argued Keedy. 'It's more likely to be about the Salvation Army, isn't it?'

It was an organisation that he knew a great deal about because Marmion's brother, Raymond, was a member of it. They had once investigated a murder at the hostel run by Raymond Marmion and his wife.

Mandeville was brusque. 'Then we'd certainly never have put it on.'

'Why not?'

'Let me show you.'

He led Keedy across to a framed photograph on the wall. It showed a young actress in the uniform of the Salvation Army, standing between a sizeable, dignified woman in her late fifties and an imposing man. Keedy recognised that the man was, in fact, Mandeville.

'We did *Major Barbara* last April because it is Bernard Shaw at his best. The heroine is in the Salvation Army. My dear wife – God bless her – took the role of Lady Britomart, Barbara's mother, and I was her father, Andrew Undershaft.'

'I see.'

'It was a case of art imitating life because the title role was played by our own daughter, Philomena.'

'There is a likeness between her and your wife,' observed Keedy.

'The point is that nobody needs two plays about the Salvation Army,' explained Mandeville, 'so we'd reject the one you mentioned. Our production was well received by the critics and my performance as Andrew Undershaft was singled out for its excellence.' He struck an attitude. 'I can still remember those famous speeches word for word. Listen to this one—'

'I'd rather not,' said Keedy, forcefully. 'I'm sorry to interrupt but you obviously don't understand the seriousness of the crime that brought me here.'

'Stealing a couple of army uniforms is only a minor infringement of the law.'

'The man who stole them took part in a gruesome murder.'

'Good gracious!'

'So, if you don't mind, sir, I'll hear your memoirs another time. Right now, all my attention is fixed on a hideous crime.'

'Quite so.'

'The lady at Pegasus Costumes mentioned a name to you.'

'I remember it well – John Morris. I know nobody of that name.'

'It could be false,' said Keedy, 'but he did mention this theatre and that is what brought me here. He was described as around my age but a little shorter. She told me that he was an ugly man who had a limp. He spoke with a Midland accent and had a certain charm.'

'I still can't pick him out,' said Mandeville. 'As it happens, we do have someone in our ranks who fits your description, having both an unprepossessing face and a pronounced limp – but she happens to be a woman.'

'Thank you for your help, sir.'

'I wish I could have been more use.'

'If, however, you do remember meeting someone who looked like the man I described, please ring Scotland Yard.'

'I most certainly will, Sergeant. You know,' he said, warming to the idea, 'it's rather exciting, being involved in a murder case, if only tangentially. I wish you good luck in your search.'

'We'll need it,' said Keedy under his breath.

Marmion was buoyant. On his return to Scotland Yard, he headed straight for the superintendent's office, eager to impart what he felt was enlightening information about the murder victim. When he came face to face with Chatfield, however, he was not even given a chance to speak. The superintendent indicated a chair.

'Sit down, Harvey,' he said, solemnly.

Marmion was worried. In all the years they had known each other, he could count on one hand the number of times that Chatfield had addressed him by his Christian name. He lowered himself onto a chair.

Chatfield took a deep breath. 'I have some news for you, I'm afraid.'

'What sort of news?'

'The serious kind.'

'You're not going to take me off this case, are you?' said Marmion in alarm.

'I'm hoping to do exactly the opposite.'

'What do you mean, sir?'

'I had a phone call from a police station in Wells, Somerset. A Sergeant Dear had been trawling through a list of Missing Persons. He recognised a name.'

Marmion felt his stomach tighten. His son had been found and that set off a whirl of emotions. As he wondered if Paul was alive or dead, he braced himself.

'Your son is in custody, I'm afraid,' said the superintendent.

'On what charges?'

'There's quite a list of them and they include being in possession of an offensive weapon.' Marmion gulped. 'Perhaps you'd like a moment to adjust to the news. I know you'd accepted that you might never hear of him again.'

Marmion gave a nod and considered the implications. It was painful for him to hear that Paul – the son of a detective inspector – was in trouble with the police. How had he lived until he had come to Somerset? What had he done in Wells to merit arrest? Were the police certain of his identity?

Chatfield read his mind. 'Yes,' he said, 'it definitely is him. He fits the description issued and has documents with his name on them. He admits to being Paul Marmion. It is your son.'

It was difficult for Marmion to adjust to the news, and he knew that his wife and daughter would have the same problem. As a family, they believed that Paul had deliberately walked out on them, never to return. Out of the blue, he had now surfaced in disgrace. Marmion made one decision immediately.

'I want to carry on leading this investigation, sir,' he declared.

'Are you absolutely sure?'

'Yes, I am.'

'I could easily draft in Inspector Gallimore.'

Marmion was emphatic. 'This case is mine.'

'I was hoping you'd say that.'

'All I need is time to contact my wife and daughter,' said Marmion. 'It's not the kind of thing I want to do over the telephone.'

'I understand. Do what needs to be done.'

Marmion rose to his feet. 'Thank you, sir.'

'I'll tell Sergeant Keedy that you're temporarily unavailable. He has a personal interest, of course. Your son will soon become his brother-in-law.'

Too dazed to reply, Marmion walked slowly out of the office.

Alice Marmion was angry with herself. Rather than inventing an excuse to part with Iris Goodliffe, she could have stayed in the West End until the shops had started to close. Instead of that, she was sitting at the window of her first-floor flat, gazing out at traffic rolling past in the fading light. A dull evening beckoned. Her only hope was that Joe Keedy would somehow contrive to see her at the end of the day, if only for a brief time. Realistically, she knew that it was a doomed fantasy, but it was the one possibility that gave her any sense of pleasure.

Forcing herself away from the window, she took out the Christmas wrapping paper she had bought and found the presents. She was soon on her knees with a pair of scissors. It was a task that occupied her mind and stopped her brooding. Before she could finish it, however, she heard a car arriving outside the house. When she looked out of the window, she saw her father getting out of the rear of the vehicle. Alice reeled. Only an emergency would bring him to her flat and it would almost certainly involve Keedy. Trembling with fear, she raced downstairs. She flung open the door and saw the grim look on her father's face.

'What's happened, Daddy?' she asked.

'Thank heaven you're here!' said Marmion.

'Is it Joe?'

'No, Alice, it isn't.'

The relief she felt suddenly turned to a mixture of shock and foreboding.

'It's Paul, isn't it?'

'Yes.'

'Has he been found alive?'

'Oh, he's very much alive.'

'What do you mean?'

'Jump into the car,' he said, 'and I'll tell you. We need to discuss this at home with your mother. The superintendent has given me time off to do so.'

'Where is Paul?'

'He's in trouble.'

Claude Chatfield delayed passing on the news. He was anxious to listen to Keedy's report of his trips to Pegasus Costumes Ltd and to the Camden Town Arts Centre. Once he had heard the full details, he told the sergeant about the reappearance of Paul Marmion. Keedy was astounded.

'I thought he'd gone for good,' he said.

'So did the inspector.'

'How did he take the news, sir?'

'It shook him up badly,' said Chatfield. 'In a sense, it's like someone coming back from the dead. As a father myself, I sympathise with him. I know how strong the bond is between parent and child.'

'Where is the inspector now?'

'I gave him time off to speak to his wife and daughter.'

'That was kind of you, Superintendent.'

'It wasn't kindness that prompted me. It was practicality. I need him to stay in charge of this investigation. That is why I made allowances. He'll be back as soon as he's discussed the situation with Mrs Marmion and their daughter.'

'It's a conversation that I would have liked to be involved in.'

'Your place is here, Sergeant.'

'It could make such a big change to their lives.'

'That's not necessarily true,' said Chatfield. 'When the police in Wells realised that he was on the list of Missing Persons, he begged them not to get in touch with his parents. Fortunately, they knew where their duty lay.'

'Is he still being held at the police station?'

'No, he was too disruptive. He was taken before a magistrate and remanded to Shepton Mallet prison. Imagine how the inspector felt on hearing that his son is a criminal.'

Keedy was more interested in Alice's reaction than in that of her father. He had to master an urge to go to her at once and offer support, but that was impossible. There was a murder to solve, and his energies had to be focused on that.

'So,' said Chatfield, 'our killers got their army uniforms from a costume hire company, did they? What about their motorbikes?'

'That's the next thing I need to find out.'

'I'm sorry you had slim pickings at that theatre.'

'It was an education for me, sir,' said Keedy. 'I learnt that *The Master Builder* is a play by someone called Ibsen. And I had the pleasure of meeting a man who had actually played the character onstage.'

* * *

Roland Mandeville arrived back home to a cordial welcome from his wife. They lived in one of the better areas of Camden Town. Over a glass of gin and tonic, they were able to chat. Cassandra Mandeville had the remains of an almost dazzling beauty. However, she still retained the effervescence and love of the theatre that had first attracted her husband to her.

'How did you get on, Roland?' she asked.

'I was shaken rigid.'

'Why?'

'I thought I was meeting Sergeant Keedy to talk about the theft of two army uniforms. It turns out that those costumes were worn by men who committed a murder. The uniforms were part of the killers' disguise.'

'What a chilling thought!'

'He asked me if I knew a man named John Morris.'

'It's not a name that I remember,' she said, frowning.

'It's one that was given at Pegasus Costumes.'

Mandeville went on to give her the description of the man being sought. His wife pursed her lips and shook her head. Like her husband, she could think of nobody who came close to fitting the description.

'While you were out,' she told him, 'Desmond called.'

'What did he want?' asked her husband, grimacing.

'Can't you guess?'

'I'm afraid that I can. Desmond is demanding to know what the final play in next year's spring season will be.'

'That's right.'

'We haven't decided yet, Cassie.'

'What you mean is that you have, but it has to be ratified by the committee.'

'No, I'm still hovering, to be honest. Desmond only wants to know our choice in the hope that there is a part in it for him. I made sure that there is not. Desmond Cooper can single-handedly ruin any production. That's why I try to keep him off the stage and serving drinks in the intervals.'

'Is it still a choice between *Charley's Aunt* or Pinero's *The Magistrate*?'

'Yes – which would you choose, Cassie?'

'Whichever one has a delicious role for a tubby old woman,' she said with a giggle. 'If Desmond is going to push himself forward, then so am I. It's months since I had a starring role and I'm a born actress.'

'You don't need to tell me that, my love,' he said, fondly. 'You belong on the boards. I tell you what,' he joked. 'Why don't we put on Shakespeare's *Antony and Cleopatra* and play the lead roles? We could both show our mettle in that.'

'Show our mettle?' she repeated. 'I'd be too busy hiding my fat bottom.'

She went off into peals of laughter. When she finally stopped, Cassandra took a sip of her drink and became thoughtful.

'I'd rather forgotten him.'

'Who are you talking about?'

'John Morris,' she said.

'But that's not his real name.'

'I know. It's just that I'm wondering if I might have come across him, after all. Give me that description of the man again.'

* * *

181

Ellen Marmion was just about to draw the curtains in the living room when she saw the police car arrive outside the house. She was at first pleased that her husband had somehow found the time to slip back home, then she watched her daughter getting out of the vehicle as well. Concern made her rush to the front door. Opening it wide, she embraced Alice then looked enquiringly at Marmion.

'I'll tell you inside,' he said.

The three of them adjourned to the living room. Before he spoke, Marmion made sure that his wife was sitting down. Alice sat beside her on the sofa.

'Paul has been found alive,' he said.

'Oh, my God!' exclaimed Ellen, bringing both hands to her face.

Alice put an arm around her shoulders. 'It's bad news, Mummy.'

'Yes,' said Marmion. 'He's in custody.'

'Where?' demanded Ellen. 'And what has he done? It's not something really serious, is it? Paul hasn't . . . ?'

'It's serious enough, Ellen. He was arrested in Somerset.'

'What was he doing there?'

'If you let me speak, I'll tell you all I know.'

'It's ironic, isn't it?' said Alice, bitterly. 'Only yesterday, Mummy and I agreed that Paul had disappeared for ever and that we had to accept the fact. No sooner do we do that, than he pops up again.'

Any pleasure the commissioner gained from the apparent progress in the investigation was overshadowed by the news about Paul Marmion. He was sympathetic.

'It's every policeman's nightmare,' he said. 'Having a son in trouble with the law is more than an embarrassment.'

'It might be even more painful if it was a daughter, Sir Henry.'

'Ah, yes, I suppose it would. As the father of daughters, you would feel ashamed if it happened to you. Not that it ever would, of course, because you've brought your children up to respect the law.'

'Inspector Marmion did the same with his children.'

'What went wrong?'

'His son was a victim of the war.'

'Yes, I remember that he was wounded at the Battle of the Somme.'

'The major damage appears to have been psychological.'

'Then we're bound to feel sorry for the lad.'

'He's more than a lad, Sir Edward. Paul is a fully grown man now. He has somehow managed to keep himself alive all this time. The sergeant who contacted me from Wells said that he looked and smelled like tramp.'

'Oh dear!'

'To his credit,' said Chatfield, 'the inspector is not insisting on being allowed to dash off to Somerset. He's putting his duty first and continuing to lead the case.'

'I call that a blessed relief.'

'We just have to hope that this business doesn't affect his concentration.'

'He's the most committed officer we have,' said the other. 'You and he are on a par in that regard. The difference is that you operate solely from here whereas Marmion goes out and faces recurring dangers. I'm not sure that even you could do that with the same record of success.'

Chatfield looked bilious.

Making the use of the telephone in Marmion's office, Keedy was ringing garages in the London area that sold motorcycles. He was less interested in those that had been sold than in two that might have been stolen together. When he put the receiver down, he ticked another name off his list. Before he could move on to the next one, the telephone rang.

'Sergeant Keedy,' he said, picking up the receiver.

'Ah, wonderful,' said Roland Mandeville, 'they've put me through to the right person. Mandeville here – we met earlier today.'

'I recognised your voice immediately, sir.'

'I take that as a compliment.'

'How may I help you?'

'Well, I'm hoping it's a case of my helping you or – to be more exact – of my wife helping you. When I got home earlier, I gave her the description of one of the men you're after.'

'John Morris.'

'At first, my wife had no memory of someone who looked like the false Mr Morris. After a while, however, she changed her mind.'

'You have a name?' asked Keedy, hopefully.

'I'll let Cassie talk to you herself,' said Mandeville.

Keedy heard some whispering at the end of the line then a woman spoke up.

'Sergeant Keedy?'

'Good evening to you.'

'I'm Cassandra Mandeville and I help my husband to run the theatre you visited earlier. What he omitted to tell you is that we are dedicated to the arts in general, not simply to the theatre. Musicians, singers and dancers perform regularly onstage and artists are not neglected.'

Keedy was intrigued by her voice. It was deep, fruity and vibrant, each word enunciated with resounding clarity. He could well imagine her playing a member of the nobility in a play by Bernard Shaw.

'I organise the art exhibitions in the foyer,' she explained. 'Talent is not confined to those whose paintings are hung at the Royal Academy. It abounds everywhere. We display work with artistic merit that not only interests the visiting public, it sometimes induces them to buy a painting.'

'Excuse me interrupting,' said Keedy, 'but I don't see what this has to do with a suspect in a murder case.'

'Our last exhibition was over two weeks ago. I believe I might have met John Morris there.'

'What makes you think that?'

'It was a very casual contact,' she told him. 'He was a man in his thirties with an unbecoming face and a limp. The moment I talked to him he dispelled my misgivings about him.'

'How?' asked Keedy.

'He was so complimentary about the exhibition.'

'What did he say to you?'

'How much is this?' she replied.

'I'm sorry, Mrs Mandeville, you've lost me.'

'I was on duty there. I knew the prices of everything.'

'Did he want to buy the painting?'

'He was thinking about it. When I told him how much it was, he went in search of the artist to see if he would lower the price.'

'Can you remember what the painting was like?'

'Of course, Sergeant – once seen, nobody could forget it.'

'Was it so striking?'

'To be candid, it was rather nauseating.'

'Why was that?'

It was a depiction of Christ on the cross,' she replied, 'standing amid the carnage of the Battle of the Somme.'

For a couple of minutes, Ellen Marmion was too stunned to reply. Face pale and body frozen, she tried to cope with the enormity of what her husband had told her. Having written her son out of her life, she found that he had just written himself back into it. While his abrupt departure had left her feeling she had failed as a mother, the threat of his return awoke deep fears rather than maternal tenderness. Paul had reportedly become an itinerant criminal, living rough, working his way from county to county and stealing what he could not get by begging.

Marmion exchanged a glance with his daughter. Both had experienced the same reaction. It was one of shock, if not disgust, tempered by the fact that, whatever he had done, Paul was still part of the family. There had to be pity as well as regret. At such a low ebb in his life, he needed them more than ever.

Taking out a handkerchief, Ellen dabbed at her tears.

'How can they be certain that it is him?' she asked.

'He had Paul's papers,' replied Marmion.

'He might have stolen them.'

'The prisoner matches the description we gave of our son.'

'I'm still not convinced, Harvey.'

'Then there's only one thing for it,' he suggested. 'I'm too entangled in this case to go to Somerset myself but you can go in my place.'

'I'll go with you, Mummy,' Alice volunteered.

'Would you be able to get permission from Inspector Gale?'

'I can ask her. If she refuses, you can get Superintendent Chatfield to speak to her. It may not come to that. Gale Force let me go last time and I'm in her good books for once.' She turned to her mother. 'We'll go together, Mummy.'

Ellen was uncertain. 'I'm not sure that I want to.'

'Why not?'

'I suppose . . . I suppose that I'm afraid of what I might find.'

'One look is all you need to see if it's Paul,' said Marmion.

'Yes, but what sort of look will he give me in return?'

'You stay here, Mummy,' said Alice. 'I'll go on my own.'

'That's unfair on you,' said Ellen.

'Well, someone has to find out the truth.'

'He may not even agree to see us, Alice.'

'I think I see the trouble here,' said Marmion, gently. 'In your heart, you're almost afraid to learn the truth. When there was a sighting of Paul before, the pair of you went with high hopes. Both of you believed that Paul was working on the farm just outside Coventry.'

'Well, he definitely had been, Daddy,' said Alice.

'Yes, I know, and he might still have been there now if he'd behaved himself. But he stepped out of line and became interested in the farmer's daughter. There was no way he could stay after that,' he continued. 'Do you see my point? We all felt that Paul was still part of the family then. Now, we're not so sure.'

'We can't pretend he doesn't exist,' said Ellen.

Alice gave a wan smile. 'That's what we agreed to do yesterday.'

'I know and it was wrong of us.'

'Does that mean you'll come to Somerset with me?'

'I need time to think it over.'

'If you prefer, I can delay the visit by a day or so.'

'You heard your mother, Alice,' said Marmion. 'Give her time to take it all in. The news has knocked me for six, and I don't mind admitting it. Ideally, I'd be on a train to Somerset right now, but I can't just abandon this investigation.'

'We know that,' said his wife. 'It was kind of the superintendent to let you come home. If you had simply rung me from work with this news, I'd have been in a terrible state.' She squeezed Alice's hand. 'Having you both here with me has . . . well, I was going to say that it softened the blow but it's still painful enough.'

'Take time to think it over, love.'

'I'll stay, if you want me to,' offered Alice.

'I do,' said Ellen, tightening her grip on her daughter's hand.

Marmion glanced at his watch. 'I'll have to go, I'm afraid.'

'Yes, of course. Please ring us if there's . . . any other information.'

'I will.'

After kissing his wife and his daughter, Marmion let himself out of the house and climbed into the car. Ellen and Alice were left to discuss the latest news.

'What do you think, Mummy?' asked Alice.

'I'm not sure.'

'That makes two of us. Daddy was right. It's not as easy as last time, is it? When we went to the farm near Coventry, we were dying to see Paul again. That feeling is no longer there, somehow.'

'I don't have feelings of any kind, Alice. I'm just numb.'

'We have to ask ourselves a simple question.'

'What is it?

'Would we rather that it was Paul – or that it wasn't?'

Ellen shrugged. 'I wish I knew,' she said.

CHAPTER TWELVE

Keedy had spent so much time on the telephone in Marmion's office that his ear was buzzing. He was glad to be interrupted by the inspector's return and was on his feet at once.

'How did Alice take the news?' he asked. 'Did she send a message for me? What did the police in Wells say about Paul? Is it true that you told Chat that this case took priority? Did he put pressure on you? Is Alice thinking about going to Somerset with her mother? What exactly is happening?'

'Let me get my breath back, Joe,' said Marmion. 'The last couple of hours have been rather hectic for me.'

'Then come and sit down.'

Keedy vacated the seat behind the desk so that Marmion, weary and careworn, could take his seat. The inspector needed a few minutes to regain his concentration.

'I'm his father, Joe,' he said, eventually. 'I want him back home where we can look after him. But I must be realistic. It may never happen. Paul has rejected us as a family. We can hardly force him to come back to us.'

'And even if you could,' said Keedy, 'there'd be endless difficulties. If Paul has been living rough, he will not fit back easily into normal life.'

'There's no such thing as normal life for Paul. He must be one of many rudderless soldiers invalided out of the army and sent home with damage we can never understand, let alone try to heal.' He slapped the desk. 'Right, that's enough about family problems. Let's get back to the job we are paid to do.' He glanced down. 'I see that you've got a list of garages here. Most of them are ticked off.'

'That means I've contacted them,' said Keedy, 'but to no avail.'

'What else have you been doing?'

Keedy told him about the visits he had made, then moved on quickly to an account of his telephone conversation with Cassandra Mandeville. He was hoping that she might accidentally have met one of their suspects. Marmion was curious.

'It's a long shot, Joe,' he said, 'but we've been lucky with those in the past.'

'If it is the man we want, he must live in or near to Camden Town.'

191

'Why?'

'The Arts Theatre is well known in the area but less so outside it. They have limited funds so are unable to advertise widely. In other words, the people who go to their exhibitions tend to be local.'

'What interests me is this painting of the Battle of the Somme.'

'It sounds weird to me,' said Keedy, pulling a face. 'Paul actually fought in that battle and he never mentioned seeing Christ on a cross there.'

'Was that painting actually sold?'

'No, it wasn't.'

'Why not?'

'Mrs Mandeville said that most people were rather horrified by it. When a vicar came in, he called it obscene and wanted it taken down. He had an argument with the artist about it.'

'Who won the argument?'

'Mrs Mandeville did. Having accepted the painting for display, she defended her decision fiercely. I've only spoken to her on the phone but I'd think twice about having a row with her. She's the sort of woman who always gets her way.'

'I've got a daughter like that,' said Marmion, grinning. 'Be warned.'

'There was another reason why the painting didn't sell. The artist was asking far too much, apparently.'

'What was his name?'

'Colin Voisey.'

'Any idea where he lives?'

Keedy opened his notepad. 'I made a point of getting his address.'

* * *

After a long discussion with her daughter, Ellen Marmion finally reached a decision.

'I'm simply not ready to go there tomorrow, Alice.'

'Then I will have to visit the prison instead of you.'

'I'd rather you didn't.'

'One of us has to go, Mummy.'

'It's a trip that we must make together. I feel that it's my duty to go,' said Ellen, 'but I need a full day to get up the courage.'

'You don't need courage to visit your own son,' said Alice.

'In this case, I do.' She shuddered. 'Isn't that a terrible thing to admit?'

'Given what's happened, it's . . . understandable. I've had a few tremors myself. Let's think about the day after tomorrow, shall we? If it's possible, that is.'

'I don't follow.'

'Well, we can't just turn up at the doors of Shepton Mallet prison and ask to be let in. We'll need permission in advance. Daddy will have to organise that.'

'What if Paul refuses to see us?'

'He's within his rights to do that, Mummy.'

'We'd have had a wasted journey.'

'It's a risk I'm ready to take,' said Alice. 'Maybe we're looking at it the wrong way. We are trying to reach a decision that really belongs to him. Does he want us back in his life again?'

'It's highly unlikely.'

'It might also be very upsetting for him. Paul will feel ashamed to have let us down the way that he has.'

'I doubt if he has any sense of shame left, Alice. Remember what your father told us about his behaviour at that police station in Wells. Does that sound to you as if he cares what he does?' She heaved a sigh. 'We could be going all that way just to get a slap in the face from him.'

'I can't believe that.'

'I still can't believe the way he tormented Sally Redwood, but that's exactly what he did.'

'Yes,' said Alice, 'and he had no sense of shame afterwards.'

'He laughed about it.'

'That was so unlike Paul. When we were growing up together, he could be mischievous and wayward, but never cruel. He is different now. Perhaps we need another full day to think it through,' said Alice. 'At the moment, we're simply reacting quickly to a complete surprise.'

'I agree. We deserve time to let it sink in.'

Alice smiled. 'Is there any chance of food while we do that?'

'Are you hungry?'

'I'm starving, Mummy.'

'Let's see what's in the larder.'

'I'll be happy to do the cooking.'

'Then I'll be happy to let you,' said Ellen, gratefully. 'At the moment, I'm not sure that I could do anything properly. I'm still trying to come to terms with what's happened. And I'm so grateful that I've got company.' She put her arms around her daughter. 'Honestly, I've never needed you so much, Alice.'

They hugged each other for several minutes.

It was dark when the police car nosed its way through the streets of Camden Town. When it reached its destination, it pulled up at the kerb. Marmion and Keedy got out and looked at the dingy street around them. From what they could make out in the gloom, the houses were small, terraced and in dire need of repair. Evidently, art was not a lucrative source of money for Colin Voisey.

They walked along the street until they reached the address they sought. It was a basement flat in a house in the middle of the row. Marmion chuckled.

'What a disappointment!' he said.

'Why?'

'I always thought artists starved in garrets. This one lives in a basement that must get little natural light.'

'Let's find out, shall we?' said Keedy.

They opened the iron gate and went down the steps. As soon as they knocked on the door, they heard a shout of annoyance. Since nobody came to let them in, Keedy banged even harder. The protests were even louder, but they had at least aroused attention.

The door swung open to reveal a tall, dishevelled, scrawny man in his forties.

'Who the bleeding hell are you?' he demanded.

'We're detectives from Scotland Yard,' said Marmion.

The artist stiffened. 'Painting a picture is not against the law now, is it?'

'No, it isn't, Mr Voisey.'

'How do you know my name?' asked the other, warily.

'We're interested in your work,' said Keedy. 'That's to say, we'd like to look at a painting you exhibited recently.'

Voisey relaxed. 'Why didn't you say so? People who admire my work are always welcome. It's a pity there aren't more of them.' He stood back. 'Come in.'

Entering the living room, they were grateful for the light from the gas lamp. It allowed them to take a closer look at Voisey. He had a shaggy beard tinged with the same paint that they could see on his hands. A rag was dangling from his pocket. Pulling it out, he wiped his hands with it.

'I know what you're thinking,' he said, appraising each of them in turn. 'Why do I work down here in the dark? It's because it suits the kind of pictures I paint. They belong in the shadows. I could never create them in broad daylight.'

'Is this what you do for a living?' asked Marmion.

'It's what I do out of love. My stall in the market is what I do for a living. Art is my true vocation. Selling fruit and veg allows me to follow it.'

'We're really interested in a painting that was on display at the Arts Theatre here. I'm told that it features the Battle of the Somme.'

Voisey narrowed his lids. 'Why pick that one?'

'My son was injured in that battle.'

'Really?'

'I took him to see the film that was made about the battle.'

'Yes, I saw that as well. It was terrible. Our lads were killed like flies.'

'Could we see your painting, please?'

'Only if you're thinking of buying it,' said Voisey.

'We are, we are,' pretended Keedy. 'At least, the inspector is, because of his association with the battle through his son.'

'Wait here while I get it from my studio.'

Voisey shuffled out and gave them a chance to study their surroundings. They were in the middle of a low-ceilinged room that was more like a junk shop than a place where anyone would choose to live. The only thing on which it was possible to sit was on an old leather sofa with an abundance of cushions, none of which matched the others in size or colour. For the rest, the place was given over to an array of items that ranged from a pair of china peacocks to a grandfather clock. Its tick was loud and sonorous.

When he returned, Voisey was carrying a large painting in a black frame. He placed it under the light so that it was shown to its best advantage. They stared at it with mingled curiosity and revulsion. The battle itself had been created with some skill and reminded them of images from the film. But their gaze was fixed on the golden cross that rose above the dead and dying soldiers. Nailed immovably to it, Christ was sharing in their agony.

Keedy was astounded. 'I can see what Mrs Mandeville meant.'

'She's a true lover of art,' asserted Voisey. 'I know that she hated it, but she recognised its quality. When others criticised it, she defended me to the hilt.'

'We're told that someone tried to buy it off you,' said Marmion.

'That's right. He came and found me at the refreshments table.'

'How much were you asking?'

'It was a fair price – fifty pounds.'

Marmion gaped. 'How much?'

'You heard.'

'Did he try to haggle with you?'

'Yes,' said Voisey, 'and I felt insulted. You can see how much work went into the painting, not to mention the skill. A labourer is worthy of his hire, gentlemen. An artist deserves respect.' He turned on Keedy. 'How much would you pay, sir?'

'I certainly couldn't afford fifty pounds, I'm afraid. It would take me years to save an amount of that size. It's an extraordinary piece of work, Mr Voisey, but it's far too expensive for me.'

'They all say that,' muttered the artist.

'Tell us about the man who wanted to buy it.'

'He knew nothing about art.'

'Did he make you an offer?'

'Yes, he did, and it was insulting.'

'How would you describe him?' asked Marmion.

'Why do you wish to know?'

'Because the sergeant and I are leading a murder investigation. We have reason to believe that the man who showed interest in your work may have been involved in that murder.'

Voisey goggled. 'Really?'

'Mrs Mandeville has given us a good description of him, but she did not get as close to the man as you obviously did. Also,' Marmion continued, 'she was on duty at the exhibition and distracted by the crowd.'

'That man was a killer?' said the artist in disbelief.

'He may have been. That's all we can say.'

'Then I'll do more than describe him.'

'What do you mean?'

'I can draw a portrait of him in pencil. Would that be of any use?'

'It might well be.'

'Then let's talk about money beforehand.'

'Why?'

'You can't expect me to work for nothing,' said the artist, plaintively.

'And you can't expect us to buy a pig in a poke,' argued Keedy. 'We'd need to see it before we could assess its worth. And don't you dare dash off a sketch that is nothing like the man you met. We can always show it to Mrs Mandeville for confirmation.'

Voisey was offended. 'There's no need to do that,' he said, earnestly. 'I'm an artist. I paint the truth. You'll get what I saw, I promise you.' He looked from one to the other and sucked his teeth. 'Could you manage a fiver?'

Claude Chatfield had a justified reputation for starting work at Scotland Yard early in the morning and for finishing it well beyond the appointed time of his departure. When he held another press conference, he had been on duty for over thirteen hours. Questions from the reports came at him from all sides but he remained calm. Sir Edward Henry had watched part of the event. When it was all over, he took the superintendent aside.

'You should have been a cricketer,' he said.

'I dislike sports of any kind, Sir Edward.'

'That's a pity. You played like an opening batsman. No matter how fast and furious the questions came, you kept a straight bat.'

'I just hope they have the grace to print what I told them.'

'We'll see,' said the commissioner. 'Any breakthrough yet?'

'There's a possible one. Inspector Marmion and Keedy have gone to interview someone who may have met one of the suspects.'

'That's reassuring news.'

'I stress the word "may". It's best to remain cautious.'

'Where exactly have they gone?'

'Camden Town.'

'That's better than charging off to the seaside without notice,' said the commissioner with a ghost of a smile. 'Did anything come of the Brighton episode?'

'It's a matter of opinion. Marmion believed that it did. I disagreed.'

'Going back to the press conference,' said Sir Edward, 'I couldn't help noticing that three different reporters asked why they couldn't question Marmion as well as your good self.'

'If you heard those questions, then you know my answer.'

'You dismissed the idea out of hand.'

'Marmion is far more use gathering evidence than being interrogated by the press. It can, as you know, be a gruelling process.'

'Yet he's always coped well with it in the past.'

'The decision stands, Sir Edward,' said Chatfield, meeting his eye. 'There's something that you seem to have overlooked.'

'What's that?'

'The inspector's son is in prison on remand. If that information gets out, Marmion would be under heavy fire at a press conference. He needs to be protected from that at all costs.'

'What chance is there of a leak?'

'You know what the pay rates are for lower ranks, Sir Edward. Someone might be tempted to make a phone call to a national newspaper to see how much his information might be worth.'

The commissioner nodded. 'It must be embarrassing for the inspector.'

'And for his daughter,' said Chatfield. 'She's in the Women's Police Force. If the word spreads, she may come in for some ribbing from her colleagues.'

'What about the son himself?'

'Sadly, I don't think he cares two hoots about his family.'

The prisoner lay contentedly on his bunk with his hands behind his head. When he heard a key being inserted in the lock, he stood up at once. The door opened and a prison officer came in with a tray of food. When it was placed on the little table in the cell, the prisoner gave it a cursory glance.

'It looks better than the horse shit they served in Wells,' he said.

During the drive back to Scotland Yard, it was too dark to see anything of the portrait they had bought from Colin Voisey. When they eventually returned to Marmion's office, they were able to scrutinise it properly.

'Voisey is very nifty with a pencil,' said Marmion, noting the detail. 'We have to admire him for that.'

'Yes,' said Keedy. 'I agree. I think it might be a good likeness. All the features that Mrs Mandeville and the lady at Pegasus Costumes picked out are there.'

'I'm interested in his clothing. He's quite well-dressed.'

'Neither of the two ladies said much about that.'

'All in all,' said Marmion, 'my fiver was money well spent.'

'Are you going to give Chat the bill?'

'Only if this sketch turns out to be of any use. It might be worth taking it across to the police station in Camden Town. Someone might recognise him.'

'Let's look through our own records first,' said Keedy. 'If he has a history of offending, we may have his photograph in our files. If not, I'll go back to Camden first thing in the morning.'

'I'll hold you to that, Joe.'

'Are you going to show it to Chat?'

'I'll have to,' said Marmion, 'but I won't mention that we had to pay to get it.'

'Thank goodness you had enough money on you. I'm almost skint.'

'Solve this crime and you can demand a pay rise.'

'Is there any point?'

'None at all.' They laughed. Marmion studied the portrait again. 'Voisey certainly has an eye for detail. Those eyes are so dark and menacing,' he noted. 'He could well be one of the killers. Voisey deserves credit. He's a clever artist.'

'I didn't think so when he showed us that painting of the Battle of the Somme. Frankly,' admitted Keedy, 'it turned my stomach. I can't believe that he had the cheek to ask fifty pounds for it.'

'That was only a starting point. He was ready to haggle.'

'Even at half that amount, it would be ridiculously overpriced.'

'Maybe that was his intention, Joe.'

'What do you mean?'

'Voisey loves that painting,' said Marmion. 'You could see that it was special to him. He wants to keep it. When someone shows an interest, he gives them a ludicrous price to frighten them off.'

'Mrs Mandeville told me that he had other paintings on display and that a couple of them sold for modest amounts. But the one featuring that cross at the Battle of the Somme scared most people away.'

'Not this chap,' said Marmion, looking at the portrait once more. 'From what you told me about him, this is close to a photograph.'

'I think that's true.'

'What do we know about him, Joe?'

'He's capable of murder and likes paintings filled with violence.'

'Then who, in the name of God, is he?'

The man with ugly features was seated at the table, counting out the last of the money. His friend soon came into the room. Older and stockier, he had the furrowed brow of someone who took life seriously. He glanced at his companion.

'How much is there altogether?' he asked.

'There's nearly two hundred in cash plus the jewellery, though why a man living alone needs so much jewellery, I don't know.'

'It's too late to ask him.'

'We're not thieves. We needed to convince the police that we were just to confuse them. It's time to get rid of it.'

'I agree.'

'I've just realised something,' said the younger man with a smile. 'With this much money, I could afford to buy that painting I liked.'

'The money is not ours,' his friend reminded him. 'You know what we agreed. We keep enough for our expenses and the rest goes to charity. As for that painting, you told me you rejected it.'

'I did.'

'Why?'

'It wasn't worth the asking price.'

'What appealed to you about it?'

'I liked the message it sent out. It was bold and assertive.' He sat back in his chair. 'What shall we do with all those photographs we took from the house?'

'We put them in a sack and drop it in the canal.'

'And then what?'

'We wait for our orders.'

'That could take time.'

'There's no hurry.'

'There might be if the police pick up our trail.'

'Fat chance of that happening!' said the older man with a derisive laugh. 'You saw the morning papers. The coppers are hopeless. They're running around in circles like headless chickens.'

'I've heard about Inspector Marmion. He never gives up.'

'Forget him. We're in the clear and ready for another assignment.'

'Where will the next one be?'

'I don't know but I hope it's easier than this one. It took us ages to find that bloody doctor. He covered his tracks well.'

'We got him in the end.'

'It's because we stuck at it,' said the other. 'There's no escape from us.'

Though it was almost nine o'clock in the evening when they went to the superintendent's office, Chatfield was still there, studying reports of other investigations. When Marmion and Keedy entered, he looked up with interest.

'Well?'

'We have something to show you, sir,' said Marmion.

'I hope it's worth looking at.'

'It is,' confirmed Keedy. 'It's a portrait of one of the killers.'

'Let me see.' He took the paper and examined the portrait at length. His eyes flicked up at them. 'It's well drawn.'

'Voisey is a good artist,' said Marmion, 'but, like so many of them, not good enough to make money at it.'

'What took you so long?'

'We spent a lot of time with him, sir,' said Keedy, 'then we did what you'd have wanted us to do?'

'Oh?'

'We came back here and trawled through the files to see if we could find a photograph that looked like the man in front of you.'

'And?'

'The cupboard was bare, Superintendent.'

'We don't think that he has a police record,' added Marmion.

'He may not have been successfully prosecuted,' said Chatfield, 'but he could still be known to the police in Camden Town.'

'Inspector Marmion has already asked me to go there tomorrow morning,' said Keedy. 'What we don't know is if he's a resident in the area or someone who just stayed there until he and his accomplice had committed the murder. Camden and Edmonton are not a million miles apart, sir.'

'Neither are they exactly next-door neighbours, Sergeant.' Chatfield set the portrait aside. 'We need more than a hasty sketch from an impecunious artist.'

'I think it could be a good likeness, sir.'

'You might even release it to the press,' ventured Marmion.

'They've got enough to go on,' said Chatfield, fussily. 'I saw to that. I have doubts about this man being a suspect. If he is not, we will have wasted valuable time going down a blind alley. If, by chance, he is – and my reservations remain – then a glance at this portrait of him in the papers will send him scuttling away from Camden Town in a flash. We must never give warnings to villains,' he said, handing the portrait back to Marmion. 'It hands them an advantage.'

'Wise counsel, sir,' said the other.

'I agree,' added Keedy, dutifully.

Before he dismissed them, Chatfield had a question for the inspector.

'I take it that you've spoken to your wife and daughter about . . .'

'Yes, sir. Thanks to you, I have.'

'And what have they decided to do?'

'I don't know,' said Marmion. 'If I manage to get home in time, I'm hoping to find out if they have made a decision.'

* * *

Having her daughter there for two consecutive nights was a treat that Ellen had not enjoyed for a long time. She was doing the best to make the most of it. Instead of debating endlessly the possibility of a visit to Shepton Mallet prison, they ranged over several subjects. Chief among them was the forthcoming marriage.

'What did Joe think of the house?' asked Ellen.

'He liked it, Mummy, much more than I did.'

'Was this the one you spotted in the evening paper?'

'Yes,' said Alice. 'We couldn't find a time to see it together. I went first and Joe sneaked a few minutes to pop in for a quick look.'

'What was the result?'

'He really liked it, but I didn't.'

'Why was that?'

'It had the smallest kitchen I've ever seen and no garden. There was just a yard at the back, filled with bins and a pile of junk. Also,' said Alice, 'there was a smell as if a drain was blocked.'

'Why did Joe react so differently to you?'

'A small kitchen didn't put him off because I'll do all the cooking. And he was glad there was no garden because it meant there was no grass for him to cut. As for the stench, someone could fix that.' Ellen laughed. 'What's so funny?'

'You sound just like me and your father. We look at the same thing from completely different angles. Not that we were able to own a house straight away, mind you,' recalled Ellen. 'After the wedding, your father moved into our house. A lot of awkward adjustments had to be made with my parents. When we did finally move out, my father was delighted, and my mother begged us to stay.'

'But you both wanted your independence.'

'Yes, we did.'

'So you know why it means so much to me and Joe.'

Ellen brought up a hand to stifle a yawn. 'I'm tired,' she said, glancing at the clock on the mantelpiece. 'Have you seen the time?'

'I'm usually in bed much earlier than this.'

'It's not a usual day, Alice.'

Getting up from the sofa, they were about to leave the room when they heard a car pull up outside. Ellen was delighted.

'That will be your father,' she said.

'I'll be glad of a word with him before I go to bed.'

'I'm so weary, I may need him to help me upstairs.'

They heard a key being inserted in the front door, then it opened wide. When she heard two voices, Alice was delighted. Her father had brought Keedy with him. She ran out of the room and into his arms. Marmion closed the front door.

'I brought you a present, Alice,' he said.

Keedy laughed. 'I've been called worse.'

'It's such a wonderful surprise,' said Alice.

'Yes, it is,' said Ellen, joining them. 'Hello, Joe.'

'I've been invited to spend the night on your sofa,' he told her.

She headed for the stairs. 'I'll get blankets right away.'

'How is the investigation going?' asked Alice.

'I'll let Joe tell you,' said Marmion. 'I'm off to bed.'

'Good night, Daddy.'

She took Keedy into the living room and kissed him. He pulled her close.

'This is the best thing that's happened to me all day,' he said. He looked down at the sofa. 'If I remember aright, it's not very comfy to sleep on.'

Alice laughed softly. 'You may not get much sleep.'

CHAPTER THIRTEEN

For those in law enforcement, there was no rest. Crime in Camden Town took place all day and night, so its police station never closed. It was five o'clock in the morning when a figure crept along the street with a small bag in his hand. Approaching cautiously, he reached the police station, eased open the door and pushed the bag inside. Then he sprinted off into the darkness. The desk sergeant had heard the door open and shut. When he came to investigate, he saw the bag and picked it up. Taking it back to his desk, he tipped out the contents. His jaw dropped involuntarily.

'Where the hell did all this come from?' he asked.

He was looking at a small pile of jewellery.

After an early breakfast at Marmion's home, he and Keedy were picked up by a police car and driven towards central London. A good night's sleep had revived Marmion but Keedy seemed as if he was only half-awake. For the first stretch of the journey, he let Marmion do most of the talking. He then made a conscious effort to join in the conversation.

'I agree with you, Harv,' he said. 'They made the right decision.'

'It was Alice who actually made it. Ellen took time to come round to the idea. My daughter can be very persuasive when she wants to be.'

'I've already found that out.'

'Drop me off at Scotland Yard,' said Marmion, 'then continue on to Camden Town.'

'I don't hold out much hope.'

'Why not?'

'Those men are professionals. Look at the way that they got into Dr Tindall's house. They did their homework beforehand. It's the reason we found no trace of them in our files. They've so far got away scot-free.'

'That will soon change.'

'I hope so, Harv. By the way, are you going to ring the prison?'

'No, I'll ask Chat to do that. Superintendents carry more weight.'

'What about Inspector Gale? Someone needs to explain to her why Alice is not available today.'

'I'll do that as soon as I reach my office.'

'Use your charm.'

211

'What charm?' asked Marmion with a hollow laugh.

'Oh, I've just thought of something,' said Keedy. 'Suppose the prisoner refuses to see them?'

'I can't see that happening, Joe. In my experience, anyone locked up behind bars usually jumps at the chance of a change of scene, if only for a short time. Apart from anything else, they like to stretch their legs.'

'But a prisoner can't be forced to leave his cell, can he?'

'That depends on the circumstances.'

'What if his mother and sister have come to visit him?'

'There's always the chance that it's not Paul,' insisted Marmion.

'They'd have to see him to make absolutely sure.'

'No, they wouldn't, Joe.'

'What makes you say that?'

'If he refuses to see them, then we know one thing for certain.'

'Do we?'

'Yes – it definitely is Paul.'

Breakfast was served by an impassive prison officer who made no comment. The prisoner ran an appreciative eye over the items on his tray.

'That looks good,' he said, cheerily. 'I came to the right place.'

Alice Marmion was annoyed with herself for having overslept. It meant that she had missed seeing Keedy leave. She blamed her mother.

'Why didn't you call me?' she demanded.

'I did, Alice, but you obviously didn't hear me.'

'Nobody told me that they'd have to be off so early.'

Ellen was philosophical. 'That's police work for you.'

'Oh, I'm so cross with myself.'

She attacked the boiled egg with her spoon. As she ate her breakfast, Alice slowly relaxed and accepted what had happened.

'I'm sorry, Mummy,' she said. 'It's my fault. I should have got up in time.'

'You're up now, that's the main thing.'

'Gale Force will be up as well. She'll soon be wondering where I am.'

'Your father promised to smooth her feathers.'

Alice spluttered. 'Then he's in for a shock. Gale Force doesn't have feathers. She's covered in spikes like a hedgehog. Yes, and she snuffles like one sometimes. If Daddy tries to stroke her, he'll get a nasty surprise.'

'Your father is more tactful than you know,' said Ellen. 'He'll have Inspector Gale eating out of his hand.'

'Count his fingers when he comes home. He might have one missing.'

'Alice!'

While her daughter carried on eating, Ellen sipped her tea reflectively. Her face was soon shadowed with doubt.

'I still don't know if we made the right decision,' she said.

'There's no point in delay, Mummy. That would give us an extra twenty-four hours of sheer misery, wondering if it is Paul. Remember what Daddy and Joe said. We must find out the truth as soon as possible.'

'I suppose so.'

'What's happened to that confidence you suddenly had last night?' asked Alice. 'You couldn't wait to get off to Somerset.'

'Things are different in the daylight.'

'Not for me. I'm going, even if you pull out.'

The telephone rang in the hall. Ellen leapt to her feet at once and ran out.

'That will be your father to tell us if the prison will let us in . . .'

The car drew up outside the police station in Camden Town and Keedy got out. After looking up and down the street, he went into the building. The desk sergeant was glancing at a morning newspaper. When he saw Keedy, he put it away. The sergeant was a stout, grizzled man in his late fifties with a world of suspicion in his eyes.

'Can I help you, sir?' he asked.

'I hope so,' said Keedy, producing his warrant card and holding it up. 'I'm involved in the investigation into the murder of Dr Tindall.'

'I read about that,' said the other, his manner changing at once. 'It's not often that I'm shocked but I was when I learnt the details. The poor man was executed.'

'We're anxious to speak to someone from Camden Town who may be of interest to us. As far as we know, he has no previous convictions, but you might just have come across him.'

'What was the name?'

'We don't have one.'

'That's awkward.'

'What we do have,' said Keedy, taking the portrait from his pocket and unfolding it to put on the desk, 'is this. We're assured that it's a good likeness.'

The sergeant's eyebrows arched in approval. 'It's certainly a good drawing,' he said. 'This was done by a proper artist.'

'I'll come to him. Take your time – have a good look.'

Picking up the portrait, the sergeant held it near his face so that he could squint at it. It was almost a minute before he spoke.

'No,' he said, 'I'm sorry. I've never seen him before.'

'Are you certain of that?'

'I've got a good memory, Sergeant Keedy.'

'Fair enough.' Taking the portrait from him, Keedy folded it up and put it back in his pocket. 'Let's move on to the artist, shall we?'

'What artist?'

'His name is Colin Voisey.'

The sergeant chuckled. 'Oh, we know Colin very well.'

'Has he been in trouble?'

'He's spent the odd night in one of our cells, drunk as a lord.'

'I'm surprised he can afford it.'

'Last time we had him here was over an argument in the market. A customer claimed that some of the fruit Colin sold him was rotten. That was like a red rag to a bull. Colin threatened to kick lumps off the customer. They both ended up in here.' He peered at Keedy. 'What's your interest in Colin Voisey?'

'He drew that portrait I showed you.'

'Did he?' asked the other. 'He's got more talent than I thought.'

'There's someone else you might have come across,' said Keedy.

'Who's that?'

'Mrs Mandeville.'

'Oh, yes,' said the other, grinning. 'We've certainly come across Cassie Mandeville. She puts on a pantomime every year in the Arts Theatre. I took my granddaughter to the last one and she's still talking about it . . .'

Having enjoyed their day out together, Iris Goodliffe was looking forward to seeing her friend again so that she could thank her. She was therefore nonplussed when she was told by Inspector Gale that Alice Marmion was not there.

'Why not?' she asked.

'It doesn't matter,' said the older woman.

'It matters to me, Inspector. We walk the same beat.'

'Today, you will have a different partner.'

'Is Alice ill?' asked Iris. 'She was fine yesterday.'

'I'm not at liberty to tell you the reason why she's unable to be here,' said the inspector. 'When I spoke to her father, he stressed that it was a private matter.'

'There are no secrets between Alice and me.'

Thelma Gale glared. 'Stop pestering me.'

'I'm curious, that's all, Inspector.'

'Direct your curiosity at the streets you're about to walk. I've assigned Jerrold to your beat.'

'Oh, no!'

216

'Is there a problem?'

'I like Jennifer Jerrold,' said Iris. 'I like her a lot but . . . she's not the person I'd choose to spend most of the day with.'

'You don't have the option of a choice,' warned the inspector. 'You go wherever I tell you and with whom I select. Is that clear?'

'Yes, Inspector.'

'In fact, I've been thinking of putting you with Jerrold on a permanent basis.'

Iris was aghast. 'You can't do that!'

'I can do whatever I wish.'

'Alice and I are best friends.'

'That's one of the reasons I'm splitting you up. Walking the beat is more of a social event for the two of you. You probably spend most of the time exchanging gossip instead of concentrating on the task in hand.'

'That's unfair.'

'Jerrold will be a steadying influence.'

'Alice and I have proved our worth as a team many times.'

'You'll do even better in harness with Jerrold.'

'But Jenny and I don't have the same . . . understanding.'

'That will come in time.'

'There's no earthly chance of it happening,' said Iris in despair. 'I've nothing against Jenny. She's a nice woman. But – if I may be honest with you – she's too religious for me. She's always talking about her church.'

'Good,' said the other, crisply. 'A brush with Christianity might help to rub some of those rough edges off you. Now get out there and do your job.'

* * *

While he and Sergeant Keedy ventured outside Scotland Yard, Marmion had a small team of detectives who remained, for the most part, back at their base. One of them was Detective Constable Clifford Burge, a powerful, thickset man in his thirties with a face that even his best friends would never call handsome. He had already proven his worth when he dealt with some feral gangs terrorising the district where he had grown up. Marmion valued him highly. Once Burge was given an assignment, he worked tirelessly at it.

When he came into Marmion's office, the inspector was glad to see him.

'Good morning, sir,' said Burge, smiling.

'I hope that that look on your face means you have something for me.'

'I may have.'

'Sit down and tell me what it is.'

'Thank you,' said Burge, taking a seat and flipping his notebook open. 'You asked me to look at this case and try to find something similar in the files.'

'And did you?'

'I believe so.'

Marmion waved an arm. 'The floor is yours.'

'Right, sir.' Burge cleared his throat then launched into his report. 'Several months ago, a solicitor in Bristol was hacked to death in his office. He had been castrated.' He gave a grim chuckle. 'Even an angry client wouldn't go that far.'

'What did the police report say?'

'They believe that two men were involved but have no idea who they were. The search continues,' said Burge, 'but there is an interesting piece of information that came to light. The victim had a brother in the army – a Captain Tait.'

'So?'

'He committed suicide some time after his brother was killed.'

'Has any connection been made between the two incidents?'

'The police are still speculating, sir.'

'I'm sure they are,' said Marmion. 'Is that it?'

'No, Inspector. I telephoned the police in Bristol and asked for more detail about the case.'

'Good man.'

'It should arrive by post today.'

'I look forward to seeing it. Making a judgement without more detail would be foolish but, on the surface, there is a resemblance to the case in hand. First, a lawyer and now, an orthopaedic surgeon. Does someone bear a grudge against middle-class professional men?'

'I haven't finished yet, Inspector.'

'Oh, I'm sorry. Do carry on.'

'There's somebody we have to slip in between those two cases. The landlord of a pub in Stafford was murdered several weeks ago. Unnecessary violence was used. In this case, the head was cut off – and so was something else.'

'I can guess what it was,' said Marmion. 'Any leads?'

'Not really, sir. The police have drafted in additional manpower, but they have not dug up anything significant yet. And yes,' Burge went on, 'I did try to get more detail. I got in touch with a Superintendent Ash in Stafford. He was very helpful.'

'Put what he told you in a report so that I can read it.'

'I will, sir. If I keep on looking, I may find other similar murders.'

'Then do just that.'

'It's the degree of brutality that links all three cases.'

'That's true,' agreed Marmion, 'but that's not enough in itself to prove that the same killers were at work in all three cases. Why should anyone jump from Bristol to Stafford then on to London? Since the war started, most people have stayed where they are and kept their heads down. As for the excessive violence, I'm afraid that that, too, is a legacy of the war. It has pushed people to extremes. What used to be a fist is now a knife or a broken bottle. Well, look at those gangs you tackled for us. That turf war was incendiary.'

'Those lads were ready to kill,' recalled Burge. 'I couldn't believe some of the weapons we collected.'

'Thankfully, they've been taken out of action.'

'What shall I do next, sir?'

'Wait until the information arrives from Bristol then compare the details with those of the Stafford murder. I want a written report of both investigations.'

'Yes, sir.'

'Oh, and a word of warning,' added Marmion. 'Don't bank on the three crimes being the work of the same offenders. We've had close similarities before between cases that turned out to be unrelated.'

'I'll bear that in mind.'

'Off you go, then – and well done!'

* * *

Faced with a long journey, Ellen Marmion was determined not to spend it agonising about her son. Accordingly, she took a library book with her to read on the train and Alice bought a magazine from the bookstall at the station. As it was, the only seats they could find were in a full compartment, so a private conversation was impossible. Though Ellen tried hard to concentrate on her romantic novel, her mind kept gravitating towards her son. When Marmion had contacted her earlier on, he told her that Superintendent Chatfield had not only secured permission for the two women to get into Shepton Mallet prison. He was even able to pass on the news that – having been contacted by the governor – the prisoner had agreed to meet them.

What had at first been a source of optimism had now become one that made her increasingly uneasy. Even if the prisoner was her son, she was going to meet a stranger. It was a long time since they had seen each other and Paul would have changed in every way. While he may have agreed to see two members of his family, he might refuse to do so out of spite once they had arrived. It was a risk they had to take. And there was also the possibility that the prisoner was not even her son, and that he had used the invitation to meet the two women simply to enjoy some momentary freedom from being locked in his cell. If that were the case, Ellen wondered how she would react. Would she feel anguish or relief?

For her part, Alice was dividing her attention between a recipe in her magazine and warm thoughts about Joe Keedy. Time went quickly for her.

* * *

221

The two policewomen had walked side by side for several minutes without exchanging a single word. It was unusual for someone as garrulous as Iris Goodliffe to remain silent. At length, it was Jennifer Jerrold who spoke first. She was a lanky, fair-haired young woman with a pretty face, now disfigured by a frown.

'Have I done something wrong?' she asked, tentatively.

'No,' said Iris, 'of course not.'

'I get the feeling that you're cross with me.'

'That's not true, Jenny.'

'Then why haven't you spoken since we set out?'

'My mind was on other things.'

'In other words, you were thinking about Alice.'

'Yes, I was. I still can't work out why she didn't turn up this morning. We spent the best part of the day together yesterday, so she had plenty of chances to warn me that she was not feeling well or that she had another reason for staying away today. It's so unlike Alice.'

'The inspector says that she is the best policewoman we have.'

'It's true,' said Iris. 'It's a pity that Gale Force doesn't tell her that to her face. She never stops criticising Alice. I think she is jealous because Alice has got a father who is a detective inspector and because she's engaged to Sergeant Keedy. In other words, she rubs shoulders with real policemen.'

'We're real policewomen,' said Jennifer, proudly.

'Yes, but we don't have the power or the experience that men have.'

'All I know is that Alice saved me from resigning.'

'Thank goodness she did,' said Iris. 'In doing so, she proved what a good detective she is. Because she found out who was stalking you, you are still here with us. That's a bonus.'

'There's more to it than that. Because I felt that someone was watching me all the time, I withdrew into my shell. I can't tell you how horrible it was,' said Jennifer. 'My confidence drained away completely. How could I enforce the law when I was feeling like that?'

'It must have been an ordeal.'

'Because of Alice, I'm a new woman. I can't thank her enough.'

'I'm the same, Jenny. She has been a rock to me. When I had . . . problems, it was Alice who gave me moral support. That meant so much.'

Jennifer smiled. 'She's done something for the two of us as well.'

'Has she?'

'Yes, Alice has got the two of us talking to each other at last.'

They burst out laughing and walked on purposefully.

As soon as he returned to Scotland Yard, Keedy went straight to Marmion's office. The inspector glanced up from his desk.

'Take a pew, Joe,' he said. 'How did you get on?'

Keedy sat down. 'It was worth the visit,' he replied.

'Tell me why.'

The sergeant recounted the long chat he had with the duty sergeant at Camden Town police station. The man had been unable to recognise the face in the portrait. What he had been able to do was to tell Keedy how much Roland Mandeville and his wife contributed to the community. Keedy looked up from the notebook.

'I've saved the best bit to the end,' he said.

'I'm all agog.'

'Earlier this morning, someone sneaked up to the police station in the dark and left a bag inside the door. When it was opened, it was found to contain an assortment of jewellery. I'm no expert,' said Keedy, 'but it looked like the expensive kind.'

'Did the duty sergeant have any idea where it came from?' asked Marmion.

'No, he didn't.'

'Had there been any recent robbery that involved the theft of jewellery?' Keedy shook his head. 'So where did it come from?'

'I could hazard a guess.'

'Don't jump to conclusions, Joe.'

'Well, we know that valuables were taken from Dr Tindall's safe.'

'But we don't know which valuables,' stressed Marmion.

'Think about it,' urged Keedy. 'A man who keeps photographs of his late wife would be bound to keep her jewellery as a souvenir, especially as he had paid for it in the first place.'

'He may also have paid for her clothing, yet we didn't find a single dress hanging up in the wardrobe. And please do not tell me that the killers took those as well,' added Marmion. 'They may have enjoyed wearing an army uniform, but I fancy that they'd draw the line at ballroom gowns.'

'You're missing something, Harv.'

'Am I?'

'One of those men has been traced to Camden Town.'

'He's been traced to an art exhibition there, maybe. It does not prove that he lives in Camden. He might have been passing through the area, or he may have come off a barge moored in the canal. He might have been visiting a friend who does live there, and he happened to notice what was on at the Arts Theatre. No,' said Marmion, 'there are far too many "mights" here.'

'You may change your mind when that jewellery is valued.'

'Why is that?'

'We've already discovered that Tindall was a wealthy man. He would have bought stuff of the highest quality for his wife. If a jeweller puts a high valuation on it, I think it came from that safe in Edmonton.' Marmion looked dubious. 'It's a reasonable assumption.'

'Then why am I unable to make that assumption?'

'You're starting to sound like Chat.'

Marmion grinned. 'Insults will get you nowhere.'

'Let me remind you of something else,' said Keedy. 'Because we specialise in homicide, we rarely look closely at other crimes being investigated. If there is a big jewellery heist, however, we would get to hear about it, if only from the gossip in the canteen. Can you think of a recent case that was worth talking about?'

'No,' conceded Marmion, 'I can't.'

'Then don't just dismiss my theory.'

'I'm not dismissing it, Joe. I'm glad that you've woken up in time to think straight again. In the car on the way here, you were barely awake. A bag of jewellery has really brought you alive. From my point of view, that's good news.'

'Fair enough,' said Keedy. 'I've said my piece. I won't badger you any more about that jewellery.'

'Thanks.'

'What have you been up to here?'

'I've been considering what may turn out to be some new evidence.'

'Where did it come from?'

'I asked Detective Constable Burge to search for a lookalike crime.'

'Did he find one?'

'He may have found two,' said Marmion, 'though that has yet to be confirmed. Burge is a good detective. I'll be interested to discover what he has unearthed.'

After a long, tedious, and uncomfortable train journey, Ellen Marmion and her daughter endured a lengthy wait at the railway station before a bus finally arrived to take them to Shepton Mallet. As the vehicle struggled along bumpy roads, they were reminded how spoilt they were by living in the nation's capital where taxis, buses and an underground system made travel relatively easy. The one advantage of the second part of their journey was that they were able sit at the rear of the bus and converse freely without being overheard.

'I'm beginning to wonder if we'll ever get there,' moaned Ellen.

'Don't say that, Mummy. My nerves are shredded enough already.'

'I'm having second thoughts.'

'It's too late for that,' said Alice, firmly. 'We have to know the truth.'

'The fact is that Paul has avoided us like the plague.'

226

'I'm not sure about that. I wonder whether he's just too embarrassed to come back.'

'Embarrassed?' echoed her mother. 'By what?'

'By what he sees as his failure to build a new life. That must have been part of the reason why he left. Paul wanted to find something else,' said Alice. 'He knew he was causing all sorts of problems for us and we were probably doing things that maddened him.'

'I felt that sometimes. He hated being mothered.'

'Perhaps he's changed his mind.'

'There's only one way to find out, Alice.'

The bus eventually dropped them off in the middle of Shepton Mallet and they took their first look at the historic town. It was a world away from the crowded streets and permanent hubbub of the capital. After taking directions from a uniformed policeman, they walked to Frithfield Lane and found the prison. By comparison with the major prisons in London, it was small, but nevertheless forbidding. The idea that Paul was being held behind the high perimeter walls was a chilling one for both women. As they approached, they tried not to look up.

Getting into the prison took time. They were questioned at length, asked to produce proof of identity, and stared at by burly male officers. Eventually, they were taken to the governor's office. After introductions had been made, they sat down.

Gerald Scarman, the governor, was a tall, angular man in his fifties.

'How was your journey?' he asked.

'It was something of a trial,' said Ellen.

'When I spoke to Superintendent Chatfield yesterday, he told me that your husband was a detective inspector at Scotland Yard.'

'That's right. He is. Did he tell you that my daughter was in the Women's Police Force?'

'No, he didn't,' said the governor, turning his attention to Alice. 'I applaud you, Miss Marmion. In times of crisis, it is a case of all hands to the pump, even if some of them are soft, feminine hands.'

'We believe that Paul agreed to see us,' said Alice.

'Ah, well, he did at first, but he seems to have had a change of heart.'

Ellen was horrified. 'We've come all this way for nothing?'

'Not necessarily. The chaplain is talking to the prisoner. He can be very persuasive. What we want to avoid, of course,' said the governor, 'is having to drag him kicking and screaming from his cell. That's hardly the mood you want him in for a family reunion.'

'But we don't yet know that it is my brother,' said Alice.

'The prisoner was happy to confirm it. There is no doubt on that score. We will just have to wait to see if the chaplain can work his magic. Meanwhile,' he went on, 'may I offer you some refreshments?'

CHAPTER FOURTEEN

Claude Chatfield disliked criticism, especially when it came from the commissioner. Because it was delivered by Sir Edward Henry in such a polite, gentlemanly way, it somehow had more impact than a blistering tirade. The morning newspapers had given more extensive coverage on their front pages to the fate of Dr Tindall but – by means of misquoting the superintendent – had somehow conveyed the impression that Scotland Yard was baffled and had made virtually no progress in the investigation. The commissioner had, in effect, blamed the superintendent. As he walked off to his office, Chatfield was in no mood for conversation. When he was confronted by

Marmion and Burge, therefore, he waved them aside with an imperious hand.

Marmion stood his ground. 'We need to speak to you, sir,' he said.

'Come back this afternoon.'

'This is important.'

'Don't you understand an order when you hear one?'

'As you wish,' said Marmion, moving aside. 'We'll have to take the information to the commissioner.'

'Don't you dare go above my head,' snapped Chatfield. 'And who are you?' he added, noticing Burge for the first time.

'Detective Constable Burge, sir,' replied the other.

'Are you part of this ambush?'

'It is not an ambush, sir,' said Marmion. 'We are simply trying to bring you what may turn out to be crucial information. If you have more important things to deal with, of course, we'll seek an opinion from Sir Edward.'

There was a long pause as Chatfield considered the threat.

'Follow me,' he growled.

He swept off down the corridor. Marmion winked at Burge and followed the quivering figure in front of them. Once inside his office, Chatfield swung round to issue a challenge.

'I need good news for a change. Give it to me.'

'It concerns a case in Bristol, sir,' said Marmion.

'Then I've no wish to hear about it. My only interest is in a murder that happened right here in London.'

'The men who killed Dr Tindall may have been active in Bristol beforehand.'

'And in Stafford, for that matter,' said Burge.

'We're talking about two remarkably similar murders, sir.'

Burge nodded. 'And there's a distinct echo of them in Dr Tindall's case.'

'You've been distracted,' said Chatfield, acidly. 'I can forgive someone like Burge but a man of your experience, Inspector, should not be led astray so easily.'

'Both murders feature brutality on a scale comparable to that in our case, Superintendent. To be more exact,' Marmion went on, 'both victims were hacked to death and castrated – just like Dr Tindall.'

'We believe the killers were making a point,' said Burge.

'They made the same one in Edmonton.'

'The inspector has told me what the post-mortem report revealed. It's very much in accord with what happened in Bristol and Stafford.'

'What are you trying to tell me?' asked Chatfield.

'If you care to sit down, sir,' said Marmion, 'we will explain.'

'I can hear perfectly well standing up.'

'So be it.' He turned to Burge. 'You take over.'

'Well,' said the other, 'this all came about because of an initiative launched by Inspector Marmion. He believes that the men who killed Dr Tindall were experienced. He therefore asked me to search for cases with the same modus operandi. I began digging in the recent past. The first murder that jumped out at me occurred in Bristol months ago. The victim was a respected solicitor in the city – Meredith Tait. They are still searching for the men who butchered him to death . . .'

When they left London, the last thing that Ellen and Alice expected to do was to sit in the prison governor's office, drink tea, nibble biscuits and wonder if they would get to see the person calling himself Paul Marmion. Scarman was pleasant and attentive. He was particularly interested in what being a policewoman entailed.

'My daughter is somewhat younger than you, Miss Marmion,' he said, 'and finds it rather embarrassing that her father runs a prison. It's something she never dared to mention when she was at school.'

'I'm proud of what my father does,' said Alice.

'Rightly so, Miss Marmion.'

'This war has given us precious few benefits but one of them is that it has enabled women to play a more active role in society.'

'I couldn't agree more. As a matter of fact . . .'

Whatever he was about to say died on his lips because there was a knock on his door. Scarman opened it to admit a prison officer who delivered a message in an undertone. After apologising to his visitors, the governor went out.

'Paul has turned us down,' said Ellen with an air of finality.

'Let's wait to see what the chaplain does.'

'He's had plenty of time to persuade him and he's failed. If you want my opinion, I think that Paul is playing games with us. He agreed to see us to bring us all the way here, then refused to leave his cell. He's probably sitting in there at this moment, laughing at us.'

'He's not that callous.'

'He is now, Alice.'

'We talked ourselves into believing that it is really him.'

'It is – I sense it.'

'Well, I'm starting to think that it's not my brother at all. It is someone he met along the way who got hold of Paul's papers. That is why he is refusing to see us face to face. We'd expose him as the fraud he obviously is.'

'All I want,' said Ellen, 'is to learn the truth. Is it really Paul?'

'No – he'd never treat us like this.'

'I'm horribly afraid that he would, Alice.'

Her daughter's face puckered. 'I blame myself for persuading you to come here,' she said. 'You wanted another day to think it over and you were right.'

'There's no need to be sorry,' said Ellen. 'I needed a good push from someone, and you gave it to me.' She looked around. 'This place gives me the shivers.'

'Imagine what it must be like to be locked up here.'

'I can't bear to think about it.'

Ellen sat up in surprise as the door opened and the governor came in.

'Your son has agreed to see you, after all,' he said.

'What a relief!' she sighed.

'Why did he change his mind?' asked Alice.

Scarman smiled. 'I did say that the chaplain was persuasive.'

She got to her feet. 'How do we know that it is Paul?'

'It seems that he anticipated that question, Miss Marmion. That's why he sent a message to both of you.'

'What is it?'

'He asked to be remembered to Sally Redwood.'

Ellen gasped and glanced at Alice. It was him.

Remaining on his feet throughout, Chatfield listened carefully. Clifford Burge referred to his notes throughout and marshalled his argument well. Marmion slipped in the occasional rider. The superintendent's face was so motionless that it was impossible to fathom his reaction. When it came, it was cold and clinical.

'Granted,' he said, 'there are surface similarities between the Bristol and the Stafford cases, but that is all they are. You should have started by listing the differences between the two, instead of the coincidences.'

'Both victims died in the same way,' Marmion reminded him.

'They appeared to have done, Inspector, but bear this in mind. Murders across the board have become more vicious. In the last century,' said Chatfield, 'poison was often the chosen weapon. It is far more likely to be a gun, a knife or a meat cleaver now. For some depraved individuals, it is not enough simply to kill. They have the urge to butcher the corpse until it is unrecognisable.'

'That is what happened in both cases,' said Burge.

'I know, but take a closer look at the victims. One was a solicitor with a glowing reputation while the other ran a pub in the Midlands. In the first case, theft was involved. Solicitors are well paid,' said Chatfield. 'When they opened the safe in his office, the killers knew that there would be rich pickings. Robbery played no part whatsoever in the second case. That is hardly surprising. What was there to steal in a pub except a barrel of beer?'

'In both cases,' said Marmion, 'their purpose was to kill. It was the same in Dr Tindall's case. The killers dumped the jewellery they stole at a police station.'

'That's purely hypothetical.'

'It came from a safe in Edmonton.'

'What proof do you have?'

'We can place one of the killers in Camden.'

'That's guesswork.'

'I believe we can see a pattern, sir.'

'Then let me tell you what I believe,' said Chatfield, icily. 'Neither of the cases that Burge has found are linked in any way with what happened to Dr Tindall. That has unique features that separate it from the Bristol and Stafford murders. Nor am I convinced that the same men chose to kill a solicitor in one part of the country and a publican in another. What were their motives?'

'They were obeying orders, sir,' said Marmion.

'From whom?'

'I don't know.'

'Then come back to me when you do.'

'I will, sir. That's a promise.'

'Can I add an interesting piece of information, sir?' asked Burge.

'Please do,' invited Chatfield.

'I told you that the solicitor's brother, Captain Tait, committed suicide.'

'Yes, he shot himself.'

'What I didn't mention was someone in the Stafford case. The police interviewed a woman named Molly Roper, who had worked as a barmaid at the pub for some years. From what I can gather, she had a small stake in the business. Superintendent Ash told me that she was devastated by the murder.'

'I hope this digression has a point,' said Chatfield.

235

'Mrs Roper's husband was fighting in France. He was killed in action. That, at least, is what his wife was told. Ash learnt more detail about his death. He discovered that Sam Roper, the husband, climbed out of the trench against orders and ran towards the enemy.'

'That sounds like a man who wanted to be killed,' observed Marmion.

'Not to me,' argued Chatfield. 'I think he simply went berserk out of sheer frustration. I can understand that all too easily. If you are stuck in a trench under constant bombardment, it must be like hell. Every day is the same – mud, rats, the stench of death, the noise of bullets and bombs, the sheer terror of it all. You must yearn to escape somehow, no matter what the danger is.'

'There's something I haven't told you yet, sir,' said Burge.

'Well, get on with it, man.'

'Captain Tait and Sam Roper were in the same regiment.'

Chatfield was silenced. His jaw dropped.

'Explain that away, sir,' said Marmion. 'If you can, that is.'

The visitors were taken to a cold, bare, cheerless room. Apart from a table and three chairs, there was no furniture. The whitewashed walls had faded badly over the years. There was a distinct smell of damp. Ellen and Alice sat beside each other on one side of the table. The third chair was opposite them. The governor stood behind the two women. There was a long delay. Ellen's heart was beating faster all the time and she was afraid that the sight of her son would be too much for her. Alice, too, was suffering, certain that Paul would reject them and even resort to abuse. The longer they waited, the more the women suffered.

When the door was finally unlocked, a prison officer led in a young man whose wrists were handcuffed behind his back.

'Paul!' cried Ellen, jumping to her feet.

'It's not him, Mummy,' said Alice, holding her arm.

'Yes, it is,' said the prisoner, defiantly. 'You ask Sally Redwood.'

Ellen stared at him. He looked like her son, though his face was largely obscured by his beard. Alice had no doubts.

'His voice gives him away,' she said to the governor. 'This man is only pretending to be my brother.'

'Alice is right,' agreed Ellen, sadly. 'I was mistaken.'

'Get him out of here,' ordered the governor.

As the prisoner was pushed out of the room, he was cackling.

'I'm sorry that we were tricked by him,' said the governor, 'but your visit was not in vain. You helped to expose him as the arrant liar that he is. We can now add an extra charge against him.' He saw the whiteness of Ellen's face. 'Are you all right, Mrs Marmion? Can I get you something – another cup of tea, perhaps?'

'No, thank you,' she said.

'We just want to get out of here,' added Alice.

'Yes, we do. I feel the need for fresh air.'

'There is one thing you might do for us, please.'

'What is it, Miss Marmion?' he asked.

'Make him tell you where Paul is. He obviously met my brother, but he has not explained when and how. We want the truth.'

The governor nodded. 'Leave it to us.'

* * *

237

Back in his office, Marmion was explaining how the superintendent had rejected the idea of three related murder cases. Keedy rolled his eyes.

'What else could you expect from Chat?'

'We'd have liked a fair hearing from him, Joe.'

'Was he in a bad mood?'

'Yes,' said Marmion. 'He shot down every theory we offered him. Burge was quite upset. He worked hard to collate all that information.'

'What are we going to do with it?'

'Follow in the direction it is pointing us.'

'In other words,' said Keedy, 'we defy the superintendent. I've no argument with that. We've done it before when he's been bone-headed.'

'What stands out in all three cases?'

'Sadistic violence.'

'That is present, I admit, but the link between them for me is the army. The Bristol case was linked to the suicide of an army officer. Another suicide occurred on the battlefield before a publican was murdered in Stafford. And,' Marmion went on, 'I need hardly remind you that Dr Tindall was working in an army hospital. In his case, we believe the killers were disguised as soldiers.'

'I'm convinced of it.'

'Put yourself in their position, Joe.'

'I don't follow.'

'Well, it's highly unlikely they happened to live in Camden Town – or in Bristol or Stafford. What would they have done?'

'Move into each of those places in turn to familiarise

themselves with it,' said Keedy. 'Look at the amount of preparation needed for Dr Tindall's murder. They might have watched him for weeks.'

'How would they do that?'

'They'd find a base nearby.'

'Exactly,' said Marmion. 'They would have rented a small house or bedsit.'

'What would that entail?'

'Think hard.'

'Ah,' said Keedy, realising. 'You want me to get in touch with estate agents in Camden Town and adjoining districts.'

Marmion grinned. 'You've read my mind at last.'

'I've had plenty of practice over the years.'

About to reply, the inspector looked at his watch instead.

'What's up?' asked Keedy.

'They should have reached the prison by now.'

'I'd forgotten about that.'

'I hadn't. It's far too important to forget.'

'You're right.'

'I just hope that Ellen bears up under the pressure.'

'What are you expecting?'

'The truth, Joe,' said the other. 'I want to know exactly what my son has been doing since he ran away from home.'

On the bus journey, they sat in silence. Ellen was too stunned to say a word and Alice was simmering with rage. They were on the station platform before they finally broke the silence.

'It was my own fault,' admitted Ellen.

'That's not true, Mummy.'

'I dared to hope. I dared to believe that Paul would be at the prison, and that he would be touched by the fact that we had gone all that way to see him. Instead of that, we were humiliated by that . . . dreadful young man.'

'He enjoyed it,' said Alice. 'That's what made my blood boil. First, he deliberately kept us waiting then he played a cruel trick on us. How could anyone behave that way?'

'I thought it was Paul. He fooled me at first.'

'I knew that he was an impostor as soon as I saw him.'

'Oh, I feel so disappointed, Alice.'

'I'm just furious,' said her daughter. 'When he mentioned Sally Redwood, I really hoped it was him, but it was simply a means of taunting us.'

'He must have heard about Sally from Paul, who probably boasted about what he did to the poor girl. I daresay the two of them sniggered about her.'

'I'm afraid that might be true.'

'Who is that wicked young man, Alice?'

'I wish I knew.'

'Did Paul choose someone like that as a friend?' asked Ellen.

'I hope so, Mummy.'

'That's a terrible thing to say. He is a criminal. Are you happy that your brother is close to someone as revolting as that?'

'I'd much rather he was Paul's friend than his enemy.'

'I don't understand.'

'How do you think he got hold of Paul's papers?' asked Alice, worriedly. 'If he was not a friend, he might have killed to get his hands on them.'

* * *

When the younger man got back to the house, he put the food on a shelf in the larder. His companion came into the kitchen.

'How did you get on?' he asked.

'The market was as busy as ever.'

'Did you see that so-called artist?'

'Yes,' said the other. 'He was selling fruit and veg as usual. I asked him how much he would charge for a couple of apples and that painting I fancied.'

'What did he say?'

'His price is still stupidly high.'

'Nobody will ever pay that much,' said the other with contempt. 'He's not a real artist. He's just a market trader who dabbles in art.'

'Voisey thinks it's the other way round.'

'He's simply playing at being an artist. I should know.'

'Yes, you make a living at it.'

A sudden noise startled the younger man.

'Relax,' said the other. 'It's only the letter box.'

He went into the passageway to pick up the mail. When he came back, he was opening an envelope. His friend was hopeful.

'Is it from him?'

'No,' said the older man, reading the letter. 'It's from the estate agent, reminding us we leave at the end of the week. Someone will come to pick up the key.'

The gates of Edmonton Military Hospital were opened so that two ambulances could drive in. Looking down from the window of his office, Major Palmer-Loach clicked his tongue. Neil Irvine was standing beside him.

'Is this another batch from Cambrai?' he asked.

'Yes – they keep coming.'

'Casualties were appallingly high, Howard, but that applies to the Germans as well. Our tanks drove them right back.'

'It seemed so at the time perhaps,' said the major, sadly, 'but reports are now coming through that suggest the Germans have recovered much of the territory they lost to us. Meanwhile, this hospital is having to find beds for those wounded in the battle.'

'You sound weary. That's unlike you.'

'I'm not so much weary as pessimistic,' said Palmer-Loach. 'I just can't see an end to this war. We keep winning ground we are unable to hold and losing good men by the thousand. It is so pointless.' He turned away from the window. 'I'm sorry, Neil. I'm talking like a civilian and not like the soldier I've been for all these years. Victory will be within sight one day and we'll celebrate it together.'

'I'll hold you to that, Howard. We'll raise a glass to the Gordon Highlanders. I've a cousin serving in that regiment. They fought at Passchendaele, an even bloodier battle than Cambrai.'

'Scots regiments have distinguished themselves.'

'They always do. Oh,' said Irvine, remembering something. 'Any word from Inspector Marmion?'

'No – he's been eerily silent.'

'I'm sorry to hear that.'

'He did warn us that it would take time.'

'He also said that he'd keep in touch.'

'When he had something of moment to report – that's what he meant. Evidently, there has been no real progress. But I remain confident that there will be in due course. Marmion is tenacious,' said the major. 'I have faith in him to solve the murder of George Tindall and put all our minds at rest.'

On the train journey back to London, there was no need for a romantic novel or a magazine. All that Ellen and Alice wanted was to be left alone with their thoughts. The visit to Shepton Mallet had been more than a disappointment. It had raised the possibility that Paul might not even be alive. Ellen struggled to hold on to the idea that her son was safe and well. There was something so vile and knowing about the prisoner they had met. He had deliberately made their ordeal more difficult to bear, agreeing to meet them for the sole purpose of shattering their hopes. Now that Alice had put the idea into her head, Ellen was in agony. Paul was dead. He had been murdered by someone who stole his identity and used it as a way of tormenting his mother and his sister.

Alice was trying hard to believe that her brother might still be alive, after all. Paul had somehow managed to keep well clear of the police, knowing that his family would have reported him as a missing person and that a description of him would have been circulated to every police station. Arrest meant that they would know where he was. Paul had wanted to avoid that at all costs. Alice had assumed that her brother had drifted from place to place, searching for casual work and, if driven to it, begging for food. What she had never considered was the sort of people he might meet along the way. Now that she had done so, she realised just how dangerous a life on the road could be.

The impostor they had met at the prison was an unapologetic criminal, taking anything that he could get his hands on. He must have wormed his way into a friendship with Paul and got him to talk openly about his family. When she first saw the prisoner, Ellen had believed it was her son. Alice was not deceived for a second. What she noticed was the way that he leered at her. It made her wonder what exactly Paul had told him about his sister. At all events, the visit to the prison had been an ordeal from start to finish. She clung to one slim hope – that Paul was alive. Alice now had to convince her mother that it might be true.

While he had been unfairly misquoted in some of the newspapers, Claude Chatfield saw the benefits of publicity. There was an immediate response. Those who manned the switchboard at Scotland Yard took several calls offering information regarding the murder. Some of it was clearly bogus, aimed at confusing the police investigation, but a lot of reliable facts about George Tindall also came in. From time to time, it was collated and taken to the superintendent's office.

He was busy separating the wheat from the chaff when he was interrupted by a detective constable. The man held out a sheet of paper.

'What's that?' asked Chatfield.

'It's a telephone number, sir.'

'If it's another hoax call, you can tear it up right now.'

'I'm convinced that it's genuine.'

'Let me see.'

Chatfield took the paper and read the name on it. The impact made him reel. When he recovered, he snatched up the receiver immediately.

* * *

Keedy was restive. Instead of being out in pursuit of suspects, he was stuck in Marmion's office, ringing estate agents in turn. Time and again, he spoke to someone who was unable to help him, leading him to believe that the suspects might be living nowhere near Camden Town. After another call proved fruitless, he slammed the receiver down.

'Steady on, Joe,' said Marmion. 'That phone is a vital tool for us. Don't smash it to bits.'

'I'm sorry, but it's so frustrating. I'm getting nowhere.'

'How many costume hire companies did you contact before you found one that gave you vital evidence?'

'Quite a few,' admitted Keedy.

'I rest my case.'

'I'm sorry to complain, Harv, but this is getting on my nerves. I'd much rather be in Camden Town, searching for them.'

'Where would you start? You'd be like a blind man in a dark cellar.'

'I could take that portrait of one of the killers with me and show it around. At least, I'd have the feeling of doing something.'

'You are doing something,' said Marmion, 'and it's important work. Grit your teeth and keep going. Who knows? The next estate agent you speak to might be the one who can actually help us.'

'I've been telling myself that for the last half an hour.'

'Perseverance is a virtue.'

Keedy sighed. 'If you say so . . .'

The door suddenly opened, and Chatfield came in.

'I've been on the telephone,' he announced.

'So have I, sir,' complained Keedy, 'and I'm getting nowhere.'

'As a result of the newspaper coverage, information has been coming in from all over the place. This is a summary of it,' he went on, handing a sheaf of papers to Marmion. 'There are people who worked alongside Dr Tindall in Brighton and others who knew him as a medical student in St Thomas's Hospital.'

'Thank you very much, sir,' said Marmion.

'It will help to fill in some of the gaps.'

'They're not gaps – they're chasms.'

'Whatever you're doing, I want you to drop it at once.'

'Why?'

'You and the sergeant must go to Kent immediately.'

Marmion was taken aback. 'Has something happened?'

'I spoke to a woman on the telephone,' explained Chatfield. 'She was in such a state that I couldn't make out what she was saying at first. When I did manage to calm her down, she made a remarkable claim.'

'What was it, sir?'

'She said that she was George Tindall's wife.'

'But his wife is dead,' said Marmion.

'She sounded very much alive to me.'

'What name did she give, Superintendent?'

'Eleanor Tindall.'

'That was the name of his late wife.'

'He kept photographs of her all over his house,' recalled Keedy. 'For some reason, the killers stole them.'

'How convinced were you she was telling the truth?' asked Marmion.

'Completely,' affirmed Chatfield. 'She provided so much detail that it was impossible not to believe her. She was in great distress. Only two weeks ago, Mrs Tindall saw her husband alive and well. He paid a fleeting visit to her.'

'What's her address?'

'It's on the top page I just gave you – so is her telephone number.'

'Well,' said Keedy, 'this sounds promising.'

'Go by train to Tonbridge and take a taxi from there.'

Marmion was puzzled. 'Why on earth did Dr Tindall tell everyone that his wife had died?' he wondered. 'That's an extraordinary thing to do.'

'I agree,' said Chatfield, 'but we are dealing with an extraordinary man.'

CHAPTER FIFTEEN

When their train stopped at Reading station, other passengers in their compartment got out. Ellen and Alice were able to talk freely and release emotions that had been bottled up throughout their journey.

'I thought that we'd never be alone,' said Ellen with relief.

'I felt the same, Mummy. We've had to suffer in silence.'

'Being able to talk to you like this is a luxury.'

'How are you feeling now?' asked Alice.

'To be honest, I feel more depressed than ever. I could not believe that anyone could be so cruel. He dragged us all the way there on purpose. If he can do something as wicked as that, he's got no conscience.'

'He will pay for it, Mummy. As a result of what he did, time will be added to the length of his sentence. In torturing us, he gave himself away. They know that he was lying about his identity now and will do their best to find out who he really is. Anyway,' said Alice, 'forget about him. We still have our freedom. He's going to be locked up for a long time.'

'Do you really believe that he did kill Paul?'

'No, I don't.'

'But you thought he was capable of it.'

'That was my immediate reaction.'

'What has changed your mind?'

'I've been thinking,' said Alice. 'If he had murdered Paul, he wouldn't have been stupid enough to see us because he knew that his deception would be revealed immediately. How he got hold of those papers, I have no idea, but they're worthless now and that didn't worry him.'

'Nothing did,' said Ellen. 'Even though he was handcuffed, he seemed completely at home in that prison. Obviously, it is not the first time that he's been locked up. It may well be the story of his life.'

'Let's hope that Paul was not led astray by him.'

'You know what they say about birds of a feather.'

'I refuse to believe that my brother would sink that low,' said Alice with sudden passion. 'He had his faults, but he was brought up to know the difference between right and wrong. Have more faith in him.'

'I wish that I could,' said Ellen, uneasily.

'What do you mean?'

'Running away from home is wrong. Refusing to contact your parents is wrong. Deliberately letting us suffer is wrong.

Paul might have been able to tell the difference between right and wrong once,' said Ellen, sharply, 'but he's forgotten how to do it now. We've lost him, Alice.'

They sat at the kitchen table over the remains of their meal. The older man was reading a newspaper. When he broke off, he tapped the photograph on the front page.

'Look at him,' he said. 'Tindall was a handsome man in his prime.'

'He wasn't very handsome by the time we finished with him,' said the other with a snigger. 'He got what he deserved.'

'We stopped him for good – and not before time.'

'What does the article say?'

'Oh, it's full of threats by someone called Superintendent Chatfield. He reckons that his detectives will soon run the culprits to earth.'

'Is that what we are – culprits?'

'We are much more than that,' said the older man, seriously, 'but this superintendent would never understand why. He thinks we're no better than wild animals.'

'What evidence do they have?'

'None at all, Brian. The police know absolutely nothing.'

'Nevertheless,' admitted the other, 'I'll be glad when we move away from here. I'll feel safer then.'

'We're perfectly safe where we are.'

'I'm not so sure now. We're strangers here, remember. People still give us funny looks in the street. What if someone reports us to the police?'

'Calm down,' said the other. 'I thought you liked this area. Where else would you have found that painting you liked so much? In art galleries, all you can do is look. At that exhibition in the Arts Theatre, everything was for sale.'

'The only painting I wanted was too expensive.'

'You could always steal it,' teased the older man.

'We don't steal. That's why we gave that jewellery back.'

'I wonder what the police thought when they found it.'

'They'll know something funny is going on. It's one of the reasons I'd like to move on.'

'We rented this place until the end of the week,' said the other, calmly. 'It's been perfect for us. I hope we find somewhere like it when we move on and leave the police floundering yet again.'

As they alighted from the train at Tonbridge station, Marmion and Keedy headed for the exit. They soon joined the queue at the taxi rank. Keedy was sceptical.

'Are we certain that this woman really is Mrs Tindall?' he asked.

'Who else might she be?'

'Some people love making fake calls.'

'Not in this case, Joe,' said Marmion. 'Chat would never be fooled like that. If he says that she is genuine, then I accept that she must be. I'm just surprised that she lives in Kent.'

'But we knew that he owned a house here somewhere.'

'He used to own one. I assumed that he sold it when he moved to Edmonton. We were told that he wanted to get away from a place with so many associations with his late wife.'

'There is no late wife. Mrs Tindall is alive and kicking.'

'Yes – and he even found time to visit her recently.'

'Whatever is going on?' asked Keedy, bemused.

'I think the doctor must have been leading a double life.'

'How did he manage that? I can't afford to live one on police pay.'

'I've just remembered something,' said Marmion. 'We were told that he owned a property in Brighton.'

'Yes, we saw it – that large flat of his.'

'I'm talking about the house we visited.'

'Hipwell Manor?'

'Yes, that's the place.'

'It was a big mistake. We got kicked out straight away.'

'I know. Mrs Langford was furious with us.'

'I'll never forget that look on her face.'

'Do you remember what she threatened to do?'

'Yes,' said Keedy. 'She was going to complain about us to Chat.'

'Then why didn't she?'

'She must have changed her mind.'

'I doubt that, Joe. There must be another reason.'

'Her letter might have got stuck in the post.'

'When we left her,' recalled Marmion, 'she was in a mood to deliver it in person to Scotland Yard. She claimed that we'd violated her privacy, yet all we did was to ask a few simple questions.'

'Some women are like that.'

'Mrs Langford is not one of them, Joe. I've got a strange feeling that we haven't heard the last of her somehow.'

'No,' said Keedy. 'When that husband of hers gets back from his latest deployment, she'll probably set him on to us.

That means we'll have the Admiralty on our tails – and all for asking a few simple questions.'

Before they left Scotland Yard, Marmion had delegated the job of ringing estate agents to Clifford Burge. Having already contributed evidence to the investigation, Burge was delighted to be trusted with an important task. Unlike Keedy, he was not disheartened by lack of success. As he drew a blank with one estate agent, he simply moved on to another. The sergeant had started with companies based in or near Camden Town before shifting slowly away from it.

Burge followed his example, moving slightly north, then east and then south before completing the circle by pushing to the west. When he telephoned someone in Acton, he finally got a positive result.

'I may have found what you wanted,' said the estate agent. 'It's a three-week rental in Camden Town that terminates this weekend.'

'Could I have the address, please?'

The man gave him the details and described the house as small but with a garden at the rear. It was something the client had stipulated.

'I'd like his name, please,' said Burge.

'It was Anthony Brown, sir.'

'Did he give you his home address?'

'No,' said the other, 'but there was a sort of rustic burr in his voice. The rental address is as follows.'

Burge jotted it down. The estate agent anticipated the next question.

'He paid the full amount in advance, sir. He came here and paid in cash.'

'Can you recall what he looked like?'

'He was an older man, perhaps in his late fifties. He was well-built and wore a suit. He gave no reason for moving to Camden Town for such a short time. I assumed he had business in the area. He was anxious to view the property before handing over the money.'

'Any distinguishing features?' asked Burge.

'Yes, he had a beard. He was quiet, polite and had the kind of eyes that seem to look right through you. Oh, and he was broad-shouldered. Somehow he didn't look as if he belonged in a suit.'

'Do you have any idea what he did for a living?'

'If I had to guess,' said the estate agent, 'I'd say that he had something to do with the land. He was definitely not a city person.'

The taxi took them to a country lane near Hadlow and the driver agreed to wait until the detectives had finished their business there. Marmion and Keedy appraised the house. It was a sprawling cottage set in the middle of a garden large enough to boast a lawn tennis court. They admired its charm and serenity.

'It's idyllic, Joe,' said Marmion. 'I'd move in tomorrow if I could.'

'You hate gardening.'

'I'd expect you to do that in your spare time.'

Keedy laughed. 'What spare time?'

Before they reached the front door, it was opened by a nervous young maidservant who all but curtseyed to them. As they entered the house, she told them that Mrs Tindall was unwell and being looked after by her mother. When they removed their coats and hats, the servant hung them on pegs in the hall. She then conducted them into the lounge.

Eleanor Tindall was seated on the sofa with a blanket draped across her lap. She was a beautiful woman in her thirties turned into a pale, fragile shell of her former self. Sitting beside her was the person from whom she had inherited her good looks. Romilly Staynes was a handsome, well-dressed woman who had retained her figure into her early sixties. When the detectives entered the room, she rose at once to introduce herself and her daughter, speaking in a clipped, educated voice. Marmion performed introductions in return. Keedy, meanwhile, was glancing around the room and taking note of the expensive furniture and fittings.

As the three of them took their seats, Romilly explained that her daughter was still reeling from the shock she had received, and that the detectives had to be gentle with her.

'I'm fine now, Mama,' said Eleanor.

'Let me do the talking, dear,' suggested her mother. She turned to Marmion. 'You can guess what I'm about to ask you, Inspector.'

'Yes, Mrs Staynes,' he said, 'and the simple answer is that we are absolutely certain that the deceased is Dr George Tindall.'

'But he wasn't a doctor,' protested Eleanor.

'What did you think he was, Mrs Tindall?'

'I can't tell you that.'

'Why not?'

'It's . . . classified information.'

'That is what we were tricked into believing,' said Romilly, spitting the words out. 'The simple truth is that my daughter married a man who deceived her in the most appalling way. What we need from you, Inspector, is a promise that we will be protected from any intrusion by the newspapers. Above all else, my daughter needs privacy. She sustained a fearful blow – and so, of course, have I.'

'What about your husband, Mrs Staynes?' asked Keedy.

'He died some years ago. If he had been alive at the time, the marriage would never have taken place. He had a nose for bounders.'

'That's not what George was, Mama,' pleaded Eleanor. 'He loved me truly. I still think that a grotesque mistake has been made.'

'Unfortunately, we made it.'

'To answer your question, Mrs Staynes,' said Marmion, 'I am unable to guarantee complete immunity from the press, but there are ways in which we can help you in that regard. What we don't understand is why Dr Tindall and his wife chose to live apart.' The two women exchanged a rueful glance. 'Sooner or later, the truth will come out. Furthermore, it would help our investigation if we understood how your daughter came to meet and marry George Tindall.'

Alice Marmion waited at the bus stop with her mother so that she could wave her off. They were both reassured to be back in London again.

'It's funny, isn't it?' said Ellen.

'What is?'

'On any other day, it would have been a pleasure to visit a lovely town like Shepton Mallet. When we first got to meet, your father and I sometimes went for a walk in the country. The peace was wonderful and there were always animals to see in the fields.'

'It might have been the same for us today, Mummy. We went at the wrong time to a place we would otherwise have enjoyed. It was so pretty – until we saw its prison.'

'Let's put that all behind us, Alice.'

'I agree.'

'It's caused us enough heartache already.'

'Are you going to ring Daddy when you get home?'

'No, I won't do that.'

'He'll be dying to know what happened.'

'I can't interrupt him in the middle of a murder investigation,' said Ellen. 'Besides, I'm not supposed to contact him unless there's an emergency.'

'That means he won't know what happened until he gets home late.'

'Oh, I think he will. In fact, he may already have been told.'

'How?'

'Superintendent Chatfield may have spoken to your father. It was only because of him that we were able to visit the prison. I'm fairly certain that the governor would have contacted the superintendent to tell him all about our visit.'

When he discovered what he felt was to be crucial information, Clifford Burge had wanted to pass it on immediately so that he could accompany Marmion and Keedy to the address in Camden Town. Unfortunately, they were no longer in Scotland Yard. He was therefore forced to report to Chatfield instead. The superintendent listened carefully but was unconvinced.

'Remember your mathematics,' he warned.

'What do you mean, sir?'

'Things have to add up properly. You put two and two together and ended up with twenty-seven. If I had a dunce's hat in here, you'd be wearing it.'

Burge was deflated. 'That's unfair, sir,' he protested. 'I spent a long time on the telephone to get that address and I still think it could be significant.'

'Why?'

'Our suspects could be living there.'

'What are the chances of that?'

'I'd say that they were quite strong.'

'Well, I'd say that they were minimal. Sergeant Keedy has an obsession that those men are living in Camden Town, but he has no conclusive proof that it is true. All that you established with your phone call is that an estate agency in Acton rented a property in Camden. It was a perfectly legal transaction.'

'It was also a strange coincidence.'

'We're back to your faulty mathematics again.'

'The inspector believes that our suspects would have found somewhere to stay weeks before they actually committed the murder.'

'I agree with him,' said Chatfield, 'but why stay some distance away from Edmonton when that is where they should have been doing their reconnaissance?'

'I don't know,' admitted Burge.

'Start asking estate agents if they have rented property in Edmonton recently. That's a much more promising line of enquiry.'

'I was only following orders, sir.'

'Then let me give you some more to obey. One – forget about Camden Town.'

'Yes, sir.'

'Two – don't get infected by Sergeant's Keedy's overenthusiasm.'

'That's unkind, sir.'

'Three – don't bother me again unless you have cast-iron information.'

'It may still turn out to be exactly that,' insisted Burge.

'Four – abandon hopeless positions like the one you're in now. I'm sorry to be so harsh on you,' said Chatfield. 'You have the makings of a good detective. I expect big things of you – once you've learnt that brainwaves of the kind that some of my officers have from time to time bear no comparison with factual evidence gathered by means of hard graft.' He gave a steely smile. 'Pass that message on.'

Marmion and Keedy were spellbound by the story they were told. It was essentially a confession by Eleanor, though her mother interrupted her so often that it began to seem like a joint effort. With his notebook perched on his knee, Keedy was having trouble keeping up with the narrative.

It had all started before the war when Tindall had met the two women at a dinner party. He had sat between them and, with wine flowing, had ample time to ingratiate himself with them. The friendship forged there had developed slowly. What he had told them was that he was the administrator of a large hospital in Birmingham and that he was only able to get away from time to time. While his main interest had been in Eleanor, it was obvious that he had charmed the mother as well, conscious that he could make no headway without her approval.

Social events always involved the three of them. They went to plays, concerts and operas together. The fact that he insisted on paying for everything worked in his favour. When he visited the house, Romilly made sure that he spent time alone with her daughter. The friendship between them deepened into love. Then came the bombshell. Tindall told them that he could no longer deceive them. His job as a hospital administrator did not exist. It was a convenient mask for the work that he really did with British intelligence.

'First,' recalled Eleanor, 'he swore us to secrecy, then he told us about work he'd done abroad. War seemed inevitable at that point so – because he was fluent in German – he was about to be sent behind enemy lines.'

'He then told us,' added Romilly, 'that we had become his closest friends and that it had pained him to go on deceiving us. When he confided in us that he would have to disappear from our lives, we were thunderstruck. George had seemed everything I had ever hoped for my daughter.'

'We had . . . talked about marriage,' murmured Eleanor.

'But he felt that the burden on us would be too great to bear. He would be away for long periods, unable to remain in constant contact.'

'I didn't mind that,' confessed Eleanor. 'In fact, I felt rather excited by the idea of a secret marriage to a wonderful man, facing danger for the benefit of his country. I was ready to accept him on those terms.'

'To my chagrin,' said Romilly, 'I agreed. I let my only child marry someone I admired as the secret agent he claimed he was. How reckless could a mother be?'

'What did you tell your family and friends?' said Keedy.

'We told them as little as possible,' replied Romilly. 'It was a quiet wedding. They were married in a civil ceremony and spent their honeymoon in the Lake District. A couple of weeks later, war broke out and George disappeared.'

'How often did you see him after that?' asked Marmion.

'No more than a dozen times or so. Often, it was only for a couple of days. On their first wedding anniversary, he managed a full week.'

'It was heavenly,' said Eleanor. 'Or so I thought at the time.'

'Do you have any children?' asked Keedy, softly.

'We have a son, Peter. He's almost three.'

'Imagine the kind of shock that awaits him,' said Romilly. 'The day will come when he has to know the truth about his father. He will carry the shame of it for the rest of his life. George was a barefaced liar. I find myself quite unable to have any sympathy for the way that he died.'

'Mama!' exclaimed her daughter.

'We have to be honest.'

'Even so . . .'

When he saw tears forming in Eleanor's eyes, Marmion decided that it was time to bring the interview to an end. After a few more questions, he thanked both women for being so open with him and promised to keep in touch with them. He and Keedy then left the house.

'What did you make of that, Joe?'

'I can't wait to see the look on Chat's face when we pass on the information.'

'He'll be outraged,' said Marmion. 'He believes strongly in the sanctity of marriage – and so, for that matter, do I.'

Keedy was amused. 'Am I being warned by my future father-in-law?'

'It's more of a gentle nudge than a warning.'

'Fair enough.'

'Unlike Dr Tindall, you'll be married in the sight of God.'

'As it happens,' said Keedy, seriously, 'it's what Alice and I want more than anything else.'

Back at his desk, Clifford Burge was still feeling bruised after his argument with the superintendent. His frustration was compounded by the way he had been mocked, then summarily dismissed by Chatfield. Hoping for praise, he had met with condemnation instead. He felt certain that he would get a more sympathetic hearing from Marmion.

Until the inspector returned, Burge decided to take a second look at the evidence he discovered about the murders in Bristol and Stafford. What linked them was the suicide of two men in the North Staffordshire Regiment. Captain Tait had shot himself and Private Samuel Roper had deliberately broken cover to run towards enemy fire. Burge knew that they were by no means the only soldiers to commit suicide. Men who lost limbs or suffered disfiguring injuries had elected to die by their own hand rather than lead what they feared would be miserable lives. Those with severe mental problems or permanent shellshock also found death a tempting alternative to what lay ahead.

It was not in the interests of morale – at home as well as in the ranks – for the British Expeditionary Force to give full details of suicides. The terse telegrams sent to waiting families on the Home Front made no mention of the intolerable pressures that had forced someone to take his own life. They had died in action, an honourable way to serve their country. That was all that parents needed to be told.

The suicides he had located were two among many. Other soldiers had shot themselves or used enemy ammunition as a means of escape from hell. Yet the two deaths in the North Staffordshire Regiment continued to burrow into his mind. They were connected in a way he was unable to comprehend. Checking his notes once more, Burge gave the two victims his full concentration, convinced that they might somehow hold the key to the savage murder of George Tindall.

When evening shadows darkened the streets of Camden Town, the two men felt able to leave their hiding place without fear. They walked side by side along a high street now largely deserted. The older man turned to his companion.

'How do you feel now, Brian?' he asked.

'All the better for knowing we'll soon leave,' said the other.

'I was beginning to get bored with this place.'

'I can't wait to go.'

'Even though you can't take that painting with you?'

'I can live without it.'

'The main thing is that we obeyed our orders to the letter.'

'And we got away with it.'

'Remember to offer thanks in your prayers.'

Turning a corner, he led his companion towards the church.

As they walked across the concourse at Charing Cross Station, they were able to have a private conversation at last. That had been impossible in the taxi that took them to Tonbridge and the train that brought them back to London.

'What are you going to tell Chat?' asked Keedy.

'You were the one taking notes, Joe. I'll rely on you to give him an accurate account of what we learnt.'

'He's going to be appalled.'

'I agree,' said Marmion, 'and with good cause. Chat has got daughters of his own. The idea that one of them might suffer the fate of Eleanor Tindall will be horrifying to him.'

'If he'd been Eleanor's father, this would never have happened. He would have been suspicious of George Tindall from the very start. Unfortunately,' said Keedy, 'the poor woman didn't have a father.'

'That was one of the reasons Tindall was attracted to her.'

'It was easy to see why. Eleanor was beautiful, intelligent and came from a good family. The only problem was that hawk-eyed mother of hers. Tindall had to win her over first and he obviously did that.'

'I felt sorry for Mrs Staynes. She knows she failed her daughter.'

'It's the child I worry about,' said Keedy. 'There's going to be an awkward moment in his life when he learns what a ruthless man his father was.'

'Chat will be quick to make that point, Joe.'

'Is there anything you're not going to tell him?'

'Yes, there is.'

'What is it?'

'Attractive as she was,' said Marmion, 'I don't believe that Eleanor would ever be enough for Dr Tindall. He was a man of great cunning and, I fancy, great appetite. The tricks that he played on one woman would work equally well on others.'

Keedy was startled. 'You think that he had another wife?'

'I'd go even further, Joe. I believe that we may have met her.'

Donald Hepburn was a tall, dignified man in his sixties with long, curling grey hair giving him a slightly leonine appearance. He paced the lounge at Hipwell Manor, shifting between fury and concern. Above his head, he could hear footsteps in the main bedroom. When they began to descend the stairs, he rushed into the hall.

'How is my daughter?' he asked.

'I've given Mrs Langford a sedative,' said the doctor with a sad smile. 'Sleep is what she needs more than anything else.'

CHAPTER SIXTEEN

As soon as they got back to Scotland Yard, they went straight to Marmion's office. An envelope was propped up against the inkwell on his desk. Slitting it open with a paperknife, he read the message.

'Who is it from?' asked Keedy.

'Cliff Burge.'

'What does he want?'

'He thinks he's found something interesting,' said Marmion, 'but, when he discussed it with Chat, his theory was shot down in flames.'

'We've all had that happen to us,' moaned Keedy.

'Read this for yourself.'

Marmion handed him the letter and waited for his response. It took only seconds before the sergeant's face lit up with pleasure. He read on to the end of the letter then waved it in the air.

'This is wonderful news,' he said.

'And how was it achieved?'

'Cliff Burge used his intelligence.'

'There's something you've missed out, Joe. He used his intelligence by ringing estate agents until he found the right one. Then he got vital information. In other words,' said Marmion, 'he persisted at a task that you found boring.'

Keedy spread his arms. 'I admit it freely.'

'It's the boring tasks that often deliver the goods.'

'I'd love to put this new information to the test.'

'It's exactly what I want you to do,' said Marmion. 'Find Burge and get the full details from him. If you think his discovery merits acting upon, take him with you to Camden Town.'

'Don't I need Chat's permission?'

'Let me worry about the superintendent.'

'Won't he ask what I'm doing?'

'No, he'll be far too busy coping with the shock of what we discovered in Kent. Chat will be wondering how he can keep the full truth out of the newspapers. Think of the headlines,' said Marmion. 'Murder victim turns out to be a cruel confidence trickster – the press would love a story like that.'

Eleanor Tindall was sitting up in bed, reading wistfully through a pile of letters she had received during her courtship. They were so affectionate and touching that she could still not wholly believe her future husband had exploited her. Their intimate moments together were memories she had treasured. Could they really have been so many mirages? Were all his promises grounded in deceit? Had Tindall's joy at the birth of their son simply been an act for her benefit?

While she tried desperately to persuade herself that he had really loved her, she remembered the visit of the two detectives. They told her things about her husband that shattered her fantasies. Yet even as she kept telling herself to accept the harsh truth, she kept reading the honeyed words of his letters.

When the door suddenly opened, she was startled. Her mother had just come into the bedroom. It took Romilly only seconds to realise what her daughter was doing. Snatching the letters away from her, she walked across to the fire crackling in the grate and threw them one by one into the flames. Romilly's teeth were exposed in a silent snarl. She ignored Eleanor's squeals of protest and watched the false promises curling up the chimney in smoke.

It was uncharacteristic of Claude Chatfield to sit in his chair and listen to a report without interrupting it with endless questions. But the story that Marmion told him had rendered the superintendent speechless. He took a long time to absorb all the details. There was a note of incredulity in his voice.

'Can all this be true?' he asked.

'Mrs Staynes and her daughter gave us an honest, unvarnished account.'

'My heart goes out to them. What must they have thought

when they saw that photograph of Dr Tindall in the newspapers? It came as a hammer blow to them.'

'They're still rather dazed by it all, sir.'

'The pair of them were bamboozled for years.'

'Tindall knew exactly how to worm his way into their affections,' said Marmion. 'I don't believe that they were his first victims.'

'What makes you think that?'

'He was obviously so confident and practised.'

'It's the wife that I feel the greatest sympathy for,' said Chatfield. 'After years of what she believed was a happy marriage, she learns that it was a complete sham.'

'Her mother suffered as well, sir. She blames herself for not protecting her daughter better. When her husband died, she took the duty of care onto her own shoulders. Mrs Staynes struck me as an intelligent, loving, watchful woman. It says a lot for Tindall's manipulative skills,' Marmion contended, 'that he was able to convince her that his attentions were entirely honourable.'

'You make him sound like a puppeteer.'

'That is exactly what he was, sir. He controlled their movements by twitching the strings. His wife and mother-in-law were ready to endure the many constraints and absences because he made up for them when he came back into their lives again.'

'And it was always at a time of his choosing,' said Chatfield, bitterly.

The superintendent fell silent. As a devout Roman Catholic, he had a clear idea of the virtues of family life. He could not understand how a talented man like George Tindall could jettison every principle of fatherhood and, indeed, of sheer decency. While it was necessary to discuss the ugly details of the case with Marmion, he would never dare to do so with his wife.

'One is bound to feel sorry for any murder victim,' he said, sonorously, 'but I feel that my sympathy for Dr Tindall is beginning to wane.'

'He was a vicious predator, sir.'

'Bigamy – if that's what we may have here – is a disgusting crime and a heinous sin.'

'I couldn't agree more, sir.'

Chatfield went off into a kind of trance as he considered the implications of Tindall's behaviour. When he had finished, he looked at Marmion as if seeing him for the first time. His memory was jogged.

'Oh,' he said, 'forgive me. I have a message for you. The governor of Shepton Mallet prison was kind enough to telephone me.'

'Is he holding my son in his prison?'

'No, Inspector.'

Marmion was relieved. 'Then who is using Paul's name?'

'His identity is still unknown.'

'What exactly happened at the prison?'

'To find that out,' said Chatfield, 'you will have to speak to your wife.'

When she alighted from the bus, Ellen Marmion still had to walk several blocks to reach her home. Her fear was that she would bump into Patricia Redwood once again. The most memorable thing about her visit to Shepton Mallet was the jeering reference to Sally Redwood. It had been made by the prisoner and it proved that he had met her son. Ellen was horrified that Sally's name had been used in the crude banter between two young men who were living rough. Much as she disliked the mother, she felt sorry for the daughter and was glad that Sally was unaware of what had happened.

It had been a long and disappointing day. When she got to the house, Ellen promised herself, she would make herself a cup of tea and flop into an armchair. The streets were cold, dark and deserted. Because a blackout had been imposed, there were no friendly gas lamps to guide her home. By the time she finally got there, her feet were sore. Letting herself into the house, she went straight to the kitchen, filled the kettle and set it on the stove. When the kettle had boiled, she used some of the hot water to warm the teapot. Minutes later, she went into the living room with her cup of tea and sat down.

Only then did she realise that she was still wearing her hat and coat. Before she could laugh at herself, she heard the telephone ring. Putting her cup aside, Ellen hauled herself out of the chair and went into the hall. She put the receiver to her ear.

'Hello . . .'

'It's me, love,' said Marmion. 'How did you get on?'

It took Keedy only a couple of minutes to decide that Burge's argument was compelling. The two of them left the building at speed. As they sat in the rear of a police car, Burge was worried.

'Does the superintendent know about this?' he asked.

'He will do when we take two prisoners back with us.'

'We can't be sure that we will,' said Burge. 'I don't want to give him another chance to rap me over the knuckles.'

'Don't worry, Cliff. I take full responsibility for what we do.'

'The superintendent was so contemptuous. It made me feel that all my research had been a waste of time.'

'I take the opposite view – and so does the inspector. The information you discovered about that regiment could be vital.'

'I've learnt a bit more about them,' said Burge. 'The Prince of Wales's North Staffordshire Regiment has been involved in some of the toughest battles in the war – the Somme, Passchendaele and Cambrai, for instance. They've suffered huge losses.'

'We need to find out even more about those two cases of suicide,' said Keedy. 'Right now, however, our priority is that house in Camden Town.'

'Do you know where it is?'

'No, but we can get directions from the local police.'

'One thing puzzled me about the place they rented.'

'What was it?'

'The man insisted that it had a garden at the rear. Why was that? They can't plant anything in the short time they are there.'

Keedy chuckled. 'They weren't thinking about gardening,' he said. 'They wanted a second exit in case people like us come knocking on the front door. We must split up, Cliff. While I do the knocking, you watch the back of the house.'

'Wonderful!' said Burge. 'I'm dying for some action.'

Though they sneered at police attempts to track them down, they nevertheless took precautions. While they were in the house during the day, they glanced through the front and back windows on a regular basis. At night they took it in turns to sleep for four-hour shifts, with one man on sentry duty in the front bedroom.

'What will you miss most about this place?' asked the older man.

'The painting I wanted to buy.'

'You can wave goodbye to that – unless you have fifty quid.'

Brian laughed. 'I don't have a fraction of that.'

'It's a pity you couldn't take a photo of it.'

'That would be pointless. It wouldn't be the same in black and white. What made it special were the colours Voisey chose.'

'I will miss the feeling of safety we have here,' said the other. 'We didn't really have that in Stafford. We were always on edge. I was glad when we finished our business there and moved on.'

'I liked the place. That pub served good beer.'

'We were there for a higher purpose than drinking beer.'

Brian nodded. 'Yes, I know.'

'Never forget it. We were doing God's work.'

When they stopped at the police station, they not only got directions to the house. They acquired two uniformed constables as well. The four passengers squeezed into the car and the driver followed Keedy's instructions.

'You were right about that garden,' said Burge, impressed. 'The duty sergeant said that there's a lane at the bottom of it.'

'That's their escape route.'

'We'll block it off.'

'Be careful, Cliff. These men are dangerous.'

273

'Yes, but we'll have the advantage of surprise.'

'That's true.' Keedy spoke to the driver. 'Get a move on.'

It was a relatively short journey. Turning into the street, the driver stopped the vehicle outside the house number they'd been given, then got out with the others. The five of them moved forward in the dark. After they had sized up the house, Keedy sent Burge off with the uniformed policemen to the lane at the rear of the property. He and the driver gave them five minutes to get in position. During the wait, Keedy's excitement was building. The promise of action was one of the things that had drawn him to the Metropolitan Police Force in the first place. He felt a surge of adrenalin.

'Right,' he said. 'Let's go.'

He and the driver walked up to the door of the house. Keedy used the knocker with as much force as he could, then waited for a response. None, however, came. Because the blinds were drawn, he was unable to see whether there were lights on inside. He banged on the door with his fist.

'Police! Open up!'

The driver joined in the shouting. After a while, the door opened wide to reveal Clifford Burge. He shrugged his shoulders.

'When we reached the garden gate,' he explained, 'it was wide open. I'm sorry, Sergeant. They got away.'

Alone in his office, Marmion was trying to digest what his wife had told him about the visit to the West Country. He was immensely grateful that his daughter had also been there. Her support and practicality would have been an asset to her mother. Even though he was preoccupied by the demands of his job, he never forgot Paul and frequently wondered what he was doing. The fact that his son had not, in fact, committed a series of crimes in Wells gave him solace. He was less comforted by Ellen's description of the young man who had clearly known Paul. Evidently, his son was moving in dangerous company.

His mind was still fixed on Shepton Mallet when the telephone rang.

He picked up the receiver. 'Inspector Marmion . . .'

'Ah,' said a hesitant voice, 'I was hoping to speak to you in confidence.'

'Do you have information regarding the murder, sir?'

'In a sense, I do.' There was a lengthy pause. 'My name is Donald Hepburn. I understand that you and a Sergeant Keedy came to Hipwell Manor and met my daughter, Caroline.'

'That is right, sir. We called on Mrs Langford some days ago.'

'You were given rather short shrift, I gather.'

'We were not made to feel entirely welcome,' said Marmion, tactfully.

'Caroline regrets that now.'

'We took no offence, sir.'

There was another pause. Feeling sorry for him, Marmion tried to make the conversation less painful for him.

'I believe I know why you have contacted me, Mr Hepburn,' he said, 'and I assure you that this is a private conversation between the two of us. Nothing of what you say needs to be made public.'

'Thank God for that!'

'It might interest you to know that Mrs Langford is not his only victim.'

Hepburn was rocked. 'Really?'

'We are learning some strange things about Dr Tindall.'

'Is that who he is?'

'Yes, sir.'

'He didn't even tell us his real name,' complained the other. 'When they were married in a register office, he was posing as a Michael Langford. He had documents that seemed to prove his identity.'

'How is your daughter now?' asked Marmion, quietly.

'She was hysterical when she learnt the truth, Inspector. We had to call in the doctor to give her a sedative. Look,' he went on, 'I hope that you will accept my version of events. Caroline could never withstand being questioned by you. She has been wounded far too deeply.'

'There will be no need for us to speak to her, Mr Hepburn.'

'That's a huge relief.'

'I suspect that you are able to tell us all that we need to know.'

Hepburn took a deep breath. 'The situation is this, Inspector . . .'

Roused by the noise in the street, one of the neighbours came out to investigate. He was a short, tubby old man in a dressing gown and slippers. Keedy explained who they were and asked if they might step inside his house. Glad to get out of the cold, the old man led the way. Keedy and Burge followed. When all three of them were indoors, Keedy took the folded portrait from his pocket and opened it out.

'Do you recognise this man, sir?' he asked.

'Yes, he's been living two doors away for weeks.'

'Do you know his name?'

'He told us it was John,' said the other, 'and his friend is Anthony.'

'John Morris and Anthony Brown,' said Keedy, thoughtfully. 'Those are not their real names, sir.'

'Why not? Are those men criminals?'

'Oh, yes and they need to be caught as soon as possible.'

'What can you tell us about him?' asked Burge.

'Not very much,' admitted the old man. 'Most of the time, they just stayed in the house. The only time I bumped into the younger one was in the market. He didn't really want to chat.'

He went on to tell them the little that he knew about the two men who had been his neighbours until that evening. He added one significant detail.

'They rented the house and a lock-up garage two streets away.'

'What did they want that for?' asked Keedy.

'Their motorbikes . . .'

It was the second conversation they had had about betrayal and it was just as upsetting for Claude Chatfield as the first. Marmion's account was slow and measured. He paid tribute to the father's courage in coming forward to explain how he, his wife and his daughter had been duped by a man he now knew as Dr George Tindall.

'What did they believe his name was?' asked Chatfield.

'Michael Langford.'

'Did he claim that he was a hospital administrator this time?'

'No,' replied Marmion, 'he invented another role for himself as a captain of a destroyer who spent most of his time at sea.'

'But from what you tell me about the father, he seems like a highly intelligent man. Why was he taken in so easily?'

'Oh, he had grave reservations about Tindall at the start. It took years before he accepted him as a suitor for his daughter. At that point – after Tindall had sworn him to secrecy – he believed that she was about to become the wife of a brave man who was engaged in the war at sea. Mr Hepburn was so proud of him that he gave them Hipwell Manor as a wedding present.'

'I do wish people were not so gullible,' said Chatfield. 'I'd never have been persuaded to believe in that nonsense.'

'You are a trained policeman, sir. Suspicion is part of our stock-in-trade. It is unfair to blame hapless victims. They were exploited by a master of his art.'

'He was a master of his art as a surgeon as well.'

'There's no disputing it.'

'Wasn't that enough for him?'

'Apparently not, Superintendent.'

'The man was incorrigible.'

'I did tell you that Eleanor Tindall was not the only one,' Marmion reminded him. 'There could be others, though they may be too embarrassed to come forward.'

'Why do you say that?'

'We have to be realistic, sir. There may well have been relationships where Dr Tindall felt that matrimony was unnecessary. In other words, he could get what he wanted without a marriage proposal.'

'That's disgraceful!' hissed Chatfield.

'It may have been the reason why he rented the flat so near to the hospital in Brighton where he worked.'

'Are you telling me that he was entertaining women there while he had a wife just down the road in Hipwell Manor?'

'Technically, Mrs Langford was not really his wife. That honour – if I dare call it that – went to Eleanor Staynes. The second marriage was bigamous.'

'Is there no end to this man's lust?'

'We may never know.'

Chatfield was fuming. Leaping to his feet, he marched up and down his office several times before he controlled himself. He looked at Marmion.

'You say that you had doubts about Mrs Langford?'

'I did, sir.'

'How did they arise?'

'She was far too anxious to get us out of the house,' said Marmion. 'If she had been more cooperative, we would have gone on our way and forgotten all about her. The big mistake she made was to show us a photograph of her husband.'

'Why was it a mistake?'

'Her change of tone was too sudden, sir. One minute she was trying to throw us out, the next, she was taking the photograph off the piano and thrusting it at us. It worried me for some time,' confided Marmion. 'Then I began to wonder if she really was married to the bearded man she pointed out, or simply using the photograph of someone else in a bid to remove our suspicions.'

'Your instincts were sound,' said Chatfield, managing to make the compliment sound more like a reproach. 'Thank you for telling me all this. We must be as discreet as we can about Dr Tindall's . . . entanglements.'

'He was so irresponsible.'

'I can think of a stronger word than that for his antics. He has fathered at least two children. Imagine the shock that awaits them in due course.'

'He may have left them something in his will.'

'Nothing can make up for the damage and misery he has caused. Thinking about it makes my stomach heave. Let's talk about something else,' he decided, changing tack and lowering his voice. 'I take it that you spoke to your wife?'

'I did, sir.'

'How did you find her?'

'I don't think she's fully recovered from the experience. It may take time to adjust to it. My daughter will have the same problem.'

'I meant to tell you what Inspector Gale said about her.'

'Oh?'

'When I explained to her that Alice needed a day off to visit someone in prison who might be her brother, the inspector agreed instantly. She said that your daughter was the best policewoman under her command. That's high praise.'

'It is, indeed,' said Marmion. 'I'm pleased that one member of the family is getting some recognition for their efforts.'

Turning on his heel, he left the room quickly.

Keedy's anger at their failure to make two arrests was tempered by the fact that they had tracked the suspects to their hiding place. That was an achievement. He and Burge started a thorough search of the house. While the sergeant went from room to room on the ground floor, his colleague did the same upstairs. After a few minutes, Keedy was alerted by a shout from above. He trotted up the staircase.

'I'm in the front bedroom,' said Burge.

Keedy joined him. 'Why have you got the light off?'

'I want to show you something.' He pointed to a hole cut in the blind. 'They took no chances. When the light was off in here, they could keep watch through that hole without giving themselves away.'

'No wonder they made a run for it,' said Keedy. 'When one of them saw five men coming out of the gloom towards the house, he guessed who we must be. They had their bags already packed for an emergency dash.'

'What did they leave behind?'

'Almost nothing, Cliff – just a couple of things in the larder.'

'They must have sprinted down the garden.'

'Thirty seconds was all they needed, and we were stupid enough to give it to them. Bugger!' exclaimed Keedy. 'I'm so annoyed we let them slip through our fingers. We knew they were professionals. We should have made allowances for that.'

'What about that lock-up garage?'

'We won't find any clues there, Cliff. It will be just like this house – nothing at all to give them away. Remember what the estate agent told you about the man who rented this house?'

'He looked powerful.'

'I fancy that he might well have served in the army. That is why they escaped. Everything was planned with military precision. Even though they felt safe here, they probably alternated as sentries. It's what saved them.'

'Where are they now?'

'Haring along on those motorbikes with a big grin on their faces.'

Burge sighed. 'So much for my hope of some real action.'

'I was fired up for it as well.'

'What are we going to tell the superintendent?'

'We have to tell him the truth.'

'I don't relish that.'

'It was my decision to come here,' admitted Keedy, 'so I'll bear the brunt of Chat's anger. You'll come out of it much better.'

'Why?'

'Well, it was your hard work on the phone that helped to find their hideaway. Chat is bound to give you credit for that.'

Burge was dubious. 'Is he?'

'Ah,' said Keedy, changing his mind. 'I see what you mean. Perhaps you ought to wear a bulletproof waistcoat just in case.'

During his long tenure as commissioner, Sir Edward Henry had introduced many improvements at Scotland Yard and built a reputation as a man with a steady hand on the tiller. He was at heart a realist and knew that major crimes were never solved easily. When he went to the superintendent's office that evening, all that he was hoping for was news of progress in the murder investigation. In the event, he was given far more information than he had expected.

'Tindall was married twice?' he gulped.

'The inspector believes that the two unfortunate women

may not be the only victims of his carnal appetite.'

'Are you telling me that he had some sort of harem?'

'Some of the details made my hair stand on end,' confessed Chatfield. 'I feel that we must keep these unsavoury discoveries out of the newspapers.'

'Quite so, Superintendent. We must protect the unfortunate victims.'

'Inspector Marmion gave me a full report earlier on. He has dealt very tactfully with the two families who got in touch with us.'

'Were there children from these marriages?'

'I'm afraid so. The first wife had a boy and the second – who is not legally his spouse, of course – produced a girl.'

'Dear God!'

'The inspector spoke at length to the latter's father. According to the gentleman, Tindall – or Langford as he called himself – had always seemed so considerate towards his family.'

'It's a pity his concern for others didn't keep him within the bounds of the law,' said the commissioner. 'The War Office holds Tindall up as an example of dedication to duty in that military hospital, yet the fellow is nothing but a rampant Lothario.'

'Let us not deprive him of his due reward, Sir Edward,' advised Chatfield. 'His surgical expertise has saved lives. On that account, we owe him respect. As for his private life, however . . .'

'We must put that aside. I agree with you. What I came for is something that will show the War Office that your detectives are getting closer to the men who committed the murder. May I report that they are?'

'You may,' said Chatfield, conjuring up a smile behind

which to hide his misgivings. 'Tell them that my detectives are getting closer every day to the two suspects responsible.'

CHAPTER SEVENTEEN

Keedy and Burge returned to Scotland Yard empty-handed. They told Marmion about the abortive raid in Camden Town. The inspector was very unhappy about what he was hearing.

'Enthusiasm got the better of us,' admitted Keedy. 'When we raced to the house in the car, the noise of the engine must have alerted them. By the time we got on to the pavement, they were probably running away.'

'It was the reason they rented a house with a rear exit,' explained Burge. 'The garden gate was wide open when we got there.'

'Didn't you search the streets for them?' asked Marmion.

'We tried, sir, but they'd already escaped on their motorbikes. The local police station sent out two cars to scour the area, but the suspects had a head start.'

'Had they left anything behind them?'

'Two apples and some tins of baked beans,' said Keedy. 'We searched the place from top to bottom.'

Marmion was dismayed. 'You should have parked streets away,' he said, 'and sneaked up on them.'

'We know that now. Because we were too hasty, we lost them.'

'And you probably threw away the one chance you had of catching the pair. This is unlike you, Joe. I'm disappointed.'

'I'm to blame as well, sir,' confessed Burge. 'When we had the support of those two constables, I was raring to go.' He grimaced. 'Do we have to tell the superintendent that we failed?'

'There's no way we can hide this from him.'

'I was afraid you'd say that.'

'It was my call,' said Keedy.

'Yes,' agreed Marmion, 'but you were acting on my instructions. We'll speak to Chat together and keep Cliff out of this.'

'I deserve to face the music as well,' offered Burge.

'There's no point in all three of us getting a reprimand. Besides, you provided the crucial address. That needs to be recognised.'

'Thank you.'

'Keep your head down and say nothing.'

'Yes, Inspector.'

'Just pray that we come out of Chat's office alive,' joked Keedy. 'By the way, I showed that portrait to one of the

286

neighbours. He said it was a good likeness of the younger man, who called himself John Morris.'

'It's a common enough name,' said Marmion.

'So is Anthony Brown. There must be hundreds of men in London with that name. You can see why they both used an alias.'

'It's further proof that they are experienced.'

'And very brave,' said Keedy with a chuckle. 'Who else would want to live on a diet of apples and baked beans?'

'We're learning more about them all the time,' said Marmion. 'Morris is the one who likes scary paintings and Brown may have served in the army.'

'We need a lot more than that to run them to earth.'

'We found them once and we can find them again.'

'How do we do that?' asked Keedy.

Marmion puffed out his cheeks. 'There must be a way somehow.'

Romilly Staynes sat on the edge of the bed with an arm around her daughter, offering what comfort she could. As a result of the revelations about her husband, Eleanor was close to despair. Every so often, a memory helped to ease the pain.

'I can't believe that my marriage was completely hollow, Mummy.'

'No,' said Romilly, 'I accept that. There were good times. The problem was that they were few and far between.'

'What was George doing when he wasn't there?' asked Eleanor.

'It seems that he was working in a hospital as a surgeon.'

'I wasn't thinking about his job. Where did he live? How did he spend his free time? Was he alone or . . . did he have someone else?'

'Don't ask such questions, darling. It only makes things worse.'

'I must know the truth.'

'And you will,' said her mother, 'in due course. Now is not the time to torment yourself. There is a long way to go before the police investigation is complete. Only then will we know the full truth.'

'He told me that I was the only woman he ever loved.'

'I think you should try to forget anything he ever said to you, Eleanor. That's why I burnt those letters of his. They were full of lies.'

Her daughter brooded. 'I should have spotted the signs,' she said at length.

'What signs?'

'It happened more than once,' remembered Eleanor. 'We moved here because George knew that I wanted a big garden. When I told him that we could potter about in it together, he made it clear that he would never actually do anything like digging or even mowing the lawn. I couldn't understand why he emphasised that.'

'His hands,' said Romilly, realising. 'A surgeon has to protect his hands. He was ready to play tennis with you, but he could not risk doing manual work.'

'Why were we both so blind, Mummy?'

'It was because he made us trust him,' said Romilly. 'He worked on the pair of us slowly and cunningly. I was taken in by him just as you were.' She bit her lip. 'There may well be horrid revelations to come. We must brace ourselves for that.'

'People will laugh at us.'

'We must ignore them.'

'Do you think we should move away from here?'

'No,' said her mother, decisively. 'Our family and friends won't laugh. We will be drawn closer to them. Besides, where would we go?'

'I've no idea.'

'We must wait until the whole thing blows over.'

'But it's never going to do that, is it?' said Eleanor.

Romilly sighed. 'No, I suppose not.'

'The stigma will be there for ever.'

She burst into tears and her mother hugged her close for minutes.

'Do you know what I really hate him for?' said Romilly.

'What?'

'If George had been honest about his work as a surgeon, I would have admired him. He was saving lives.' Her eyes flashed. 'Yet he ruined ours.'

When he and Keedy faced the superintendent in the latter's office, Marmion had no opportunity to give the full account he had rehearsed. As soon as the failure to catch the suspects was admitted, Chatfield swooped like an eagle on Keedy, digging in his talons with relish.

'You let them get away?' he demanded.

'I misjudged the situation, sir,' said Keedy.

'Five of you against two of them – and they escape without

a scratch.'

'They were alert and prepared for anything.'

'That's more than I can say about you, Sergeant. I cannot believe that an officer of mine was so inept. It's almost as if you wanted them to escape.'

'That's not true at all, sir,' said Marmion, interrupting. 'The fact is that the sergeant and Detective Constable Burge did actually find out where these men were hiding. That took intelligence and persistence.'

'It's a pity those qualities were singularly lacking once they got to Camden Town,' said Chatfield. 'The operation was a disaster. Keedy and Burge must take the blame for that – but you were responsible for encouraging them, Inspector.'

'And I'd do the same again. All the evidence pointed to the fact that the suspects were hiding in Camden Town – a claim that you rejected with scorn.'

'That's right,' added Keedy. 'When Burge told you that he had found their address, you sent him packing.'

'I also told him to take no further action,' said Chatfield, vehemently.

'I felt that you were wrong to do so, sir.'

'An order is an order.'

'I chose to disobey it on this occasion,' said Marmion, 'because it meant disregarding sound evidence. If we had listened to you, we would never have confirmed that those men were hiding in the very place Burge had identified.'

'I may have made a slight error of judgement,' confessed Chatfield, 'but it pales beside the idiocy that the sergeant showed this evening.'

'He rushed in where he should have crept up, but you have to applaud his bravery. The sergeant and the others were unarmed. Yet they were ready to tackle men who were proven killers.'

'We have armed officers at our disposal. They should have been used.'

'Impossible,' declared Keedy. 'You'd already dismissed the idea that the suspects were at the address we had. If we had appealed to you for armed support, we'd never have been allowed to leave this building.'

'It all comes back to your intransigence,' said Marmion.

'Be quiet!' snapped Chatfield.

'If you had had the sense to—'

'Quiet, I said!' yelled the other.

There was a tense silence. Chatfield took time to compose himself.

'Earlier on,' he told them, 'the commissioner asked me for signs of progress in this case. Because I trusted my officers, I told him that everything was in hand. What is he going to say if he learns that an inspector blatantly defied my orders and a sergeant, who had the suspects cornered, allowed them to get away scot-free?'

'If you wish to take us off this investigation,' said Marmion, stoutly, 'we will appeal to the commissioner. He will appreciate the amount of intelligence we have already gathered.'

'And he has always supported us to the hilt,' Keedy reminded him.

'What is your decision, sir?'

Chatfield looked from one to the other. Their threat was not an idle one. The commissioner's faith in Marmion was unshakeable. If the superintendent chose to take the inspector off the case, Sir Edward Henry would demand to know why.

'Get out and do your job,' snapped Chatfield.

'Can we have more of a free hand?' asked Marmion.

'It would make things so much easier,' said Keedy. 'If we have to come to you for permission whenever we want to take action, we're hampered.'

'What do you say, sir?'

'I remain in charge, Inspector,' affirmed Chatfield.

'We accept that. All that we ask for is some . . . leeway.'

The superintendent sniffed. 'I'll think about it.'

It was a small concession but an important one. The balance of power had shifted slightly. Marmion and Keedy left the room with a spring in their step.

Since she had had two days off work in succession, Alice Marmion made sure that she reported for duty early the next morning. Thelma Gale was pleased to see her.

'Welcome back,' she said.

'Thank you, Inspector.'

'I gather that the prisoner was not, after all, your brother.'

'No,' replied Alice. 'He was simply using Paul's name.'

'Your father was considerate enough to ring me as soon as he'd heard details of what happened. He stressed how taxing an experience it had been for you and your mother.'

'That's true.'

'Are you sure that you feel able to go out on patrol today?'

'It's kind of you to ask,' said Alice, surprised by the kindness in the inspector's voice. 'I'm not only fit for work, I'm anxious to keep my mind occupied. Otherwise, I'd spend the whole day worrying about my brother.'

'You won't be able to forget him completely, I'm afraid.'

'Why not?'

'Iris Goodliffe is certain to bombard you with questions about your absence yesterday. You know how inquisitive she can be.'

'Iris understands the situation. I'll be happy to confide in her.'

'She was partnered by Jennifer Jerrold yesterday.'

'The two of them would have got on well together.'

'That's not what Goodliffe said – but I'm sure she'll give you full details.'

'Yes,' agreed Alice with a grin. 'I'm sure that she will.'

Breakfast at Hipwell Manor was a muted affair. Donald Hepburn buttered his toast and looked across at his daughter. She was pale, drawn and listless. Head down, Caroline was picking at her food but eating little of it. Her father was concerned.

'How do you feel now?' he asked.

'I just feel so stupid,' she replied. 'I can't think properly and it's an effort to move. All I want to do is to stay in bed and cry.'

'I can understand that but it's not the answer. Also, it is out of character. You have always been so strong and independent. Nothing seemed to get you down. You must fight back, Caroline,' he urged. 'It's what we must both do.'

'I know, Papa.'

'It will be a different life from now on. Adjustments will have to be made.'

'Adjustments?' She gave a weary laugh. 'Is that what you call them? My husband has been murdered and I have discovered that I might not even have been legally married to him. I have been living under a false name for years and our daughter, it now transpires, may be illegitimate. How can I adjust to things like that?'

'It will take time.'

'Everything I believed in has been shattered to pieces.'

'You still have people who love you and you still have the most beautiful daughter in the world. For her sake – as well as for your own – you must fight against despair.' He reached out to take her hand. 'I know that your whole world looks black and pointless, but it will not always be like that. We must show some fighting spirit.'

'It's been drained out of me, Daddy.'

'I don't believe it,' he said. 'It's been bruised, perhaps, but it's still there to be called upon. Have you forgotten that tennis tournament you won?'

'It was years ago.'

'Your mother and I were so proud. When you came back on court for the deciding set, you looked exhausted. As soon as the ball was served at you, however, you came back to life with a vengeance and completely overpowered your opponent. We'd never seen you play so well.'

'This is different,' she said. 'It's not a game. It's a form of death sentence.'

'Caroline!' he exclaimed.

'It's true. Everything I valued has fallen apart. I've lost my husband, my reputation, my place in society and my will to live.'

'Don't talk like that. It's frightening me.'

'I'm sorry,' she said, 'but that is how I feel. I simply can't believe that it will ever be any better.'

'You just need care and attention to get over the shock.'

'I also need to apologise to you.'

'Why?'

'I was the one who let Michael into the family. You never liked him.'

'That was only at the start. I am ashamed to say that I lowered my defences. I came to be impressed by him. I'm the one who should apologise to you, Caroline,' he said. 'I should have sensed that there was something funny about him. Michael Langford was rotten to the core.'

'That was not even his real name.'

'He lied to you about almost everything.' Releasing her hand, he sat back. 'That conversation I had on the telephone with Inspector Marmion was one of the most difficult I've ever had in my life. I had to summon up all my courage to lift the receiver. I am so glad that I did, however. The inspector was kind and understanding. He actually managed to soothe me.'

Caroline was penitent. 'I feel so ashamed of the way I spoke to him,' she said. 'I just wanted to get him out of here. I still thought my husband was alive then. I was beastly to both of the detectives.'

'They'll forgive you,' he said. 'What you must do is to start forgiving yourself for things that were not really your fault. We are two of a kind – we were both victims of a clever impostor. Now that he is gone, we can live a better, more honest life.'

'I hope so,' she said.

But there was no conviction in her voice.

* * *

After sifting his way through a mound of material, Keedy went off to Marmion's office. As he entered the room, he saw that the inspector was on the telephone. Keedy mimed an apology and offered to leave. Marmion indicated that he should sit down. Within a few seconds, he replaced the receiver.

'Sorry to interrupt,' said Keedy.

'We'd almost finished. I got in touch with the hospital again.'

'Did you talk to that major?'

'No, I wanted another word with Dr Irvine,' said Marmion. 'Insofar as George Tindall actually had a friend, Irvine was him.'

'Did he have anything interesting to say?'

'Yes, Joe – he told me about Tindall's time in France.'

'I'd forgotten that,' said Keedy. 'He worked in a field hospital, didn't he?'

'It may be the link we need. However,' said Marmion, 'before I start theorising, let me hear what you found.'

'Reading all the letters that came in, I was staggered. Dr Tindall had a secret life. Most of the information came from women in his past who preferred to remain anonymous. I suspect that some of them were nurses.' He handed over a letter. 'This is from one in that Brighton hospital who thought she was engaged to him.'

Marmion gave it a glance, then handed it back.

'He's left a trail of disappointed women behind him,' he said.

Keedy squirmed slightly. Before he became engaged to the inspector's daughter, he had enjoyed a full social life and was noted for his success among nurses. Marmion gave him a long, hard look.

'But there was a lot of praise for him as well,' added Keedy, anxious to move the conversation in another direction. 'I read letters from some wounded soldiers. When they were sent to Edmonton Hospital, Dr Tindall not only saved their lives in the operating theatre, he kept an eye on them throughout their convalescence.'

'In other words, he was a saint as well as a sinner.'

'Nobody can be both.'

'That's what he found out in the end,' said Marmion. 'There's a price to pay for taking advantage of young women.'

'Are we sure that that is the reason he was murdered?'

'I'm ninety-nine per cent certain.'

'You mentioned a theory.'

'Let me tell you about it . . .'

Alice was glad to be back at work again even if it meant pacing the streets in a fine drizzle. Iris Goodliffe was thrilled to see her again and was primed with questions. She was fascinated to hear about Shepton Mallet prison.

'What was it like inside?' she asked.

'I don't think you would have enjoyed it.'

'Did they show you the place where they hang killers?'

'No, they didn't, Iris. We were not there for a tour. We just wanted to meet the prisoner named Paul Marmion.'

'Yet it wasn't him.'

'It was very much like him, and my mother jumped to her feet when they brought him in. Then she realised that it was not Paul.'

'Was she disappointed?'

'Mummy was in the same frame of mind as me,' said Alice. 'She just wanted to get out of there.'

Iris broke off as she noticed a blind man waiting patiently at the kerb. Putting a hand on his elbow, she waited for the traffic to stop before she took him to the safety of the opposite pavement. They exchanged a few words. When she came back, she was giggling.

'What's so funny?' asked Alice.

'He said that, if he was twenty years younger, he'd marry me.'

'That's your first offer of the day, Iris.'

'He loved the sound of my voice – that's what he said.'

'Blind people tend to have keen hearing because they have to rely on it so much. He could tell from the sound of your voice how kind you are.'

'He was such a cheerful old chap. In his condition, I'd be angry.'

She fell in beside Alice and they strolled on at their usual speed.

'This is just like old times,' said Iris, happily. Her face then crumpled. 'I had Jenny Jerrold yesterday.'

'That's what Gale Force told me.'

'I'm very fond of her but all she could talk about is what happened in church last Sunday. She even told me what hymns they sang. Gale Force was threatening to team the two of us together permanently, but I begged her not to. Jenny will be much happier with someone else.'

'I daresay that she will.'

'She kept wondering where you were.'

'You must have guessed that the most likely reason was to do with my brother,' said Alice. 'Did you tell that to Jenny?'

'No, I kept it to myself. It's our secret.'

'Thank you. I appreciate that.'

'Besides, Jenny is easily shocked.'

'She would have been shocked by the sight of that prisoner. He was so uncouth, Iris. I can't believe that Paul would have fallen to that level.'

'How did he get hold of your brother's papers?'

'I've been wondering about that,' said Alice. 'Somehow I don't think that man stole them. He and Paul must have exchanged their papers. There is a worrying message for us in that. My brother is somebody else now.'

Joe Keedy listened patiently as Marmion developed his theory. He had claimed earlier that the army was the connecting link between the three different murders. He now provided more detail to bolster his argument.

'Those men were not acting of their own volition, Joe,' he said. 'They were given orders to kill.'

'Who gave them?'

'Someone at the Front.'

'Dr Tindall had no connection with the North Staffordshire Regiment.'

'Yes, he did. That is why I was keen to speak to Dr Irvine again. He told me that Tindall spent time working in a field hospital during the Battle of Loos. One of the regiment's battalions was involved in that.'

'So?'

'That could be the link we need.'

'It sounds unlikely to me,' said Keedy. 'The newspapers said that it was a hellish battle for us and for the French. Casualties

299

in both armies were enormous. If Tindall was tending the wounded, he would have been seen as a hero. He might even have been singled out for a medal. Who on earth could possibly want him killed?'

'That's what we have to find out.'

'How?'

'We must find out where the regiment is stationed and go there.'

Keedy laughed. 'Has nobody told you there is a war on?'

'We've done it before,' said Marmion. 'When we had to arrest two soldiers at the start of the war, we went all the way to France and back. We thought nothing of going into a war zone.'

'Things have changed a lot since then,' said Keedy, seriously. 'They use tanks and poison gas and bigger shells now.'

'I'm aware of that.'

'We could be committing suicide.'

'Not if we take sensible precautions.'

Keedy shook his head. 'I'm uneasy about this.'

'There's no alternative. If we want the truth about Dr Tindall's murder, we have to cross the Channel.'

'That means we could be attacked by German submarines or aircraft.'

'We'd have the protection of a convoy,' said Marmion.

'I'm not so sure.'

'We have to find out who is controlling those two assassins – because that's what they are. They escaped you yesterday, Joe. Don't you want a second chance of catching them?'

'Yes, I do,' said Keedy, eyes glinting. 'I want it more than anything else.'

'It's settled, then.'

'What about—?'

'Leave Alice and Ellen out of it,' said Marmion. 'They accept that we sometimes have to take risks. Also – they trust our judgement.'

'There's one snag, Harv.'

'I don't see it.'

'Chat would never let us go, surely?'

'He will if we supply him enough evidence.'

'But we simply don't have it yet.'

'That is why you and I are going to Bristol straight away.'

Keedy was mystified. 'Bristol?'

'Yes, Joe,' said Marmion, rising from his chair, 'and while we are there, Cliff Burge will be making enquiries in Stafford.'

'Whatever for?'

'Wait and see.'

'This is madness!'

Marmion grinned. 'Sometimes we have to resort to that.'

Claude Chatfield had finally found something that warmed his heart. As he read that morning's edition of *The Times*, he saw that he was not only quoted correctly he was praised for his record of success in solving murder cases. His eye ran down the column until it reached something that made him freeze. It was the commissioner who was quoted this time. While he applauded the superintendent's efforts, Sir Edward Henry went on to say that they depended on the brilliance of detectives like Inspector Marmion. Scrunching up the newspaper, Chatfield put it aside.

There was a tap on the door and a detective constable came in with an envelope in his hand. He gave it to the superintendent.'

'Inspector Marmion asked me to deliver this, sir.'

'Why couldn't he speak to me in person?'

'He and Sergeant Keedy are no longer in the building.'

'Where have they gone?'

'That letter may help to explain, sir.'

The visitor left and closed the door behind him. Tearing open the envelope, Chatfield was astounded by what he read. When there was another tap on the door, he was unwelcoming.

'What is it this time?' he barked.

With a look of surprise on his face, the commissioner came into the room.

'Oh, I do beg your pardon, Sir Edward,' said Chatfield, writhing with embarrassment. 'I was expecting someone else.'

The commissioner frowned. 'So it seems.'

'Can I help you in any way?'

'I sincerely hope so. I've heard disturbing whispers.'

'Pay no attention to gossip, Sir Edward. It's always unreliable.'

'That's why I came here. I'm counting on you to deny the accusation.'

'What accusation?' asked Chatfield, warily.

'Well, the story is that the suspects were identified as living in a house they had rented in Camden Town. Some of your men went off to investigate and picked up reinforcements at the local police station.' His eyelids narrowed. 'Does any of this sound likely to you?'

'Please go on.'

'There's not much more to say beyond the fact that the operation was bungled. With two killers at their mercy, your

302

men somehow contrived to let them escape. Is there any truth in this nonsense?'

'I'm afraid that there is, Sir Edward,' croaked Chatfield.

'I refuse to believe that Marmion was involved.'

'The inspector had no part in the raid. Sergeant Keedy was in charge.'

'Then I suggest that you send for him so that I can hear the full story.'

'Unfortunately, he is not in the building.'

'Then where is the man?'

'According to a letter from Inspector Marmion, they will be out for most of the day pursuing a line of enquiry. What that is, Sir Edward, I can't rightly say.'

'Then I have to tell you that I'm displeased,' said the commissioner. 'Not to put too fine a point on it, I am extremely displeased. Why was I not informed about the failure of the attempted arrest and why are you incapable of explaining where officers under your command are at the moment?' He saw the newspaper on the desk. 'Ah, you have read *The Times*, I see. No doubt you have been basking in the praise lavished on you. It is as well that the reporter was unaware of yesterday's fiasco, or you and your officers would have been pilloried. Good day to you.'

Leaving the room, the commissioner slammed the door behind him.

Chatfield buried his head in his hands.

CHAPTER EIGHTEEN

Paddington Station was busy when they got there. Marmion and Keedy noticed the prevalence of women in the uniforms of the Great Western Railway. It had become a feature of all railway stations during the war. Female porters, carriage cleaners, ticket collectors and messengers abounded. Jobs that had routinely been given to men were being done just as efficiently by women. The detectives looked on with approval. They were less impressed, however, by the long queues of passengers.

'Why is there such a shortage of trains?' asked Keedy.

'That's the wrong question,' said Marmion.

'Is it?'

'You should be asking why the price of train tickets has shot up. We're being asked to pay more for what is a reduced service.'

'That's not fair.'

'Blame the war, Joe. It's changed everything.'

The queue that they had joined eventually made its way to a platform.

'Why do we need to go all the way to Bristol?' said Keedy. 'Couldn't you have spoken to somebody by telephone?'

'That's what Cliff Burge did, and they would only release basic details of the case. The report they sent him added very little. If we want the full facts, we need to talk to a detective involved in it.'

'He got a bit more detail from the police in Stafford.'

'That's why I sent him there,' said Marmion. 'With luck, he may be able to get the full story of the murder of that publican.'

'What surprises me is that the killers were so merciless in all three cases.'

'Why is that so surprising?'

'Well,' said Keedy, 'one of them obviously has Christian principles.'

'I doubt that.'

'Think about that painting he wanted to buy.'

'I try not to, Joe. When the artist showed it to us, I thought it was revolting. Who would want to hang that on a wall?'

'John Morris – or whoever he really is.'

'Then he has a perverted idea of art.'

'You have to admit that that painting sticks in the mind.'

'It doesn't stick in my mind,' said Marmion with contempt.

'There's something else,' recalled Keedy. 'When he hired the army uniforms from Pegasus Costumes, Morris said that they'd be used in a play.'

'I know – *Soldiers of the Cross*.'

'There is no such play.'

'How do you know?'

'The woman at Pegasus Costumes had never heard of it. Nor had Mandeville.'

'What are you trying to say, Joe?'

'I wonder if that's how they see themselves.'

'Who?'

'The killers, of course.'

'You've lost me.'

'Well, we call them cold-hearted assassins,' said Keedy. 'What if they believe they are on some sort of crusade as Soldiers of the Cross?'

Having spoken to Detective Superintendent Ash on the telephone, Clifford Burge had been given a false impression of his appearance. When he met him in person at the police station in Stafford, he was taken aback.

'Is there anything wrong?' asked Ash.

'I was expecting someone bigger, sir.'

'It's the deep voice. People expect me to be fat and jolly. In fact, I'm a skinny chap with a big nose who happens to sing in the bass section of the police choir.' He laughed. 'You, on the other hand, look exactly the way you sounded.'

'Is that good or bad?'

'It's good.'

They were in a small room used for interviews. After arriving by train, Burge had gone straight to the police station and was delighted to find Ash on the premises. The superintendent was a tall, rangy individual in his forties.

'Who sent you?' he asked.

'Inspector Marmion of Scotland Yard.'

'I've seen that name in the papers.'

'You've also seen details of the case I told you about. The inspector believes there are similarities with the murder of that publican here in Stafford.'

'I'm not sure about that.'

'Exceptional violence was used.'

'I've seen quite a few cases like that,' said Ash. 'The most recent was a month or so ago. It concerned two soldiers in a military hospital. There had been a feud between them, apparently. Shortly after they were discharged, one of them killed the other with a bayonet. They counted over fifty stab wounds and both eyes had been gouged out.'

Burge shuddered. 'What happened to the killer?'

'He took his own life.'

'Let's talk about the death of that publican, Charlie Ferriday.'

'I gave you all of the details about that.'

'Not quite all,' said Burge. 'There was something you held back.'

'It was speculation rather than hard evidence. What did you make of the case?'

'I think that Molly Roper was to blame. From what you told me, she and Ferriday were close.'

'They were business partners of a sort.'

'I think there was more to it than that. If she got involved with Ferriday, she might have written to her husband to tell him. I can imagine the shock it must have been for someone marooned in the trenches. Just think,' said Burge. 'He must have been in a terrible state. His wife had betrayed him. What was there to bring him home after the war? The shame would have been unbearable. It's no wonder he decided to end it all by getting himself killed.'

'That's a good guess,' said Ash, 'but there are two things you don't know.'

'What are they?'

'Molly Roper was devoted to her husband. When she worked at the pub, she did what all barmaids do and flirted with the customers. I know because I drank there occasionally. But that was as far as it went. The only man for her was Sam Roper.'

'You said there were two things.'

'The second one was Vera Ferriday. She was Charlie's wife and kept a close eye on him. If anything had happened between him and Molly, she'd have known about it straight away and brained him.'

Burge was puzzled. 'But I thought . . .'

'It wasn't Molly who told her husband she had committed adultery.'

'Then who was it?'

'We're still trying to find out,' admitted Ash. 'He did it deliberately, knowing full well how Sam Roper was likely to react. In effect, the man who wrote that letter killed Sam. Can you see what else he did?'

'Yes,' replied Burge, shocked. 'He also got the publican murdered as well.'

'Nothing happened between him and Molly Roper. The men who sliced off Charlie Ferriday's head killed an innocent man.'

When they got to the police headquarters in Bristol, they noticed how old most of those in uniform were. It was the same everywhere. Having lost so many younger men to the army, forces all over the country were compelled to supplement their numbers by asking retired officers to return to work. While Keedy was inclined to be critical of the elderly officers, Marmion admired them for responding to the call. Their experience, he contended, made up for their lack of speed and mental agility.

They were at first delighted to discover that Inspector Hugh Griggs, who had led the investigation in which they were interested, was available. When they met him in his office, however, they changed their minds instantly. Griggs was a flabby man in his forties with dark eyes set in a pasty face, and with an abiding air of resentment. Marmion thanked him for information already provided but pressed for more detail.

'Why are you bothering me?' asked Griggs. 'There's only a surface similarity between your case and the one that I'm concerned with.'

'I disagree,' said Marmion. 'We believe that Mr Tait was killed by the same two men who murdered Dr Tindall.'

'That's rubbish! What proof do you have?'

'The modus operandi is identical.'

'And there's a third case we tracked down,' said Keedy. 'It involves a cruel murder in Stafford. That followed the same pattern.'

'There is no pattern,' insisted Griggs. 'What happened here in Bristol is quite unique. Meredith Tait was killed immediately before his safe was rifled. As I told Detective Constable Burge when he first got in touch with me, it was a clear-cut example of murder for gain.'

'How close are you to an arrest, Inspector?'

Griggs glowered. 'We continue to gather evidence.'

He went on to explain that the victim was a lawyer of good reputation who had been adopted as a parliamentary candidate at the next election. Since the death of his wife, he had looked after their two children. The visitors listened to the detailed account of how and when Tait had been murdered. Marmion asked the first question.

'Mr Tait had two partners and, presumably, there were a number of others who worked in the building. How were the killers able to get close to him?'

'I don't accept that there were two of them,' said Griggs. 'One man arranged a meeting with him but, because he could not get to Bristol during working hours, he asked if Tait could possibly see him in the evening.'

'Is that recorded in the appointments diary?'

'Yes – the meeting was at 7 p.m.'

'What was the name of the client?'

'Mr James Smith.'

'Do you know why he was so keen to see Mr Tait?' asked Keedy.

'He wanted representation in a case involving a contested will.'

'Were any details given?'

'No,' said Griggs, irritably, 'but, according to Tait's secretary, a large amount of money was at stake. It was the kind of case in which he specialised. Tait was expensive to retain but he usually won any battles in court. In essence, that is it. Having inveigled himself into a private meeting with Tait, the bogus client killed him and ransacked the safe.'

'It's difficult to believe that a lawyer could be so unguarded,' said Marmion. 'Most people in his position would make sure they had someone else in the office.'

'When they spoke, James Smith obviously persuaded him that he was exactly what he claimed to be.'

'There's something you're not telling us, Inspector.'

'I sent the details to Scotland Yard. You must have read them.'

'We have. What's missing is a link between the murder and the subsequent suicide of Captain Tait.'

'We can only assume he was devastated by the death of his brother.'

'You're far too clever to work on assumptions.'

'I'm a busy man, Inspector. Instead of answering questions from you, I need to be out with my team, leading the hunt for the killer.'

'There are two of them.'

'I know this case inside out – you don't.'

'That's exactly why we need more detail.'

Gregg was dismissive. 'Well, you'll have to get it elsewhere, Inspector.'

'If you don't help us, I'll have to complain to your superior.'

'You will not solve your case by being here in Bristol.'

'No,' agreed Marmion, 'but we might be able to give you some useful information regarding your own investigation. If you assist us, we will assist you. It's called cooperation. I recommend it.'

It was good to be back on his farm again and to find that his livestock had been looked after in his absence. When he had spoken to both of his farmhands, he walked across to the large shed and unlocked it. He surveyed his workplace with pride. Sizeable pieces of timber of various kinds were stacked against one wall. The floor was covered in sawdust and there were wood shavings around the sculpture of an angel on which he had been working before he had gone to London. He was still admiring his work when his nephew came into the shed.

'They've finished milking the cows,' said Brian.

'You should learn to do that.'

'I'm no milkmaid.'

'If you live on a farm, you have to turn your hand to anything.'

'I do miss our adventure in London,' said his nephew. 'And I miss those motorbikes we stole.'

'We didn't steal them, Brian' emphasised the other. 'We simply borrowed them then returned them without a scratch on them. That means we have clear consciences.'

His nephew looked around. 'I'd forgotten what a wonderful place this is,' he said. 'Look at all these chisels. Do you really need that many?'

'Yes, I do. Each one does a separate job. I've used well over a dozen of them when working on this.' He pointed to the life-sized angel with wings spread. 'I'll have a chance to finish it now.'

'Unless we get some more instructions.'

'There is that.'

'What if we don't?'

'Then our work is done,' said his uncle. 'I start living as a sculptor again and you help me to run this place.'

'I'll miss the excitement. What about you?'

'I feel the same,' admitted the other.

'To be honest, I hope it never stops. We get the thrill of doing our Christian duty, and the world is rid of someone who deserves to die in pain.'

'That's the bit I love.'

'My favourite moment is when we say a prayer over him afterwards.'

Claude Chatfield had been tied up in meetings all morning. Still smarting from the way that the commissioner had spoken to him earlier, he went in search of the driver who had taken Marmion and Keedy away from Scotland Yard. When he finally tracked the man down, he pointed an accusatory finger.

'Where did you take them?' he demanded.

The driver was baffled. 'Who are you talking about, sir?'

'Inspector Marmion and Sergeant Keedy.'

'Oh, I see. The thing is, I've driven a lot of people about today.'

'Those are the only two that interest me.'

'Then the answer is Paddington Station.'

'Why were they going there?'

'I overheard the inspector talking about Bristol.'

'Bristol, for heaven's sake!' cried Chatfield. 'They are investigating a crime that occurred here in London.'

'I thought they were following orders, sir, and the same goes for Constable Burge. I gave him a lift this morning as well.'

'Why? Where was he going?'

'Stafford.'

'I can't believe this,' yelled the superintendent. 'Why didn't they have the decency to tell me? What use are my officers in Bristol and Stafford? I need them here, solving a murder in Edmonton.'

They had met people with the same attitude before, senior detectives in the provinces who had a grudge against Scotland Yard because of the prime position it occupied in national law enforcement. Hugh Griggs was typical of the breed. He believed that he could lead a murder investigation as well as anyone, and he hated to be diverted from it. Failing to get rid of his visitors, he was forced to give them details about the case that he had so far refused to pass on to Scotland Yard for fear of interference.

'Captain Richard Tait had been on active service for over a year,' he said. 'He was a good officer, highly rated by his superiors. He seemed to cope with the rigours of war extremely well.'

'Yet he committed suicide,' said Marmion.

'He and his wife had no children. They had always been devoted to each other. Mrs Tait wrote to him regularly. Then one day . . .'

'Ah,' said Keedy as Griggs fell silent, 'I could hazard a guess what happened. Captain Tait had a letter from her that upset him.'

'That's right.'

'Did she tell him that she was pregnant?'

'Mrs Tait denies it, but I don't believe her. What is certain is that she was feeling very lonely. That made her vulnerable.'

'Vulnerable to her brother-in-law, I suspect,' said Marmion. 'That would have hurt Captain Tait more than anything. He must have felt trapped abroad in the middle of a battle while his wife was being unfaithful to him in Bristol.'

'The next thing we know,' said Griggs, 'Meredith Tait is murdered.'

'How did his sister-in-law react?'

'She collapsed and had to be rushed to hospital.'

'Did she recover?'

'Yes, she did – but she lost the baby she denied that she was carrying.'

During their beat, there were places where they stopped for a brief respite. They reached the latest of them and came to a halt. Iris Goodliffe was pensive.

'What are you going to do after the war?' she asked.

'That depends on who wins,' replied Alice.

'There's no doubt about that, is there? The Battle of Cambrai was a triumph for us. It's the only battle in the whole war for which the church bells were rung. That was a signal that the end was in sight.'

'I don't think so, Iris. According to the newspaper I read, the Germans are hitting back. They're not finished yet.'

'What a pity!'

'We've had so many false dawns in this war that I've stopped getting my hopes up. The fighting will be going on well into next year.'

'How many more British soldiers have to die before it's finished?'

'Too many, I expect,' said Alice. 'To answer your question, I think that I'll go back to teaching.'

'I'm not brainy enough to do that.'

'You've been trained to work in a pharmacy. That shows how intelligent you are. Why do you always have to belittle yourself?'

'I don't know. I just never feel good enough, somehow.'

'You do this job well.'

Iris laughed. 'Gale Force doesn't think so,' she said. 'She has a new complaint about me every day.'

'Ignore her.'

'I wish I could.'

'When the war is over, you can wave her goodbye.'

'I'll be sad to wave you goodbye,' said Iris with an edge of desperation. 'We will stay friends afterwards, won't we?'

'Of course, we will.'

'Can I come and see you at your school?'

'Maybe,' said Alice, guardedly.

'You obviously have a gift with children.'

'I love watching them grow up and develop.'

'Well, you won't be doing that for long.'

'What do you mean?'

'You'll have children of your own, surely?'

'I don't know,' admitted Alice. 'Joe and I have not really talked about it. I suppose that it will happen one day and, yes, I'd love to be a mother.'

Iris sighed. 'Being a mother is yet another thing you'll be good at.'

'I could say the same about you, Iris.'

'There's no chance of that happening,' said the other, gloomily. 'Who would want to marry me?'

Iris was back to her familiar theme. It was time to cut her short.

'Let's move on,' said Alice, leading the way. 'At our next stop, we get our free cup of tea. If we're lucky, we might even get a biscuit . . .'

After a long conversation in Bristol with Inspector Griggs, they made their way back to the railway station. On a cold, windswept platform, Marmion and Keedy reflected on what had happened.

'Griggs has got a huge chip on his shoulder,' said Keedy. 'He saw us as the enemy, not as fellow police officers.'

'We broke down his resistance in the end,' Marmion pointed out. 'He was amazed when we gave him clear proof that two men were involved in the murder of that lawyer.'

'Our big achievement was to convince him that the same killers were behind the death of Dr Tindall. He now realises that he is not dealing with an isolated event.'

'No, it's only the first of three linked murders.'

'Solve one and we solve all three.'

'I don't think Inspector Griggs would like that. He'd hate us to get credit for the capture of two people whose killing spree started in Bristol.'

'It's no time to be territorial,' said Keedy.

'Our time here was well spent. Even Chat must accept that.'

'Do you think he'll agree to our demand?'

'No,' said Marmion. 'We may have to go above his head.'

'He'd never forgive us.'

'We can live with that.' He raised his voice above the noise of the approaching train. 'Well, our work is done here. I just hope that Cliff Burge had equal success up there in Stafford.'

* * *

On the way to the sewing circle, Ellen Marmion had been wondering once again where her son was. There were periods of time when she was able to push Paul to the very back of her mind, but the trip to Shepton Mallet had changed that. Her maternal instincts were given a new intensity. She wanted somehow to assure him that they still loved him and accepted his desire to live apart from the family. They might even be able to help him financially, in a small way. With Christmas at hand and the coldest months of the year to follow, Ellen feared for his health and safety.

When she got to the sewing circle, however, all thoughts of Paul were instantly banished. She heard that one of the other women had received a telegram from the War Office to inform her of the death of her son in the wake of the battle of Cambrai. That became the main topic of conversation as they sewed or knitted garments to keep the soldiers warm throughout the winter. Ellen was grateful to be able to care about someone else's son for a change. It was a crushing blow for the family but at least they knew where he was and what fate had befallen him. There was a degree of comfort in that.

They had agreed to meet in a cafe not far from Scotland Yard so that they could pool information before reporting to Superintendent Chatfield. When they arrived, they were pleased to see that Burge was already there. They joined him at his table and ordered refreshments. Marmion gave him a highly edited account of their meeting with Inspector Griggs then it was Burge's turn.

'It was an eye-opener,' he confessed. 'On the basis of the outline facts of the case, I made some foolish assumptions . . .'

Referring to his notebook, he told them what had happened and how Superintendent Ash had made him look at the Stafford murder from a totally different angle. Marmion and Keedy were intrigued.

'What I didn't have,' said Burge, 'was local knowledge. He had the advantage there. He knew the people involved and was certain that nothing had happened between Charlie and Molly Roper.'

'So the publican was completely innocent,' said Keedy. 'That means the killers were acting on incorrect information.'

'Someone lied to Sam Roper. He believed them.'

'The same goes for the person who ordered the killing.'

'When we find him,' vowed Marmion, 'we'll tell him that.'

Burge was agog. 'According to you, the orders came from France.'

'Then that's where we have to go.'

CHAPTER NINETEEN

They were seated in the workshed, enjoying a glass of cider and looking back over their achievements. Their narrow escape in Camden Town had been alarming at the time but was now a source of laughter.

'I'd love to have seen their faces when they realised that we'd gone,' said the sculptor. 'They were clever enough to find us but too stupid to catch us. I really enjoyed the moment when we took to our heels.'

'Well, I didn't,' complained his nephew. 'Scarpering like that made this artificial foot of mine hurt like hell.'

'Sorry about that, Brian.'

'Last time I had to run for my life, I wasn't quite so lucky. It was during the Battle of Loos. When the bullets were flying, I didn't move fast enough, and my foot was shattered. That put paid to my army career.'

'At least you fought in a real battle.'

'You did the same in South Africa, surely?'

'No,' said the other, 'none of the battles were on the same scale as Loos. I was based outside Johannesburg as part of the 15th Brigade under General Wavell. We had skirmishes galore in the first phase of the war with the Boers but that was it. The truth is that, when it came to real action, I had far more excitement in Bristol, Stafford and Edmonton.'

'We had three triumphs in a row.'

His uncle raised his glass. 'Here's to the next one.'

'He must be delighted with our work.'

'Approval from above is more important,' said the other, looking upwards. 'Our orders really come from him. We are soldiers of the cross, empowered to wreak God's revenge.'

Claude Chatfield had had many arguments with Marmion over the years, but none had been as fierce as the one in which they were now embroiled. Every accusation hurled at the inspector was either firmly rebuffed or deftly avoided. Every demand from the superintendent was bravely challenged. At the point where Chatfield realised that he was losing the debate, Marmion issued his ultimatum.

'We must go to France,' he asserted, 'or this murder will never be solved.'

'It's out of the question.'

'Is it, sir? Because it has an interest in this case, the War Office has hounded the commissioner and he, in turn, has been hounding you. Let us exert pressure in return. If the War Office wants Dr Tindall's case to be solved, it must give us the means to solve it.'

'And what are those means?'

'Safe passage to and from north-east France and an order to the commanding officer of the North Staffordshire Regiment stationed in Cambrai, requiring him to give us all the help we need.'

'You'd be going into a war zone.'

'The sergeant and I have taken that into account.'

'I can't guarantee that the War Office will agree to your demands.'

'Then they need to be offered as polite requests,' said Marmion with a teasing smile. 'You'd do that much better than me. We leave it in your capable hands.'

Chatfield came close to frothing at the mouth.

Alice had been glad to get back to work and to see her colleagues again. When she came to the end of her shift, she left the building with Iris Goodliffe beside her, chatting amiably. They did not, however, stay together because Alice saw that Joe Keedy was waiting for her. Leaving her friend, she ran forward into a warm embrace.

'What a lovely surprise!' she said.

'Let me walk you to your bus stop,' he said, offering his arm.

'Yes, please.'

'I'm sorry to pop up like a Jack-in-the-box.'

'It's a wonderful treat for me.'

They walked on until they were out of earshot of the others.

'There's something I need to tell you Alice,' he said.

She was perplexed. 'Why are you so solemn?'

'You'll soon understand.'

Ellen Marmion replaced the receiver and rushed into the living room to sit down. Her heart was racing, and she was shaking all over. Though her husband had tried to break the news gently, it still rocked her. He was planning to go to France with Joe Keedy in the hope of making an arrest. It seemed an act of madness to her. Why risk their lives by crossing the Channel, then going to the very place where a massive battle had so recently taken place? It was an almost suicidal decision.

She gave herself time to absorb the news. From the moment she had first met him, she knew that Marmion would always put duty before personal safety. While he would exercise discretion in the face of danger, he would never walk away from it. Ellen feared that he would put his life at risk simply by sailing to France. British ships were targets for enemy aircraft and submarines. There was little defence against either. Her husband might not even reach land. Even if he did, he would be going on to an area devastated by the latest action on the Western Front.

The war had been a geography lesson for Ellen. When her son's regiment was in France, she had followed its movements with the aid of a map. As he travelled through Picardy, her husband would now be going past the Somme battlefield where Paul had fought, been wounded, and lost his best friend. It was a cruel coincidence. Her thoughts turned to her daughter. If Alice had heard the news, she would be suffering as well, terrified that she might lose both her father and the man she was due to marry in the new year. It was a frightening possibility. All that Ellen could do was to close her eyes and offer a silent prayer.

Though he had grave misgivings about their trip, Claude Chatfield sent them off with his best wishes, hoping that they would return safe and well. Notwithstanding his occasional clashes with Marmion, he admired the inspector's bravery and determination. The commissioner was even more impressed.

'I applaud their courage,' he said. 'Marmion's attitude is commendable – one has to follow the evidence, wherever it might take one.'

'I just wish it were not taking them to France,' sighed Chatfield.

'The War Office has been criticised for its slowness but that was not the case here. When I stressed the importance of their mission, arrangements were quickly made to get them across the Channel.'

'Thank you for using your influence, Sir Edward.'

'I was delighted to be able to do so. And yes, I know that they are taking a massive risk. But have faith in them, Superintendent. They have been to France before in hostile conditions and they made two significant arrests. I'm sure that they will achieve their objective again.'

It was the second time that they had been in a troop train heading for the south coast. On this occasion, however, they were not going to Brighton to conduct some interviews. Marmion and Keedy were on their way to Dover with reinforcements dispatched to repair some of the huge gaps in manpower that were the legacy of the Battle of Cambrai. The detectives could only imagine how the young and untried soldiers were feeling. Like them, Marmion and Keedy were fully aware of the dangers of joining British forces at the Western Front.

There was a lengthy wait at the port and, when their ship finally arrived, they had to let the wounded be unloaded before they could board the vessel in their place. Crossing the Channel on a cold, blustery, December night was a grim prospect, but they accepted the situation without complaint. Of more concern to them was the fear and anxiety they had created in Ellen and Alice. Until their safe return, the women would have long, anxious, sleepless nights. Both men felt guilty.

The young lieutenant tasked with looking after them had managed to find some protective clothing and helmets for each of them. Keedy joked that he would like a rifle and bayonet as well. Cabins were reserved for the officers. The remainder of the soldiers were assigned to the large public rooms. Freedom of movement was allowed but the majority preferred to stay indoors, away from the fierce wind and the stinging salt spray. Since the ship was running dark, those who ventured out on deck had to move cautiously and keep one hand on the rail. The detectives were among them.

'How are you feeling, Joe?' asked Marmion.

'I feel glad that I didn't join the navy,' replied Keedy. 'My stomach is heaving.'

'You'll get used to it.'

Marmion looked up. 'I thought I heard the sound of an aeroplane.'

'Was it one of ours or one of theirs?'

'One of theirs, I think, but it's not going to waste its bombs on a target like us that they can't see. My guess is that it's heading for London, with a lot of friends to back it up. If it drops its load over the capital, it's bound to hit something.'

'Listen to that,' said Keedy.

'Now that the German plane has flown past, all I can hear are the ship's engines and the sound of the waves battering us.'

'Listen more carefully.'

'What am I supposed to hear?'

'Someone is singing.'

It was true. When Marmion cocked an ear and concentrated, he could hear the strains of a song written the previous year and achieving almost instant popularity. Wind and waves tried to silence it, but they heard the words clearly.

> *Roses are shining in Picardy, in the hush of the silvery dew,*
> *Roses are flow'ring in Picardy, but there's never a rose like you!*
> *And the roses will die with the summertime, and our roads*
> *may be far apart,*
> *But there's one rose that dies not in Picardy!*
> *'Tis the rose that I keep in my heart!*

The invisible singer had a beautiful tenor voice, ideally suited to the sense of yearning in the lyrics. Marmion and Keedy were not the only men on deck who felt tears coursing down their cheeks.

Alice's pleasure at the unexpected appearance of Keedy had quickly dwindled into concern. The fact that he and her father were about to head for France set off a peal of alarm bells in her head. Despite Keedy's assurances, she was fearful. As soon as they parted, she decided to go to the family home to be with her mother. It was a time when they needed each other.

The moment that her daughter appeared, Ellen clung to her in desperation. Though they spent long hours together, there was little conversation. When midnight chimed, they were seated on the sofa, looking at the dying embers in the grate. Neither of them had the urge to go to bed.

'What are you thinking, Mummy?' asked Alice at length.

Ellen turned to her. 'I'm wondering where they are.'

'Somewhere safe, I hope.'

War paid no attention to the time of day. When the ship docked in Calais, they could hear the distant thunder of artillery. Men and equipment were quickly unloaded. Marmion and Keedy found themselves in the back of a car that was part of the long convoy that set off into the night. Cambrai was over ninety miles away, but they saw nothing of the countryside in the dark and besides, they slept all the way there. When they eventually woke up, they had reached the British encampment. They got out of the car in the gloom to see a vast array of tents and a haphazard display of tanks, armoured cars and ambulances. Soldiers were moving about everywhere. There was no sense of triumph after their success on the battlefield. What the detectives felt was an abiding sense of fatigue.

Someone was ordered to take them to the area where the North Staffordshire Regiment was based. Once there, Marmion handed over the letter he had been given by the War Office. It earned them enough time to have a wash and shave to smarten themselves up. They were then given breakfast and shown to the quarters of the commanding officer and told to wait.

After an hour of twiddling his thumbs, Keedy became restive.

'They've forgotten us,' he complained.

'We have to be patient, Joe.'

'But we are on serious business.'

'Nothing is more serious than war,' said Marmion. 'We're here to talk about three murders. Compare that to the huge losses in the Battle of Cambrai. They run into thousands. We have to keep things in perspective.'

'Are they just going to ignore us?'

'There's no question of that happening,' Marmion assured him. 'The letter from the War Office will open doors for us. That is why I handed it over straight away. It not only demands that we are given cooperation, it gives exact details of why we are here. It will save a lot of explanation.'

Keedy was unmoved. 'I still think they've forgotten us – on purpose.'

Ten minutes later, a tall, stately man in the uniform of a Lieutenant-Colonel came into the tent. Now in his late fifties, he had deep-set eyes and a black moustache fringed with grey hairs. Julian Fulton introduced himself and studied them in turn.

'I'm not sure that we can help you, Inspector,' he said. 'The battle we have just fought comprised ten days of utter carnage. It's more than possible that the person you seek is now buried in a war grave.'

'We believe him to be an officer,' said Marmion.

'Officers fell in profusion along with their men.'

'It's the relationship between the two that interests me, sir.'

'It rests firmly on discipline, Inspector.'

'Is it true that, when men are killed in action, the officers who commanded them often write to their families to offer sympathy? That was certainly the case,' Marmion went on, 'in my son's regiment. He fought at the Battle of the Somme.'

'I'm sorry to hear of his loss,' muttered Fulton.

'He's not dead,' explained Keedy. 'He was only wounded.'

'Ah, I see. To answer your question, Inspector, it is the practice for officers to contact the families of those who fall in battle. In this regiment, they are sometimes helped by our chaplain, the Reverend Wilshaw. He has a gift of offering a few comforting words to grieving families.'

'Then the chaplain may be a good place to start,' said Marmion. 'May we speak to him, please?'

'I'll send someone to find him, but you may have to wait. He is always in demand. Harry Wilshaw is an inspirational man,' said Fulton. 'You will never have met anyone quite like him.'

Braving the icy wind, the Reverend Harold Wilshaw finished conducting the latest of a long line of burial services. After a brief chat with those beside him, he headed briskly for his quarters. He was intercepted by a messenger.

'Lieutenant-Colonel Fulton sends his compliments and asks you to join him.'

'Do I have time to change?' asked Wilshaw, indicating his surplice.

'It's an urgent summons, Reverend.'

'Then I'll come at once.'

While they waited for the chaplain to arrive, Marmion and Keedy learnt something about the battle. Lieutenant-Colonel Fulton was honest with them.

'Cambrai is a an important rail town for the Huns,' he said, 'and an essential part of their supply line. Attacking it was vital.'

'And you did just that,' said Keedy, impressed.

'It was a pyrrhic victory,' admitted the other. 'We smashed a hole in the German defences and shattered the myth that the Hindenburg Line was impenetrable, but there was a terrible price to be paid. We sent 476 tanks into battle plus six infantry and two cavalry divisions. They cut through the Huns like a knife through butter.'

'How many of the tanks did you lose?' asked Keedy.

'About two-thirds of them. Many of those that survived need repair.'

'But you made big territorial gains,' noted Marmion.

'We did indeed,' said Fulton, 'and we were rightly praised. But we were not, alas, able to hold all the land we occupied. Success can bring problems. In this case, it exposed our lack of manpower. We captured some 11,000 prisoners, giving ourselves the headache of keeping them safely locked up.'

Before he could elaborate, he saw the chaplain enter the tent. Clutching his Bible, the newcomer shared a benign smile among all three of them. Wilshaw was a slim, striking man of medium height with a luminous face that made him seem ten years younger than he really was.

'Thank you for coming, Harry,' said Fulton, amicably. 'These gentlemen believe that you may be able to help them.'

As the detectives were introduced, Wilshaw gave each of them a firm handshake, looking them in the eye as he did so. Fulton then withdrew, leaving the others to sit down and exchange a few pleasantries. Marmion then took charge.

'We are investigating three murders that occurred back in England,' he explained, 'and they are linked together by this regiment.'

Wilshaw was surprised. 'Really?'

'We wondered if you knew any of the victims.'

'It's possible, Inspector. What were their names?'

'The first one was Captain Tait – that's Richard Tait.'

'No,' said the chaplain, shaking his head. 'That's not a name I recall.'

'Lieutenant-Colonel Fulton assured us that you had an amazing memory.'

'It's kind of him to say so, but I have met thousands of soldiers during the years I have been chaplain. You can't expect me to remember all of their names.'

'You ought to remember this one,' said Keedy.

'Why?'

'He committed suicide by shooting himself.'

'Then you are quite right, Sergeant,' said Wilshaw, seriously. 'I should have remembered him. I wish that he had turned to me. I am trusted to keep secrets, you see. Officers are there to lead, not to show sympathy. Men find it difficult to reveal any worries or weaknesses to those in command. If they come to me, they are able to open their hearts.'

'That must be a consolation,' said Marmion. 'As a man of the cloth, you are more approachable.'

Wilshaw chuckled. 'Not everyone thinks like that,' he conceded. 'To some of the coarser types, I am a figure of fun. I endure their mockery without turning a hair because I know that the majority trust and respect me. What they are desperate for is someone who will listen instead of merely barking orders at them.'

The detectives were impressed by him. Wilshaw embodied dedication. To maintain a Christian presence in the regiment, he was ready to undergo multiple dangers and discomfort. Marmion remembered that his son had spoken well of the chaplain in his regiment. Such men were priceless assets.

'Even the atheists turn to me sometimes,' said Wilshaw. 'They rail against the sheer futility of this war and ask me why God is allowing it to happen. I usually manage to convince them that there is a sense of purpose in what he is doing.'

'I wish you could convince me,' murmured Keedy.

'Let's go back to Captain Tait,' said Marmion.

Wilshaw nodded. 'I'm trying hard to place him.'

'He came from Bristol.'

'Then that makes him unusual. For obvious reasons, we recruit largely in Staffordshire. It may be that the captain had a prior connection with the county, of course, but I've no idea what it was. And I still have no memory of him, I fear. Why did you bring up his name in the first place?'

'His brother was brutally murdered.'

'Good heavens!'

'It's the reason we're here,' explained Marmion. 'The death occurred in Bristol, but we believe that it was ordered by someone in his brother's regiment.'

The chaplain blenched.

Having made the effort to arrive early on the previous day, Alice Marmion turned up for work fifteen minutes late. She knew that explaining that her bus had been delayed was not an adequate excuse. If someone were a mere five minutes late, Inspector Gale would seize on the opportunity to berate them. As she entered the building, therefore, Alice gritted her teeth in readiness.

The inspector swooped down on her and took her into a side room.

'I'd like a word with you,' she said, quietly, 'and you don't need to tell my why you're late today. To be candid, I didn't expect to see you at all.'

'You've been speaking to Superintendent Chatfield,' guessed Alice.

'He felt that it was important to explain your situation.'

'I'm grateful to him.'

'You seem to be displaying the courage I expected of you.'

'I have duties to perform. It never occurred to me to let you down.'

'My thoughts are with your father and Sergeant Keedy,' said the other, 'but my principal concern is with you, Alice.'

'Thank you, Inspector.'

'Let me give you some advice. It is only natural that you wish to confide in Iris Goodliffe. In this case, I feel that would be unwise. She would fear the worst and talk endlessly about the danger they face.'

'I'd already decided to say nothing to her.'

'That's very sensible of you.'

'I'm here in the hope that work will keep my mind off the situation.'

'That's the second time this week that you've told me that,' said the other, smiling. 'I hope that it doesn't become a habit.'

'So do I.'

'Two crises in one week are enough for anybody.'

'I agree.'

'How do you feel?'

'I feel that I'm ready to do what I've been trained to do,' declared Alice. 'I will not be distracted, I promise you. Today will be just like any other.'

When he gave the chaplain the outline details of the case, Marmion watched him carefully. Wilshaw seemed genuinely horrified and tried to probe for more information. Marmion suggested that he might not wish to hear exactly how the lawyer had been killed.

'A strong stomach is a necessity in my job,' said Wilshaw, stoutly. 'I have seen death in many forms and know how hideous it can be. In this case, I am sorry that Captain Tait did not seek me out. I might have been able to still his demons.'

'What we can't understand,' said Keedy, 'is why the brother was killed and the wife was spared. Both were at fault.'

'Indeed, they were. Marriage is sacred. It must be respected as such at all costs. The brother may have died but Captain Tait's wife has not escaped punishment. For the rest of her life, she will suffer torments of loss and regret. Unhappily,' the chaplain went on, 'the situation is all too common.'

'In what way?' asked Marmion.

'Well, I could cite dozens of cases where a wife's adultery has driven men in this regiment to extremes. Mail from their home is vital to the morale of our soldiers. They like to know that they are loved and remembered. However,' explained the chaplain, 'we do not filter bad news out of any letters. If something serious has happened at home, men are entitled to know what it is.'

'We can imagine their situation.'

'It's heart-rending to see at close quarters, Inspector. Soldiers feel trapped and helpless. When they hear of wives or girlfriends who have gone astray, they are at their wits' ends. And there are other shocks sometimes. Only a few weeks ago,' recalled Wilshaw, 'I was shown a letter by an officer in which his wife told him that the house had been burgled and that his precious collection of Roman coins had been stolen. Worse still, his beloved dog had been shot.'

'He must have been so frustrated,' said Keedy.

'That's an understatement, Sergeant.'

'What happened to him?'

'He is still here, haunted by the thought that he was not at home to protect his wife and property. We simply can't grant compassionate leave in such cases.'

'No, I suppose not.'

'My apologies, Inspector,' said Wilshaw. 'I was digressing. You spoke of three murders. Which was the second one?'

'It concerns a Private Samuel Roper.'

'Ah, now that's a name I do remember.'

'Did you know the man?'

'Oh, yes. He confided in me that his wife had been unfaithful. What really upset him was that the man in question had been a close friend of his, the landlord of his local pub. They had grown up together. Roper told me that – until he got the news –

the first thing he had wanted to do when he got home was to go fishing with this friend, Charlie Ferriday. I gave Roper what little advice I could,' said Wilshaw, 'and he went back to the unit. Foolishly, I flattered myself that I had taken some of the sting out of his pain. The next day, I was told that he had suddenly clambered out of his trench and run directly towards enemy lines. He was cut to ribbons by German machine guns.'

'Charlie Ferriday was hacked to death in Stafford,' said Marmion.

'I deplore what he did,' said the other, 'but I am shocked to hear that he was murdered as a result. How did you get to know of this, Inspector?'

'We looked into cases that had elements in common with the one we were investigating.'

Wilshaw was startled. 'That was enterprising of you.'

'The sergeant and I went to Bristol and talked to the officer in charge of the case involving Captain Tait's brother. While we were doing that,' Marmion went on, 'a colleague of ours went to Stafford and spoke to someone with a detailed knowledge of this second case.'

'What makes you think that the cases are connected?'

'The similarity is unmistakable. Mr Tait was dismembered, and Ferriday was decapitated.'

Wilshaw was horrified. 'How gruesome!'

'The two killers left their autograph on both victims.'

'How do you know that there were two of them?'

'We have clear evidence of that,' said Marmion. 'We know their names or, to be more exact, the aliases they use.'

'John Morris and Anthony Brown,' said Keedy.

'The sergeant even found out where they were hiding.'

'It was a house in Camden Town. We came close to catching them there.'

'Your detective skills are quite remarkable,' said Wilshaw, looking from one to the other. 'Who was the victim in this third murder?'

'We'll come to him in a moment,' said Marmion. 'There's something about the case in Stafford that we need to explain. When we first heard about it, we concluded that Ferriday, the publican, had seduced Samuel Roper's wife.'

Wilshaw nodded. 'That's exactly what Roper himself told me.'

'He was wrong.'

'How could he be? He had a letter from Stafford.'

'Was it written by his wife?'

'Well, no,' said Wilshaw, 'it was not. It was sent by a friend of Roper's, who felt that he ought to know what was going on behind his back.'

'Did he show you the letter?'

'It no longer existed. Sam Roper was so angry that he burnt the letter with his cigarette as soon as he had read it. By the time he came to me, he was in a manic state. The next day,' said Wilshaw, 'he decided there was no purpose to his life, so he put an end to it.'

'What action did you take?'

'I felt obliged to write to his wife and tell her what happened. It was not for me to chastise her for what she had done. I merely offered my sympathy and gave her the facts, knowing that she would draw her own conclusion.'

'You gave her the facts as you saw them,' corrected Marmion, 'but they were false. Roper did not die because his wife had

337

slept with Charlie Ferriday. The police in Stafford are absolutely certain that the publican had not seduced Mrs Roper.'

'Then why was Roper so certain that he had?' asked Wilshaw.

'His letter came from someone who wanted him to suffer by making him believe that the wife had betrayed him. The police in Stafford have yet to identify the man but they believe it was someone with designs on Molly Roper herself.' The chaplain was stunned. 'You see how malign a letter of that kind can be. It led to the death of a decent man and the misery of an honest woman. Mrs Roper lost a husband she worshipped and a man with whom she had worked happily for years, and whose own wife is still wondering why he was butchered to death.'

'You can see why we are so keen to catch the men responsible for the murder,' said Keedy. 'They have killed three victims to date. We are determined to prevent them from adding another name to the list.'

'More power to your elbow, Sergeant,' said Wilshaw, sternly. 'What was the name of the third victim?'

'Dr George Tindall.'

'And you say that he was linked in some way to this regiment?'

'He is a renowned surgeon, by all accounts,' said Marmion, 'and felt the urge to help in the war effort. He worked in a field hospital near your regiment when they were engaged in the Battle of Loos.'

'That was rather a torrid time,' sighed the chaplain.

'Did you ever meet or hear of Dr Tindall?'

'I'm afraid that I didn't.'

'Yet you must spend a lot of time among the wounded and meet large numbers of the medical team.'

'I do, Inspector. It is an aspect of my work that is important to me. It means that I have rubbed shoulders with countless patients, doctors, nurses and stretcher-bearers. This surgeon, George Tindall, may well have been in the field hospital when we fought at Loos, but I have no memory of the man.'

Before the chaplain could say anything else, an orderly came into the tent, apologised for the interruption, then explained that Wilshaw was needed desperately.

'I'm sorry,' he said to the detectives, 'but I must go. Someone else is on the point of death and asking for me. I don't expect to be long.' A thought struck him. 'Why don't you come to my quarters in twenty minutes or so. I have a record there of all the soldiers I have advised or helped in the past. Captain Tait's name may well be among them. If I am not there, just step inside.' He moved off. 'Please excuse me.'

Wilshaw left with the orderly. Marmion turned to Keedy.

'What did you make of him, Joe?'

'I think he's the nearest thing to a saint that I've ever met.'

'He's certainly found his true calling,' said Marmion, 'but I'm surprised that he couldn't remember two of the names I put to him.'

'I can suggest why he didn't recall Dr Tindall.'

'Can you?'

'Yes,' said Keedy. 'Perhaps the doctor was using a different name. I'm thinking about that second wife of his. She knew him as Michael Langford.'

Marmion was dubious. 'Would he dare to give the army a false name?'

'He had the cheek to do anything.'

* * *

They were together in the workshed again. While the sculptor continued to chip away at the wooden angel, his nephew looked at the one bare wall.

'That would be a perfect place to hang it,' he said.

'What are you talking about?'

'That painting I wanted to buy.'

His uncle glowered. 'I wouldn't have it anywhere near me,' he said, breaking off from his work. 'Every time I looked up at it, my toenails would curl.'

'But it's a religious painting.'

'It's the work of a bungling amateur. He should stick to selling fruit and veg in the market and leave real artistry to people like me.'

'You know,' admitted the other, 'I never really took your work seriously until I was saved. And that only happened because I was stuck in a field hospital in Loos. It was pandemonium in there. Doctors and nurses were darting about everywhere as new patients came in. The only person with the slightest interest in me was the chaplain.'

'He did you an enormous favour. Before you joined the army, you were turning into a real criminal.'

'I couldn't help it,' pleaded the other. 'After my apprenticeship as a locksmith at Chubbs, the temptation was too great. I had a knack for opening just about every lock I came across in Wolverhampton. So why not make use of it?'

'It was against the law, that's why. Frankly, I was ashamed of you. It's why I urged you to enlist. I thought it might bring you to your senses.'

'A German bullet did that. You can't make a quick getaway with an artificial foot. I was at a low ebb in that field hospital.

And then,' he went on, face brightening, 'I met a miracle worker. He wiped away my former life as if it had never existed and gave me a better one.'

'Serving God and doing his bidding.'

'That's when I came to work for you and realised what amazing skill you had. I understood why you did so much work for churches.'

'And the occasional monastery,' boasted his uncle. 'I carved a new lectern for one of them. It was the most satisfying commission I ever had.'

'The most satisfying things I've ever had were the ones I shared with you. It all started when the chaplain came into my life. I swore to him that I would do absolutely anything he asked me,' said Brian, 'if it involved serving God. He took me at my word.'

'And he put you to the test, Brian. After keeping in touch with you by letter, he was ready to trust you. That's why he asked you to go to Bristol on a mission. You had the sense to involve me.'

'I knew that you had strong religious principles,' said Brian, 'and I needed to have your advice. You not only encouraged me to do what I was asked to do, you agreed to help me. That made all the difference.' He smiled. 'It's funny, really, isn't it?'

'What do you mean?'

'Well, you saved me from a life of crime and gave me a job here – yet you urged me to commit three murders.'

'They were not crimes, Brian.'

'Other people would say that they were.'

'They don't understand. We were God's executioners, obeying his command and ridding the world of sinners who had no right to live.'

* * *

Having taken directions, they went to the chaplain's quarters. When they entered, they found him on his knees in prayer in front of a crucifix that stood on a small cupboard. Marmion and Keedy felt embarrassed at having interrupted him. Before they could step out of the tent, however, Wilshaw got to his feet to give them a welcome.

'Don't go,' he said. 'I always pray after I've just watched somebody die. Thankfully, I was in time to say a few parting words to him before he slipped away.'

'You talked about checking your records,' said Marmion, 'to see if the names of Captain Tait and Dr Tindall were there.'

'I'll do that in a moment, Inspector. First, I must ask you to confirm what you told me about the person I did remember – Samuel Roper. Is it true that the man who, allegedly, seduced Roper's wife was, in fact, innocent of the charge?'

'He was completely innocent,' said Marmion.

'How can you be so sure?'

'One of the detectives involved in the case knew Ferriday and went to his pub occasionally. The publican and his wife were a devoted couple. Mrs Roper had worked happily with them for years. She was equally devoted to her own husband and proud that he had enlisted in the army.'

'I see.'

'Ferriday was killed in the same way as the others,' said Keedy. 'It's the reason we've been able to link all three cases.'

'And you came close to catching the killers, you say?'

'Extremely close.'

'We've gathered a lot of information,' added Marmion. 'We have a good description of each of them and it has been passed

342

to police stations throughout the country. It's only a matter of time before we catch them and find out who has been giving them their orders.'

'And what sort of person do you imagine he would be?' asked Wilshaw.

'He's a man to whom adultery is an anathema.'

'It's one of the Ten Commandments – "Thou shalt not commit adultery".'

'There's a commandment that comes before it – "Thou shalt not kill".'

'There are exceptions in some cases,' argued the chaplain.

'Someone obviously believes it,' said Keedy. 'He thinks that adultery has to be punished by death, as if it's a crime.'

'It's more than a crime, Sergeant – it's a sin.'

'We suspect that one of the killers had military experience,' said Marmion. 'It's highly likely that he served in this regiment.'

'Then why isn't he still in uniform?' asked Wilshaw.

'He could have been invalided out of the army,' replied Marmion. 'People who actually met him told us that he has a pronounced limp. It might be the result of a war wound.'

'I see.'

'One person did more than simply describe him,' said Keedy. 'He actually drew a portrait of the man.'

'I have it here,' said Marmion.

Taking it from his pocket, he unfolded it then showed it to the chaplain. Wilshaw's face whitened and he turned away.

'I've never seen this man before.'

'Are you quite certain?' asked Marmion, watching him closely.

'Yes.'

'Look me in the face and tell the truth.'

Wilshaw forced himself to look at Marmion. As he met the inspector's gaze, he began to wilt. He ran his tongue over dry lips. Tears formed in his eyes.

'When you came in,' he confessed, 'I was not praying for the man who died while I crouched beside him. I was praying for forgiveness.'

'That's what I guessed. We like to think that our detective skills guided us to you, but I daresay you view it differently. You believe that God brought us here.'

Wilshaw shivered. 'When did you suspect me?'

'You gave yourself away when you realised how painstaking our work had been. We not only tracked down your accomplices, we came very close to catching them. I saw your face twitch when you learnt that.'

'The mistake was accidental,' pleaded Wilshaw. 'I swear it. Mr Ferriday should still be alive. I could not believe it when you told me that he had been beheaded. That was not what I instructed. What sort of monsters have I let loose?'

'The kind that kill for the sake of it,' replied Keedy. 'And they got a weird religious thrill out of it.'

'You did know Captain Tait, didn't you?' said Marmion.

'Yes, I did,' confessed the chaplain, 'and I had no qualms about what happened to that brother of his. He deserved to die for such an act of betrayal,' he went on, voice rising. 'And Dr Tindall deserved to die as well.'

'You had no right to make those decisions,' said Marmion.

'God directed my hand. Don't you understand? Holy matrimony had been abused. The sinners had to be punished.'

'Ferriday was no sinner,' Keedy reminded him. 'He was wrongly accused.'

'I freely admit it,' said Wilshaw, 'and I'm ready to accept my punishment.'

'And what about Dr Tindall? Why did you order his assassination?'

'Tindall was a scourge. Brilliant as he was, he had a darker side to him. One of the nurses he seduced became pregnant by him and the other, a faithful wife, was tricked into betraying her marriage vows. It destroyed her. I remember her weeping piteously. Unable to face her husband, she drowned herself.'

'Why didn't you challenge Dr Tindall?' asked Marmion.

'He'd already gone back to England,' said Wilshaw, scornfully. 'He told me that he was desperate to see his wife – a woman he had betrayed at least twice.'

'So you gave orders for him to be tracked down.'

'It took time,' said Wilshaw, 'but I had two men at my command, imbued with the same beliefs as me. They found him in the end. Tindall exploited women at will and treated marriage as if it were meaningless. He had to die.'

'The same is true of you,' said Marmion.

Before he could seize him, Wilshaw began to cough violently, bending forward as if he were about to vomit. Taking out some keys, he unlocked the cupboard and extracted a bottle of pills. He removed the cork and tipped the pills into his hand. When he tried to put them in his mouth, however, he felt Marmion's strong hand on his wrist.

'Let me go!' he cried.

'You won't escape that way,' said Marmion, shaking the chaplain's wrist until he dropped the pills. 'Handcuff him, Sergeant.'

Keedy stepped in swiftly to obey the order. Though he did not resist, Wilshaw kept pleading with them.

'Let go of me,' he begged. 'I acted in good faith and made a ruinous mistake. I'm prepared to suffer the consequences. If I swallow those cyanide pills, I will not only die, I'll do so in excruciating pain, as did Meredith Tait and George Tindall.'

'And Charlie Ferriday,' said Marmion, bitterly.

'That is what I regret most. I had an innocent man killed.'

'What will your regiment think about you when they realise what you did?'

'I shudder at the thought, Inspector. I beg you to give me those pills. You will save yourselves the trouble of taking me back to face trial. It's the best way.'

'Let me ask you one question, Reverend. Are you married?'

Wilshaw reacted as if he had just been punched in the stomach.

'I was,' he whispered.

Seated in the superintendent's office, Sir Edward Henry listened to the report with an amalgam of admiration and horror. While he was impressed at the way that Marmion and Keedy had solved the case, he was sickened by the behaviour of the chaplain.

'The man was a veritable monster,' he said.

'According to the inspector,' Chatfield told him, 'the Reverend Wilshaw was held in the highest regard.'

'How could anyone look up to an ogre like that?'

'He did good work, Sir Edward, there's no denying that. On first meeting him, Marmion and Keedy thought that he was a species of saint.'

'A saint!' exclaimed the commissioner.

'He will never be able to instigate murders again.'

'What about his two assassins?'

'I am confident that we may soon hear of their arrest,' said Chatfield, beaming. 'I will then have the pleasure of informing the police in Bristol and Stafford respectively, that we have solved a murder case for them.

Conscious that the men they were after would not surrender easily, Marmion asked for two armed officers to be assigned to him. He had found the address of the farm in the chaplain's diary along with the names of the killers who had been his henchmen. The driver took them out of the maelstrom of the capital and off into the wilds of Herefordshire. When they eventually reached the property, they parked a short distance away and walked up the path. The first person they met was one of the farmhands, a stocky, middle-aged man in the process of mending a fence. He told them where they would find the owner and his nephew.

'I didn't realise they were related,' said Keedy.

'You take the nephew,' ordered Marmion, 'and we'll tackle his uncle.'

When they split up, Keedy and one of the supporting officers went off to a row of pigsties. The man feeding the pigs from a large bucket moved with a limp. When Keedy nudged his companion, the latter took out his revolver. They closed quickly on the suspect.

'Brian Gullard?' said Keedy.

'Who are you?' asked the other, turning to face him.

'I'm Detective Sergeant Keedy from Scotland Yard and I've come to arrest you for the murder of Dr George Tindall.'

The man blinked in surprise. 'I don't know what you're talking about.'

'I think you do,' said Keedy, taking out a pair of handcuffs.

Gullard responded by hurling the remains of the pig swill at him before taking to his heels. Angered by the mess over his coat, Keedy went after him. Gullard was determined to escape but his artificial foot hampered him badly. The detectives soon caught up with him. When he saw a patch of thick mud ahead, Keedy timed his dive to perfection. He landed on Gullard's back and sent him head first into the mire. Before he could move, Gullard felt his arms being pulled behind him so that the handcuffs could be clipped on to his wrists. He writhed madly.

'Look at the mess on my coat,' said Keedy, standing up. 'I ought to send you the bill from the cleaners.'

Marmion, meanwhile, had entered the shed with the other armed officer and saw the sculptor working at his bench. The man guessed at once who they must be and why they had come. Turning to face them, he had a thick chisel in one hand and a mallet in the other. He was clearly prepared to use them as weapons. Marmion's companion drew his gun.

'I'd advise against it, Mr Hooke,' said Marmion, quietly. 'Detective Constable Neill is an excellent marksman.'

'What do you want?' grunted the other.

'First of all, I need to pass on some news. Your good friend, the Reverend Wilshaw, was arrested when we confronted him recently in Cambrai.'

Hooke was shaken. 'I don't believe it.'

'There will be no more orders to kill for you and your nephew.'

'Who are you?'

'My name is Detective Inspector Marmion and I've been leading the investigation into the murder of George Tindall. He was the third of your victims after Meredith Tait and Charlie Ferriday.'

'They deserved to die!'

'The same, I fear, may be said of you and your nephew.' He looked at the wooden angel. 'That's a wonderful carving. It's a pity you won't be able to finish it.'

The man reacted instantly, hurling the mallet at Neill, and knocking the gun from his hand. With the chisel raised, he ran towards Marmion, but the inspector had anticipated an attack. Swooping up a handful of sawdust, he threw it into his face and blinded him momentarily. All that the sculptor could do was to slash away wildly with his weapon. Marmion and Neill moved in swiftly to overpower him and take the chisel from his hand. The prisoner was soon handcuffed.

Keedy came into the shed with the other prisoner.

'We did God's work,' said Gullard, defiantly. 'We were soldiers of the cross.'

'Yes,' added his uncle. 'Our orders came from above.'

'So did ours,' said Marmion. 'You'll be able to meet the superintendent.'

It was Saturday evening and all four of them were enjoying the luxury of a meal together. Now that the murder of Dr Tindall had finally been solved, Marmion and Keedy were able to relax slightly. When the meal was over, they moved to the living room. Ellen and Alice wanted full details of the arrests and how the killers had tried to justify what they had done.

'We have had difficult cases before,' said Marmion, 'but this was the most testing. I hope we never have to go into a war zone again.'

'I found our visit to Herefordshire more dangerous,' said Keedy. 'My overcoat will have a permanent smell of pig swill.'

'It will remind you of an important arrest you made.'

'The most important arrest was that of the chaplain. He set himself up as judge and jury. And he had two executioners at his beck and call.'

'The Reverend Wilshaw had been married,' said Marmion, 'but his wife was unfaithful to him. It was a wound that would never heal. It warped his mind. He found solace in ordering the deaths of men who had seduced married women.'

'It's all over now,' said Keedy. 'We can actually have free time again.'

'Oh,' said Alice, 'I'm so glad about that. We can start looking forward to Christmas. I feel that it's going to be really special this year.'

'So do I,' said Keedy. 'We deserve a treat.'

'It won't be such a treat for Ellen,' Marmion pointed out. 'There's all the cooking and preparation to do.' He turned to her. 'That's right, love, isn't it?'

'What?' she asked, coming out of a daydream. 'I'm sorry. I didn't hear what you said.'

'We were talking about the wonderful Christmas we'll all have.'

'It won't be wonderful for all of us.'

'What do you mean?'

'There'll be an empty chair at the table,' she said, quietly.

After thanking the driver for the lift, Paul Marmion jumped off the cart, pulled on his haversack and began to trudge towards the nearby village.

EDWARD MARSTON has written over a hundred books. He is best known for his hugely successful Railway Detective series and he also writes the Bow Street Rivals series featuring twin detectives set during the Regency as well as the Domesday series and the Home Front Detective series.

FINALIST ... ICTION
LONG... RIZE

'Gayl Jones is a literary legend. In novels and poetry, she has reimagined the lives of Black women across North, South and Central America living in differen... *Palmares* revinvents seventeen... ty, beauty, humanity and chaos. ... ture, the kind that changes your understanding of the world when reading it' **Fowler**, *Guardian*

'Gayl Jones conjures with deep intimacy and immediacy a brutal world that is centuries past but fully alive with spirit and mystery. Page after breathtaking page, her prose is intricate, mesmerizing, and endlessly inventive and subversive. *Palmares* is absolutely stunning!' **Deesha Philyaw**

'Tremendous. A masterfully absorbing, mythic work from a vital voice. The gods have conspired to gift us a new book from Gayl Jones, and my what a gloriously eddying read' **Irenosen Okojie**

'*Palmares* enfolds the reader in a bygone world, with a glance to our own, and has a great whispering lushness that is both magical and panoramic' **Diana Evans**

'Mercy, this story shimmers. Shakes. Wails. Moves to rhythms long forgotten. Chants in incantations highly forbidden. It is a story woven with extraordinary complexity, depth and skill; in many ways: holy ... After suffering the author's absence for far too long, we – the witnesses longing for texts like hers, the borderline sacred – can rejoice at her return' **Robert Jones, Jr**, *New York Times*

'An intricate, imaginative story of love and brutality ... After a two-decade absence, Jones is back with a formidable novel steeped in history, magical realism, trauma and triumph' *Observer*

'Astonishingly rich in character and incident, filled with magic and mystery' *The Times*

Palmares

GAYL JONES

virago

VIRAGO

First published in Great Britain in 2021 by Virago Press
This paperback edition published in 2022 by Virago Press

1 3 5 7 9 10 8 6 4 2

Copyright © 2021 by Gayl Jones

The moral right of the author has been asserted.

*All characters and events in this publication, other than those
clearly in the public domain, are fictitious and any resemblance
to real persons, living or dead, is purely coincidental.*

A CIP catalogue record for this book
is available from the British Library.

ISBN 978-0-349-01524-8

Text design by Wilsted & Taylor Publishing Services
Printed and bound in Great Britain by Clays Ltd, Elcograf S.p.A.

Papers used by Virago are from well-managed forests
and other responsible sources.

Contents

Palmares

ALMEYDITA

Mexia

MEXIA, HALF BLACK AND HALF INDIAN, was said to be the concubine of a Franciscan priest, Father Tollinare. It was a rule that Franciscan padres were to take only old black women for their housekeepers, but Father Tollinare had taken a young woman, and not a preto, and so it was said that she was not only his housekeeper but his woman, his mistress. She was beautiful, more beautiful than a caboclo, with dark smooth skin of both the black and the Indian, so that her complexion was like red clay. She was plump but small-waisted, the ideal for a woman then. She wore a black string around her plain muslin dress, to show off her small waist and accentuate her hips. Her hair was shiny like the Indian's, but stood tall and thick on her head like any preto's. Her cheekbones were higher than any I've ever seen, and her large, round eyes were mostly melancholy, but sometimes they'd sparkle. She never spoke to anyone. I had never heard her speak even to the Father. Perhaps if what people said was true, she spoke when they were alone together, at those intimate times, but what if not then? What if she did not speak even at those moments? What of it?

To me she seemed a good woman, and I'm sure she knew the Portuguese as well as anyone in Bahia, better than most. I heard Father Tollinare once call her Silent Spirit.

Father Tollinare lived in rooms attached to the chapel of the casa grande. The walls were thick and white and there was little furniture, only a hard bed, a table, a long rosewood bench, and many chairs. A painting of a longhaired, dark-skinned Christ was on the wall, his eyes large and melancholy as Mexia's. In looking at the painting one is drawn to the eyes first and then outward to the rest of the man. He had long dark lashes, dark curly hair and beard, and a high forehead. He could have been a dark mulatto or an Indian. His nose was medium sized and rounded, not sharp and pointy like the Europeans'. When I first saw the painting, I thought the eyes were Mexia's, but then Father Tollinare explained to me that that was the Christ. He didn't explain then that his own Christ was as pale as himself and that the dark one was to better lead us dark ones to Christianity.

I was too young to understand the tale of the priest and his concubine, but no one on the plantation showed any moral outrage toward either Father Tollinare or his woman – it was only outsiders. It is said that once, for instance, two of Father Tollinare's superiors from Rio came to visit and stayed there expecting to be angry and offended, but had ended up themselves developing some attachment to the woman and respected her reserve and dignity. When they left, it is said, they both bowed carefully to the woman and had looked at Father Tollinare with what could only be described as envy. I'd not seen this for myself, but had heard my mother and grandmother and other women who sat about in a hut in the senzala smoking long pipes and talking.

'They looked at her as if she was something sacred,' one woman said.

'Yes, and at him with envy.'

'It wasn't envy. Priests don't have envy. They don't have emotions.'

'Love of God then.'

'I'm no Christian. They looked at her as if they wanted to take possession of her their own selves. What're you looking at me for? I'm no Christian.'

'What's the matter with her? She never talks.'

'But she does no harm to anyone.'

'You can see in his eyes how he loves her. Not like a senhor de engenho.'

'He couldn't. Priests are only supposed to love God. It's just an evil tale.'

'I know a priest who sent his sons to Europe to study.'

'Sons did you say?'

'Sim. He can't bear it when she's not there. He has to see her, even if she's silent as a fig.'

'I bet she talks to him. I bet she talks to him those times of sim sim sim sim.'

'I wonder if she loves him.'

'Look at Almeydita, how she's watching with her ojos grandes. Come and sit beside me, menina. What d'you think?'

4

'I think he loves her.'

'She doesn't know what it all means.'

'Sim, she does. You know sim sim sim sim. Here's coconut milk and cinnamon.'

I was seven and I was a slave. I liked Father Tollinare because he had taught me how to read. He brought black, Indian children, and white ones from the casa grande into his rooms and taught us all together the catechism and how to read from the Bible. Sometimes the woman Mexia would be there, sweeping or making a sweet out of manioc flour. But she never spoke.

Once I entered the room early and alone. Father Tollinare had not come yet. But Mexia was there mixing something with molasses, Brazil nuts, manioc paste, cinnamon, clove, and fruit. I stood watching her, and when she finished, she gave me a little bowl of it to eat. She handed it to me with such gentleness, but didn't speak to me.

I learned to read and write between the ages of seven and nine years. I learned some geography and all the Bible stories and lives of the saints. Some places in Bahia not even the children of the brancos are taught anything, so I considered the years with Father Tollinare to be fortunate ones.

Father Tollinare was a tall reinol, born in the Old World, with a high, broad forehead, and big hands sticking out of the sleeves of his cassock. During the studies, he'd pass one worn Bible around and we'd read the stories, and he'd shake his head when we dropped letters off the ends of words, and he'd say, 'In Portugal they say it this way.'

'But here we say it this way,' I protested once. He looked at me sternly. He told me to give the book to Rafael. I did, swinging my legs and string down at the dust on my feet. Rafael read the passage over and put in the missing letters.

Father Tollinare smiled and said, 'That's the way it should be done.' I started to say again 'But that's not how I hear them say it in Bahia. The pretos or brancos either.' Instead I said nothing. I was afraid that if I spoke a second time, he might scold me and send me out. I was silent because I wanted to know how to read and write the words, even if I continued to pronounce them a different way.

In dreams I would always hear myself challenging him, though.

'If you were in Portugal, how'd you say that?' he'd ask.

'I'm not in Portugal.'

'Read that word.'

'I don't know it. I've never heard it.'

'What's the meaning of it?'

'If I heard it, I'd know.'

But mostly it's the woman Mexia who stays in my memory. When I was seven she was the image for me of what it might mean to be a woman in this world.

I remember when I was sitting in the corner eating my bowl of sweet mixture that Mexia had given me, the Father came in and tapped me on the forehead.

'What's good, Almeydita?'

'This is.'

'I mean what does it mean to be good? What does it mean to be good in the world?'

I looked up at his round gray eyes but said nothing.

'How do you know what is good for life and for the soul?' he persisted.

I admitted I didn't know.

'Do you think you'll find your spiritual place in this world?'

I didn't answer and he tapped my forehead again. Then he went and sat at his long wooden desk and opened his catechism. He had a slender, delicate nose. Mexia left the room and came back bringing him a washbasin and a linen towel. He said nothing to her. He didn't say thanks. He didn't even smile. She handled his big hands in the washbasin, massaged the tips of his fingers and his palms. She looked at him but didn't speak. As I watched her, I could see myself as a tall, silent woman, but I couldn't picture a place for myself. I kept watching Mexia standing over the huge man in the dark cassock. His nose seemed too slender and delicate for his size. I watched them and pictured them in a field of sugarcane. She stood with her back to him. He had his hand flat against her back and was whispering something close to her. At first I couldn't imagine what he was saying, then I heard him say, 'Sim. Sim. Sim. Sim.'

When Mexia finished washing his big hands, she turned, saw me and looked as if she'd forgotten I was there. I wondered if that was what the Father meant when he spoke the word 'epiphany.' She turned her eyes from me and went out.

As soon as the other children came inside and took their seats, Father

6

Tollinare got up from his desk and stood in front of me first with the huge Bible. He said my name several times before I took the Bible and began to read, leaving off the end letters. He shook his head, but this time he didn't scold me. Instead he simply passed the book to a young Indian girl who kept all the letters as she saw them. I felt he must've understood that I could have done the same thing if I'd wanted to. I felt arrogant in my small defiance.

After the schooling, I entered the hut of my mother. The hut was in the senzala some distance from the big house, behind the cinchona trees. My grandmother was sitting in her hammock making a basket. My mother sat in the corner cutting cassava and shelling ground nuts.

I asked my mother, 'Do you believe Father Tollinare makes love with the woman Mexia?'

My mother frowned deeply, then she said, 'Priests don't make love with women. Priests make love with no one.'

My grandmother laughed. 'They love the holy virgin,' she said. She laughed again. 'I haven't known one priest who didn't love the holy virgin.'

My mother went on cutting cassava. My grandmother kept laughing. 'Is Mexia a holy virgin?' I asked.

'No,' said my mother.

My grandmother laughed again. I looked at her and smiled because people said my grandmother was a crazy woman.

'Hush and come help me shell these nuts,' said my mother. 'Hasn't the priest been good to you?'

I smiled at my grandmother, then I sat on the ground beside my mother, who pushed the basket of ground nuts toward me.

'Tomorrow we'll go for a walk, Almeydita,' said my grandmother, 'and I'll tell you all about sim sim sim sim. I'll tell you all about what takes place between a man and woman. I'll take you to the place of the men and women.'

My mother gave her a scolding look.

'I'm a crazy woman. I can take her anywhere,' my grandmother said.

That night, in my hammock, I dreamed I was Mexia. I washed his hands in the basin but they turned as dark as my own and then he took my little hands in his big ones. His face was still large and red with the delicate nose that quivered and he was wearing strange clothing like the wings

7

of butterflies or some rainbow-colored fish, but his large hands were my color and he kept holding mine in his as he whispered to me.

'Mexia, why don't you ever speak to me?'

I, as Mexia, said nothing.

'Why're you such a different woman? Why're you so strange? Why're you so contrary? Why don't you ever talk to me?'

Still I didn't answer.

'You know why you're here, don't you?'

I looked up at his gray eyes.

'Because of all the others I felt that you had a greatness of spirit. But now I'm not sure. Now I'm not too sure. Now I'm not so sure at all. Say something. Eh, you're just a creature like all the others. But I love you. Don't you believe that? I love you so much. Why don't you say something to me, woman?'

But I kept standing there, saying nothing. Then his look changed.

His nose still quivered, but it was a different sort of quiver. 'Well, I'll sell you to Father Cordial. He wanted you. I'll sell you to Father Cordial or Father Conto. I can't abide strangeness.'

All that I heard in my dream, although he'd never said a word to her in my presence.

'Talk to me, Mexia,' he snorted. Then he said the same thing tenderly.

I remained silent.

'What're you doing here? Don't you know you're a danger? Don't you know you're a danger?'

He put his hand on my shoulder. It was a soft hand, as white as lace. 'Every day you become more dangerous. But every day more wary and elusive.'

I'd never heard him say a thing to her, nor had I ever heard those words before, yet I heard him say them in my dream, as clear as day.

'Speak to me, Mexia. I know you're an intelligent woman. I know you're not a dumb creature, like the others.'

8

The Place of the
Men and the Women

Tomorrow when you go to visit Pao Joaquim you must say nothing, you must observe silence before him. You must be like a little sphinx, do you hear me? A little sphinx. And he'll give you a blessing.'

I said yes that I'd be just like that.

'Today I'll tell you a little tale. Come, help me gather palm leaves for your mother. The priest selected you as one of the bright ones, so you're seeing another little world. You've got nothing to do but smile at strangers and curtsy and let all the women with loose hair lie in your lap while you rub lice from their hair. Isn't that your only little experience in this complex world? Rubbing lice from the heads of white men's daughters?'

I grabbed at the low branches, she at the tall ones. She'd only a string of cloth across her belly. I looked sideways at her hanging breasts and the rippling muscles in her thighs as she reached up on tiptoe.

'And to run with their little chamber pots and to fill the whale oil lantern and polish rosewood. All you'll remember of this age is a big goose-faced man in a cassock and a whale oil lamp.'

I jumped when she said 'goose-faced' because I'd never thought of Father Tollinare as anything but a big handsome man, except his nose seemed too small for his face, that's all. Well, perhaps he wasn't handsome. Perhaps he was a funny-looking man after all. Then what did Mexia see in him? Did she scratch the lice from his head while he lay in her lap?

'That's all you're remember of this age,' she repeated, reaching to a taller branch. 'And stories of enchanted Mooresses with charms hidden in their hair.'

I grabbed a palm frond and dropped it in my apron.

'Ah, when you grow up, though, you'll wander from place to place, an old storyteller perhaps? But tomorrow, my dear, you must say nothing. Absolutely nothing. You must stare at him with your large, soft eyes and say nothing. You must be the truly silent one,' she said shaking the palm leaves.

She shook one down at me and I stuffed it in my apron. Mine was a tiny apron, almost full now.

9

'He'll give you a blessing.' She looked at me closely. 'You won't be afraid of him, will you?'

'Afraid?'

'Of Pao Joaquim. You won't be afraid?'

'No.'

'Some fear him. They've learned not to fear the old priests, but they're afraid of their own healers.'

I looked around in the palm grove. Here at a long bench and a clearing encircled by palm trees, I imagined lovers meeting secretly.

'Is this the place of the men and the women?' I asked because I'd never been here before and it did seem like a magic place. Now I looked around at it expecting magic. She laughed softly, and sat down on a rock.

'To you,' she began, 'I seem like an ordinary old woman, don't I? But there've been some times in my life when others have seen me with fascination, with enchantment, as if I were invested with some magic, that magic you're seeking now, and I've entered their imaginations.'

I looked at her, holding the palm leaves in her own large apron. I didn't know how I saw her. Some said that she was only a crazy woman, but a crazy woman who knew magic, which made some difference. Me, I'd never seen her work any magic.

'Ah, and I've also been a valueless thing. I've had no value for some, while others I've carried through fascination and terror. But listen, menina. The imagination is broad. It ranges. But everything happens in this complex world, and some say it's all right.'

Now I felt sure she was playing with me, and I laughed. Because at other times she'd shown me her special craziness in her stories, and I'd laughed. But now she didn't laugh along with me. She looked at me in a hard silence.

'Every woman wants a man who values her,' she said and added, 'Even in these circumstances. We may be slaves but we don't have to *be* slaves.'

I looked at her, my eyes still round with delight, but I felt that in my laughter I'd missed something, that there was something that she'd told me while I was laughing and that this completed it. I wondered why we sat on a mere rock and not on the long bench.

'Listen. I have been everywhere, from Tamararca, to Pernambuco, to Ilheos, to Rio, to Bahia. I'm like cane. I'm everywhere. What you see though is an ordinary woman, a basket maker, but didn't you see me tell

Ainda that it was that bone keeping the circulation from her feet? Didn't you see me work on her? Didn't I heal her?'

I nodded because I'd seen Ainda rise and dance the batuque with the others, and in the morning she'd gone to the cane fields with a red rag tied around her head, telling everyone how something had stopped the circulation in her feet for a whole year.

'Didn't I chase the devil away?' she asked.

I nodded.

'And didn't I touch Goncalo's forehead and cure him of his craziness?'

I looked at her. She smiled.

'You want me to cure my own? Ha. Ha. Shall I cure yours?'

I shook my head and smiled and kicked my feet in the grass. I shook the palm leaves in my apron and stared at the distant hills, the dark and green land, one of the ridges jutting out like the head of a green cobra.

'Here we've got the best fruit in the state.'

The master and a stranger passed. The master glanced at my grandmother, the stranger at me. I smiled. Or perhaps it was not at us they were looking, but merely in our direction.

'You dry the leaves first, and then you tear them apart, like this,' my grandmother said. 'And when you're out in the field, you chew on a cane stalk and it'll give you energy . . . and kill the hunger.' The last thing she said softly so the master wouldn't hear.

'Have you found out who's been setting the fires?' asked the stranger.

'Quem e aquele desconhecido?' I whispered.

Grandmother shook her head, but she cocked her ear to listen.

'No, not yet,' replied the master, 'but mulher or homem . . .'

He said something so softly that he couldn't be heard.

The two men left the palm grove. I saw the stranger turn to look at me, again. Yes, it was at me he looked.

'I'll show you how to make bowls out of palm nut shells,' said my grandmother in an ordinary voice, then she closed her eyes and leaned against a palm tree. 'I see a black man sitting on a horse.'

'Pretos can't ride horses. It's against the law. I know that.'

'Hush. All black men and women will gain liberty here. Between the rocks I see abandoned plantations, but there's a white man lying on a hammock. Oh, there's a white man lying on a hammock, eating a mandacaru.'

I knew that only brancos rode horses, but anyone could lie in a hammock and eat a mandacaru but pretos couldn't do it just anytime they wanted. Abandoned plantations? Freedom? Was that why they called her a crazy woman, to speak always of such things? I stared at the hill that stuck out like the head of a green cobra. A tapir peeked out at me from under a low branch.

'I see people dancing in the streets of Bahia. Pretos and brancos dancing. But there's one old crazy woman going around saying, "Is it true I'm a free woman? Is it true I'm free?" And an old crazy man comes up to her and says, "As long as you're with me." Then they dance the batuque. And there's a white man lying in a hammock eating a mandacaru. There's a white man eating a mandacaru.' She sang the lines, then she said, 'But me? I'll tell you what I'll remember. A slow whisper without any tenderness and the penitents of St Sebastian slashing themselves with pieces of broken glass.'

'Will you be there on the day of our freedom?'

'We'll all be there,' she answered. Then she laughed. '"Is it true I'm a free woman?" Oh, I'll be out in the street with everyone dancing the batuque to the sound of African drums.'

I laughed at her. I rubbed the large soft leaves of the palm tree and stared at the hill.

'There're a variety of snakes,' she said, as if she'd seen my mind. 'I'll show you the magic that can be done with a magical one.'

I looked at her and frowned. I looked again at the strange place she'd brought me to, waiting, holding onto the palm leaves in my apron.

'That man behind you,' she whispered suddenly, pointing, and leaning into my ear. 'He's the one I brought you here to tell you about. His name's Rugendas. I wanted to tell you about me and Senhor Rugendas.'

I looked behind me, but there was no one standing there. I looked back at her. She was still leaning into my ear and staring back over my shoulder at him. I looked behind me again, but I still saw no one.

'His name's Senhor Rugendas,' she said, still looking behind my shoulder, but leaning forward now. 'Your mother would remember him. It took me a long time to make any kind of peace with his world or his spirit. But still it's no kind of peace. I did my duties, but I did them without any feeling. You hear me laugh, don't you? But I'm without laughter. I'm an old woman without any laughter. But I have laughed.

I have held laughter and fear in the same fist.' She picked up one of the palm leaves from her apron and held it in her fist. She shoved her fist out in the direction where Senhor Rugendas was, then drew it back. But still I saw no Senhor Rugendas. 'Haven't I, Rugendas?' she asked the man who wasn't there, or whom I didn't see.

She waited though as if he would answer, then she looked back at me. Then she turned her eyes on Senhor Rugendas again. Her eyes threw daggers at him, then she looked back at me.

'Yes, he's seen me hold laughter and terror in the same fist. Rugendas came here feeling that it was a land of promise and wasn't it that for you, mapmaker? But me, I wanted nothing from this place. I'm an old woman without any laughter, but I can still bite blood from an onion, can't I, Rugendas? Yes, he knows I can. See how he loves me and fears me too? He's looking at my breasts now. They're not so high as they once were, Senhor.' She moved the upper part of her body; her breasts shook gently. '"You're a strange one," he told me. "You're a strange one," he said. "No," I replied. "I'm like any other woman." But to him, he couldn't see me as the men in my own country would have. He saw a strange, exotic creature.

'No, he didn't see me as a full and human woman. "Pick one and I'll bring her to you. See how quiet she is. She's yours. You hear that? Come to the land of gold and women. They're always open, these women. Do you hear that? Everything comes from God."'

She shook the palm leaves again and her breasts gently. The nipples on them jutted out and looked like fruit. 'He asked me if I felt like I was a new woman here. A new land, a new woman. No I didn't. Not my land of promise, I told him. I walked with the other women. They let him see me plainly. Didn't you see me plainly, Rugendas? Couldn't you draw a map of me?' She pinched her nipples and they jutted out more. 'But it was me you chose. I kept all my feelings away from you. I hid them. A new world for you, Rugendas. A new brave world for you. And this one wants me to tell her about tomorrow. Do you want me to tell her I'm not tomorrow's woman? But I'll be dancing with all the others. I was afraid to be a woman, then, afraid of my breasts and belly. Afraid of the touch inside my hand. I see you laughing. They'd open your mouth so they could look inside. They'd open your mouth and pinch your nipples.'

I started to pinch my own nipples, but she struck my hand away. 'In those days too I was afraid to look at myself, afraid of my own eyes.' She looked at me. I encircled my apron with my hands.

'I'd travel with him. He went around drawing maps and I'd travel with him into the interior of the country. I'd ride behind him on horseback, holding onto his back. Only in the interior of the country. He liked my silence and detachment. I was silent and detached. That was me and he liked that, as he went about his work, his drawings, his calculations. He'd look at me and say all the time, "The woman isn't talking. Why does the woman not talk?" But he liked it. And me, didn't I stare into the face of the monster. Oh, I don't mean him. By their standards, he's a handsome man. Aren't you, Senhor? I mean the monster of time. Yes, and tomorrow … Rugendas is displeased when I speak of the future. He only wants me to speak of the past. Isn't that so, Senhor?'

She looked at him. I tried to see him but could not. I twisted and turned on the rock, but he was perfectly invisible to me.

'The final act is always an act of mutilation and blood. No? Of recognition and tenderness, he wants me to say. Ha. He knows it's not so. What do I want from you, Senhor? Nothing. What does a woman like me want from a man like you? Nothing, Senhor. I would travel with you, wouldn't I? Lean over your shoulder and study the new maps. You don't want me to leave you? I'm yours anyway, aren't I?'

She leaned over my shoulder as if to listen.

'He says that we're close now, spiritually close. Ha. Do you hear that? That now he acknowledges the spirituality in this creature of God like any other woman. Ha. Hear that? But now he doesn't want me to tell you about the future, and he claims the past too.'

She straightened her shoulders and looked at him. Her nipples no longer jutted out. They were rounded. But her breasts were no longer hanging. They were round and firm. Was it magic?

'He doesn't want me to speak of the future and he claims the past too,' she repeated. 'Do you believe, Rugendas, that a man and woman can be made perfect?' She cupped her hand to her ear and listened. 'He wants me to tell him I love him. No, I don't say such things with ease and I won't say them, not to the likes of you, Senhor.'

She wrinkled her forehead and stood up. Really, she was not an old woman. She was only thirty years older than me, thirty-seven then, but she called herself an old woman, and my age made me agree with her.

'I've introduced you to Senhor Rugendas,' she said, as we left the palm grove and entered the road leading toward the senzala. 'Ha. Ha. He feels that we're spiritually close. Spiritually close, did you hear that?

'Those are his words. He acknowledges my soul. When we entered the palm grove, he said, "The beautiful woman has come." Did you hear him? I know charms. I carry charms in my hair. He thinks I'm the same dark stranger I was then. But I'm not the same menina I was when the mapmaker bought me and tried to make me say sim sim sim sim. Did you hear that? Listen. He said he'd be pleased if the old woman would stop talking. That's what he liked in those days, my silence. But I talk now, don't I, Rugendas? Don't I, Senhor? Spiritually close. Ha. Ha. That's for you.'

She touched my hair.

'This is my gift to you, Almeydita,' she said, as we stood in the road.

She touched my hair and my forehead. 'And tomorrow Joaquim, Pao Joaquim will give you a blessing.' I looked up at her and smiled. 'Rugendas. Ha. Ha,' she said, nodding her head and staring in front of her. We continued walking. 'He's displeased when I talk of the future. But I've stood in the face of the monster of time. I've stood in his face, Rugendas.'

I wanted to look back to see if he was following us, to see if I could see him more easily on the road, but I was afraid to. I feared to see him and I feared that again I wouldn't see him.

'Is he a spirit?' I whispered.

'Is who a spirit?'

'Rugendas.'

'Rugendas a spirit? Ha. He feels we are spiritually close. Ha. Ha. That's what he feels, that's what he says he feels.'

I laughed too, stroking the large soft leaves.

'Rugendas a spirit,' she kept repeating and laughing. 'What maps have you drawn on your new world of the spirit?' she inquired. 'Well, perhaps we're closer now in spirit,' she added with a chuckle.

Pao Joaquim

IN THE HUT OF PAO JOAQUIM I'm silent. I stare across at him and he stares at me with his strange eyes. I hold my hands in my lap staring at him, then he motions for me to rise and I do. He is wearing a mask. He stares out from it with his strange eyes. As I go out, my grandmother lowers her head and enters. When she returns, she touches my shoulder. 'Come and go for a walk with me,' she says.

In the road a black man comes riding by on a horse. He sits very tall and straight in the saddle. I've never seen a black man on a horse before, because here it's against the law. So why is he sitting up there? I've never seen a black man sit on a horse before, and I've never seen any man sitting on a horse like he does. He's wearing a white muslin shirt and ordinary cotton pants, cotton they call Sea Island cotton, cotton they call Egyptian cotton. His skin is dark and smooth and he has a beard, a beard like the one on the mask of Pao Joaquim. When he gets to us he stops and holds his hand down. My grandmother takes it and he tries to pull her up on the horse. 'No, it's not the time,' she whispers.

He sits tall with his shoulders back and says nothing. I think he's looking at me, but can't tell. He jerks the stirrups and rides on. I start to look back at him, but my grandmother holds my head forward and we keep walking. We walk on a flat wide road.

'He always wore a wide hat and he gave me a smaller narrower hat,' my grandmother said.

She picked up two small stones from the road to jingle them in her hands as we walked. 'I'd hold onto his waist and ride with him that way all the way into the interior. We didn't travel into the city, because then there'd be evil stories, and he thought he could shield me. But no man has such power. In the interior, in the solitude of forest and jungle, that was my place. I was his woman, but I was my own too. He knew I was my own with my own power, different from his compasses and mathematical reckonings.'

'Who? That man?' I asked. I wanted to look back, but stared ahead.

'Rugendas, I meant.'

'And that one?'

She ignored my question. 'One day we were riding and I was holding his waist, Rugendas, and the horse was prancing. And we came to this enclosure, like a huge stable, and there was a black man inside sitting on a donkey. He was wearing a vest and no shirt and a wide straw hat and leaning forward with his back hunched. The donkey's ears were pricked up like he was listening for something. Then when the black man saw us – we were well upon him before he saw us – but then when he saw us, he turned his back to us. Rugendas tried to lead the horse into the enclosure. Was it a slave pen? I don't know what it was. A barn or a slave pen out in the middle of the forest. Every time Rugendas tried to lead the horse in, the horse wouldn't move. Smart horse. He stood with his leg up, with his knee pointed, as if he'd go inside, but didn't. I held Rugendas tighter around the waist. I felt as if there was something inside the enclosure I couldn't see.

'Something beside the man on the donkey. I couldn't take my eyes off him, the man with his back to us. Now he was sitting straight and tall as an arrow.

'Then the black man began to turn his horse around – yes, in the time we were looking and not seeing, the donkey had turned into a horse.

'There was a woman with dark eyes sitting in front of the fire looking up at the man on the horse, a white man was lying in a hammock, a black man was leaning against a bale of hay putting the finishing touches on a saddle that he'd made. The white man in the hammock saw us and started rising to greet Rugendas. And the black man turned around slowly, but before he got completely around, Rugendas's horse took fright and galloped away.'

We were walking in the wide road between the casa grande and the palm grove, but we didn't enter the place of the palmeira trees where she had taken me before, where there was the man that only she saw. We walked back and forth on the long road, and she didn't speak for a long time, and then as we neared the banana grove where the black men were working, I was sure she was saying things not meant for me. I watched the men bare to the waist and wearing only their cotton trousers. Some worked on the ground while others climbed into the banana trees.

'Then we went everywhere. I could never learn that tongue though. He called me something that meant black girl. Was it the same? Nigger. And it could be said to anyone, not just me in particular, but he came looking for me that time, not just anyone. Mr Rugendas they called him in his country, not Senhor. Have you seen her?'

'Seen who?' I asked. I imagined myself climbing to the tip top of one of the banana trees.

'I left her with the woman who owns the place. No. I have her papers. What's been done with her? Not just any woman.'

She was talking that talk now. I listened, looking from her to the men in the trees, but I could understand nothing. It was all nonsense to me. A peacock strutted near us with its bright feathers.

'No, not just any woman.'

'Pavao,' I mumbled to the bright bird.

'What place did you bring her from? It doesn't matter. We have a woman here. But Mrs Dumpling has taken her into town with her. Mrs Dumpling, the English woman, she told me about all her husbands, all along the way, what this one was like and what that one, but still she was a free woman and always would be, as free as a duckweed. She liked this new country, she said, it was just like her. Is that your man, the one that left you with me? She asked. We saw him, waiting. As we got nearer she kept saying what a free woman she was, rubbing it in, you know, because I wasn't. Rub the lice from her hair. Rub rub rub rub. Do you want me to buy you from him? I was thinking I'd like to. You're a good companion.

'But no, he wouldn't sell me because I was the one he was waiting for all that time. And she told him too the country was just like her. And they ate together, while I stood in the kitchen. I watched them from the kitchen. I kept watching them. She was a handsome woman in a green silk dress and wearing a hat with feathers and red shoes. I'd never seen a woman dress like that, except the whores in Rio, but she wasn't a whore, she was a free woman. She'd look solemn at some moments and burst into laughter at others. She had a space between her teeth, but it didn't distract from her handsomeness, it added to it. Handsome I'll call her, because she was no beauty, not even by their rules. I could tell he found the woman interesting. Oh, yes. And there was wine on the table, which they drank freely. The solemn expression, and then the laughter. She swore something by St Thomas, but I couldn't hear exactly what it was.'

'St Thomas?'

'Santo Tomas.'

'"I ain't always such a reveler," I heard her say, again solemn. He asked her why'd she come to that country. She was silent, then she talked about all her men, how all of them enchanted her.'

'Enchanted Mooress.'

'Then Mrs Dumpling said, "I don't dally, I give myself whole, but not to any every man." He was silent and she looked solemn for some moments, then she burst out laughing again. She could see me in the doorway, I knew it. "See how jolly I am," she said loud where I could hear. "And I sing like a nightingale." She sang him a ballad, a *romance*, about the English countrysides and lovers and mystical creatures that appeared and disappeared. When she finished she said she wished God would bless his soul. I thought he'd stay with her.'

'Pavao,' I said to the bright bird who strutted near my feet. I reached down and touched his feathers.

'I kept thinking when we first rode up to the inn – they had inns in that part of the country – I hadn't liked the eyes of the woman. He was talking to her now and suddenly she just sat staring at him. The innkeeper, watching them too, came up and asked, "What's wrong with the woman?" Rugendas said he didn't know. But I knew exactly what it was. She just kept staring. "I don't know," said Rugendas. "She just started staring like that." "Come and look at the woman," the innkeeper said. "She's gone mad." Someone touched her forehead and the side of her face. Everyone was looking at her, except for Rugendas who was looking at me. A doctor was sent for, but even he couldn't discover what was wrong with the woman. The doctor claimed it was called epilepsy, that she'd had herself quite a fit. Oh, he said a number of strange words for it. But Rugendas just kept looking at me.

'"What weed did you give her?" he asked when we were alone. I didn't answer.

'"Is that what you'll do to me?" he asked.

'I was silent. In the morning, she recovered and food was taken to her room, she was quite famished, and Rugendas and I rode into a new territory, where there weren't any inns at all.'

'Tomorrow they're going to send me away from here to a Negro asylum,' my grandmother announced matter-of-factly to my mother and me. She sat in her hammock eating a mandacaru while my mother was spreading manioc paste on banana leaves, and I stood in a corner of the hut slicing bananas. In another corner of the hut were baskets woven from palm fronds.

My mother looked toward her, waiting for her to explain. 'They say I'm the one whose been setting the fires.'

My grandmother's own hut had burned down and that's why she

had moved in with my mother and me. I couldn't imagine her setting fire to her own hut. One of the fields had burned and they had to put out a small fire at the side of the master's house, the casa grande. One man claimed he saw my grandmother sitting inside the hut while it was burning, and furthermore, he said he saw her light the fire and then go inside and sit.

They might have believed the first part of his story, if it had not been for the second. He was sold with some slaves on their way to North America, for the crime of telling lies and my grandmother was brought to the hut of my mother. Then a cane field burned and next, one side of the master's house.

The next day they put my grandmother into a wagon. I ran up to her. 'When I first came here, I was a crazy woman,' she explained. 'They said when I first came to this land I was crazy. Ha ha ha ha. They wanted to put me into a Negro asylum then. Now look at me. You have to be crazy in this land.'

She kissed my forehead and jaw. My mother came up behind me and held my shoulders and kept me from plunging forward, into the wagon too.

A Disillusioned and Sadistic Man

WHEN I SAW THEM TOGETHER, it was as if the dreamed had stepped out of itself and plunged into the world. They stood with their backs to me, and so instead of coming out into the clearing I squatted in the bushes. She seemed taller than him, her back broader and darker than it had seemed whenever I'd see her inside the chapel. He held his hand, as I remember, fist against her back.

'I beg you to understand,' he was saying. 'I'm not a sadistic man, I'm a disillusioned man. I beg you to understand me.'

She did not answer, nor did she turn around. Was it really her, I wondered then, or was it some other woman? No, the muslin, the small waist.

'I don't know what kind of woman you are,' he said with anger, his hand still on her back. 'You've become a symbol of something to me. You're like a religion.'

She said nothing.

'Why do you make me say absurdities? I enjoy no favors, none, except what the eyes see.'

He put his hand against her small waist. The other hand disappeared in front of her.

'What will you fix for me tonight, Mexia?' he asked. He looked like a man in fever, but it was a fever that he relished. 'Something with a fine flavor, something made with almonds and lots of sugar and lots of cinnamon ...' He sniffed at her hair as if it were that sweet thing. 'I'm not a sadistic man,' he repeated softly, whispering against her back. 'You won't make any sound, will you? Nothing. Something smooth and mouth-watering and full of flavors and yams and meat. I know it's you who's been setting the fires. Some delicacy to preserve a man's spirit. Something wholesome and delicious. I'm disillusioned. Rolls with jelly mango, coconut. I know it's you who's been setting the fires. I know it's you ... I wanted you to come out and enjoy the air with me, but always you're silent, and you begin to disappear. I can't bear to have you away. You're like some rare, nocturnal bird. Why do you lead me to say such things? You're a woman of nobility and dignity and energy. Mexia, ah Mexia, Paixao. These are the rules of the game? But there's an exception to every rule. Estas são as regras do jogo? Noco ha regra sem excecao. Ah, Mexia, no harm done, is there? I'm not a sadistic man, I'm disillusioned. I know it's been you setting those fires.'

As she was about to turn, that was when I fell flat on the ground.

When I raised myself up again, they were gone. After that, she seemed even more mysterious too, and there was a mingling of fear mixed with affection for her. For him, I felt suspicion and pity. But I told no one it was her setting those fires.

And still sometimes at night as I lay on my hammock, I'd make up my own conversations and actions for them, but always they'd have their backs to me.

'Am I more understandable now?' he'd ask. Silence.

'I'm not a sadistic man; I'm a reminiscent man.'

Both words I'd heard, but I didn't know their meanings.

Silence. He touched her small waist. 'You're so callipygous.'

I'd seen the word once in a romanceiro. Father Tollinare took the book from me and handed me a catechism.

'I like the way you're constructed. I like a woman built just so.' Silence.

'I tell you you're not a wench, you're a lady. Your Negro and Indian ancestry is not imaginary, but that's got nothing to do with worth. It's insignificant. You belong to the better class of mulheres.'

Silence.

'I like the aroma of your hair, like cinnamon.' Silence.

'Will you fix me coconuts and oranges, mangoes and cacao, yams and cinnamon, and coconuts, coconuts, coconuts, coconuts? Mexia, you're a sacred being. I don't have the same feelings about color as the other senhores. To me you're a sacred being. Perhaps it's my theological up-bringing and my ... the fact that I'm from the Old World. Please forgive me. I'm a disillusioned man. Why do you keep so quiet? Why are you such a danger?'

At this point in the dream of daydream, whenever she'd turn I'd wake up. But somehow whenever I saw the woman, I'd stand in affectionate awe of her, and yet feel at the same time that she was dangerous, 'spiritually dangerous,' a phrase I heard Father Tollinare say often. How all those words entered my dream I don't know.

'I know you've been setting those fires,' he'd whisper against her hair.

The Book Room

THERE WAS A ROOM in the back of the one we learned to read in. I used to imagine that it was the room where Mexia and Father Tollinare spent time alone together and where she talked. Once I dreamed that I opened the door of the room and instead of finding Father Tollinare and the lovely Mexia there, I discovered the ugly sea monster hipupiara with his sharp teeth and pointed ears and claws. I stood still, almost as if I was in a trance, unable to speak or scream, staring at the water devil, who had large, almost human eyes but a horrid pointed animal's face, breasts like a woman, but the rest of him a hairy fish. And then Mexia placed her hand gently on my shoulder and pulled me away and shut the door. I knew it was Mexia even though I did not turn to see her. The animal brayed behind the closed door.

'Come away,' said Mexia. 'You're not the captain's son; you're his slave. Do you think you're Baltesar?'

Baltesar Ferreira, the son of the Captain of Sao Vicente, had killed such a monster over a hundred years ago. My grandmother had told me the story of the water devil who ate the secret parts of children. Of everyone, but especially he liked the secret parts of children, she said. 'They killed one in 1564, but do you think that was the only one? Do you think in the big, mysterious sea there was only one hipupiara?'

I found a sword in my hand and shook Mexia loose. 'I may not be the captain's son, but I'm as brave as he!' I declared and opened the door, but the monster was gone.

But on waking from my dream I was not so brave, and the dream kept me for a long time from discovering what was behind the door, until one day when I was there early, and both Mexia and Father Tollinare had left the room. So I dared to open the door. But there was no monster, only walls and walls of books, more books than I'd ever seen or imagined in the world. Then it seemed so to me.

I walked down the two wooden steps, entered the room, and turned in circles. Shelves and tables of books. I lifted one and then another.

Among the titles were Robert Boyle's *The Skeptical Chymist*, Rene Descartes's *Discourse on Method*, Galileo's *Letters on the Solar Spots*, Moliere's *Le Misanthrope*, Milton's *Paradise Lost*, John Bunyan's *The Pilgrim's Progress*, Gine Perez de Hita's *The Civil Wars of Granada*, Miguel de Cervantes's *Don Quijote*, Soror Maria Agreda's *Mystical City of God*, Pero de Magalhaes's *The Histories of Brazil*. There were so many books I can't name them here, but there were hundreds of volumes, not only in Portuguese, but in French, Italian, Latin, Greek, and English. I opened the book by Magalhaes to see what he said of our country, but on the very first page I read the following:

I have read the present work of Pero de Magalhaes, at the order of the gentlemen of the Council General of the Inquisition, and it does not contain anything contrary to our Holy Catholic Faith, nor to good morals; on the contrary, many things well worth reading. Today, the 10th of November, 1575.

Francisco de Gouvea

And beneath that was written:

In accordance with the above certificate, the book may be printed and the original shall be returned with one of the printed copies to this council, and this decision shall be printed at the beginning of the book together with the above certificate. At Evora the 10th of November. By order of Manuel Antunez, Secretary of the Council General of the Holy Office of the Inquisition in the year 1575.

Liso Anriques   Manual de Coadros

I stared at the approbation almost as long as I'd stared at the monster. Then as I began to read the verses and the prologue to the reader, I felt a hand on my shoulder. I turned to look up at Mexia whose look was solemn, worried, afraid. She took the book from my hand and put it down on the table, then she drew me out of the room and closed the door.

'Those aren't for you,' she said softly, the first line of words she'd ever said to me. 'If Father Tollinare had found you, it'd have been your time of troubles like it was mine.'

'Did Father Tollinare find you in there?'

'Yes.' She looked down at her fingers.

She sat down on a bench and I sat down beside her. 'What did he do to you?'

She wouldn't answer, but continued to stare at her hands. Her fingers were very long and delicate, but the fingernails were short and ragged.

'I want to read more than the lives of saints,' I said.

'So did I,' she said gently.

'Do you suppose if I asked him kindly, he'd allow me to read some of them?'

'You wouldn't understand most of them,' she said.

'Well, I'll learn to understand them,' I protested.

'Not so loud,' she whispered. 'If he ever knows you were there, there'll be trouble.'

I pouted. She stroked my head.

'Even he thinks the books are dangerous.'

'Like you.'

'Like me? What like me?' she asked.

'Dangerous,' I said.

She clucked her teeth. 'Some of them belong to him, but others belong to his uncle, Father Froger.'

'Then I'll ask Father Froger.'

'He was burned over fifty years ago in France, for witchcraft.'

She was looking at me oddly now, but when I caught her at it, she looked away.

'What did he do for witchcraft? How can a holy father be a witch?' She looked as if she wanted to laugh.

'I don't know the whole story,' she said. 'Perhaps he was angry only because when I was in there I discovered the wrong book. There are right books and wrong books. The one I found was an unpublished book by his uncle. He talks about witches, but claims that there are no such things, that witches, or rather the things that witches declare they do and see are merely the hallucinations of melancholy women. That's why they burned him, as a witch and a friend of witches. That's why Father Tollinare . . .'

I waited, but she wouldn't continue.

'Do you think his uncle was a witch?' I asked.

'He was a strange and different man, that was his only crime,' said Father Tollinare entering the room and spying us. But he didn't look at me; he looked at Mexia with hard eyes. 'One can believe anything, no matter how impossible.'

He kept staring at Mexia as if he were trying to discover something hidden at some depth. With a look of fright, as if he were the sea monster hipupiara, she got up, holding her skirts and ran. She wore a full dress, like the brancas. Father Tollinare looked at me fiercely, then threw the book he was carrying down on the bench beside me. It was the life of St Mary Magdalen, the beautiful woman who washed the feet of Jesus. I'd already read the book many times. It was illustrated, but the Christ inside of it was a white man with blue eyes and blond hair, not like the man on Father Tollinare's wall. But my grandmother had already explained to me by then that the Christ on the Father's wall was to attract the Indians and Negroes to Christianity. 'Either that,' she declared with a laugh, 'or the white one in the book is to attract the Englishmen and Frenchmen and Dutch and Finns to it.'

I stared at the longhaired penitent kneeling at the feet of Christ. Did I hear him whisper, 'Why are you crying? Don't you think God knows who to bring together? Don't you think he knows what to arrange?'

I sat there in silence, for it was then that I discovered places that Father Tollinare would not allow me to go in my learning, and I wondered what my real education would have been if he'd allowed me to be alone in that room of books.

The next time I tried to get into the room, the door was locked. 'Almeydita, you sly one, read from the life of St Mary.'

I began, 'To know what great love is . . . '

Lorraine Alsace

DO THEY BURN WITCHES HERE?' I asked my mother.

'What do you mean, burn witches?'

'Mexia just told me that Father Tollinare is the nephew of a priest they burned for witchcraft.'

My mother gave a short hum. Sitting in the corner of the hut, she wove a large hammock with cotton threads. I had taken over the task of weaving the baskets from palm and banana leaves, and sat on the floor with one between my knees. I wondered whether my grandmother was weaving baskets at the Negro asylum. I'd asked my mother about the place but she'd refused to divulge any information. I knew that there were many Negro asylums scattered about Brazil because slaves were always going 'off' in one way or another. Slaves who weren't crazy, but simply intractable were sometimes shipped off to a Negro asylum. Sometimes, I learned later, women slaves who were 'unapproachable' were sometimes sent there.

'Mexia talked?' my mother asked.

'Yes. But I think she got herself into trouble. I never saw Father Tollinare look so angry.'

'Priests get angry. But the son of a priest burned for witchcraft.'

'Nephew.'

'I bet he's the son,' she mumbled.

Then she gave a short hum.

'In England they hang them,' she said.

'What do they do here?'

'The Portuguese, eh the Portuguese, they don't do anything, here or in Portugal. They're like the Spanish. They're too busy hunting Jews and Moors. In Spain, a witch wears a Jew's hat.'

'Are we Moors?'

'We've got a touch of Moorish blood. We're Sudanese with a touch of Moorish blood.'

My mother gave another short hum.

'Is grandmother a witch?' I asked, for that hum sounded exactly like hers.

'A witch?' she repeated.

It was then that grandmother peeked her head in the door. I'll swear it's so, but mother says I was merely daydreaming.

'A witch? I wouldn't be a witch,' she said. 'A sorceress is the thing to be. A witch is nothing.'

'Mother, don't talk so,' my mother said, but she swears it's not so, that I was merely daydreaming.

But I remember it exactly like that. I kept looking at my grandmother.

She winked at me. She said, 'But a curer of those who have been bewitched is the best thing to be.'

'Belief in witches is unchristian,' said my mother.

'Well, I'm no Christian,' said my grandmother. 'Old or new.' Then grandmother laughed and hummed. 'Witches is how Christians settle unsettled times.'

I asked her what she meant.

'May I tell her about Lorraine Alsace?'

'I don't believe there was such a woman.'

She looked at her mother, frowning, then went back to twisting the cotton threads, her fingers quick and agile.

Why does she insist it's not so?

'The hallucinations of a melancholy woman,' my grandmother explained and winked at me. How could she have known?

'Your mother doesn't believe anything,' she said to me. 'Doesn't she know there are things in this world which she hasn't seen and doesn't have any knowledge of? Doesn't she know there are wonders in the world, strange and frightful wonders?'

'I know the difference between possible and impossible things,' said Mother.

'Would you say it was impossible that the horse trader could have found you again, without my magic?'

My mother bit her lip in silence. I look from one to the other. Was that why she insists it's not so, because Grandmother mentioned the horse trader? She lifted up the hammock she was making. She pulled on it to test how strong the threads were.

'Alsace,' I said, to remind my grandmother of the tale she promised.

'Alsace was a Moorish woman who turned up in Bahia de Todos os Santos many years ago, a traveling woman, an itinerant singer and very beautiful. I was a young woman myself then. As soon's she showed up many strange things began to happen. But only natural things, heavy rains, storms, fishing troubles. But because the woman was there and from one of the dark corners of the world, they blamed the occurrences on her.

'Then one night someone claimed they saw her rubbing devil's grease on her hair and body, and they captured her and imprisoned her. When she was in prison, a guard swore that he saw a big, black bearded man in the cell with her, kissing her on the lips. When she was confronted by the fact that the devil was in there, she told them, "Indeed, there was no man there, but if one was, wouldn't it've been natural for him to've been a black man with a beard?" They took that to mean a confession that the devil had indeed been with her. I myself was standing on the street when they were taking her to be executed. I myself. She saw me and touched my hand. I was standing on the street, because I'd been sent by my master with some ambergris for ...'

'I don't believe the woman passed on any powers to you, Mother.'

'Don't tell the 'nina that.'

'The horse trader's here, isn't he? Didn't he know the exact place and time?'

My mother was silent.

'How was unsettled times settled?' I asked.

I'd stopped weaving the basket to listen. Now I sat up in my hammock that had become too small for me.

'Ah, after her execution, there were more heavy rains and storms and fishing problems, but there was no Moorish woman to blame for it, so they blamed it on the laws of nature.'

'But your grandmother claims that she caused things this second time, with powers that Alsace had passed to her.'

'She was only the medium of the gift, not the source of it.'

Mother hummed then she said, 'I don't believe she was here. I don't believe in Alsace, because they don't let Moors in the country.'

'Don't you think she'd have her ways?'

'Did the black bearded man come to you?' I asked. 'Is that the one we saw?'

'What black man?' My mother looked at her. My grandmother jumped in the air with excitement.

'Your mother doesn't believe in the invisible world,' she explained, 'or the powers of anyone except the Portuguese and the Dutchmen. Maybe an Englishman or two.' She twisted her hands in her hair and went out.

I swear it's so, but Mother swears it's not. She does say I asked her about the witch and the black man.

'We saw a black man riding on a horse,' I told her. 'Who is he?'

'It's not for you to know,' she scolded. 'Some way she's gotten you to share her visions.'

'Then she *is* a witch!' I exclaimed, clapping my hands.

'Hush. Come here and hold this.'

I went and held the new hammock while she twisted the cotton threads.

The Gathering of Turtle Eggs

B UT THE GIRL WITH THE TURTLE EGGS, she said was real. It was before my grandmother had been sent off to the Negro asylum. We found this young girl. Years later, when I saw my grandmother again, she told me that the young girl was Alsace, come round again, but then I only knew that she was brought to my mother's and grandmother's hut. She was found wandering alone on a beach and she was very sick. She was very thin with dark skin and glossy hair and huge black eyes, and indeed did look like the enchanted Mooresses in the storybooks. My grandmother – did she recognize her then? – placed her in her hammock, but with all her magic she couldn't determine what was wrong with the girl – or refused to tell us.

Anyway, my mother went to the man who'd found her and asked him where she was and what was around her when she was found. He said, 'On the beach, just the beach. Piles of sand and bits of rock and little dead fish and a basket of broken turtle eggs.'

Grandmother came back and said that maybe the girl had been with a crew who'd been gathering turtle eggs.

'To eat?' I wrinkled my nose up. I liked nothing with turtle, not even turtle soup with garlic.

'No,' she said. 'They make oil out of it. Turtle butter. Very expensive and very good. She must've been traveling with them, the poor dear, and got sick and they left her behind.'

She treated the girl not like some stranger, but someone she knew. I didn't know the tale of Alsace at the time though and Father Tollinare didn't believe in reincarnation, claiming it to be a devil's trick. Anyway, the girl stayed with us till she got well. My grandmother never discovered what it was she had, or never told us. She just gave her soups, even turtle soup, and herbs till she got better. But the girl never spoke and she'd back away whenever anyone but Grandmother came near her. Even when my grandmother would hand her a plate of rice and bacon she would go into the corner and away from everyone and eat it. Her eyes were as shiny as pearls. I saw her touching my grandmother's hand, but I didn't give it any significance then. I thought it was merely to thank her for the help she'd given. Did my grandmother need more powers? New ones? Was that why Alsace had come again?

Master Entralgo – some people swore behind his back that he was not a branco but only considered himself to be one – sent someone to inquire of the health of the girl. When she was well, he said, I was to bring her to the master. And so when she was well, she walked with me in silence, and kept her arms folded.

'What's your name?' Entralgo asked.

When she didn't answer, I spoke up for her. 'I don't know her name, Sir,' I said. 'She's spoken to no one.'

'I'm asking her what's her name.'

She refused to answer.

'And how'm I going to tell if you're dangerous or not,' he said with a snorting chuckle, 'if you don't speak?'

The girl still refused to answer, her hands hugging her arms. 'Whose slave're you then?'

No answer.

He watched her with annoyance. I thought he would swoop down and strike her. 'Well, if you belong to no one else I'll take you.'

'I belong to me,' she said in a little voice.

He laughed. I waited for him to swoop down on her. 'And did you belong to you before we found you?'

The girl wasn't much older than I myself, perhaps ten. But I liked her.

No one had ever spoken to Entralgo like that. Not anyone I knew. 'Where're your free papers, wench?'

She said nothing. Wasn't she too young to be a wench?

Still she didn't answer, and still I expected him to swoop down on her with his anger, but he merely laughed. Why? What power did she have? I had no idea that this was Alsace.

'You're an uppity little wench,' he said.

'I'm not from the same world as you,' she said.

'And what world do you come from, wench?'

I kept staring at the girl, who was looking at him directly, not out of the corner of her eyes, as I only looked at brancos.

'If it's the devil, then he owns you,' said the man.

'No, I'm from a place there.' The girl pointed eastward.

Entralgo said, 'Take her back to your grandmother till I decide what's to be done with her. A Negro asylum for this one, I'll guess.'

The girl turned a moment before I did. I'd been expecting him to swoop down on her, but he hadn't. Whatever he planned to do to her, I wasn't sure, but I knew he planned something. The girl and I walked back. I wanted to ask her why she behaved in such a manner, but I didn't dare. When we got back to the senzala, to our hut, I told my mother what had taken place. She shook her head and clucked at the girl, saying that it was a wonder Entralgo hadn't stripped her bare and beat her there and then.

When I told my grandmother what had happened, she merely looked at the girl and smiled.

Now I was sure that since she'd spoken, she'd continue to speak to us, but she didn't. She seemed more withdrawn than before, taking her food into a corner away from us. She spent whole days alone and in silence. I kept waiting for Entralgo to decide what to do with her. When he did not, my mother began to give her bits of laundry to take down to the stream and wash, which she did expressionless.

And when I took her to school with me, Father Tollinare had started to pass her the catechism, then realizing that she was not a regular student, was about to take the book from her, when she took the book and began to read, quickly and intelligently, as if she'd been born to it. She read in a manner that Father Tollinare much regarded, leaving all the endings on all her words.

'Where'd you learn to read like that?' asked Father Tollinare, in amazement.

The girl hunched her shoulders but didn't answer. Mexia, who'd been in the room, had stopped and looked at the child.

'That was wonderful,' said Father Tollinare. I'd never heard him fawn over anyone so, not even the brancos.

Although I was said to be a quick and agile reader, still Father Tollinare complained that I exaggerated some of my words while leaving whole syllables off of others.

'That is perfect, child,' he said. 'What's your name?'

'She doesn't have a name,' I answered quickly. I don't know why I said it. It just popped out, as if someone had impelled me to.

Father Tollinare looked at me with impatience, then back at the child.

'I am called Selvagem,' said the girl.

'Savage! Who'd call you that? You're very intelligent.'

'She's from Sudan,' I said quickly, before she could say anything. 'From East Africa.'

Father Tollinare looked at me. You could say that I was looking at myself too, for in truth I didn't know a thing about her.

'I want you to come here again and again,' he said to the child. 'Do you write?' he asked eagerly. 'Do you know how to copy the scriptures?'

The girl nodded. Father Tollinare clapped his hands. 'But come tomorrow and show me what you can do. I can see you're a very intelligent little girl.'

She came the next day and copied the scriptures, but Father Tollinare scolded her for putting things in there that weren't there. She kept putting things in there that were ... well, forbidden. He couldn't understand why she didn't copy what she saw. What it was she put into the scriptures, he wouldn't tell us, but he began to look frightened by it, and quickly took the writing papers away from her and tore the papers up.

'I can see you're very intelligent,' he proclaimed. 'But such things are forbidden. Such things are dangerous.'

'That part and that part are my own creation,' she said.

He extolled her intelligence, but he said again that such things were forbidden, were dangerous, were unholy. He told her what was in the scriptures, and if she saw anything else there, why she imagined it, or it was the work of the devil. The girl replied with nothing, but she didn't return the next day nor the next; she refused to speak to anyone and drew further into herself.

Once I asked her what turtle oil was used for and she said for light. I asked her if the ship she'd sailed on was a pirate ship. I'd heard tales of pirates.

'Your master, was he a pirate?' I asked.

She'd come with me to the palm grove where we gathered palm leaves. She didn't answer, but looked at me as if I were a fool to ask such a question. But I liked her anyway.

And Grandmother treated her with a special kind of tenderness. Once she commented that if the girl were from anywhere it was from her own country because there it was considered a virtue for a woman to be quiet, but she admitted that now in this New World she didn't consider silence very virtuous among women. 'Ah, but then wasn't I the truly silent woman?' she said. Was it Rugendas she spoke to?

The girl's eyes seemed to get larger whenever my grandmother spoke to her. I knew now it was because Grandmother shared the secret of her identity. That is, if she's to be believed. I know my grandmother would stare at her often. 'What should we do?' she'd ask. I thought then that she was asking what we should do with the girl, because she couldn't be fathomed. But now I suspect that she was addressing the girl. Once when she asked that, the girl came and kissed my grandmother as if she recognized her suddenly, then she went out into the yard.

When the girl didn't return for a time, my mother went out to find her. She found her, she said, but she didn't bring her back; she took her instead to Father Tollinare. My grandmother said that she'd committed suicide, that she'd eaten earth, so much of it, and in that way had committed suicide. Some others believe that it was Entralgo that stuffed her with earth and killed her.

'But why?' my mother asked, believing I suppose the first thing.

But my grandmother was again the truly silent one. She refused to explain, nor did she tell us who the girl really was, but when we were alone she told me that that was the way that lessons were learned in the world. I had no idea what she meant.

Antonia Artiga

I SUPPOSE THE FIRST THING was true, because when Master Entralgo discovered he couldn't have his way with the girl, he took things out on Antonia Artiga. Everyone said she was a drunkard and a thief, although what she stole or continued to steal I don't know. My grandmother swore that it was one thing she stole and only one thing, but that Entralgo (she never called him 'Master,' not even when speaking face to face with him), but as soon as he learned about the girl, Entralgo beat this Antonia Artiga. It wasn't as if he hadn't beat her before. He'd always beat her for this one thing she'd stolen as if she'd stolen it again and again. And if anything else drove him to annoyance, he'd beat her for that too.

We were sitting in the palm grove where Grandmother had first spoken to the invisible Rugendas. This time, however, she spoke to no one. We sat in silence until we could hear the woman scream. It was loud and long. That's the way she'd do it. One loud long scream and then she'd be silent for the rest of the time. He'd beat her publicly, once a week, and like I said, any other time that he was irked. The rest of the time she'd go about her work in the cane field, like any other woman. In the evening she'd sit in front of her hut, sitting very straight and proud, chewing on a cane stalk and drinking rum she'd made herself. Then she'd commit some crime again or someone else would do a thing that riled him and he'd go and grab Antonia.

After her beating, my grandmother would visit her or some other woman who knew about medicine and rub salve on her wounds, then the next day, early in the morning, she'd be out in the fields cutting cane with the other women, as if she'd never been beaten.

'What did she steal? What does she keep stealing?' I asked.

'She doesn't keep stealing. What she stole she only stole one time. Such a woman only needs to commit one crime. He goes on beating her

34

for the same one. But that's not why he's beating her now. A man like that can take one reason or another.'

I looked at her, but she wouldn't explain in words that I could understand. After a moment, she got up and began picking certain leaves, and then I followed her out of the palm grove and among the cinchona trees. She scratched off some of its bark and drew sap from it.

'Come on,' she said. 'I'll go see about her. She's more stubborn than a goat, but a man like that can take one reason or another.'

I walked beside her up the road. We stood in the senzala watching while they untied the woman from a post. My grandmother left me standing there and walked with the woman into her hut. I went into my mother's hut.

'Why does he beat her in public?' I asked.

I knew he beat other women, but none of them in public. Besides Antonia, only the men were beaten in public. When my mother didn't explain, I climbed into my hammock.

After a long moment, she said, 'It's considered indecent to beat a woman out of doors.'

I waited for her to explain further, but she wouldn't, as if she wanted me to make the connections she refused to make. 'Make the understanding for yourself,' was a phrase I often heard my grandmother say. But I sat there with my mouth open waiting for her to make the understanding for me.

Grandmother came in smelling like cinchona salve and told me to shut my mouth before I swallowed a goat.

Entralgo Comes to
the Medicine Woman

HE KEEPS PROMISING HER he'll ship her to Corricao's,' said Grandmother as she climbed into her hammock and took up a basket to weave.

I shuddered, because I knew that Corricao's was the place where they breed slaves. A few of the slaves on our plantation had been born at Corricao's and disgusting things were whispered, even into the ears of children. I started to ask Grandmother why some slaves had to work harder than others, and why some were even forced to do disgusting things. Perhaps Corricao wouldn't buy Antonia, I was thinking. Perhaps he wouldn't buy a drunkard and a thief, as she was called.

As I was about to speak, a tall house servant loomed in the doorway. I eyed him because they had just started talking to me about going to Pao Joaquim and I knew that Pao Joaquim could be any of the men, behind his mask. But this tall house servant didn't look fierce at all. Still, it was the mask that could make anyone fierce.

'What do you want?' my mother asked the man.

'Master Entralgo wants the other woman.'

Mother looked at Grandmother, wondering what she'd done wrong again. Grandmother sat on her hammock weaving, looking nonchalant, then she looked up.

'What does he want?' she inquired, not of him, but of Mother.

'You must come,' the man told her.

Grandmother shrugged. 'I've done nothing,' she said. Then she got up from her hammock. 'Almeydita, I want you to come with me and carry my basket.'

I picked up her basket which had various medicines in it, as if it contained treasures.

'He didn't send for Almeydita,' said my mother.

'No, he didn't send for the little one,' said the man.

'What little one?' I pouted. I straightened my shoulders and placed my hands on my hips. Could this be Pao Joaquim? You don't defy Pao Joaquim.

'But I want her to come with me.'

'All right. Do what you will. You'll do it anyway.'

I walked behind my grandmother and the tall man, carrying the basket of charms and potions. When we reached the casa grande, we were taken into the music and sitting room. Entralgo was surrounded by all kinds of musical instruments and paintings. Indeed, I hadn't noticed Entralgo at first. But he had hung a hammock up and was lying in that and eating a mandacaru.

'Why've you brought that little girl?' he asked with anger.

He looked as if he were ready to swoop down on me. Did I remind him of Selvagem?

'She won't understand what language we speak in,' retorted Grand-mother. 'Or why you've sent for me.'

'Then tell me why I've sent for you, Old Witch?' he asked, throwing the mandacaru onto the carpeted floor. A servant whom I hadn't noticed came and scooped it up and put it in a basket. He waved the servant out and raised up somewhat to look at her out of hawk's eyes.

'For a gift I might give,' she replied, looking at him steadily, and not from the corner of her eyes.

'There's no gift that such a woman as you might give to such a man as me.'

'So you have no need of me,' she said, turning.

'What did you bring?' he asked, motioning toward the basket.

'Do you think I can touch the eye and heal it without medicines?'

'What eye?'

'I thought it was the eye that needed to be healed. Isn't it the eye that's somewhat bloodshot?'

'No, it's not the eye,' he said. 'I've heard that men go to you for such problems, though, and though you're not exclusively concerned, not wholly concerned with such matters, you've been very helpful and have cured such problems. And that many times after you've healed the eye it gives no more trouble. It works as it should.'

I looked at him, wondering why he was now talking about the eye when he had just said it was not the eye. And he looked like he had two good eyes.

'Yes, that's true, yes,' she said. 'I recommend coffee mixed with clots of menstrual blood of the desired woman, very strong coffee, much sugar. Some say it's the blood of a mulatto woman that's the best, but I don't agree.'

He sat looking at her with his mouth slightly open. 'Do you want to poison me?'

'If you have trouble getting the menstrual blood, the other remedy I'd recommend is fresh air, plenty of exercise, not the kind you get beating Antonia ... '

'Careful, Witch.'

'A change of food, plenty of vegetables and fruits. But besides that, Sir, I don't know what to recommend. As far as magic goes, Sir, I'm not very skilled.'

'And not at all crazy either, I wager. Send the girl out.'

'Sir, I'm not one of those magicians who can simply touch the eye and heal it.'

He tossed his hand into the air and told my grandmother to get out, although after that one began to see him walk more and ride around less in his hammock, carried by servants. And I recall that Antonia began to be beaten not so frequently as before.

'What did that devil want?' my mother asked when we got back inside.

'Me to teach him how to be the master.'

'What? What craziness is that? I've never seen more master. Has Antonia seen more master than that one?'

'To teach him to conquer himself,' said Grandmother, going back to her weaving. 'To teach him to master himself.'

Mother shook her head. 'I don't know what you mean.'

'He believes I have some sexual magic, but I told him I hadn't any.' My grandmother gave a deep laugh.

Mother, silent, looked at me then at her. 'He wanted you to cure him?' She looked at me again.

'No bad blood,' my grandmother said. 'A lack of power.'

My mother gave a sigh of relief. I didn't know what it was about then, but learned later that the superstition was that only virgins could cure bad blood, and only black ones, though myth had it that there were very few of those.

My mother nodded, but still kept looking at me.

'She stayed outside,' Grandmother said, although she did not explain that it was only in understanding that I'd been outside.

Gold

WHAT'RE YOU SELLING, SIR?' my grand-mother asked the itinerant peddler, whom we met as we walked along the road gathering cashew nuts.

'Wigs, silk stockings, wine, olive oil, and wheaten flour.'

'Wheaten flour?'

'Yes, and tobacco, brandy, rum.'

'I'd like some wheaten flour.'

The man, who was wearing high boots and a broad-brimmed hat, didn't move to get her any of the wheaten flour that was in the cart that he pulled along behind him. Finally, she reached into a hidden pocket in her skirt, took out a little bag and sprinkled bits of gold powder into her hand. When he saw it, his eyes lit up and he jumped down from his horse and went quickly to the side of the cart and got a bag of wheaten flour. He opened a bag that he carried at his waist, and she emptied the gold powder into it.

'You see me today but you won't see me tomorrow,' said the man.

'And why's that?' asked grandmother, holding the bag of wheaten flour in her fist.

''Cause I'm on my way to the gold mines at Minas Gerais. If I don't find gold I'll still be a rich man.'

'How will you be a rich man if you don't find gold?' I asked. 'How's that?'

''Cause he'll charge outrageous prices,' said my grandmother. 'Isn't that so, Sir?'

'Sim, I'll charge outrageous prices,' he said with a laugh, going his way.

'Where'd you get the gold?' I asked as we walked back to the senzala.

She explained that when she'd gone into the interior of the country with Rugendas, into the sertao, they'd met Indians who lived in cities, not like the tiny mission villages along the coast, but real cities, and these Indians made many things out of gold, except that gold meant nothing to them.

'Were they Tupi?'

'No, the Tupis live near the coast. I don't know what names they have in the interior. Gold didn't mean a thing to them, though. They saw the tools that Rugendas carried, and exchanged their gold for his tools.'

'Gold didn't mean a thing at all to them.'

I asked her why she'd spent some of it on wheaten flour.

'It's enough for wheaten flour,' she said, 'but not enough to buy freedom. Did Rugendas have to buy his?'

A Conversation with Antonia

WAIT A MINUTE, LITTLE GIRL,' she called. 'Come here, menina.'

It was a Sunday and a holiday and she was sitting out in front of her hut, drinking rum. I'd been walking along the road as I always did on holidays. I'd gone to the palm grove where my grandmother had taken me. I'd still discovered no mysteries there nor had I seen the invisible Rugendas. I was on my way back to my mother's hut.

'Come over here, menina,' she called again.

I went over and stood in front of her. She was a tall and big woman but not a fat one. She wore one of her breasts covered but the other free. A hard-drinking and hard-working woman, she took no nonsense from anyone, and I wondered why she took it even from the master. Although she was a slave and he was the master, she still seemed to me, even then, a better woman than he was a man. She took a gulp of rum and stared at me in silence. Her eyes were bloodshot but sparkling.

'I'd like to invite you into my hut to talk to me,' she said. I shook my head and backed away from her.

'I like you, menina,' she said. 'Hasn't your spirit ever been attracted to someone?'

I nodded, though I only guessed at what she meant. She stood up and I followed her inside. She took her clay jug of rum with her. Her hut was very small with only one short hammock, which looked as if she couldn't stretch out fully in it, many multicolored mats that she'd woven from pieces of Sea Island cotton, clay jugs along the wall, some decorated with pretty designs. She motioned for me to sit down on one of the mats, while she sat on another one. She lifted the clay jug and took a swig of rum.

'Sim, who knows why the spirit attaches itself to someone?' she said. 'It's just the way and you don't know why.' She took another swig of rum. 'What do you think of my face? Do you think it's ugly or beautiful? Or can you tell?'

Another one for the Negro asylum, I was thinking, as I watched her.

She didn't frighten me, but I stood as far away from her as one could in that tiny hut. It was true she had one of those faces that could be different things for different people. Was she ugly or beautiful? It was difficult to tell. Her most generous features were her ears, which stuck out from puffs of fluffy black hair. The rest of her was cat-like, a small nose and mouth, slit-like but attractive eyes. And there were little marks on her face, like scratches, patterns that I'd mostly seen on the faces of old people and newly arrived Africans.

She gave a little laugh as she looked at me. 'What d'you think of me? Do you like me?'

'Sim.'

'He thinks I'm in the hands of the devil, that Entralgo. He thinks I've bewitched him,' she said. She tilted her head to the side and gave a short jerk. My eyes widened. 'That's why he sent for the Old Witch ... That's what he calls her, not me.'

I stood against the wall of the hut.

'You don't know whether I'm ugly or beautiful?' she asked.

I shook my head no.

'And don't you know whether I'm good or evil either?'

'They say that you're a thief and a drunkard.'

'Oh, do they? Yes, they do, don't they? So am I good or evil?'

I said that I couldn't decide.

'Well, after you have decided that, you must decide what punishment or what reward you'll give me.'

'How can I reward or punish you?' I asked. I felt like the little one the tall servant had called me.

She looked at me for a long moment.

'No, I'm not beautiful,' she said suddenly. 'And I'm not ugly either.' She drank another swig from her rum, then she gave me a look like Entralgo had Selvagem when I thought he would swoop down on her. Then she wiped her right hand across her mouth, then up and down her right thigh. Her thigh had scars and scratches on it too. Her eyes seemed to grow smaller as she looked at me.

'D'you think I'd bewitch a man?' she asked. 'D'you think I could do it? I'm not very beautiful. But he thinks I bewitched him and so he got your grandmother to unbewitch him ... Do you think the master takes care of me?'

I asked her didn't he take care of all of us, since he owned us.

'Owns us, eh? We're in a foreign land, menina. It's not our own. We're in a foreign land that's not our own. What land d'you live in?'

'The same as you.'

She clucked. 'Why my spirit's attracted to you, I don't know. But you won't be able to forget about me, either. He thinks I've enchanted him and so he got your grandmother to disenchant him. It's she wanted me to tell you that, as if she couldn't tell you well enough her own self.' She swallowed more rum. 'I'm a generous woman and I'm not wicked. I'm only unmanageable. There are things I won't swallow. Things I won't swallow, you see. No, not a bit. I've got no magic charms.'

She arched her back.

'I heal fast, only because of the help of your grandmother, but me, I have no magic charms. I'm just an ordinary mulher, not wicked. There are just things I won't swallow.'

She leaned toward me and I backed into the wall. If I could have become the wall, I would have.

'See that woman?'

I peeked out her door. It was Mexia there in the road. Yes, I nodded that I saw her.

'Her eyes are as meek as a cow's, as meek as a cow's. Do you know what relationship there's between her and the old priest?'

'Sim,' I said meekly.

'Is she good or evil?'

I tried to remember Father Tollinare's question.

'Yes, you know it, but you won't say.'

I tried to remember how Father Tollinare had phrased it.

'She's got some power over the old priest or he's got some power over her. But she's a fool and a simpleton. Nobody should be as yielding and pliable as that.'

I felt as if she were talking about a different woman, not the Mexia that I knew, but I nodded anyway.

'She doesn't know she's in a foreign country that's not her own. She thinks it's hers too. They call me a drunkard and a thief, but I'm not so drunk as that, and I can't steal a land that's not my own.'

She took a new swig of rum, swirled it in her mouth, and swallowed. She put her hand to her lips and belched, without excusing herself. 'I don't know why, but the spirit's a funny thing. Mine's very jolly when I see you. Do you know why everybody calls me a drunkard and a thief?'

'No.'

'Because he started it. Entralgo. He started it so everyone took it up, whether they knew it to be true or not. I drink, yes, because I'm in a foreign land that's not my own.'

I stared at the scratches on her thigh.

'But I've stolen nothing,' she continued. 'Now he's got two new names for me. Now he calls me a madwoman and a murderer, but I dare him to spread that about. I dare him to.' She slapped her hand across her thigh.

We looked at each other for a long time. She arched her back again, then she came forward and caressed me and said again that she didn't know what moved one spirit toward another.

'Your grandmother told me to tell you all this. I wouldn't have otherwise. Of my own nature, I don't speak such things.'

Then she apologized for keeping me too long, although I felt I could have stayed longer then. 'May God keep you,' she whispered, then took her eternal swig of rum.

Dr Johann

ACAIBA, BRING ALMEYDITA.'
My mother brought me outside. I stared at the green hills but not at the white man who was standing in front of us.

'Is this the one?' Entralgo asked him.

The stranger was a young man, about twenty, although he seemed older to me then. I stared at the green hills and then at the man from the corner of my eyes. He had high cheekbones and full lips, his dark eyes slanted downwards. I looked at him fully. He was more beautiful than handsome and there was something womanly about him.

'Yes,' he nodded, looking at me. He wasn't really smiling, but he looked at me in a full way that made me feel he was not from this country.

Now I might describe his look as a mixture of curiosity and tenderness.

Still I'm not sure. It was one of those kinds of looks that changes meaning with time and place. Certainly, he was not from this country.

'Dr Johann wants to paint her,' Entralgo said to my other. 'Bring her to the veranda.'

We went onto the veranda and then followed them into the place with thick white walls and oriental carpets and Dutch chandeliers. I was taken into the interior of the house, the part of the house where the doctor was staying, toward the back, a room with Dutch windows facing the orchard.

Most of the house was dark and damp and I was glad for the sunshine. 'Do you want the other wench to stay?' asked Entralgo.

Dr Johann looked at my mother. He gave her a different look. 'Yes,' he said. 'I might want to include her too.'

I'd never seen a man like him before. A master would give you a bold look but not a full one. I assume now that it was not simply because he was not from this country, but because he was an artist. He explained to my mother and me – he spoke to us directly – that he had seen me in the yard and that my face had interested him, particularly the huge eyes – he called them 'dark, intelligent' eyes, not the sort of eyes that you'd describe a slave as having, and he had wanted to paint me. But he added that I had a miserable body, so skinny. Entralgo interrupted to say that I was fed well and lazy enough – 'All of them are lazy enough,' he added, meaning both my mother and grandmother too. He said that we were all useless as field hands and too haughty for our own good so he'd set us to weaving baskets and making hammocks and such. 'But a more well fed or lazier bunch you'll never see,' he said.

Dr Johann didn't reply to his harangue, he simply told me where to stand to get the best of the light, while he stood behind a long board, a canvas I learned, and held a brush and a smaller board full of an assortment of many different colors. He told my mother, who stood back watching me, that she might stand closer near me. Entralgo stood by looking serious, then bewildered and curious, then disgusted.

'But, Senhor, there are so many white women in the house,' said Entralgo.

'I have seen so many white women,' replied Dr Johann. He put on a bored expression.

Entralgo stood by watching, then grunted and left. Every now and then as he worked, Dr Johann would come to me and touch my hair and run his hands along my jaw and touch the lids of my eyes. His hands were soft and I found myself waiting for him to stop painting and come and touch me. My mother stood in silence and watched him with some wariness until he finished that day, and then the next day and the next I was taken there, while my mother would stand waiting. Then one day it was not me that Dr Johann wanted but my mother.

'Leave Almeydita here,' Entralgo's messenger said when he came to our hut. 'Dr Johann wants you alone today.'

'Almeydita can watch as he paints me,' my mother hastened to say.

'He wants you alone,' repeated the messenger, looking at her sternly.

Mother left with him. When she returned she was very silent.

'Did you see the painting of me?' I asked with excitement. 'Has he finished mine?'

She stared at me, then she said, 'He wanted your face and eyes, but my body.'

Her solemn face had made mine turn solemn.

'Will he paint you tomorrow?' I asked.

'Yes,' she said. Then she knelt in the corner of the hut, lifting rice in her hands.

I pictured Dr Johann coming to her and touching her as he'd done me, her jawline and her eyelids. She was silent, standing stiffly and solemn. I wanted to ask something, but she was too silent, and she wouldn't look at me. I watched her preparing the rice. I peeked out the door of the hut and saw Dr Johann sitting on a rock painting a man who was standing holding a basket and a woman who was balancing a basket of bananas on her head. I tried to imagine the painting he'd done – with the face and eyes of a young girl and the body of a woman. Dr Johann looked over his canvas. I half-imagined that he saw me, but his eyes returned to his canvas. I pulled back inside and my mother handed me a plate of coconut and rice and onions.

Tempo, the Horse Trader

HE WAS A MAN WHO KEPT HORSES, not for white men but for himself. He lived outside of the plantation in a square hut made of mud bricks and straw. Whenever I'd go with my mother to the stream with the other women, I could catch glimpses of Tempo on the side of the hill with his five saddle horses, or four or three, that he rented out to people, or exchanged with men who were traveling distances on the road and needed fresh horses.

Because he wasn't a branco, he couldn't ride them his own self, although he was free. At the stream, I'd kneel with my mother, rinsing clothes after she'd washed them, wringing them and putting them into a basket. I'd beg my mother if I could race up to the hillside and see him.

'See who?' she'd always ask, although she knew who I meant.

'Senhor Tempo, Senhor Tempo,' I'd say impatiently.

'Go ahead,' she'd say with a slight smile.

I'd rush up to the hillside and he'd be waiting for me and smiling.

Always he wore a loose gray-white shirt and gray-white trousers and carried a pole or stick. He'd help me up on one of the horses, and he'd hold the bridle and we'd walk around the small barn where he slept in straw alongside the horses. Because I was a menina, he thought he could bend the laws for me.

'How old are you now, Almeydita?' he'd ask, although I kept telling him the same thing, or it seemed like I always told him the same thing. He knew perfectly well my age.

'I'm eight,' I'd say, stroking the horse's mane. Once it had been seven, once six, once five that I'd said, but it was always the same question.

Then he'd be silent and we'd walk around and around the barn until my mother lifted her arm and waved. Then he'd help me off the horse, holding me by my thin waist.

My mother had never come up there with me and had never that I could remember spoken to the man, yet whenever I would leave he'd say, 'Give Acaiba my best thoughts.'

I'd smile and he'd nod at me and I'd rush down the hill to the woman gathering up laundry. Then we'd go to another place and I'd help my mother hang the wet clothes on bushes and low trees. If I'd been older I might have noticed a certain look my mother had whenever I'd return from Tempo. She'd be silent but there'd be that certain look, and once when we returned to our hut she spoke aloud.

'He's the only free man I know,' she said. She was silent, then she said, 'Or maybe he just thinks he's a free man. Maybe he just thinks he's free.'

A Man Comes to Ride a Horse and Work on a Dictionary

FTER DR JOHANN ARRIVED, my mother was brought to work in the household, in the casa grande. I was many times there working along with her and so got to see many visitors. Since there were no inns in our part of the country – and indeed in most of Brazil there were no inns – those with letters of introduction and visiting dignitaries were allowed to stay at the casa grande; those without letters of introduction, if they were not thieves or ruffians were allowed to camp on the outskirts of the plantation or in the fields surrounding the senzala. Therefore many of the visitors were not even relatives of Entralgo, but having letters of introduction from noblemen and viceroys and other senhores de engenho, a caudilho or cornel, fazendeiro, or ouvidor – more were welcome as if they were, as plantation owners did in those days, and were given guest rooms. Rubber gatherers, cowboys, muleteers, slave-hunters, bushwhacking captains, tropas de resgate and the like had to camp on the outskirts of the plantation or near the senzala.

Well, this one senhor was a short, dark-haired man with blue steel eyes. When we first saw him, everyone was told to come out into the yard and even the family of Entralgo was brought out sitting in hammocks, except the women and the girls of course were in covered hammocks.

Immediately the visitor jumped onto one of the horses and began to ride. Grinning like a lunatic, he stood up on the horse's back as it galloped at full speed. Then stepping down as if he were falling, but holding onto the horn, he pulled himself up again. Next he jumped from one side of the horse to the other, climbed under its belly to the other side, disappeared several times behind the horse and appeared again. He did other stunts and acrobatics. His expressions brought laughter, his tricks delight. My grandmother had once told me that her mapmaker, Rugendas, was capable of such stunts.

When he jumped down from the horse, everyone applauded, the master most raucously. I went with my mother to prepare the meal. After dinner I was told to bring the visitor water, a glass of strong beer, and a Portuguese cigar. He was sitting at a mahogany writing table bending over some papers. I was surprised to find a man doing such stunts bending over papers. He didn't look like a simple licenciado. Most scholars had squinty eyes, and his, though they squinted some to look at the papers, flashed clear and generous when they looked at me. He wasn't exactly a polished man either, but he wasn't as coarse as a muleteer. He motioned for me to set the water, beer, and cigar on the table. His look was cantankerous.

'I tell him that a dictionary of the Brazilian language should not be only academic Portuguese words, but should include Indian words and contributions to the language by Negroes and others.'

I look at him. I'd never heard a branco speak to me in such a way, not even Dr Johann. When he noticed I didn't understand him, he explained.

'Father Tollinare and I, you see, are working on a Brazilian dictionary. He feels I'm making it imperfect by the impure words I wish to put into it. So we finished it in the strictest most unadulterated Portuguese, but now I'm doing my own supplement, you see. Now I'm collecting as many of the "impure" words and phrases as are common only to this New World. When one is in a new world one must have new words, you see. Certainly the contributions of the first Brazilians should be here, at least the first ones that we know about, and what the Negroes brought here along with the Portuguese. You see what I'm saying? Why are you looking at me so? Do you think I'm a funny man?'

I shook my head.

'Do I look like a man of learning, then?'

I shook my head again.

He said he was a self-taught man and he mentioned places he had traveled to, places in New Spain, and in the Old World too – Paris and London. I wondered if self-taught meant that he was a man of as much learning as Father Tollinare. I wondered whether he had read forbidden books.

'Did you like my riding this morning?'

'Sim.'

'Well, you've seen the only two things that I'm good at, putting together dictionaries and doing stunt rides. Well, in New Spain I'm good at *juego de canas*. Do you know what that is?'

'No.'

'Jousting, my dear. It's done on horseback and it's like throwing javelins, except it's done for sport at holiday and we only use lightweight canes.'

'Are you from New Spain?'

'No, I was born and bred right here.' He gulped his strong beer, lit the Portuguese cigar, and took a few puffs. 'I don't know anything else. Oh, I know a thing or two about the world and a thing or two about the imagination, but it's not stuff you can use really except in a book or two. I'm a very timid man.'

'You don't act timid.'

'Sim. Dictionaries and stunt riding. I do one thing because I do the other. I balance my timidity with a show of recklessness, but it's all very controlled, every bit of it. I'm not at all spontaneous really. Long, patient, difficult work. And that's from a well-traveled man but a man who also has a disposition for leisure, strong beer, and a good cigar.' He nodded, smoked, took another huge swallow of beer. 'If it were up to me, perhaps, I wouldn't be so well-traveled. My father, now that's a lover of adventure and novelties. It's he who taught me to stunt ride while my mother wanted me to be a licenciado at some great university in Europe. My father's an archeologist. He's somewhere in Africa or India now and my mother's traipsing with him. Me, I came back here because I wanted to make something of the New World. So I say this is important work. Do you think dictionary-making is important work?'

I said I didn't know. I wondered whether a dictionary could include forbidden words, but I didn't ask him.

'Is it important? Well, I make claims that it is. You use a word, but me, I isolate, analyze, explain, give history to it. My father thinks it's some silliness I've gotten myself into, some estupidez, some obsession. Even Father Tollinare and I have disputes on what are the highest and most imaginative words. I say one thing and he says the other, and he wants to ban some words altogether; he doesn't want those in the Old World to see the new one as a prurient or vulgar place. But if the words are here, I say use them. He says one thing and I say another. I say one thing and

49

he says another. It's not just imagination that's meaningful in a word, it's the preservation of tradition. That's the important thing. The purpose of a dictionary, he says, is not to say what words are in use, but what words should be in use. He'd transport the whole Portuguese language here, if he could, not taking into account what changes would be naturally made, how one comes to terms linguistically with new geography and experiences. When I was in Portugal they laughed at the way I spoke my native language. Perhaps that's what obsessed me, and even Father Tollinare complains that I don't talk much like a lexicographer.'

'What's a lexicographer?'

'Why, a compiler of dictionaries. That's what I am. Didn't I say so? I don't talk much like one, you see, and I don't have letters of credence from a university. And in Portugal they laughed at my native tongue, called it barbaric. So I'm making my own little supplement on the New World Portuguese. Do you hear what I'm saying? A maker of dictionaries. For my father, that doesn't begin to be anything for a man to do, a real man, a true man. He'd never understand. Do you think it's something for a man to do, even a man without letters of credence?'

I wasn't sure what letters of credence were. I said, however, I didn't know.

'A man should live within his own imagination. By that, I mean what he can imagine himself to be. How can he live beyond it?'

I kept looking at the man. His hair was so black it looked blue. 'Ah, this is a very useful expression,' he said, scribbling something on the paper. 'What if it doesn't mean literally what it says? Sometimes we use words here as we imagine them to mean.'

He didn't tell me what the word was and I couldn't make out his scribbling. Perhaps it was a word I shouldn't know. Perhaps it was forbidden.

'All of this in just one word,' he mumbled.

Since he had not dismissed me, I remained standing there.

'What is it you want?' he asked, looking at me suddenly, as if noticing I was still there, or noticing me for the first time.

'I'm waiting for you to dismiss me, Sir.'

He looked at me, then looked down at his work again, then scribbled something else. Strangely, he still did not dismiss me. He gulped some more beer and puffed again.

'How many hyphens?' he asked himself. 'I could write volumes and volumes of supplements, but Father Tollinare despises this, he ridicules it. But this is a new country. Who knows which language will develop here? Especially fertile is the linguistic imagination of the lower classes. And all kinds of words have entered our language from the Guinea coast.'

'Guinea coast?'

'Don't you know your own country?'

'I know a guinea fowl when I see one.'

'Our native expressions ... What was I saying?'

'The Guinea coast.'

'All new countries have a murderous tongue, but that's how one survives. That's a New World. Who knows, what Father Tollinare despises now might be what someday distinguishes our whole country. And if your people had their way, little black girl ... ' He looked at me, but didn't continue what he was going to say. 'I've heard free Negroes talk, the learned ones, the ones with pretensions, and they're worse than Father Tollinare.'

'Father Tollinare's from Portugal.'

'He claims that, does he? He's a Mazombo like the rest of us.'

'Macumba?'

'A Brazilian born in the New World not the Old. Of European parents of course. Macumba is the Guinea version of our Holy Faith. Father Tollinare ... this has nothing to do with religion.'

'How can a priest have nothing to do with religion?'

He looked impatient, cantankerous again. 'What I'm saying though about the Guineas who try to use a privileged language, like the criollos, their language is the most circumscribed, the most absolutely perfect, rigid, unimaginative guff. All they've learned well is the language of the Master ... '

'But you just said they were free.'

'Some are free, others merely pretentious. The language that prevents subversiveness is what I'm saying, just like the criollos and there's talk among some criollos of one day having our own country where we can make our own cigars and don't have to always import expensive Portuguese ones. Do you know that we can't even make our own cigars in our own country? No manufactured things, only raw materials. That's what a colony means. They talk of winning our freedom, but shouldn't we be free to use our own language?'

'What does a colony mean?'

'That you must import every manufactured thing. Didn't you know that? But you have never been to the coast. Raw goods go out and manufactured goods come in. It is the same in New Spain. It's a crime to even manufacture our own rum.'

'Antonia makes her own.'

'Antonia? Eh, some slave girl. Antonia? I've heard that name. The rascal, he calls her. Why, this is a world of rascals. These are the laws of import-export I'm talking about. It's all economics and the official prohibition of anything manufactured here, even the mustache cup. Shall you deny me my mustache cup?'

'No,' I said and started to rush about to find one.

'Come back here.'

I came and stood before him again. He squinted his eyes at me.

'You don't look dumb,' he said. 'You look well-fed. You look like one who always drinks the beastings. Language, let me tell you, has its own genius for rebellion or compromise. And should we always import our art from Europe, as Entralgo does even his paintings?'

I started to tell him of Dr Johann, but he was so rapid with his talk that I just listened.

'My father goes hunting for lost races and the races are here!' he shouted. 'Try to improve the ones here I say, and he calls me a discredit to the family. He's off to some magic desert and I'm here where the manioc grows. So, you see I'm a maker of dictionaries and a clown and acrobat. Do you think I'm a clown? Do you think I'm uncultivated?'

'Sim,' I answered, although I was uncertain what he meant.

'Well, this is a land of clowns, or at least exaggerated personalities. But isn't this a country enough for that? Don't we have passion enough for that? Just like you drink the beastings. Anyway, we should all take advantage of opportunities for racial improvement, shouldn't we? When I was in Europe, I married a Swiss prostitute. How's that for improving the race? I tried studying archeology, but I changed to etymology. The spoils of my father's adventures all go to museums. And my mother traipses about with him, like a woman on the edge of a storm. This dictionary-making, child, this is patient, difficult work.'

He took another swig of beer. 'Antonia, did you say? Well, Entralgo and his slave-making activities. Me, I'm a lover of language. New words for a new landscape, that's what I say. Authority and submission. Subject and object. I see you're an intelligent little girl. This word here is from the Dutch. Eh, this is a common error. And this an uncommon one. Words for a new generation. Keep the secret. Can you keep a secret?' He took another swig of beer and leaned into my ear. 'Language and politics, my child, is very interesting.' He leaned back into his papers. 'Let us return now to the previous footnote. Very interesting. Similar in style these two personal expressions. This letter. What do you think?'

'I don't know.'

Just then Father Tollinare came into the room, saw the young man had gotten quite drunk, and motioned for me to leave. When I was outside I heard him say, 'Foolish boy' and 'Foolish notion' and 'but a language of tremendous prestige' and 'off with our boots.'

And I heard the young man reply, 'But, Padre, you hyperbolize, you hypercriticize, you hyperbola, he he, you hyperborean, you hypercatalectic hyperborean, you hyperesthetic hypercatalectic hyperborean, you must confront the realities of life, the realities of language. The beatings?'

'Foolish boy,' I heard Father Tollinare say.

I did not hear anything else for my mother came, saw me eavesdropping and drew me away.

The Woman and Palmares

I'D NEVER SEEN A BLACK WOMAN dressed like her before. She rode up in a carriage beside a white man. People along the road stopped and gaped at her. Those inside came to the doors of their huts. She was dressed in a long silk gown full of pleats and folds and ruffles and there was a crucifix around her neck. Her hair was straightened and tied in a ball just like a branca's. Her neck looked very thick and deformed, but my mother explained to me that that was the kind of woolen collar that she wore in the city; it was considered very stylish, very much in vogue, although she agreed with me that it did look like some deformity, and must be very hot in this climate, but near the coast it was not so hot as here, though hot enough.

The crucifix sat between the woman's breasts. The woman herself sat very straight and tall. I looked at her feet, though, and saw that she was wearing no shoes. She was as barefoot as myself, and her toes stuck out from the full pleats. I smiled. I saw other people smiling too but I felt it was for a different reason. I myself was in awe of her. I can't describe the white man very well, because it was the woman who kept my attention.

However, I remember that he was wearing a broad hat and a dark suit. The woman's eyes were slanted upward and there was a gold comb in her hair, like a little crown. She seemed extraordinarily tall, but perhaps it was where she was riding, right in the front seat beside the man.

'Who's that woman?' I whispered to my mother.

I've not described my mother. A big-boned, handsome woman, she did not comb her hair down or tie it in scarves like some of the other women; she wore it so that it looked like the crown of a tree, high all around her head. She said nothing until she went and got her long pipe that was in the corner of the room. A long slender reed, the stem pointed downward and ended below her knees, then there was a very small bowl. I didn't know what she smoked in it, as I'd smelled tobacco and it wasn't that.

'I don't know. I've heard stories of her, though,' she replied.

'What stories?'

She looked at me without speaking and drew at her pipe. She looked as if she were thinking through something, which she didn't tell me, then she said, 'Some say she's a princess from Africa ... '

'From Guinea coast?' I asked, my eyes wide.

'From Africa,' she repeated, 'and that that white man, that branco, went and got her and brought her here and shared his wealth with her.' She puffed on her pipe, then added snidely, 'Or she shared hers with him.'

And there was something else. This she thought through, but didn't say.

'Why were they laughing at her?' I asked.

'Cause he's dressed her up to look like a white woman, a branca, eh, that's why they laugh. Cause of the way he's dressed her up.'

'If I wore a silk dress would they laugh at me too?'

'Where'd you get a silk dress?' she asked. 'Or brocades or satin or velvet too. You do good to get Sea Island cotton. Or muslin too.'

I said nothing. She took a draw from her long pipe.

'I bet she's got diamonds and gold rings. I bet she's got a velvet saddle and diamond sevigne too.'

54

'What d'you know of diamond sevigne?' she asked, and drew on her long pipe. 'Straw sapatos do you good.'

My mother and I were the ones who were sent for to come up to the casa grande to see about the new guests. I didn't know how to treat the woman except as a branca. She was sitting in a big chair in the room they'd given her. When I came in with the angel cakes I was to bring to her, she wouldn't look at me. She held her head high, but wouldn't look even in my direction. They'd given her an elegant room with Dutch furniture, but the women of the house didn't gather around her as they did when other lady guests arrived. Then the women of the house would go off into the mistress's room and gather around the new lady, sitting on pillows and mats or lying in hammocks, chewing plums or sweet cakes. But this lady sat alone and very straight in a wooden chair with her bare feet sticking out from the hem of her dress. She wouldn't look at me and there was nothing I could say to her. I thought of the slave women gathering around her and of Antonia offering her a swig of rum and my mother a puff from her long pipe. And I'd bring her a mandacaru. But I felt that it would be somehow wrong and that she wouldn't like it. I sat the tray of angel cakes down on her table and bowed to her. I curtsied properly like to any lady. She held her back like an arrow.

'Are you a slave woman or a free woman?' I dared to ask.

'I am neither kind,' she answered, still without looking at me.

In the living room, the men, my mother related to me, spoke of Palmares for the benefit of Dr Johann, who had heard stories and legends of the settlements of escaped slaves and had asked Entralgo and the other senhores native to the region to speak of it. He had wished, he said, to travel where they were and to paint them, but both the visitor and Entralgo and the other senhores present persuaded him or rather dissuaded him, saying that it was foolish, it would be too dangerous. They'd cut off his ears and feet. And they spoke also of how the Palmaristas, as these fugitive devils were called – that was their language – had had some women stolen some years ago, some comely women. No, not white women, gracas a Deus, but black ones and Indians. But stealing white women wasn't beyond those devils. That time, though, they hadn't. The savages had killed no one, that time, they'd only taken from the stores and stolen the women, but that was a long time ago, because with the aid of the Paulistas, they'd driven them further into the forests and mountains, so that kind of thing they didn't expect. Some comely women too, repeated Entralgo. He himself was just a boy, but he could appreciate ... But it would be dangerous and foolish, he told the senhor, even if he did want to keep an artistic record of the times, hadn't he gotten enough black faces already? Anyway, what he'd like to know, pelo amor de Deus, where were his white sketches of the New World? Was it only those people he wanted to depict for immortality? What did he have to show to the estrangeiros of the lovely white senhoras e senhorinhas and the interesting white senhores of the territory? All the possibilities and challenges to his talent were right there. He couldn't understand himself how Dr Johann could see any interest or complexities in those pretos. For complexity or interest a branco or a branca any day. Why didn't he paint pictures of the people in whom man's fate lay? Wouldn't that be a challenge to his artistic talents? These others, these pretos, they'd forever be a threat to Brazilian progress and civilization. He could tell Dr Johann was after all an artist of intellect and religious feeling.

'There're enough black faces around here already,' Entralgo had said. 'What, to paint new ones. No, Senhor, you don't have to put yourself in the way of danger to get any more of them. And like I said aren't there lovely and interesting white people in this territory, who'd challenge your talents more?'

'Sim, sim, sim, sim,' toasted some of the senhores present.

'The captain could direct me how to get them,' said Dr Johann. 'I know it wouldn't be an easy thing.'

Entralgo laughed and continued laughing. The captain said nothing.

'Even the captain has fought his last expedition against the Negroes. But with him it's an example of what love can do. Captain Goncalo has discovered that even Negroes are human.'

Captain Goncalo was silent. He sat stiffly in a chair. Entralgo lay in a hammock. Dr Johann sat with his arm thrown along the back of a couch.

'My wife lived in Palmares for four years,' Captain Goncalo told Dr Johann. 'She was one of the captured women.'

'You do not kill them in these wars?'

Entralgo laughed hard, causing his hammock to swing. My mother stood near, fanning him and handing him imported chocolates and bits of angel cake. Dr Johann, she said, looked at her every now and then as if she were doing something disrespectful, not for herself, but to him. She said 'him' but I did not know whether she meant Dr Johann himself or Entralgo.

'Few women are ever killed. Those Negroes who are captured are divided among the soldiers.'

'And that one he could not resist,' Entralgo said. 'And in your love for her haven't you turned her into a laughingstock?'

Captain Goncalo was silent. He cleared his throat. He stood up. Dr Johann looked at my mother.

'There'd be no guarantees for your safety if you were to go on an expedition against the Negroes,' said the captain.

'It wouldn't be *against* them,' said Dr Johann.

'And who knows perhaps a little negrita would be distributed to you if you were to escape with your life,' Entralgo said.

He opened his mouth and my mother popped a chocolate inside. Dr Johann gave her that look.

'I'd really like very much to go,' he said then. 'There's some more work I'd like to finish up here, and then I'd like it if you'd write me a letter of introduction to someone.'

'Letters of introduction to Negroes?' asked Entralgo. 'Is this the New World?'

'I don't mean that,' explained Dr Johann. 'I mean to another captain when they go on their next expedition.'

Captain Goncalo nodded and was silent. My mother felt that he was thinking about the woman even before he spoke.

'My wife tried to commit suicide twice when she was first with me.' He paused, looking at no one. 'She's not tried to commit suicide now in a number of years.'

'What? Her desire for liberty isn't so great now, eh?' Entralgo said and laughed. 'Scratch my head,' he told my mother.

My mother scratched his head and picked lice from it. Captain Goncalo was silent. Dr Johann stared at my mother. She parted Entralgo's hair, searched and searched for more lice.

'I took her back,' Captain Goncalo said. 'After the second time she tried to kill herself, we went back there only to find Palmares had been abandoned. They'd left that part and gone somewhere else and formed a new Palmares, those who were not killed or captured. "Do we continue our journey?" I asked. She'd simply sat down and began to cry. "Do we continue our journey?" I asked again. "Sim," she said, but it was back the way we had come that she pointed. It was then that I kept her for my wife. I took her legally for my wife.'

'He he,' laughed Entralgo. 'Is that a lie or a true story?'

'Weren't you afraid to go back there alone with one of their women? Suppose they'd been there?'

'They say the leader has a blonde wench,' Entralgo said. 'One of his women's a blonde wench. But perhaps she has some Guinea ancestor. I've an imaginary Guinea ancestor. Ha. Ha. Don't we all? Everybody in this country has an imaginary Guinea. No no. I can prove I'm of good blood and purely European. I'm of pure blood.'

'I always imagine that's what the woman was thinking,' Captain Goncalo said in reply to Dr Johann. 'I had taken her back there anyway, regardless of what harm might be done. I imagine that's why she came back with me.'

'It's not true, Captain, I can't believe it, it's not true,' Entralgo said, pushing my mother's fingers out of his hair. 'What's your true feeling for the woman? Dr Johann, go and paint the wench for him. Go and paint the wench for him to see what she's really like. Show him what she's really like. Use your talent, man. Go and paint the wench for him. That's what you can do for this territory, show us what the devils are really like.'

'Sir,' Captain Goncalo said to Dr Johann. 'I'm going to my room and to my wife now. I'll write you a brief introduction to a Captain Moreira who'll be leading an expedition against the Negroes very soon now, and perhaps you'll be able to accompany him. But for your own safety, Sir, I would agree with Senhor Entralgo, that you should remain in this territory, as the blacks are not very dangerous here.'

'Not dangerous,' Entralgo said with a grunt. 'Rascals every one of them.'

'Not very dangerous,' continued the captain, 'and you'll be able to collect a number of excellent faces . . . '

'But not nearly so interesting and complex . . . '

'A number of very excellent types even among the Negroes here and the various Indian tribes, the Tupi, the . . . '

'That's an idea for you,' Entralgo said. 'Have Father Tollinare take you to see the Indians. Do you think the Negroes are the only dark people here? Go see the Indians. It would be less dangerous and your safety would be better guaranteed. At least our Indians here are quiet . . . except for the men, they're always running off. Except they are such loners in the forests. They're such mavericks.'

'Yes, I'd appreciate a letter of introduction. I'll stay here a bit longer as I intended to visit the Indian groups,' Dr Johann said.

'Yes, Father Tollinare has them all in hand.' Entralgo waved his hand in the air. 'Except for the men, like I said, they're such mavericks. Living alone in the forests, the way some of them do.'

My mother watched his hand in the air. She saw Dr Johann observing her, disapprovingly, and so stared at nothing.

Captain Goncalo sat down at a huge desk, wrote a brief letter, folded it, and presented it to Dr Johann.

'It's been a great pleasure to meet you,' he said standing, bowing to Dr Johann. Dr Johann bowed and said it had been his pleasure to meet a man such as the captain.

Captain Goncalo bowed to Entralgo and said, 'Sir, I am no longer a guest in your house, nor will be from this day.'

He stood stiffly and walked out.

Entralgo laughed and put my mother's hands back in his hair. Dr Johann looked at them both, then he told Entralgo that he was going for a short walk.

'And then we'll dine,' Entralgo said, still laughing. 'But go see the Father, he'll be glad to show you where the Indians are. He knows them quite intimately.' He chuckled. 'My father had a number of them, but I prefer to do without them myself, but I have a number of the mixed variety, the caboclos. They provide some variety, you see. Some diversion for the eye.'

A High Post
in the Government

HE WAS AN INTELLIGENT, tall, and attractive young Indian. He'd been one of Father Tollinare's students many years before, and had been sent to study in Europe, first Paris and then Berlin. The older people knew of him. My mother said that she knew of him and that they were about the same age. In those days my mother was in her early twenties, though I don't know her exact age. She said that she too had been one of Father Tollinare's students, which surprised me, because she'd never given any indication that she knew either how to read or write.

She explained that she'd been among the generation of 'experiments.' In those early days, she said, they believed that the Senegalese Negro with a drop of Arabic blood was the most intelligent, and so even though her mother was thought of as 'the crazy woman,' Father Tollinare had chosen her anyway among other little girls. Still, whenever she saw me with my copybook she behaved around me shyly, as if what I was doing was something very strange.

'Your grandmother speaks and writes Arabic,' she said now, as she watched Father Tollinare parading the ground with the dark-suited young man, whose Portuguese name was Alejandro but whose Tupi name my mother couldn't remember and confessed that perhaps he himself had forgotten it if he had ever known it as a boy. 'But she would let none of *them* know. And me, she'd laugh at me when I'd read out of their books. She'd laugh and then recite long poems in Arabic. Odes, she'd call them. Qasidas. She'd sing of dark-eyed and dark-lipped people, just like us. And she'd make fun of Father Tollinare always having us pray a lot, always on our knees. She'd pound her own knees with laughter. Yet, I remember as a child she'd always pray a lot, on her own knees, and recite that strange language she refused to teach me. And *her* copybooks full of those strange scribblings; she keeps them hidden. Qasidas. I remember that thought, like my own name. She'd eat sprigs of wild onion and sing of Amru al-Qays and Labid and Tarafah.'

I said nothing. For some reason, I thought of the woman, Captain Goncalo's wife riding off in the wagon and looking haughty when they left Entralgo's plantation, looking as haughty as a branca. I imagined her with scrolls around her neck and waist instead of jewels. I imagined her hiding her scrolls in secret places, even keeping them from her husband, Captain Goncalo.

Alejandro was silent while Father Tollinare spoke loudly and with his hands. He seemed very proud of the young man and wanted to show him off. I felt eager to go for the lesson that day, thinking I'd catch a closer glimpse of the young man. And I did, for as I entered, Father Tollinare had him sitting in the front of the room, in a cane chair up beside his desk. He never spoke, but I was sure that Father Tollinare had him sitting up there as an example to us. (Later I found out from Father Tollinare that the young man had asked him who I was, after I'd read my lesson, and although I'd only met him in his silence, it had made me very proud. He was one of those people, like Mexia, whose presence remained with one.)

When class was dismissed, I left with the other children, but went back to the low window to peek at him again. He still sat stiffly, watching Father Tollinare, who made excited gestures. From that angle, in profile he reminded me of one of those still and silent Egyptian pharaohs I'd seen in one of Dr Johann's paintings. He said that it was a reproduction of a painting which he'd seen in one of the museums of Europe. I was so drawn to it that he gave it to me, but when Father Tollinare saw me with it he took it from me, declaring Egypt to be an evil world peopled by worshippers of serpents, and that the only paintings I should have were those of the Holy Virgin.

Peeking in at the low window, I could hear clearly what Father Tollinare was saying. He began to tell Alejandro that he had hopes for him with regard to a certain high post in the government. I knew that the brancos were becoming not opposed to having Indians in such high positions now, as in the early days when they considered Indians mere savages and children and though the majority of Indians were still thought mere savages and children, yet some of the brancos now, who referred to themselves as indianists, had even begun to boast of their Indian ancestors, even those with only imaginary ones. The Indian, I once remembered hearing Father Tollinare say, was what distinguished Brazil from the Old World.

Anyway, Father Tollinare began to tell him of a certain Indian, a captain-major who'd had such a grand position, and what had he done? Why, he'd done something unworthy of that honor. He'd been informed that he shouldn't, that under no circumstances, should he marry a certain preto woman, that he shouldn't tarnish his good blood with hers, but what had he done? Why, he'd done so anyway.

One priest had refused to marry them, but they'd found another who would. Some profligate. And so, the Indian, the captain-major had been dismissed from that high position in which he might have attained even greater honors.

Now that Alejandro knew that history, he said, he should not commit the same error.

'No, my boy, there are important men here who know of you, quite important men, who know of you and who have been anxious for your return. Yes, my boy.'

Certainly, Father Tollinare explained, he'd first sent him to study abroad because he expected when he returned he would enter the priesthood, but now things were changing, there were more choices, more recognition of an Indian's humanity. And everyone had heard such magnificent accounts of him, his intelligence, his moral virtue.

He'd hoped that Alejandro would by now have forgotten the woman and his affection for her. He himself had seen that affection blossoming and that's partly why he'd sent him away. Even though she has the blood of the Indian, of his own people, there is Negro blood there too, and so she is all preto, or might as well be, and if he were to marry her, why, there'd be no place in the government, no worthy position for him, no position of honor.

He himself, he went on, recognized that she was a real and human woman.

'Yes, Alejandro, as I myself recognized that you are real and human. But I'm not a man of my own century, you see. Even so, I must look realistically at my own century. I must be pragmatic. Why, years ago, I'd have been that priest who'd have not refused to marry them. I'd have been that profligate. But now I'm a pragmatic man and I must look realistically at my own century, and so you should do. Love? Certainly, for a young man of your gifts, Alejandro, a young man who has borne other burdens of your century ... Why, certainly I believe, as any righteous man, that the marriage would not be unworthy before God. But it is before men that we are speaking of now Alejandro. Mexia ...'

When he said her name I almost fell into the window. I caught my balance and listened harder.

'Mexia,' he repeated, 'is a beautiful and not unintelligent woman, and so I can understand your desire, Alejandro, any man's desire for her, I should say, but now I will be that priest who refuses.'

For there were many goods, he explained, many kinds of good, and he wanted the broad good for Alejandro, a position which perhaps no other Indian of his century would obtain. It would be solitary there, like the priesthood. But they had had such remarkable accounts of him.

Alejandro's eyes seemed unchanged throughout the long speech, and he continued to sit stiffly.

Finally, Father Tollinare stood up, stretched himself, and looked as if he would come to the window. I ducked down. He closed the shutters and spoke of the moon being especially bright. Then he must have left, for I heard the door close. Or was it Alejandro who had left? The following day, however, when we came for the lessons, there was no Mexia to be found.

The Dance

WHILE DR JOHANN WAS THERE, Entralgo gathered some of his slaves together and had them dance for him. Two of the men who were musicians were told to play, while two men and two women danced. My mother was known as one of the best dancers, so she was one of the women that Entralgo chose. In those days, as I've said, women often wore dresses that exposed their breasts or they simply wore skirts; the breasts, especially the breasts of a preto or mulatto woman, were not considered shameful. My mother and the other women were dressed in this fashion. The two men wore cotton trousers and white cotton shirts that were tied by a string at the neck and open at the front.

Other people on the plantation were allowed to stop their work and stand around and watch. There was pineapple and cassava to eat, which we were told that Dr Johann had provided for us, as a gift in return for our allowing him to paint us. This seemed an odd expression to me, for none of us had allowed him anything. Yet I partook of the pineapple and cassava along with the others.

When the dancers entered, I noticed Dr Johann's eyes widen when he saw my mother among them. He had that look again, as if she'd done something disrespectful – to him or herself I still didn't know. Then the men and women were dancing, raising their arms into the air, lifting their bare feet. A lot of the children on the sidelines raised their arms, too, as they watched, and so did I. Most of the grownups, though, just stood and simply watched. The dancers were the only ones who were smiling. The men looked as if they were delighted with the dance and with the women. The women had a similar expression; they were delighted and happy with the dance and with the men. But those who stood on the sidelines looked solemn, except for some of the children, who clapped their little hands and laughed.

I continued watching Dr Johann. His eyes kept getting darker and darker. In fact, his whole face seemed darker. He'd brought his canvas and brushes out into the yard, but instead of painting anything, he simply stood there looking. Then after some minutes, he walked toward the dancers. He stood nearest my mother, standing very still. The dancers kept dancing, but there was more tension and uneasiness in their movements, particularly in my mother's, although she tried to maintain her look of ease and abandon. Then Dr Johann stepped closer. I thought he was about to reach out and grab my mother, but Entralgo was beside him now and grabbed his arms, saying nothing. Then he nodded to the overseer, who unfolded his own arms and clapped his hands for the dancers to stop and for the people to get back to their work.

I stood there wondering about what I'd seen. The overseer scowled at me and clapped his hands. I ran to mother. I reached for her hand, but she didn't take hold of mine. I walked beside her back to the hut, my hands at my sides. She bent to enter the low door of the hut and I walked in behind her. Inside she turned to look down at me, then she touched my arm. I stared up at her, then down at the shadow of her arm on my arm.

She started to stay something, but instead she hugged me.

At night as I lay on my hammock, I saw the shadow of a man. It bent to enter the small hut. It went to my mother's hammock and touched her arm. It said it hadn't seen such dances before. It called the dance dissolute, vulgar, unreligious. It didn't want her doing such dances. I knew it was Dr Johann's shadow. He said he didn't want any woman of his to do such dances.

My mother was silent. I strained to look, but it was dark and I couldn't tell how her expression was. I could only see the tilt of her head. She raised up a bit, looking. I wondered if he too wished to see her expression.

'*Your* woman?' she asked. '*Yours*?'

'As long as I'm here, you're mine. When I leave you can go back to being your own.'

She laughed, then she said, 'No woman is her own in this country, Sir.'

He bent toward her. His shadow seemed to cover hers.

'This is a country where neither the women nor their daughters are respected. How is it in your land?'

His shadow left hers and he went out. I closed my eyes and slept. In my dreams, I thought another man had entered. He stood near her in silence, and like Dr Johann had touched her arm.

'You're still true to me, Acaiba?' he asked.

'True?' she repeated, as if that were an impossible question.

'You still believe in me, don't you?'

'Yes,' she whispered.

In my dream, my grandmother was standing in front of me wearing many things on her body – fans, palm branches, the feathers of ducks and peacocks. She was dressed in blue and white and she walked around very slowly and dignified, her head held high.

'Gold means nothing to them,' she said. 'Dignity is their most prized possession.'

Then she began to make the movements of the ocean – soft, gentle waves, then violent ones. She arched her back and made waves of her hips. She was wearing yellow flowers in her hair, and her cheeks and lips were red.

'Have you been to the house of images?' she asked.

She lifted me up from the hammock and carried me about as if I were a feather, then she replaced me.

A man came in carrying pickaxes, hammers, and other tools. He kissed her briefly and they walked out together, laughing.

Fiestas

WHEN DR JOHANN ASKED Father Tollinare to take him to see the dances of two tribes of Indians who were in that territory, my mother and I were permitted to go along with them, as well as two men, who carried their belongings and Dr Johann's canvases, paints, and other art materials.

Father Tollinare and Dr Johann walked in front, then came my mother and I, followed by the two men. We walked on a narrow path through the forest, sometimes in single file. The forest was damp and close and dark, the trees covered with trumpet vines. We walked for several hours before stopping at the edge of a clearing.

We didn't reveal ourselves to the Indians, although we could have, for these were not warriors, and they knew Father Tollinare. As always, here were more women and children than men, and they were all without clothes, and the women had long golden breasts. I stared at the women's breasts and the heavy, bulging muscles in the backs, arms, and legs of the men. The men wore cloths around their private parts, but the women and children wore nothing even there. I stood near Dr Johann as he motioned for his canvasses and charcoal and began to sketch.

Soon I began watching his drawings more than the real people. I watched him sketch the long breasts of one of the women. She was bent forward slightly, carrying a basket across her back, and holding a child's hand. Her hair was long, straight, and black, and her cheekbones very high.

Father Tollinare stood by silently, solemnly. Sometimes I would look at him. He'd watch the Indians first, then watch Dr Johann, then watch the cinnamon trees. Sometimes he'd leave us, go back a ways, then return.

Since Mexia had disappeared, he was mostly silent now.

Dr Johann drew a woman holding a child, another squatting with a baby sucking at her breasts. I wondered if the milk from golden breasts tasted golden. It was mostly the women he drew, but there was one man. In the drawing, the man didn't wear a loincloth. Dr Johann drew his navel and then his heavy private part. I thought that Father Tollinare would say something, even at this, but he didn't.

Then four men came out into the clearing, carrying shields and spears. Dr Johann stepped away from his canvas, looking startled and surprised. Father Tollinare whispered that the dance was beginning. Dr Johann watched as the men danced a pretended fight. He kept watching. I waited for him to sketch them, but he didn't.

When the dance ended, and the men sat down exhausted, it was then I thought Dr Johann would sketch them. But still he did not. Instead, he began to sketch a canoe and a running stream that wasn't even there. After that, the face of one of the women began to appear. Suddenly, she was sitting in the canoe holding her child.

We did not go into their camp. I wondered, though, what they'd have done if he'd showed them drawings of themselves. Would they have been pleased or alarmed?

On the way back through the forest, Dr Johann wondered aloud also what they'd have thought, seeing themselves.

'That you were trying to conjure their spirits,' Father Tollinare said,

66

solemnly. Then he added in the same solemn voice, 'By now they believe it's their destiny to have their spirits conjured.'

Dr Johann said nothing. He scratched his head. I pulled a wild fig from one of the trees and ate it.

At night when we were in our hut, when my mother had finished her laundry and her trip to see Dr Johann, she sat in her hammock and began to tell me of something she remembered vaguely. She said that going to the place of the Indians had made her think of it. There was a long march and she was riding on the shoulders of a man. She was no more than two or three. But that part of the memory was very clear, and the people in the march were not her own people, but the people we'd just seen. They'd allowed my mother and my grandmother to journey with them.

'I don't know what it was all about,' she said, swinging slightly in her hammock. 'I kept feeling that they were protecting us, that it was for our protection that we went along with them. Perhaps we'd just escaped from some place and had gone to them for refuge. It must've been that.'

As she talked, I pictured myself riding on the shoulders of one of the men I'd seen. Riding on his shoulder and eating a wild fig. But we weren't in a long march, not in a column. The line had formed not a column but a circle and so we were walking around in a circle. The people wore masks with sad faces, masks of people, of ducks, of horses, of strange animals I'd not seen before. I didn't know whether they were imaginary, magical animals or real ones. One man had his whole body covered with a cloth made of the bark of a cinnamon tree and he was painted with squares and triangles, but his real face was exposed. The man whose shoulders I was riding on was naked, fully, but I couldn't see his face. They began to walk faster and faster in the circle. The man asked me to hold tighter, because they were trying to protect us, me and 'the crazy woman.'

I held on as tight as I could, till I grew dizzy and let go and tumbled backward to the ground. Then he was bending over me, chanting something that was the repetition of one sound. I felt as if I were the center of a magical ritual but that nothing was demanded of me, except what destiny intended. He sang the same monotonous song again and again and his voice grew higher and higher, till it was octaves higher than any sound I'd ever heard, till it grew too high to hear. The same sound over and over. What the word meant I don't know.

Although he was bending over me, and this is the strange thing, it was still the back of his head that I saw, his straight hair, a feather, a fish-shaped gold ornament, strips of fur. I wondered how he could bend over me, and yet I could not see his full face. His voice grew higher and higher as before, then lower and more solemn. Then lower still. I waited for it to get too low to hear. But then he gave a great shout and lifted his arms in the air. Yet, it was still the back of his head that I saw, and sometimes the side of his face and one high cheekbone, but never did he turn toward me enough for me to see his full features.

Others lifted me onto his shoulders again. Although I'd fallen I had felt no pain. Again we were marching in the circle.

'Somehow I felt it was for our protection that we were with them,' my mother was saying. 'But I can't remember anything. I can't remember how we left them and got to this place. I can't remember anything about our movements in time or place. We were just here.'

She climbed down out of her hammock and went to a corner of the hut. She came back and handed me a bowl of coconut milk. As I drank it I saw myself on the man's shoulders again, marching in the circle. A woman entered the circle, one of the women with long golden breasts, and they moved around her three times. Then someone lifted me from the man's back and placed me into the arms of the man. It was a man I knew. It was Alejandro, the man Father Tollinare had sent to study in Europe, the man who had absconded – it was Father Tollinare's word; I'd overheard him say it to Entralgo – with Mexia.

'You'll have to bear with me, my love,' he was saying to me. 'I'm a silent man, given to few sentences.'

'What are you about, Almeydita? Your daydreams again?'

My mother stood over me. She picked up the bowl that was on the ground beside me. There was coconut milk all over me and my hammock and the ground.

'There's no more,' she said.

Now it was I the woman in the circle, no little girl. Then the silent Alejandro took my hand and brought me into the hut.

When Dr Johann went again to the Indian village, I didn't get to go along with them, but my mother went along with them, and when she returned repeated everything to me. At the village Dr Johann had done more sketches. My mother described one of them to me: a sketch of a man with feathers decorating his body. He was raising a wooden sword and cracking the skull of another man. The strange thing was that nothing like that had occurred while they were at the village. Not even a war dance.

'Tell me something about them,' Dr Johann had asked Entralgo as they headed back.

'They used to eat each other, but they don't anymore. Even those they loved, they'd eat. When the Company of Jesus came, they converted them and changed their ways.' Entralgo laughed and peeked at Father Tollinare and went on talking. 'They're called Tupis. I mean Tapuyas. All they used to do was eat and drink and kill. Now all they do is eat and drink. They don't fight anymore. They only eat Christian things. Now they're very courteous to each other, very loving. If only the Company of Jesus could do that for the rest of us, eh Father? But I bet, I'd swear to it – mustn't I swear? – that there's some amongst them who still remember the taste of human flesh. What do you think, Father?'

Father Tollinare, of course, said nothing. And my mother said that, although he was talking to Father Tollinare, he'd looked at her when he said that last thing, about the taste of human flesh. But she said that she herself had heard differently about the Tapuyas, that they were the enemies of the flesh-eaters and not human flesh-eaters themselves, and that they were always fighting those who ate human flesh.

'In that dance you saw,' explained Entralgo, 'they were only pretending, but in the old days it was real. Look at the wench, looking at me with eyes like a sea cow. I only tell what's true. I don't give false information. Do you still remember the taste of it? I bet if you don't the old woman does.'

My mother had said nothing to this, though she had glanced at Dr Johann who'd turned his back to her, so that she didn't see his face.

When no one was looking, she grabbed at one of the wild figs and chewed it fiercely.

What Is Happening
in Agriculture?

ENTRALGO SENT MY MOTHER AND ME into the field to carry water to the slaves there. Some of them would stop, drink water, then return to the field. Antonia came up to us, and I handed her a gourd to drink from. Her eye was red and swollen. The master, I was sure, had beat her again.

I noticed that a young white man was out in the field, working along with the slaves. However, unlike the others, he'd stop at times to examine the weeds and other plants. I remember I'd seen him before, when I'd gone to the stream on the other side of the cane field to take laundry. I carried a small load on my head. He was stripped to the waist and washing himself, even his armpits. I ducked behind a bush and waited till he'd left the stream, before I came forward to wash my clothes.

Now I asked, 'Who is that white man?'

'Maybe he's not a branco,' said my mother.

'That's Entralgo's son, don't you know,' said Antonia. 'Your master's son, don't you know.'

My mother laughed a cruel laugh.

'Not his son *that* way,' said Antonia. She straightened her shoulders, took a long drink from the gourd, then said, 'That there's his *legitimate* son, his "boy", who went off to study in Paris.'

My mother said nothing. She took the empty gourd from Antonia and scooped more water out from the barrel, then handed it to her.

'Then why does he have him work in the field like a common slave?' she demanded. 'If that's his boy-boy?'

While they talked, I kept staring at the pale boy whose brown, loose hair kept falling into his face. He wore a long-sleeved white shirt that opened at the collar, black trousers, and sandals. Tufts of brown hair peeked out at his collar.

'It's his choice,' said Antonia.

'His choice? What d'you mean by that?'

'He's come to teach his father what's happening in agriculture, new European ideas that'll help his father's crops grow larger and faster. As if they didn't grow large and fast enough.'

I watched the boy. I remembered walking down the long path to the stream and being frightened that he'd reappear again. Hairs in his armpits.

'He'll fail,' said Antonia, decisively.

'Who says that?' my mother asked. 'Why do you say it?'

'He'll fail,' repeated Antonia. She touched her swollen eye. She poured a bit of water in her palm and bathed the eye in it. 'Here he is bringing new European ideas, but is it Europe here? It's not Europe here. It's New World ideas that've got to be brought in here. New World ideas,' said Antonia.

She winked her swollen eye at me. My mother shook her head, saying nothing. Then she scooped the gourd into the barrel for another thirsty slave.

But it turned out to be true what Antonia, the so-called drunkard and thief, had said. Not only were the crops not larger and bigger, but they were smaller and more shriveled up and some did not come at all. After the disappointment, some said the son left and went back to Europe.

Others said Entralgo drove him off, that the son had wanted to say in the New World and keep trying, that he'd learn the right things to apply to Brazilian soils, but the father said no, he wouldn't allow him to experiment with his fields. Go help the farmers in Paris, he said. There're enough poor bugs in Brazil.

Still others said that the later thing couldn't have happened, because they saw Entralgo standing in the yard shaking his son's swollen and bitten hands, hands that were a dry white color and still covered with blood and dust. And so the father had to take them very tenderly.

Those who claimed the latter said that if Entralgo sent his son away, it was done out of love and for his own good.

It was Antonia, however, who said he'd called his son a poor bug, as well. And it's probably true what she said, for after the poor bug left for Europe, she had another swollen eye.

Miss Pepperell
and the Lice Scratcher

ENTRALGO'S DAUGHTER LAID HER HEAD in my lap. Her dark hair flowed to the floor, while I parted it and searched for lice. A strange white woman came into the room. She was whiter than any woman I'd seen so far in that country. She looked as if she was lost, but she kept staring at me.

Entralgo's daughter turned her head to look at her, but said nothing. I combed my fingers through her hair again, but wouldn't look again at the white woman, who was almost as white as rice. I wondered how Entralgo's daughter felt with her head in my lap. The white woman left, then she returned and peeked at us again, then she left.

'Mistress, tell me, who is that woman?' I asked.

'She's from England, from London. An introduction from the queen, no less. Well, one of the queen's retainers, but that's just as good.'

I didn't tell her that I'd never seen a woman so white before.

'Her name's Miss Pepperell, of all things. She's very wealthy and she travels. She's very wealthy, that's all my father needs to know. He said she's from a very old and decadent family in London. I heard him say so. And to her face. But she only laughed and said something about "an excess of traditions". "Not decadent," she said, "but an excess of traditions". I don't know myself what they were talking about. It was some sort of joke, of course. My father fancies jokesters. But my father says she's been to Russia and to Africa and places of that sort and now she's come here.

'She's a writer of some sort. He's never been at all fond of lady writers. He thinks they all write nonsense. But she writes travel stories, and like I said, she's a jokester, and he likes that.' She twisted her head in my lap. 'But I don't want to talk about her. Tell me a story about an enchanted black woman. That's what I want to hear.'

'I don't know any stories about enchanted black women.'

'There used to be stories about enchanted black women. My mother said she was always told stories about enchanted Mooresses. All the time.'

'The only women I know are ordinary,' I said.

She looked disgusted, shook her head rapidly back and forth, put her hand under my knee and pushed hard.

'Maybe she'll put you in her book, you're so uppity,' she said. 'She was looking at you, anyhow. Hush.'

The strange woman, Miss Pepperell, came back into the room, looked at us, at me especially, and left again.

The girl burst out laughing. 'Soon they'll come for you, anyhow,' she said.

'To the Negro asylum?' I asked eagerly.

She said nothing. She picked a louse from her own hair and flicked it on the ground.

'Who for me?' I asked, then not to sound so uppity, I added, 'Mistress, who for me?'

'A man's come here for the cure.'

'The cure?'

She laughed again, jumped up from my lap and ran out. She was wearing nothing but her blouse and bloomers. I waited for her to return, but after a while, my mother came into the room carrying a butcher knife. She grabbed my hair and put the knife to my neck.

It was then that Entralgo and a stranger entered. The stranger looked frightened, but Entralgo's face was hard and expressionless. Then he chuckled. My mother said in an even voice that unless they stopped their plans with me, she'd kill me.

Entralgo looked expressionless again. The stranger, in embarrassment asked, 'You're sure she's a virgin, are you, Sir?'

'Yes,' said Entralgo. 'Yes.' Entralgo started to come near.

'No,' said my mother. 'You'll not take my daughter.'

That was the first time I'd seen my mother behave that way. She was big-boned, but at the same time a very delicate and gentle woman.

'They say that only a virgin can cure this man,' Entralgo stated. 'I want Almeydita.'

He still looked at my mother. The stranger reached down and scratched his genitals as though there were lice there.

'I'll kill mine as surely as you'd kill yours if this were to happen. Would you give your daughter up to such a man?'

The stranger came to Entralgo and whispered something.

Entralgo said to him angrily, 'Who's the slave here?'

The stranger whispered again.

'Who's the slave here?' asked Entralgo.

I could see behind them the girl standing outside the door with her hair flowing, and a look of amusement on her face. When her father turned, she ran.

My mother took the knife from my neck and held my head against her stomach.

'Who's the slave here?' asked Entralgo again. 'Why, we'll see who's the slave here.'

When we returned to the hut, my mother explained to me what had happened. At first she intended not to explain, but I kept asking her. Then she told me that it was believed that the blood of a black virgin would cure men with certain diseases. I thought of all the ways he could get my blood. Then she explained to me about the way in which a virgin's blood is drawn by a man.

I sat on my hammock looking at her, very still, with my eyes wide.

She stopped talking suddenly, then she looked as if there was something she would tell. I kept waiting, but she refused to tell that thing.

'This is why you've not been bothered before now,' she said, looking at me. 'There are gentlemen in this territory who know they can always count on Master Entralgo for such cure.'

That was when she mixed a certain herb and gave it to me to drink. I didn't know what it was for, I simply watched her boil the water, then remove the clay jug. She put a dried root in it and covered it with a banana leaf, then she waited. When the water was very dark, she gave it to me to drink. She watched me until I had drunk it all down.

Miss Pepperell:
Her Travels in Recife and
Other Territories, 1680

Here begins Miss Pepperell's travels and travails in Recife and other territories in the wild country of Brazil, 1680,' read the first page of the notebook.

One of the women who cleaned Miss Pepperell's room after she'd left Entralgo's found a notebook and rather than give it to Master Entralgo to send to Miss Pepperell wherever she might be, had given the book to my mother, knowing that she was literate and also had a daughter who was at Father Tollinare's school. My mother gave the notebook to me because she did not read English. She'd barely learned Portuguese and Latin. But she knew that I not only read Portuguese and Latin, but that Father Tollinare, experimenting with the new generation of students was teaching us our choice of several of the 'vulgar tongues.' Because I'd once overheard Father Tollinare's telling someone how books in English, more than any other language, were often banned by the Holy Office of the Inquisition, I chose to learn that language. In those days, it was strange for a slave to be able to choose anything. So I chose that language readily.

However, it was only years later that I was able to translate the notebook fully.

The entries were not stories, not those 'vices' as the holy fathers called them, but rather thoughts that Miss Pepperell had while staying at Entralgo's and perhaps notes for future articles and letters she'd write and send to the London newspapers.

Under the first title she'd scribbled, but drawn a line through 'Tales of an English woman Abroad,' then she'd written and also drawn a line through 'In the Americas, 1680.' I'll include here a sampling of what the notebook contained, though as I say, it was only years later that I was able to translate it fully as I present it here:

Sometimes it all seems like a fine parade and comedy, even the so-called society here in Brazil. Exaggerated characteristics. But there are people here of great character, as our English men and women.

Sometimes I think, though, that if they were placed on a London street, they'd be seen as mere clowns and jesters. But I wonder, how am I seen? Mr Entralgo entertains me with chocolates and conversation.

Sometimes I can't tell the mulatto serving women from the daughters of the house. They are all a tawny people. I suppose it is because of the intensity of the sun. But it is the same as in New Spain. Often to be 'white' here is merely to consider oneself white, or to be considered so by others. I have embarrassed myself at least several times treating a mulatto woman as if she were a mistress of the house. I must add that the women, all of them, go around in pantaloons and bare feet when they are inside the house. How can one distinguish one class from the other when they are all in pantaloons?

There's been a gentleman visitor here rotten with venereal disease who wants one of the little slave girls. Disgusting. He has got none so far, and is off to another plantation. I must jot down the name of it. Corricao's. A gentleman? Did I call him a gentleman? But I've heard them whisper that even the priests are rotten with it here.

I ride on horseback. This is a country of enchantment. The Indians, at least the ones near here, are not so fearsome as those in some of the countries I have been to. They are a quite handsome people. Golden.

Entralgo sees me talking to a slave man and calls me in. I swear he was a mulatto and I thought he was surely one of the gentlemen residing here, with a letter of introduction. I did intentionally talk to another slave man, though, while Entralgo wasn't looking. I was listening to some of his remedies. There are all sorts of herbs and spices here that seem to have quite useful purposes. I wish I were a better naturalist. Entralgo says that in my country and some other countries that I've been, I may be a gentlewoman, but here such behavior can only be considered the behavior of a whore.

I have lice scratched from my head. I observed it being done. It feels quite pleasurable. So relaxing. Lice is everywhere.

As a woman, I'm shown little respect here. I used to think that peoples who hid their women respected them, but it's not so, at least not here. Or perhaps it's because I'm too much in evidence that they show me little respect. Oh, yes, I should have guessed it. Because I'm not here on the arms of a husband.

I've spoken too freely with one of the servants again and shown her every politeness. It's because of my fascination with that medicine man and she promised to take me to witness one of his purification rituals. But alas, he won't allow me to witness it. Even so, I had to explain to Entralgo that my interest is mainly in something that will go into the newspapers, that I have no personal interest in all of it. Even when I show him my sketch of the man to go along with the article 'My Conversations with a Medicine Man,' he still disapproves. He looks at me as if I'm some new scandal in the world and says I'm not the woman of good family described in my letter of introduction and whose father he remembers dining with in Lisbon.

I tell him that this is the only way that I can finish my collection of sketches on the Indians and Negroes. But he fears I'm a bad influence on his wife and daughters and takes me in hand. He speaks again of my old and decent family, but I know he really thinks it's an old and decadent one. He's as much as told me so. And to my face.

I receive a slap in the face and an accusation. All very scandalous. He concludes I'm a whore, though in the beginning he liked my wit. A whore?

His wife calls me a poor unfortunate woman. A very unsettling scene, and in the presence of Dr Johann, a likable man. He (Entralgo) says he doesn't want a woman here who might be the ruin of his daughter whom he has given every care and attention. So I must abandon my articles on the Indians and the Negro Medicine Man and the Women here. I cannot utter one word in my defense. But my fortitude remains.

I'll return to New Spain and seek sanctuary with the Barbacotes. Is that their name? Or perhaps I should go visit the Corricao plantation first. Titles for articles: A Brief Conversation with a Medicine Man, A Woman of Society in Recife, I Miss the Church of England, Chocolate and Coffee, Notes on Good Behavior in This Country, Some Questions I've Been Asked About England Here and Answers I Have Given, Are There Any Free Negroes Anywhere? My Conversations with an Indian Medicine Woman, What It Means to Be an Ungentlewoman Here, Some Anecdotes, Among Strangers, Strange Men and Women in the Americas.

Sacred River

WHEN WE LEFT THE CIRCLE and went into the hut, he lay me in his hammock. I waited, not knowing what would happen. He began drawing lines on his face – moons and half-moons, many connected squares and lines down his neck. Just above his shoulders he began drawing arrows or what resembled arrows. Then he looked at me solemnly. When he got near me, he held my hands and together we watched the blood flow from my fingers.

My mother lowered her basket to the ground, then she picked up my clothes that had fallen, and placed them back in my tiny basket, and secured it on my head again.

'I don't know what to make of you, Almeydita,' she said. 'When will this spirit stop entering your head? They'll think that you're crazy too. Do you want them to send you to a Negro asylum too?'

I held my hands around the rim of the basket, as we went down to the river.

'For the Indians this is a sacred river,' she said softly. 'But for Entralgo, it's just any river.'

I said nothing. I thought she would tell me what the river meant, but she didn't. *When I got to the water I placed the tips of my fingers in it. He helped me wash the blood from my fingers and the wounds closed instantly. He said now the marriage ceremony had been completed and he kissed me.*

When I finished my laundry I asked my mother if I might go visit Tempo, and she said yes. I raced up the side of the mountain. He did not smile at me as before. He looked at me solemnly as he held on to the bridle of one of the horses. When I saw him look so solemn, I did not run to get onto the horse, but stood very still.

'How are you today, Almeydita?' he asked.

I nodded, then I said I was fine.

'Are you the same today as you were yesterday?'

I said yes. I must have looked at him strangely.

'Don't you want your ride today?' he asked with a smile.

I waited for him to ask the old question, but he didn't.

Again, I stood very still, looking up at him.

'Aren't you going to ask about my mother?' I demanded. 'Don't you want me to tell her anything?'

He said he'd tell her himself. I must've been looking at him strangely again, for he gave me my strange look back. Then I stared down at his riding boots. Finally, I walked down the hill to where my mother was, lifting her basket of laundry onto her head and nodding toward mine.

Mercado

WHERE ARE WE GOING?' I asked, as we got into the same wagon that my grandmother had ridden away in. 'Are we going to the Negro asylum too?'

She said that we were not. She looked expressionless, then solemn. Although there was straw on the floor of the wagon, where we placed our backs was hard. Three silent men also sat in the wagon. They were not from our plantation, but we were all on our way to the same place, wherever it was to be.

'Where are we going?' I pestered her again. She didn't answer.

'You're going to market,' said one of the men.

My mother looked at him but didn't change her expression.

'What would you like?' he asked. 'National or international travel? Would you like to go to North America, little girl? How about Cuba?'

'Russia,' I said. 'Or England.'

My mother looked at me. The man laughed.

'What about back to Africa?' he asked. 'What about back to the Old Country?'

'They don't sell you back there,' I said.

He laughed again. I looked at him closely and then I remembered. I'd seen him once before when my mother had been allowed to go into town with Entralgo's wife who was going to visit her cousin but taking her own servants with her. We'd seen him crossing the street. He was wearing a dark coat and a white ruffled shirt and dark trousers like a white student or licenciado would wear, and he even wore buckled shoes. Though he was wearing only cotton trousers with a rope belt now, I knew it was the same man. Entralgo's wife had laughed when she saw him and so did the black driver. Later, when I asked my mother why they'd laughed at the man, she explained that they always laugh whenever a black man dresses 'out of his color.' It had been the first time I'd seen such a black man, and I'd turned my head all the way around to look at him, but I hadn't laughed.

'Why?' I'd asked.

'I don't know,' she confessed.

'You didn't laugh,' I said.

'No,' she replied.

Entralgo's wife had asked the driver who the silly man was. The driver answered that he was a black schoolteacher in the town. The mistress had laughed again, for on the plantations there was no such thing. She'd never heard of such a thing. The driver explained that he was a tutor to many white students in the town. The mistress laughed again, a deeper laugh, and exclaimed that such an absurdity could happen only in the city, which she considered an immoral place anyhow.

I glanced at my mother, who did not seem to recognize the man. Every now and then, though, as we journeyed, I'd sneak another look at him. He was wearing dark trousers and a plain white shirt, but was as barefooted as any slave.

The wagon stopped in front of a long barn and we were told to go inside. Before we'd left the plantation, they'd taken our garments and given us two wide pieces of cloth. My mother didn't cover her breasts with it, only the lower part of her body. Her breasts were large and firm. I too put my cloth around my waist and knotted it, but it hung below my knees.

The three men sat on the floor of the barn with others who were already there. My mother remained standing and so did I. A strange white man came to the doorway and peeked in at us. I crossed my arms about my chest, as if I were a branca, even though I had no breasts then. I looked at my mother. But, like I said, in those days it was not shameful for a preto woman to show her breasts. I myself had only learned shame while in the casa grande. My mother did not cover her breasts as I had done, although she was the one that the stranger watched, and the only one.

He had dark slick hair like Dr Johann, and I began to wonder whether Dr Johann knew that my mother and I had been taken away to market and whether he himself would come to purchase us. So I imagined it was Dr Johann standing there considering what price he'd give for us, instead of the stranger. In my mind, I questioned him.

'I heard you say that when you left my mother would no longer be your woman. But she's the one who's leaving, who's being sold away, even before you've had your chance to. How do you feel about her now, Sir? How do you look at her now? Is she still your woman?'

He wouldn't answer, although he kept watching my mother as if she were the only one there, or as if there was some power she possessed that drew his eyes to her.

There were straw mats on the floor that the three black men had sat down upon. One was filing his toenails with the edge of a small stone, the other was chewing on a piece of reed he'd picked up from the floor. The third man who looked like the black schoolteacher I'd seen crossing the street in town sat with his knees drawn up, his arms across his knees, his face in his arm, staring at the ground. None of them seemed to know that my mother and I were there. They didn't look at us at all.

It seemed strange that they'd let my mother keep a certain wide hat and long earrings that she was wearing, and that she said a certain man had given to her. I don't know what certain man she meant. If it were Dr Johann I'm sure she'd have said so. But she kept them almost as if they were charmed. I watched her and then I looked at the white man again, who was still watching her. He kept staring at her face, her breasts, her smooth round shoulders. She still didn't look at him, and her eyes seemed vacant. I don't know how long it was that he stood in the doorway, his arms folded. He was wearing a loose white shirt and trousers, but of a fine, well-cut material. I didn't think it was stranger than a kind of hat my mother was wearing, but it was not a slave's hat.

Finally, the man who stood in the doorway left, and then in the evening another man came to get my mother, for she'd been sold. Before she left with him, she put her face against mine. I could feel her soft breasts against my shoulder. I could smell the oil in her hair.

Behind her the stranger reappeared in the door, and the man who'd come for her pulled her away from me. Her eyes remained vacant as though she'd pushed them beyond tears. I stood very still as the water dropped from my eyes. The black man who'd been the teacher and who had his head in his arms looked up at me, then he patted the ground beside him. I went and sat down, but he said nothing to me. He put his hand on my chin and touched the side of my face and wiped the tears away, but still he said nothing.

I sat with him a long time in silence and then I heard something that sounded like, 'They drink the hair of Indians,' but it made no sense and must've been those words you form when you're sleeping. Every now and then the man would reach out and touch my shoulder, but he wouldn't speak to me.

'Where are the new Negroes?' I heard someone call. Others came and stood in the doorway.

'The woman was sold, but the little girl, she's still ...'

'The brutality of existence,' the man whispered, touching my shoulder and leaning toward me.

'The brutality of existence,' he repeated. 'That's what I'll call myself when they ask my name again. Brutalidade da Existencia. I'm no longer Matoso. If they ask you, "Who's this man?" you must tell them, "Brutalidade da Existencia."'

I was the one who was pulled up from the ground. I looked at him as I was going, but his head was on his knees again and he wouldn't look at me.

'Brutalidade da Existencia,' I said, but he wouldn't look up.

I was put into the same wagon I'd been brought here in. As we traveled, I recognized the landscape. It wasn't to a new place I was being taken, but to an old one. I was put into the hut of my mother. I waited to be told what had occurred to me, but no one came, and so I climbed into my hammock and fell asleep.

Virgin of the Stones

I WAS LYING IN THE HAMMOCK when he came back into the hut. He'd washed the lines from his face and neck and had oiled his whole body until it was slick and shining. This time he didn't make my fingers bleed, but climbed into the hammock with me.

'Is this the same girl?'

'Yes, she's the same one.'

82

'And a virgin?'

Something hard and soft and firm scraped against my belly. Then I felt my mother's breasts against my shoulder again.

'What's wrong with the girl?'

'What do you mean?'

He began to curse. I felt him moving between my knees.

'I can't enter her. She won't be entered. It keeps pushing me out. It's like trying to penetrate a stone.'

A finger on my stomach, touching me between my legs. The man cursed again, said the names of holy saints, called on the Virgin of Solitude, then said Entralgo's name.

'What's wrong with her?' he repeated.

He got out of the hammock; it swung heavily. The two shadows of men left the hut. I touched myself between my legs, but felt no stone there.

'I'll have her examined. I'll have the old woman examine her.'

The man cursed again, saying that he'd waited for that one because he'd wanted that one. He'd wanted it to be a pleasure as well as a cure.

But he'd waited long enough.

'I'll have the old woman look at her.'

'Why's it that only a black one can cure such a malady?' he asked.

He cursed again, and then he called the name Corricao. I'd heard that name before, but felt certain it wasn't the name of a saint.

Entralgo was silent, then he said something that I couldn't make out.

'In the condition I am in at the moment ...'

' ... then it is best that you leave.'

In the morning, an old woman whose name I didn't know and who refused to have anyone call her anything, except 'old woman' if it was necessary arrived (and the story was that even when she was young she refused to be called anything at all, except 'woman,' when that was necessary). I was silent when she entered and I was silent too when she spread my legs open and began to touch me.

'Am I going to die?' I asked.

'No, you're not going to die,' she said sternly, although she looked at me as if she knew something that I didn't. Then she left the hut and returned with a bowl and cloth. First she wiped my stomach and then she wiped the parts between my legs carefully again and again.

Entralgo entered while my legs were spread. I tried to close them, but the old woman without a name held them open. Entralgo looked between them as though he were seeing nothing, or something that he'd seen many times. Then he leaned forward as if seeking something.

'What's wrong with her?' he asked. The old woman was silent.

He waited, but didn't press her.

'It's a rare thing,' she said when she was ready to speak. 'I've only seen it once, though I've heard tales of it. Perhaps some have a name for it, but I don't. There's something that has made the muscles here so they won't give.' She touched. 'So they won't give at all. See how they contract tighter when I ... If there's a name for it, I don't know it.'

Entralgo was silent. I tried to shut my legs, thinking that he might try to touch me there too, but the old woman held them open. She cooed at me.

'Does it sound strange to you?' she asked Entralgo.

He kept staring at the place he'd seen many times, and then at the place where he sought something. Finally, he asked, 'When she's a woman, will she grow out of it?'

'I've only seen it once, and heard tales of it. But they say it's a condition that stays with a woman.'

Entralgo said nothing. He got closer to me and touched me himself.

I squirmed, but the old woman held me. When he was satisfied there might be some strange truth in what she was saying, he left. Though before he left, he gave me a look I couldn't read. But it was still the look of someone seeking something.

'He's gone to wash his hands and then he'll go to the chapel,' said the old woman. She wiped me again and then pushed my legs together. 'I've seen this only once,' she said, looking at me closely. 'I've heard tales of it and I've told tales of it. When I tell my tales, I tell them that it's what the gods do to protect certain women whom the devil desires. But I didn't do this. I'm not responsible for this. Who did this? Who gave you the secret plant? Who knows the secret plant but me?'

Vision and the Woman
Without a Name

SHORTLY AFTER MY MOTHER HAD BEEN SOLD, Tempo disappeared from the mountainside along with his saddle horses. Now I took my mother's huge laundry basket down to the stream, except now there was no play, no bounding up the hillside to speak with Tempo, or ride one of his horses.

I carried my laundry down to the stream and squatted beside the old woman without a name. She must've read my thoughts, because she said, 'Tempo no longer keeps his saddle horses on the mountain.'

I nodded.

'Who'll make you race to the sky now?' she asked.

'No one,' I said.

The woman laughed.

I saw a man and woman on the side of the mountain, and the man embraced her. But by now I was used to such daydreams and paid them no mind.

'Did you think they were strangers?' she asked, looking at me askance, as she scrubbed her own laundry. 'Can't you tell when a man and woman have come a long journey together?'

I looked at her. She was a thin dark woman with straight gray hair. Perhaps she was part Tupi, I don't know. I looked back at the side of the mountain. The man and woman were not there. I moved the clothes back and forth in the stream.

'A man has many spirits and so does a woman.'

I said nothing, but now I felt that I was beside my grandmother again, and wondered why they'd not taken this other crazy woman away.

'A madwoman and the daughter of the daughter of a madwoman,' she said, reading my thoughts again.

'Has he followed her? Has Tempo followed my mother to the other plantation?' I asked hurriedly. 'Is that why he's not here? Did he love her dearly and follow her?'

The woman without a name laughed. 'If a man disappears, he must reappear somewhere.'

I rinsed a girl's underclothes. One of Entralgo's daughter's. In my mind I saw Tempo on the side of another mountain and my mother racing to meet him. Then he got on one of his horses, lifted her to the back of it and they rode off.

The old woman looked at me, not askance, but fully. 'Come on and shoulder your burden,' she said. 'It's time to get back.'

She lifted her basket of clothes onto her head. I raised my own. I held my hands on the sides of the basket. She walked with hers sitting freely. Her hair was so straight I wondered how she could balance it. I stared at the muscles in her legs. They were the muscles of a younger woman. As we walked, I kept straightening my basket.

'When you become a woman,' she began.

'What?' I asked.

She didn't answer. We followed the other women and watched the steam rise from trees. When the clothes were dry, we folded them into baskets.

There was one thing that the woman without a name would never mention, and that was when she had come to examine me. She behaved as if it were not a thing that had happened in the world.

Even when I asked her what was Entralgo seeking, she pretended not to know.

Dreams

WHY IS IT THAT YOU HAVE NO NAME?' I asked her.

'Oh, I'm sure that I've got one, but it's unknown to me. But what've you come for?'

She was sitting on the floor of her hut smoking a long pipe. I sat across from her.

'What have you dreamt?' she asked, before I told her why I'd come.

'Three white men in a boat and the other boat had seven black men.'

'The black men had round heads and wore white loincloths. The white men were wearing white hats and white suits. The two boats were close to each other and the men were looking at each other. Then there were two white men sitting at a table and two white men standing. They were dressed in dark suits. Three black men naked, except for cloths around their loins, were standing in front of them, waiting. The black men had marks on their faces, stars and dots. Their faces were solemn. They didn't speak the language of the men they stood in front of. I saw the side of one of the men's faces. His cheeks, his temples, his forehead were painted. When he turned toward me, I saw the marks from his head to the tip of his nose.

'He looked at me without seeing me, and then he turned back to the men at the table. I felt he'd been a man of power somewhere.'

She was silent, then she said, 'Describe them.'

'What?'

'The scars on the man's face.'

'Long slashes, a six-pointed star with dots between the points, a half circle with long slashes inside.'

I made the marks on the ground. She watched but said nothing.

'I'm an old woman who's lost her name and has no memory of such markings,' she said. 'I'm no interpreter of dreams.'

'They told me ...'

'How old are you, Almeydita?'

'Fifteen.'

'An age where you bind your breasts ... But me, I'm no interpreter of dreams. I could sound out your future in your voice, in your eyes, when you are older, read it in the lines of your forehead. But I'm no interpreter of dreams. What do you see now?' she asked, looking at me and holding my chin.

'Nothing?'

'A man touching the side of my face, my hair, my shoulders.'

'I knew it,' she said. 'What is he telling you?'

'He says that I still have the dreams of a slave. That now I'm in that place and I'm free.'

'I knew it. But tell me which place, what place are you in?'

'He says only "that place". I look away from him. I feel as if I've strings on my thighs. No, they're scratches.'

'Like in the Old Country?'

'No, scratches from branches, from walking through the forests, a great distance. He tells me that my mother and my grandmother ...'

'What?'

'I don't understand what he's saying.'

'What do you hear?'

'I don't understand what he's saying.'

'What do you think you understand?'

I say nothing.

'What else does he say?'

'The same thing. He repeats it. That I am in that place and a free woman ... I look at him, study the side of his face, the marks that have been put there. I don't know their meaning. These are not scratches. But scarification. Like you said. Like in the Old Country. I want to know their meaning. I ask him, but he won't tell me.'

'Do you see the white woman, the branca?'

'White woman? Which white woman?'

She waits.

'Yes, I see her. A black man, a big one, brings her into camp.'

'What camp? Are you sure it's a camp?'

'I don't know. It looks like a camp. In this part. But over there, there are houses.'

'Who's she? Who is the woman? Tell me more about her.'

'She's a branca yes, but she's dressed like an African woman. She's wearing an African garment.'

'What else?'

'That's all. The man again, touching my face. What else? I don't know. Ah, yes. A black man and woman in a boat facing each other.'

'Tell me more about the white woman.'

'Only that I see her walking and she has long hair and is wearing an African garment. And there's a tall black man beside her.'

'The one who's touched you?'

'No, another one. A ruler. He seems to be a ruler. His hair is long, it sticks up tall on his head.'

'What else?'

'Nothing else. Yes, there are many palm trees.'

She keeps her hand on my chin. 'Have you entered the dance with the other women?'

'I'm running. I enter the dance with the other women. Young women. I have no breasts.'

'You're a woman and you have no breasts? Already you are binding them.'

She touches the cloth around my bosom and puts her hand on my forehead and jaw.

'I watch their breasts and their round protruding bellies, and the dark between their thighs. I can't explain what I don't have. A man follows me into the dance of the women. A young man. On the outside is a naked old man with a white beard. The women, every one of them but me, must touch the beard of the naked old man. I want to run from the place where the women are dancing, but the man won't let me go. He says he wants to kiss my belly and squeeze my knees. The women shout and dance in a circle.'

'Where've you learned this dance?'

'From the Dutch and the Portuguese, they say.'

'What's the dance for?'

'The sacrifice of women. Women taken prisoner. I run.'

'Are you a woman now?'

'Yes. The man tells me I must leave the new place ... The women dance in a circle, holding a rope to their shoulders and waists. Now I'm a girl again. My mother braids my hair. She pushes her palm into my back.

'I'm frightened. She pushes me into a long room full of men waiting to buy us. "I want to remember my knees riding on his shoulders, my small hands wrapped around his chin," she says. "I want to remember the men with shoulders like birds."'

'What? What are you saying now?'

'"The Indians found us and took us with them on their big march. The white men came, killed the Indian men, took the Indian women. I held my chin against my mother's head. They didn't kill us because we're useful and could be sold for much money. It was the Indians who were no longer of us."'

'You've taken me from the future to the past, my child. Where are you now?'

'At a place where they wear the skin of anteaters and wood piercing their lower lips.'

'You're still here, my child. You are back here now,' she said, rubbing my arms.

I opened my eyes. She told me I would soon be leaving that place, Entralgo's plantation, and taken to a larger place.

'But still one doesn't enter or leave any place easily, or from will,' she said, smoking her long pipe. 'Not when one is a slave.'

She grew very silent, then she reached out and took my arm, in anger. I had never seen such silence before, silence with anger at the core of it.

'So I'm the one you come to when you've dreams to tell,' she said. 'But soon you'll go to another woman. Soon you'll take them elsewhere. Soon you'll take your dreams to a woman who has a name. A name, yes, but a name which is not her own.'

She laughed, then she held her arm up. I stood up and left her hut. When I was outside, she called me from the doorway, 'Almeyda!'

I turned.

But she only wished to say my name, my new name. I was not the little one now, not Almeydita. But Almeyda, the woman.

Madonna with Child

I WAS TAKEN TO A LARGE PLACE with three arches over the doorway. The center arch that ran over the door was narrow and there were two wide arches over the windows, on either side of the narrow door. I didn't notice this until I was sitting. Then I looked up and saw a Madonna with child over the doorway. And there were points of light over the doorway too.

I was afraid to look up at the people. There were many people. A white man stood in the center of the room with his hair in a braid. He wore a tall white hat and a long white coat. He was the only white man in the room. A mulatto sat at a narrow table counting money. He was not dressed as elegantly as the white man, but he had on trousers and a vest. A black woman dressed like a branca and wearing a long white dress and red shawl sat in a chair near the doorway with a basket of fruit in her lap. I heard people say that she was the woman of the white man who was standing.

The rest of us sat on mats on the bare floor. I sat beside a woman holding a baby. I watched her. I watched the baby. And there was a woman standing with her hands on her hips. I followed her eyes to a man painting pictures on the wall. In the picture I see the faces of the people around me. Dr Johann, I wonder. I raise up to peer at him. But even from the back I know it's not Dr Johann. And he'd have his canvases. No crude painting on a wall. But I see the face of the woman standing. When she first entered, I saw anger in her face and then she sat down calmly, to wait with the others.

After a while, I lay on my stomach and watched the baby put his fingers in the woman's mouth. A man entered. The man in the white hat came over to where we were sitting and lifted a young boy, and brought him to the man who inquired his price. He spoke loudly.

'How much?'

He was told a price. 'As much as that, eh?'

He touched the boy's chin and the place in his pants where his genitals were.

'As much as that, eh?' he repeated.

Then he went to the table where the mulatto was counting money.

He handed gold coins to the white man who then gave money to the mulatto. The man who'd purchased him took the boy and left. I rose from my stomach and sat on my knees. I turned and saw my face among the pictures on the wall and the man who'd painted it turning to watch me. No, not Dr Johann at all. A wild, scoundrel's face, but shy eyes.

I don't know how long I sat there. No one spoke. The men and women sat watching each other and saying nothing. Resting on my elbows, I was lying between a certain silent man and woman. Every now and then the baby would look at me with his round quiet eyes. He looked as if he knew everything that was going on.

'I was one of the Ambassadors sent to him from Palmares,' the man said to the woman.

I looked at him intensely, as I'd heard the name of that place.

'There were two other Negroes. I stood behind them. I clasped my hands before me, but I didn't fall on my knees as the men before me did. That's why I wasn't killed, but sold into slavery. Do you think that's why? Me, I think so. Because I didn't fall on my knees, that's why. There was a black man dressed in boots and a long coat, a feather in his cap, serving as interpreter. I don't remember which man was governor then. Perhaps it was de Almeida. I don't know. My memory's gone.'

The woman was silent. She touched the baby's head and continued to look at the man.

'There you'd be a free woman,' he said. 'There I'd have my memory again.'

I looked at his black hair and the wrinkles under his eyes. I couldn't tell his age.

'I want to feel that place in my bosom,' the woman said. She held the baby against her heart. The man looked at her, his eyes larger, solemn.

'I'm not the man to ask. Nhouguge is not the one. My memory's gone. I've only the muscles in my back and arms. My arms reach for cane. They don't reach for a woman anymore. Eh, that would be the place for you, and you'd wear your freedom in your eyes.' He scratched his chin. 'Perhaps I was de Almeida. I don't remember the one who was governor, but the one whose name I don't remember sent me to this place. Perhaps it was de Almeida.'

I put my hands to my ears. The baby began to laugh. The woman looked down at him and kissed his head. The man who'd been painting me came and bent down. No, he was not Dr Johann. Not with his rascal's face, and his eyes weren't so shy up close.

'Come and sit by me,' he asked.

I got up and walked with him over to the mural.

'I want to get the lines of the eyes better,' he said. 'What were they talking about?'

But he was as inquisitive as Dr Johann and he asked a thing instead of demanding it.

'A place called Palmares,' I answered. 'A place where black men and women are free.'

He raised an eyebrow, but said nothing.

'Do you know the place?' I asked him, for I realized now that he was not a dark-skinned branco, but a mulatto.

'It's near the forest of Alagoas,' he said. 'Go into the Mundahu valley and come out again. Do you know the Barriaga mountain range?'

'I don't know those places.'

'Well, maybe they'll search you out,' he said. He looked at me carefully. 'They have spies everywhere. Perhaps one will take note of you.'

I said nothing.

'I am Antalaquituxe,' he said.

It was a Tupi name. Perhaps he was made up of everyone in this New World.

I told him my name was Almeyda.

He said nothing. Up close he did not seem like such a scoundrel. And his eyes were shy again. I sat down on the ground and looked up at him as he drew the mural. He was dressed like the other black men, loose white trousers and a shirt open at the front.

'They look like perfect hieroglyphs,' he said.

'What?'

'Your eyes.'

He put his hand to my chin and turned my face to the side. 'And from the profile you look like bastet.'

I frowned, looking at his long nose and chin. It was only his huge eyes that were really handsome.

'What are you calling me?' I asked meanly.

'Bastet. The Egyptian goddess. The goddess of love and joy. Or would you rather be Oshun, Shango's wife?'

My frown softened, but I still looked at the ugly man with suspicion. I'd heard of the Yorubaland warrior Shango from my grandmother, and though he'd been a brave and generous and loving man, his end had been tragic. I thought of the saints in Father Tollinare's stories, who dreamed and prayed for martyrdom. Their heroic dreams, their dreams of prophecy delighted me, but their dreams of martyrdom frightened me. I thought them silly.

Antalaquituxe painted my eyes larger than they were in reality and my eyes stared out into the room of people.

'Why've the white men made you do this? Paint all of us?' I asked.

'Why's it always the white men?' he asked with anger. 'Why do you think it's the white man's idea?'

I was silent. I looked at him. He looked at me. No, not a scoundrel's face. His expression softened. He continued painting.

'Are you a spy of Palmares?' I asked.

'I'm waiting to be sold the same as you,' he replied.

He drew the dark lines out until they touched my temples.

'I'm just passing the time doing this,' he said. 'Someone will buy you quickly, but this frog-faced man will be here a while.'

I saw a shadow on the mural and turned. The man in the white hat was standing over me. Behind him was a white man waiting to examine me, and to offer a price.

'This is the one that I was told about?' he inquired.

'There've been others who've inquired of her, even Corricao, the breeder, but I've explained to them the situation ...' He winked at the man.

The man waved his hands in the air, looking disgusted. 'I grow cassava, and if she has good hands, that's all I need.'

'Hold out your hands,' said the man in the white hat. I held out my hands.

'It's too bad, because this one is such a beauty.'

The man who grew cassava said nothing as he examined my palms and the backs of my hands.

He didn't even ask my price, but when he was told it, he gave money at the table and I was taken out of that place.

'What is your name?' he asked when we were outside.

'Almeyda,' I told him.

'Like the governor,' he said matter-of-factly.

'Not with an "i", with a "y"', I said.

He looked at me. I'd forgotten that most slaves did not even know how to spell their own names and that it was best that they shouldn't. I looked down at my hands.

'I grow cassava,' he repeated, and climbed onto his horse.

For a moment I thought that he would reach down and pull me up behind him, and I started to lift up my hand, but his horse pranced forward, and I trotted along after.

'I see you are one of Father Tollinare's experiments,' he said quietly. 'I see you will have to learn your proper place in the world.'

Cassava

HE TOOK ME TO A BLACK WOMAN who dressed me in a long skirt and white blouse and tied a white rag around my head. She fixed the blouse so that it hung off my shoulders. Then she stood back and looked at me. She looked at my eyes and my shoulders.

'You're very pretty,' she said.

Then she went to a corner of the small room and took from a box a string of beads with many different colors on them: yellow, red, black, blue, green, turquoise, white. She put them carefully around my neck. They hung down below my waist. She put them around my neck again, so that they doubled. She looked at me.

'There,' she said, smiling.

She was tall with a thin waist and pretty eyes and her white blouse fell lower off her shoulders, showing the tips of her breasts. At that moment she was the woman I wanted to be when I became one.

I looked down at the floor that was not tile but ground packed hard together. I looked back up at her and smiled. She didn't give me shoes as she herself was not wearing any. She touched my shoulder and told me to come with her. I followed her to a barn with a wheel and a hot furnace.

There were rollers connected to the wheel. Standing over a white stone pot were two young women dressed like the woman I'd followed, and there was an old woman in a long dress that did not show her breasts but came high on her shoulders. On the other side, a woman was baking bread over the fire, while a man knelt beside her, feeding coal into the furnace, and shielding his eyes. He was bare to the waist and had only a cloth around his loins. A man in striped pants and vest and a big white hat came to us when we entered. The woman stood looking at him without smiling. He pointed to two men who were sitting on baskets cutting cassava. The woman nodded. Both men were dressed in white loincloths, but one was wearing a feathered hat. The woman took me over to them and sat me down on a basket.

'Watch how they do it,' she instructed.

'She's too young for the knife,' the man with the feathered hat said.

He looked at me with hard eyes. The other men went on cutting.

The woman gave me a bundle of branches and told me to cut the roots from them. She wasn't smiling now; her eyes were very solemn. I thought I'd angered her. I looked down at the ground.

'When they need more hands, they'll show you how to do it,' she said.

'Take her over with the women,' said the man in the feathered hat.

I didn't look at him. I cut the roots from the branches with shaking hands. He shoved a basket in front of me. I put the thick starchy roots in.

'When it is full, give it to me,' he said. I nodded, but didn't look up at him.

When I finally looked up, the woman who'd brought me there was over by the door getting ready to leave. The man in the striped pants touched her bare shoulder and she waited. And they stood talking. I couldn't hear what they were saying. I watched her long back, where the blouse fell from her shoulders almost to her waist. The man with the feathered cap slapped my fingers and pushed my head down.

'Mind what you are doing, girl,' he said. 'Here you will learn.'

The other man looked up at him, but said nothing. I cut roots from the branches. I couldn't keep my fingers still. I didn't see when the woman left. I was afraid to ask when she would return. The man in the striped pants stood with his foot on a basket, watching us work.

I looked back at the man shielding his eyes from the fire, then I looked down at my work.

The Woman Whose Name
She Does Not Know
in the Beginning

WHEN THE LONG DAY WAS OVER, the woman who'd brought me there, came for me. I followed her back to the place I'd first been taken. The house where she lived wasn't a part of the main house; it was some yards in the back of it, behind a clump of trees. It wasn't a hut but a square out-building made of plaster, although its floor was packed dirt like any other hut and its roof was made of thatch. The walls inside were clean and white and smooth and she had a little wooden dressing table and mirror.

Another hammock was strung inside, a multicolored hammock like her own.

'You'll sleep there,' she said, 'until you're used to the place, and then you'll sleep with the other women.'

Her voice didn't seem to have the same kindness as it seemed to have before. Still I liked the straight way she stood, the way she stood with her head very high, as if she'd control of her own life, or took responsibility for it. I didn't think those thoughts in those days, though. I thought merely that she didn't stand like a slave, but like a free woman, like a senhora from the big house.

She went to the dresser and began to brush her hair, then she rubbed an oil into it, and into her face as well. There was the heavy smell of incense and coconut.

Not knowing what to do, I remained standing.

'Go on and sleep,' she said kindly. 'Aren't you tired? You're standing there like you're made of wood. Go on. You won't have long to rest, before I shake you in the morning.'

I watched her oil her shoulders and breasts till they were glistening like her face and hair and bright eyes. Then I climbed into the hammock. My stomach growled and rumbled.

'You're hungry?' she said. 'Didn't they feed you?'

'They gave me some cassava bread.'

She reached under the dresser and came up with a bowlful of dried coconut, which she handed to me. I took a handful.

'Here,' she said, and gave the bowl to me.

I didn't know what to think of her. She moved so easily from a voice and show of kindness to one of anger and impatience, from soft eyes to fierce ones.

'When you're finished, put it on the dressing table. That's imported, from England. I'm going to sleep.'

I started to tell her that I'd seen a woman from England who looked like a ghost with a red mouth and red cheeks, but she'd climbed into her hammock and turned her long back to me.

I finished half of the bowl of dried coconut meat and then tiptoed over to the dressing table. I set it down with a louder noise than I'd expected. I waited for her to complain, but she didn't. I went back and lay down in the hammock, picking little bits of coconut from my teeth.

'If I wasn't here, would you live here alone?' I asked, forgetting that she was a woman I didn't know.

She said nothing to me at first, so that I thought she must be sleeping, then she said, softly, with her back still to me, 'Yes.' Then there was silence. Then she said in an even softer voice, 'Until a new young girl is purchased. First they are taken to Old Vera and then brought to me.'

'Old Vera?'

'The old woman. Weren't you taken to the old woman first? The old woman? The healer? He always takes the new ones there first.'

'No,' I answered.

She said nothing. For a long time there was silence before she said into the silence and not to me, 'Perhaps it's an ailment of spirit, then. Perhaps it's that.'

I didn't know what she meant. 'Do you know of a place called Palmares?' I whispered.

She didn't answer at all.

I turned onto my stomach and soon fell asleep.

'Is that the girl?' I heard someone ask. 'Is that her?'

'One of Father Tollinare's experiments,' said another. 'And hasn't yet learned her proper place in the world.'

I didn't know whether I was asleep or awake. But I fell asleep and I dreamed of Palmares, where one's true place in the world was said to be the same as any free man's or woman's.

Fazendo and the Indian Woman Who Was Not Touched by Mascarenhas

WHEN MY HAMMOCK BEGAN TO MOVE back and forth, I woke. It was morning. The woman was standing over me, her face solemn. She was holding a piece of fruit, what is called the mandacaru. I took it and thanked her. Without a word, she went to the mirror to brush her hair. It was very long and thick.

'Why do you brush your hair so much?' I asked, chewing the mandacaru. Again, I spoke to her as if she were not a stranger.

'Because I've got charms in my hair,' she said with a smile. Her teeth were very white. Her face and shoulders were no longer shiny but very smooth.

I was silent.

'Haven't you heard that?' she asked. 'About charms hidden in the hair?'

I shook my head.

She turned without smiling and said, 'Come on.'

I followed her to the place I'd been the day before, although today it seemed hotter, the heat from the furnace reaching even over where I sat, yards away. I sat down to cut roots, but there weren't any branches. Then I realized how strange it seemed, that branches had been picked as well as the roots. I sat watching the woman speak to the man in striped pants, then she left without saying a word to me. What would I do? I watched the woman at the furnace and the man shielding his eyes. I watched the woman standing over the round pot with her arms deep in cassava paste. Then the man in striped pants came over to me.

'I'm called Mascarenhas,' he declared. I said nothing.

'Do you know what these men are doing?' he asked.

I looked at the two men and the one in the feathered hat looked at me evilly, but continued cutting cassava even when his eyes were raised on mine.

'Yes,' I said, looking back at Mascarenhas.

I didn't feel as shaky as I had the day before. I sat calmly. I tried to keep my eyes expressionless.

'Can you do what they're doing without making your hands bleed?'

'Yes, I can do it,' I boasted and looked evilly at the man in the feathered hat, who returned the evil look, then I turned expressionless eyes to Mascarenhas. I said, 'Yes,' again, but the second time I wouldn't look at the man in the feathered hat.

Mascarenhas handed me a small knife. The man in the feathered hat began to laugh at this, then he was silent. I wouldn't look at him. He shoved a basket of cassava under my feet. I began to cut one without looking up at him. I wouldn't speak to him the next day nor the next, nor would he say a word to me, but when one of my baskets was finished, he'd shove another under my feet.

Three times a day, Indian women would enter carrying bundles of cassava. They were naked to the waist. One of the women I'd see sitting at the door of her hut with a small light-haired baby at her breast.

Whenever this woman would enter, as silent as the other women, Mascarenhas would laugh and say in the woman's presence, 'Me? I did not touch the Indian woman.' She wouldn't look at him and always carried her head down.

I didn't know what this meant, but every day the white man in the striped pants would say that. 'Me? I did not touch the Indian woman.' But I would see her sitting in front of her hut, her straight black hair against her shoulders, the baby sucking at her breast. I never heard her speak a word to anyone, not even to the other Indian women. I didn't realize then how strange it was, but there were no Indian men there, only women. Later I learned that the men refused to live there and were scattered in the forests; and at certain times certain ones would return to their women, and it was in that way children were conceived by them. I didn't know if this was true, because I'd only seen the Indian women there.

Of the Indian woman that Mascarenhas taunted, it was said, 'She has forgotten her language and refuses to learn that of the masters.' But I didn't feel she'd forgotten her own language. I felt that she simply refused to use either her own or that of the masters.

Each day I'd feel the man in the feathered cap looking at me with hard eyes, cutting his own cassava without looking at what he was doing.

After several days, he said, 'I am called Fazendo.' He looked at me coldly.

'I am Almeyda,' I replied, without turning my eyes to him. It was the first time I'd not put the 'ita' on the end.

'Fazendo, she's too young for the knife,' Mascarenhas said laughing. 'I'm afraid she might bleed.'

I looked at no one. I cut the cassava. I looked down at the ground. I carried my basket to the women when I'd finished. I didn't want my shoulders to be seen. I wanted to forget the language I had learned. I went back and sat silently, cutting cassava, until the woman entered and came and touched my shoulder. I started out with her still holding the little knife.

'Give that to me,' Mascarenhas said. 'I've told you always to give that to me.'

I handed him the small knife and followed the woman.

The Wife of Martim Aprigio

I SAT ON THE HAMMOCK and watched her brush her hair.

'Have you ever heard of a place called Palmares?' I dared to ask her again.

She turned and looked at me. She was very still. Her dark eyes looked fierce. Her hair was still swept back from the brushing. I felt afraid of her and yet I waited for her to speak. She began brushing her hair again, and climbed onto the hammock, still brushing it.

'I'm no longer a free woman because of that place,' she said. She stopped brushing and held the brush tightly in her lap.

'I thought women became free because of it,' I said, watching her.

One side of her face remained still, while the other began to move, to twitch, the eye, the jawline.

'No, I'm no longer free because of it. But there are women there who're free as long as they stay there.'

'Did you leave?'

'No. I was never at that place. I was free outside of it. I had my own house. I'd always been free. I was never a slave. Never. That's why even now I can hold my head as high as any woman. I was the wife of Martim Aprigio, a respected man, an engineer, and I was a respected woman, and we didn't always live in this country. After we were married, we lived in Holland for a long time. But after a while, Martim became like a crazy man and said a man wasn't free if he couldn't live anywhere. And so we came back here. But here we had to have papers to show our respectability.

'Martim Aprigio, a man who'd lectured in the Netherlands and Germany and England and France and at Russian courts, and who was even hired for projects by the czar. That Martim Aprigio.

'But here, we always had to show our papers. Me, I got used to it.

'He didn't. The necessary papers and letters of introduction. In a wild country such as this, even noblemen carry letters of introduction. But free papers? No, he wouldn't get used to that.

'And then there was this man we helped, whom we gave food and drink. And it turned out that he was a spy for the escaped slaves at Palmares. They have their own spies, you see, everywhere. I didn't know it. I thought he too was a free man, a friend of my husband's, and I treated him with every kindness. But my husband knew who he was and what he was doing, and that a man could be executed for such a crime and a woman, and a woman captured and sold into slavery and . . .'

She did not go on. During her talk, she'd turned away from me, and it was only the still side of her face that I saw as she resumed her talk.

'He, Martim I mean, never told me how he came to be free and to be educated in foreign countries. He'd never tell me. But me? My mother was what they call "a maker of angels", an abortionist. All sorts of women came to her, even the wives of wealthy and important men. And there were enough of important men's wives. It's a horrible thing. When I was old enough to know what it was that got our freedom, why . . . No, I said nothing. I suppose anything to win one's freedom. But I walked about the house in silence, only silence.' She turned to face me, both of her eyes very wide. 'She stopped it, and began to sell angels. She sold little cakes that they call angels. And one day this black man, unlike any black man I'd ever seen in my whole life . . . He wore a dark suit, but he didn't wear it as some men, as if it didn't belong to him. It was his and his own life was his. I hadn't seen such a man ever, and I still haven't seen any.

'When my mother saw him coming, she'd pushed me up to the counter. I sold him a little angel, and he kept coming back and began to court me. He said he wouldn't be in this country long and wanted to marry me and take me with him. I didn't even know how he'd got to be the way he was, for he never told me, and then when we were in Holland, in Amsterdam, I saw the honor with which the people treated him. And it was not a false honor, not the false honor I saw him sometimes treated with here, when he'd show his letters of introduction. No, it was not a false honor, but real . . .

'He said he would be executed for such a crime. They took him one place and me another . . . But all my life I'd been protected from such evils as that and such evils as I've experienced here in this place. But I won't lower my head from it. I'll walk the same way that I did when I walked in the courtyards of noblemen.'

She straightened her shoulders and began to brush her hair very hard. I stared at her high smooth forehead.

The next day I learned the difference between the sweet cassava and the bitter cassava. Wine was made from the juice of the sweet cassava, and bread from the starchy root. The juice of the bitter cassava was poison and every bit of it must be squeezed and baked out. Cassava branches were cut and then replanted for new cassava plants. If the branch of a cassava plant were cut and the roots were kept in the ground, the cassava root would stay whole and good and could be dug up many years later and eaten. I learned to make war flour by toasting dry cassava. War flour would last for a year, but fresh cassava flour would only last for two days.

Dream of Feathers

THE WIFE OF MARTIM APRIGIO soon sent me to live with the old woman and the rest of the women who worked at the cassava barn. They lived in a very large hut with rows of hammocks. Although they never spoke of her, I felt the distance there seemed between them and this woman who once had been free. I also wondered what it was she did besides provide a place for the new women (I called myself a woman then) to stay.

I only remember her taking me to the cassava barn in the mornings.

And I learned that she was the only black woman who would stand speaking to Mascarenhas. The others met him with silence, although he'd speak to them freely, that is when he didn't think that they were working properly or fast enough. Mascarenhas's skin was a dark red, even though he was a white man, or considered himself to be one. It looked as if it had been baked over the furnace like the cassava bread.

Now I came and went with the rest of the women. It was said to be a large plantation, although it was only a corner of it that I saw, and didn't feel I could roam freely as I had at Entralgo's place. In fact, here I'd not even seen the master and learned that the man who'd purchased me was not the master but a man named Sobrieski, a Polish shoemaker who sometimes acted as the master's agent, and who did most of his business from the master, whose name was Azevedo, but of whom no one ever spoke. No one had ever taken an order from him directly, and he stayed, as far as I could tell, within the thick walls of his mansion and when he ventured outside, he was carried around in a curtained hammock.

Although I'd heard that some masters would have their slaves carry them about, I'd not grown up with that, as Entralgo strolled about his plantation freely, giving orders and punishments, riding his horse through his cane fields and orchards. It was only the women who he kept sheltered, and it was said that he'd whipped one of his daughters almost to death for letting a stranger see her standing at the window. The girl had only been three or four, and it was said that there were still scars on her body, and they said that he would regret it later when it came time for her to marry, for it would lessen her price. At first, I hadn't understood it, when they used the word 'price,' since the daughters of Entralgo were free.

'Who is that pacha?' I asked, the first time I saw the curtained hammock.

A group of women were crowded in the doorway watching. 'Pacha?' asked one of the women. 'That's the master himself.'

'What is his name?'

'Azevedo it is.'

'Has no one ever seen him?'

'The old woman Vera has seen him.'

'The old woman has seen everybody.'

'Yes, even when he comes out into the yard he rides in a covered hammock.'

'I saw his hand once. He was eating grapes and he threw a handful of seeds out from behind the curtain. A very delicate hand too.'

'Does he have a wife and children?' I asked.

'No, Vera says he doesn't,' one of the women said.

I wondered if I'd ever see him. Vera came to the doorway and there was no more talk of Azevedo. I wondered why none of the women were ever with any of the men I'd seen, for on the Entralgo plantation one often saw men and women together. But I'd only seen three men after all. There were the two men who cut cassava, and the one who threw coal into the furnace. I asked one of the women about this. She said nothing at first. In fact, it was many days before she answered my question. We were returning at night from the cassava barn and I was walking alone. She left the other women, came back and walked with me.

'There's something wrong with all the women who work on this part of the plantation,' she whispered.

I said that there was nothing wrong with me and tried to hold my head as high as the wife of Martim Aprigio.

'We're none of us able to have children,' she explained. 'It's either from mutilation or nature or age.'

I was silent, then I looked at her.

'My reason is the first one,' she said solemnly. 'But I won't tell the story. It's a horror and I refuse to tell horrors to anyone. There are enough of those in this wicked world.'

I said nothing. I noticed how small the steps were she took, as we walked behind the other women. She had a very tall and slender body and she stooped to enter the low door of the hut when we arrived there.

As soon as we were inside, she raised herself onto her hammock and closed her eyes.

'Almeydita.'

I'd not been called Almeydita for a very long time. I turned and the old woman Vera was looking at me. 'I hear you've dreams to tell,' she said.

I'd told no one of the dreams and daydreams I used to have. In fact, I'd had no daydreams here.

'I'm the one you come to if you've dreams to tell,' she said, then she climbed into her hammock and slept.

I climbed into my hammock and went to sleep and dreamed.

In the morning, a Sunday, I followed her into a low doorway. There was the smell of wood burning. She said that white men were in the forest making a canoe. I started to say that the smell came from inside the place she'd brought me to, but she looked at me, and I did not speak. She sat on a mat and gently pulled me down beside her.

'Almeydita,' she called the old name again.

I looked at the gray in her hair and the gold rings in her ears. There were small brown specks in her eyes. Her cheekbones were high and her eyes were like almonds. There were wrinkles in the corners of her eyes and on her forehead. She looked at me with her lips pressed together, then she smiled.

'Tell me your dreams,' she said. She was solemn again.

'Is Vera your real name?' I asked.

She raised her eyebrows and made the wrinkles in her forehead deeper.

'And what does the real name of this woman have to do with you?' she asked.

'Because someone told me that your name was not your own.'

'Is anyone's?' she asked.

She felt the upper part of my arm for no reason I could see, except that it was very thin, then she removed her hand.

'And will you refuse to tell me the dream without the name?' she said, and smiled.

'No,' I replied. 'They were wearing feathers on their heads and blowing horns.'

'Who?'

'Black men. Pretos. They came down from the top of the mountain on two sides and they were wearing white trousers and no shirts and their heads were full of feathers. Some had feathers on their hats like the white man and others had bands around their heads and feathers sticking out of their bands. There was so much noise and shouting. Some were beating drums, some were blowing horns, some were playing flutes and trumpets. They had swords and bows and arrows, torches, axes.'

'Were there rifles?'

'No. Not even the white men. The white men had swords too.' I stopped and looked at her. She nodded for me to go on.

'On the top of the hill there was a fence surrounding it made of wood with sharp points. I only saw part of the fence. I couldn't see what it was surrounding. But the men. All these men coming down from both sides of the mountain. They were preparing for a great battle it seemed. The white men were afraid and turned back.'

'What was certain?'

'What do you mean?'

'Which men were certain?'

'I don't know what you mean.'

She didn't explain. She stood and pulled me up.

'As long as you're here, you must tell your dreams to me.'

She had branches on her head and flowers. Flowers and leaves on the branches. A branch on each side of her head. Two bands wrapped around her head to hold the branches, and she was wearing a wide necklace with many colors. She'd grown into a beautiful young woman dressed this way, and there were moons painted between her breasts.

Painted with red paint, red moons facing each other. And her breasts were large. I'd never seen breasts so large. The breasts were large and there was a big space between them that the red moons filled. She wore bracelets on the upper parts of her arms, and there were little branches hanging from the bracelets. These branches had leaves but no flowers.

And her eyes, her eyes were bright and looked as if they were slanted all the way up to the sky.

'You've not forsaken the principles of your religion,' she said.

I didn't understand her. It was dream language that I didn't understand. She took my arm and we sat down on the ground again. She was old Vera again.

'You're a woman,' she said to me softly.

Then she wasn't there and I was sitting in the doorway of a house that wasn't my own. There were red lines on my forehead and cheekbones. I was within myself and outside as well. I was weaving something. A blanket? Yes, I was weaving a blanket with many colors in it. My shoulders were round and not sharp and awkward and angular. My breasts were round. I was wearing a wide necklace and bracelets on my arms. I was wearing earrings and my eyes were painted, dark lines around them. There were two baskets and a big shell for cigarette smoke, but I was not smoking. There was a guitar and a mandolin hanging in the doorway. I looked up at a man who was carrying a sheaf of arrows, a very tall man. We were not talking. I watched him remove his jacket.

'Now you're dreaming the dream of a woman,' she said, an old woman standing in front of me, touching my upper arm.

I said nothing.

'Grandmother,' I whispered. 'Is this the Negro asylum?'

'It is Ituiba,' she said quietly.

'What?' I asked.

'My real name. It is Ituiba,' she said. 'That's my real name, not Vera. Come.'

I followed her outside where there were white men carving a canoe.

It was the morning of the next day and I followed her into the cassava barn. I kept waiting to grow tired, but I felt through the day as if I'd rested the whole night.

An Obsessed Man

ONE DAY I SAW THE COVERED HAMMOCK. Two men carried it tied to a long pole, and there was a heavy rug of some kind slung over it, so that it covered him completely, and I wondered how he breathed, as I could not see the slit on one side. It left from the back of the mansion and traveled down to the little thatched house where I'd first stayed. Then it couldn't have been but five or ten minutes before the hammock came out again. I'd felt faint and Vera had asked Mascarenhas to let me stand in the yard.

When the hammock left the little house, the men who carried it walked a few yards, and then stopped as if someone inside had commanded them to, although I, at a little distance from them, had heard no one. Then the men continued and carried the hammock into the back of the house.

I'd not been back inside for very long when Sobrieski came inside the cassava barn and said something to Mascarenhas. Then it was Mascarenhas who came to me and told me to go with Sobrieski. I handed him my knife and followed the slender and silent Polish shoemaker. It was into the back of the mansion that he took me, and through a long corridor.

The master sat on a hammock. There were ruffles around his collar and ruffles that hung from the sleeves of his dressing gown. Sobrieski left, closing the door. I stood in the center of the room and stared at hands that were as plump as sausages but as delicate as lace. His dark gray eyes were sunken in puffy jaws. He kept staring at me.

'Why do you look at me with your strange eyes?' he asked.

I didn't answer. I was barefoot, and there was still cassava juice on my hands and dress and feet.

'Why do you look at me so strangely with those eyes? Come nearer.'

I walked nearer, but was still not very close to him in the long room. 'Why do you look at me so?'

I was still silent.

'I've not had a woman in this room for a very long time. I'm not a common man, you know. I'm a strange man, an unusual man.'

I still stood watching him.

'I haven't dined with a woman in a long time,' he said.

I kept looking at him, his jaws and fingers uncooked sausages, his eyes hidden in his face. He called out a name that sounded like Pita and one of the men who'd carried his hammock entered and stood very stiffly, waiting for orders.

'Bring ham, coconut milk, sugar loaf, rice, pears, biscuits, wine, ah fish,' he said. 'And tell Sobrieski I want him to fit the woman for a pair of shoes. Sandals. Any other kind will be difficult for her now. Have you ever worn shoes? Didn't Father Tollinare ever put shoes on his little experiments?'

I shook my head.

'Sandals for now,' said Azevedo.

The man nodded and went out. He didn't look at me at all. I remember only the wife of Aprigio had been wearing shoes – sandals. But I'm sure she hadn't been barefoot in the courtyards of noblemen.

'A man should be with a good woman every now and then,' he said.

At first it had been curiosity that made me stare at him so, for I'd thought all masters were as lean and well-proportioned as Entralgo. Now I stared at him in fear.

'Sit down,' he said. 'It's been a long time since I've had a woman to look at me like that. Your eyes are lovely, my dear.'

He pointed to one of the many mats and huge many-colored pillows on the floor of the room. I remained standing.

'I'm not a common man, you know,' he repeated. 'I'm an unusual man. I've kept to myself my whole life until now, not even servants in the house, no servants in the house, not a woman. I cleared all this ground myself, no help none, a man all alone, and planted the first cassava, sugarcane, bananas. No slaves for me. I built this house for myself, no help, by myself, all by myself. I'm not a usual man. You look at me now, eh? Well, I wasn't the same man you're staring at now, my dear, being carried about. No. And hiding from people? Well, they'd have hidden from me. But there was no one here but me then. Nobody. A man alone. I built this house by myself, cleared the forest. You're not looking at a usual man, my dear. Sit down.'

I remained standing.

'I built all these grounds with my own hands.'

He waved his hands in the air. I couldn't imagine him building anything with them.

'You're not looking at the same man,' he said. 'It was only after it was done, after everything was built, that you people came here. It was only after I got to be an old man that I needed servants in the house. And no woman. I didn't need a woman here at all, not even a Tupi, and haven't dined with a good woman in many years.'

Pita entered carrying a long tray which he sat on the floor. He left and came back with another long tray full of all the things that Azevedo had ordered him to bring. Pita left again, and returned with another man.

Together they arranged the long cushions and then lowered Azevedo's hammock to the floor. They placed a mat and pillows for me, but I remained standing. This time Pita looked at me, and looked away.

'Sit down,' Azevedo said to me. Pita glanced at me again.

'Come, my woman,' Azevedo said, waving his hands across the tray of food.

I remained standing. Pita looked at me and kept his eyes on me. I went to the pillows that had been laid for me and sat down across from Azevedo.

'I'm done with you. I don't need anyone else,' Azevedo said, and Pita and the other man left, closing the door.

Azevedo sat looking at me, then he waved his hand across the trays again. 'Take what you want, my dear.'

I took nothing. I still stared at him, at his small gray eyes. He reached down and picked up a piece of smoked fish and held it out to me. He kept holding it out. Although I didn't take it, he wouldn't put it down.

There was something in his face that made me feel as if I should take it, but I couldn't. He still held it out.

'I am not a common man,' he said. 'You're not looking at the man I was then. If you were looking at the man I was then, you'd not refuse me, not even you.'

I suddenly reached out and took it. He smiled and reached down for another piece. He ate it in small quick bites. I held mine in my hand for a long time, and then ate it slowly. He held out other things to me, which I took. I'd never had so much food at one time, though I'd often seen the masters eat like that. Some things on the tray I'd never eaten before, and some things I'd never even seen before. I took what he handed to me until my stomach began to feel strange, and I held it. I wondered how the masters ate like that without their stomachs complaining.

'What's wrong?' he asked.

'I'm not used to eating so much.'

'Mascarenhas doesn't feed you?' he asked.

'Yes, but it's mostly the same things again and again. Cassava bread and cassava pudding.'

He handed me a bowl of coconut milk. 'Here, drink this. It will help,' he said.

I took it and drank and set the bowl back down on the tray. Then I wouldn't speak again. I sat very still and wouldn't speak or look at him. I felt ashamed for eating with him.

'Now you are fed, you would deny me.'

I pretended not to know what he meant. Perhaps I didn't know. I wouldn't look at him. My stomach felt very unsettled, and I held it. I wasn't sure whether it was the shame or the food that unsettled it.

'Look at me. I want to see your lovely eyes.'

I looked at him. He put his hand under his coat and kept looking at me.

'I am not a usual man,' he said slowly. 'Why are you watching me with such eyes? Speak to me. Say something. This isn't an ordinary man that you're looking at. No. I came to this place alone and cleared the land by myself.'

He stared at me with gray eyes deep inside his face. His hand moved back and forth and up and down inside his long coat.

'I came here alone and built this house for myself and alone, see how thick the walls are and how cool it is inside, it's as big and good as any you've seen, alone, with nobody, I cleared and planted, a man alone, ah yes, I didn't need a woman here, no, I didn't need a woman in this place, ah yes, why are you looking at me with such lovely eyes?'

He kept his hand inside his coat and rose up slightly. Then he settled down in the hammock, and seemed to sigh. His gray eyes got wider, and looked at me fully.

'You're like a woman who never moves. You never move and have stopped speaking. Are you of flesh and blood?'

Suddenly, here was a knock at the door and Sobrieski said his name.

Azevedo told him to enter. He came in and bowed to Azevedo, then began, without a word, to measure my feet for sandals. Then he left quickly without a word. He had light-colored flat hair, and was dressed in a white shirt and trousers more like a slave's than a master's, although the first time I'd seen him he'd worn expensive looking clothes, and I'd been certain he was my new master.

'The leatherworker claims he's some kin to me,' Azevedo said with a smirk. 'That we're brothers by a different father but the same woman.' He laughed out loud. 'We're all brothers by the same father. Ha ha ha ha. Aren't we all?' He paused. 'Speak to me.' He waited. 'Is your stomach still unsettled?'

I didn't answer. He'd taken his hand from his coat and wiped it on a cloth. Now he put it back inside. 'Speak to me,' he whispered. His eyes looked pleading. Then he stared out, expressionless. 'You think I'm an ordinary man. But you're looking at what I am now. Ask the old woman, ask Old Vera. Ask her what this man was then and that's what she'll remember, all she'll remember, because I haven't let her get a glimpse of me in years and so that's all she'll remember, because that's all she's seen. Ask her what I'm like, my dear, and she won't speak to you of the man you're looking at, because she's never seen this one.' His hand went back and forth. 'I built it by myself and I kept it, and then her with her slanted eyes, no, not like now, huge almond eyes, and her breasts like sweet cassava. In those days, mind you, I could eat cassava all the time. Old Vera. But it's the same as me. All you see now is the old woman, afraid to show her bosom, but then, in those days she was too handsome, too handsome. I never needed any woman, and then I never needed any other woman.'

I stared at him and started to rise, but he waved his other hand at me while the one inside his coat moved up and down, then back and forth.

'When I first brought her here I had flowers everywhere, everywhere.

'And she'd put them all over. She'd put them all over her body, on her arms, around her ankles, around her head, flowers, banana leaves, cassava branches.'

I looked at him, my eyes wide, for he was describing the woman I had seen.

'She wasn't afraid of her bosom then. Sweet, ripe cassava. She was too handsome. And I was no ordinary man myself then. You look at me now, but you don't remember what she remembers. When I first came here, I worked like a slave myself, a slave and more, cleared my own land, built this house. I went for years without the touch of a woman. No, you're not looking at the same man she remembers.' He stopped moving his hand and stared at me, then he began to move it again. He raised himself up and seemed to stay there, almost floating atop his hammock, his hand still inside his long coat.

'She said that it was I who made cruelty here. That it was I who made it, as if it didn't already exist in the world. I who made it ... There's a code of silence between us now. But she'll know. She'll know that I've been with a good woman. She'll know it. She has her ways of knowing such things.' His whole body seemed to settle again.

He removed his hand from his coat and wiped it on the cloth.

'What did you do?' I asked.

'What?' He spoke quickly.

'What cruelty to her? What did you do to her?'

'Cruelty? Me? What did I do to her? It's what she did to me is more the question.'

He sat and stared at me. He put his hand in his coat, then removed it and wiped it on the cloth again. He looked at me for a very long time. He raised himself up again, in anger, I thought, then he peered at me calmly.

'I brought her bottles of red wine from Europe. I had a gold necklace sent over, a wide gold necklace that had once belonged to an Egyptian princess, or could've belonged to one. She claimed she was Iararaca – is that the name of it? – the great magic serpent, the mystical serpent. She said yes she was one.' He stared at his hand as if it were Iararaca, and then he wiped it on the cloth again. 'I treated her like a lady, but I should've known what she was from the beginning, and what she'd do when she had her chance to do it.'

'What did she do?' I asked.

'Destroy. She tried to destroy everything. All I'd built. Everything.'

'Burn it?' I asked, thinking of my grandmother.

'Burn? What do you mean burn? Did she tell you? Did she betray me in that too? A code of silence we had.'

'No, she didn't tell me.'

'Are you another Iararaca? I won't put up with it.'

I shook my head.

'Burn?' he asked. 'She tried to burn. Burn all the grounds, cotton, sugarcane, cassava, banana trees. And to burn this, to burn this.' I thought he would put his hand in his long coat again, but he waved it in the air. 'She tried to burn this mansion with me inside of it. Burn it while I was right here inside. Burn it to the ground. My cruelty? Ah, and now she's afraid of her own bosom. Why do I tell you all this?' He peered at me. 'Did she send you here? I've not had a woman in this house. Did she send you here?'

'No, you did, Sir. You sent for me.'

'Cruelty? I'm not the one who brought the cruelty. I left her for dead. I walked away from her. But she healed miraculously. Plants she knows, herbs, her magic,' he said with contempt. 'Or maybe she is old great Iararaca. But it wasn't my cruelty, not mine. Did she tell you it was mine?'

I shook my head.

'She healed miraculously, and so we have a code of silence, and the old serpent doesn't enter here. I've watched her grow old, but me, all she remembers is the man bending over her with the machete and what pain she felt, if Iararaca is capable of that. But that's the man she remembers, and I've kept it so. But her. Does Iararaca grow old? I left her for dead, lying against the house she tried to burn, with me inside. But I came out in time and saw what the witch was doing. And we've a code of silence, and she doesn't know of the man you're seeing now. She only remembers that one ... Did she send you here to spy on me?'

'You sent for me, Sir.'

He looked at me and wiped his hand across his chest as if he were slashing with a machete. I've heard of such sexual punishment for women, and my grandmother had said that she'd seen it done, the breasts of an unfortunate woman cut off. It was whispered that Entralgo had once tried to do the same thing to Antonia but that Father Tollinare had forbidden it.

'The man was drunk and angry at someone and the woman got in his way, and so he cut her breasts off. There wasn't any crime she'd done.'

My grandmother had told me that story when my mother was away, because my mother didn't like her to tell me such stories.

'She won't always live in this little world,' my grandmother had replied. 'They're not all Entralgos. There are Corricaos too.'

Yes, that was the first time I'd remembered hearing the name of the slave breeder Corricao. It was said that he bred even his own daughters and the daughters of his daughters, but I'd never seen him. But whenever grandmother told such stories or mentioned the names of such masters as that one, my mother would look at her with anger and had even once said, referring to my grandmother's insanity, 'And maybe she'll not always be sane, but she is now, and I want to keep her that way as long as I can.'

My grandmother had said nothing then. I looked at her and smiled and made her smile too.

'My cruelty?' Azevedo was still asking when I emerged from my reverie. 'It's only that I didn't recognize the serpent in the woman. That was my error. But I won't make that error again.' He flung his hand into the air. 'But she'll see. She'll see I've been with a good woman again. You're not as handsome as her though.'

His head settled against his heavy neck and he fell asleep. I sat there for several hours, it seemed, until he woke and ignoring me asked Pita to go for Sobrieski to take me back.

When I entered the hut, it was the old woman's eyes that stared at me without stopping. Had he been right? Had she made use of me to see him for herself? It was rumored that witches could do that, use the eyes of others to see whatever and whoever they wanted to see. Had I seen everything she'd wanted me to see? Had I heard more than she'd wanted? Thinking she had, had he broken their code of silence?

I kept waiting for her to say something to me, but she never did, except here were times when she would stare at me for a very long time. I wouldn't look at her at those times, and when I did look, my eyes would not go beyond her flat and covered bosom.

New Sandals

THE NEXT MORNING when I came to work, new sandals had been left beside my stool. I left them sitting there and didn't try them on. Fazendo, one of the men who cut cassava, continued to look at me evilly throughout the day. The Indians entered as usual to bring bushels of cassava, and when a certain woman entered, Mascarenhas, as usual, would say, 'Me? I didn't touch the Indian woman' except this time he added, 'Me? I'm not the one. I didn't make a present of new sandals.'

I said nothing, but I felt shame again, although nothing had occurred between the master and myself. I stared ahead of me, and nodded when the woman set the basket of ripe cassava by my feet. This time I looked up at her. Her eyes were not staring blankly as they usually did, she was staring straight at me, her flat long hair hanging down on all sides. I didn't know what to make of her expression, and glanced quickly away from her.

'Me? I didn't touch the Indian woman. You think I'm the one? I didn't make a present of new sandals either.'

I glanced at him expecting him to be looking at me, but he wasn't. He was staring straight ahead, standing in the center of the cassava barn, with a long whip I hadn't as yet seen him use.

I felt Fazendo's eyes on me, but didn't dare look at him. I wondered if the same were true of the men as I'd been told of the women who worked there. There were only three men among us, and the two servants of Azevedo that I'd seen. Azevedo had called me one of Father Tollinare's experiments, but did he have his own cruel experiments?

When the day was over I dropped my little knife beside my basket. I looked at the sandals and started to leave them there. I sensed Fazendo waiting to see what I would do. I lifted them up quickly by the leather straps, not knowing why I'd done so, and left, walking behind the other women.

'Me? I'm not the one . . .'

I imagined his sly eyes on me. Outside, Fazendo's hand slid against my arm. I didn't look at him, although I let him walk beside me.

'Do you stay now with those women?' he asked.

'Yes.'

'You don't know if the shoes fit.'

I looked at him. He wasn't watching me, but looking ahead. I stared at the smooth line of his jaw and his thick hair.

'So you've seen him,' he said. 'So you know what he looks like.'

'I've seen only as much of him as you.'

His eyes narrowed at me. 'He'll send for you again. He'll send for you anytime.'

'There won't be any other time,' I snorted. 'I'll escape and go to Palmares where I'll be a free woman.'

He laughed, but looked at me strangely. 'Who told you about that place? What do you know of that place?'

'No one told me. I'll be a free woman and no one can touch me there.'

He laughed again. 'Oh, there'll be plenty to touch you there, my dear.'

I frowned.

'If I wanted you for myself,' he said, 'why I'd go to Mascarenhas. But you've nothing. You've nothing for a real man.'

'And isn't he real?'

'Who, Mascarenhas? I have my doubts.'

'No, the master.' I pointed to the mansion. 'Isn't he real?'

'You're the one who's seen him. But I have my doubts about that one too.'

Then he stopped walking. I stopped a moment, but seeing he had nothing else to say to me and had meant for me to go on, I continued.

When I got to the door of the women's hut, I looked back and saw him waiting. Then he turned quickly and I entered the long hut. The old woman Vera's eyes were on me as I set the sandals on the ground, and climbed into my hammock. She looked at the sandals as though she would burn them.

The Stranger

A STRANGE WHITE MAN came riding into Azevedo's plantation. He was riding a skinny, pointy-eared horse, and there was an umbrella over his head. Everyone else after looking at him went about their business, but me, I stood and watched the strange skinny man on the skinny horse. The Indian woman who spoke to no one was sitting in her doorway holding the light-haired baby on her lap. The man kept looking around at people. He looked at me. It was Sunday and I too sat outside my hut, weaving and reweaving and reweaving the same basket. He rode straight to the Indian woman and got down from the skinny horse. His own face was very long like the animal's, and sallow. He got down from the horse, folded his umbrella, and knelt in front of her on one knee.

'My mistress, my lady,' he said. 'Don't you appreciate the aspect of a man of good character who would live his whole life in your honor?'

She continued to watch him but said nothing.

'Who would protect you from any danger and just now has traveled a long and treacherous journey to come to you?'

I heard a few suppressed giggles while others went about their business, weaving or carving, or other of their own work they spent the holiday doing. Even Old Xavier, who was known as the wizard and was Old Vera's rival on the plantation (those who were not satisfied with Old Vera's cures would go to Arraial Xavier and vice versa), had brought out his small bottles of tonics and was exchanging one for a bag of ground nuts a broad-shouldered man was handing to him. He too acted as though the stranger were not there, continuing to examine his bottles, to taste samples which could cure everything from maculo (diarrhea), to the 'white man's disease,' and there were some bottles that were for love-sorcery, to cure what Xavier called 'diseases of the heart'; he even boasted of having medicines to cure soul ailments.

Watching Old Xavier, I'd lost the beginning of what the stranger said, but heard only the words 'perpetual adoration' as he continued on his bent knee. Then before he stood he reached for the woman's hand and gently kissed the back of it. She allowed him to, and then returned her hand to hold the baby more securely.

Suddenly, I couldn't tell whether the man was Portuguese or Indian or Negro, and the hat he was wearing didn't allow one to see the texture of his hair. He said nothing else to the woman, but rose in silence, got up on his horse and rode away the same way he'd come. The woman remained sitting as if nothing unusual had happened.

I was the only one who continued to watch her. For a moment, I was uncertain whether this was one of my waking dreams or whether it had actually happened. And I had become afraid to ask questions of the old woman Vera, because she continued to look at me strangely, and had not said one word to me since I'd been sent for by Azevedo. So I kept looking at the Indian woman until the baby pulled at her breasts and began to suck, then I went over to Vera's rival, the old man Xavier, whom I discovered was also the cook for Azevedo, because he spoke Portuguese well and knew something of the Christian religion, which Azevedo expected of his house servants and those who touched his food, no matter what 'sorcery' they used outside or what concoctions they made for others.

I walked up to him and stood there for a long time without speaking.

I'd never spoken to him and was a little afraid. He had a very long neck that looked like a goose's neck. As I stood there, he squatted on the ground and drew my eyes, then he stood up.

'Do you wish to speak to me or to the one who touches the eyes without medicines and heals them? If you wish to speak to me, then you must translate your silence into words. Come on, what is it?'

'I came to ask about that man.'

'Haven't you seen a lunatic before?' He tasted from one of his bottles, squinted his eyes, and tasted again. 'He's a lunatic, that's all.'

'Who is he, where does he come from? I haven't seen him anywhere before or anyone like him.'

'Are you sure of that?' He squinted at me. 'He's a traveling lunatic. You've heard of troubadours, haven't you?'

I nodded.

'Well, he's something like that, except he's a traveling crazy man. Who knows where he's been? But he certainly comes here twelve times a year to make much ado over that woman. Twelve times a year he brings himself into her presence. Don't ask me what it's for. I accept the gifts that've been given me, and sometimes the spirits enter me and I can see the future and the past, but otherwise I'm a rational man. I'll tell you what he thinks he sees in her. He thinks her eyes reflect the universe. Ha.

The universe, mind you. He thinks her right eye's the sun and her left eye's the moon. What do you think of that?'

I watched the woman staring down at the child.

'As for me,' said Xavier, 'I don't see the universe in any woman. And if I did see it, I wouldn't believe my own eyes.' He lifted one of his bottles and smelled it, put a bit on his finger and tasted it. 'Well, I'll say one thing, he's a free man, and that's more than I can say for myself. I'm not Old Vera I'm not, who claims she's free when the soul of one of the gods enters. Me, I'm a rational man.'

He screwed on the top of one of the bottles and handed it to me.

'What's this?' I asked.

'An antidote,' he said. 'I'm a love-sorcerer, am I not? You're the one to decide what it's for and when it will be useful.'

He handed the bottle to me in one hand and held out the other one. I wondered again whether the man had been real or all in my imagination. I knew that if he hadn't appeared I would have never dared to say a word to Old Xavier.

I handed him the basket I had woven and rewoven many times.

I stared at the black liquid in the bottle. It reminded me of what my mother had made from the black root and had given me to drink. I took the bottle and looked again at the Indian woman who sat calmly in the door with her fair-haired baby.

'Maybe he's not crazy,' said Xavier, looking at the woman. 'But me? I haven't seen the universe in any women's eyes and don't intend to.'

I went back and sat in front of the squat, long building, imagining it was myself the lunatic had come and knelt before, seeing the universe in my eyes.

The Hidden Woman

I DON'T KNOW IF IT WAS OLD VERA's machinations (because I had seen Azevedo or had dared to seek out the advice of her rival Old Xavier) or whether it was an idea the master had his own self, but I was rented to a woman in the city, and it was at that time that I realized that I was destined to meet people who were repetitions and variations of my grandmother.

Sometimes when I met them I wondered whether they were indeed my grandmother, capable of doing what they said witches in the Old Country could do, transform themselves. Witches in the Old Country, they said, were capable of all sorts of transformations and transmutations. But I don't know if any of that is true. The woman herself had come for me driving the wagon and wearing a man's trousers, shirt, and hat. At first I hadn't recognized the woman as a woman, for she sat silently in the driver's seat and I on straw in the back of the wagon, although I noticed that there was a certain strangeness to the curve of the man's back. She'd covered her hair with a huge straw hat as I'd seen many wear in that country. As we journeyed into town, she never said a word to me.

We entered the wide gray streets of the city and drove around the back of the little shop. How the woman had rented me from Azevedo I never knew, as he kept himself hidden from strangers as well as most of his servants, and he seemed, as we saw no strangers enter or leave the mansion, to have no friends among the townspeople or other plantation owners in the region. I assume, though, that Sobrieski must have acted as his agent in this as other matters.

At the rear of the shop we stopped and the man, the woman whom I thought was a man then, jumped down. At the time I didn't know that there would be such another scene sometime in my life, but for quite a different purpose from my going to serve someone. I don't mean to jump ahead in my story but only to point to my suspicions of Old Vera's or perhaps even my own grandmother's machinations in this destiny. Nevertheless, the woman, acting as a man, helped me down, but still didn't speak to me, and then she opened the heavy gray door and went into the back room of the shop, which looked to be a shop where women's hats were sold.

The man said, 'Wait here.'

I waited, as the man went into another small room. I remained standing. There was a rosewood table and two hard rosewood benches on either side of it on the left side of a curtained door leading to the front. A very tall dark mahogany chest of drawers which ended only a few inches below the ceiling stood beside the table. There were two rosewood hard chairs against the wall. On the left wall was a slender hammock.

A woman who seemed to be in her early thirties came out, dressed in a plainly cut silk dress. She resembled the man and I thought she must be his sister. She had in her hand the hat he'd been wearing. I thought she must be a special servant to the hatmaker who'd hired me to work for her.

'What does your mistress want me to do?' I inquired.

She began to laugh. Her teeth were very white and her smile made her somewhat pretty, but the solemn expression she returned to me made her a plain-looking dark yellow skinned woman.

I looked at her, my expression a curious frown. I could see no one in the back room, although she'd left the door wide open. There was cloth, straw, feathers scattered about on low gray benches, but I could see no one.

'Where did your brother go?'

She laughed again and then was as quickly solemn. I stared at her, thinking surely this too was a crazy woman.

'He's not my brother. But he appears and disappears when I wish him to. He makes life easier for me sometimes, other times more difficult. But he went for you more easily than I could have, carrying a note from our mistress.'

I caught the funny way she'd said the last thing and kept my curious expression. I arched an eyebrow and stared at the hair about her shoulders, the thick fuzziness of a black woman, the flatness and looseness of a white's combined. I thought of a story I'd heard about a magic man in a lamp.

'How can a real man appear and disappear?' I asked.

'Did I say he was a real man?'

Yes, she was certainly crazy, I thought, for I'd surely seen him with my own eyes, although it was true he'd not spoken one word to me. I wondered whether mulattoes were sent to the Negro asylum or whether they had their own asylum, like the whites. She laughed and pushed her long hair up and put the hat back on. She was the man. I began to laugh.

'So it's your mistress has only one servant and she uses you for a woman and a man,' I said, feeling that I'd caught the joke and I clapped my hands, though softly, afraid the mistress might hear.

She was not delighted at all. She frowned and looked more solemn. She removed the hat and shook her hair out.

'I'm your mistress,' she said. 'I'm your mistress and the man.'

I shook my head. 'No,' I said. 'I don't like such jokes. You're a colored woman. There aren't any colored women mistresses.' Then I was doubtful, as I thought of the strange colored woman I'd seen once before, the captain's wife. Then I added, 'I've never had a colored woman for a mistress.'

'Well, I'm to be,' she said. 'At least until the festival is over.'

I looked down at the hard wooden floor and my bare feet. I still wouldn't wear the sandals, though I'd not thrown them away, keeping them on the floor when I slept and in my hammock during the day, and listening daily to Mascarenhas talk of the gift of sandals he'd not given as well as the flesh and blood gift that had not been his.

'Well, they're having themselves a parade to celebrate their Indian ancestry. Suddenly all the people in this town have got Indian grandmothers and great-grandmothers and so forth and they're celebrating them. Changing their names to Indian names, but it's just their Christian names and their mother's names they're changing, the rascals, for it's their father's name that holds the prestige for them. Do you think they'd change their prestige names?' She asked this question strangely, paused, but didn't look as if she expected me to answer, then went on, 'The only Indian names any of them know are the names for trees and rivers.' She laughed. 'So they're all naming themselves after trees and rivers. And the mayor's declaring it a special holiday, and there'll be parades and dances, and as for me, I've been commissioned to make special hats and headgear for the devils to look just like those Indians wear ... And so that's why I needed extra help.'

My mouth fell open. I'd never heard brancos referred to as devils and rascals before.

'Why didn't you get an Indian woman?' I asked.

'I've got sketches of what I want. I wanted someone who made things, wove baskets and of some ability, and you were the one they sent. Anyway, they kept telling me that their Indian women didn't make good servants.' She tossed her hat into one of the chairs. 'Does it surprise you I'm your mistress and a free colored woman?'

I nodded. 'Does the town know you? Do you fool them too?'

'The town knows me, and I've no problems here. None to speak of. My father was a carpenter and built the church and many of its ornaments. He was a respected man here. Commissioned to build a lot of the better houses.'

'A free colored man?'

'No,' she replied, as if angered that I'd think so. 'A white man, a Portuguese carpenter, and my mother was his slave.' She sounded impatient.

'She was his slave and he freed her and me. There's a lot we have to do. Come on.'

She started into the small room and when I didn't follow her she turned and looked at me meanly.

'Come on, I said. Do you think that because I'm a colored woman I don't have the right to give orders or that I won't punish you if you don't obey them?' She stood with her arms folded, her large eyes narrow.

As she turned again to enter the small room, I followed her.

My first task was to dye all the white hen feathers yellow. The peacock feathers and all the other splendid ones from parrots and macaws I was to leave as they were. I worked at a low bench with bowls of yellow, red, and green dye, while she sat at a high table with parchment spread in front of her on which were certain symbols and designs. I don't know if they had any meaning; most were abstract, although one looked like a running deer. They were designs she had seen, she explained, from Indian art, sculpture, and headdresses.

At first she'd said she'd seen them, and then she clarified that she'd copied them from a Jesuit's library. She explained that she herself had not gone into the library, as that was forbidden, but one of the townsmen had copied it, so I wasn't certain how authentic any of the designs were, whether or not I knew their meanings. Nor it turned out was she.

'I hope the rascal copied this one right,' I heard her mumble.

Mostly I enjoyed my task of dyeing the feathers and of studying the splendid designs in those that nature had painted. When I finished that task she gave me a little brush and wanted me to put certain designs onto bark cloth. She said that it was very simple and I'd be able to do it quite easily. I put a painting on them that looked like circles inside circles and other geometric patterns. Only one pattern looked familiar. It resembled my own eyes that Old Xavier had drawn in the sand.

One of the things she made was a sad mask with many-colored feathers sticking out all around it, the eyes oval and slanting down, the mouth slanting down at the corners and huge round balls for ears. Then there was a hat with feathers sticking out around the bottom edges as if there was hair hanging down. There were square patterns in the hat, some painted red, some white, and all made out of straw. She showed me how to weave the pattern into an egg-shaped basket, turned upside down. I was to make many of these hats and attach feathers to them while she made the more difficult mask, with the round ears and cylindrical nose.

On the paper there were animal heads that we'd begin to do tomorrow, she said. My task then would be simply to paint in the little round eyes.

'It's very easy,' she said.

I nodded and continued to weave the upside down baskets. 'Will there be any real Indians in the parade?' I asked.

'No, of course not. They're all rascals, didn't I tell you? Just those who claim to have an Indian grandmother or great-grandmother here and there. It's not the old days anymore. They all think they've got to celebrate their Indian ancestry instead of condemn it. Even the priest feels it's a good thing.'

A picture of Father Tollinare bending to kiss Mexia's hand flashed into my mind, then he turned into the skinny man on the skinny horse and carrying an umbrella.

'Do you have any Indian blood?' I asked, weaving my hat, while watching her attach feathers to one of the bark-cloth masks she'd made.

'No. Haven't I enough defect of blood?'

I looked at her, but she'd spoken casually and automatically, and her face didn't shift from its solemn expression, as she carefully attached feathers, and wiped the moisture from her forehead and around her nose. She didn't even look up at me, or show a familiar smirk to show that we share some feeling. I kept watching her face. Hadn't she called the brancos rascals? Whose defect of blood?

'Look what you're doing.'

She pulled the work from my hands. Only a bit of it was twisted in the wrong direction, what I'd done in the past few minutes, because I was very used to watching people while I wove. She took the work apart and then threw it back at me.

'Keep your eyes on what you're doing,' she said, a deep frown in her forehead, a line that ran in the middle very deep.

I couldn't read foreheads and tell fortunes in them like my grandmother and Old Vera could, but I felt it had some meaning, and that she must be a woman of some special destiny. The wife of Martim Aprigio had spoken of freedom, but the woman I stared across at was really a free colored woman, and I couldn't help trying to take all of her in, her movements, her turns of phrase.

'Your mother was a slave,' I said suddenly, 'before he made her a free woman?'

She nodded but did not look up at me. 'Did he marry her to make her free?'

I watched the deep line. Finally, she answered, 'No. He declared her a free woman. He declared her and his daughter free. You're a nosey one, eh. He declared us free. I'm his daughter.' She looked at me as if to say that if I didn't know that, then I couldn't remember things from one moment to the next.

I was silent, but there were many questions I wanted to ask her about her father and about her mother and about the town that had accepted her as a free woman, colored and all. We worked a whole day before she got up to bring me victuals – a bowl of cabbage and thick and pasty rice with manioc biscuits. Yes, she brought it to me her own self. She didn't say get me this and that. And she herself ate the same, except she didn't give herself manioc biscuits, she ate wheat bread. And I ate in the small room, while she sat in the middle room. She sat facing me, and though I looked into the room at her a great many times, she didn't look at me once.

When we finished eating, I told her how strange it was that she hadn't asked me to prepare the food for herself and me, since it was I who was her servant and she'd rented me.

She said proudly that she'd only gotten me for one task, to help her with the costumes and that she'd continue to do the rest of her work, for she was a woman of honor.

'It's very difficult for a free woman of color in a town such as this one,' she said, as she settled down to continue her work.

I started to say that this contradicted what she'd said earlier, but I didn't. I waited for her to continue, but she did not. After some moments I heard a bell ring and she went into the front of the shop. I heard low talking, but couldn't make out any of the words.

When she returned she sat down and said bitterly, 'One cannot even dance in the streets with a person of color. My costumes will be in the public procession, but I won't be. Nor did I want to be. I'm mostly a hidden woman, anyway. I'm not a public person. I wouldn't be a public woman, whether I were white or black. A spirit doesn't undergo a change of personality with a change of skin. But to know that I couldn't be even if I chose to. Do you know what I'm saying? There's a free man of color here who's written a play for the public procession. They're making use of his play, but not the man.'

She wore an expression that made her look ugly, twisting her mouth almost to the corner of her face. Seeing her like that made me want to turn away, but I continued to watch her. She looked as if she were wearing a mask.

'It's more difficult for him, because his spirit's not so private as my own. Should I wear gloves and one of these sad masks and join the procession anyway, Almeyda?'

I didn't know she knew my name.

'Should I make a mask for him, and we both go that way?' She waited as if I'd have an answer, but what could I say?

'Even the tooth puller's daughter will dance in the streets next week.' She bowed her head and examined one of the masks. She still wore her own mask. 'But I'm not a dancing woman, nor a public one, and I'd be a hidden woman whether white or black.'

Her expression grew easier, and she took up more bark cloth, and began to create another mask for the people who'd take part in the procession, and who'd changed their names to Indian names for trees and rivers.

I wondered about the man she'd mentioned and what their relationship was, and if they loved each other. When she'd mentioned what they'd do, I saw a masked man and woman dancing along the streets.

We worked for several more hours in silence, then she leaned back in her chair and breathed heavily. She lined up several of the sad-faced masks in front of her on the table, then pushing them away, she put her forehead down on the table.

'Are you married?' I asked.

She raised her head and straightened her shoulders.

'No,' she replied, but the tone of her voice sounded proud, even of that. Then she rose slowly and reaching into a corner, she got a folded hammock. 'Here, hold this end.'

I got up and held it. She tied one end to a hooked post sticking out of the wall, then she took the end I was holding and tied it to the hook sticking out from the other wall. Coming back around the table, she almost stumbled, but reaching out, caught the table. I rushed to catch her, but she'd already braced herself against the table. I stood awkwardly, watching her.

'You sleep in here,' she said, coming around me and standing in the arched doorway between the two rooms.

She seemed suddenly very nervous and almost afraid of me. 'You've done very good work,' she said. 'I probably won't need you for more than a couple of days.'

'Are they paying you for your work?' I asked, not knowing why I asked it.

She frowned. 'No, everyone's contributing. Everyone who has a business is contributing something.'

'How much did I cost?'

'What?'

'To rent me. How much was I?'

'That's none of your concern.'

I pushed myself up into the hammock, still staring at her. 'Don't look at me with such eyes,' she said.

I looked away from her. When I looked again the doorway was empty.

I heard her climb into her own hammock.

I stayed with her for several more days, attaching feathers to the masks she made and painting eyes on animal heads.

'What was he like?' I asked her once.

'Which he?'

'Your father. The carpenter. And your mother too. What kind of woman?' I finally got my questions out.

'And am I to tell you? Am I to tell you that?' She looked at me with narrowed eyes. 'You're such a talkative creature, and nosey too. I don't like talkative creatures with their noses everywhere. If you want to grow to be a good woman, learn to be silent and mind your own business.'

'I usually don't talk very much, but I'm always curious.'

She smiled at me, then she straightened her shoulders. 'But with me, eh? You think because you're looking at your same color, there's no distance between us, and that I'm the same as you and have no right to demand your respectful silence.'

She tied the string of her trousers, then she tied her breasts very tightly, and put on a loose white shirt. She put a cream on her lips that took a slightly berry-color away from them, then she pushed her hair up and put the large white hat on, down across her forehead.

'How do I look?'

'Like a man,' I said glumly.

'But I can't change my voice, there's nothing I can do to change my voice. So I pretend he's mute.'

'Oh.'

'Don't be angry with me. I accept my station the same as I accept my defect of blood.'

I said nothing. But again she'd spoken without changing her expression or looking at me as if we shared some special knowledge.

'I'm no tooth puller's daughter,' she said, looking perfectly like a man, with the hat making a long shadow on her face. 'No, and my father was more than a carpenter. The sculptured figures for the church he made, and many churches in the territory. If he'd stayed in the Old World and hadn't come to the New, he'd have sculptured different art. You'd have seen his work in galleries. I'm no tooth puller's daughter. Don't look at me like that ... You think because we share the same blood ...' She looked at me haughtily from under her straw hat. 'No, don't assume that, and even if I were a white woman I'd be the same one you see here, hidden in these rooms. I'd be the same woman you see standing here now. Don't think we share anything of the spirit because we share the same blood. And don't ask me again of that man and woman either. Don't ask me anything about them, because it's not your place to.'

I followed her outside and climbed into the back of the wagon. When we returned to Azevedo's plantation, Old Xavier was sitting on the ground outside his hut with his bottles arranged in front of him. The woman drove the wagon right up to him.

'Tell Mascarenhas I returned her,' she said in her own woman's voice.

Xavier nodded but said nothing. I climbed out of the wagon, but still stood near them.

'Climb down, Maria,' he said, as if she were someone he'd known a very long time.

She did as she was told and sat on the ground near him. 'Nyanga,' he called her.

He ran his hand along her forehead and the side of her neck and pushed his hand in the air as if he were shaking something away from her. Then he lifted one of the bottles that lay beside him and handed it to her.

'That will relieve the ailment,' he said.

She thanked him and stood up. She looked at me with what seemed to be embarrassment, then she climbed onto the driver's seat and drove away.

I kept staring down at Old Xavier, wondering what it was he'd given her.

'Do you believe it is only bodily ailments that Old Xavier treats?' he inquired. 'Don't you think his territory is also the spirit? Don't you think he treats ailments of the soul?'

I said nothing, because that was the answer I'd given myself, that this time he'd given a remedy for the soul.

Suddenly my legs began to tremble and I fell to the ground in front of him. I felt as though I couldn't move, felt as if I'd been drugged. I saw him placing flowers and beads on the ground in front of me.

'Accept these offerings and take them to your jeweled home in the sea.'

He kept watching me, although I couldn't straighten or stand. I stared into his copper-brown eyes. The sky behind him looked as if it were lit by candles. Then he held large banana leaves and began to rub them all over my face and body.

'Are you an African woman?' he asked.

'I am the granddaughter of an African,' I replied.

'You are the same as any woman except when the spirit of one of the gods enters. But tell me, are you an informer? Are you a spy who has been sent here to ferret out the hiding place of these renegades?'

I answered him as if I knew exactly what he was saying and why and said, 'No.'

'You are not?'

'No.'

'Well, they hung him and put his head on a pole as a warning to the other rebels. That he is no immortal man.'

'Oh, yes, he is immortal, as his soul has come into all of us.'

'Are you a woman alone?'

'Yes, in the beginning. They attacked a small town and then the plantation and declared us free.'

'Were you afraid?'

'Yes, but I trust fear. No one has the right to determine the liberty of others. To make them free or to keep them from freedom.'

'Are you any other woman?'

'I'm Almeyda.'

Then the Indian woman was standing there, rising above me, candles in the sky behind her.

'The whole right side of her face looks swollen. May I lift her up?'

'No.'

'Do you think it's erysipelas?'

'No.'

'May I lift her up?'

'Where?'

'Into my bosom. She sought protection in an Indian village, but the Indians themselves captured her.'

'Was it this one?'

'Perhaps this one.'

'No, they were protecting us,' I said. 'I was riding on his shoulders. His helmet was made of anteater's skin.'

Xavier kept rubbing the banana leaves all over my face and body, and then he lifted cassava branches, scraping them all over me.

'Is it an ailment of the spirit or of the soul?' asked the Indian woman. 'He gave her biscuits and a pair of shoes and so she informed on the hiding place of the rebels.'

'No!' I shouted. 'No!'

Xavier kept scraping the cassava branches up and down my back and thighs, my whole body twisted, my face turned up to him.

'Did you see her in the Holy Week procession?'

'Yes, and they don't allow colored women.'

'It's difficult for a colored woman to live in such a town,' I said.

'Do you trust fear?'

'Yes.'

'Did you make a mask?'

'I put feathers along the edges of them.'

'Did you see the man who came to visit me? He's the godfather of my child.'

'Father?'

'Godfather.'

'Barbacoeba's his name. He came first and stayed with the wife of Martim Aprigio and then he saw me and knelt down and said he'd never seen such a beautiful woman. He didn't know where such beautiful women came from in such a country. Aren't you the enchanted Mooress, your lips tinted with berries, the blue of the sky on your eyelids?'

I couldn't tell if I was the one speaking or the Indian woman. 'Lips tinted with blood?' asked Xavier.

'It's not only my people who've made such sacrifices or have come into strange lands to live off the flesh and blood of others. Oh, it's the gods who rest on the old stone and know everything. I'm a silent woman in the worst country. Why does she look at me with such eyes?'

'Why does she look at us with such eyes?' Xavier repeated. 'Has she come to solve the mystery of this place?'

'Only the gods rest on the stones and know everything. You have said it.'

'Look how her shoes are wide open.'

'I'm not wearing any.'

'Why does she look at us so?'

'Yemanja? Is this the goddess Yemanja?'

'I'm Almeyda. Didn't I say so?'

'Have you shown her how to rise up out of her body? Have you presented her with a supernatural gift?'

'It's only the gods who sit on the stones and know everything.'

He kept rubbing cassava branches on me, till the leaves had broken off, then he lay the naked branches on the ground beside me. My body sore, and blood raised in places.

'Any man can raise blood,' said the Indian woman. 'But have you shown her the other?'

Xavier placed an amulet around my neck, an amulet made of seeds and trumpet shells. He rubbed an oil over my arms and thighs and the wounds healed. What was left, he lifted my head and made me drink. I rose into the sky, floating above the candles. Then when I was back beside them lying on the banana and cassava leaves, they lifted me and carried me into the long hut where the women were and lay me on my hammock. They carried me easily, for I was very light.

'The next time I come I'll come in a form that will please you,' he said, and he bent and kissed my mouth.

Xavier and the Indian woman walked away. I lay there. Then the old woman Vera was standing silent above me. I tried to raise up, but couldn't. Though the scratches on my body were healed, I could still feel the sting of them.

'They say that we're rivals but we're not,' she confided. 'We work together.'

I said nothing.

'He won't keep you very long now,' she said.

'Who?'

She laughed hard.

'Azevedo,' she said. 'Does anyone else make such a decision here?'

I still couldn't move and stared up at her. Then I asked, 'Why won't he keep me?'

'Because he's afraid of what you know, afraid of what you saw, afraid you'll tell me. He's afraid of me knowing it. It's less you than me he fears.'

Her eyes got larger, rounder. She had a habit of widening her eyes at certain times when she spoke to someone. And when she did it, it was like a light, a spark, or a spirit jumped out from them. Now the light jumped out. I shut my eyes to avoid her penetrating stare.

'But didn't you already see?' I asked.

'Yes, I *see*.' I could still feel her above me. 'He thinks I don't see what he's come to, that I don't know. He thinks only he sees this old woman, peeking out of his slit. He thinks I can't see the man that's in that covered hammock. Every way he hides himself from me, but do you think I can't see?'

I wanted to see the eyes of the woman now, but dared not open my eyes to look at her. She began to laugh again, but then grew very silent.

'He thinks you'll repeat what he said of me. Does he fear that? As if I couldn't repeat him word for word and sentence by sentence, nor tell you every rise and fall of his voice. Every rise and fall of his voice. He thinks I didn't see that? He thinks I can't see him now, eh? He's never hidden from this woman. No. I see what you saw with your own eyes that day, and more than you saw. Do you hear me? I see what you saw with your own eyes and more. Strange symbols he'd put on paper and say that was his science. Strange symbols I'd write on the ground, and say that was mine. Should I tell you my story? Should I make my case?'

I opened my eyes and looked at her.

'He says I'm one of the witches they brought from Africa, but I won't claim anything. Should I say I wasn't even there when the fire started?

'Well, I was healing someone, burning coca leaves to rid a young girl of demons, rubbing ash on her eyelids. He claimed he saw me running away from the house. Others claimed they saw me too. But wasn't I there, forcing the young girl to stare into the fire?'

I nodded.

'Telling her she was a new woman, telling her over and over again she was not the same, burning coca leaves, forcing the girl to be a new woman. Wasn't I curing someone?'

I nodded again.

'But he says he saw me and that I leaped into the air and ran as fast as a serpent. And how could I be two places at one time? How could I be curing that girl and destroying him in his house at the same time? Didn't the girl see me? Didn't I force the smoke into her nostrils and paint her eyelids? So I'm one of the witches that came from Africa, eh, but didn't I cure that girl?'

I nodded yet again.

'Didn't I share some of the knowledge of the heavens with her? How, then, can I be two places at one time?'

Did I sleep? I opened my eyes and she was not there but there was the smell of burning coca leaves.

The Shoemaker and the Sadism of the Senhora

DID YOU RENT ME OR BUY ME?' I dared to ask the silent Sobrieski.

He said nothing as we walked across a banana grove toward a long squat building. Near it under palm trees were three slave huts, smaller and not as well constructed as the ones on Azevedo's plantation – though this could not rightly be called a plantation.

'I have only two other slaves,' he said, though it did not seem as if he were speaking to me, but I walked slightly behind him and so could not see his eyes.

'I work hard like a slave myself,' he said.

He certainly dressed like one, I was thinking. I waited for him to go on talking but he said nothing.

As we drew near the buildings, I thought he would point to one of the huts for me to enter, but instead he kept walking and I followed him into the back doorway of the long squat building – that I later learned was both his house and workshop. As soon as we got inside I saw two slaves sitting at a long wooden table covered with straps of leather. Lined along the walls were sandals and high top European shoes. One of the men, who was sewing leather into a cylindrical shape looked up at me. The other, who was pounding leather and had sandals piled up to the side of him, did not. In one corner were piled saddlebags, but I saw only one saddle, a very expensive-looking one among the rows of shoes.

Sobrieski went inside, but I stayed in the doorway. 'Sit down,' he said.

'Capao, show her how to string the sandals,' he said to the man who was pounding leather.

Capao looked at me grimly and stopped what he was doing. I sat down in one of the chairs near him, but not very close. 'Sit here,' Capao said.

I sat closer. Sobrieski left the workshop and disappeared into the next room.

Capao took a flat piece of leather and a long strap. Holes were already in the leather, so I did not have to worry about that.

'Here and here and here,' he said simply, showing me what to do, then tying the end of the strap, and pulling it tightly in his teeth.

'Do you see how to do it?' he asked.

I nodded. He handed the other one to me, then watched as I made his movements, though not so quickly as he did, and finished by pulling the string between my teeth, except that it felt that my teeth also were being pulled, as I was not used to using them in labors.

He laughed.

'What?' I asked.

'You squinch up your face so. You put all your face into it.'

'There,' I said, putting it down.

'Good,' he said, pushing a pile of flat bottoms of different shapes and sizes over to me, and a bundle of straps. 'That is your job now.'

He went back to his pounding and stretching leather.

I did another one. At the end of several, my teeth felt as if they were out of my mouth. I told him so.

He handed me a metal clamp. 'Here, put it in here.' Then he pulled on it.

'Better?' he asked. I nodded.

He went back to his work.

'Am I being rented or did he buy me?' I asked Capao.

'How should I know? I am a slave the same as you. Do you think the master shares his business transactions with me?'

'Well, do you know how long I will be here?'

'Forever? And what business would it be of yours or mine?'

I started to say something, but he rapped the table in front of me.

'He likes silence from his workers. Do you want to get in trouble your first day?'

I said nothing. I pulled one of the flat soles toward me and strung it.

After I had completed those, he tossed them into a corner, and showed me the proper stitching for more intricate looking shoes.

'You learn very quickly,' he said.

I pricked my finger and there was a bloodstain on the leather. I wiped it away on the back of my hand. There were footsteps and then silence.

Sobrieski looked over my shoulder.

'Not so far apart,' he said. He grabbed what I was doing, stitched and returned it.

I stitched again. He said nothing, watched me a while longer, then went into a corner of the workshop, sat at a desk, on which were saddle-bags. He dipped into a bowl and began to rub some kind of oil on them. Every now and then he would get up and stare over my shoulder, but would say nothing. In his corner, he began to cut shapes into huge pieces of leather. The man sitting next to Capao, and who had said nothing the whole time I was there, began to sew buttons into the thick leather.

I felt her before I saw her – a woman holding a baby and standing in the door. I looked back at her and I was the one she was looking at hard. I looked back at the work I was doing, but I still felt her eyes on my back. I pricked my finger again, staining the leather. Capao glanced over at me, but said nothing. He had begun his stitching now, more complicated and intricate than my own. He slid a very black cloth over to me, for me to wipe the leather. The woman still stood in the doorway and then I heard a strange sound. I glanced back and saw that she had undone her blouse and taken one of her breasts out and the baby was sucking on it. She had a strange look on her face as she watched me – for it was me she continued to watch and no one else, as if I were the only one in the room and even her husband was not there. Her hair was a very pale and flimsy brown and I could not tell what her strange expression must mean. None of the men turned to look at her, not even her husband, who continued to cut pieces of leather. After some moments, though probably fewer than it seemed, I turned back to what I was doing. She was very much younger than Sobrieski. She seemed to be in her mid-twenties while he appeared to be in his early forties. I do not know the meaning of the woman's look or the very slight smile that was on her lips – but it was not the kind of smile one takes for kindness or interest, but a very slight though self-conscious smile that made me afraid of her.

Then my fingers were slapped and Sobrieski grabbed the leather from me. He took a pen knife from his pocket and slit the stitches I had made, made several stitches, then tossed the leather sandal back on the table.

I turned and saw the woman, still eyeing me – a deeper smirk. 'Agostinha,' Sobrieski said.

She disappeared from the doorway. We worked again in silence until the woman placed bowls of rice and cassava in front of us and banana leaves to roll the mixture in. Then we stopped and Sobrieski disappeared into the exterior of the house.

'She fears you,' Capao said.

'What?'

'Don't you see the woman is afraid of you,' he said. 'She wonders of what her husband might come to see in you, and so she is afraid.'

I said nothing. Then I said, 'I am afraid of her.'

'For what reason?' he asked.

'The way she was looking at me. I was afraid of her.'

'Then we have two women who are afraid of each other,' Capao said as if he were making a joke.

I stared down into my bowl of rice and cassava. 'I am afraid of that woman,' I said.

Capao sat stroking his forehead and saying nothing. He touched my shoulder. I pulled away from him.

'Aren't you more afraid of the man than you are of the woman?' he asked.

I said nothing, then I said I was not afraid of any man, and he began to laugh.

'How are you doing, Pedro the Third?' he asked the man next to him. Pedro nodded, but said nothing.

'Pedro the Third won't speak to anyone. He stays silent. He thinks that silence will free him.' Capao chuckled.

Pedro the Third took a handful of rice and ate it in glum silence. 'Who knows why he is called Pedro the Third?' Capao said. 'Neither his father nor his father before him has had such a name. Why is he not Pedro the First?'

I looked at Pedro the Third who scraped his fingers with his teeth.

'Do you know why he is in such a state?' Capao asked.

I shook my head no.

'Because he fought against his own kind, that's why. He was in the military, in another territory, and they sent him on expeditions against escaped Negroes. And he captured many, many, and informed on many.'

He waited for me to speak, but I was silent.

'They decorated him for all the niggers he has captured. Ha. Ha, but now he is a slave himself. The niggers captured him and cut out his tongue and put an "f" on his forehead, for fugitive. And that is why you see him in the condition that he's in today.'

Pedro the Third did not look at either one of us. And there was silence for a very long time. I thought of the evil that the man had done and the evil that had been done to him.

'How do you know all this if he has not spoken?' I asked.

'It was I who put the "f" on my own forehead,' Pedro the Third said. 'I painted "f" on my own forehead.'

Capao began to laugh. I did not like the joke that had been played. 'Are you still afraid of the woman?' Capao said.

'I am afraid of no one,' I said glumly.

When Sobrieski returned, I sewed in silence. When it was time to go outside I followed Capao and Pedro the Third. Sobrieski did not go with us. I had expected that all three of us would have a hut, but Capao and Pedro the Third walked into the same one. I stayed standing outside. When I did not follow them in, Capao came outside.

'What are you doing?'

'Waiting to be told where I'm to sleep.'

'There are three hammocks hanging in this one,' he said, pointing to the one he had just entered. 'There is red meat hanging in that one, and in the other tanned hide. What will it be? Choose as you wish.'

He went back inside. Silently I followed him.

After I had been there a week, the wife of Sobrieski asked her husband why I couldn't do chores for her while the men did chores for him. She could not understand why he had me in there with the men and I was never getting any stitches right; she said why couldn't I help her, with the laundry and the housework and other things that were women's work.

I did not hear her say these things of course but soon it was that in the mornings I would do the things she wanted done, taking the laundry down to the stream, baking cassava bread, polishing the rosewood furniture with coconut oil. She would only speak to me to tell me what thing it was she wanted me to do, and she would always find a great many things, and sometimes I felt that she was putting clean clothes in with the dirty ones. In the afternoon my hands would be shaking from the work she had demanded. Then there were more occasions where Sobrieski would slap my fingers, and she would stand in the doorway smirking with the baby sucking at her breast. But again in the day, I would say nothing to her and she would say nothing to me except to make her orders of my chores for the morning.

Once when I was down at the stream washing clothes I heard footsteps and here she was, coming toward me and carrying a basket. I thought she was bringing more work but she set the basket down away from me, upstream, but I could see the top of the baby's head and hear his sleeping noises. She stood there beside the baby, away from me, and not saying anything, looking out into the clear water as if she were contemplating something.

Then she began slowly to undress, first taking off her top garments, so that her large breasts dropped out, then she took off the rest of her clothes. She swam, she played, she bathed. I continued to wash the clothes, the dirty ones and what looked like clean garments. Then she was suddenly up there beside me, her light hair out about her shoulders, her white shoulders and breasts out of the water.

'Almeyda, it's nice in here,' she said. 'Why don't you take your clothes off and join me. There's room enough for two women.'

I did not know why she said the last thing she did the way she said it. 'This is how I used to see the Indian women bathing,' she said, 'looking like enchanted Moors.'

'Come and get in,' she said, looking at me now with hard eyes. 'It's so comfortable. One feels as if one's whole spirit is being healed.'

She stayed in front of me, till I could no longer scrub clothes.

'I'll bet you'd look just like them, just like an enchanted Moorish woman,' she said. 'I bet you'd look just like them. Come and get in the water. Do you want me to pull you in? Do you want me to tell my husband that you won't behave? Do you want him to beat you?'

Slowly I began to take my clothes off as she watched me.

'You look just like them,' she said, as I stepped into the water. She kept her eyes on me. 'You look like an enchanted Moorish woman like in the storybook. Except your hair's not long, except your hair's so awfully short.'

Her own hair was floating on the water now.

'I always wanted black hair,' she said. 'Like the woman in the storybook. But my husband likes my hair, he does. I'm not a Polish woman. I'm a full-blooded Portuguese woman,' she said proudly.

I said nothing. I had not gone far into the water, but stayed with my back against the bank.

'Doesn't it feel as if your spirit is being healed?' she asked.

I did not answer. Again she played, and swam, and sprinkled water on her breasts and arms. Then she was in front of me again and turned her back to me and sat in the water.

'I've got lice in my hair. I think there's lice in my hair,' she said. I put my fingers to her loose hair and searched for lice.

Then I felt a sharp stone graze my thigh. I reached down and grabbed my thigh as she sprang from the water and the water reddened. I turned to see her tossing her clothes into the basket with the baby and running into the forest, disappearing. Still holding my thigh I climbed further down into the water, and sat against the bank. I washed the leg. It was a long but not a very deep cut. I tore some of the linen and wrapped it. I put on my clothes and rinsed the few pieces that were left. I started to throw the torn undergarment into the stream, but instead put it back in the basket. Near the house, I flung everything onto low branches to dry in the sun and wind.

When I finished I walked into the hut but not knowing there was blood on my dress.

'Is it your time?' Capao asked, when Sobrieski was not present.

'What?'

'There's blood stains on your dress. What goes?'

I was silent.

'What goes, woman?'

'I cut myself on a stone,' I said. 'When I was down at the stream. I fell against a stone.'

'Where?' he asked, frowning.

'Just my thigh. It's not very bad. It doesn't hurt.' He said nothing.

'Did she send you to wash the laundry and her hair?'

'What?'

'I saw the woman coming back with wet hair.'

I said nothing. He looked at me. I looked away.

'I'll make a salve for you to put on it,' he said, and went back to his work. 'Cuts can be dangerous.'

I said nothing, and stitched the leather with shaking fingers.

This time I did not think she would appear but she did, holding the baby against her breasts and watching my back. Had she tried to raise the stone higher? I wondered. Did she know it was only a scratch on my thigh or had she done me some greater harm?

She left the doorway and came back without the baby. Her hair, still damp, was down about her shoulders. She started to brush it.

Her husband did not look back at her. I continued sewing the thick leather.

The next time I was alone with her she held a piece of broken glass.

I was in the kitchen, wringing the moisture out of cassava paste, getting ready to bake it. I felt her and turned and she was holding a piece of broken glass.

'This is a devil of a thing,' she said. 'My husband ordered me a pretty glass vase from Lisbon, and it arrived broken. I thought I'd gotten all of it up. But this is really a devil of a thing. I'm glad the baby didn't crawl onto it. In my own country, glass seems so pretty, but here it just seems a devil of a thing.'

She went to dispose of it, but each day I waited to feel the cut across my face, or the slash in some more secret place, but nothing happened, nor did she come down to the stream again. But each afternoon she would stand in the doorway while her baby sucked at her breast, and after she put him down, she would begin the new thing – brushing her long hair. Had it been her threat to show what she would do to me if given any reason? Yet if she did fear that her husband would take notice of me, it was needless, for he went about his shop as if I were not there, the same way he went about it in her presence, yet she would continue to watch me as if I were the only one in the room, and as if her husband were in some danger of my charms.

Once a day Sobrieski would stand and watch our hands as we worked. If something was done wrong, he would slap the fingers that did it or rap the table. Always, I was the only one who would sometimes put a stitch wrong. And as Capao had said he expected us to observe silence as he himself did when he worked. For Pedro the Third it was no burden, as he neither talked when Sobrieski was there or away. And at night when we lay in our hammocks, he spoke not a word.

But there was one time when Capao drove into the city with Sobrieski to take a wagonload of shoes to be sold in a shop there, and as we continued to work in silence, Pedro the Third said, 'Do you wonder why this man stopped talking?'

'You have told me,' I said. 'That you informed on your own people and captured them.'

'And performed all horrible cruelties against them without once seeing my own face. I was in Portuguese service. They were not my own people. I did not see my own face anywhere among them.'

'Did the white men turn on you and make you a slave after you had served them?'

'No. I made myself a slave.'

'You made yourself?'

'I did not go into the military thinking that it would be fugitive slaves I would be sent after. No. First we were promised our freedom if we would enlist, and what did I think? I imagined exploring all parts of the world unknown, and what if there was danger? It was the places unknown. But what places unknown!' He thumped his head and then his heart. 'Here and here.'

Then again he was silent and continued to go through his days without saying one word to me or to anyone in my hearing.

Mr Iaiyesimi

A BLACK MAN STOOD IN THE DOORWAY, and a woman stood shy behind him. They were both dressed in expensive European clothes. The man was very large with broad shoulders and very dark smooth skin, and the woman's skin was dark and soft and was very delicate looking, but she wouldn't come from behind the man.

Sobrieski did not see them as he sat in the corner, but then he saw them and got up hurriedly.

'Are you ...' he began.

'I am Mr Iaiyesimi.'

He stood stiffly and spoke with dignity. I'd never seen such a man and I thought of the one the wife of Martim Aprigio had spoken of and imagined this was him. It was only years later that I discovered that this was indeed him and that they were not what they seemed, but spies for the rebels. Then, however, I simply stared at them like they were curiosities.

Although Mr Iaiyesimi spoke to Sobrieski, he didn't look at him, but over his shoulder at me.

'Yes, yes,' said Sobrieski. I had never seen him behave so excitedly. He began to make exaggerated motions with his hand.

'Mr Sobrieski?'

'Yes, yes.' He ushered them inside. The woman still lingered behind.

'Come in, Zaria.'

Sobrieski took them over to his desk. Mr Iaiyesimi was carrying a box that he set down on the desk.

'This is not your concern,' Sobrieski said, and we went back to work. 'There are the bark cloth shoes that my company makes. And this is vegetable fiber.'

'You say it holds even in rainy climate?'

'Yes. These I'll leave with you. We've purchased a shop in Porto Calvo, and have taken a house there.'

I felt as if he were looking at me and when I turned he was, as was also the woman, who stood shyly near her husband. I looked down at the work I was doing – embroidery work on a pair of special sandals for a rich woman in Porto Calvo.

'What house have you rented?' asked Sobrieski.

'The house and shop both from a Dutchman named Lantz.'

'Oh, yes. What do you think of our town of Porto Calvo?' Sobrieski spoke to him as if he were a white man.

Mr Iaiyesimi was silent.

'My wife and I, they laughed at us until they found out we were of royal blood in another country and that I'm the owner of much land and many factories and many slaves. Now we're treated with respect suitable to our position. By those who know. Mainly the town's businessmen, of course.'

'Yes, yes,' said Sobrieski.

'But it's of little consequence. I don't think my wife and I will spend very long in this place, to suffer the insults of strangers. But eventually we'll get a white man to manage it, although sometimes it's taken me moments of ponder to decide who is who in this land.'

He looked at me then, although I was certain that I couldn't be mistaken for anything else. Besides him and his wife, though, my skin seemed to take on a lighter shade, but beside Sobrieski's it seemed as dark as anyone's.

'This country is not unlike my own, Sir, as far as the climate goes, and what I hope to do is to introduce certain building materials as well as my shoe manufacturing. Because these Dutch houses are nonsense. But I don't feel it will be accepted. "It's not Africa, Sir," said one of the fellows. "But neither is it Portugal or Holland," I told him. Or better, it's France or England they want to see here. My wife and I come into the city and it's not Mr Iaiyesimi and his wife they see, but buffoons and clowns. And they're surprised at how tender and shy my wife Zaria is.'

'Who is this woman?' he asked, pointing at me.

Sobrieski looked uncomfortable, then he explained that I was one of his servants, one of his slaves.

'In my country, she would be a woman of quality,' said Mr Iaiyesimi.

He continued to look at me, and so did his wife, while Sobrieski stood by with a look of much discomfort.

'So, they see my black face, they think it is the same one they see here,' said Mr Iaiyesimi, still looking at me as if the two men Capao and Pedro the Third were not there. Pedro continued his work in silence.

Capao continued his with a frown.

'Well, she looks fierce and intelligent enough,' said Mr Iaiyesimi, with a deep sigh. Then he turned to his own woman and clasped her shoulder. She still looked at me, but with shy curiosity and not like most women whose husband had spoken of another woman in such a way. 'Well, Zaria, if my plans were not unsettled I would purchase her for you. What would you say to that?'

Zaria nodded. I did not know the meaning of it all then, as Mr Iaiyesimi turned to Sobrieski. 'Mr Sobrieski, it's been a pleasure,' he said, with a slight bow. 'Please let me know your decision about the matter.'

Sobrieski shook his hand and nodded, but now he was looking at them with curiosity and confusion. Mr Iaiyesimi left without explaining anything.

'Get back to work, you,' said Sobrieski.

Men from the Quilombo

As I sat cutting and sewing leather, I thought I heard the scream of a woman. I don't know why, but I pictured the Indian woman with her back on the ground, then I pictured Mr Iaiyesimi's shy and tender wife, Zaria.

Then I saw the man again at the cassava barn shielding his eyes from the fire as he opened the small door to put more wood into the furnace. I saw the tall woman holding cassava bread over the furnace. All the women's arms were white with cassava flour, the white rising past their elbows, their hands sticky and white. I saw Azevedo with his machete. Then everyone looked to the door.

Four black men stood in the doorway, two holding knives, one a sword, one a musket. I was the first to see them. The man holding the musket steadied it at me. I was silent. Then Capao and Pedro saw.

Sobrieski saw and remained at his table, although he looked quickly at the direction his wife might be, but she was not standing here. I wondered how the scene might have been if she'd been standing there with the baby at her breast.

'Who else is here?' demanded the man holding the musket. 'There is a white woman and a baby,' I said.

'Araujo, go see.'

Araujo went into the next room and came back, the woman walking in front of him and holding the baby. She looked frightened, and for the first time did not look at me.

'Do you wish to come freely with us and be free men and a free woman?' the man with the musket asked. 'For if you do not come freely, you'll be slaves wherever you go.'

No one said anything.

'It is to Palmares,' Pedro said knowingly.

The man with the musket said nothing, then he came and took my arm.

'Do you go with me of your own will?' he asked.

'Yes,' I answered.

He told the men to follow if it was their will. Capao stood but Pedro the Third remained sitting.

'Araujo,' said the man, still holding my arm tightly. Araujo put the sword under Pedro's chin.

'Come. And it is not to your freedom that you go.'

The two men had tied Sobrieski and the woman with leather straps and lay the baby on the table on a pile of soles.

We followed them, walking in a column. Two of the Palmares men were in the lead, two others behind us. Araujo held the sword to Pedro's back. As we walked through the dense forest over tangled vines and palm leaves, I kept waiting for signs of blood, but saw none. We marched through the heavy forest, everyone as silent as Pedro.

When we arrived at the place called Palmares, I saw the old woman Vera, and two of the younger women from Azevedo's plantation, one being the wife of Martim Aprigio. It was the old woman Vera who winked at me. When I got close to the old woman, I asked her what happened and why hadn't more come to be free here. She said that Mascarenhas had been killed, and the men who'd not wanted to come they had murdered. After that, I wondered why they hadn't murdered Pedro. She said that Pita had come and the Fazendo had stayed.

'Did they kill Fazendo?' I asked.

'No.'

'You just said they . . .'

'Fazendo said that he wanted to stay with his woman.'

'His woman? What woman?'

'The Indian woman.'

My eyes widened. 'And Azevedo. Is he dead?'

She laughed, then she said, 'I wasn't there, but I'm told that they went through his mansion taking everything they wanted, gold, silver, provisions, arms, and ammunition. All he did was sit in his hammock and watch them. He said nothing, but I'm told that he asked them to finish him and perhaps that's why they didn't, because he asked them to, because it was his will. And when they refused, he asked them to send him Iararaca, send him the mystical serpent, send him that one to stare at him and finish him.'

Her eyes widened, and the light jumped out. The man, Pedro, who'd refused to come was marched off before the rest of us.

'He wasn't killed,' I said to Vera. 'He refused to come and they didn't kill him.'

'Didn't they kill him?' she asked.

We still stood at the entrance where the caltrops and spiked pieces of wood rose up from the ground. They hadn't yet taken us into the village surrounded by palm forests, but we could see the many large and small huts and many comfortable and fine-looking houses, and a large palace where we were told King Zumbi lived. And there were gardens and fields. We stood there for what seemed like hours, the man with the musket standing near us, and another standing on a high rock looking down on us. At the edge of the village was a very high cliff that dropped down. When we entered, they didn't take us very far when we were told to sit down in a circle and we made sort of a camp at the entrance to the village. I tried to breathe in being a free woman, as I was told would happen here, but instead I felt uncertainty and danger, although in the distance I saw only black men and women and a few Indians walking about. I stared at the banana groves.

Food was brought to us by a very tall broad-shouldered woman. She was silent as she walked among us, and she looked at no one as she bent from the shoulder to hand us the dishes of onions, baked fish, rice, cassava bread, fried bananas, coconut, and fresh cow's milk, which I do not remember ever having, and did not like its taste, but drank it as I was very thirsty. I kept staring at the woman who served us with lowered eyes. She was dressed not unlike us, but in the distance there were some men and women dressed in Portuguese and Dutch clothes, some which I later learned were spoils from their raids, while others were from an ordinary and quite regular trade they carried on with certain Pernambucans. This, of course, was not official and was in defiance of the laws and of the government which had resolved to destroy Palmares. Many Pernambucans, I learned, sent their slaves as agents to trade with us or they themselves met with the Palmares agents. These Pernambucans were in that way also protected from our raids.

But I did not know all that then, and it was too early for me to speak of 'us' and 'ours.' I spit out the cow's milk, and grabbed a coconut.

The man with the musket was soon relieved by a man with a bow and arrow. However, he was dressed in a Portuguese military uniform, which made me want to smile, though I kept my face without any expression.

Then I lifted up the coconut and drank.

I thought of Father Tollinare's question years ago about what my true place was in the world.

'Do you think you'll find your spiritual place in this world?'

'Palmares!' I shouted. Then I whispered to the woman beside me, 'Who is that pacha?'

'Pacha? Why that's King Zumbi. That's Zumbi himself. That's Zumbi himself. That's the king of Palmares himself.'

'Don't talk to me of kings,' said another of the women. 'It's freedom I want to hear.'

'Then you've come to the right place,' I said. 'For Palmares and freedom are the same.'

'Come? Come? Come? Did you say?' asked another. 'Why, they dragged me here. Is that what freedom is?'

I lifted up the coconut and drank.

QUILOMBO

Ritual of a Stranger

I THOUGHT WE WOULD BE MADE to sit there through the night, but I heard hoofbeats and raised my head to see a man riding into the village on a horse, sitting very straight and tall, a very broad-shouldered, handsome man. He drew nearer and stopped at our camp, looking down at us, though his eyes caught on me. I felt we were strangers and not strangers, for he seemed to be the same man I had seen many years before, who had stopped and spoken to my grandmother once when we were walking on the road. He sat the same way and his hair was long and bushy and hung down in the same manner. But if he were that man I felt he would have been much older and not simply by the ten years he seemed to have on me. But it was the man, I kept thinking. It was him, and he had looked at me with the same eyes as I was seeing now, though he looked at me as if he were seeing me for the first time. He jumped down and went to the man who was carrying the bow and arrow and dressed like a Portuguese military man.

'These are the new women?' he asked, though I felt unnecessarily.

'Yes.'

'Who is this new woman?' he asked, nodding toward me, but speaking to the guard.

The guard said that he had not yet been informed of the names of the women, nor which were free, nor which were slaves.

My eyes widened. The man stared down at me. 'I am called Almeyda,' I said.

'Like the governor.'

'Not like the governor,' I said. 'I spell it differently. With a "y."'

'You *spell* it differently,' he said. He seemed to be mocking me, but then he asked, 'Do you read and write?'

'Yes,' I said.

'More than your name?'

'Yes.'

'We may have good use for such a woman,' he said to the guard. 'She is free.'

I thought he would go to the other women, but he did not. He climbed back onto his horse and rode into the village. After some time, the woman who had served our camp came to me and bent down.

'Come with me,' she said.

As I rose, Old Vera touched the calf of my leg. I looked back at her, but we did not exchange words. Then I followed the tall woman.

Conversation with a Slave

I FOLLOWED HER TO A SMALL HOUSE that was on the edge of the village. Behind it was a cocoa grove, and behind that more spikes sticking out from the ground. She ducked to enter and I followed her.

The house was small, but with a thatched roof. Inside there was a single room; a very pretty oriental rug on the tiled floor, a hammock; there was a European table and several chairs and someone had hung a picture on one of the walls, of a stream and palm groves. If one looked closely one could see miniature pictures within the picture: some ships, a three-walled house with a man and woman sitting in a hammock, a strange little picture of a cat breaking the neck of a serpent and a tiny crocodile riding the back of an ibis.

I stood in the middle of the room on the rug and felt its softness against my heel.

She remained standing as if she were waiting. I remembered seeing my mother standing that way waiting for Entralgo to speak to her, and I had stood myself that way before Sobrieski. She stood with her eyes slightly lowered, but still on my face.

'Is it true we are free women here?' I asked, not knowing what to say, and uncertain about that matter, though I had been totally certain about it before I arrived here.

'It is true you are a free woman. I am a slave.'

I stared at her. Her eyes were still lowered and she would not look at me directly. I saw her bowing to me again as she placed the food. She was a handsome woman but not pretty and had a broad face, broad in the middle, but tapered at the chin and a high forehead and very high cheekbones.

'Is there anything you would have me do? Is there anything you need?' she asked.

'No.'

I kept looking at her. Though she still didn't look at me, I felt her discomfort.

'Master sent me to take care of you until you know your way around here.'

'Master?' I asked. 'There are no masters here. We are all the same people. We are all free,' I said, though I remembered the man had said Pedro would come as a slave. Then I asked, 'Didn't you come here on your own free will?'

'I didn't know where we were being taken. There were women captured and we were brought here. Some were brought to be free women and others slaves.'

'But they did not ask you if you chose to come?'

'Oh, there was *choice*,' she said. 'There was *choice* when we got here. Those women who were *chosen* by certain men were free. Women like you. They captured me only to be a slave again.'

'You must be wrong. If you are a slave I am one,' I said, though I knew the man on the horse had said I was free.

'No, there is a man who has chosen you. You will not be a slave. The men see me and look away.'

She raised her eyes to mine, but did not keep them there.

She went away and came back carrying a plate of cassava, rice, and pears. She placed the dish in front of me. I had not sat in one of the chairs, but on the carpet.

'All my life I've heard stories of this place,' I said. 'I was told black people were free here. I longed to escape here to be free.'

'You *are* free.'

I said nothing.

'I will go now,' she said. 'Unless there is something you wish for me to do.'

'No,' I said, rising.

'What is your name?' I asked.

'Nobrega.'

'I am Almeyda.'

She widened her eyes, looking at me. She said nothing, then turned and left quickly.

I sat back down, holding the bowl of rice and cassava against my lap.

The Wife of Martim Aprigio, Reunited with Her Husband

MAY I COME IN?'
I stared up at Martim Aprigio's wife. She was wearing a long dress with ruffles around the high collar. She was smiling, but though her eyes were bright there also seemed to be a sadness in them.

'I am going to my husband,' she said.

'What?' I asked, thinking that he had been executed.

'He's alive and living in Porto Calvo, which is not very far from here. Perhaps sixteen leagues. But he's there and a free man. He built a bridge for them or something and now they are all over him. I don't know how it came about but I am told he – that he continues to be instrumental in helping the people here. I mean, in Palmares. He is an agent. It will be dangerous, as what he does, if discovered is still forbidden and a criminal act. I don't know. He was taken one way and I the other and I did not think I would see him alive again. It was someone of the Macombo, one of the smaller settlements, that rescued him.'

I stood up, and I kept looking at her in amazement.

'When I told them – as I always tell anyone, as if I myself have no name, and will never have another one – "I am the wife of Martim Aprigio," they knew him! And they said they would be taking me to my husband. I will be a free woman, living with my husband again.'

She hugged me and then she ran outside.

The man who had been riding on the horse and who had asked my name was waiting outside. This time he was standing by a wagon. He helped her up and then climbed to the driver's seat. She waved at me and I lifted my hand. The man did not look at me.

When Nobrega came in the evening, bringing me water, fruit, and oils, I asked, 'Was the man, the man who came in on the horse – was he Martim Aprigio?'

'No, Martim Aprigio lives in Porto Calvo.' I waited. She said nothing else.

'Who was he then?'

'His name is Martim too. Martim Anninho.'

'Does he live in Porto Calvo too?'

'No, he lives here.'

'Is he a slave or a free man?'

'A free man,' she answered. She looked at me as if she were going to say something else, but didn't.

'What?' I asked.

'Nothing,' she said. 'I can't say anything else about him.' She looked at me. 'Except he's the man who has chosen you. He's my master.'

I said nothing, and she left.

A Man Is Brought Back;
An Old Woman's
Stories of Brutality

IF I WAS THE WOMAN HE HAD CHOSEN, it was a very long time before I saw him again, and when I did see him he did not even speak to me.

The next day in the morning Nobrega came to take me down to one of the running streams where the women went to bathe in the morning.

There were two other women there who told me their names were Francisca and Antonia, and Old Vera was there sitting on the edge washing herself between her legs. She raised her skirt and knotted it but did not remove her blouse.

I undressed and got into the stream. 'Aren't you coming in?' I asked Nobrega.

'No, I can't,' she said.

Nobrega stood on the edge holding my clothes.

'Put them down and come in,' I asked. 'It's very nice in here.'

'No, I can't,' she said, then, 'I've already bathed. I bathed very early.'

I said nothing. I soaped my shoulders with a good smelling soap she had given me and then soaped the rest of my body. My thigh was still sore from the sharp stone.

Nobrega stood looking at me strangely, then she lowered her eyes.

'What do they grow here?' I asked. 'I saw fields in the distance.'

'Cacao, manioc, corn, sweet potatoes,' she said.

I raised up out of the water and she handed a cloth to me. 'You look like the African Queen of the Waves,' Old Vera called, as I stepped out of the water. 'What blessings do you have for an old woman?'

'To always be loved,' I said.

'Where is your necklace?' she asked.

I had worn the necklace of cacao seeds and trumpet shells into the water, but when I touched my throat it was not there. I got back into the water, ran my hands along the shallow bottom, but could not find them. I got out again. I felt as if I had lost something that was magic.

'Perhaps they dissolved away,' the old woman said, looking at me. She stood on the side of the bank oiling her legs.

I dried myself again, and Nobrega, laying my clothes down on a stone, began to oil my back and shoulders. She started to oil the rest of me but I took the bowl away from her, and rubbed the back of my own thighs and my belly and breasts. The palms of my hands were white from the cool water. My arms seemed very long and dark in the long white sleeveless dress she had given me.

'Wait for an old woman,' Old Vera said, as she climbed to meet me. 'Wait for an old slave.'

I turned back at her with deep surprise.

'You're not an old slave now?' I asked. 'You're a free woman?'

'I'm an old woman,' she said, still holding the hem of her dress, then she let it drop. 'I'm an old woman,' she repeated. 'Ech, I've watched many generations lie in their hammocks, and scratched lice from the heads and genitals of every one of them. But none can follow me through *that* space. None can go there.'

I looked at her, not knowing what she meant. Nobrega walked in front of us.

'Are there fish in that other lake?' Old Vera asked.

'Yes, in abundance,' Nobrega said.

'Are you a slave?' I still wanted to know.

'That handsome one said perhaps they'd have use for my magic as long as their king does not know about it. He does not favor such things.'

'Is he ever seen?' I asked.

'Yes, he is seen,' said Nobrega.

We passed a sentry box and entered a small wood.

'Let me rest,' said Old Vera, sitting on a stone.

I sat beside her. Nobrega stood; not knowing what to do, I said, 'Sit down,' patting the side of me. 'We are the same woman, we are one woman.' Still she would not sit down.

Old Vera began to talk. 'Do you know what he did? I did not tell you what he did. Afterwards. After I healed. He called me an old serpent then. But after that, the only women he would purchase were mutilated women, who had been punished for crimes or suspected crimes, or for no reason. From jealousy. One woman, jealous of her slave's beauty, burned her with hot irons between her legs and left her for a dead woman. It was Azevedo who purchased her, said, "Here, fix this one up. Cure this one with your devil's magic, your serpent's magic." And another mutilation and another. All sexual atrocities. All aimed at the groin or the bosom; but women whose facial beauty was untouched – those are the ones he would purchase. "Here, Old Serpent, heal these." All mutilated women. Those were the ones. But all the men there. Perfect. Whole men. You see. And all those beautiful mutilated women. But the mutilations unseen. "Here, cure this one, heal these ones. Draw the pain out." All the mutilated ones. They got so they saved them for him. Every new atrocity. "This one for Azevedo." "I hold this one for Azevedo. If she lives long enough. Ha. Ha." "See if you can cure this one, Old Serpent." "Are you still unfinished? Don't you have the cure?

'"Haven't you had enough experience? Here's another one. It's not lack of knowledge. Here's one for you. Here, I'm afraid to look at this one. From what I've been told. Here, you look." All the mutilated women, mutilated in impossible ways it seemed. And whole men. No men, except the whole ones. And all the women with the handsome faces and ...' She stopped. 'You did not see. You saw and did not see. You saw and did not see those women. "This one won't last the night." But she did. They walked around him taking what they wanted. Gold, ammunition. The Palmaristas, when they liberated that place. "Send the old serpent to finish me." But then I'd *see*. He thinks all that long time I did not see. You saw and did not see, Yemanja.'

Why did she call me by that name?

The old woman got up and we walked through thick underbrush, past one of the lookout towers and into a stretch of woods. Nobrega gasped. The man, tied to a tree, raised his eyes to us. He was tied to a tree; his legs looked like bloody bags.

He gave out a curse, then he began to talk softly to us. 'For God's sake take pity.'

'What happened?'

Nobrega spoke. 'He deserted to return to his old master and they brought him back and crushed his legs. Crushed all the bones in his legs. They'll let him hang like that until the evening and then chop his head off.'

The man cursed and then again asked us to have pity on him for the Lord's sake.

'Go on, women,' the man standing on the parapet called out to us. 'It's not your concern. Go on.'

'Let me talk to the women. Let me talk to some good women for the last time, in the name of God.' Then he cursed at the man and tried to raise himself up on his legs but could not, and his feet were twisted almost to the back, since the bones in his ankles were also crushed.

'What shall we do?' I asked.

'Kill me,' he said.

'Go on, women. It is not your concern what is done here. Go on, I say.'

'We'd better do as he says,' Nobrega said.

I started to go with her, but Old Vera reached down for some leaves that grew at the base of the tree, and popped them in the man's mouth. He looked at her with his eyes very wide and began to chew slowly.

Old Vera pushed my shoulder and told me to go on. We stumbled through thick underbrush.

The Free Woman and the Slave

IF I AM THE WOMAN HE HAS CHOSEN,' I asked Nobrega, who had brought me fruit and cow's milk and who was oiling my hair. (I said that she could oil and brush it only if I oiled and brushed hers in return.) 'If I am the woman he has chosen, why has he not spoken to me? I saw him sitting with other men, and he did not see me. He saw me, but would not say so.'

'I can't say why,' she said.

'And this king, whom they call Zumbi. I have not seen him. Does he stay hidden?'

'Perhaps you have seen him and not known.'

I said nothing, thinking perhaps the man who carried himself with importance whom they had told me was Martim Anninho, was in fact King Zumbi.

'Is he the king?' I asked finally.

'Who?'

'The man you called Anninho.'

She laughed. 'No, he is not King Zumbi.' She laughed again.

'He carries himself with such importance. I have never seen a black man carry himself so.'

She said nothing. When she finished braiding my hair she remained standing with her hands to her sides.

'Now, you sit down,' I said, getting up.

'No, I cannot,' she said.

I took the brush from her and asked her again to sit down. This time she did and I began to oil and brush her hair.

'Do not tell anyone,' she said. 'Everyone must keep to his own place.'

'Did you commit a crime?' I asked her.

'No, I am not a criminal. Perhaps I simply gave fatal herbs to a man like Old Vera did.'

I dropped the bowl of oil. She jumped up to clean it up, and then not letting me finish her hair, she wrapped it in a cloth.

'What will they do to her?'

'I was told she got away with only a reprimand, a warning, because she is new and did not know the laws here. But me, I knew them well.'

She started to say something else, but did not. 'Was he a man you knew?' I asked.

'What?' she asked, tying the scarf very tightly, letting the ends hang across her shoulders.

'The man you freed from such torture?'

'Yes, I knew him,' she said. 'I knew him.' She looked at me fully for the first time. 'I saw them when they brought him back. He had not wanted to stay here. He did not leave to go back to some old master.'

'Was he a slave here?'

'No, he was a free man. But for him it was a difficult freedom. He wanted to be free. Not in a perpetual fight for it. He didn't mind taking responsibility for his own freedom. But he wanted out of the whole place, the whole country. But the ones here captured him and brought him back before anyone out there did. I saw his eyes when they brought him back. I saw him and stared at his doom. Oh, I could not pass that man easily,' she said.

She had gotten up as much of the oil as she could, then she said she would come back with something, and got up and left.

'For God's sake, have some pity,' I heard the man say.

Zumbi's Women; Small Talk on Mulatto Women and the Virtues of Reserve and Silence

I SAW ALL THREE OF ZUMBI'S WOMEN before I saw him. I had gone down with Nobrega to the stream and saw three women there. One was very white, the other a bushy-haired mulatta, and the third a dark round-faced woman with short hair and sad eyes and rings in her ears. Three women stood on the bank watching them. I started to get in but Nobrega told me to wait.

'Those are Zumbi's women,' she whispered.

I stood watching them, mostly staring at the white woman. I thought at first that she was also a mulatta, but then I realized she was really a white woman.

'The white one?' I asked without completing it.

'Yes,' she said.

'Let's go back some,' she said.

We sat on a rock at the edge of the wood, until the women got out of the stream and dressed, helped by the three women on the bank.

I stared at the mulatta who had short curls all over her head, not the long hair of most mulatta women I had seen, not long down her back. It was only the white one who wore her hair long down her back. Then when the women were dressed, and shawls were placed around their shoulders, they paraded past us with serious eyes and did not look at us.

'When he first brought the white one here, some whispered against him. Others said no she was part Indian, that she looked like an Indian and so it was not wrong. But everyone knew she was a white woman. Me? I don't like her to look at me. I don't like her eyes. Once she tried to make her skin brown like ours, and he beat her, at least people say it was him that did it, but who knows in this world? The black one is the most reserved. I thought she was mean, but she is just reserved and quiet. The white one I don't like to look at. Did she have a serious expression when she passed or did she laugh like she had some secret?'

'They all looked serious,' I said.

'I'm afraid of her. I don't know why. I won't look at her. Some of the women have gotten used to her and say she acts the way she does because she feels we don't like her. What way does she act? I don't know. I don't know how white women act. She made her skin dark and tried to learn our dances, falling to the ground. But she wouldn't cut her hair. No. No.'

I said nothing.

'The mulatta is the friendliest,' she said. 'And isn't her hair nice, just like a cushion. Her waist is thin and her hips are large and she's shaped just like me, except her breasts are so small, aren't they? And her skin's got a lot of milk in it. She's the friendliest and she likes to paint her eyes. Once when I was down at the spring to get water, she came down there. It was not for water to carry, but for her own thirst. She looked at me and smiled and cupped her hands to drink. But she did not speak. But still she seemed so friendly. I don't like her the best though. I like the black one. Did you see the shadows under her eyes? She has a hard time. Did you see the mark of the tribe where she came from? It's under her chin. It's very distinctive. I like her the best, though at first I thought she was mean. It was just reserve and silence. In the place where she came from it is a virtue for women to behave so, especially royal women. It will give them youth and a long life.' She was quiet, then she said, 'I wonder which he finds the best to make love with. I have heard white men say that mulatta women are the women to make love with. That is what they believe.'

'Color is not contagious,' I said.

'What?'

'That's what they sing where I came from, the masters' sons to little mulatta girls.

'"I want your love, mulatta, Color is not contagious, So I want your love."'

She said nothing, and we rose and went to the stream to bathe.

The Name 'Almeida'

WHY DO YOU HAVE THE NAME ALMEIDA?' she asked, as we were returning. 'Who would name you after such a false governor?'

'My name is not the same as Don Pedro de Almeida,' I said. 'When I first heard of him I said too, "Why am I named after such a man?" But my name has a "y" in it, not an "i" as his. Still I don't know where my name came from. Or what it means. I looked it up in a priest's dictionary. I couldn't find it. I found "alma," that's "soul." But also it's like "almejar," "to covet." I don't like that. "To agonize." I don't like that either. But "to long for, to yearn for." It also means that.'

She listened but said nothing.

'Tell me about him, this de Almeida. How was he false?' I asked.

'I was not here,' she began, 'but it was when Ganga Zumba was king and he sought peace with the governor de Almeida. He sent representatives to prostrate themselves before his feet. That was in 1678, fifteen years ago, before I came here. It was all very strange, but it is all the same to me. I am always in the same state, in an "independent" state or outside of it. Inside or outside I am the same woman. The servitude is constant. But the representatives told the governor that we never desired war, no more than any other man, that we were the same as other men and fought only to save our lives. He said that those born free in Palmares should remain free, others would be returned to their owners, if a treaty were given. He wanted some site provided for the free men; it did not matter if the independent state of Palmares was no more, as long as there was some place provided, they would serve the flag the same as other men. It was the new governor, Aires de Souza though, who finally extended peace, freed the Palmaristas. But it was all false, he did not demobilize the detachment of soldiers, and then what did he do? He began to give land to those men who had fought against us.

'Began to give our land away. That was when Zumbi revolted, and together with some men killed his uncle, Ganga Zumba. Is that the name of the old king? Zumbi said the Portuguese have not the only claim here, that we either continue to fight or face extension, *extinction*, that is the way it will be and always will be ... But I am not a free woman. It is not my matter. I have no free ground to hold.

'Every ground I walk on is the same. Why should it matter to me if Palmares is no more? I walk on the same ground wherever I go. I am the same woman wherever I go.'

I said nothing as we entered the road leading to my house.

Black Beans, Brazilian Style; Iararaca, the Mystical Serpent Visits and Almeyda Is Made Whole Again

DID YOU MIND AN OLD WOMAN'S TALES of brutality?' she asked.

'No.'

'Every journey is preparation for another one.'

I said nothing. We sat on the rug in my small house, eating black beans and rice that she had prepared and brought to me.

'Do you still have the dreams?' she asked.

'I haven't dreamt in some time,' I said.

'It is because you are here now and think you are a free woman,' she said. 'Free to resist slavery. Free only to resist it.'

I said nothing.

'Did you see the white woman?' she asked.

I looked away from her. 'Yes, I saw her,' I said.

'Has the man touched your face, has he touched your hair and shoulders?'

I said nothing and did not look at her. She was repeating my dream to me.

'Where is the man you have chosen? Where is the man whose woman you have become?'

'I have chosen no one. I am no one's woman.'

'Do you want to be his woman?'

I said nothing.

'Tell me yes or no now,' she said.

I looked at her. I said yes. I felt as if there were a serpent crawling down my back, between my legs. I tried to pull at it.

'You are uncomfortable.'

I kept moving and twisting and trying to be rid of it. It was stuck there, and then it crawled up my belly and between my breasts, and then I did not feel it.

'Iararaca has positive meaning. There is always some positive meaning whenever Iararaca is near,' she said.

I felt it along the back of my neck and she grabbed it and shook it loose and then rubbed it across my forehead and under my chin.

Then across my thighs back and forth, then she touched my head again, the center of my forehead.

'Do you feel you are a whole woman?'

'Yes.'

'Do you feel you are a whole woman or a mutilated one?'

'I was mutilated for my own protection.'

'Do you feel you are whole now or mutilated?' she asked with anger and impatience.

'Whole,' I said timidly.

Then we were looking at each other, and she took Iararaca from me and wrapped him around her head, then she rose.

'Tell me, Almeyda, how does a woman find her spiritual place in this world?'

I said nothing and she left me sitting there.

Martim Aninho;
The First Meeting

NOBREGA CAME TO THE DOORWAY. I was sitting on the rug drinking cocoa.

'Aninho is coming,' she said.

'He is coming?' I asked. It had been weeks since I had even seen him.

'Yes, he is on his way here.'

Then she said softly, 'He has complained of your friendliness with me. He does not like it.'

'I am my own woman,' I said.

Aninho stood in the doorway, tall and straight shouldered. He looked at Nobrega and she left quickly. He looked at me.

'Let's go for a walk,' he said.

'Where?' I asked.

He looked angry. 'Just a walk.'

I put my cup down and went to the door.

We walked through the palm grove until we reached the place where the wooden pikes tipped with iron stuck out of the ground. We went no further. I stared at the side of his face, then up at the clouds in the blue sky.

'The free women here feel you shun them for a slave,' he said.

I said nothing.

'Those who escape here on their own are free. Those when we bring against their will are not. Those who go against the laws here are slaves again. Those who desert are executed. Murder, adultery, theft, desertion are punishable by death. That is the way it is.'

I said nothing. I had looked forward to our first visit, and now I was not pleased.

'I want you to be my woman,' he said.

He looked at me. I stood close to him but said nothing. I wanted to ask him why he had not spoken to me before this time, and that once when I saw him with a group of men he had shunned me.

'What do you say?' he asked.

I said nothing.

'Why do you look so sad?'

'People tell me I always look this way.'

He touched my short hair and my forehead. He touched my shoulder.

He asked if he might kiss me. I shook my head no. He said nothing. He looked out into the heavy forest. I studied the scars on his cheeks and forehead. One was shaped like a star and the other a half circle. His eyes looked very solemn. I touched one of the scars on his jaw. He turned and smiled at me. We kissed.

He put his arm around my shoulder and we walked back to the small house.

I sat down on the carpet and he asked why didn't I sit in one of the chairs. They were Dutch chairs, gotten during the time when they were at war not with the Portuguese, but with the Dutch. I said they were nice chairs but I was not used to sitting in chairs. Then he sat down on the carpet and folded his legs. He wore a white shirt and string-tied pants but he was not barefoot. He was wearing tall boots that came to his knee, but made of a flexible and thin leather.

We sat in silence. I rose nervously and got a bowl of coconut and pears and set it between us.

'How did you first come here?' I asked.

He said nothing, then he said, 'I rode in the same as you saw that morning, on horseback. They were suspicious of me for a very long time and thought I was a spy for the government and would inform on them. They sent me through difficult tests.'

'What tests?'

'You would not want to hear.'

'Not hear?' I asked. 'Perhaps I will see worse.'

'I was sent in search of a certain enemy, to come back and place his head on a pole. You see, I was very much distrusted in the beginning.'

'I have not been sent for anything.'

'You are a woman.'

'I have heard here that the women fight along with the men.'

'Fight, yes.'

'But none are distrusted? You expect none as informers?'

He laughed. 'Are you an informer? Should I distrust you? Anyway, if a man is captured by either side he is killed. The women are never killed. There are always other uses.'

I said nothing.

He said, with seriousness, 'There is a certain woman who is a spy for us in the town. You will meet her soon. But I have known few women to be executed by either army. I have known women to be executed by other women.'

I still said nothing.

'Speak to me.'

'I'm not a ready talker.'

'What do you think?'

I did not answer.

'We have a strong system of vigilance here. Spies in the towns, on the roads, at points wherever travelers and strangers gather. We have our own informers. We are a very organized group. We have garrisons in other mountains, and sometimes certain Indians join forces with us. Though certain others have been in the attacking armies. Did you come with any weapons?'

'No.'

'Have you held a sword, bow and arrow? Do you know how to shoulder a musket?'

'No.'

He frowned. 'Well, you'll learn those things. In that house over there,' he said, pointing. I rose to look over his shoulder. 'There is a woman called Indaya, Indaya Matroa; one of our best fighters. An old woman now, but an instructor to younger women. I will send you to her. The only way we maintain our freedom here is through resistance.'

I said nothing.

'That will begin tomorrow, and you will also be given some field to cultivate.'

'I have never worked in a field. I have always worked ... inside places.'

He shrugged. 'There are women who will show you. Nobrega will show you how to do that. Perhaps sweet potatoes.'

I did not speak.

'What did you do when you were found? What type of work?'

'I worked in a shoemaker's shop.'

'We have a tannery here and a shoemaker's shop, but there are no women. Here the women do the cultivating.'

I said nothing. I started to say I was the only woman in that shoemaker's shop, but I did not. Again I saw the shoemaker's wife standing in the doorway.

'Did you make those sandals you are wearing?'

'Yes. I only made sandals, and did sewing and embroidery, and when things needed to be ornamented by painted designs. But no boots and nothing with heels,' I said.

'You don't speak readily?' he asked, with a laugh.

I laughed. I was staring not at him, but at his boots.

'I was wondering why you always seem to be studying my shoes. Aren't these well-made, the pegs and screw in the right place?' he asked, with a laugh.

'They're very well made,' I said, staring at the wooden heels. There was silence.

'You tell me you read and write?' he said. 'Where did you learn that, at the shoemaker's shop?'

'No, a long time before that. When I was young we had a Franciscan priest at the plantation who taught all the young ones, not just the master's children. But everybody at one time.'

'I'll show you what is necessary in writing passes and letters of introduction. But never write them unless there is authorization from the king. Otherwise you might unwittingly help a deserter.'

I nodded.

'From a Franciscan?' he said and laughed then he said, 'When I learned to write I would not even have been allowed to speak to a Franciscan.'

'I used to be afraid of the Jesuits,' I said. 'The Indians in our territory used to burn pepper and salt as exorcism when a Jesuit came near, because their ancestors blamed all the new diseases on the Jesuits. I used to be afraid if I saw any Jesuits.'

He laughed. 'I meant any Christian. My father only prayed to Allah, and taught me to do the same. I learned to write from him. First in Arabic and then in Portuguese.'

'My grandmother could write in Arabic, but she kept it all to herself and we only heard it when she prayed. But she refused to teach my mother or me.'

He said nothing, then he said, 'I think it is an advantage to read and write in any language. The woman Indaya shares my religion, but even here we must read the Koran in secret and not speak the prayers too loudly. But my father refused all his life to be converted, and told me that I must not deny the name of Allah to my own children.'

'You have children?' I asked. I did not add, 'And a woman?'

'No. But I'm telling you that I am a Muslim and that I won't refuse to give Allah's name to our children.'

I looked at him, then back down at his shoes. 'I have not said I would be your woman.'

He went on as if I had not spoken. 'My father, he wanted to kill any Christian, black or white. It didn't matter. They were all the same. He felt that we must conquer this land and abolish the Christian religion in the name of the only God, Allah. Blacks and whites who converted would be spared. Not a black nation, but a Muslim nation. Mulattoes were to be the new servants and slaves. He did not accept this war of black against white. It was only the holy wars that had meaning. It was only in the name of Allah that one killed others ... Are you a Christian woman?'

I said nothing. I thought of the dark-skinned Jesus on Father Tollinare's wall, and how it had been put there to attract dark people to the faith. Except then I had only loved to look at the picture. I shrugged my shoulders.

'He believed one fought for the love of Allah, and that it was Allah and only Allah who gave liberty to men. All dignity and worth comes in the name of Allah, and it should only be in Allah's name that we find dignity and worth, and that we should take part in and progress in this New World only through Allah and always through Allah.'

I said nothing, then I asked, 'What do you believe?'

'I believe in Allah always, but I do not fight the same holy wars as my father, not the *same* ones.'

I was silent.

'Is your father here?' I asked.

'No. My father taught me to feel no kinship with these people. We are the same skin, but because of Allah, we do not share the same spirit.'

'But you are here?'

'Yes,' he said, standing. 'I must be going.'

I stood. He kissed my cheek and said yes I was his because Allah had given me to him.

Another Reunion; How One
Uses the Long Sword

I N THE MORNING, Nobrega came with fried cassava and berries. 'After your bath,' she said. 'I'll show you the field we're to cultivate together. The soil is rich here and very fertile. We'll be growing sweet potatoes. It's a very delicate plant and must be handled carefully.'

I said nothing. She stood near while I ate. Then she threw a cloth about her shoulder and we walked down to the stream, then into a large field that was divided among several women. She showed me what to do to keep certain diseases away from the plants by sprinkling on them the juice of another plant.

'They will be ready to get and store soon,' she said. 'Again there are certain things that must be done to prevent spoilage.'

We spent the morning weeding and applying a mixture to the soil.

At lunchtime she baked some of the sweet potatoes over coals and we ate and rested.

'You say you have seen King Zumbi?' I asked. She nodded.

'What is he like?'

'He is a man of great valor and ability. And he has never trusted the Portuguese as his uncle did.'

She told me again how before she came here Zumbi's uncle Ganga Zumba had been king. He had accepted the governor's message. That if the quilombo of Palmares would surrender, everyone would be given protection, a new place for houses and fields to cultivate. Their women and children who were prisoners from other wars would be given back to them and they would retain their dignities and their positions, nothing would be lost, they would be like other men and have the protection of their country's arms and serve their country's flag as other men and they would be the same as other men.

'Except they added "All would remain who had been born free."' She spoke as if she were telling me all this for the first time, and I listened as if it were the first time.

'This took most of what they said away. How many had been born free? And would they have respected the freedom of those born free here, as the law of the country says the child of a slave is himself or herself a slave. Zumbi's uncle accepted it, and would have gone to shake hands with the white men, but Zumbi killed his uncle and himself became leader, to fight for the freedom of everyone here, to fight for more than our lives, saying one does not gain worth or dignity bowing to the flag of another man.'

She said the last thing as if she had not spoken before of her servitude on any ground, or perhaps there was something in the way she said it that I did not detect.

I thought about the white woman and mentioned her.

'Ah, the Reina Blanca. They say she is the daughter of one of the families who live in the forests near Porto Calvo. But women, women are never considered in these matters. Women are not the same. Men look at them and do not see nations in their eyes.'

'But you are afraid of her,' I said. 'You said so.'

'*I* am afraid of her.' Then she laughed. 'But she receives the protection of *arms*.' She laughed again.

I said nothing. Even he had said that the women were always captured. And I thought again of the strange black woman, the captain's wife.

'And women, when they desert, are they punished by death?'

'I have not known a woman to desert,' she said. 'Not in the time I have been here. But once they said there was such a woman, a Zerifina. But she had refused any man here. She was tracked down and brought back and hanged. They crushed her legs the same as any man's. And she cursed them but she did not ask them to have mercy in the name of anyone. Instead she asked for a smoke, a cigarette, and she sang songs, and laughed and joked with the women. They crushed her legs in the morning and hanged her in the evening.'

'Why did she desert?'

She said nothing, then she said, 'She refused a very important man here, to be his wife, and so he made her his slave. That is why she deserted, because she could not be a woman alone here and free.'

I said nothing, looking at her.

I asked, after a silence, 'Were you in love with that man you freed from torture?'

She frowned, then said, 'I cared for him, but I was not the woman he chose. He chose me *then*. He saw his doom and he chose me *then* when he cried, "Have mercy."'

Again she was silent. We ate the sweet potatoes in silence and then walked back. She took me to the house Anninho had pointed out, where the woman they called Indaya lived.

'Here is where you learn acts of combat,' she said, taking me to the door and leaving me there.

The woman in the shadows said, 'Come in, Almeyda.'

'Do you have any memory of me?' she asked, standing and moving out of the shadows.

'Yes, Grandmother,' I said and embraced her.

She hugged me and called me a Palmarista woman.

Indaya and the Old Ghost That Never Leaves

HOW LONG HAVE YOU BEEN HERE, Grandmother, and how did you come?'

She sat down in a chair made of wicker. I sat on a large pillow. 'Ah, it is the same time they took me away. I escaped and wandered into the woods here. They found me wandering in Rio Mundahu valley. They know I am crazy, but in a hard fight I know how to wield a sword well. The first time, it was not from experience but from imagination ... They say I wandered into this camp, my eyes wild and my hair wild.'

'Grandmother.'

'What?'

'You said they found you wandering in Rio Mundahu valley, and now you say that you wandered into the camp.'

'Did I? Well, who knows what's true? I have been to the little Palmares and the big one. I have been in the mountains of Cubatão, São Paulo, Lellon, Rio de Ianeira – is that how it is named, I can't remember – Maranhão, Matto Grosso. I said I must see all of the quilombos, every place where the black man is free. But free only if he takes weapons up and defends it. That is the sadness, Almeydita; that is the sad part. And they, they are defending *their* freedom by taking weapons against us, by destroying these quilombos. As if white men cannot exist when black men are free. They need our slavery to exist. But there are some who

172

trade with us in skins, in gold, in ammunitions, foodstuffs. There are always some who trade and some who fight; isn't that so, Rugendas?' she asked, looking over her shoulder. Still I did not see him – the white man, the mapmaker. 'Some who hate and some who love. Isn't that so? But I have known some who love the night before and murder the next day. Isn't that so? Rugendas, even you told me of your friend Tovor who took an Indian woman into his hut one night and the next morning tossed her dead body into Rio de Ianeira. Is that the name? Even you told me that. But it does not matter. Is it every river and any one? We've all been through it, riding in the same boat. Ha. Ha.'

'Were you here when the woman they call Zerifina was hanged?'

'Ah, poor woman, it was not freedom of the body but freedom of the spirit she wanted. "Ah, Indaya, laugh and sing with me. Laugh and sing with me before I die."'

'Why did you change your name from Teodora?'

'Because here I picked it and I could call myself any number of names. Names without end. Acutirena, Taboca, Subupira, Osenga, Amara, Antalaquituxe. Ha ha. Isn't that so, Old Map Maker? I'll take the name Luiza Mahin in the next hundred years if it pleases me. Won't I, old soul? If it pleases me?'

'Is he a man who pleases you?' she asked. 'That one they call Anninho?'

'Yes,' I said.

She said nothing.

'He speaks your language,' I said. She nodded, but again said nothing.

'Why did you refuse to teach my mother and me?'

She said nothing. Then she said, 'Don't you like these enormous streets? There are one thousand houses, a Catholic church, and a council chamber.'

I looked at her without speaking.

'I came here with nothing except my old tongue,' she said.

'Your old tongue?'

'My old language. That is all I brought with me.'

'That is more reason to give it.'

She was silent, then she said, 'Ah, I could have told you stories in that one. But another time we'll be walking together and I'll tell you of the loves of Boabdil and Vendaraja. "For of all the Moorish ladies Venda-raja he loves best." Isn't that so, old ghost who always returns?

'Or is it that you never leave, Rugendas? It's not the task of slavery that brought me fear. I too know how to hold a thousand years in a second. Ha ha. Or to chain one soul to another?'

She jerked at her hair.

'When he was first alone with me, he grabbed my hair. "Is this your own hair?" he asked. I said, "Yes." "What?" "Yes," I told him. He kept his hand on my hair all the time. Every time we were alone. He had just come to this country. He had not seen women like us. "What are you, an old Dutchman or an old Portuguese?" I asked him what kind of man he was and he said, "I'm a Dutchman" or was it Portuguese? Oh, if I could have told him what kind of woman I was in just one word without him linking every horror with it. Should I say "I'm a Sudanese" and say it with my head up? And what would he have seen? A sensual demon? But he had just come to this country and he'd stare at my dark arms and shoulders. But now I belong to no one. Ha ha. Now I'm no one's woman. What are you doing touching my old shoulders? Keep your hands in your own hair.'

She pulled away from the man she saw.

'This is my granddaughter. Yours? No. Always mine. I stood in the doorway. She didn't see me. I watched her walking with him. Did you see them too? I watched his tallness, his broad back, his deep eyes. I watched them drawing shadows across the ground. Don't look sad because you can't make shadows anymore. You've made one across my heart. I watched them enter the hut together. Are you pleased with the man?'

I answered, 'Yes.'

'Do you remember,' she asked, looking over her shoulders, 'when you'd hold me, I'd watch my shadow dancing on your cheekbones. Don't look sad, old ghost, take mine. Share mine. They call me the crazy woman. It is the same in every generation. Do you remember the time I dressed you up like a little angel?' she asked me.

'Yes, there was a little boy too dressed up like an angel and an old man playing a guitar. It was the fiesta da rainha.'

'He tried to kiss you. I said no. I said no, old spirit. He thought he had some right to love you. I said fine, but don't do that, you can't do that.'

I remembered she had grabbed me up and snatched the wings off me and took me to my mother's hut. They had called it the act of a crazy woman.

'When did he die?'

'Who?'

'Rugendas?'

'Who? Rugendas, dead?' she asked, looking around, and starring behind her. Then seeing someone there, she seemed to smile with reassurance.

She rose and went into a corner and brought out two long swords, handing me one.

'Straighten up.'

'No, like this. And if you are in the field when it happens, your hoe becomes the sword, like this. Toss it up this way, from the crook in the elbow.'

My back and arms were sore, and there were two small cuts on my arm when we sat down to cassava, rice, cacao seeds, nuts, and bananas. She had poured rum over everything.

'Anninho gave me this good rum,' she said.

We ate bits of pineapple and drank cups of water. 'You have grown to be a beautiful woman,' she said.

I said nothing. Her skin was still as dark and smooth as I remembered, except for tiny lines around the eyes, sticking out of the corners like points on a star.

I scratched a mosquito bite on the inside of my elbow. She pulled my arm away and looked at it. She went out and came back with a leaf, poured salt on it, rubbed it across my arm, gave me the leaf to chew. We were silent.

'Rugendas, aren't you a Dutchman?' she asked suddenly. 'It's a Portuguese name, but you came from the Dutch, didn't you?

'Someone came into camp yesterday wearing Dutch trousers. A black man. Where did he get them? I looked at him again and again and then I went out to speak to him. "Where did you get those Dutch trousers? Where did you get those Dutch trousers?" He wouldn't answer. "Did you kill a Dutchman?" I told him to give them to me. I said I could wear them. I said I used to wear Dutch trousers, in the old days when the Dutchmen were everywhere and I was a young woman and smoked tobacco. He wouldn't answer me because somebody told him I was crazy and he didn't have to answer me. But then they had that little war, and didn't I wield my sword well?

'Rugendas, aren't you a Dutchman?' She looked over her shoulder. 'Did you kiss a Dutchman? Let me stare at your eyes. There were many women of spirit of my generation who would have killed a man for that. Don't you think I wanted my own spirit and would have it back? There were many women who would have killed a man for that.'

'Charcoal, sulfur, niter. It tends to pick up moisture so I keep it here ... But me myself I prefer the long sword or a good hoe.'

'Where is your mother? I have been afraid to ask.'

'She was sold to another plantation,' I said sadly. 'I have not seen nor heard of her in many years.'

'Well, we have had one miracle,' she said, touching my shoulder. 'We have found each other again in this lifetime ... And Tempo?'

I frowned and stared at her.

'Well, he went away when she did, but some say he followed her, that they're together.'

She laughed. 'Don't you think an old African knows how to join one soul to another? Don't you think an old African knows?'

Paraiu Baptizes and Marries

I STOOD IN THE DOORWAY, watching them at the edge of the palm grove decorating a small palm tree hut with palm and banana leaves and flowers.

When Nobrega came I asked her what it was the men were doing.

'It is preparations for a wedding. There will be a marriage ceremony.'

'Who is getting married?'

She shrugged as if she did not know, and I went to the river.

She gave me a very strong smelling oil to put on my body. I dressed and we walked back to the house. As we neared, Anninho stood in the doorway, with a man they called Paraiu, who was part Indian and part Negro.

Nobrega did not come to the door with me but said goodbye, and walked to the end of the village where she shared a house with other women.

'This is Paraiu, who baptizes and marries,' said Anninho, pointing to the man.

I opened my mouth but did not speak.

'Come inside,' he said, standing away and holding my arm. 'Usually these are public ceremonies, Almeyda, but I ...'

We stood at the far end of the house in the shadows. Paraiu read from a book that was not the bible, in a language I had not heard for many years.

Then I knelt with him and bowed as he did and said with him that Allah was the greatest.

'Now we must have the Christian one,' he said, when we were standing.

I looked at him but said nothing.

Paraiu stood in front of us and spoke a language that I understood. Then, when it was completed, Anninho put a necklace of cacao seeds and trumpet shells around my neck. I stared at the necklace but said nothing, and then we walked down to the hut decorated with flowers, palm and banana leaves, and spent the night there.

'Why did you also have them perform the Christian ceremony?'

'You refused to tell me what you believe, or whether you are a Christian woman.'

He got into the hammock and raised me up to lie beside him. 'What is it?' he asked.

'Nothing ... Nothing.'

Old Vera moved the serpent over my thighs ... 'Whole spirit, whole soul, whole body whole spirit' ... She wrapped it around my forehead. She kissed the center of my forehead.

'You're a beautiful woman, Almeyda,' he said. 'You are very beautiful.'

He spoke of my body and of my spirit. He kissed me and touched my hair. I watched my shadow dancing.

177

The Harboring Forest

I MIXED GREEN PEPPERS, palm oil, and shrimp. It was evening and our first real dinner together. When I finished I handed him a tin plate and sat down with mine.

'You seem more at ease with me now,' he said. I looked at him but said nothing.

'*We* are more at ease,' he said. 'But the times are not.' He was silent, then he said, 'I would have liked a long courtship with you.'

He watched me. I tried to act at ease, but had trouble finding my mouth. He laughed and reached out and touched the side of my face, wiped a piece of rice from my jaw. I smiled and stared down at my plate.

The women sat in a circle. One of them had a baby sucking at her breasts. A white man came and bent over the woman and brushed her hair back from her forehead. She was a pretty woman with black eyes. He kept looking at her and then he touched the baby. 'No, Almeydita,' the woman screamed. She moved the baby away from her. There was blood on her nipple. The white man backed away. He kept backing away from her. 'Oh, no, Almeydita.'

'What is it?'

'Nothing.'

I lay with my arm across my forehead, then I leaned over and kissed him.

'How do you feel?' he asked.

'Fine.'

He said nothing, then he said, 'I have to go into town tomorrow. Into Porto Calvo. I'd like you to come along.'

I looked at him, fearful. He laughed, touched my side.

'It's all right. We'll be safe. We'll go at night. There's trading to do, skins and leather goods to trade for ammunition.'

I still looked at him.

'There's a free black woman who owns a store. We are safe there. She gets weapons for us. We take things she needs.'

'How does she get weapons?'

'She has her ways.' He frowned, then raised an eyebrow. I said nothing. He kept his hand on my side.

'You'll go with me?' he asked.

'Yes,' I said.

I saw myself walking into a heavy forest, standing at the entrance of a small town. I touched Anninho's shoulders. I stared into the dark corners of his eyes.

The woman squatted on her toes, and moved the baby to her other breast while she sopped the blood up from that one.

'Don't you want me to know you?' the white man asked, still standing away.

'I have no memory of myself, so why should you have any?'

He came near, pulled the baby's hair, and she raised blood on the other nipple.

'Oh, Almeydita, please. Well, it'll have to be milk and blood. It'll have to be milk and blood then.'

Luiza Cosme

AND WHAT COULD I DO when the white man take my gold, but go to the courtroom and sit there. I had already say what he had done. I had say it and went there and sit there with them looking at me with accusing eye as if I had done something wrong. As if I were the bad one, the demon. I will tell you what it came to be. It came to be me asking him for not to punish me for the wrong he had done to me. Do you understand? I am a black woman. My mama is a black woman. My papa is a black man. That is what it all come back to. It return to the same thing again and again.'

She was a beautiful woman with strings of trumpet shells around her neck. Anninho took the skins we had brought into a small back room and brought out large 'grain' sacks.

Luiza stood against the counter. We were in half darkness, the moon shining into a small window near the ceiling at the right side of the counter. She took my arm and I followed her into the back room where there was a tiny whale oil lamp and where sacks of grain and beans and skins lay about.

'Some thing never change,' she said, sitting on one of the grain sacks. I remained standing.

She was wearing a white blouse hanging off her broad shoulders, and a full print skirt. She wore a shawl, not around her shoulders, but around her hips.

'It came down to me asking them not to punish me,' she said, 'when it had started with what he had done.'

Anninho had taken all of the special sacks out and had come back in. He stood looking at her but said nothing.

'Who is the woman?' she asked him.

He told her my name was Almeyda. She looked at me, but said nothing. Then she unfastened a leather bracelet she was wearing.

She handed it to me.

'Here, wear this. It bring you luck. You need luck in this world.'

Luiza fastened it to my wrist. A leather bracelet trimmed with cacao seeds and trumpet shells.

I said nothing at first, then I said thank you.

'Anninho would say there is no such thing as luck. It is all Allah,' she said with a smile, looking at him.

'You have found a silent woman, Anninho. You have found the right one. This man hardly ever speak,' she said to me. 'But silence, they say, bring happiness.'

'They did nothing to the white man?' Anninho asked.

'No. Nothing. When it was over, I was afraid to go out into the street. He was the same man leaving as he was when he enter there. But me? I leave without dignity. I'm the different woman. He say that my earrings are immoral, immoral, immoral, not suited to my birth. I tell them I do not wear them in public as the law say. I only wear them here on the inside. But they will not make dirty the name of a white man for something to do with a black woman. Oh, no. And he the same man today that he was yesterday. He is the same. I am the one who will not see myself again ... I am a black woman ... I am a free black, you say? Ah, I have no freedom. You in the quilombos have freedom because you have the freedom to fight. The arms you see are real. The muskets tied across your enemies' shoulders, they are real, the swords they are real. Every day I must fight what I cannot see. Except sometimes the *arms*.' Her look was hard. She moved her hair away from her ear. The tip of her ear had been cut off. 'You see this?' she asked. 'I get this from resisting *arms*.' She let her hair fall back. 'I must go. I promise to go to Aprigio's house tonight.'

'Aprigio?' I asked. 'Is it Martim Aprigio?' She looked at me, and then at Anninho.

'His wife,' I explained. 'I knew her at the last place I was a slave.'

'The free blacks meet at his house,' Anninho said. 'They spy for us when it is necessary.'

The woman looked at him as if there was some secret they had.

He nodded to her.

'A black whether he be born free or born in chain does not live with-out danger or always possibility of it ... We help our brothers and sisters who wish to escape to you in Palmares, we help others who want to buy freedom, and have opportunity. Some say they will buy they freedom from no man because it is not a thing to buy. All of the one who meet at Aprigio, they are in place like me where they see and hear everything. They see and hear even what cannot be seen and what do not speak. Do I have ordinary eye?' she asked Anninho.

He shook his head.

'No, no. But when it become too dangerous we all have a place in quilombo, is not that so, Anninho?' she asked.

Anninho nodded.

'I go,' she said. 'And you and your woman must go with care and Allah blessing.'

She nodded to us and went outside. Anninho took my arm and we walked outside into the darkness.

Going back we did not both ride on horseback. He helped me up and I rode with the 'grain' sacks. Anninho walked alongside wearing a wide-brimmed hat.

'Who is the woman?' I asked when we had entered the road.

'Luiza Cosme,' he said. 'Didn't I say her name?'

'No.'

'She always puts herself into dangerous circumstances, and yet she has stayed free. But she is a woman.'

I started to say something.

'Here we must be silent.'

There were two white men in white shirts coming toward us both on horseback. The brims of their hats were wider than Anninho's.

Without a word, they rode past him.

'Anninho?'

He kept walking without saying anything.

Nobrega, or How to Become a Free Woman

HE IS A FREE MAN,' Nobrega said while she roasted sweet potatoes at the edge of the field. I sat under a cassava tree. I had told her about the two men on horseback and how strange it had been that they had not stopped us on the road, though before we left I had assumed he had forged papers.

'Perhaps they knew him as he is a free black, or perhaps they were traders.'

Anninho himself had refused to talk about the men.

When we got back he had taken me first to the small house and then had gone on with the load of ammunition and then he had returned and sat silently in one of the straight chairs, bending over a book that I recognized as the same book Paraiu had married us from and that was handwritten in letters I did not understand – and what looked more like illegible scribbles of a madman or woman than real words.

Then as we lay together he had touched my eyelids, tracing the lines upward.

'Are you tired from the journey?'

'Yes, a little.'

'So am I. A little. Your eyes look like an Indian woman's.'

I said nothing. He kept his hands about my face, touching my cheekbones, my temples, then traced circles around my breasts. We lay together for a long while before he kissed me and we made love.

'I love you, Almeyda,' he said.

I said nothing, holding his back and shoulders.

I dreamed I saw them coming down the mountain wearing feathers on their heads and carrying swords and drums. They came down from the top of the mountain on two sides, all black men, carrying spears, torches, axes, playing flutes, horns, trumpets. I stood behind a fence surrounded with sharp points. I was the only woman there. And then I saw the white men, wearing plumed hats and carrying swords. The black men had sure expressions on their faces but the others, the white men, had puzzled expressions. I could not tell whether it was surprise or fear.

Nobrega handed me a hot sweet potato on banana leaves.

'You always act as if you are afraid of me,' I said.

'I am not afraid. I am a slave here.'

'You are no different from me,' I said.

She sat down on the ground setting her sweet potato on the ground between her knees. She watched me but said nothing. Then she said, 'I am a slave. You are a free woman.'

'We are the same,' I said.

'You do not understand,' she said. 'When I was brought here I did not want to take on any man. I am the one who refused. But I did not try to escape like that unfortunate woman, Zeferina. I remained here and I remained a slave.'

'Why did you tell me it was no man wanted *you*?'

'I won't explain.'

I looked at her, frowning.

'You seem very lonely,' I said.

'So do you.'

I frowned, looked at her, lifted a piece of hot potato to my mouth.

'We are the same,' I said. 'There is no difference.' Then I asked, 'If you accepted someone, then would you be free?'

'I know the ways to make myself free,' she said with anger.

I said nothing. We stared into each other's eyes. 'But you said, you told me you loved that man?'

When they brought him back and tortured him so he forgot who he was and forgot who she was and thought she was another woman. She had walked by him like that day and he thought she was someone else and started speaking to her as if she were that woman and he sang to her a little love song and in the next breath he cursed her and said she must have mercy on him.

'Don't abandon me. I've loved you as well as any man.'

'But you said it was because you had mercy on him that you put him out of his torture that they made you a slave. Now you say it is because you refused the men here. Tell me, Nobrega, which is true?'

'They are both true. One story is no different from the other one,' she said with a smile, tearing the skin from the sweet potato, and eating it.

A Woman Hanged for Adultery

THEY BOUND THE WOMAN'S HANDS behind her and branded the letter A on her forehead and someone had pulled the gold earrings from her ears so that there was blood on her earlobes and running down her neck. I had not seen them do any of this but before she was to be hanged, she was paraded through the streets of the quilombo. I watched her from my grandmother's house. My grandmother did not come to the doorway.

'What has she done?' I asked.

'Adultera,' my grandmother said.

I watched her from the beginning to the end of the street. I kept waiting for her to cast her eyes down, but she did not. She walked with her head high and her back was as straight as an arrow. She did not hold it as a haughty woman or even as one who felt that she had been wrong, but – how should I put it? – as if even in this she would keep her dignity and some decorum.

'What is her name?' I asked.

'Ambrosia. But what is your concern?'

I said nothing. Her voice seemed harsh in a way I could not explain, but one that made me afraid to turn and see how her eyes were looking.

'Do you want to go see what is done to a woman whom a man marries in good faith and she betrays him?'

'No,' I said, shaking my head.

'She is hanged as a traitor.'

I still said nothing. Her voice seemed so strange. Even when the woman was out of sight, I still stood in the doorway with my back to her.

'Why are they hard on such a woman?'

'Hard?'

'To be killed for it.'

She laughed. I turned staring into eyes I had not seen before. 'He married her in good faith,' she said.

'Did she have her choice? Perhaps she would have chosen another man?'

'That *any* man should have any choices?' she said. 'That *any* black man should have any choices in such a country.'

'But the woman?'

She looked at me with the same eyes. 'In my country if such a man as Acutirene had chosen me . . .'

'But this is another country.'

'Well out *there*,' she said, shooting her arm in the direction of Porto Calvo. 'Out there, there are *none*. No choices for a man or woman.'

I said nothing.

'Are you displeased with your man?' she asked.

'No.'

'Is he the one you would have chosen if you had had some choice?'

'Yes.'

She said nothing else as if that were the end of it.

I remained standing in the doorway. There were some who had gone out into the streets now and were walking in the direction they had taken the woman.

'Such a woman won't put her head down for anything,' she said as if she'd read my thoughts. 'Even when her neck is broken it won't fall.'

I had not chosen to follow, but found myself walking in the direction they had taken the woman. I stood at the edge of a small clearing. Sunlight shown on the woman's shiny dark face. She remained silent and solemn.

Once I thought that her eyes stared straight at me and I looked down. There was a woman who stood beside me, rubbing her toes back and forth in the dust. She kept rubbing her toes back and forth until she was swinging her leg, one hand on her hip. Then she gave a sharp laugh. I looked over at her and it was almost like I was looking at the woman's sister. She had the same almond shaped, slanted eyes.

'Suppose she's a virtuous woman?' she asked.

I looked at her again. Her face was very dark and shiny and her cheekbones very high.

'I'll bet she's one of the virtuous ones. Look at her, she's not making any sound. Well, maybe that's the spirit of truth. I sang, yes I did. I sang at them, and laughed in their faces. She seems to be looking for something. What makes a woman look for something? See the way she's looking around like that? But still no sound. The rope finds her neck now. How do you find a virtuous woman? Her throat's full of saliva and the prick of a knife. She sways her head to the side, looking for something. But still no sound. And still those eyes, those beautiful eyes. I snapped my fingers to music, and sang them a dirty song and laughed in their faces. That's what they do to a woman who betrays a man. But me, I had no one. I wanted to find all the wonders of the New World, not just this place. And me? I laughed in their faces and sang them a dirty little song and snapped my fingers, and scratched my armpits at them. But now she looks at us as if we weren't the same blood, as if we didn't share the blood of this continent and hold it in our eyelids. I laughed at them showing my gold tooth. I swear to God that's what I did. The whole earth around here is full of dead men's bones. A land dancing in a circle dripping blood from its teeth. Now she can't hold her shoulders up, and look how her slender neck is broken, and look how her pretty head falls over, her eyes shining like black almonds. This is how Americans create themselves ... You are quiet even for you.'

'What?' I look down.

'Go on and look at the woman.'

I look at the woman, her head against her shoulder, her eyes rolled back.

'See how the blood of a continent drips from her eyelids. But doesn't she have lips that heal?'

I stare at the woman and the backs of the crowd. When I turn to *her* again, she is gone.

'There was a strange woman there,' I told my grandmother when I returned.

'A strange woman?' she asked, looking at me. 'It is not such a strange thing that one has done – But this has been her day of reckoning.'

'No, another woman who was speaking as if she too had been hanged like that.'

'It is the phantom of Zeferina,' she said without looking up.

She sat on a mat and scribbled something in Arabic letters. I sat down and stared at her.

'So you have seen her,' she said. 'It is nothing. Old spirits wander through here all the time. We are all part of the same world.'

She looked over her shoulder. 'What about it, old mapmaker?' I looked but saw no one.

'You know Zeferina, don't you? How does a spirit court a spirit?'

She looked at me and smiled and then was silent. I stared at the lines in the corners of her eyes, noticing for the first time that one of her eyes slanted down, the other slanted up. But if it had been that way before, wouldn't I have noticed it? Perhaps it was the way her head was tilted.

But no, she straightened it, and one still slanted down. She gave a short laugh and continued writing in Arabic letters.

A Fanatical Man

IT SEEMED AS IF ANNINHO was always on the roads, conveying messages, getting information, and as a free man he must have been very useful. Most of the time he did not take me with him, but sometimes he did. There was a man who lived not far from Palmares – in the forests.

'Come I must go see German,' he said. 'Come along.'

I thought we would ride, but he said it was not very far, and I walked beside him, until we got to the narrow paths when I walked behind. Vines carpeted the path and clung thickly to the sides of trees.

'Who is German?' I asked once, but when he did not answer I remained silent. Perhaps he had not heard me. When we got near the clearing and could see fresh sunlight, Anninho said, 'Do not let the women frighten you ... He is a madman, but he is useful.'

We came into the clearing and saw the long mud and grass hut. But it was not the mud and grass hut that I watched but five Indian women lined up in front of it, one, the oldest sitting and smoking – the young ones busying themselves with their fingers, making mats. The old one occasionally mumbled something but in an Indian language. Their skin looked redder than it should have been and as we drew nearer, I became frightened. Anninho took my arm, but said nothing. The women's skin looked raw, even their faces, as if it had been rubbed with bark or some grainy fiber. There was fresh bleeding over what looked like older scars – the skin of red crocodiles. I wanted to ask something, or to just make some sound but I could tell by Anninho's manner that he did not wish for me to. All of the women were silent, as if they felt nothing. The young ones did not look up at us, going on with their work. The old woman looked at us, silent, puffing on her long pipe.

'Where is German?' Anninho asked her.

Before she could answer, a voice came from the dark interior, 'I'm in here, man of good faith. I too do not believe in the Christian god.'

'You don't believe in any god,' Anninho said.

We walked inside. Anninho bowed to him and he returned the bow. I could not see the man's features, as he sat in the shadows, but he was a little, slender man. His movements seemed crooked, disjointed.

Anninho sat on a mat and motioned for me to sit down beside him.

'Who is the woman?' German asked.

'My new wife,' Anninho said.

German gave a short laugh. 'Well, you have my blessing,' he said. Anninho was silent.

'You should not have brought her here at this time,' German said. 'My outlandish appearance.'

'*Their* appearance,' Anninho said.

'Shall I have one of my servants fix you something? Is there anything you would like? Any food or drink?'

Anninho said, 'No.'

'See how I put up with him?' the man said, good-naturedly to me.

I smiled, but said nothing. I was still uncertain though of what I had seen. I looked from Anninho to the man in the shadows.

'What excuse do you have for coming?'

'What excuse do you have for sending for me?' Anninho asked.

'Why is she looking at me so?'

'Almeyda? She can't see you. Get to your business.'

'It's no business, it's a story. It's always some story your king wants told.'

'Tell your story, German.'

'Will your woman mind sitting with my women?'

'German is playing games again,' Anninho said. 'Go and sit next to the old woman.'

'I'm no gamer. This man's a gamer,' German said to me, as I rose.

I stood still for a moment, thinking he would say something else, but he did not.

I went out and sat down beside the old woman, who looked at me but said nothing.

'Do you want to go for a walk?' she asked suddenly. I looked at her.

'You are afraid? Don't be afraid of me. I'm Turi. One drop of Arabic blood, no other. Come and walk and talk with me. I'm an old woman.

'What harm can I do? I did not do this thing to these women. I would not do such a thing. And you go in there? Come and go for a walk.

We won't go far. I want to gather some kurumikaa leaves to put on these women.

'Do you want to go with me? Where we go, you can still see the hut from there.' She looked at me. 'How can an old woman go very far in the body, though my spirit has been places you haven't seen? My father was a paje. He taught me what to do. Come on. *He* will still protect you.'

She took my arm, and we rose and walked behind the hut and to the edge of the clearing and near a small stream. I expected her to begin picking leaves from a certain plant, but she did not. Instead she sat down on a rock and told me to sit down.

'You do not know the man you went in there to see,' she said. I could not tell if it were a question or a statement.

'No,' I said, then I said it was my first time to come here.

'I knew that,' she said, then, 'He is the devil, he worships the devil, the devil and all his works through time,' she said. 'I do not believe in the Christian god either, but I believe in some god. Do you see these trees around here, aren't they blessed? Do you think He blessed them and disappeared? No, He is still here, and He knows my words before I do.

'And His eyes never close. Do you know the peacock? It is the male peacock with all the eyes on his feathers, and the royal colors. That's a blessed creature. Didn't God bless that one with beauty? But the devil can make something beautiful too, to trick a person. I will get the kurumikaa leaves when you go, so the women will heal well. I want to talk now and tell you things. You are very beautiful, but don't worry. I think it is the "eye" that looks on you kindly. Do you know I have one drop of Arabic blood and no other? I am a very intelligent woman. I pray a lot. You know, in the old days, I never had seen a black woman before. No one had ever seen a black woman. That is why the African woman was captured. Those Indians had never seen one before, so that is why they tied her to a tree and tried to rub the black color off. They rubbed and rubbed but it would not come off. Was this not a woman? Was not this stranger human? They had not seen one before, so they skinned her and stuffed her with straw.'

She looked at me, her eyes very wide. I closed my eyes, and opened them. She still looked at me, her eyes with some question.

'We did not see the husband of the woman. Did he hide and watch them make the straw woman? He must have watched it to know what was done to her. He did not rush out and show us a man we had never seen.

'What would my man have done? Would he have rushed for me among strange savage people who had never seen a brown woman? But he did not. Now I have seen all kinds of people, every color. White with Negro features. But then they did not know Africans. Skin the color of the bark of some tree, but very smooth. Now I have seen everyone, but then there were no Africans here. Now I have seen everyone. We are all savage people who do not know what to do with strangers. And now what does that man do? He captures Indian women. Some he sells, others he keeps for his own women. Me he has kept because I am the paje's daughter, and cure them as fast as he can destroy them. If I am the paje's daughter, why don't I give him some poison? He captures all the Indian women he can. If I am the paje's daughter, why don't I poison him? Once a month he ties them to a tree and rubs their skin till it bleeds. I heal it fast. I keep an infection from coming. But look what he has done to the beauty? They go about their work. They look at me and say, "You are the paje's daughter." But what can I do? I heal them fast. I make it so there is no pain.'

She looked up and I looked too to see Anninho standing against the back wall of the hut.

'Go on with your man,' she said. 'I will gather my kurumikaa leaves.

'What can a paje's daughter do but tell the story? I do not do the devil's work. I pray all the time. Maybe the eternal ear will hear.'

I said goodbye to the woman, saying something about perhaps seeing her again. She said something about her spirit's journey.

I walked up to Anninho and he took my arm.

'Did you hear his story?' he asked when we left the clearing.

'What?'

'Did the old woman tell you German's story?'

'Yes,' I said. 'You know it?'

He said, 'Yes.' I waited but he did not say anything nor did he tell me the story German told him. When we got back to our house, he left me at the door, saying that he had a message for the king.

A Visit and
a Draughtsman's Plans

IT WAS NIGHT WHEN WE TRAVELED to the place. I rode behind Anninho on the one horse. Anninho moved the horse easily through the narrow paths of the forest, through swampland where we saw a shy tapir who ran and hid behind a bush. It is said that tapirs are so shy that they hide during the day and only graze at night. And I have never seen one in the daytime.

We left the swampland and rode along the bank of a river, and then through a wide valley. We rode up a small hill at the top of which was a building which looked like both a mansion and an unfinished castle, with high stone walls and towers. It did not look like something that belonged in the country of Brazil.

'Why are we going to see a white man?' I whispered. 'Does he have something to trade?' The word 'traitor' suddenly came into my head.

'He's not a white man,' replied Anninho in low tones. 'He's Sudanese the same as I am. Maybe a drop or two of Arabic blood. He helped to design the parapets and lookout towers in Palmares. They call him a Moor, but he's Sudanese.'

Anninho gave several low whistles as we entered the wall. A light was lit in one of the ground windows. Anninho dismounted and helped me down. We walked between mangrove and palm trees up to the tall door.

There were many bottles of water on the ground outside the door. The man let us in in silence. I could not make out his feature in the darkness, but he was as tall and broad-shouldered as Anninho. There was a wide entrance hall with many mats on the floor. He led us through an arched doorway into a large room with tile floors – red, green, and white. There was English and Dutch furniture, and oriental rugs. The man was wearing black trousers and a long-sleeved white shirt. I still saw only the back of him, his round bald head. He still had not spoken. When he turned I thought he was the handsomest man I had ever seen. His baldness gave his forehead a higher, broader, majestic, otherworldly look. His eyes were jet black, intense, sparkling. He seemed a serious man, but one who could jump quickly to humor at the proper occasion. His nose was long, but rounded and his lips smooth and full. There were slender lines around his eyes and mouth. He looked to be in his middle fifties though with the 'sense' and vigor of a younger man. His complexion was dark but with a touch of red.

Anninho and I sat in two chairs he pointed out to us. Tall-backed chairs. He sat in a similar one across from us, and crossed his legs. Though the floor had very elaborate, polished tiles, there were no wall decorations, except for a few Arabic inscriptions near the ceiling.

'If I call any man my master and teacher it is this one,' said Anninho, as a way of introducing the man.

The man looked at him with a barely perceptible twinkle and then looked at me.

'This is Almeyda?' asked the man.

'Yes,' Anninho replied.

They said nothing to each other for a long time. I felt awkward and uncomfortable, but they didn't seem to, as if their pleasure was in seeing each other.

'Did you bring the draughts?' asked the man after a moment. I think he said 'draughts' but I might be wrong.

Anninho pulled up the loose sleeve of his shirt. Papers were tied around his arm. He undid the strings, and he and the man moved their chairs up to a low table, leaving me sitting alone, as they bent over several drawings. I could not make out the meaning of everything they were saying. But I will record as much of it as I remember in the way that I remember it.

'This is the shape of the hull?' asked the man.

'Yes.'

'The smallest beam I ...'

'The length is almost ten times the beam.'

'That's impossible.'

'It's not impossible. For speed, ease of movement ... I've combined some of the features of a warship and a merchantman here ... These are my calculations of its speed and stability under different sea temperatures and weather conditions. Here's a table of the different speeds.'

'What's this?'

'Different loads. Heavier weights here ... The first ship can be bought or hired but the others should be privately built ... The difference between a shipowner and a shipbuilder, a shipowner who's also a shipbuilder. You know my feelings on that matter.'

'What does this mean?'

'This can be shortened or enlarged by detaching this. You see? And it will have to be armed for protection from pirates.'

'And slavers,' said the man, raising his eyebrows. 'That goes without saying.'

Silence.

'I'm naming it Zumbi, the first one. All of this is for extra speed, rapid turning ... But merchant shipping – that's the only way. That's what the world is about. Participation in trade rivalry. That's what the New World's about, and the old one. They're always looking for new types and features. We'll have all the crew. A number of black whaling men I've been in contact with. Do you know how many of the whaling men are black? And you've heard from that black shipowner in Massachusetts.'

'Yes.'

'Well, we've got to take the risk if anything is to come of anything. Aprigio's giving all his energies to Dutch shipbuilding interests. He could train the shipwrights, and I the marine architects and designers. But he has no faith in it. It's all Palmares, and their meaningless raids. I don't mean that. I understand the usefulness of that. But I'm very tired. Do you know what I mean? We have to develop something outside of that. Instead of wasting energies.'

'Land is always important.'

'Yes, but you don't understand.'

The man said something about the others not all having the 'freedom of movement' of Anninho, and perhaps himself.

Anninho was silent. Then he said something about intelligent men having to waste their intellect and energies on things that other men took easily and for granted.

'But Aprigio would say it's necessary. And he does it ... So there's you, myself, Cuffee in Massachusetts, Alsace on Madagascar Island, Barcala when he returns to Holland, Mr Iaiyesimi and trade with the West African coast.'

'There'll be others,' said Anninho.

The man bent over the plans again. He questioned something. 'That part of the design is experimental now. But Aprigio agrees we should try it. There's a need for a new approach ... They're always spying for new designs – their marine architects will get it soon enough when it's afloat ... but why merely copy what's already been done without contributing some new feature ... This is the approximate scale of feet ... sections, sail plan, deck plan ... Note the shape here ... just the underwater portion ... Studied lines of a fish quick, agile, graceful ... some scientific approach ... No decoration ... no carvings ... sure it's the style but we're more concerned with performance than style ... Phineas Pett's masterpiece, an outstanding achievement for his time but hampered by the style, so forget the century's style, all meaningful design ... Look at this ... But the key is to begin building our own craft as soon as possible. Start with the hired one and then move to this. The merchanting of course the first level, but if we get into conflict with any slavers ...'

'What does Aprigio think of your calculations?'

'He's studied the plans. He thought this was impractical, and I modified it. But he has no real faith. Even though he himself studied with a master builder. If it had been a Dutchman who had approached him five years ago he would have said it was possible.'

'I think he's a man of integrity. A very honorable, a very worthy man.'

'Yes, that's true. But such a man rides easily into ...'

'He just doesn't take his freedom for granted, not as long as there are others ... None of us can afford to take it for granted.'

Anninho was silent, then he said something about some using their freedom for grander visions.

'What do these geometric patterns mean?' asked the man.

'Something I want to be painted on the upper part of the hull.'

'The great mystery, eh?' asked the man, looking at Anninho with piercing eyes, his lips curling slightly. 'What else are you quietly developing?'

Anninho was silent, though he too smiled slightly.

'Could you make me copies of the draughts?' asked the man. 'I'd like to study them more.'

'You still have your doubts.'

'No, not in the idea. It just seems that so much time is wasted in building.'

'Parapets but not ships.' He paused. 'We'll start with the hired one from the Massachusetts man. But in the long run our own designs will matter. I'm thinking of the future.'

The man agreed, though he still seemed uncertain or reluctant. 'Aren't you a believer?' asked Anninho.

'Everything comes from Allah,' said the man, but he still looked as if there was something he had not resolved.

'International trade,' said Anninho as if he were proposing a toast. Then he looked seriously at the man.

'It's not impossible.' Then he said something about his father's 'holy war' and what he would think of his contacts with a Catholic, a Yoruba ancestor worshipper, an Olurun worshipper, and a Black Puritan from Massachusetts. Then he repeated, 'It's not impossible.'

'Nothing that can be imagined is impossible,' said the man. 'But the trick is to realize it.'

Anninho nodded, saying nothing, then the two men stood, and moving toward each other clasped hands and embraced. The man said what might have been a short prayer and then the man took some beads from around his neck, which had been hidden under his shirt. Attached to the red beads were square, leather amulets. He handed this to Anninho, who thanked the man, calling him Mualim.

Anninho placed the amulet around his neck and replaced the plans under his sleeve, promising to get copies to the man, then he reached for my hand and I stood. The man looked at me kindly but did not say goodbye.

'I keep good hopes for the future,' said the man, as we left.

'Allah is great,' said Anninho.

When we were outside, Anninho placed the amulet around my neck, and mounting, lifted me up on the horse, in back of him.

'I am involved with Palmares,' he said. 'But you see, I am involved with something beyond that.'

I said nothing, though I did not fully see.

The Return and a Discussion on
New Musical Discoveries

ANNINHO SPENT SEVERAL DAYS, with his other journeys and responsibilities, copying the draughts and then returned to the man he had called Mualim. This time the man was not alone, but in the large room with him were Mr and Mrs Iaiyesimi, the Nigerian trader and his wife. The woman stood quietly, dressed in a purple silk, robe-like dress. Her husband wore a long white cotton green-striped robe and a green fez. The woman took me aside and said that we should go into the music room and leave the men alone, but she did not seem to recognize me as the same woman that she and her husband had noticed when they had come to the shoemaker Sobrieski's shop some months before. If she did recognize me she did not say so, nor did her husband.

We went into a small room where there was a harp, a harpsichord, a thumb piano, and a long strange wooden instrument, and many cushions. I sat down on one of the cushions, but the woman, who seemed very silent and shy, lifted the wooden instrument, and began to finger the holes along its length, but without making a sound.

'What's that?' I inquired as she sat on the harpsichord stool.

'A clarinet,' she said. 'It's a new musical instrument. It was just invented seven years ago, in 1690. It's a present my husband and I presented to Mr Oparinde.'

'I thought his name was Mualim,' I said.

'No, no. That's some title his religion gives him. It means teacher, I think.'

She began to play a strange music, and sang a song, and then played again. The song was in a language I do not know, so I cannot say the words of it, but it was sung with much expression, as if she were telling me something, or talking to someone else. She played again, slowly at first, and then a faster more energetic rhythm, with many sounds mingling, though I cannot really describe it. When she finished she spoke of her and her husband's traveling in Europe, and going to a big hall in which people on a stage were singing songs that told stories and that she had just sang one of them. She liked the 'arias' and as they had stayed there for three years, she had learned some of them. Then she started talking about the dramatic song-dances that she remembered as a child, the masked dancers, and the blending of dance, music, and drama that reminded her of that, or that that reminded her of, except for where and how they were required to sit to observe it, and the absence of the drums. But every movement, every gesture, every sound had a meaning.

'Supply international market,' we heard drift from another room.

'I haven't met any intelligent Americans,' said a voice which I took to be Mr Iaiyesimi's.

Then there were bits and pieces of sentences. Though I could not hear everything, there seemed to be some connection, or mistrust, or something.

The wife of Mr Iaiyesimi, whose first name I did not remember, and who did not tell me, sat studying the harpsichord keys. I could not tell if she was also listening. I wondered what kind of man Mr Iaiyesimi was. What had enabled him to travel around the world, making trading contacts? Was he a prince or a king? When other Africans traveled internationally it was in the holes of ships, though it is told that there were African explorers with early expeditions. I wondered what the men were planning and what it would mean. How did they plan to reconstruct their world? Hadn't I seen Mr Iaiyesimi converse as easily with the Polish shoemaker Sobrieski as he was conversing now with these men? Who was this strange African woman, his wife, who knew European music and played it with such ease?

'It's a very ecstatic experience, like a religious one. Everyone is possessed,' the woman was saying.

'It's here for the taking,' I heard from the other room. 'There are always threats of disintegration . . .'

'It's called opera,' the woman was saying.

'What do you mean, how will the world respond?' from outside.

'Still it would be easier to simply hire a merchant vessel and an escort ship.'

'I'm concerned with what it will mean over time. In the future.'

'An ecstatic experience. A possession,' the woman said.

Then Anninho and Mr Iaiyesimi appeared at the door, and we each went with our husbands.

We left through the entrance hall, but I did not see Mualim or Mr Oparinde as we were leaving. Mr Iaiyesimi and his wife said goodbye and got into a carriage. My husband lifted me onto the back of his horse but he was silent as we rode back. Though in the silence I felt there was anger. If other visits were made or other discussions held, other plans, I did not know of them, nor even the full meaning of those I was in some proximity to.

A Medicine Man Is Banished

MY GRANDMOTHER RUSHED INTO MY HUT and told me to come to the door.

I came seeing a man being hurried along the street, dragged along, with much noise, and being beat by ropes. The man was very silent, perfectly silent, but the men dragging him made noise, and continued to flog his bare back and arms, and where his trousers were rolled up, the calves of his legs.

'What has the man done?' I asked.

'That is what they do to medicine men and witches,' she said. 'They are not permitted here.'

'Are you a witch?'

She looked at me. 'I have a knowledge of medicines and herbs. I'm a medicine woman,' she said, nonchalantly.

'How did they find out what he is? Did someone tell on him?'

'There are numerous spies. Someone, I think, overheard him speaking about the fate of Palmares, and trying to work his medicines to prevent such disaster, and they told the king. He did not deny it. He confessed. He spoke of his hope for Palmares, that he might be able to help. But the king said such beliefs are the weakness of the State, and had him banished.'

'Not killed?' I asked.

'No, not killed,' my grandmother said, staring at the man, who as he passed our doorway glanced our way. My grandmother nodded to him with reverence. I looked on with curious eyes.

'He's not a witch but a diviner,' my grandmother said, when he had been taken further down the road. 'He divines destruction and he offers cures to prevent it. But they say it's witchcraft.'

I said nothing, hearing the noise and the silence of the man.

'We won't hold the ground for a very long time,' my grandmother said.

'Does he have a wife?' I asked suddenly.

'A wife?' she repeated. 'No, that man is without a wife. Why do you ask?'

'I wondered how she was feeling.'

She was silent, then she said, 'Perhaps there is some Palmarista woman, who is not exhibited in public.'

Many watched, and for a moment I thought I saw that special woman, standing with her hands in her hair, and suddenly her hands were at her sides, and all the time she remained perfectly silent.

'They will continue to fight,' my grandmother said, 'but the ground is not meant to be held.'

She made a long shadow across the door as she went out.

When she returned she said again that he was not a witch but a diviner. 'They say it's witchcraft, and so they won't attempt his occult stratagem.'

A Woman Not Exhibited in Public

WHY I WAS DRAWN TO THE WOMAN I cannot say. I waited until one could hear no more noise, and then when the woman turned and went back to her hut, I followed her. Inside she sat on a reed mat, with her forehead in her hands. I stood in the doorway, until she felt or saw my shadow and looked up. I had expected to see tears, but her face was very dry and very solemn.

'What do you want?' she asked.

'I don't know,' I said.

She frowned a bit, and kept looking at me.

'I know that you're his woman, and that you love each other,' I whispered.

'Come in,' she said, standing up quickly.

I came in. She motioned for me to sit down on the mat she'd been sitting on. I sat down.

She remained standing, her hands to the sides of her face.

'How do you know what I am to that man?'

I told her my suspicions, a fleeting gesture, my grandmother's comments.

'Ah,' she said, looking down at me.

She put her hand to her hair. We looked at each other in silence. I was thinking of Xavier, the old medicine man I knew when I was younger. I was wondering what it would be like to be the woman of a man who knew all kinds of magic. Why did I say they loved each other? I did not even know the woman. I had never spoken to her. I wondered if Xavier had had a woman whom he did not exhibit in public.

'What is it?' she asked.

'Nothing,' I said.

'What do you want to tell me?' she asked.

'Just that I am sorry about what happened.'

'I'm glad you've come. Now I can tell him someone came to comfort me. What is your name?'

'Almeyda.'

'Almeyda,' she repeated. 'My husband will be pleased and he will reward you for being my friend and coming to comfort me.'

I wondered how he could reward me not being here and no one knowing what had become of him.

She sat down on another mat.

'Just sit with me. We don't have to talk. I don't care to talk. I'm glad that you've come.'

We sat together silently for a very long time. Then she began to talk slowly. 'He will come, even if the gates are guarded and the doors are locked. He'll look at me and we'll both be free. We shall amuse ourselves, in spite of all of this. We'll surround ourselves with each other. Again and again we'll take each other for husband and wife. No meaningless ritual.

'I'm grateful that you've come. And he'll be very glad of it. He's a great man and will reward you. Did you know he can write the future? Yes, he can write it out in full. I've seen it happen. He knows they'll be surrounded on all sides. But who'll listen? He'll give you a gift. Yes. A supernatural gift. Though with Indaya you needn't worry. I'll see him again soon. When we see each other we will laugh, and congratulate each other, and speak about how good it is to be in our native country.'

I looked at her, but said nothing.

'My husband is a good man,' she said. 'He's a preserver of life.'

She smiled at me. 'He'll come and take me away from here, and we'll laugh in our native country … Do you know I've never laughed here? I've wanted to, but I never have.'

She climbed upon her hammock.

'I want to be alone now,' she said, 'but I'm grateful that you came. Come tomorrow and I won't be here.'

I went out, asking myself, was the woman crazy? But the next day when I went there, she was not there. When it was discovered that she was missing, an expedition was sent in search of her, but she was never found.

Pedro the Third

I AGAIN SAW THE MAN called Pedro the Third, who had worked in the shoemaker's shop along with me. I had not seen him in the several months since we had been brought to the quilombo and then I saw him walking down the street in front of my house, carrying a big bag of coffee. Anninho was not there as he had gone into town on some business. Though in my mind I saw him and the woman they called Luiza Cosme in a secret meeting at this man Martim Aprigio's house – the wife of Martim Aprigio and others gathered in a back room.

When I saw Pedro I went outside and stood. When he did not look toward me I called his name. He turned and stopped, but said nothing to me.

'Pedro, how are you?' He said nothing.

'I have not seen you in a very long time.'

'Did you think I was dead? Did you think they had murdered me?'

I said nothing, though I had worried at not seeing him, and thought perhaps he had tried to escape, or they had learned of his military past, and he had been strung up in the horrid way that other man had been -- though since that first discovery I had not seen with my own eyes any others who had deserted and were captured and brought back.

He seemed at first to be afraid to be speaking to me and then he got closer, though he was silent, waiting for me to speak. A man passed on the street and glanced at us. He frowned but kept walking.

'They disapprove of the wife of Martim Anninho speaking to me,' he said, then he laughed. 'Or do you still say you are your own woman?'

He had heard Capao ask me one night if I had been anyone's woman before I had come there.

'I have been and am my own woman,' I had said. 'I lay alone in my own hammock.'

'*Your* hammock,' he had said. 'Not *your* hammock. Not your own soul. I could ask *him* anytime, or he could say, "Here, Capao." Anytime. His tongue has been cut out,' he said of Pedro. 'He claims he did it to himself. He claims he cut it at the roots his own self.'

'He speaks. I heard him.'

He had laughed then, and then I did not know what he had meant. 'Capao will tell any lie,' Pedro had said.

'I've hunted for such men as these,' he said now. His face looked ashen. 'My captain gave the orders and I went. They think I do not know if I am a white man or a black one. I remember. Sure I remember. I killed some, captured others and made them slaves again. Why do you always want to know that? Why do you want to know that? She looked a bit like you, that's why I didn't want you there. I'd go to visit her, not to stay with her, because they didn't want the black soldiers to sleep in the barracks with the other men, and so those who had women would go to them. I'd lay with her. And after we made love I would tell her. Why I chose to tell the woman I didn't know. But I would tell her how many I had killed and what horrible things – what mutilations I had done and had to do in the name of the army, and how many I had captured and brought back to be slaves again. But one night she said to me, '"You said those of you who would serve in the militia were given your freedom. It was part of the exchange?"

'"Yes," I said. "You know that."

'She said nothing. She kept looking at me and would not take her eyes off.

'"You know I will be here when you return. You know I will be here again and again. But do not tell me those things you have done or the things you must do tomorrow."

'I did not go back to her nor did I go back to the others. I deserted them both – the woman and the military. I cut my own tongue out. I branded fujao on my own head. I let them hunt for this fugitive.'

I said nothing. We kept watching each other. I kept trying to remember how much of the story had changed, and whether this was the true version.

The man who had passed us before passed by again. 'Get along, Pedro. Get along, man,' he said, without looking at either one of us.

Pedro walked on down the road and I entered the house to wait for Anninho's return.

An Observer
in Porto Calvo

ANNINHO CAME BACK carrying a bag of coffee like the one I had seen Pedro carrying. I thought at first that the man who had passed us on the street had said something about his wife standing in the doorway talking to a certain slave. But he said only hello to me and set the bag down in the corner and there was no mention of the incident.

'Did you see Luiza Cosme?' I asked.

He looked at me for a moment, then he said, 'No.' He said he had merely gone into town to observe what was going on, and it was easier for him alone than if he had taken me with him.

He sat down at the table, and moved the lighted candle and books and papers toward him. Some were maps, some writings, his own and other people's, in both Arabic and Portuguese – some were not words, but small drawings, others numbers and figures.

I sat on the hammock, sewing straps into a pair of sandals.

Occasionally I would look at him; sometimes he would seem unaware of my presence. Other times he would look at me and smile.

'You went there only to observe?' I asked after a long time. 'What is going on?'

He looked at me, at first not speaking, then he said, 'I wanted to see what is going on with the local militia.'

I stared at him without speaking. I had heard them only speak of danger and horrors; and when I was growing up it had been the tales of horror, somewhat distant brutalities of existence. I had only seen one man and one woman hanged with my own eyes, and my grandmother had shown me the dried ears and feet of an enemy, the first one she had slain, and had told me stories of other exploits; and there had been the old woman's tales and Pedro's, and there had been the tale of the straw woman, and the sight of the women healing.

He watched me, then he said, 'They are making preparations to destroy Palmares again. Another expedition will be sent. When I don't know, but it is better to think it is every minute. It is better to think every second is the second.'

I said nothing, then I asked, 'Is it coffee?'

'What?'

'Is it coffee?' I asked, pointing to the sack.

'No.'

He poured over the maps again, began to make little marks and signs.

'It is not the visible world but the invisible one I am most drawn to,' he said, looking up at me. 'And that I would devote myself to completely if I were given my choice in this world.'

I said nothing. The sandals I was making were not made of leather but vegetable fiber.

'A new expedition will be sent very soon,' he said, looking up at me and saying it as if it was something he had just heard.

A man knocked at the door, a dark-skinned man of royal bearing. He came in without being told, bowed to me without speaking and then walked up to Anninho.

'This is the passage,' Anninho said.

The man said something to him in a tongue I did not know. Anninho replied back in the same language. But it did not sound like the Arabic one I had heard him and my grandmother speak. Even when she refused to teach it to us, she had referred to it as a language that literary men spoke. She had said that there were few among even the colonists who could read or write the language they spoke. She had said it in an arrogant way, and still even now treated it as though it were a forbidden and sacred language.

The man stayed there for close to an hour and they poured over books together and spoke together in that language. Then the man bowed to him and bowed to me and left.

'Is that ... was that the man they call Zumbi?' I asked hurriedly.

Anninho laughed. 'No,' he replied. 'I sent for him because he is one of the few who still understands an African tongue. But he has also been known to use the language of Virgil and Horace.'

I looked at him, not knowing what he was talking about. 'Latin,' he said.

I nodded, thinking of one of the books Father Tollinare had that he had refused to instruct us from.

'He is renowned for his knowledge of dead languages as well as living ones.' He laughed. 'And also for his casting of love spells.'

'What?'

'He was driven from Porto Calvo not because of his learning, but because there were nine women – nine white women – who accused him of casting love spells and making them do things. At first he had been celebrated for his learning, a curiosity, but then one woman, then another claimed his eyes made her do things. First he was sentenced to a special jail and then to perpetual imprisonment. It's a funny story when he tells it. How in court they made him cover his eyes, the women afraid to look at him when they told their stories.'

'Was it true? Had he made them do things?' I asked, for the man seemed to have very 'strong' eyes.

'Perhaps,' he said with a shrug. 'Or perhaps only what they themselves wanted ... He escaped and came here. He has a number of women, but none has *complained* of his love spells,' he said with a laugh.

'Do you have ... a number of women?' I asked.

'How many do you see?' he asked.

I said nothing.

'I only have time for one,' he said, smiling a bit, and looking at his studies. Then he glanced up again. 'There were many women in my family – wives of my father.'

'Where is he now?' I asked.

'He felt there were not enough believers in Allah. I don't know where he is. The last thing he'd done was left all of his women, including my mother, and tried to convert a tribe of Indians to have them wage a holy war with him ... I don't know nor does my mother.'

'Where is your mother?'

'I won't talk of her. I won't talk of her to anyone,' he said. 'That is something I don't do. I'll stay with you as long as you love me, but she'll remain unknown.'

His look made me glance away from him.

In silence, I sewed the vegetable fiber sandals while he made marks on the pages, wrote strange figures, traced new lines on the maps, then he rose, and said, 'Come on, I must see someone. This time you may go. I need your company.'

Whale Oil

I RODE BEHIND HIM ON HORSEBACK, holding him around the waist. His broad shoulders tapered to a narrow line. His stomach was flat and hard. Though he had said he wanted my company, he did not speak to me in the whole time we traveled.

He stopped outside of an old tavern on a road somewhere between the Palm Forests and Porto Calvo, perhaps eight leagues from the town.

He jumped off the horse and said, 'Wait here for me,' started in but on second thought came back, held his hand up and helped me down.

When I was down, he tied the horse to a post and I followed him inside. It was a tavern, but when we got inside there was no one at the wooden counter or the tables near the window. In the corner only sat a man with a brown and red scarf wrapped around his head, clumps of straight black hair sticking out; there was a patch over one of his eyes. His one eye seemed fierce and 'possessed' – if that is the proper word for the mad, dark mystery some eyes seem to have. He looked at Anninho but stayed at the table. Anninho walked me to another corner and told me to sit down. But instead of sitting with me, he walked over to where the man sat, and sat down, without speaking.

The man said something softly about 'the woman' but I could not make out what it was, and I did not hear any answer from Anninho.

It seemed that they sat there for a long time in silence and then they began to whisper and when the whispers grew louder, I still did not know what it was they said, for it was in yet another foreign tongue – French or English or Dutch – but not Portuguese. I had learned a little English, but this did not sound like the English I knew.

Anninho spoke in very level unemotional tones. The man did too at first and then his words grew passionate, excited, 'possessed.' Once he even rapped on the table, then he got up and started across the room – that was when I saw that his left leg was wooden, and there was only that sound as he walked slowly. When he passed me, he glanced but only for a moment. Behind the counter he poured two wooden mugs of beer. He started to pour a third, but Anninho called, 'She doesn't drink it.'

The man picked up the two mugs and walked back across the room slowly, the tap of wood on wood. He stared out of his one fierce eye.

He set the mugs down heavily, then sat down.

Again here was silence, then the foreign language – Anninho's even-toned. The man's, even-toned in the beginning, then possessed.

'Allah,' I heard Anninho say, then he was talking steadily in the other man's language.

After what seemed like several hours the man again got up and walked across the room, came back carrying a small keg; barely larger than his hands. He set it down on the table beside Anninho. Anninho took it and rose. Anninho walked over to where I was and tapped me on the shoulder. When we were standing, the man was looking at me out of his fierce eye but said nothing. He said something to Anninho again in his language. Anninho nodded firmly, but said nothing. Then we left.

He got onto the horse and then reached down and pulled me up. 'Who is the man?' I asked.

'A crazy man,' he said.

He placed the small keg in one of my hands, then took the reins. 'What is it?' I asked, holding it in my fist.

'Whale oil,' he said, and he was silent the rest of the way, and did not speak of the man even when we returned home.

Of the White Woman
from Porto Calvo and Other
Women, Black and White

I stood in the doorway watching the men return. They had some black and mulatto women with them and one white woman. Anninho walked behind the others. Some had spears, others bows and arrows, some swords, some firearms. A few men were carrying both swords and firearms, the firearms having been taken from the sugar plantation. One man walked with a limp, but no one else was wounded. Anninho did not look toward me as they walked past in the wide road. I did not go out to him, but went back into the house and began work on a new pair of sandals. By now, I had a pile of sandals in one corner of the house.

Later, Anninho came with sugar and rum. We kissed and then sat down. He took out a silver necklace and handed it to me. I shook my head and said, 'No.' I fingered the one made out of cacao seed and trumpet shells. He laughed. He put the silver one back in his pocket. We sat at the table in silence. I wondered if the necklace had been taken from that woman I had seen.

'What will they do with the white woman?' I asked.

'Nothing.'

'Nothing?'

He lifted his elbow and said, 'She will be held for ransom. She is the daughter of a rich man in Porto Calvo.'

I looked at him without speaking.

'*They* imagine things we are doing to her. She is in her own hut, guarded. She is the same woman she was when we brought her here. She is as whole as she was when we found her.'

He said everything without raising his voice and without any feeling, then he looked away from me.

'One of Zumbi's women is a white woman,' I said.

He nodded but said nothing. He spread his maps and books out on the table. Then he said, 'What does it matter? A woman is a woman.'

I looked down at my hands. At first I had had no opinion of her or feeling toward her, but I had passed her this morning. Her long hair was parted in the center. She was wearing many layers of beads. I could not bring myself to look at her, though I could feel her eyes on me. I had kept my head down. I glimpsed her black skirt hitting against her ankles and then I passed.

I went back to the sandals I was making. After a while, Anninho stood up.

'I'm going out,' he said.

I nodded. I tossed the sandals into the corner with the other ones and lay down in the hammock. I dreamed that Anninho and I were standing together and the woman came. I would not look at her, but he watched. I touched the beads on my neck. They were gone. I thought she was wearing them, but I was afraid to look. Out of the corner of my eye I saw circles and circles of color around her neck.

'Who is that woman?' I heard Anninho ask. He was not talking to me.

'She came here yesterday. Zumbi has taken her for his woman. I didn't think he would want that kind of woman. But a woman's a woman, I guess.' I heard the voice, but I did not know who was speaking.

Anninho said nothing. I could feel him watching her. She started to sing. I was afraid because her voice was beautiful. I stared down at the ground. I left them. Anninho stayed watching her. I walked down the side of the mountain, hearing her voice.

Color is not contagious. A woman's a woman.

When I awoke, I could still hear the woman singing. Anninho came back. He stood watching me, then he climbed into the hammock and lay down beside me.

It is not often in this world that such a thing happens.

What?

That a man and woman return to each other.

'What will they ransom the woman for?'

'Muskets, gunpowder, gold.'

A Slave Captures a Slave
and Redeems Himself

PEDRO THE THIRD CAME TO THE DOOR of my hut. He stood in the doorway as if he were waiting for me. 'I am no longer a slave,' he said, 'and am free to talk to you as any man.'

'What do you mean?' I asked, coming to the door, frowning because of the thing that had happened when he had stopped on the road to talk to me.

'I'm a free man,' he said, both hands on his chest. 'And can speak with you the same as any other man.'

I stood looking at him, feeling cautious. 'How can you be a free man?' I asked.

'Don't you know the law here?' he asked. 'That if a slave captures a slave he redeems himself. Isn't that the way?'

I said nothing. He was looking at me with large eyes.

'I'm a free Palmarista man,' he almost screamed, leaning into the door.

Someone walked by on the road and looked over but went on.

'A slave capturing another slave. That's my profession and has always been. Except now I capture a slave for my own freedom. Then I used to capture a slave for the Portuguese, but now it's for my own self. Isn't that something for old Pedro?'

Why had he called himself that? I stood looking at him, a tall, mustached, quite handsome man.

'Isn't that something? That's what I like in a woman. No answers. I had a woman. I'd tell her all of it, every bit of it. And you, Almeyda, you'd say nothing to all that, wouldn't you? Each time, if you were the woman, I'd come back after an expedition, telling you. And you'd say nothing.

'Wouldn't that be fine for an old slave catcher. But her – her look accusing me. And yours? What does yours do? Everything in the eyes, and yet they're silent now. Unspeaking. I'm a free man, and if you weren't taken, I'd choose you. But you're that man's woman.'

I nodded, but said nothing.

'I wanted to come and tell you how I redeemed myself. A slave catches a slave. That is how one buys his own freedom here.'

He kept looking at me strangely.

He asked me, 'Where is your husband?'

I said I didn't know. Perhaps he had gone into Porto Calvo on some business.

'That is how I redeem my existence,' he said. 'That is how I get my manhood back. And do you believe the spirit of the man returns as well? What will I do with my freedom? Well, I'll fight along with the others to maintain it, but not as their servant, but their equal, a man knowledgeable in the ways of the military. I'll be of some use. Don't you feel it is right for a slave to capture another slave and redeem himself?'

I was silent.

'What shall I do with my freedom? Freedom now to capture the slaves whom *I* choose, and do what *I* choose with them. Isn't that something? Doesn't that give a free man something to do? Isn't that a way to exercise my freedom? I was tired of being a slave, otherwise I wouldn't have gone after him.' He laughed, but out of anxiety. 'What is your opinion on the subject?'

I said nothing.

'Well, it is the way of the nation. Another man's freedom depends on the slavery of yet another. How many slaves must I capture to get the maximum freedom? Are you in disagreement? Why do you look at me so? Do you think I am a crazy man? A silly man? Ah, I am not the man who puts his own freedom in danger to help rebels. If I were that man, do you know what I'd do? I'd leave this place and exercise my freedom daily. Buy your freedom, take you with me. My regards to this place. Have our little world. Travel about *my* country, the cities, the backlands, by horseback, by canoe. See *my* country in ways I am longing to see it. That's what I would do if I were that man. See *my* country. And what kind of knowledge does he have? Is it some knowledge of the stars? Is he an astrologer? Does he know the sea? Some knowledge of the oceans? Is he a geographer?

'Is that the word? I see him with his little books and figures, his maps, his secret codes, his knowledge of languages. His secret codes. Or perhaps he's not here to do these people any good, but a spy for *them*? Is he a traitor?'

I shook my head, but said nothing, and thought of the man he had met in the tavern.

'No, he is no traitor. He is no spy for the military. But I'd go about my country with you, and then to another one and another across all the oceans. Look how they fight for a limited existence, some little piece of independent ground. But what if there are no other choices? You exchange one limited existence for another. But here I am within the confines of it. But when I was a military man, first I fought in the wars against the Dutch, and then when there were no more Dutch to fight, what is it they do? I am sent in the punitive wars against the Negroes. Ha. Ha. And I did it, in exchange for some little freedom. Some mobility, some trek across *my* land. But if I were that man, I'd go to the very heart of my country. What is the heart? Perhaps I am there. Do you think I am there? No, but they call us the scabs of the country, and it is their duty to remove the scabs. I'd see all sorts of people. Do you think our country is an interesting comedy or a tragedy? What do you think is the essence of it?

'What are the emotions of the ordinary people? The extraordinary, the freakish even? What are the hopes of men in other countries? I'd take my new freedom and do things with it, learn whatever secrets there are. Or do you think that I live in the big secret now, that I'm in it now? Ha. Ha. Why don't you take my dream of existence to that man? Without dreams you will receive nothing. And without them, what do you receive? Tell him to take his freedom by the collar and pull it about where he wants to go.'

He paused, waiting for me to speak, but I said nothing. He looked for a moment like he wasn't being clear enough. He looked like he wanted to be clear enough, to say something I would remember.

'But that man, that man of yours, perhaps it is here he wants to be because he does have such choices. Is he a historian? Do you think he is writing about us?'

He paused again and waited. I said nothing.

'But he comes to hear no one's story. He is a man of few words, and does not mingle well. How can he be a historian? He must be an astrologer. He must have some enchantment with the stars. He must set down such things as the stars are doing.' He shook his head with sadness. He looked like he wanted to say something memorable, but couldn't find the words. He shook his head again. 'I am a free man today. I was beginning to think it would not come. Do you think I thought it would be something I could see? Do you see that woman? I've noticed her for a long time, but she's free. Do you think I should trust her? Do you think that is the only place my freedom will take me?' He laughed with despair. 'Is that where the road leads to with the least difficulty? If I hurry, do you think she will talk to me?'

I said I didn't know.

'Well, I must hurry anyway,' he said, stepping away from the door. 'For I see your husband advancing.'

He hurried away from the door and I saw him run to catch up with the woman. I did not look to see how she greeted him, for Anninho came in the door.

'What did he want?' he asked.

'He came only to tell me that he had his freedom. He captured another slave and so they gave him his freedom.'

He nodded but said nothing, still looking at me.

'We were slaves in the same place,' I explained. 'The shoemaker's ...'

'Well, he has a gift for talk,' he said. 'I was at the lookout post and saw him standing here a good long while.'

A Praise of Heroes
and a Paid Informer

I WENT WITH MY GRANDMOTHER to view the man. I did not know where I was going, but my grandmother said that everyone must go out to view the conspirator. This was to be a warning to potential conspirators. This man, it was said, was a paid informer, whose job it was to ferret out the hiding places of renegades. He was one who had been trusted. He had taken part in all the raids on pack trains, sugar mills, and plantations. He had been a slave and had purchased his own freedom. I could not believe my eyes when I saw the man. It was Pedro the Third. I left my grandmother and drew closer till he was looking at me.

'Almeyda,' he said.

People looked at me. They had first tied him to a tree. In the evening he would be hanged. He tipped his head to me.

'Have you come to praise the hero?' he asked. I heard a man curse and spit in his direction.

'That is why you are here, in praise of the hero,' he said, sarcastically. He kept staring at me.

'Do you know that you're all a threat to Brazilian civilization,' he said. 'All of you. The whole history of this place would be different if it weren't for you. I wish you'd leave me alone. Or are you trying to find yourselves in me? Look at me. I don't know where I'm going. Where will I be tomorrow? Yes, you've all come to praise the hero.'

Someone spit in his direction.

'Almeyda, have you come to find yourself too? Do you think you're a traitor?'

I said nothing. Now the eyes of the Palmaristas were on me.

'Let this be a lesson to all potential traitors,' he said. 'But this is my greatest work,' he whispered. 'A triumph of imagination.' He began to laugh. 'I've got no right to determine your liberty, but haven't I determined mine? Almeyda, after this is done, I'll go all about *my* country. *Mine.*

'Anywhere. I'll visit the South first, then the Northeast, then the rest of it. Study the political, military, social history. The memories of the people. Mine. And the intimate histories. I'll find myself in everybody. Ha. *My* country. *My* freedom. How far am I from Porto Calvo?' He waited as if he expected an answer from me, then he went on, 'Sixteen leagues? I'll be there tomorrow. Then in the mountains, canoeing on the rivers. No need to fight with guns and spears and knives. Always protected. All the time.

'And then I won't move my lips not at all, just watch all of you. I'll be watching all of you. The whole panorama of my country. *Mine.* I'll go to any tavern in any territory. I'll go to the theaters, the churches, into the big houses, into the innermost chambers. I won't say a thing. Not even "This is me, Pedro." No, not a word. I'll wear a gold halo of feathers. I'll wear enormous rings on my fingers, satin shoes, armbands. I'll climb hills. I'll go to other countries. I'll go from city to city. Always the stranger. Always free. I'll hear *your* conversations, all of them, but never a word from me.

'I'll be in out-of-the-way places and in-the-way places. Everywhere. Always see the new and different, in the world and in me too. No, I won't be the same Pedro. I'll move from one vocation to the other. I'll be my own man forever.'

Did I actually hear him talking? Had he really spoken? I did not see him when they hanged him and placed his head on a pole. I did not see it until after it was done and my grandmother drew me away.

'Did he say anything? Did you hear what he said?' I asked her.

'No, he was silent the whole time,' she replied. 'He was silent, but he couldn't take his eyes off you.'

Malaria Fever;
Dreams of Escape and Capture;
of Zumbi, the Chieftain

Circles under my eyes. I run into the stream. I paint cacao on my eyelids. My grandmother rubs oil on my forehead and shoulders, gives me leaves to chew.

She lifts my arms, tells me to breathe this way and this.

Is it true that in that place beautiful women paint their bodies and are allowed to go naked?

What place? She takes the leaf from my mouth and gives me another to chew. Swallow this one.

In the old days it was the Dutch and now it is the Portuguese. They are building a fence around the outside of ours.

What fence? What do you see, Almeyda?

A fence. There is no other way. They want me to go to Parahyba with them. He wants me to follow him through that space.

Anninho comes in and touches my forehead and eyelids.

Have they cut us off now? I was in the circle with the other women.

She doesn't know what she's saying, my grandmother tells him. It's dreams and senseless talk.

He touches my breasts and stomach. I stand with him on a deserted beach and then in a place in the mountains. We walk through a palm forest.

Look at me, Almeyda.

Will you take me with you to Porto Calvo? No, you're dreaming.

Did you see the strange man and woman come into camp? Why did they come now?

I'll draw the poison out with bark from a cabbage tree, says my grandmother.

Why did they come now?

Anninho, keep away from your woman at this moment. Do not lay with her. She has the fever.

Anninho, where are we going now? Did you see the strange man and woman? I'm told they are brave warriors. Hold on to the spirits of such men and women.

He lifts my head and she rubs oil on the back of my neck. I swing the moon up on my shoulders and climb over fallen trees and roots. I am covered with dirt and mud. We walk in the river. My blood comes. We crawl under roots to sleep hidden on the ground. My hair has not been combed.

Grandmother, is here an absolute future? An absolute past?

Absolute? Unchanging.

Soft cassava, soft banana, on the back of my tongue. Anninho cuts his shoulder on a sharp stone. I sew it up with hard brown threads. He stands over me, silent. I wipe the blood from his shoulder.

Is the future absolute? What is she saying, Indaya? Senseless talk.

Vera, you've come.

Old Vera touches my shoulder with sunlight. Are you a spirit or a woman?

She is carrying the sun on her dark shoulders and touching me with it.

Here, stand over here and protect your woman. But do not lay with her.

I see these things, Anninho. Is the future absolute?

Zumbi, the chieftain, bows his head and enters. His broad shoulders touch the sun. They say he is immortal.

What is the name of this woman?

Almeyda.

Does she prophesy the future?

Almeyda, the war will always be needed. War of swords or consciousness.

I see these things happening.

Is Almeyda the one you have chosen? Is Almeyda the one? Yes.

A man in a hammock with his woman. Two white men enter carrying rifles and they have a striped Indian with them, his body filled with striped tattoos. They enter even while the man is with his woman. He stands up, his arms held out to protect his woman, to cover her naked body.

The sun red and gold stands on his dark shoulders. He looks as if he is all shadow.

Are you a man or the spirit of one? I will not tell you the rest of the story. Ah, I won't tell you the rest of that sad story.

Is this the one you have chosen? Yes.

Did you see Old Vera appear and disappear?

Anninho turns his back to me, whispers to someone, then turns back, touches my head again, kisses the side of my mouth.

My grandmother fed me crushed pineapple and more leaves to chew and a heavy oil to drink.

Do not lay with her tonight. I have two sleeping rooms and a kitchen. Luiza, did you get your earrings back?

What is she saying?

Four snakes' heads beaten together in buttermilk and powdered scorpion ashes. A butterfly alights on my forehead.

Almeyda, what do you want? Liberty, safety, solitude.

Is this the oil that protects? Yes, put some more on her.

It's Iararaca come to visit. Put him on her forehead, to draw the fever out.

Can't you see the fever rise out of her body? Take him away now.

He's tasted the fever and now it's rising out of her.

Old Vera and my grandmother rub leaves all over my body and give me others to chew.

Anninho, I said I have two sleeping rooms. He turns and goes out. Zumbi?

There's no Zumbi here.

They're holding him by the hair. Is he a man or a spirit?

They burn coca leaves. I see large ants, scorpions, snakes. I walk over sharp stones, a creek, deep swamp. I feel hot days, cold days, heavy rains.

We stand on the edge of a camp. Anninho circles a point on a map he has drawn.

She is quiet now.

They lean down, touching my head.

Anninho, an older man, enters. No, it's his father. Are you the woman?

Are you the general of arms? Where's Anninho?

I sent him away, so he won't observe what two old women do. Some sorcery?

Herbs that preserve health. He touches my forehead.

The blessings of Allah. Where's my son? I must speak with my son. Where is he?

Across the street. I have two sleeping rooms. I have heard there will be another expedition.

But we know the territory better, the layout of the land. The forest is difficult to penetrate.

What to do now? Await the enemy.

They are building a new line of defense. Pits full of spears. Some to pierce the feet, others the groin, the throat. We have our own observers in the town. Now they have Indians with them, and blacks. Shall I use a knife? A hatchet? A shovel? A scythe? A sword? A hoe?

Old Vera is holding a long pipe and begins to puff from it. More coca leaves. She waves the smoke under my nose.

Leave me alone with my granddaughter. She has no experience in wars. I want to bless her and pray alone.

A LEAP
THROUGH TIME
AND SPIRIT

Oranges and Fresh Butter

WHEN I AM WELL, Anninho brings me oranges and fresh butter.

First I saw his shadow standing outside the door and then he entered.

He kissed my forehead and mouth.

'Did you see your father?' I asked.

'What?' he said, frowning.

I said that his father had come in with many people. But he shook his head and said it was not so, that I must have seen his father through my fever and delirium. Then he lay the oranges and fresh butter beside me on the hammock, and went back into the street. There were two shouts but I could not make out whose voices or what was said. Then I heard plainly:

'I can leave this place anytime I want to. Why do I stay?'

It sounded like the voice of the old man Xavier, the medicine man.

Once when I had had menstrual trouble I had gone to him for some remedy. I sat on the mat with him outside his hut. He had taken me inside, touched me in places, rubbed my palms, then he had brewed me a tea to drink that did the work in three minutes.

'What kind of root is it?' I'd asked.

'Maybe it's no root,' he'd said. 'Maybe it's scorpion dung.'

He was playful like that about his remedies, teasing me with all kinds of ingredients, though most times he was solemn and serious and guarded about the matter; and there was a certain young man whom he taught the real ingredients.

'How do you feel?' he'd asked.

I'd told him that I felt very fine now.

'I should take an herb and leave this place,' he'd said. 'I don't have to stay here, you know. No, Xavier does not have to stay here, he can leave this place anytime he wants to. But one day Wencelau (where he got that name I don't know) – but one day he will take over, and Xavier will take off,' he'd said, laughing. 'Wencelau will have the workload and old Peixoto will be free. Peixoto's my name too. A man has to have a name for his body and a name for his soul too, that's what I feel. Old Peixoto will be free, and watch how he'll leap through time then. Ah, I do it now, but I always come back. I return here. So many need healing. But watch how he'll leap through time and space then, ha ha. Drop me off a cliff and see how I'll soar.'

He'd looked at me and spread his arms out, and I'll tell anyone he was a bird, then he became a man again. I'll tell that to anybody.

'I'll go through real time and I'll go through legendary time, imaginary time,' he'd said with another laugh, pointing his chin at me and looking up. 'Watch Peixoto make his leaps and bounds and move through time. He'll move through names too. How do you like Alves, Pecanho, Ribeiro, Garostazu? I could leave here now,' he said, looking at me firmly, 'but I'm not. So many need my healing. I'll have other names, but I won't tell you. And I'll have different shapes and forms. But I'll have the same eyes. That's how you'll know me.'

I sleep and dream that I am looking at Anninho's eyes. 'What is it?' he asks.

'Your eyes haven't changed,' I say.

'What?' he asks.

'Nothing,' I say quickly, then I ask him if the soul peeks out through the eyes as they say it does.

Xavier is standing before me smiling now.

'I'm all shapes and forms,' he says, 'but my eyes haven't changed. Don't you recognize Peixoto? Don't you remember Peixoto?'

'Yes,' I say, but it comes out funny, it comes out sounding more like 'Yis.'

He takes both my hands and pulls me up off the hammock, and we are out in a flat, wide, sunny field. He begins to turn me around and around as he turns around, making a circle.

'How do you like me now?' he says again and again. With each turn he changes, but I can't make out any of the faces. Then he's a blur, but

I don't feel dizzy. He disappears, but still I'm not dizzy. Around and around in a circle with him.

'Do you like me now?' the invisible man asks.

'Yes,' I say.

Around and around till we lift off, and I see the field and feel the sun against my forehead, then there's my whole country, and my continent, and the round ball.

'Watch how the universe expands and contracts,' he says. 'Watch how we go away from each other and come back.'

Then darkness, the sunlight on my forehead and face again. Anninho standing there smiling.

'I told you I could leap through time and the spirit,' Peixoto says. Anninho touches my forehead and jaw.

'You sleep and dream and I always come back,' Peixoto says. 'Do you want to go down into the ocean and look at the turtle grass?'

'What's the matter?' asks Anninho.

'Nothing.'

'One more time,' says Peixoto. 'See how that part of space moves away from us and this one returns. Now into the sea.'

I hold Peixoto's hand and he dives down to the bottom. 'Are you having a good time?'

'Yes.'

'You're such a good woman. I enjoy being with you.'

He makes circles and loops and strange patterns appear. I see colors of the rain.

'Now you seem relaxed and calm. Do you like this place?'

'Yes.'

'Do you see the figure of a woman circling there? She circles and circles. Let's join her.'

They begin to speak quietly in a language I don't know or don't remember. They speak as if they're old dear friends. Then the woman swims away.

'Who is the woman?'

'Your idea is as good as mine. I see beauty everywhere. Somehow I always find it, or it finds me.' He smiles gently. 'Now let's enter the school of fish. We must get to the middle to avoid being eaten. We've gotten to the middle, haven't we? It's not the middle, it's the *center*. And how well we see each other. How well we hear. How well our spirits meet. Do you think we're dreaming together or is it real?'

'I've heard that sometimes one can enter the dream of another.'

'Ah, yes.'

The Return of the
White Woman to Those
to Whom She Belongs

I STOOD IN THE DOORWAY and watched them take the white woman out of the village.

'Drop her off the cliff,' I heard one woman say softly, then continued to watch the procession in silence.

I walked out into the road.

'Did her father agree to the ransom?'

She looked at me quickly and said, 'Yes,' then was silent.

The white woman sat in the hammock holding her head down, and with her hands folded in her lap.

'Look at her,' the woman said, again softly. 'Holding her head down like she's been wronged, like some horror's been done to her. I know myself that she's the same woman leaving as she was when she entered here. They say her father will pay so much for her because he sleeps with her himself.'

'Stop talking vulgar,' a man standing nearby said.

'You know yourself about the white man who lives in the forests who sleep with his daughter.'

'Yes, they say he does,' the man replied. 'But he's a wild old crazy man.'

'And this man?'

'He's a rich man from Porto Calvo.'

The woman gave a derisive laugh. The man laughed too.

I stood watching until they carried the woman out of the gate. A hand on my shoulder. I turned quickly. It was Anninho. He put his hand around my waist and we walked into the house.

'Did you negotiate with the man for the return of the girl?' I asked.

'What man?'

'The one in the tavern.'

He looked at me, then he said, 'No. That man had nothing to do with that woman.'

The Bashful Woman,
or Our Lady of Solitude

THERE WAS A WOMAN who lived in one of the huts. She was a solitary, bashful woman who spoke seldom and only about necessary things. When she first came to the quilombo, the Palmaristas mistook her silence for arrogance, until it was discovered it was not arrogance but bashfulness, and then her silence was respected by some, tolerated by others, ridiculed by a few, but still not understood. She had come as a free woman, not as a slave. She had walked one morning into the quilombo. A house had been provided for her. In all the time she had been there no man had taken her for his wife or she had taken no man. They said she was too bashful to approach. Every time a man came near her she would hold her head down and jump, just a bit, as though she had distemper. Her house was between the high rock watch post and the coca grove. Sometimes I would see her standing among the cocoa trees staring at the ground, deep in thought. It was said that she was the first one who had gone to the church and painted first Our Lady of Solitude a dark color, and then she began to paint all the saints. Every one she painted except Sao Benedito, who was already black. If she had any story besides her silence and what she had done to Our Lady of Solitude and the other saints, nobody knew it. But whenever anyone came near her, she would hold her head down and jump a bit.

Anninho's Plans to Leave
Palmares and the Question

I STAY HERE BY CHOICE,' Anninho said, looking up from his calculations and draughts.

'I am a free man,' he said, standing. 'I've stayed here by choice, but now I want to leave and take you with me. I've thought it over and now I've decided. Perhaps it is knowing a life unlike my former, solitary one. But I have decided and now I must act.'

I said nothing.

'I'll go to Porto Calvo tomorrow and get the things we'll need for our journey,' he said.

I was silent.

'I want you to trust me, Almeyda.'

Silence.

'I'll go to Porto Calvo and then I'll come back for you.'

I turned away from him, saying nothing. He got up and touched my shoulder. I nodded without looking at him.

'Tell no one our plans. As far as anyone knows, it is another errand for the king.'

He kissed my forehead and went out. I sat on the mat wondering about his visit to the Mualim or Mr Oparinde, their discussions with Mr Iaiyesimi, and his strange visit to the tavern and conversation with the seaman. Was all of that tied with his decision to leave Palmares now, at a time when they most needed everyone to stay and fight against the Portuguese? I had not heard him mention any of those people again. He did not discuss such matters with me, though I observed his moody silences, and the greater attention he began to give to his papers. Or was his decision to go simply for our personal protection? But didn't we have a responsibility to others as well as ourselves? I thought of my grandmother. But she had been through several of their wars already, fighting like the other women, along with the men, in wars against the Dutch and then the Portuguese. I thought of her long sword, her musket, her preparations of gunpowder, her prayers, and who knew what occult stratagems.

After a while I raised myself from the mat, and taking Anninho's fishing pole, went down to the river, to catch fish to serve with the cashews and pears I had gathered earlier.

I fried the fish in coconut oil and butter and put it on a platter of banana leaves, surrounding it with sliced pears and cashew nuts. When Anninho returned, his face was beaming. I fixed his platter and then my own. We sat down on the mats.

'Did you catch these or did Nobrega?' he asked.

'I did,' I said. 'They were so small, though, that's why I prepared them like that, so they'd look better. It was so funny.'

'What?' he asked.

'When I took them out of the water, they puffed up so,' I said laughing, and puffing my cheeks out.

Before I could lift the fish to my mouth, Anninho shoved my hand away from my face, and shoved the platter out of my lap.

'What are you trying to do, woman, kill us both?'

'I don't know what you mean, Anninho. What are you talking about?'

'Don't you know anything?'

'I don't know what you mean.'

'Those are mayacus. Very poisonous fish. Just a mouthful. And there's no remedy.'

He looked at me with anger and collected the poisonous fish and took it outside to dispose of it. When he returned he was silent. He sat down in his hammock.

'You didn't know what you were doing?' he asked.

'No, Anninho.'

He looked at me. 'If it hadn't happened now ...'

'I didn't know. I didn't know the fish was poison.'

He was silent, then he said, 'If you felt you would rather kill us both, then ... it's no desertion, it's an exercise of choice. I'm a free man.'

'I didn't try to kill us,' I insisted.

He looked at me, where I sat on the mat on the floor, then he got up, held the back of my head, and kissed my forehead. Then he lay back down on the hammock. I do not know to this day whether he believed me.

'Come and lie beside me,' he said after a long time.

The Cycle

I AM BEING SENT INTO TOWN TOMORROW to get fire-locks and gunpowder for the expected war. You will come with me,' he said.

'Won't they suspect something? You know what punishment deserters are given.'

'I know. I have given such punishment.'

'They say it is dangerous on the road now, even for a free man and his woman.'

'You have nothing to fear. I'll protect you with my own life.' I said nothing.

'You want me to stay here and fight. There are many ways to fight.

'But they destroy one Palmares, we scatter, we form another one. That one is destroyed. We scatter, those who are not captured or killed, we come together again. New fugitives come to us, and free blacks like myself who will risk their own freedom. Generations of destroyed villages, new villages, and new destructions. I know the cycle by heart. Garrostazu ...'

'Garrostazu?'

'The medicine man who was banished. The medicine man, the diviner, the witch doctor, the warlock, the shaman. He says that this will be the final Palmares. I am an educated man, and I believe him. I saw it written.' He paused a long time looking at me. 'He has reckoned it his way and I have reckoned it mine.' He paused again. 'I want to go my own way. I want to take you with me. I want you to be safe, protected. But you don't want to stay with me. You want to be Zumbi's woman.'

'What?'

'You said his name again and again.'

'When did I say it?'

'During your fever. And again when you were dreaming.'

'I am no other man's woman, Anninho. I want to be no other man's woman. I'll go with you, wherever you go.'

An Invisible Man;
Malaria Fever

WHY ARE YOU WALKING HERE? It's not safe for a woman alone to be walking here.'
'It was safe yesterday.'

The man on the rock stares down at me.

'What do you see from where you are standing?' I ask, looking up.

'All the way to Porto Calvo.'

'Can you see my husband?'

'You are Martim Anninho's woman?'

'Yes.'

'Sure I see him, standing, talking to some other men, laughing. Now he looks angry. Now the woman who has silk for hair passes. The men look at her.'

'Does *he* look?'

'Only a glance, as they all give her. She is King Zumbi's woman.'

'Do you think she's beautiful?'

'When he looks at your eyes, how can he look at any other woman? But it's not my duty to tell you which way your man is standing or which way he's looking. It's my duty to watch for the enemy.'

He puts a cigar in his mouth.

'Almeyda.'

I turn to see my grandmother.

'Who were you talking to?'

'The man on the rock.'

'What man on what rock? There's no man there.'

'What?' I look up.

'What will become of you?' she asks, touching my shoulder. 'There's no place else to go. When we are born, we have been everywhere.' She pats my shoulder. 'Poor Almeyda, what will you do?'

She is holding a papaya; the sweet smell drifts up. 'Come home with me,' she says, taking my arm.

In her house, she rubs oil into my hair and gives me a cup of hot chocolate to drink.

'You think you're a woman now,' she says, her fingers on my hair-line. 'But you don't know your place in the world.'

'My spiritual place, like Father Tollinare says?'

She pierces holes in my ears and places gold rings through them.

'Hold your head up higher.'

Anninho comes to the door and watches me. 'Who is this woman?' he asks.

'This is Almeyda. Don't you know her yet? She has been with you all along. What cause do you fight for?'

'The cause is always one. To be free and human.' Grandmother oils my stomach and the backs of my thighs.

'How do you feel, Almeyda?' Anninho asks.

'Fine.'

Anninho keeps watching me.

'Tell me about your Dutchman,' I ask my grandmother.

'That was centuries ago. I can remember nothing.'

'What was his name?'

'Lintz. Was it Lintz?'

'No, it was Rugendas.'

'A Portuguese name?'

She washes my face in the juice from a leaf. Her eyes grow dark.

'When it was time to kill him I killed him.' She gives me tea to drink.

'He would have done the same for this woman,' she said. 'He would have done the same thing for this one.'

She puts her hands on my shoulders.

Anninho touches my hair, my forehead, the spaces under my eyes. 'I was dreaming that I had the fever again and that my grandmother was attending to me,' I tell him.

He puts his hand against my face. 'Do I feel warm?' I ask.

'No.'

I lay my forehead on the inside of one of his elbows. He strokes the back of my head.

'I want to take you to a place where you'll be treated with some dignity, where we'll both be treated with some dignity.'

'Here we are so treated.'

'A perpetual conflict. A cycle of destruction and resurrection and destruction? Why do you resist me?'

He touches my hair.

'Already there are too many shadows about your eyes. When I first saw you, you looked like the sun's woman.' He combs his hands through my hair. 'And your hair was longer, thicker.'

'Yes, but it's the fever. Not Palmares.'

He touches my forehead. I touch his. He holds me and says my name.

Almeyda's Farewell

MY GRANDMOTHER SMILED AT ME when I entered, but did not speak. I sat quietly against one of her huge pillows. She came near me and sat without speaking. She looked at me boldly, as if she were studying me, but still did not speak.

'I have watched your man come back and forth this way all morning,' she said. 'And the others I have watched them digging pits to trap the enemy.'

She burst out laughing, looking at me with her huge eyes.

'What is it?'

She didn't answer. She got out a small bowl of coconut oil. 'Here,' she said, handing it to me. 'Oil your old grandmother's wild head before you go.'

I looked at her quickly. She placed one of her huge pillows for me to sit down on, then she sat between my knees. I parted her hair and oiled her scalp and strands of thick hair.

'Did Anninho tell you?'

'No. I have only to look at either of you to know what you are doing. If you're captured . . .'

She didn't go on. I said nothing, smoothing back her hair with my palm.

'It will be cruel,' she said. 'By us or them, a difficult punishment.'

When I stood, she also stood, and held both my shoulders, then embraced me and kissed my forehead.

'Perhaps it's best that you go,' she said. 'It's the time of destruction.'

'What?'

'I'll fight the fight,' she said, then smiled. 'You won't get to see an old woman wield a sword.'

'Do you feel we are traitors?' I asked.

She said nothing. She touched my hairline, then embraced me again.

'Here,' she said, reaching for a bunch of yellow papers tied together with a string. 'This is a record of my travels and worst memories and spiritual adventures. But you can't read it. It's written in Arabic. Too bad, but there's no more I can give you to take with you on your journey.'

I took the papers. She frowned and kissed my forehead again. She walked me to the door. I turned to say goodbye again, but she kept me from seeing her.

The Journey —
Preparations

ANNINHO THREW THE LEATHER BAGS across the horse's back. 'I have been in territories where a free black man cannot even ride a horse,' he said. I said nothing. One of Zumbi's messengers neared us. He looked at the horse, saying nothing. Then he said, 'We are told that they may have more than a thousand men and Indians.'

'Are Indians not men?' asked Anninho.

The messenger ignored him and punched the saddlebags on the horse. I waited for him to peer into them, or ask what we were carrying, but he did not.

'What word did King Zumbi send?' Anninho asked.

'No word. It is expected that Luiza Cosme will have some word for him and you should be careful to get it.'

Anninho frowned but said nothing.

'Why have you need of her?' the messenger asked.

'I have permission to take her.'

The messenger smiled but said nothing. 'King Zumbi says for you to be careful on your journey,' he said, turning. 'You are one of his most treasured and respected men.'

When the messenger left, I said softly, 'It would be foolish to go now.'

'We will be sure to go to the woman Luiza Cosme,' was all he answered.

A Visit to Luiza Cosme,
and the Return to Palmares

ANNINHO WAS HARD AND SILENT on the road. There was no one who stopped us. I had put grandmother's papers into one of the leather bags and held onto his back.

We went to the store near the edge of the city. This time I noticed a raised X carved into the dark wood over the back door. Anninho knocked softly, but there was no answer. He knocked softly again, still no answer. Then we heard soft steps from the corner of the building. I touched Anninho's arm. He pushed me behind him and grabbed the small sword at his waist. The woman came around the corner, seeing us, startled.

'It is Luiza,' she whispered.

She was wearing loose trousers and a short waistcoat. Her hair was piled in a high cushion on her head. She looked at Anninho solemnly, but smiled at me.

We went inside, Luiza leading the way.

She closed the door, but did not light a candle. Again, the moon showed through the high window.

'I have just come from Aprigio's,' she said.

'I was told you would have a message for Zumbi,' Anninho said. His voice was hard and even. There was no warmth. He stood stiffly.

'No. No more than he knows already. The governor is putting together a new expedition. Bandeirantes and Indians in the bunch. How long will it be? A day? A week? A month? Nothing that he does not know. Nothing that he does not expect any day.'

'So there is nothing you have for Zumbi?' he asked.

Luiza looked at him but did not speak, then she answered, 'No. Aprigio will send someone if there is any news ... When I come from

Aprigio's I go to pray to São Benedito. He is the only one I pray to these days. He is the only one I speak to. Some of his jewels have been stolen. They say the criminal says in his defense that it is not right for a Negro to wear such precious jewels, even a Negro who is a saint. And they do nothing.'

Anninho said nothing. I did not speak.

'They want to carry the stupidness of this world even into the heaven. Oh, I have tales to tell. But you are a silent man tonight.'

He still did not speak. He touched her shoulder and she touched the side of his arm. I wondered then how they had known each other and looked down at the floor. I thought of his admiration for her and for her 'dangerous existence.'

Then we were going. He took my arm. 'It is good to be a silent man,' Luiza said.

Is it to the mountains? I did not ask him. No, it was back into the palm forests the way we had come.

When we returned, I placed the yellowed papers into my grandmother's palm. She handed them back to me.

'Now you will see how an old woman defends her blood,' she said, her cheekbones growing higher.

A Messenger from Aprigio

THE MESSENGER FROM APRIGIO had been wounded in the shoulder. They had found him unconscious near the entrance. My grandmother came out and told them to bring him into her house.

'Come with me, Almeyda,' she said.

She washed his shoulder, and crushed some dried leaves and packed it into the shoulder and bandaged it. Then she wiped his forehead and the blood from his arms and fists. He was still unconscious.

Anninho and others gathered near the door. Grandmother told them to go away. All but Anninho left.

'And you?' she asked.

He smiled at her, bowed and left. One of Zumbi's messengers entered. 'Has he spoken?'

'No.'

He went to the man.

'How long will he stay this way?'

'I don't know.'

'When he's conscious, send someone to the king.'

'Yes,' she said.

The messenger left. She touched the man's high forehead. He looked no more than thirty, of mixed blood. His hair was short and curly. His shirt and trousers were smeared with blood and dirt. His nose and chin were angular, but his forehead and jawline were soft and rounded. My grandmother put her hand under his head and lifted it slightly. She rubbed oil in his hair.

Almeyda's Conversation
with the Young Man;
His Message Told

SHE TOLD ME TO KEEP AN EYE ON HIM. She put on her sandals and went out. I sat by the low hammock and dampened the cloth again, wiping his forehead. In his sleep, he twisted away from me. I put my hand on his arm and held him gently.

He opened his eyes suddenly.

'I am sent to the captain named Zumbi.' He looked at me as if I was not there.

'Sir, they are sending a regiment of more than ... I am afraid Palmares ...'

I wiped his face with the damp cloth again. His eyes were wide and glassy. I took one of his hands.

'They are sixteen leagues from Porto Calvo. Bandeirantes from São Paulo. Domingos Jorge. The Paulistas have reached Pernambuco.'

He closed his eyes and slept. When my grandmother returned, I was still holding his hand. She came over to him and touched his forehead.

She touched him in his armpits.

'He says the Paulistas have reached Pernambuco,' I said.

She went to the doorway and called someone and repeated the message, then she came back inside and told me to go to my own house, she would look after the man.

When I came to the house, Anninho stood in the doorway.

'I want to protect you. I want to put you in the least danger.' I said nothing.

He pointed to a sketch he had drawn. 'You know this?'

I nodded.

'I have built an underground hut of mud and bushes. If it is possible we'll meet here. You see it well?'

I nodded.

He burnt the sketch on the edge of a candle.

We lay down in the hammock; he put his head against my shoulder. 'Do you want me?' he asked.

'Yes,' I said.

I kept waiting for him to touch me, to take me in his arms, but he did not. Then I felt that perhaps I'd only thought he'd asked me that, that I had only imagined it. I touched his forehead and his hair. He kept his head against my shoulder.

'You will remember this place, Palmares?' he asked.

'Yes,' I said.

'The Rio Mundahu valley is very beautiful.'

He kept his head on my shoulder and fell asleep.

Barcala Aprigio,
the Brother of Martim;
a Young Brazilian Writer

MY GRANDMOTHER STIRRED HONEY and ginger together and gave it to him in small spoonfuls to take. He tightened his mouth at first, but then opened it.

'Who is that woman?' he asked as I came into the door.

'That is my granddaughter Almeyda,' she said, without turning.

He kept looking at me. Then he raised a paper and began reading it to my grandmother, as if he were continuing something that they had already begun. It was written in Portuguese but he spoke with the accent of a Dutchman, saying the following things:

' . . . but only the offspring of the white men and black women – these are the beauties of this continent. Their bodies have a natural grace and they have huge dark eyes. They are the real beauties of this continent . . . But the dances, I have never seen such jerks, such lascivious movements – the passions of the devil released. I have never seen such devilry before. It makes me blush when I think of our own women . . .'

Then he was out of that voice but still reading, 'What are the true emotions of this continent? Who can tell what the true emotions are? Do we go back only to hunger, thirst, sex, and blood?'

He looked up at her. 'It had to do with the Dutch experience in this continent. I lived in Holland a long time with my brother, but it was here not there I wanted to write about and somehow combine here and there.'

'Who is your brother?' I asked, coming near.

'Martim Aprigio.' I nodded.

'We have a young Brazilian writer in our midst,' my grandmother said solemnly.

'The book I wrote was at first celebrated in Holland; they even wept over it. But here they condemned my use of sex in the writings. There were complex relationships I was trying to deal with between black and white, rich and poor. They did not know I was a mulatto, but claimed I knew nothing of such relationships and the work was very immoral and decadent. And besides, I did not write in "pure" Portuguese but a "bastard" of it and my inclusion of the occult demonstrated without a doubt some connection with devilry. My brother had hoped that I would stay in Holland, but I decided to return here. Of course I was treated with more respect and dignity there, but then I did not know firsthand what was happening here in Brazil, and although I felt there was some spiritual validity in what I was saying about my own country, I realized I did not present ordinary days and normal traits of personality and feeling. But isn't the whole country one of exaggerated personality and feeling, much of it taking the form of sexual atrocities ... Yet, I often wonder what it would be like to return to Holland and be treated with dignity again ... Now it is my brother Martim who wants me to stay.'

He looked at me and asked me to come closer. I did. He stared at me.

'Do you think I have come to witness the final destruction of this place?' he asked.

'I don't know,' I replied.

My grandmother looked at me but said nothing.

'Forgive me for observing you so strangely,' he said. 'I am still learning how to look at my own women, the women of my own country. I think you're quite beautiful. I'm wondering who you were in your other life.'

'The devils are running through the forest,' someone yelled. 'They're here! They're not two leagues from here.'

'What's the most horror you've seen?' he asked, as Indaya grabbed the long swords and a musket and he raised himself up.

Escape, or a Supernatural Intervention

I REMEMBER ONLY FOLLOWING my grandmother outside. She pushed me to the ground and I saw her cut into the belly of a man. As she did so she called out, 'Allah!'

'Stay close to the ground,' she whispered, and I felt a heavy weight against my back. But when I reached behind me, there was no one there. Still I felt it. I tell you, it's true, and not the delusions of a melancholy woman.

I stayed close to the ground. Was it hours, or months? I know now it was months, but how could I have lost time? I remember nothing. All I remember is when Anninho took my arm and pulled me up.

'You fools,' a commanding voice declared. 'Why have you let them overtake us? Why have you let them build their stockade next to ours? Who was on watch last night?'

We moved swiftly through some dark labyrinth until we arrived at the place in the ground Anninho had prepared for us to stay. It was close to a gameleira tree that Anninho had dug an underground hut and covered it with vines, branches, palm leaves, and grass. He lifted a mat of grass. He jumped down and helped me down. He covered the entrance. It was dark inside, and we crawled into a corner where he had piled small sacks of manioc, yams, cucumbers, coconuts, peanuts – but mostly yams and peanuts. He had pounded stakes into the ground to string a hammock, and we felt our way. He helped me up and rested beside me.

We stayed hidden for several weeks. Anninho would leave when it was dark and return with handfuls of wild vegetables and fruits, and sometimes wild flowers that he would present to me. Once he stayed out all night and did not return before dawn. I lay in the dark all night, fearful for him. I lay in our hammock with my knees drawn up to my chest. At dawn he lifted the mat and jumped down. He came and stood near me. He said that he thought it safe to go further this time. He wanted to find out all that he could. He said that Palmares was deserted, that the Portuguese had taken many prisoners and divided them as slaves among themselves. He didn't know how many had escaped, though he had seen the bodies of many who had thrown themselves off of cliffs, and had escaped that way.

'Zumbi?' I asked.

He said nothing at first, then he sighed deeply.

'Some say he escaped with about twenty men, others say he has been captured and beheaded ...'

I stared at him.

' ... and his head hung in a public place to prove to us that he is not immortal.'

I lowered my head. We did not speak. I lay back down. Anninho came softly and stretched out beside me.

'Where are we going?' I asked.

He shook his head, saying nothing.

After a while he said, 'Already he's become a legend.'

'What do you mean?'

'They are saying all kinds of things. Some are saying that when they discovered King Zumbi on a cliff at the edge of the palm forest that he metamorphosed himself and became a bird and flew off. Others say that he simply flew as a man. Others are saying that his great feat was to jump from the cliff, to commit suicide rather than be taken as a slave. And there are still others who say that he removed himself to another place and time and that he'll return again to lead his people ... Garrostazu prophesied that Zumbi, the spirit of Zumbi, would return again and again, but he fears it will be destroyed again and again. When his spirit cannot be destroyed, they destroy the body that carries it.'

I was silent.

'Zumbi escaped with about twenty men and they found their way to a cabin on Barriaga Hill, but one of the men betrayed them, and that same one, it is said, held King Zumbi's hair while a Portuguese soldier beheaded him.'

'Who?'

'I don't know. It could have been anyone of them. Some blame a mulatto.'

I was silent, then I asked, 'Do you believe that if they had not banished the medicine man, that he could have prevented such disaster?'

'No, I don't believe it. I believed he was correct in his prophecy from the beginning, but I don't believe that his remedies would have had any effect.'

I thought again of the strange experience that I had had.

'No, I don't believe in any occult stratagem,' he said. 'I cautioned Garrostazu to maintain his silence and reserve, to work his remedies in secret if he felt he must. Perhaps in another world it would have mattered, but here it doesn't.'

I looked at him. I wanted to tell him about my strange experience.

Was it some occult stratagem? I held my silence.

'The prophecy I believed, but not the remedy. But he *knew*. He blessed my amulet anyway, even if I did not believe. "And what if it is

only in the *mind*," he said. "What if I possess no medicine, and it is only
an act of the *mind*, then go with that, my friend,' he said. But he should
have kept his divinations to himself. Praise Allah that banishment was
all he got for it.'

The Tapuyan Woman
and the Discovery

I N THE MORNING there was the sound of rustling above
the entrance to the underground cave and then a low
bird's whistle like a tui.

'Come on,' said Anninho.

'What is it?'

'Just come.'

We climbed out of the hammock. Anninho lifted me up by the
hips, and someone outside grabbed my hands. I drew them back at
first, but then relaxed, as Anninho knew what was going on, even if I
didn't. As I was pulled up I saw the brown muscular legs and thighs of
a Tapuyan woman. Woman? There was a bow and arrow slung across
her shoulders, and her hair was cut short like a man's. Her face was
broad, her cheekbones very high. She was silent as she lifted me easily
and I stood on the ground next to her. Anninho climbed out of the
hole and nodded to the woman, and we followed her through dense
forest and into a clearing where there was a long wooden house that
looked like a warehouse. We went inside, where there were rows of
hammocks, but no one in them. We sat on mats and another Tapuyan
woman, with very long, very clean and well-combed hair, braided in
the front but falling about her shoulders, came and served us fish and
pineapple. Her lower lip was pierced and a small stone placed in the
hole. I stared at her, though I did not mean to. The Tapuyans near the
plantations where I had lived had been discouraged from 'mutilating
themselves' by the old custom. Particularly the younger ones. I was not
used to seeing such a young and handsome woman with a stone placed
so, though I had seen older Tapuyans with stones and holes in their

faces. After she had served us, she left us and went to a corner at the back of the room.

'Not mayacus,' Anninho said to me with a short laugh.

'I would not serve you mayacus,' said the woman, who had been silent all the time. 'I would not poison you and your woman.' She looked hurt. 'You are a very honorable man. Very kind.'

'No, no, Maite, I did not mean ...' He explained to her what had happened.

She smiled broadly, but did not laugh. Then she looked at me as if she too were puzzling over my intentions. I felt foolish and looked down. The woman got up and came back wearing a shawl made of anteater's hair.

'Ah, you have been many places since I last saw you,' said the woman to Anninho. 'What hardships have you endured?'

'Ah, I have been luckier than most.'

'Ah, they are not so valiant, nor so enlightened as you are. Ah, if my ancestors had been so!'

I watched them, but it seemed as if it were not a real conversation but a ritual one. Then Anninho stood and bowed to the woman and she stood and bowed to him. The other woman, whose hair had been well-combed before, came out from the corner with disheveled hair and kissed Anninho's hands.

I nodded to both the women and we left.

'Why does that woman look and behave like a man?' I asked.

'She's taken a vow of chastity, like the Catholic nuns do. Such women don't have men, but they must look like men, cut their hair like a man, and do the things that men do. They hunt like the men. In the old days, they went to war along with the men. They have serving women. Now that one lives alone with her "woman."'

'Do they ... ?'

'I don't know,' he said.

We walked on. Anninho kept his arm about my shoulder. Vines and gameleira leaves covered the ground.

'Are we going back underground?' I asked.

He said, 'No. Maite has not seen any Portuguese or Tapuya soldiers in many days ...

'We're supposed to meet the others in the Barriaga Hills. How many escaped, I don't know ...'

'Tapuya soldiers?'

'They recruited some Tapuyan soldiers to fight along with them. They know the forests. And it's my suspicion that the strategy they used was Tapuyan strategy, though Velho will take the credit for it.'

'What? I don't know what you mean.'

We came to a clearing and a small stream and sat down on a stone. 'I have known of Tapuyan battles in which the Tapuyas build stockades next to the stockades of their enemies, and gradually move the stockades up closer, until they build the final stockade next door to the stockade of their enemies, and in that way they prevent their escape at the same time that they are able to overrun them, or at least fight with them hand to hand. But to the Portuguese their wars were all confusion, with no leaders, and no strategy.'

'Who is Velho?'

'He's the Portuguese who led the attack against Palmares.'

'They're all the same to me,' I said. 'I don't know their names, nor do I want to.'

He frowned. He was silent. Then he said, 'If it ever became time for you to document this time and place, wouldn't you want to know the enemies' names the same as our own?'

I was silent. He touched my face, then he went to the stream and took his shirt off.

'Do you want to bathe here?' he asked. I shook my head.

'There may still be Portuguese around,' I said. 'Perhaps the Tapuyans have also taught them how to hide from us.'

'They have captured their niggers and are gone,' he said. I slid the shirt off my shoulders but kept the trousers on. 'Is that how you bathe?'

I said nothing. He had unbuckled his trousers and was in the stream.

I took off my trousers and walked in. The water was warm, drawing the sting from the scratches and bites on my legs. He held me close for a moment. I thought he would make love, but he did not. He held me against him for a long time and then he turned me around and rubbed the water against my shoulders and rubbed the backs of my legs. I stared up into an iuca tree.

We did not hear them till they were upon us. They stood around the back silent, Tapuyans, Bandeirantes, and Portuguese soldiers. Was one of them a black man? One was almost as dark as me. A Tapuyan? A Hausa? A dark-skinned Portuguese? The Bandeirantes and Portuguese soldiers had muskets, the Tapuyans spears and bows and arrows. I stood close to Anninho, but he pushed me behind him. The captain walked to the edge of the bank and pointed his musket. Anninho put his hand behind him. I took it and we came out of the stream.

A Tapuyan speared our clothes and tossed them to us. He had tattoos on his arms and thighs. His head was shaped like a diamond. I stooped quickly to pick up my clothes.

'No,' said one of the Portuguese soldiers, a young man of about twenty.

'Let the man dress first,' he said.

Anninho did not stoop for his clothes. He stayed standing, rigid. The young man pointed his musket at Anninho.

'Tell them you are a free man,' I said. Anninho was silent.

Someone lifted me onto a red blanket and carried me into the forest. I only saw iuca trees and gameleira trees.

In the Barriaga Mountains

Someone was touching me, touching my breasts. Were they still there? Did I dream they were cut off and I saw them thrown into the river? I feel the sun on my forehead, and then the cool shadow of a hut, the smell of oranges and coconut, the taste of rum.

'Where did you find her?'

'The river bank.'

'Anninho?'

'I didn't see him. Look what they've done to her. It must have been the mud that stopped the bleeding.'

'Wash the mud from her hair.'

A damp cloth against my hair and forehead. I see two shadows on the wall, the side of a man's face, a woman's cheekbones. A hand touches my shoulder. A hand rubs the soles of my feet. Another pain against my chest, cold water, leaves.

'What is that?'

'A medicinal plant.'

'What is it called?'

'Ipecacuanha.'

'Why have you kissed it?'

'It is not my kiss, it is the kiss of Iararaca, the mystical serpent.'

'Isn't there blood enough? What are you doing, Luiza?'

'Luiza.'

'She says your name.'

'Luiza.'

'Yes, it's me, Luiza Cosme.'

'Luiza.'

'Yes, it's me, and this is Barcala who has brought you here.'

'Isn't there blood enough?'

'This is a woman's menstrual blood. It's not the same blood. It has power in it. An old woman taught me this.'

'What's become of Anninho?'

'Anninho was not seen. Did you see Anninho?'

'I saw no one but the woman.'

'Anninho.'

'She still calls him.'

'She must be in great pain and yet ...'

'It is the juice of the Ipecacuanha.' She touches my forehead.

'What are you doing now?'

'Go for a walk, Barcala. This is woman's work.'

'What of the others? Do they know the place?'

'Yes.'

'And the family of Martina Puerreydon? Will they come?'

'Yes. Go for your walk.'

Hand against my forehead. Long fingers. A rough palm. She kisses my forehead and chest.

'Believe in the lips that will heal,' she says.

She touches something to my lips. The taste of wine.

'Wine drunk before the universe began. It is the same wine.' She puts bits of something in my mouth. I turn my face away. Is this the fruit dipped in menstrual blood?

'Will you go with the others to the New Palmares, or will you stay?'

'Drink from the wine that was here before time was.'

She raises my head and I drink. I see the front and back of her at the same time and the two sides and the top of her head and the soles of her feet. Lightning jumps from her eyes.

'When you are well, I'll take you to the woman Zibatra. It takes a mystic to know one. You'll deny it, but weren't you rescued?'

She scratches her fingers through my hair.

'This is a woman passionately loving her husband and waiting for his return.'

She traces a pyramid on my forehead. 'Listen to an old woman.'

'Where is Luiza?'

'Luiza? I'm Old Vera, don't you know me?'

'Luiza Cosme was here.'

'I've always been here,' she says. 'I'm the same woman today as I was when they first brought you here.'

Barcala's Conversation with the Printer's Slave

NOW WHEN MY CHEST HAD HEALED considerably and I sat up, Old Vera would continue to rub my chest several times a day with a salve she had mixed, and she would place bits of crushed tobacco under my tongue. I would sit in an old wicker chair in the corner of the square hut, that had both a sleeping room and a kitchen. For some reason, I said nothing to no one. Though people would come in and out and some would bow to me, still I said nothing. Did the Portuguese cut your tongue out as well? Old Vera would ask. Did he cut the woman's tongue out as well? Why have you stopped talking? She would ask. Still I would sit and watch people enter and leave, and wait for her to rub the salve where my breasts had been, and to place the crushed tobacco under my tongue, and to listen to Old Vera rebuke me for my silence. Someone had given me a man's trousers and loose blouse to wear.

'Is it Aguirre Beltran you've brought?' she asked when Barcala entered with another man.

He was very tall and a tan color. His arms and legs were long and straight, and there seemed to be no curves to his body. His hair was short and curly, his forehead high, his mouth small but his lips full. His lips curled down slightly and he seemed to be frowning, and his brown eyes sparkled. He looked at me with surprise, his mouth seemed to open slightly, then he nodded. I must not have acknowledged his nod, for I sat there, with my hands folded in my lap. He turned awkwardly and looked at Barcala, who said nothing. Then Barcala told him to have a seat. They sat at the wooden table. Old Vera brought them bread and chocolate, then she sat on a mat near me.

'So your master has died and they won't let you take over the printing shop,' Old Vera said, loudly, to the men who had entered.

My eyes widened. Had I seen or spoken with this man before? I stared at his broad shoulders. His head looked small for the shoulders which were straight across and angled, though the rest of his body was slender.

'Yes,' he said.

Barcala explained – Was it to me? And where had I heard this already? – that Beltran had been freed by his former master and that the printer's shop had been given to him, but it was the law that no black man own a printer's shop. Had the master known that?

'What will be done with the shop?' Old Vera asked.

'It will be sold to a white man.'

'Who will get the money?'

'The town.'

'And what will you do?'

'I want him to come back to Europe with me. The two of us, who can stop us?'

'So you have decided this is not your place after all?' Old Vera asked.

'Why should I stay here? There is no more Palmares. We were the lucky ones not to be destroyed. I want to be a free man again. Such things we could do there, Beltran, the printer and the Brazilian writer. But here, what is there to do but shovel dead men's bones and suck blood from the teeth.'

He spoke of bringing Brazilian society into the things he would write abroad, the relationships in Brazilian society between black and white, rich and poor; he also spoke of it as being a continent of the occult. He would take things of Brazil with him. But he wanted to be treated with dignity again. The quilombos were destroyed. He spoke of his brother Martim, whom he called a man of culture, spoke of the collection of scientific and historical works Martim had left in Holland when he had decided to return to Brazil, of engineering projects he had directed in Holland, Armenia, and Southern Russia. But his brother had argued that such things should not be said simply of him, but there should be thousands like him, as there were thousands of Englishmen and Frenchmen one could say those things of every day, and it was not those 'ordinary' things that distinguished a man, but qualities of personality, of character, of intellect, and spirit. But still he praised his brother for those professional things he had accomplished, for such men as he could not take such things for granted . . .

There are other things he said of that nature, but it is difficult for me to remember the exact wording of such talk.

'Is Martim Aprigio going back to Europe too?' I asked.

Everyone turned and looked at me as if I were strange and had said something strange.

'No. That is what I have been saying. He intends to stay. If it were possible he would stay until all such men as him can take for granted the things that he does. But look what time is wasted, what energies, what qualities of personality, of character, of intellect, and spirit are dissipated. But this one, this man, no I won't stay.'

They continued to look at me, especially Beltran, who looked as if he would say something to me, but did not.

'I have seen all I have to see here,' Barcala said. 'Let Martim waste his life and his woman's life here. I don't have centuries to wait.'

'One only wastes one's days when he refuses the truth,' Old Vera said.

'Tell me the truth,' Barcala asked.

Old Vera was silent, then she turned to me and her eyes widened and sparks seemed to jump from them. I swallowed the tobacco under my tongue.

'I will go with my brother and his wife and the family of Martina Puerreydon and the other fools as far as Parahyba and then I'll return to Holland or to Southern Russia,' Barcala said.

'And you'll write articles and stories and Beltran will print them?'

'That's the idea,' Barcala said.

Old Vera laughed. 'A man of culture,' she said. 'And don't you believe I'm a woman of culture?'

In the meantime Old Vera had gotten an onion and a piece of bread and sat eating it, pouring salt on the onion. She took a bite.

'I know the power of blood, and of the spirit, and of plants, and of old Iararaca, who moves from place to place, through time and the spirit. Am I not a woman of culture?'

He was silent.

'Will you write in Dutch or Portuguese?' she asked.

'Both, I suppose,' he said.

'Well, only you can make such a decision,' Old Vera said. 'Perhaps God has sent you here to look at this outrage and then go away and write about it. It is only through God that such as you appear ... Poor Almeyda sees nothing, or refuses to tell what she sees. Did the Portuguese cut out your tongue too?' she asked again.

Barcala stood up and put his long hands in his hair. He paced back and forth and seemed to be possessed of some passion. He put his hands to his sides and left his hair standing. He pulled at the beard he had grown.

'Oh, but that's what I mean,' he said. 'It's not just that, not just the outrage I want to speak of. Sure it will be there. I'll climb into the well of horrors and drop to the bottom. I'll suck blood from my teeth. But this is also a land of great beauty. I don't just want to write about my, *our*, relationship to white men, but to the universe itself. Why should they get in the way of everything? I want to go somewhere where they're not my main concern. I want to write about everything. The whole universe.' He paused and mused. He swung around and pointed at me. 'And I want to take her with me.'

My mouth flew open. Old Vera said, 'Hear that?'

Barcala kept looking at me. I looked at him for a while and then my eyes dropped.

'She thinks she's not a woman because of *that*?' Barcala whispered. 'She thinks no man will want her. That is how they punish the likes of her. How dare they!'

I stared into my lap, but said nothing. I felt my chest tighten.

'Do you want to go to Holland?' Old Vera asked with a laugh. 'Do you think that's your fate?'

I said nothing.

Barcala brushed his hair back, looking at me, as if he had asked the question and was waiting for an answer.

'Don't you like his hair out?' Old Vera asked. Then she said, 'This is the kind of woman who'll wander in solitude until that one returns.' She laughed. 'You've never seen a woman like her. Do you believe that?'

Barcala said nothing. He still looked at me.

I shook my head. Old Vera laughed. Beltran stared at me with a look of surprise.

'I'd go with you,' Old Vera said. 'But I'm an old woman with no hair.'

She bit into the onion and laughed again. 'It is through God that one moves through time and the spirit,' she said. 'Barcala thinks you are very beautiful, but you're the first woman of color he's ever really looked at.'

Barcala opened his mouth and began to speak, but decided to say nothing.

Old Vera looked at me and laughed.

A Man of Wealth and Light Skin and a Woman Convicted of Casting Love Spells

I WENT OUT WITH OLD VERA to gather berries and birds' eggs. That was the first time I had been out since I was brought there. When we returned a solemn man was sitting at the table. He was dressed in a black shirt and black trousers. He was sitting alone. Old Vera entered as if it were a natural thing to see him there, but I hesitated. 'Come on, child,' she said, and then she greeted him. He greeted her and said his name was Sobremonte.

'Oh, you're Sobremonte,' she said.

I entered and closed the door. Old Vera sat the baskets of berries and ostrich eggs in a corner.

Sobremonte sat in silence. He was a short, slender man of African descent it was plain to see, but his skin was very light. And his expression, or something made me feel that he was a man of wealth as well as light skin.

'And what has this land done to a young mulatto's hopes?' she asked.

He turned and stared at her, as one stares at a stranger who has discovered some secret.

'Who is the man with clear blue eyes?' she asked.

'Are you a fortune-teller?' he asked, looking at her. 'Or have I met you somewhere before? Has Barcala spoken to you of me?'

'I have neither met you nor has Barcala spoken of you. But have you sought redress for the wrong?'

He said nothing, then he said with sarcasm, 'I am an irredeemable person from a long lineage of bastardies and the priesthood is inviolate. It would be eternally ruined with an infusion of my blood.'

'Have you ever seen a mulatto priest, Almeyda?' Old Vera asked me.

'No,' I said.

She laughed.

Barcala came in. 'Sobremonte, my friend,' he said, greeting him and shaking hands. 'What word do you have from my brother?'

'They should be here before dark, and the family of Martina Puerreydon.'

'And has he sent me no message?'

'He says you are a poor devil,' Sobremonte said.

'We are all poor devils,' Barcala said.

'Do you see the woman with blood in her teeth, surrounded by dead men's bones? Do you come when she beckons you?' Old Vera asked.

No one said anything, then Sobremonte said, 'This woman knew me before I even spoke my name. Or did I speak my name? Yes. But she knew details of my life. You told her I would be here?'

'I have not seen Old Vera, but Old Vera has seen everything.'

'It's most vexing.'

'Most vexing? See how the man talks,' Old Vera said with a laugh.

'I have seen Old Vera in a trance, reciting lines from books in academic Portuguese, and knowing things it would seem impossible for such a woman to know in such a place,' said Barcala.

Everyone turned to Old Vera but she disclosed nothing. After a while she said, 'It is only through God that one travels through time and the spirit.'

Barcala had a twinkle in his eye. 'In her younger days,' he said, 'she was convicted of casting love spells.'

'Love spells?' Sobremonte asked.

'He would not know of such things,' Old Vera said.

'But don't forget. I am from a long lineage of bastardies,' Sobremonte said.

'What became of me?' Old Vera asked, wanting Barcala to continue her story.

'You were whipped and sentenced for ten years and imprisoned. So they thought. But the next day someone saw you standing outside the prison. And they checked and you were gone.'

'How did you escape?' asked Sobremonte.

'That's it. No conventional way. She claims it was some herb she took, but she won't tell me its name.'

'I ate it and then I was free.'

'But love spells? How did you do harm in that?' asked Sobremonte. Old Vera was silent.

'It was the white women of the town who accused her. It seems that all their men were looking toward that young woman. And they were sure she had cast love spells. Surely not her beauty or those delightful eyes.'

Old Vera's eyes danced and sparks jumped out. Was it only I that saw this?

'Look how the old woman's eyes dance?' Barcala said, but had he seen the other? 'Isn't that how you charmed all the men of the town?' he asked.

'I charmed no one,' she said. 'They charmed themselves.'

'But with your help, ha ha,' laughed Barcala.

I remained silent, watching the old woman's eyes dance and sparks jump from them.

'This one has become solitary and secretive,' Barcala said.

Old Vera's eyes widened and the sparks flew. 'She was always like that,' she said.

Garrostazu

ONE MORNING I TOLD OLD VERA I was going for a walk. 'Shall I come with you?' she asked. 'No. No. I'd like to go alone, I think.'

'Barcala will go.'

Barcala looked up from his writing.

'No. No,' I said. 'I'd really like to go alone.'

'Fine,' she said.

Barcala said something about the woman talking. I walked outside.

I walked to the place where we had picked berries and then sat on a rock. After a while, I got up and wandered near the cliff. I thought of the men hurling themselves off of another cliff to prevent being captured, as Anninho told me some of them had done. How many of them had done this? Had there been women among them? He had only spoken of the men, or had I assumed only the men had done it. I wondered now if there had been any woman to hurl herself off of the cliff. Or had they all allowed themselves to be taken prisoner? I wondered what Luiza Cosme would have done and where she was now. I wondered about my grand-mother. I had not wanted to think of her or what might have become of her. I saw her hurling herself off the cliff along with those men who had done so. But I could never see her reach the bottom. Why hadn't I asked *him*? He had come back and I had not even asked him, 'What of my grandmother? Did you see her? Did you see Indaya?' But if she had been among any that he had seen he would have told me so. She is captured by someone who does not know what he is getting. I thought of her laugh and laughed too. Ha. Ha. She is captured and divided among them but the one who gets her does not know who he is getting.

After a moment I got up and seeing the entrance to a cave walked into it. I did not go far before I saw a man in a white shirt, sitting with his back to me. His broad shoulders tapered to a thin line.

'Anninho? . . . Peixoto?'

He turned and smiled, but it was not Anninho, though I had seen him before. Was it the man we had gone to visit, the tutor? But he had been bald-headed and this man had a head full of thick hair, though he was the same age as that other one.

'Are you the enchanted Mooress everyone is talking about and looking for?'

I said, 'No.'

'How do you know?' he asked. 'How do you know if you're enchanted or not?'

He got up and came near me and stood in front of me. He took my hands and kissed them. He kissed the side of my neck and touched my arms.

'Do you think I'm the enchanted Moor?' he asked.

'I haven't heard any stories of enchanted Moors, just enchanted Mooresses,' I said.

'Do you ever wonder why not?'

'No.'

'Almeyda ...'

'How do you know me? Who are you?'

'I am called Garrostazu,' he said. 'Don't you know me?'

'Yes, I've heard of you. You're the medicine man, the diviner, whom they banished. Is this where you've been living all this time, in this cave? Where's your wife?' I looked around.

'She's at home,' he said, with a laugh. 'No, I haven't been living here. I came to see you.'

He kissed my neck again.

'I'm sorry the only gift I could give you was a loss of memory. But perhaps that is no gift. To remember only the tender moments and not the horrific ones.'

He kissed my hands.

'Still there were things that seemed difficult or impossible. Do you remember the battle? But I was banished, wasn't I? No one believed.

'Only Anninho. Anninho believed the prophecy, but not the remedy. And what could I do without belief? I did everything possible to prevent the final acts of mutilation and blood. But what can a medicine man do without belief?'

He held my arms and looked into my eyes and kissed my forehead. I felt as if he were showing me not only his own kindness, but that it *was also for someone else, as if he were carrying another's message of tenderness and concern.*

'Please tell me what's become of Anninho,' I said.

He was silent, then he said, 'I can't tell you.'

I looked at him. He kissed my hands again. 'I can't tell you about Anninho,' he said.

'Can you tell me where I'll find him?'

He was silent.

I said, 'Anninho told me that you believe that King Zumbi is immortal, that he'll return again.'

He nodded solemnly. 'Yes, he'll return again. His spirit will return again, but he'll be destroyed again.'

'Is there anything that can prevent his destruction?' He didn't answer.

'Don't you know?'

'He'll return again, and be destroyed again, but the last time he returns he will have learned.'

'Learned what?'

He didn't answer, then he said, 'Anninho felt that I should have prepared my medicines in secret and in silence. But that's not the type of man I am.'

He kissed my hands again and pointed me toward the entrance of the cave.

When I returned to the cabin, Old Vera kept staring at me, as if she could not take her eyes off of me.

'What is it?' I asked.

'I don't know,' she replied. 'I'm not the Azande woman.'

'What are you talking about?'

She shrugged her shoulders and I shook my head and sat down on the hammock.

Zibatra

WHEN I RETURNED FROM A WALK, Old Vera was sitting in the corner in the dark. I thought it was Old Vera and I started to greet her, but stopped for it turned out to be another woman.

'Who are you?' I asked.

'I'm Zibatra.'

I couldn't tell if she said, 'I'm Zibatra' or 'I'm from Zibatra.'

'But that doesn't matter,' she said. 'You're Almeyda and you're a Catholic. There's a woman here who has suffered the same pain as you.'

She meant Old Vera. We had both had our breasts amputated, as our punishment. A slave's crimes of defiance.

'Have you seen Old Vera?' I asked.

'You are the first to enter,' she said.

She was wearing a long dress with a fringe of velvet. I could only see the fringe of velvet sticking out of the shadows. She seemed very tall, and her thick hair was done up. I could see her outline but not her features.

She was too tall and her face was too long for Old Vera's. 'What do you want of me?' she asked.

'Of *you*?' I asked.

'Do you want to hear about your past or your future?'

'My past,' I said with hesitation. That sounded safer.

'Here's a woman who wants to speak to you,' she said. 'She's half Indian and half Negro, and she's wearing a rosary.'

It was Mexia she was speaking of, but I didn't remember the rosary. 'She asks you what do you want. What else is she trying to say? I can't hear her plainly. Do you see her now?'

I saw Mexia's eyes staring out of the woman's face, glowing. 'Yes, that's her,' I said.

'What is she saying to you?'

'She's silent.'

'Yes, and one speaks the truth in silence.'

The eyes disappeared. Had I really seen Mexia's eyes in this woman?

'Another woman wants to speak to you, but she's a bit crazy, or so they say.'

I saw my grandmother's wild hair sticking out on the top of her head.

'I don't know any mapmakers, do you?' she asked. 'You are a woman passionately loving your husband, but your mind needs to be mended. Do you think so? Do all conquerors have the right to stare into the face of the vanquished? And break the seal of God? Ah, let the woman waste her sum of days if she's a mind to. She wants to know who the woman is wearing the Dutch trousers ... Wallada drink this wine, for the love of God.' She laughed. 'How does a spirit court a spirit?'

I heard my grandmother's voice in her voice, then I saw Mexia's eyes again.

'A woman of quality comes to speak to you. Where is your captain?'

Zibatra's velvet hem changed to silk, and her feet were bare. Could she really transform herself into many women?

'Didn't he do his job? Didn't he rid the land of all the black ones? And you? What's become of you? Doesn't he still kiss your dark neck?' The smell of eucalyptus. I say nothing.

'Doesn't he have the right to stare into the face of the woman and break the seal of God? How many ways can they mutilate a woman?'

'Here's another woman who wants to talk to you. She wants to talk to you. See how straight her back is? Here she comes, singing a dirty song, laughing in the face of her murderers.'

'Zeferina?' I whispered.

'Why are they laughing at the dark woman?' She spoke in Zeferina's voice, and then Luiza's.

'Dance on the peacock's belly. Who are you and what do you want of me? Is it right to remain tender in a time of cruelty? The blood of the whole continent is in my veins. Open your eyes and see me. Spread your arms and touch me. It takes a mystic to know one. From now on call me Brutality of Existence. I'm in a market where I see a mother sold.'

Now there are man's legs peeking out of the shadows. White trousers, black ashy feet.

'From now on that's what my name will be. Where are you taking this woman? Come here, child, and this man will comfort you. Lay your head on my shoulder. I am also a servant of existence. Any more from your past?'

'No,' I said.

'It gets harder and harder to stay in the past, doesn't it?' she asked.

Bare slender feet of a woman. 'Here's a woman who's a slave while you're a free one and you have the same color and the same blood. She won't look you in the eye.'

'Nobrega,' I said.

'The moon is riding on her shoulders. Ah, but she's got a better memory than you. Here's a woman who puts oil in your hair and you share a bit of her soul.'

'Mother?'

Slender feet in sandals, shadow of a wide-brimmed hat, breasts showing.

'She kisses you and gives you a dark liquid to drink. The kiss that heals, the magic powder that protects. The navel of the woman bends across the sky, eating the sun at night, giving birth to him in the day. Who did this thing? Who mutilated you?'

She touches the center of my head.

'See how the sparks jump from her eyes?' Now she's Old Vera in Dutch trousers.

'How do you judge the immortality of any man? Shall I bring you fish and chocolate?'

Now I remember. Two slashes of a machete.

Almeyda's Reveries

Y*our face looks like the whole country.'*
I say nothing. Had she turned herself into a circle, her ankles touching her neck?

'Do you think it takes a mystic to know one?' I don't answer. She sits up very straight.

'Here's an Indian woman who wants to speak to you, her baby sucking at her breast. What is it you wish to say, my dear? Look how unhappy and lonely she seems, but the baby sucks her fine breasts and laughs. There, there, little boy. There. There. Are there others here? Any others? We're all hundreds and hundreds of years old. See how Almeyda looks around for all of you. Want to introduce yourselves?'

Her hands around a clay bowl. She drinks.

'Here's a woman from a mission. You know, I don't like to mix

my own memory here. This is your story. And this one, isn't she a true picture of this continent? Scabs on her bosom, the blood of the whole continent running in her veins. But why not? Why not? Push your blouse aside so she can see.'

I do not and a wind comes and pushes my blouse up.

'The two of you return. Oh, loved one, the only gift I can give you is the blood in your veins. And here's a fool who wants to speak to you. See how wide his eyes are. But I rescue the fool and send him away. And here's a man with his ear slashed. I mend it. Ah, yes.'

'What?'

'I'm asking this gentleman how he is, the one your grandmother is caring for. He says he's better. He's come here to witness the destruction of Palmares. Isn't he a poor devil? But we'll join again, I tell him, and form a new Palmares. Yes. Oh, I know this one. She looks at you so sadly and with such concern. Past. Heavy forest. Do not tell her her future. Here's a woman who makes something from toasted kurumikaa leaves. To drink?

'To rub in the skin? Don't worry, sweet one.' I stare at her shining hair.

'Here's a woman come to mend a mind deranged. And here's an enchanted Moorish woman.'

I feel sunshine on my face, then darkness again. I feel as if my body's bound in a cloth, then I'm free. The woman has one glowing eye.

'Here's a woman who boasts of her spiritual prowess, and here's a bitter heart. There's an old mapmaker. He thinks his eyes see farther than anyone's. The memory in my blood is as deep as the memory in yours, Sir. There's a woman wearing a mask of feathers, and now a boy's clothes, but they won't let her march in the festival. Carnival of exaggerated souls. A young Indian, a handsome man. But they tell me he's denied the position of magistrate because of his wife's blood. Oh, here's an old storyteller, look at him, medicine man, look at him. He wants to please you. How are you, Sir? Almeydita, look at this one. Her cheekbones go all the way up to the sky. You still believe King Zumbi

261

is immortal, don't you? I told you the Portuguese soldiers got him, they grabbed him by the hair and cut his head off and put it on a stick so his people would not think he's immortal. Don't you believe it?'

'No, others say he jumped from the cliff and flew away with some of his men, and perhaps women too. They were afraid of his immortality.'

Now I'm silent again. Perhaps all our words will have some value. 'Let's go this way. It's a bit steep, but we have to go there. They're behind us. Take my hand. See, it wasn't hard.'

A column, men and women. A long line, each person behind the next. Each person following someone, a bundle on their heads or strapped to their shoulders. That's the way it is.

'Here's a woman who knows how to speak with her own blood. How do you feel? Are you rested?'

'I have seen the river bleed.'

'Don't speak of it, Nzingha ...'

'I'm not Nzingha, I'm ... '

'Do you remember when I came and sat by you? You said nothing, but then I knew how it would be with us. I haven't forgotten you. My soul runs through the streets and forests and you're here.'

Here's someone carrying the dried feet and ears of an enemy. Love and horror in the same country. I see a woman with a broadsword. She presents it to different people, who carry it about to others. Perhaps I only dreamed I escaped after the defeat of Palmares. Perhaps it's only a dream. Perhaps I'm still in the valley of Mandahu with all the others, my breasts amputated and covered with mud.

The battle was real. But perhaps the escape, the hiding in caves, in forests, in underground huts a dream, a fantasy of history and imagination.

'Don't you see the woman, yourself, you, Almeyda, her breasts floating on the river, her consciousness still full of magic? Come closer, look. Remember the landscape, the hills, the mountains, the cliffs, the rivers, the dark rich land, the best fruit in Brazil. The ceremony of dreams. This picaresque story is yours. A dream, fantasista. A thatched hut.

'Here's something to kill the hunger.'

I see drums and swords, men wearing feathers on their heads, bows *and arrows, coming down from the top of the mountain, on two sides, a dream, malarial fever.*

Almeydita, her breasts gone. Is this how one punishes a desire for liberty?

How long did you live in Palmares? Four years.

How could it have been four years? Four months it must have been. To be against our people is the policy of the state.

What do you know of Zumbi?

I know that he had little faith in the promises of the Portuguese, that he rebelled against his uncle Ganga Zumba and killed him, or so they say.

Where do you think you are? I don't know.

Where do you think he is? Somewhere concentrating his forces.

Haven't I told you his head is on a pole in a public square.

The straw woman appeared, bloated with straw, straw coming out of her mouth.

Yes, I'm a real woman, she said. Eternally real. And this is the man who might have altered the history of a nation.

Someone's mixing a dish of almonds and cinnamon.

Some man is here discussing 'the wart of fugitive Negroes.' Has the wart formed again? 'An example of resistance without parallel.'

I see Negroes taken prisoner and distributed among the Portuguese soldiers. And here's a man holding biscuits and a pair of shoes, ham and a sugar loaf. Fish and rice.

And this man, his job is to ferret out the hiding places of renegades. What's your name, old woman?

Veridiana, but they call me Old Vera.

In the procession there are clowns and dancing girls, soldiers, prostitutes, kings, queens, goddesses, a few saints, some idiots, a carpenter, a mapmaker, an engineer, a bridge builder, a journalist, a tavern keeper, a blacksmith, a tooth puller's daughter ... and there's Pope Innocent VIII riding on the witches' bull, riding on old Summis Desiderantes ...

The procession stops, for behind the pope, they are leading a woman. A woman who looks familiar to me, though try as hard as I might, I can't place her. Is it Mexia, or the adulteress, or is it Antonia? Is it all of those women in one woman?

They pause and a chair is placed for the woman and she's commanded to sit down.

'Where's the Jew's hat? Who brought the Jew's hat?

There's a great deal of bustle and noise until the Jew's hat is found, and it's passed down the line by the men who stand around the woman, until it's placed upon her head. The woman sits in the chair without any expression, as if she were beyond expressions. Her lower lip is pierced and a stone is inserted into it. It's been put there, not as if the woman has desired it, as if it were a custom of her country, but to purposely mutilate and disfigure her. Her eyes are quite large and handsome and she has a mole on her cheek, a large fleshy mole.

The ones surrounding her are all men. Five are white men wearing judges' robes and powdered wigs. The other five are black men, some with elaborately painted faces, others wearing masks. They look to be witch doctors or medicine men.

'The white ones are witch hunters,' says Zibatra, as if reading my thoughts. 'The black ones are witch doctors and the white ones are witch hunters. Now you'll see the workings of the African and European witch craze at the same time. Ha. Ha. Is this your past? It must be yours, it's not mine. It must be yours. They're all afraid of her, that's why they gang up so. Look at that one, fingering the mole on her face, like it's some strange fruit. What do they want?'

The white man, a very tall, blond-haired, fleshy man, with an English accent says, 'This must be the place where the devil sucks.'

'Blood or milk?' asks another, with a French accent.

'It could be blood, it could be milk,' says the Englishman. 'Sometimes milk will do, and other times the little devils need blood.'

'How many imps do you have?' asks another man, with an accent I can't place.

'Is she the witch or the witch's apprentice?' asks one of the masked men from Yorubaland.

'I think she's the apprentice,' says another masked African. 'But it's all the same.'

'Hausa,' says Zibatra.

'Why did you put her there in the place of a Jew or a Moor?' asks the Spaniard. 'I'd rather examine a Jew or a Moor. Why should a witch replace a Jew? They're the ones to examine, not this uninformed Negro.'

'He's right,' says the Italian. 'Have you read Giovanni Antonio Andreoni's "The Synagogue Undeceived"?'

'Let's get on with the witch trial,' says the Dutchman. 'Witchfinder General, you ask the first question.'

The Africans are silent, observing the woman. They converse among themselves in secret, while the Europeans speak loudly and move in closer to the woman.

'It's an endless process,' says the Englishman. 'There'll be witches till the end of the world.'

'There were witches at the beginning of the world and there'll be witches at the end of it,' says the Hausa.

Then I notice that the white men walk about as if they don't see or hear the Africans.

'Either that or the Africans have made themselves invisible,' says Zibatra, again reading my thoughts.

The white men go on speaking:

'The witness said she rubbed herself with devil's grease and made herself invisible.'

'Another said the woman wandered into her dreams.'

'Another that she changed herself into a lion and a serpent. People say she works only in secret and in the darkness, never in daylight.'

'They're afraid of the daylight. They're all very solitary women. It's at night when they revel and have their secret meetings. It's at night when they enchant. It's at night when their little imps come and suck. Don't you see the extra teat on her face? Usually they're hidden in some secretive place. But hers is there, plain as day.'

'Yes, that's true, Sir.'

When the woman's eyes seem about to close, he slaps her. 'Don't sleep. How many imps do you have?'

The woman is silent. 'I'll put the boot to her.'

'No, sleeplessness and lack of food should get her confession.'

'I don't think it'll work. I've seen them dance all day and night and not get tired.'

'Give her the water test.'

'No, the water test is only for white witches not black ones.'

'If I'd known it was going to be a black witch, I wouldn't have come. Black witches aren't my concern. I say hang her and be done with her.'

"The Bible says to burn them. That's the only way. Otherwise they'll come back.'

'In England we hang them.'

'A black witch can't be hanged. If you hang them they'll still have control. They'll get stronger.'

'Answer me about your imps.'

'She won't confess. I'm an authority on witches. And I tell you they're all the same. A witch is a witch. You were seen with a black man on a horse, were you not? What are the names of your imps?'

Almeyda, what story do you refuse to tell? Who are you, Zibatra?

I'm a woman from another time and another world.

A goatskin draped about her shoulders. Mask of feathers. Laughing. The smell of almonds, coconuts.

I am a spirit keeper, not a spirit catcher, no not me. I don't eat souls. Do you think they'll start a new Palmares?

Here is a woman who forgets nothing. Speak so your words may endure forever. Speak to this man. Say something to him. Speak so that he will know you.

The man looks at me. Is it Anninho? He comes toward me. I feel my mouth being opened, and his lips against mine. Then he is not there.

But when he returns, he is carrying flowers.

Josef de Azarza, or a
Fate Remains Unknown

WHEN OLD VERA ENTERED I was sitting in my corner in silence. She said as she had begun to say now, 'What's wrong with the woman?' which had become her way of greeting me. I nodded to her, but remained silent.

'This old woman has been hunting,' she said. Were they squirrels she tossed on the table, or dark rabbits? She stood looking at me.

'Yes, this one has become solitary and secretive now,' she said. 'Even her spirit eludes me.'

'There was a strange woman here,' I said.

'Yes, and what strange woman besides these?'

'She said her name was Zibatra. Do you know such a woman?'

'I don't *know* such a woman,' she said.

'Have you heard her name before, or maybe she is from a place with that name?'

'I have heard many names. Where is she now?'

'I don't know. She left.'

'And was it a frightening experience for you or a humorous one?' she asked, turning away from me.

'A fearful one. But I tried not to show it. At first I thought it was you in disguise.'

'Perhaps I know such a woman,' she said, not turning to me. Was she skinning the animals she hunted? 'Yes, she was a strange woman. A strange woman of strange women. Intelligent. Her body is as agile and elusive as your spirit. Yes, I have heard tales of such a woman who wanted to remain unknown but there was a certain Josef de Azarza who desired her and wished to know her. But each time he tried to know the woman her body would fly out from under him. Do you think it was some herb that she knew?' she said with a laugh. 'You see, this Josef de Azarza, a landowner, got four of his men slaves to hold her down. She said no she did not like such a humiliating position, but they held her down anyway. But this time it was not her body that flew up but that of Josef de Azarza. Do you think it was some herb she gave him?'

She turned toward me, holding one of the skinned rabbits. I shook my head.

'To this day his fate remains unknown and she remains unknown,' she said with a chuckle and went back to her work.

'I know what you're thinking,' she said without turning around. 'But this one has been known.'

She thumped something. Her chest?

'This one has been known ... And he thought he was in hiding. He thought I left him alone. Ha. Ha.'

She breathed deeply. 'Was it your past or your future you wanted to know?'

'My past,' I said softly.

'Did you think that was safer?' she asked. I didn't answer.

'You won't tell me anything,' she said. 'But that doesn't matter. Do you know what it's like when the voice of a god speaks through a person? That's the real talking. These dialogues of the spirit. That's when we really learn to speak, and that voice goes outside time.'

Art and Leisure

IN THE DAYS THAT WE WAITED for Barcala's brother Martim and his wife, and for the family of Martina Puerreydon, Barcala would sit in the early mornings at a table writing something. I had told him about my grandmother's notebooks in Arabic, and he said he knew that language well and would translate the writings for me but he said that that would have to be when he was in another country. I said that I no longer had the notebooks, that I had returned them. That was when he produced the yellowed papers and said that my grandmother had given them to him to keep.

'Did you see her? Where is she? Is she all right?'

'I don't know. I don't know where she is. She gave them to me one moment and the next moment I didn't see her.'

He looked at me strangely. I kept watching him. Then he began writing feverishly again. I asked him once what it was about and he said it was about an intruder. He did not say anything else and I didn't ask him.

He had very little paper and it was strange to see a man show such love for paper, saving every scrap. He said that when he finished the mono-logue he would give it to me to read. Unfortunately, he said it was only a secondary thing; it did not get into real actions, but only the speech of a certain character, and the relationships came only in speaking. Maybe, he said when he was in another country he would have time to put it on the first level. He said the kind of art he wished to write could only be written at a man's leisure. He had seen enough of the old woman with blood in her teeth and the sepulcher of dead men's bones, the silent old woman grinning at him, her gestures saying, 'Come, Barcala,' but never a voice he could trust.

He said he had spent some years with her and found her out. It was always in struggle. He had wasted days with the woman. The skulls all around her were all the same color, and it didn't matter if the flesh around them had once been red or black or white or yellow. He believed in the spirit, that was the source of everything. But the woman was speechless. The closer he got to her the more exaggerated her traits, her personality in pantomime. And she had faces that could be taken off and put back on and shaped and reshaped.

Well, he said, his brother would spend more years struggling with her, and present that fine woman, his wife, to the whore. No, there were no ordinary days here. He'd go anywhere where there were ordinary days. It was the same on the whole continent and the one above it. Oh, perhaps it was these kinds of days that provided the material for an art, but not the medium to produce it in. He wondered about the places where there was nothing but niceties. Were men treated with dignity? Did they treat each other with dignity?

So he and his brother would go different places after the destruc-tion of Palmares. His brother would join with others and seek a new Palmares, a new place of perpetual struggle. Would it be a new place to be destroyed in?

'Why are you looking at me so?' he asked. 'Why are you looking at me with such eyes? Are you thinking, "Not destroyed." Do you still believe in the immortality of such a man? And *him*? Which *him*, you ask. Well, let's say it's all of them, every one of them and your man too. Talk to me, Almeyda. Why are you looking at me with such eyes? Do you think I'm any man? Are you any woman? Where will you go? Oh, you're the woman who'll not leave this place and will waste your days in waiting. Yes, you're that one. And have stopped talking. Maybe you're the eternal symbol of sadism and masochism on this continent. What the writers speak of. How can I record the words of such a woman when there are none. I must learn some new method, some method applicable to the soul of such a woman, for digging in. Shall I use sex? No. Some means of psychic horror?

'Tenderness? But I haven't shown an excess of it? Talk to me, Almeyda. I'm not used to such a woman. Shall I stay here with you? But you won't notice. It's *him*.'

I said nothing.

'Perhaps you're all of them. The fantasy of a lover I could never have. You're hopeless. Would you let me kiss you? No? You're as quiet as the moon. Look how I make hand monsters on the wall with moonlight. Shall I stay here with you?'

Still I did not speak.

'Am I making sense or nonsense? But even if you wanted me, the consequences are different for a woman. Am I making sense? When I first saw you, all these images passed before me. I told you that I grew up never seeing such tall, dark women. Did I ever tell you that? Maybe I never told you. And you fascinated me in a way I can't explain. They took me to Europe as a boy and I grew up there, so for me, you're the exotic woman. I came here to meet a mysterious woman, and so I did. I watched Old Vera rubbing you with her medicines, crushing leaves and mixing it with honey and your own menstrual blood. I've seen you and I'm still here. And I've seen the old woman take the shape of tigers and lions and flowers and fish and trumpets, and I'm not afraid. But I've wasted a sum of days here, and you want to keep me, staring into your eyes. Are they the eyes of a madwoman? See how they make slits now and now they're huge and round and lovely. I'd like to get a brush and paint you. I'll paint you in my mind. My writing now is mostly history – about people, events, and conversations. But eventually I'll get outside space and time. Speak to me. What are you? Your hand to your mouth now. What are you hiding? It's down, you smile at me. The first time you've shown me a smile. Now a sneer? No. A smile, and genuine. It's good to see it. But still no words for me? How shall I translate that smile? And it's you now who makes the shape of a lion? Agile and wary. What did she say of you? That you've had the chance to be a mystic and drink from the eternal vine, but you refused it. Can you get it back, reclaim that sum of days? But you're a laughing head now. At me? No?

Yourself? And now your forehead is ornamented with painted design. A pyramid? A bird? Your hands move so quickly I didn't see. But did they move? No, I'm not a crazy man or even a true romantic. And what's that? An eye? Another one? It's Old Vera playing tricks on us. Yes, it's Old Vera, making patterns of light move about you, and you can't see yourself. Am I changing too? Do you see things I don't? A man you've seen before and loved? Has she made me *that one*?'

'Anninho,' I started to call, but kept my silence.

'You look beautiful and happy. No harm done. Do you think I'm a fool and a false artist? An illegitimate artist? Can't a man decide whether he wants to paint his mother or his country or the world or the universe, and how? Say something to that. But no. I keep asking the woman and she won't speak to me. Give me your hand. No? Am I in love with you? So the patterns keep changing. Now the bird's elongated, distorted, mutilated and now she's whole again and staring at me with that incredible, magnificent eye. What kind of woman are you? A screen to lay with patterns on? What spirit makes the hand monsters on your forehead and now lovable creatures? Give me a kiss. No? So I'll go to another country, and in my leisure make a full description of the woman. You say nothing, but you understand. Or perhaps it's all my presumption. And what do the gods presume. No, with them it's what they *know*.'

'Hush,' said Old Vera.

'No, let me speak to her. I'll change this man's world, though we live in the same one, my brother and me. He'll stay here to help create this new Palmares, and I'll change my world from a dangerous one to a fortunate one. Here I'm a dangerous man, and remain accused, but there I'll be a decent and respected man, or so's my hope. What kind of man do you think I am? You say nothing, but you understand. You didn't say whether you still believe in his immortality. But you won't tell me. How might I set you talking, Almeyda? What is the right, the eternal question to a woman? Old Vera says that certain spirits have chosen to seek you out, but you deny them. You refuse and abandon them. Are they face to face with you now? Why do you tremble? But now the tremble's stopped, you're calm again, your forehead in total colors. The reproduction of what soul?'

He paused. I thought Old Vera would tell him to hush again, but now, sitting in her hammock, she leans forward, with interest.

'So they intend to form a new Palmares?' She nods.

'I'll go with them, then go my own way. Anyway, Old Vera, you've

271

predicted the destruction of that one. I'd like to take this woman with me, but she won't come.'

'You knew that before you started speaking.'

'This is a land of saints and devils. Words still have magic for me.'

'I see how you look at her,' said Old Vera. 'Perhaps you shouldn't look at her that way. You're tired. Lie down in your hammock and sleep.'

I don't know whether she's speaking to me or the man. Is it true he stood speaking to me so long? Now I see him lying calmly across the room in his hammock, staring wide at the ceiling, his chest moving up and down, heavy, now calmer. Does he close his eyes and sleep? Now he's up and writing something. I drift in and out of sleep. Is it some herbs I've drunk to cure the wounds on my body? Has it had some effect on my spirit? Now I see him, a handsome, bearded man, resting, his broad chest moving gently. Did he really speak to me?

The Force of Imagination

I HEARD THEM OUTSIDE THE HUT before they entered, though the only voice I recognized was Barcala's. I could make out none of the words. Now for some reason Barcala had started calling me 'The Madwoman' and whenever he would introduce me it would be as 'The Madwoman.' I heard him say, 'Only "the madwoman" is inside.' There was another voice, a deep man's voice and a delicate woman's voice, but I could not make out what they were saying. Then the door burst open and they entered.

I closed my eyes against the first burst of sunlight and then opened them. My eyes first focused on a very tall, broad-shouldered man in an elegant dark suit and short cape. His eyes were as black as ebony and large. He had a high forehead like his brother Barcala, for I knew this to be the brother I had heard so much of but never seen. He wore his hair brushed back and long. He was darker than his brother – a ruddy, dark red-brown complexion. He had a medium-sized, rounded nose and full lips and wore a beard and mustache. He looked straight at me. He nodded but did not speak.

'Almeyda,' the woman said and came and kissed me. Her shoulders were rounded and graceful and looked as if they had been polished. She was wearing gold earrings, a green silk dress, and her hair had flowers in it.

'Don't you recognize me?' she asked. 'I am Martim Aprigio's wife.'

I held my arms out to her and we hugged and I kissed her but remained silent.

She stood back and looked at me with a sad expression. 'Barcala told me what's been done to you. I am very sorry.'

I was silent, but looking at her, I felt, with affectionate eyes.

'Come have a seat, Joanna,' Barcala said. 'She won't speak to anyone.'

That was the first time I'd heard her name. Joanna looked at me sadly, then walked and sat down at the table. Her shoes and the hem of her dress were covered with mud and leaves.

'So you intend to flee to Holland,' Martim said to his brother. He took a seat, but Barcala remained standing. 'Well, poor devil, I'll be sorry to see you go.'

Barcala said nothing then he said, 'I'm no more a poor devil than you are.'

'Why is it always "poor devil"?' Joanna asked. 'Why isn't it "poor angel"?'

The men said nothing. There was silence for a long time. Barcala stood in the same place for a long time. Occasionally he would look at me. Was it with reproach?

His brother sat very straight in his silence, and Joanna occasionally looked at me with sad eyes.

'Look at the madwoman,' Barcala said.

'Well, she'll feel better when we get to the new place,' Joanna said gently.

'She's not going, neither there, nor with me to Holland,' Barcala said.

'Where is she going?' Joanna asked.

Martim had turned to look at me, but said nothing. 'She's going to stay right here,' Barcala said.

'Will Old Vera stay?' Joanna asked.

'No, Old Vera's coming along. But this one is a determined creature. She won't budge.'

'Alone?' Joanna asked, looking at me.

'Oh, maybe she's waiting for someone,' Barcala said, brushing his hands in the air.

Joanna parted her lips to say something, but did not. There was silence again.

We heard the sound of birds.

'That's right. I want some gaiety about me,' Barcala said, clapping his hands. He was still standing. 'That's right,' he said, as one bird called after another.

'How much gaiety can you handle?' Martim asked.

'Oh, a great deal,' Barcala said matter-of-factly and aloof. He looked at me again, with reproach, but said nothing. Then, 'And how long will you wait? But you won't answer ... Why don't you turn the place into an inn? A Spirit's Inn. They're sure to come in and out then. I'll help you change the place around.'

I said nothing.

He started to say something, then looking despondent, turned to his brother. 'Tell me, is it presumption or destiny?' he asked.

'What do you mean?'

I felt that Martim was a man of as little conversation as Barcala was of much.

'I mean, dear brother, you've been an actor, an engineer, an astronomer, a rebel,' he said. 'Is it presumption or destiny? Have you become what you've presumed you could become or is it simply destiny, or does one chance to be at the proper place and time?'

Martim said nothing, though he was looking at his brother strangely.

Then he said in a studied voice, 'I've never really thought of it, but I suppose it's a man's fate what he becomes, or a woman's fate,' he said, looking at his wife, with a curious look on his face.

Barcala brushed back his hair, and held it. 'That's because you were raised by nuns. This one was raised by nuns. That's why he dresses the way he does. They used to dress him up in little gentlemen's clothes, and the boys about the city would rail at him, throw rocks and taunt, and once they caught him and tore his fine clothes off, and said he should wear something more fitting of his birth and position. A horse blanket I think they gave him. Was that fate?'

Martim was silent.

'You didn't say you were raised by nuns,' Joanna said.

'It was whispered that we were the children of a local priest and a black woman,' Barcala said. 'The priest gave Martim his schooling and Martim gave me mine. For which I am grateful. But was it fate or a man's own disposition? Do I speak like a fool and a clown? I'll dye my face purple. But no. It's the force of man's imagination. Oh, you'll say it was fate that we were given our freedom, sent abroad for our schooling. But no, it's one's man's imagination versus another that takes a man from place to place and through time and the spirit.'

My eyes widened, but I said nothing.

'I believe in the force of the imagination,' Barcala declared. 'I'll spend years in that struggle. While you make your oaths and war, I'll make mine.' He paused. 'Almeyda, am I a fool and a clown?' he asked, looking at me.

I shook my head.

'No? Or don't you know?' I said nothing.

He looked down, despondent again, then raised his head. 'Anyway, it takes an act of the imagination to talk such talk at such a time, between destructions.'

'You honestly believe the new place will be destroyed as the old one was?' asked Martim.

'Old Vera says so.'

'But Old Vera is going with us.'

'Ha ha,' he said. 'And that's the real force of the imagination.' He was silent, letting his hands drop.

'Or maybe what's a man's fate *here*,' he said, looking at me, as if I would understand, 'is the force of a man's imagination *there*.'

'Some things lie beyond a man's choice and imagination,' Martim said.

'Ah, but the thing is not to accept the difference.'

'What?'

'Between the things that do and don't,' Barcala said with a laugh.

Martim's Plan

JOANNA SAT NEAR ME, but saying nothing, respecting my silence, while the men, her husband and his brother Barcala and the two men, the printer's slave and the mulatto "priest" sat at the table talking.

'And what is your strategy, Martim, what is your plan?' Barcala asked Martim.

'Well, to become a part of the New Palmares,' Martim said.

'And what is it you really want, what do you really want, what is it you see for the future, what is it that makes you remain here?'

'There are hundreds of quilombos scattered about in the mountains of not only Barriaga, but in Cubatāo, São Paulo, Lellon, Rio de Ianeira, Maranhão, Matto Grosso, and even unknown, unseen places, independent African states. If we could get the hundreds of them to come together, that would be my future for Brazil. Independent African States. Oh, the Portuguese can have their territories, and we have ours. One man's existence should not depend on the extinction of another.'

Barcala began to laugh. 'But it does, doesn't it, brother? We know that every site is initiated with blood. So you'll take the mulatto priest and I'll take the printer's slave. What does that mean? And what about the unseen populations? How will you see them, how will you know them?

'Will you know them when they are exhibited in public, as King Zumbi was, with their heads on poles?'

Martim was silent.

'Why do you laugh at such serious matters?' the mulatto priest asked.

'Because he knows that he himself is in a dangerous position,' Martim said. 'And his *sight* is initiated in blood.'

Barcala said nothing, staring down at the backs of his hands. 'Once a woman I was courting read the backs of my hands. She looked at the palms and showed such fear, that I turned them over and said, "Read the backs of them."'

'How could she read the backs of them?' the printer's slave asked.

'There's nothing, you see,' Barcala said with a laugh.

'Poor devil,' Martim said.

'We used to eat fruit every day, and sleep well every night,' Barcala said. 'It was all very good,' and then he looked at me. 'No woman loved a man as well.'

'I want it to be all very good here,' Martim said with a sadness. 'Well, it must have some meaning, it must make some sense,' Barcala said, still looking at me.

'It's without any reason,' the mulatto priest said.

'Well, I'll devote myself to matters of life,' Barcala said with a smile. 'And be without any reason.' His smile changed to a frown and he grimaced at the backs of his hands. 'And what is your plan?' he said, looking at his brother. 'And it's more fantastic than in a book. Do you think real men and women can accomplish it?'

'They'll have to.'

'I'm a man of little faith.'

'With the help of God,' Martim said.

'Oh, I have great faith in God but little in people,' he said, still grimacing at the backs of his hand. 'And even less in the unseen populations,' he said, looking at his palms, as if he were trying to see them.

'Admit Martim has a great spirit,' the printer's slave said.

'I admit I have little spirit for the talk any longer,' Barcala said rising, then he looked at me. 'And *her* strategy, her ideal? Her ideal is the truly silent woman. Is that your plan, Almeyda, the eternal truly silent woman? Oh, don't you wish!' He looked at his brother and said, 'Yes, he has a fine one,' and went out.

The Narratives
of Barcala Aprigio

The following are narratives written by Barcala Aprigio. I have decided to include them here in this history, although it was not until years later that I had the opportunity to read them. He never had them printed as he was dissatisfied with them. They were written, he said, during his passage from Brazil to Europe. I have not had the opportunity to read any of the printed manuscripts, those written during the years abroad, though in one of his letters he translated a piece that had appeared in a French newspaper. The critic spoke of having admired the writings of Barcala Aprigio until he had 'got religion,' as the critic said. Barcala 'the mystic,' he declared, was not nearly so entertaining as Barcala 'the profligate.'

I received the letter first and then I was delivered a box of hand-written manuscripts.

(I purposely do not include here where I was or what I was doing those later years, as I would prefer to relate that in another history.)

On a slip of paper inside one of the manuscripts the following list was scribbled:

The rarer ipecacuanha A freakish memory Mystical unity Man and the Universe

What he meant by this, I don't know. But here are the narratives:

THE FAMILY OF MARTINA P.

Goncalo P. annulled the marriage of his son Valdes to the young Martina without even seeing the woman, only knowing she was a mixture of blood and parentages, perhaps 'a whole series of bastardies,' in fact the blood of the whole continent ran in her veins. Knowing this, he knew she was not the woman for his son, who was 'of clean birth and purely European origin.' His son, in the woman's favor, said that she was a highly educated woman, and though her mother was of pure African blood, her father was a mulatto geologist and physician, the son of a wealthy Scandinavian physician and a Bahian woman. 'A profligate mulatto,' his father had said, attempting to strike down any good thing he might say of the woman. He told his father that she was a fascinating and intelligent and beautiful woman. 'And even if she is the prettiest on this continent, you do not need to marry her,' his father had said. The son persisted in saying that he would marry the woman.

'You are crazy,' his father said.

'Why is it that I am the lunatic and not you?' the son had asked.

The father looked at him, saddened that his son would want to marry a woman of such low degree.

'She's not a woman to speak of,' his father said. 'What about these women of good families, old and respected families? Many admire you.'

'It's true she's not to speak of, but not for your reasons. I would trade whole populations of such women for Martina.'

His father could not believe his ears. 'Women of good blood,' he said.

The son laughed, and made a joke about all the 'bad blood' since the Dutch and Portuguese came.

'What claims does she have on you? I can't understand your lunacy. Is she a love sorceress as well as the daughter of a profligate mulatto, working some danger on you? Why this woman? I say no to it.'

'You have not set eyes on her.'

'Nor do I intend to, nor upon the children of her children, who, if in God's power, will not be yours.'

He stood firmly before his son who straightened his shoulders and left the house.

'Can you remember anything? Can you remember anything since you've met this woman?'

The son married the woman, and the father, hearing of it, and having connections among the officials, had the marriage annulled, arranged for the woman to be stolen and sold into slavery (he himself buying her through an agent, to make sure it would be done). The son, thinking the woman had been unfaithful and all of the things his father had called her, left and went to North America, avoiding such women.

One day the father, Goncalo P., was walking about his plantation and saw the woman (since he had arranged to purchase her through his agent he had not laid eyes on her before). He asked his overseer who she was, saying that he did not remember such a woman, and that he did not know of any slave woman of such refinement. Upon hearing her name, his mouth fell open, but being fascinated by the strange beauty of the woman, he took her as his mistress. He felt he too had lost himself, but he could not help it. Eventually, he slayed his wife so that he could bring his mistress into the house to be with him all the time. 'There is no such woman,' servants heard him say until he moved them out of the house, so that he could be alone with her. He hid his wife inside one of the thick walls of the house. He stayed with the woman for five years, having two children by her.

Finally the son returned from North America and went to visit his father to tell him he had been right about such women and to make friends with him again. Before he got to his father he saw the woman Martina.

He went up to her. He wanted to strike her. He had his hand drawn back, but seeing her eyes, he stopped. He began to wonder what she was doing there. He asked her to forgive his look and his cheap clothes. He asked her to ignore what he had just done. He said for the last five years he had felt so isolated, but he had never traveled before, and he had tried to make that take the place of any experiences of being loved.

'What do you want, Valdes?' she asked.

Did he detect bitterness, and for what? Hadn't she left him and denied him his dreams? Wasn't he the one who had never really escaped the woman? Hadn't she stayed in his memory and imagination?

'What do you want of me?' she asked.

'First I want to know what you are doing here.'

She explained what had happened, with a slowness and nonchalance he could scarcely believe. She explained that their marriage had been annulled without his knowledge of that fact, and how she had been stolen and sold to his father, and how his father had murdered his wife and taken her into his house. She brought out the two children who were his brother and sister.

He scarcely looked at the children but continued to look at the woman who was still beautiful and fascinating, the same round eyes that seemed to take him to some mysterious region. (These were his words and thoughts), and in his rage, on account of the jewel he had lost (again his words), and her degradation, he ran to his father, and without even greeting him, slayed him and hid him inside the thick walls of the house, where, if such things are possible, the bones of his old wife, laid immediate claims on the man.

Then the son took the lovely Martina (who to his eyes had not changed in all that time) into the house to live with him, and in the five years that they remained together, had two children by her – another boy and girl. He had wanted to sell his father's children, but the woman would not part with them, loving them dearly, and so he let her keep them. He did not marry the woman this time, but merely lived with her, and then he grew tired of the woman, and began to feel that she might not have been as lovely as he had considered her to be, or as fascinating; in fact, she seemed to him a taciturn, unimaginative woman. So he went back to North America to the delights of the wilderness. (His vocabulary.) It was then, and for no other reason, than that the woman, Martina, seemed to have taken over the plantation, that the people began to realize and to whisper that they had not seen the old man Puerreydon nor his wife for many years. The old wife's disappearance they had never noticed, because she was not a woman given to public appearance nor did her husband like to exhibit his wife in public. Then when the old man went unnoticed, they excused themselves by saying it was because the son had returned and they had assumed that he had taken over the plantation and that the father, as such old men often did, had merely hidden himself inside his huge mansion. As for the woman, they thought the son had inherited her too along with the other property. And now for this 'property' to be running things, they began to take notice. What had become of the old man and the wife? And even though they knew the son had gone to North America, they asked what had become of him too? Perhaps if the woman had given them some notice they might have lessened their suspicions, but as she did not and was content with her children, and seemingly with the whole order of the universe, as if she felt it revolved, or was resolved in the children, the people were very suspicious. What had become of the Puerreydon family? First they began to ask questions, and then when they attempted to search the mansion, Martina fled with her children and was discovered by the author –

A fascinating, intelligent woman, whose family revolve around her like a planet. The beautiful Martina. What would be the consequences of loving such a woman? She claims she will be no man's wife, and will go to the New Palmares with her children. What will become of her there?

'There is no such woman.'

THE FLYING DUTCHMAN'S SLAVE

She was neither a medicine woman, nor a witch, and yet people feared her, and let her do as she pleased in the town. It was not because of the woman herself but because of the woman's ancestry. It had something to do with her great-great-grandmother. And if it were not that woman's spirit they feared, it was certainly that other spirit, for Anna Bejerano herself did nothing. She was rather a shy, inoffensive, peaceful woman, who kept to her house and made sails for the fishermen of the town. It might seem strange that they would fear the woman and yet eagerly take her their sails that needed mending and buy new ones from her, but though they distrusted the woman, they thought her sails had some magic and would protect them, so that although she was feared and shunned by the town and its people (which did not set badly with her as she was a shy woman to begin with), she was respected by the fishermen.

She was the wife of no one, and rarely appeared in public places, but spent most of her days in her workshop or going silently to market. The several generations of the Bejerano women lived unmolested in the town by both the masters and the slaves, making sails, going silently about. And though none of them had taken a husband, each had strangely around the age of twenty years become pregnant and gave birth to a daughter, by whom no one knew, though everyone supposed some sailor. Then when the girl was grown, the mother would leave town, as if she had suddenly got her wings, her freedom. They whispered that Anna's mother had left and become a wandering storyteller, while the one before her had left and gone across the sea and had become a singer and teller of tales in Syria, or some foreign port in the Far East. But no one knew really what had become of the women, and such stories were passed down, mostly by the women. The men felt it was their business only to leave the women unmolested, but not to talk of them.

It was the great-grandmother's story that caused them to regard Anna in such a strange way. The great-grandmother, Old Zurara, as she was called, had been known only as a sail maker's slave, but the sail maker had gone insane and told strange tales about her. He had gone insane and told strange tales, saying that she was not to be liked or trusted, or unfortunate things would happen in the town. People said at first that it was the man's lunacy speaking. She had been sold to the sail maker by a Norwegian sailor. She was treated like an ordinary slave whose master has taken leave of his senses, and sold at a public auction, along with a boat and some new sails. She was purchased by a printer, who suddenly, and for no explained reason began to write and publish anti-slavery literature as well as to rail against unfaithful women, as he suspected certain women of the town as being, though he called no names. Then some men who were displeased with the literature, and though they saw their own wives implicated and dishonored, broke all the presses, burned the printer's shop down, and drove the man out of town.

After that was all done, some people began to look at the woman strangely, but others treated her like an ordinary slave and sold her at a public auction, but before she was sold she was imprisoned in a slave pen. It was then that certain women in the town began to throw themselves into the sea. First they dreamed that they saw a man rising out of the sea. He was not a handsome man but they felt a strange attraction to him. They would keep having the dream until they would, finding it unbearable, throw themselves into the sea. This happened to women who were considered respectable and faithful wives. And men, fishermen, would speak of seeing a strange ship that seemed to be watching and waiting, but that they could never get near it, and speak with its captain. And whenever they saw it, they would have little luck in fishing.

The woman was taken out of jail when it was time for the next public auction, but people were afraid to buy her and she was looked upon as more than an ordinary woman. But fearing that more women would throw themselves into the sea, and more men would see the ghost ship as they had begun to call it, they gathered money and purchased the woman's freedom and got a house for her near the ocean where she could continue her sail making.

At first the fishermen were afraid to buy any of the woman's sails, but then one man, a foreigner, who knew nothing of the woman, ripped one of his sails, and had her mend it, went out, and came back boasting about the town and in the taverns about what luck he had had and what a fine catch. Whether or not it was due to the woman, and he did not claim it was, the townspeople suspected it of being, and the woman got more business than she could have imagined, though everyone stayed clear of the newly freed woman otherwise; and their women had no more dreams.

Then it was when Zurara was a young and beautiful woman, yet no man bothered her, and still her belly rose. One man claimed that when he was walking home one late night when it was the full moon he saw a man and woman rising out of the sea in each other's arms, and he swore that the woman was Zurara, though the man was unknown. People were afraid to believe him and claimed it was the full moon making patterns on the water, or that it was a dream, or the moonlight had caused his lunacy. But Zurara was pregnant and the child grew making sails with her mother, until she too was a beautiful young woman, and the mother left to wander, and she stayed making sails until Anna was born and a grown woman. But as long as the woman went unmolested, the women of the town did not throw themselves into the sea and did not dream of strange irresistible men, and if there was any dreaming to be done, it was the dreams of the men for Anna Bejerano, the great granddaughter of the flying Dutchman's slave.

Does a man come who does not know the legend, and seeks to marry the woman? Put the author himself into the story. He wants to take the woman for his wife, but sees her rising out of the sea, embracing another man. She becomes pregnant and tells him that all the generations must be the faithful love of this doomed captain. Another metaphor for the continent? The Dutch were here before the Portuguese. The flying Dutch.

Do you think the women of the town, long ago, made up such a story to prevent their men from spending all their time around such women? Still they stare at the woman, though they say nothing to her.

THE WOMAN WHO WANTED
THE RETURN OF HER LOVER

'I am a man who would not like to marry forever,' he told the woman, and so he never married her.

So the woman went to a macumbeiro, a love sorcerer, and began to keep a turtle under her bed and fed it on cow's milk, asking each day that she be the only woman to have the lover.

It so happened, however, that the same macumbeiro, on the woman's visit, had fallen in love with the woman, and as soon as he had given her the remedy to make her to keep the lover, he had also told the woman that she would need to drink coffee mixed with sugar and clots of menstrual blood, and another ingredient, which he gave to the woman but did not tell her what it was – the latter being the remedy to enable him to keep her and to be rid of any lovers she might have, and for himself to never be rid of this wonderful woman and to experience the most passionate nights with her.

So it happened that the lover committed some crime, and his master, a sadistic man, tied the lover to two canoes going in opposite directions.

When the macumbeiro heard this he sent for the distressed woman. 'I have kept my lover, but . . .'

'I know the story,' he said.

He kept looking at her, wondering why it was that his own remedy had not worked. He was certain that with what he had given her, no woman could resist loving him.

The woman had something in her skirt that she gave to him. It was a turtle.

'I'm afraid of this,' she said. 'Afraid to keep it and afraid to destroy it.'

The macumbeiro took the turtle with his right hand and put it on the table.

'The milk he liked, but the coffee . . .'

'*You* were supposed to drink the coffee,' he said in despair.

'Do you think that's why?' the woman asked in horror. 'Is that why it happened? It's all my fault. I didn't understand.'

The macumbeiro in his anger that things had not gone his way, told the woman yes it was her fault.

So the woman, in a deep depression, left, and committed the same 'crime' that her husband had committed, upon which the sadistic master bound the woman to two canoes going in opposite directions.

The macumbeiro stood watching. In the evening the turtle came to sleep beside him and bite his hair.

The macumbeiro, after some weeks of this, began to evoke the woman by evoking her memory through dreams and daily reveries. And the power of imagination of the macumbeiro is so that when he dreams of her he can evoke her actual as well as spiritual presence. Though he gets the woman there, however, he can never get her to express any strong feeling or emotion.

'Speak to me, Floriana.'

But she will not. Still it is enough for him to have corporeal glimpses of her in all of the complete beauty he remembers.

The turtle grows jealous of the woman, and one night plucks out the eyes of the macumbeiro, so that he can no longer see her, so that she cannot jump outside of his dreams and reveries into the 'real' world.

But still he continues to dream about her and it is his internal vision of the woman that continues to absorb him.

Now at this point the turtle has been staying there long enough and is intelligent enough to discover the meaning and purpose of many of the herbs and potions, and so he takes one that will enable him to finally be rid of the woman, and have the exclusive attention if not the love of the macumbeiro.

So that night while the macumbeiro is sleeping, the turtle enters the dream and slays the woman, and at the same time restores sight to the man. So now the turtle is able to be with the man both in his dreams and in his waking.

It is at this point that the macumbeiro commits a crime for which the sadistic master would surely bound him to two canoes going in opposite directions, which he does. But when the macumbeiro is bound, he looks onto the bank, and sees the turtle, poised at the edge of the bank, ready to drink from the water.

PORT OF TRANSFER

I show my free papers to the captain and pay my fare. The printer's slave is allowed aboard, as my servant recently purchased. I show him some abuse and harsh treatment, so that there are no suspicions. I discuss 'regulating the behavior of slaves' with the captain. The gold more than the free papers allows me freedom of movement, though 'my slave' must stay below in the cabin when not in my company. They think I am a wealthy sugarcane planter from Recife, as it is known that there are a number of mulattoes among them. Still there is some talk as always of the 'arrogant mulatto.'

Slaves carrying loads of tobacco, sugar, cotton, dried meat, cacao, nuts, coffee, brazil wood on board to be shipped to Portugal. One I step aside for. He glances at me. Intelligent, sullen eyes. A Bantu from Angola. He looks at me as if I am an enemy. I stare away from him at the hills, other Negroes carrying hundred and two hundred pound loads of manufactured goods, textiles, and ironwork from the warehouses down to the ships – the churches, convents, town houses, public buildings in the distance. Along the coast to the starboard they are constructing a small ship. None of the ships they build here are large or seaworthy enough for international trade, but only for coastal trade. I think of Anninho's plans.

Even the Portuguese do not build such vessels here. I feel that Amsterdam would be the best place for constructing.

A Dutch merchantman unloads pepper and Chinese silks and tea.

A Portuguese merchantman unloads five puny, giddy but marriageable women – one standing a bit apart from the others, wide-eyed, apprehensive. They are all wearing gaudy silks and remind me of parakeets. She looks as if coming here was her most daring act or most desperate one. Now she stares at one of the wonders of the new world – a chain gang being led away from the slave unloading dock. Ankle and wrist chains and iron collars fasten the necks of the men, the women's hands tied with ropes and handkerchiefs. A man is flogged for some commotion. All of the Portuguese women are calmly watching now. Blood covers the man's arm and the side of his face, the skin raw and red and swollen around the chains. When they are past, the other women turn away and chatter. That one's eyes follow them up the hill away from the sea. A gentleman with a sword at his side and a glittering rosary around his neck descends from a carriage. He reads a paper and two of the women come forward. They all enter the carriage and it drives away. A man on horseback, wearing high jack boots, and a broad-brimmed straw hat, bends down and converses with the woman who stands apart. She shakes her head. He says something else to her. She shakes her head again, and then allows him to help her up onto the back of the horse.

On deck now the captain converses with a soldier and a planter. 'Brazil doesn't exist for itself, but for Portugal,' says the soldier. 'Everything's in Portugal's interest. If it didn't exist for Portugal it wouldn't exist.'

'If it didn't exist for Portugal it would exist for some other nation,' said the captain. 'The French or the Dutch or the English. Your only military objective is to keep the colony for the Portuguese.'

The soldier says nothing. I wonder if he was one of those who had fought against Palmares.

'Me? I have no intention of being humble in the face of the Portuguese or anyone else,' says the planter. 'I have a very large estate, no small holding, a large estate and many Negroes, large productions, a large stake in this country. I'm a Brazilian. I have no intention of being humble to anyone. That's what it means to be a Brazilian – not to be satisfied with a peasant's life.'

'They'd humble you soon enough if you weren't in the country's interest. Most of your cattle are shipped to the Portuguese market.'

The planter doesn't reply. He smokes a cigar and stares at the two remaining Portuguese women.

'One of them for you, Macao?' asks the captain with a laugh.

'They don't last long,' says the planter, and he spits.

I watch the slave unloading dock, the edge of the dock being converted into the porch of a thatch-roofed clearing house. On the dock-porch sit two white men at a table. Now a small rowboat from one of the ships comes up carrying about five Africans, some wearing short white trousers, others loin cloths, all with no shirts. A white sailor sits in the boat, holding a musket and a long sheet of paper. The Africans, who are not chained, one by one grab hold to the post and climb up onto the dock. The sailor finally climbs up carrying the paper which he hands to one of the men.

I go one level below the deck where the sailors' hammocks are hanging like cocoons from the ceiling. I pass sailors, sitting on trunks and boxes, conversing with women who are allowed on board while the ships dock, drinking rum and gorging themselves on fresh meat, fresh fruits, and vegetables, having spent so long eating salt meat and biscuits.

One of the sailors wraps a costly Chinese silk about the shoulders of one of the dock women. Another sailor takes a swig of rum and spits out, 'Them that don't lead a seaman's life, don't know what hardships is!'

As I go to the next level, the Bantu with the sullen, intelligent eyes is ascending – a slave of one of the Bahian merchants. I wonder if he or any of the new arrivals I had seen on the unloading dock will find their way to the New Palmares.

Also included in the manuscripts that Barcala Aprigio had sent to me, some of which seemed to be based on African Brazilian tales or reminded me of the tales the old Africans used to tell, was an experimental tale called 'Lice Scratching.' I laughed at the title and went on to read the following:

LICE SCRATCHING

There is no one else here. No company. I lie in my hammock on my stomach. No view of the garden. He has some Russian nobleman as a guest and other distinguished visitors. Beefsteaks and tea. Should I call the woman to search for lice and pomade my hair? Portuguese pomade. That English woman goes in and out as if it were all decency, and back and forth to him. Or pork they are having and wine. That time I was in the wine cellar. I got my answer. No invisible girl. I said nothing. Bananas, bananas, bananas. If he'd caught some Negro disease. When he came to me I said, Go to the devil. I could have knocked the woman, that other woman I heard how she murdered the mulatto girl and what did that do?

But me? I still have her come and scratch the lice from my hair.

Touching my hair. But to him I said, Go to the devil. I thought of that way I'd reward him. She goes in the streets. I'd reward him that way.

Hand me some grapes, and take her hand. You're my woman too. Should I call her? Bring me chocolate and sweetmeats. What kind of conversations do they have? Go to the devil, I told him.

I heard that story about the man who murdered his wife so he could devote all his time to his mistress. Such things happen. Now he's silent with me. Anyway, he was then too. What are they talking about? Some investment. Afterwards, he brought me a peacock, a fine male one. But I said, 'Don't you know that peacocks and pigeons bring bad luck on a house?' But such a pretty bird and he spread his wings for me. Wings.

Feathers. He flew up into one of the trees and one of the servants had to get him to take him away. I could see his eyes too, looking at the bird.

How then can something blessed with such beauty bring that on a house?

My silent husband. I've heard where they've loved the son and the father. Loved? Maybe it's because it's the first hand they see. They say it's a black hand we all see on this continent. The first hand we see is a black one. To be born an enchantress. The tales they would tell of enchanted Moorish women over and over. Then see them as better than we are. All the danger of this country. I wonder if there are any astrologers in there. That time I went to that astrologer with my cousin Olinda. He didn't know it. A scientific and realistic man he said he was that time. He couldn't talk the kind of talk the other men did; he said he wasn't a romantic and a sentimentalist.

Before we got married, he said he wasn't good with courtship talk; a rationalist he said he was. But that astrologer, he would have called that a woman's silliness. Still he predicted *that* man, didn't he? His dark hands. A Greek he was, or an Egyptian, Olinda said he was, one of those. Why are they always the ones to know such mysteries? If he hadn't predicted that man I ... Still all the same he reminded me of the priest. There wasn't any difference except I didn't have to tell him the bad things I had done.

You stay silent and they tell.

If the walls weren't so thick. Conversations he has with them. What does a Russian say? I wonder how one sounds in Portuguese.

Conversations. Then a woman goes and talks to a priest. That's most of my visits and socializing. No, Sir, it isn't that because it hasn't been that for a number of years. *She* hears. That one knows everything they're saying. Well, hears it anyway. You never know how much they under-stand, or when they're pretending they do or don't understand. Look at their eyes and it doesn't tell. Mine tell everything, he said.

He said my eyes told everything. The astrologer predicted him; I know it. Some stranger, some mysterious man. Olinda said she found all men mysterious. *She* found *them*? Ha. But then it's the country that makes for that. You're never allowed to see them. They're all strangers he's got, all mysteries, because they want them that way for a woman.

What is she serving them now? She acts like she's the great mystery. Still it's the black hand that comes up first. The black hand and the black nipple. Chocolates and sweetmeats. When she finishes her work I'll call her in too. This new pomade from Portugal, I want you to put it on my hair, and bring me some of the wine they were having.

I didn't say anything in the cellar. I just stood there. Maybe she saw me, but his back was turned. I just stood there silent, and walked back up the stairs. Go to the devil I said then.

Who's playing the piano? I wanted to know why he brought that peacock. All of those customs are confused. What should a woman think or feel?

Those women they say they don't have souls, or maybe they have half souls. Then I own half of that half soul. I'll make her kneel, strike her hands together, and then come forward. The ideal woman, they say, thin waist and the rest like a cow. But a real woman's not to exhibit herself in public like a slave.

First he gave me two sons and then a girl. The sons are whiskered now, like their father. I wonder when the war will start. And my own great revolt? He brings a peacock to a respectable woman. I say I didn't want such ... He looked funny standing there though, holding the bird. He set it down and it spread its feathers. What's that? A peacock. I know what it is, but what's it for? For you. No, I told him to take it back where he got it, I wouldn't allow a peacock in or around my house. No, I said. He just thought it was a silly myth. I should have let him keep it and show him what would happen.

Not mine, it wasn't. Not for me. Such a beautiful bird, though. It spread its wings like that. At first it wouldn't turn around, and kept its back to me. They aren't so pretty that way. Then he turned around and showed me such beautiful feathers. So beautiful they are. I wonder why they say those things about them. Because they're so beautiful.

Some men don't trust a beautiful woman. But they hide them all; it doesn't matter. Except for *them*. They parade anywhere. And him, he brings a peacock to a respectable woman. Give it to that one. But still if it hadn't been for that I'd ... If I didn't like a green one he said he'd bring me a blue one. No, I said, and then it flew up in the tree. I saw it eating leaves. Eyes they have. What if all of them could see one at the same time? If there were such creatures. But no one knows what's in the world. It stood there like it knew how it looked, and then it flew up in the tree. I wonder what makes them show their feathers at certain times and not others. It's like a blessing though. An ornamental bird he called it. Why shouldn't it be for a respectable woman? But everyone's afraid of them. They say they ruin a house. All those peacocks the Puerreydons had parading about.

The smell of cinnamon from the reception hall. The Russian. I caught a glimpse of him. Black eyes. But ducked down. I heard a man killed his own daughter for letting herself be seen by foreigners. Not foreigners. Ordinary men. Any men that were not part of the family. I wonder how they treat their women. Those Cossacks. Is he a Cossack? What's a Cossack? But some kind of absolute obedience. Do they address their husbands on bended knees? Adultery punished by death. We'd be in the wine cellar, the corner where I saw them. But no, if my husband saw it, he'd come down the stairs, not go back up them. No invisible man and woman, when it's the woman. No. His sword and his rage a mile long.

And if that one caught his woman in such a circumstance. Those black eyes. I wonder what it would be like to stare into them long.

He gave her a leather bracelet. I'll bet he did. Only because they can't wear gold. Well, it goes with her position. He got the bird to spread its feathers for me and show me how beautiful it was. Was it him that got it, or do they have their own free will? What makes them do it? What makes a woman when ... Well, they spread it too. I wonder if he tells her she's beautiful there. Now I see feathers up and down her legs. Ha. An eye there. Ha. Is it green or blue? Ha. No, dark-eyed they always are. But I said no. He claims he's not superstitious, but me I am.

Always some guest. Where does he meet all those people? Some he doesn't know. They just come, and it's the custom of the country, and when that man murdered his wife he did the reckoning. I wonder if he was thinking of himself then, his own situation with that woman. Because he didn't have to tell me that story. Other things that happen in the world he doesn't tell me. But that one guest who came here, he looked like a drunken backwoodsman, but he's from a respectable family in Recife. You never can tell. I didn't let him know I saw the man. But he was standing right there. I told him he was in the wrong part of the house. The women's rooms were here.

Something made with cinnamon she's serving them now. I'll take a bit of that too. That mulatto woman that that traveling minister had. They say it happens all over the country. Always from one place to the next, though, these men are. I bet *she's* seen more of my own country than I have. The moral degradation of the country, that's what they are. What did he call them? The warts on the country, the landscape. Well, I'll call her that too. I wonder if he meant to include her with it. Well. I'll call her in here myself, and see what he sees. Do you scratch a wart? What do they say is done? She would know. Yes. What do you do with a wart?

Says she speaks French from the last people that had her. You think you are so clever, but you cannot escape. Neither can I escape. That music makes me feel as if ... I should have made myself known. Know what? What was I thinking about then? I should have made myself known. What? I should have made them know that I was standing there, that's what it was. I was looking for you, I should have told him instead of just standing there in silence.

I wonder what his expression would have been. I put them out of my mind. They were invisible. They were invisible there. Together they're invisible. When he's alone, he's visible again. I'm invisible then. They're all handsome women. I never saw one that wasn't. When they come together, something happens. They all say they're the best on the continent. I wonder how that Russian treats his woman. A nobleman he said he was. A Cossack nobleman? Do the women walk openly and alone?

What kind of fruit is she serving? And one of them has written a long, important book. About what? The dreariness of the New World? A virtuous woman remains in the house and does not speak. I wonder if he lives in a castle. Do they live in castles? What room does he put her in? Does it make echoes?

Now the music's faster. I can see myself dancing with him. How straight he stands, my hand in his. How straight. We'd talk about my dreary country and I'd ask about his. They say they're a passionate people. A people of intense passions. I suppose every country has its passions. I suppose every country does. Are there intellectual, religious passions? What other kind? But that's what they say of them, intensity and passion and one can see it in the eyes. What word would they use for this country?

I suppose a man and woman would use a different word for the same place, depending on what the customs are, the circumstances for each.

And *her*? I wonder how she sees him differently. Now he's my silent husband, irritable, cold. And to *her*? *Then* he was so many interesting people. A dangerous man, a good storyteller. I bet they're telling tiresome stories, except *him*. That vast, wild country. All but him. I wonder what stories men tell each other.

Maybe my husband is telling them that story about when he was in that battle against those Negroes. That Palmares. And this is the woman I captured. Would he speak so openly about her to those men? And even they, those Negroes, they said would capture women when they needed them, mostly Negroes and Indians but some said they saw white women there. But one never knows what one has in this country. That woman that discredited that whole family not telling them about that Negro woman in her blood. Their son wanted to marry her and she was silent about it. In time they found out and annulled it, but still the harm was done. Nobody knows who they're getting until everyone will have to have some kind of blood papers.

He doesn't know, he never will know what's in my imagination. But him, he can live in his dreams, his fantasies, his imagination, maybe even beyond them. Can a man live beyond his imagination? And then, if not, make it broader.

But then they scattered and he took the woman. I said he could have gotten better slaves than that. But he gave up some others for that one, and brought her into the house. Then I heard her singing in here. I made her stop that. Anyway, you don't know what kinds of words are in those songs. She said it was a French song. Did I tell her I thought it was some magic? She said it was French, that she was some French people's slave before she was in that place with the rebels. She called them rebels too.

But to her, it meant something different, one could see it in her eyes. I wonder if she had a man there. Someone. They said they had their own town there, their own settlement, and governed it, and had a king.

Long deep trenches. I wonder if. But there was a white woman there too. He said he saw her. Why didn't you rescue her? He didn't know what happened to her, but this one. He always saw her, though he didn't say it, I knew he always did. The whole time. But then they got them on that expedition. He said they destroyed the place that time and there wouldn't be any other problems with the renegades. Did he say renegades or fugitives? Those that weren't killed were captured, and the few that scattered it would be impossible for them to form again. He said I could go see his *head* if I stayed in the covered hammock. So I did. They said they displayed his head so those fugitives wouldn't believe he was immortal.

All those people standing out there, and some women out in the street. I asked him if he did it with his own hands. No, he said, there was another man and another who held him by the hair. So I suppose for a man such moments of excitement happen and not cruel dreariness. A woman contents herself with looking when looking's possible. So I stayed in the covered hammock and got my fill of looking.

But women are the only reasons they build houses. But for protection too. Now he is out of the military and I'm glad. His architectural studies again and all those famous men he knows. But that one, he brought that one back when he could have had a bigger share of it and some land too.

I'll call her in when they're finished. You're my slave too. I own half of the half-soul. I wonder what kind of personality he had. I watched from behind the hammock cover and it was like his eyes were looking right in mine. His jet black too. Did he see me? Looking as if he could see. And maybe he was really immortal and they were wrong, because he was staring at me out of those eyes, or I was just in the path of them. He was on that expedition for fifteen months, my husband, and when he came back he was with that girl. I said, Get the hell out. And he brought me a male peacock. Who did he think I was?

I'll call her in. I'll ring the bell for her services too. What is it, madam? she'll ask.

Bring me every bit of everything the gentlemen have had. Suppose they've all had a bit of ... Ha.

She'll go and come back.

I own half of the half-soul.

Now rub my head for lice, and here's some pomade newly arrived from Portugal.

I'll keep her the whole evening doing that, scratching lice from my head. And putting on that sweet-smelling pomade. Yes, I know how to keep your woman. Then he'll come for her and silently stare at me. Stand in the doorway. But I'll keep her. *I own half of the half-soul.* I'll keep the woman and he'll go. Do I interest you? I wonder what that Russian does with his ... women? Yes, he has them too. But a white peasant woman somewhere. In his own house, and maybe another white noblewoman or his mistress. Do they reside in the same house? Could I bear that better? Still something about the same nationality and qualities of a woman. If one that looked like me was walking about here, what would I do?

I'll call her in, yes. Does he make her smile? Make her happy? Was she smiling then? I can't remember how they were looking. I should have said, I didn't mean to disturb you. Something to make them notice. Made myself known and seen. Does that Russian make her happy and she him? Why didn't he bring her? Why didn't he bring his noblewoman or even the peasant? But they don't take their women on travels. Or has he been introduced to the wenches here?

You're such a strange man, I'll tell him, and he'd touch me carefully. But that one? Do you think he'd give her to the Russian for the night? I've never seen such a one like you before, he'd tell her. But they have black Russians, don't they? Didn't he say that? Black Russians I've heard they call them. And those Russians that look like they come from the East. But not like here. Are they just like other men? Me, he'd say he'd seen me over and over again in every country. But no, I'll say I'm as strange to you as that one. An exotic creature, here in my own country and there in yours too.

Take me there and I'll prove you've never seen one like this one. I'll prove it. Looking at his eyes that way. I'll look at him till he knows something about my strangeness. And my strange soul too, I'll say. Anybody born here has a strange soul. But I'm a whole-soul I'll tell him.

What will he be like? Some man beyond my imagination? But they all think they are. All men think they are beyond a woman's imagination, and any woman contained within theirs, always. Don't they write and paint about us? Aren't we their muses?

He goes to her. And in what small corner of his imagination is that one? Before I would have vied for a larger corner, claimed my larger corner. See how a woman lives in a man's imagination. I wonder how I would live in *his* imagination. What kinds of things would I do there? What should I ask him if we're alone? I wonder what the Cossack woman is like. Why do I keep saying Cossack? A high forehead he had. I wonder if they give different promises, men from different countries, if they have a different set of promises they give a woman, the same promises, or none at all. Those satin shoes from France he brought and that promise he gave.

But how do I know, perhaps he got them from one of those French window girls. What they most dislike, a respectable woman.

I wonder what they're talking about. Maritime trade, he said once.

And what trade? Peacocks, yes. Those men discussing maritime trade in peacocks. From Ceylon, or some place, they'll bring them. He said at first they weren't Brazilian birds. You can tell they're not. From some exotic country, those. And what is it in the air that makes them?

And how many peacocks from Java? Ha.

What was that question he asked me, that strange one, about putting ... first about what a man needs for his spirit ... then about putting a man at his spiritual ease. The difference between what a man needs for his body and what a man needs for his spirit. And what about a woman and putting her at her spiritual ease? But then that promise. Something about a man's being spiritually faithful to a certain woman. Ha. And what woman he didn't say. Ha. Fifteen months on that expedition, or was it longer? All those dreams I had about his coming back. She walked behind him. At first he put her with the other women, slave women, *half-souls*, then brought her into the house.

Cassava and rice I'll ask for and some of that wine they're having, and then lean back while she puts her hands in my hair. Searching for lice.

But still it's a good feeling. What about when it's a man? Where does she put her hands then? Always when the strangers come, the women disappear. They must believe there aren't any women here. No white women. I'll have her take my hair down, everything. It must be a different feeling for a man. Then he'll think she's an enchanted Mooress.

I wonder if foreigners know that story. Maybe it's only the Portuguese that tell it, and maybe the Spaniards. But still the Moors that were all over the country aren't the same as the Ethiopians. When strangers come, they must believe that all the women there are Negro women and mulatto girls. All the women they see. A country of Negro women and mulatto girls they'll think, and invisible women in the inner rooms behind thick walls and in covered hammocks.

Those conversations they must be having.

That time he let me watch the procession of St Sebastian. Still I can't see how they can slash themselves with broken glass. I was thinking of her then, of slashing her there with broken glass, and then when he ... What would a man do when you take away that pleasure? I told him to go to the devil and he went to her. A half-soul if any. How they did it I don't know, but all I could think of was her and what I'd do. Holy thoughts they must have to get through with it, and see their blood as His.

How large and soft he said my breasts were then. But it's all the same story. The same thing he tells her, or maybe he tells her nothing because it's not expected in the same way then. And that other man who had his wife shut up in a convent so that he could live with his black mistress. In freedom. With freedom. And how she felt locked in those small rooms. Still the same, except for no man coming. I told him to go to the devil and he brought me that peacock. The female ones don't have such feathers, it's only the male peacocks that have all that beauty.

After that first campaign he came back telling me all those stories. But it was only that last time that he brought the woman. I knew what it would be then. What was that Russian's name? Pavel? His first one. His last name I'd never get. I wonder what his woman's name is. What's a good Russian name for a woman? Some lovely long one. And he calls her by it then, or some shorter version. Or maybe it's their custom not to say anything at all to the woman. Not to call her by any name. No, everyone does, everywhere. But still maybe it's better a silent husband than some of the things he could say to a woman.

Her hands in his hair scratching the lice in both places. He said something about natural impulses of a man. What about a woman? What they were talking about this other time I overheard. He let me come in when his brother was there but that's family and not a stranger. His brother was talking about social and moral relations because he's against slavery. But it's all on account of that Indian woman he's got, living in the mountains with her the way he does. How could the Lord make two brothers so different? He started talking about how we would be seen in the future.

Looking just like a backwoodsman. If it wasn't his brother ... He was talking about people being spiritually very much alike. What does he know? I didn't want to listen any longer. If it wasn't his brother I wouldn't have stayed. He said social positions had nothing to do with the spirit of a man. Did he add, 'Or woman?' When they gave them Holy Communion did that make them have a soul?

My husband said they hadn't earned their humanity yet, because when they did the Lord would make changes. He's a good Catholic. But his brother, how did he get such ideas and talking about what we could learn from their knowledge and experience, ideas, and that they too had a moral and religious nature, but different from ours. Did he say humanity was something you had to earn?

But those dark women they'll open it for anyone. And when they first came over here all those Indian women going around naked they would open it for anyone with a bead or a piece of cloth. That's the story anyway. The tales they used to tell. Even when they'd tell Europeans about the New World. I wouldn't want to learn from those experiences. So he defends them, the half-souls, while his brother goes on expeditions to hunt them. A threat to the whole country and to civilization he says they were and still he thinks they're ... still he brought her back with him.

His brother said it was the white men that destroyed the spiritual wholeness of those other people. But no I didn't believe him, but my husband listened with good nature, though I know he didn't believe it either. He says we can't know what the truths are. That music someone's playing? Is that the truth then?

Anything without all those words to it, and memories in words. But then what about the different people with all the different kinds of music? I wonder if the Russian women have to be pulled apart. That first time with me he had to, that's why they like those others. But still the same color doesn't have the same spirit either and different nationalities. That book he's got on medical history I looked at it and it had pictures about different races and shows where Negroes and Indians are different and those yellow people, those people from the East, and their blood is different too, but still an Indian's blood isn't as bad as a Negro's, and more noble.

He looked so mysterious. If I were an English woman I could go and see him closer. That English woman. Everyone said she acted like a whore, except in her country they behave differently. She's a wellborn woman and from a respectable family. Still she wouldn't have done that with anyone, and white women are the same there, in that regard, no matter what country it is.

His brother said we had a whole sphere of things to learn from them on religion and medicine and knowledge of water and plants and the stars and other things that we call science and maybe had already learned from them but didn't know what and gave the knowledge by a different name.

He has all those crazy ideas. I think he'd journeyed even to the East and knew people from the Oriental world. Or met them here. But even if that happened a long time ago they're pagans now, and what difference does it make, because that's all that matters now. Pavel Epiphani. Why do I want to call his name that? Solovetsky, something like that. The 'sky' on the end of the name I'm sure about. Why do they call them such names? The English names are short and hard though.

It brings disorder on a country and disrespect. That's why they look at us the way they do, the Europeans . . .

They're all simplehearted people he says, but what about those rebels? All those attacks on pack trains and sugar mills . . . If that expedition hadn't destroyed them, we'd see their simple hearts. If his brother had a big house and lands and so many souls to look after and wasn't isolated with that Indian woman, he wouldn't have such ideas. If he were bound by all the obligations that his brother has . . . A moralist that's what he says he is. But wait till one of the pagans does him harm, he'll change his tune.

My husband said he's seen it happen how people can change their political feelings overnight. And we must think of the country as a whole.

He said, 'If I can't bring the Indian woman in, then I won't come in,' so he brought her into one of the interior rooms, but not with me, no thank you. Another half-soul . . .

The Russian's a nobleman and a member of some council, and the others are some important businessmen, and one's a maritime trader of some kind. Men get bored with doing nothing. They'd get bored with this.

I wonder what she's thinking now. When he was away those fifteen months. But I told him to go to the devil when he returned with that one.

I wonder if he's a cruel man, but still he's a true aristocrat. A big step from those others ...

That time he told me of how his friend, on that first expedition, collected the ears of the ones he'd killed, dried them, and carried them in a bag. But they do that to enemies in war and not just in this country.

There will always be a master class, that's what the Bible says ... All those arguments and all that talk ...

Bananas and okra I'd like. That's what I wanted that last time I was pregnant. I wonder if it's trade in sugar or something else ...

I wonder how many months on a ship he spent coming here ...

His brother said he wasn't still Catholic, but he praised the Jesuits except where the Indians were concerned. But they were better than the Franciscans, he said. My husband praised the Jesuits too, and said their plan made greater men from lesser men. Still I like all those Catholic holidays – concerts, festivals, games, processions. That's where I met him. I told him my husband was away on that expedition. What expedition? He hadn't heard of Palmares, but then he hadn't been in the country a long time. If it wasn't for that festival I wouldn't have met him.

Then I went to that one. I was mad at Olinda for not telling me she was a black woman. He'd been away for those fifteen months and he would have known it was not his ... When it's some holy day, it's not the same for a woman. I waited that other time, but on a holy day it's different ...

I like those Catholic ceremonies. They keep dreariness away from a woman. Moraze, looking at me as if she were the queen of Brazil. Olinda should have told me it was a black woman ... A maker of angels they call them ...

He gave me that strange look. I wouldn't have done it if it wasn't for that festival and the feelings I was having then. I couldn't take my eyes off him, but I'll tell anyone I was surprised to find myself in his arms.

That queen of Brazil. Some magic potion for that. She disappeared into some small dark room and then came out to me, then took me back there to make angels ...

Now she's probably pouring them all some wine to drink or strong beer ...

A silent husband and now his silent lover. He goes there fighting them all of these years and then he returns with *her*. But that's the way things are for a man, what they all do with the conquered women. That's the story of conquest. That story she told about the Moorish woman and the enemy having the right to see her. But then there's some way of communicating they have without conversation, because they don't speak in the way we do anyway. Well, I've never learned to communicate with those people anyway, and that one seldom smiles. But then I should have thought of a man's loneliness those fifteen months, the woods anyway full of Indian women – all those dark women they could want, and even if not, accept that as part of his profession.

I can't get out of my mind that woman slashing her mulatto slave girl with glass down there. Now that's some communication. More than I could say. Still I wouldn't want to see it afterwards. But they say she laughed after that, like she got a good feeling in that. But what made her crazy was the man stayed with the girl even after that, even after she was mutilated down there, as if he truly loved her, though he had others too. He kept that one and all that time she thought he would discard her, and that it was just for that ... And that priest who was trying to pretend that woman was his spiritual companion ... Still I think he kept her to prove something to *that* woman, and not because of her.

If he had been in one of the wars with the Dutch I wonder if he would have taken a Dutch woman and brought her home. They used to call them 'lead feet' – why I don't remember, but I heard my father call one of those Dutch 'lead feet,' or maybe it was the only Dutch men they called 'lead feet' and not also the women.

But still those friars no matter what they say have a weakness of the flesh the same as any other man. A weakness for the flesh. Because if she was, then we're all spiritual companions and not companions of the flesh.

The queen of Brazil. That remedy she gave me to take with me afterwards. I still remember how it tasted. I took some of it and threw the rest out, and took that doctor's medicine. I let her do what I could see with my eyes and feel, but that other, no telling what she might have put in it.

They'd all make themselves the queens of Brazil if they could. Like the leader of those renegades called himself a king. I still can't get those eyes out of my memory either. I like the ones that are trained not to look at you. This one, she doesn't look at you straight, always out of the corner of her eyes. I prefer the ones with short, matted hair. It's some magic potion she used and then had it straightened some way. I remember that old slave I had who let me touch her hair. It felt like a sponge. When I was a child it was – not now I wouldn't have asked to touch one of their heads. But then I did and hid my fingers in there. An old woman I thought she was then, but they had to send her away, they said, because of her dreams of revolution. I didn't know what they meant. I was a child. And if it was only dreams of revolution and she did nothing?

Some manioc cake and couscous I always see and remember that old slave. And that feeling I had then with my hand in her hair. Then she went on rubbing my hair and getting the lice out. I guess that's why I still like it now and always get one of those women to come and rub my head.

And I remember the first time he pushed my legs open . . .

That time those other women came and I called all my black slave women and each one had a girl and we all sat there getting our heads rubbed and talking.

But those men were in the next room talking about their adventures.

I'd like to have gone back on that ship with him and traveled through Europe and then come back here when he came on other business. And what if there had been women on *that* expedition?

Sometimes I'd like to travel through my own country. Those black women get to travel. No one minds them and they come and go anyway. If they aren't slaves . . . And some of them are free women . . . But a woman is nothing anywhere.

When I was in the confessional I was thinking if I confess it all to him, why shouldn't he confess to me too? His weakness for the flesh? Because everyone knows the story about that priest in Porto Calvo, who when those young penitent girls would come in, he'd seduce them right there, and that's the way he used his confessional. I was thinking of that and trying to see his eyes too. They still whisper about how he received that package of mercury, what they use to cleanse their blood.

Dried meat and salt cod and mercury they said he received from Portugal, and everyone knows what the mercury is for. I just told him part of it, how my imagination started to work. But Father I did nothing, I told him. Suppose I had told him all of it? Maybe he would have dropped his robe and . . . I tried to see his eyes, but I stared into my palms. It was only a sin of thought, I told him, and described to him how those festivals and ceremonies excite me. He said they're meant to excite the soul . . . Still I wanted him to know what it was like.

I wanted to see what his eyes were saying.

Alcantara. He said my name then. He must have known that it was a memory and accumulation of fantasies. But that's what memory is, an accumulation of fantasies, because you never know what reality really is.

And history too could be an accumulation of collective fantasies, our own and everyone's . . .

But he said if things kept up the way they were it would be better if the country did not have memories . . .

He said that one day they'd free all the slaves, that was his dream . . . How could a sane man dream that?

That look made me feel strange inside and I wonder what it would have been if I had told him about what had really happened with that man who kept changing, whose eyes looked like they kept changing from one moment to the next. It wasn't just my imagination, my fantasy . . .

I remember that bare room mostly. A stove, a low hammock, some mats. The stove for brewing potions. That plant she had growing, the way she went to it, touched it, and stood there as if she were communicating with it without any words. Yes, she was talking to it, silently some way, and then she looked at me again with those eyes like she thought she was the queen of the country, or what I thought that she was thinking.

Then she was talking out loud to it, saying its name. Ipecacuanha, she said. Softly she kept saying it, looking at the plant as if it had some soul, and not caring who would laugh at her. She would do it, even knowing someone might laugh. But I didn't. I kept looking at her and that strange plant she treated with such affection, as if there were some sort of bond between them. Some mystery and affection. Then she did tell me that it was a mystical plant and had much power. Then she started telling me about the power most plants have generally, a grander range of power than most people do or think, and about the power that God gave them, and what they can do for and to human beings. How they can heal or destroy, how they can get into the mind, how they can affect a man or woman's spirit. Over and over she talked about the power God gave them and how they can communicate in all those ways with a man's or woman's spirit.

Something she said about one's perceptions and possibilities. And this Ipecacuanha she said was her spiritual companion. I didn't laugh because I was in her hands then, but I'll laugh now at that silliness. And when she was done she gave me some magic plant, toasted it and crushed it and mixed it with something and put it in a bottle. I took a little of it but no telling what it could have done if I'd done what she said. Her spiritual companion. Ha!

Those young boys some of them have their first sex with a mandacaru.

Their spiritual companions? Ha! Like what that priest said about that woman. I wondered if it was a man or woman plant. Did she speak to it as if it were a man or a woman? Her hands caressing it.

Ipecacuanha.

She spoke like she could call it across time and space.

Ha! And she wore a leaf of it in her hair for a charm. I listened to that silliness then, because I was in her hands. She stood very straight, like her position was a dignified one, speaking with such seriousness, like she was a queen. Singing a praise song for that plant.

Ipecacuanha, she said, and maybe it was some Bantu language she was speaking then. Some Guinea language. Some pagan speech. If I'd been in the mood I'm in now, I might have asked her how many languages she knows and understands. Could she speak to it in any language, like it had its own voice and its own spirit? Perhaps women of all sorts and languages come to her to make angels ...

Still I wouldn't be thinking of those dark women all the time if he hadn't brought that one here. And someone taught her to avoid a white woman's eyes. I wonder if she looks at *him*.

I'd like to have some view of the sea. They always make the women sleep in rooms without windows. Ever since I was a girl. Always they put you in the inner rooms. I'd like a window by the sea and the smell of orange trees and lemons. A room without windows. That sounds like the title of a book.

That English woman was talking about having a home near the sea, a room full of windows, and walking about the seashore, gathering seashells, and how she liked the wide veranda. She laughed when I scattered the cinnamon leaves about, and when that girl began to rub my hair. She laughed until she'd been here long enough to get lice in her own hair. It wasn't funny then.

When we went out I rode in the covered hammock and she walked along beside me. She wanted to taste the guava and jackfruit. I remember her hard way of speaking Portuguese, the opposite way the Negroes speak it. I couldn't understand her half the time. She spoke like all the words were coming through her nose. She called herself an independent woman. But here that's just another name for a whore. Still she was more interesting than any I know. And in her own country she's considered respectable.

Except she said that the mulattoes have such magnificent eyes and how attractive they were. 'They have such an aesthetic sense,' she said. Or sensibility? Nonsense.

'It was performed by all mulatto actors,' she was telling Olinda about some play.

'All the mulattoes here are drawn to acting and literature and aesthetic things – the free ones,' Olinda proclaimed, showing off how well she knew them. Trying to impress that English woman.

I didn't join in the conversation.

That's when she noticed it, the English woman. 'This room doesn't have any windows,' she said.

And that's when I truly noticed it, and knew I'd always all my life been in rooms without windows, all the respectable girls had. That's when she started talking about all her windows and that precious view of the sea.

I don't trust a woman that talks like a man and talks to men so freely. Then I found out she was writing about us, writing about her views of all the countries she'd been in, even Africa she's traveled to. I didn't want to be in her tales of some wild and savage country, because that's the way she probably saw us. In this new world.

Once we were sitting in here and I wasn't saying one word to her. 'Brazilian women have an exaggerated desire for privacy, don't they?' she asked.

I didn't know what she meant by that and so I didn't say one thing to her, and she kept looking at me.

'I bet that's true, isn't it?' she asked.

And why is it true? I wanted to ask. Maybe I did know what she meant, but what did she know about it? What did she know about our new world? Those foreigners always have their eyes on someone, and then with one or two glances they think they know your whole story, your whole spirit, your whole world. And then they share the information with you. But I should have told her that she couldn't even see past my shadow, or even her own. A room without windows. That's what she could call her book about the ladies of Brazil.

All the ladies stayed away from her when they learned she was a writer, except for Olinda. She came like she came to show herself to her.

I've been in Olinda's house. They have that Negro slave who's a painter to paint pictures all over the walls of their drawing room and in the halls. And the paintings are mostly of Negroes. Probably all of them want to start some type of rebellion. They all have the potential for it. They all have the hearts of renegades.

When that English woman saw him she asked his name.

'Well, I don't know his name,' I said. 'It's enough for me to keep up with the name of my own Negroes.'

'She said he was a freedman. An artist and a doctor.'

'I don't know,' I told her.

But I didn't tell her that I thought there must have been something between Olinda and him. I'll think it even if she is my cousin, because she's the one who called him a Wonder Worker and a great artist. And then there's that gypsy horse trader, Burlamaqui. That might as well be a Negro. Those gypsies might as well be Negroes. She has all these foolish ideas.

Olinda took me to that black woman. And I think it was intentional that she didn't tell me. How did she know her? She probably went to her for some problem she had. She gave me some salve and something with cinnamon leaves.

I can't get that festival out of my mind. More the festival than the man. First I caught a glimpse of the beard and mustache and then that stylish long coat and his eyes looked at me so. He spoke Portuguese like he'd learned it from a book. But still he knew the names of all those plants and flowers, more than I knew. Some he said grew only in Brazil. He talked of all the trees we had – orange, lemon, guava, mango, peach, coconut. He said he liked to eat some fruit every day, that it helped a man to keep his spirits up. Did he mean spirits? I sent one of the girls to bring him some fruit.

I like a man who has stories to tell. I must have seen some tales of adventures in his eyes.

That woman also had tales of adventures. She said something then when she was talking about her view of the sea. She kept talking about her new sense of freedom. I wanted her to talk more about that man she had mentioned. Had he left her or she left him? Why was she traveling alone here? But she wouldn't tell me about the man, just about how the sea changed. Was she married when she met him or had she ever been? No, she wouldn't tell me anything about her personal life except that one vision. Or maybe he was no real man and she might have gone on and told me how he himself came out of the sea. Ha. Ha. Like those legends about men rising up from the sea, and sometimes women. And those tales the slaves tell each other. But she herself comes out of the sea, in a way, to all the places she's been.

I'd like to be that kind of woman myself, always rising out of the sea to some new place. Back to Russia with that bearded man I'd go. She said after that. After what? I was only half listening. But she said after that, it was more than the sea that changed. At first she thought it was only the sea, and then discovered that it was her own soul that had changed too. But I don't like that kind of talk anyway, and wonder if she writes like that. All that talk of souls in her voyages and all those shadows of people she sees. Because no, I don't have any special desire for privacy. Is that the answer to her question? It's the custom here.

But still a woman like that could go in front of any strange man she wanted to. Yet she's from a respected family, my husband said. But they must be glad she's on the other side of the world and not an embarrassment to them in England.

She wanted to go to the Street of the Gypsies because she said there was something she wanted to find out there and wanted me to go along.

Needless to say I didn't and I jokingly asked her why didn't she take one of the Negro women with her and she did. I wondered what she wanted there. Maybe some Gypsy to tell her fortune. They're just like the Negroes, their bright colors and strong perfumes. And the Gypsies have stories too. Have I ever heard a Gypsy's tale? They're lovers of bright colors ... I'll wear my bright shawl at festivals because everyone does ... 'Why do they have a special street?' she asked.

'Because that's their custom,' I said, 'living apart like that. And there's a street of the Jews, and one of the fishmongers.'

'Fishmongers?'

'Yes, the fishmongers have their own street,' I said, but she didn't get my humor and just frowned.

When I found out what she did, though, I stopped talking. All the women stopped coming except Olinda, but she's like a stranger in her own country.

'What is malungo?' she asked.

'What?'

'I heard a Negro call another one malungo.'

I told her I didn't know, but that's some word they use to show respect to each other. Is it that? I don't know what it really means. Something to do with their being in the same situation.

'What does malungo mean?' she insisted.

'Comrade,' I said.

And then she wrote it down in her little book. She'd have to get its true meaning from the Negroes, because I wasn't saying anything else.

'From what I've seen of your doctors in this country, I'd put more trust in the medicines of the Indians and the Negroes.'

She kept talking that nonsense. Something about their herbs and plants. I started to tell her about that woman talking to her plants. But I didn't dare.

'There must be a lot of Orientals here,' she mused. 'Do they have their own street?'

'What?'

'There must be a lot of Orientals here. There are a lot of things Oriental. The silks and tapestries.'

Then she started listing all the things here that reminded her of the Orient and even a certain shawl I had and wore to Mass all the time.

Then she started talking about a mulatto actor she knew.

'He's very intelligent,' she said. 'He takes his acting very seriously, but he's so obsessed by his complexion. He's the son of a Portuguese father and a Negro-Indian mother, and he feels doomed because he's not the right complexion. Such a brilliant man, and so handsome. When he's on stage, he creates his own private world. Even for me, when I watch him on stage, everything seems forgotten except the world he creates there. He thinks he merely amuses others and wonders why I should want to come and talk to him.'

'Yes, why should you,' I said.

She ignored me and went on talking.

'He calls himself a mere clown and acrobat, even though it was a very serious play he was doing. He thought the people watching thought it was the antics of a clown. It must be awful to carry such anxiety. An interesting man, though.'

I said nothing. I thought of that peacock he brought me. Still it was a beauty. But all those tales I heard.

'He thinks he's a failure as an actor, but I think he's brilliant.' If he hadn't brought the woman, I was thinking.

'They played everything in blackface except the ghost was painted white and looked deformed among the others.'

Go to the devil, I said. I could see him kissing her feet, her fingers, her eyes. Her eyes especially. Because they think mulatto women have such beautiful eyes. But that one's not a true mulatto, darker, it's only her hair that makes her ...

That first time I asked her to do the head rubbing and get the lice out I was surprised at myself, but still it was her I called.

Madriaga.

But I couldn't take the name back and call one of the others. I handed her that pomade from Portugal to rub in afterwards.

Black beans and pineapples she brought me that first time. The way she withdrew then, her shy little way. I almost liked her, but I think she does that trying to please him.

When I was a girl, though, I used to like coal-black St Benedicto. But that was when I didn't know. I thought that he was special then with his curly hair and beard, before I knew what he was. Still he's there with all the other saints, and those dark-skinned Madonnas you sometimes see, because the priests want everyone to love Christ, and sometimes he's dark skinned too. But if St Benedicto is their color, it's not the same spirit. It's who he is in the eyes of God.

I liked him too because he seemed so isolated in his color, so alone there, as though I felt some kinship with that one and not the others. When I was sleeping in my room without windows I'd think of him too. That was before I knew anything.

Then I asked her why she spoke to him. A whore and a public woman I was thinking.

'I write travel books and articles for the English newspapers,' she said. 'Of course on a lot of them I don't say it's a woman who wrote them, because they might not publish them then.'

I said nothing. I maintained my silence. She was wearing a hat that looked as if it had been made of peacock feathers.

When I was talking to that woman Olinda introduced me to, I felt as if new energy were flowing throughout my whole body. Moraze? Is that what she called her? Then I just wanted to get out. Have it done and be out of there. Makers of angels they call them.

'But one feels it more in the tropics, don't you think?' I hadn't been listening to her again, so I said nothing.

'Why are you so taciturn and morose?' she asked. 'I wish you'd wear that red dress you were wearing when I first saw you. So Brazilian, I was thinking. You seemed the essence of Brazil. You looked just like a Brazilian bird.'

The feathers on her hat flopping down. Go talk to Olinda, I was thinking. She could tell you the whole history of the country. Some tale of love and desire.

'Why aren't you talking? Never mind, I'm off to have my fortune told ...'

A trumpet shell necklace and gold earrings she was wearing, like she didn't know a Negro woman wasn't supposed to wear gold.

Olinda told me what I could do to get him to come to my bed again.

Something she probably learned from that woman He knows where I sleep, I said. But still she told me what she learned, probably from that woman. She told me anyway as if I wanted to hear it. Very strong coffee and much sugar and a clot of menstrual blood I was to give him. He wouldn't taste the menstrual blood, because the coffee would be so strong. I told her again I didn't want to hear it. And what kind of strange man would that make him? Some sexual magic she learned from that woman.

Something to enchant him.

That time she cooked fish in coconut milk, that was my best dish.

And that English woman looking around at the walls like she saw windows that I didn't see.

'Was it the Dutch who built those wide streets?' she asked. 'I mean, before the Portuguese came?'

How was I supposed to know that history? My father fought the Dutch and my grandfather the French, but how was I supposed to know that history?

My grandfather, they said, had a passion for horses and Negro women. I didn't know what it was then, but on St John's Eve when they had those dances ... Silver and glass I remember them polishing the whole day. The white people dancing inside and the blacks outside, their wild dances and my grandfather asked me which ones I wanted to watch, and I said the Negroes for whatever reason it was I liked St Benedicto then. So we stood out on the veranda; he was holding my hand.

'See Old Luiza,' he kept saying over and over again. An old woman out there with the others, who kept turning and showing her broad back like all she wanted to be seen was her broad back. And he kept saying her name over and over again. 'See Old Luiza,' he kept saying and squeezing my hand tighter. Then saying something about wishing he could still ride as well as she could still dance, for her old age, and something else about horses and women that I didn't understand. And she kept turning so that we could only see her broad back. And dancing like she wasn't an old woman at all.

'Why do they have all the fires?' I asked him.

'To chase the devil away,' he answered.

Then my father came outside and said something about knowing that my grandfather loved horses and Negroes, but he should bring me back inside. Then I dreamed about Negroes building a bonfire to chase the devil away. And then when I saw the devil it was my own grandfather, dancing naked and holding a basket of fruit. When the Negroes saw him, he kept saying, 'I'm St John.'

'No, you're the devil,' they said.

'I'm St John and it's my eve,' he insisted.

'No, you're the devil,' they kept saying, and building the fire higher so they could chase him away.

When I built a fire to chase the devil away they found it in time. 'What do you think you're doing? You could have burned the whole mansion down.'

'To chase the devil away,' I said.

Someone said they believe, the Indians or the Negroes I can't remember, it's white men who have webbed feet like devils. When I was older I had that dream again and he had dropped the basket of fruit. An Indian woman and a Negro woman were standing on each side of him with flowers in their hair, then they began to light the fire to chase him away.

They truly looked like the birds of Brazil.

'You can't beg it, you'll have to produce it,' I heard him say. Why he said that and what he meant I don't know.

'You can't beg it, you'll have to produce it,' he repeated, the basket on the ground.

I kept looking, trying to see his webbed feet, but somehow couldn't.

The other part of him was quivering.

One of the women, the Indian or the Negro, was holding an iron harpoon.

I remember hearing some woman say she saw one of her slaves toss something in her bath. She got out of it quickly because she didn't want to take some kind of strange wicked bath. She said you have to watch them all the time. She wasn't superstitious about things like that she said, but when the priests sprinkle you, that's a special bath, a holy bath.

Anyway, I'd like to read what that English woman would say about our country. If I'd known she was a writer, I wouldn't have talked to her at all from the beginning.

I'll have her bring me some heavenly bacon. Why do they call it that?

It's easily made. I watched her. Almond paste and eggs and butter and sugar. A spoonful or two of flour. I tried to make some, but it didn't come out right. The children refused to eat it. They said they wanted Madriaga to make it. Well, let Madriaga make it then, I said. That's what's wrong with this country. A black hand is the first hand they see. I should never have had those black wet nurses, or I should have gotten white ones. It's a black tit they all want. And their father too. But he made sure that the wet nurse was a clean woman, and she had papers saying she was clean. But. What was I thinking then?

Heavenly bacon. The nuns make it too. Maybe that's how it got its name. I told him to buy some heavenly bacon and nun's bellies. Divine pastries. Anyone can make heavenly bacon. At the nunnery they sell heavenly bacon and nun's bellies and little wooden images of the saints, even St Benedicto. But I remember that time they took those jewels off of him because they said that even a black who was a saint shouldn't wear expensive jewels.

They sell little wooden saints, Our Lady of Solitude, Our Lady of the Roses ... But when I was a little girl I'd ask for St Benedicto right out, and kept him on my pillow and slept with him at night but I can't remember what became of him. Now I don't dare ask for St Benedicto.

That first hammock we lay in had bird's feathers and tassels and palm and cinnamon leaves, and that's what we were eating then, heavenly bacon and nun's bellies, the sweetest pastries. It was like there wasn't any time, but when he was on those expeditions against the fugitives it was like time came back again and time's back now. It wasn't an easy journey to Palmares, he said, because they weren't used to the forests. They had the Indians with them though, he said, some tribes they recruited. And some Negroes. I wonder what's in their minds when they're going after their own kind. Well, maybe it's like when the Dutch are fighting the French or the French fighting the Portuguese. Because they're different tribes? No different than fighting each other in Africa where they have tribal wars and sell each other into slavery. But over here aren't they all the same? They're all thrown together, so they're the same. Except the Mohammedans – they don't like to be called that; they say it's offensive to them – but the Mohammedan Negroes seem to carry themselves with more dignity. I said I didn't want him to buy any Mohammedan Negroes because they're too prideful and they think they're superior even to Europeans.

They act as if they have freedom when they don't.

Still a dark woman has more freedom to walk about the streets than I do, because it doesn't matter to them about respectability. They don't dishonor their family. They don't scandalize everyone. The only white woman I know to do that is Aranha Gracas. On Fishmongers Street buying salt fish. 'There's that devil. There's that Aranha Gracas,' someone said of her.

'Yes,' the women riding in their carriages said of her. 'But she's a scandal. She's not a respectable woman.'

She's a beauty, but no respectable man would have her. But maybe she doesn't care. Still, a woman's respectability is the most important thing, I feel. But it was the festival putting those other feelings in me. I told him my name was Lauradia. I didn't tell him my true name. We ate coconut candy and drank beer.

If it were not for the festival and that he was a stranger and a foreigner then I would never ...

But why did I take the name of that slave woman? Her name's Lauradia.

'Lauradia.'

'Yes, master.'

He wanted her to light the whale oil lamp. He forgot her name as soon as he said it.

'Who are you?'

'I'm Lauradia, master.'

She'd fix him onions and black beans or okra and fish stew. 'Who are you?'

'Lauradia, master.'

He forgot her name as soon as he said it. That was my grandfather as an old man.

When they're done, I'll send for her to rub my head and get the lice out. What I can't stand about this climate.

Why am I always thinking about those dark women? They shouldn't occupy my thoughts. That Negro woman carrying that parasol and wearing her nails long. That Portuguese merchant who married her and dressed her up that way. They always dress them up so fancy. Like peacocks. But I laugh whenever I see them dressed like that. Still there are Indians in the interior who wear no clothes at all, and when they put them on can't endure them. A special kind of blood they have. And when we penetrate the interior of this continent no telling what we'll find and what degrees of humanity. When I was a girl, an Indian woman

313

told me about that white man, Zume, some myths they have about a white man that came to found their religion, so that it was not a surprise to them when the white man came again, because he was expected. Some secret herb she had that kept her from getting hungry and thirsty for a long time. I told my father what she said about the secret herb, and he kept trying to get the secret from her, but she wouldn't tell him. He tried to coax her, but she wouldn't tell him. 'It cleanses the spirit, and it keeps one from becoming hungry and thirsty for a long time.' He became obsessed. He wanted to make it into a drug and sell it everywhere, but she wouldn't divulge the secret. Her name was Zuma. Why was it so similar to Zume, the myth she had told me?

She would not divulge the name of the secret herb, but she became sullen. She'd go about her household duties, but became sullen and sullen with me for telling my father. I was even afraid for her to wash my hair, because I feared that she'd plunge my whole head in the basin. But she would wash it as always, first rubbing my head and scratching for lice then lowering my head into the basin, soaping the hairline and the rest of my scalp. I would squeeze my eyes tightly waiting for the plunge and feeling I deserved it for telling her secret, but ready to scream. But always she'd pull my head up, dry it in sullen silence. When it dried, she'd pomade my hair and put it up. I would avoid her eyes.

Then she disappeared and I did not see her anymore. She was replaced by a tall, slender Negro woman.

At first I did not want the Negro and I kept asking where Zuma was, and I treated the black woman as Zuma had been treating me, in sullen silence.

'Where's Zuma?' I asked her finally, when no one else would tell me.

'Zuma?' she asked and seemed surprised at me speaking.

'My Indian,' I said.

'Ah, that little girl, that poor little girl,' she said.

It seemed strange to hear someone calling her a little girl, when I always thought of her as a woman.

'That poor little girl,' she repeated. 'I guess she couldn't bear it anymore, this slavery, it was too much for her spirit.'

'She had a secret herb for her spirit, and her hunger and thirst too,' I said, and then I put my hand to my mouth. Then I stood straight like I'd seen my mother do when talking to slaves and demanded that she tell me what had happened to Zuma.

'It was too much for her spirit,' she said, looking at me with curiosity and what seemed like a sneer. 'She started eating earth, the poor little girl, and it killed her.'

After that I stopped seeing Indians and they were gradually replaced by Negroes. I thought my father had forgotten about the secret herb, but every time he saw an Indian he'd badger them about the secret plant. But they all met his questions with sullenness and silence.

'Ah, the poor little girl,' mumbled the Negro woman. 'Ah, the poor little Zuma.'

'Why are you alone here?'

'Because my husband is on an expedition going after Negroes, some fugitive Negroes.'

'A punitive expedition?'

'Yes.'

Coconut tapioca I'd like spread on a banana leaf and sprinkled with cinnamon.

Those penitents cutting themselves with glass. I dreamed of them all in a parade, one of the saint's days. They were all in a line, cutting themselves with pieces of glass. In reality, I only watched them, but in the dream I asked them what their sins were.

'A spiritual transgression,' one of them replied. 'The flesh was willing but the spirit wasn't.'

They told me all kinds of offenses and then one of them said, 'Join us.'

In the dream, I joined the procession. In the hand of God? I used to hear them say that. So-and-so was in the hand of God. Means they're crazy. A cousin or an aunt they'd say that of. I used to think they meant some fine position, until they explained what it really meant.

'I'm in the hand of God,' one of them said.

After they cut themselves with glass, they sprinkle salt on themselves afterwards.

What is my ancestry, they all want to know. Portuguese mostly, and some Spanish and Dutch. 'I wish someone would rub my head. There's lice.'

That English woman couldn't believe that respectable people could have lice in their hair. But it's the country I told her. The tropics. Then she stayed here long enough and got lice in her own aristocratic hair. I laughed at that.

'Well, it's almost worth it, to get such a good head rubbing.' That hat she brought. It would make it worse, I said.

'In this country only prostitutes wear hats.'

'In my country it's prostitutes that don't.'

When my husband talked to her, though, she put on a mantilla like the rest of us, for the Mass anyway.

Wine and cashew nuts we sat around with. Olinda wanted to hear all about Africa. The Sudan where she said she was from. Olinda's eyes wide with every tale, and who's to know what's true and what's not. These travelers who send back stories about magical serpents and wonder drugs, and sea monsters and rivers of gold. I could tell such tales myself, and create foreign princes for women to dream about in a room without windows, and maps pointing to places where they make their fantastic discoveries.

'Escape with me to the backlands.'

'No,' I told him in the dream.

'Why won't you go to the interior with me?'

He kept asking that. Then in the dream I found myself going with him into the backlands. The dark, unexplored, mysterious interior. Those priests, they'll go. The Jesuits probably braver than the rest. Whatever strange places they go, they send the Jesuits.

He kept the back of his head to me, but his feet were turned backwards, and there was only the shadow to be seen.

'Are you afraid of the interior?'

I walked on, in the dream cutting myself with pieces of glass, as the others were doing. I only saw the streams of red, but felt nothing.

'We could leave the others and head for the interior now.'

'No,' I said.

And she was talking about the savages again. 'And their language has only the numbers from one to four. They have no other numbers.

'They don't know that the world has other numbers. Anything beyond four is "many." They have no need for anything beyond the number four.'

The English woman told us about some place in Africa she had traveled to, some village, where she said she was tortured by the women of a certain African tribe. She didn't describe what kind of torture but she said she kept telling them, 'I'm not your enemy, I'm your friend.' For some unexplained reason they stopped torturing her. Or rather, she couldn't explain it until she found out they had discovered some things

316

she had written, and though they could not read it and themselves had no written language, they felt that this proved her to be a magician. However, they burned the papers and sent her on her way. 'To prevent,' said one of the tribesmen who spoke a pidgin English, 'to prevent the things she put down on it from come.' So they felt she had the power not simply to predict, but to create events. But if it had not been for the papers she said, the women would have continued to torture.

'You have such hard and dangerous work,' Olinda said after she heard the story.

'Yes,' the English woman replied.

'What were you writing about that they thought were charms?'

'Just a short history and description of the country and its people, and some notes on my impressions and feelings.'

'Oh, you're so brave,' said Olinda. 'There've been things like that to happen with the wild Indians. People who return from the interior tell such stories. But I stick to civilized countries. Isn't she brave, Alcantara?'

I nodded but said nothing.

'You're so brave,' Olinda repeated. 'You must have true faith. Do they wear clothes?'

'No, they're entirely naked. They don't do anything at all to cover themselves.'

'Just like the Indians,' Olinda said. 'Or rather, like they say they used to be before the Jesuits came and tamed them. But there are still naked Indians in the interior, they say. The men and women alike.'

'I'd like to travel into the interior of your country, but I'm not as brave as you make me out to be.'

Sometimes when I dream, I dream about that plant and its power.

'What's its name? Do you have a name for it?'

'I have no name for it. It has its own name.'

Or maybe she told me a strange name I can't remember.

'But one has to have the knowledge of how to use it,' she said. 'It is not of the same use for everyone. The same plant that creates, might also destroy. But this one, this dear one I have the deepest love for, as it is this one that helped me to reclaim my spiritual powers.'

'Does it talk to you?'

'No, it doesn't talk, not with words. But it understands my language and I understand its language.' She laughed suddenly. 'Do you think it's my master? Do you think it could be? Do you think this little plant could have power over the body and over the soul too?'

And she gave me something to rub my stomach with and something to make a strong tea with and drink.

'She is very discreet,' said Olinda of her. 'She is the most discreet.'

I'm silent, but I throw away that herb and the other remedies. No telling what she had given me. Something to make me keep going again and again to her like Olinda does. Such savage potions.

'The most discreet,' Olinda kept repeating.

A red blouse and black earring she was wearing, or were they gold? Who could tell in that shadow?

'How was it?' Olinda asked when I came out and we rode back.

'There wasn't any pain,' I said.

'What did I tell you?'

'Should I tell you my dreams too, Father?' I asked.

'Your dreams?'

'Should we confess our dreams?'

'I want to protect your spiritual welfare, sweet angel, and our dreams are part of your experiences in the world. My first duty is to protect spiritual welfare.'

'But you, Father, have also been in my dreams.'

Then I dreamed I was living in a dream. A dream inside a dream.

Some secret revolt it was, but after the dream I couldn't remember it. Perhaps I had overheard the Negroes talking in my sleep. A dream of revolts. But I couldn't remember anything. Then a woman was talking. I remember that. 'Do you want me to show you how to rise out of your body?' Was it her? That one?

The thoughts, the dreams, the feelings, the imaginings. How much of those does one take to confession. But only the dreams I asked about. If it was all of those, a priest could spend his whole time with just one person.

Or each one has his own priest. 'Is that all of it?'

'Yes, Father Tovor.'

'You're a little angel.'

Still if it hadn't been for the religious holiday and that man who

passed by with St Anthony's fire. Why they call it that I don't know.
Yes, she said she treated all kinds of things. St Anthony's fire too, I'll
bet. I wonder if they have diseases named after other saints. St Vitus'
dance I've heard that. I wonder what would be named after St Bene-
dicto. The black saint. St Benedicto's what?

Discreet, she called her.

A peacock he brought after I told him to go to the devil. Bringing it to me because of all the pretty colors. I gave it to her to take care of.

'My husband said he captured you after the Palmares expedition,' I said.

'Yes.'

'How did you get there?'

I felt silly but I wanted to ask her something about it. I didn't want to ask *him*.

'I was captured and taken there.'

'Captured? Didn't you want to go?'

'Yes. I was rescued it would be better to say.'

Then she said something about her liberators, but using the French word for it, because she had been a slave for a French family and would often use the French word for things. Liberateur? I wanted her to tell me as much as I could get from her so that I could see what he saw, but after that she was silent.

And I remember that time I went in there and found her sitting on the floor making rosaries from palm nuts. That's what she was doing, and all the children would gather palm nuts for her and she would string them to make rosaries.

I asked him, 'Do you know what your black girl is doing?'

'What?'

'Making rosaries out of palm nuts.'

He looked at me like he thought I was the strange one, not her. 'She'll sell them and buy her freedom,' I said.

Why I said that I don't know. Because he made her stop it.

But she was sitting there stringing palm nuts. She looked like a cat then the way her eyes went up, and the way she had her legs, her knees pointed up. I couldn't sit that way. I tried to do it. I bet he asks her to sit that way for him. What power do you have, Madriaga?

''A woman is nothing without passion,'' she said.

'Who said that?'

'St Benedicto,' she replied, inside the dream.

'Do you mean a woman's own passion or the passion a man has for her?'

I close my eyes and see the same dream woman, but she won't answer. She is stringing rosaries from palm nuts.

'I swallowed a bit from the bottle, but threw the rest away,' I told her.

'Who is that woman?' someone asked.

'She's a Negress slave, my husband brought her back from an expedition against some fugitive Negroes hiding in the forests. A place called Palmares. She's not real. She's an object some curandeira put in my head.'

'What is she doing now?'

'Searching for lice.'

Now I dream I'm riding on a crocodile's back, not straddling him, like when you ride a horse, but lying on my back on his back and looking up at the sky.

'Tell me more about the Palmares, tell me more about the Palmaristas,' I ask her.

But she doesn't answer. She goes on stringing palm nuts for rosaries.

THE BOOK
OF JAGUARA AND
THE APPRENTICE

Martina Puerreydon
and the Journey

MARTINA PUERREYDON was a very tall woman who came in the nighttime with four young children. A hammock was strung for her, and we all, but Old Vera, shared a hammock with one of the small children. The girl who shared the hammock with me was a pretty one with almond-shaped eyes and pretty brown curls. There were two girls and two boys. They were all different colors, ranging from chocolate to golden brown and yellow, to almost white. The youngest was four, the oldest looked eight or nine.

Martina and the children had been tired, so no one had spoken until the morning, which was when she hugged and greeted everyone and said hello to them with grace and some formality and said, on seeing me, 'I do not know that woman.' Barcala said I was 'the madwoman' but Old Vera told her my name, Almeyda, but explained that I had grown silent and wary in these months and that she had not heard two words from me. She called me a complicated soul, but Barcala, who stood before me as if in judgment called it 'cunning.' The woman looked at me with curiosity and a smile. She was dressed in white, loose-fitting trousers and a shirt and sandals, and her children who seemed to always be crowding near her, were similarly dressed.

'Do you believe in reincarnation?' she asked me suddenly. I looked at her, but said nothing.

All the children watched me with wide eyes and then when their mother turned away, they did too.

'Old Vera feels she has mystical connections,' Barcala said. He laughed.

'Tell Barcala anything and watch him laugh,' Old Vera said. Barcala looked at her but said nothing.

'Let's be peaceable,' Martina Puerreydon said. 'Today begins the new journey.'

'Or the old one repeated,' Old Vera said.

'Yes,' said Martina.

Martina was standing with her children gathered around her. Barcala was standing looking at me fiercely. The others were settled around the table. Joanna still watched me with a sad and kind expression. Old Vera sat on her mat with her legs in front of her. I sat in my chair in the corner.

'This one stays here with her spirits,' Barcala said. 'With her invisible objects and events. But how does she know they're not devils?'

'And what do you do, Barcala?' Martina asked. 'They say you are not going with us.'

'No,' he said.

Everyone waited for him to say more, but he did not.

'See, I have learned,' he said, looking at me. 'Everything is possible.

'Look how she's become a laughing head. I'll bet you're still a little imp yourself, aren't you? I'll bet it's all play and mischief, behind the silence. You're not really a morbid woman.'

He came and touched my jaw and kissed me. 'Goodbye,' he said.

The others said goodbye. Joanna hugged me. Old Vera touched my head and shoulders, and kissed my forehead.

I went to the door with them and stood watching the column of people winding down the side of the mountain. When I could no longer see them, I came back inside and sat in my chair.

1697

Jaguaribe, His Family, the Beginning of a Journey

AFTER THE OTHERS HAD GONE DOWN the side of the mountain in search of the New Palmares, I sat in the chair with a shawl wrapped about my shoulders. What had become of Anninho? I went from the chair to my hammock and lay down. I felt feverish. A recurrence of malarial fever again? Did I call it upon myself at such moments? Out of fear, desperation, loneliness? I thought of the conversation with Mexia and the phrase she had used when she told me about the uncle of Father Tollinare who had been hanged for witchcraft because he had written about it as 'the hallucinations of a melancholy woman'? They'd called him a witch and a defender of witches. I lay the back of my hand across my forehead.

When I opened my eyes I was not alone, but a tall brown man was standing above me. He raised the back of my head and gave me a thick soup which I drank with much difficulty. He lay my head back on the pillow, touching my forehead and jaw. Even though he was near me, I felt as if he was touching me from a great distance.

'How are you?' he asked. I was silent.

'My name is Jaguaribe,' he said.

He spoke with a strange accent, not like a Tupi-Guarani speaking Portuguese; he spoke a bit like Father Tollinare had spoken it and a bit like an Englishman who had come to one of the plantations I had lived on. He stood gazing at me with wide brown eyes. His face was very smooth and firm, his chin slightly protruding. Did I not know him? Was he not the young man I had seen some years ago, the Indian who had returned from European studies? He was not dressed in a black suit now, but in white trousers, a string tying the waist, and a loose short-sleeved white shirt, with turquoise designs on it, reminding me of the designs 'the hidden woman' had painted on the masks and headdresses she had made for the festival in which the townspeople had celebrated their Indian ancestry, renaming themselves for trees and rivers, which were the only Indian words they knew.

'You were with Father Tollinare,' I said. He looked at me carefully.

'Who are you?' he asked.

'My name is Almeyda. I was one of the children in his reading class. I was there that day when you came.'

I remembered eavesdropping on Father Tollinare's conversation with him, but said nothing concerning that.

'Ah, yes,' he said. There were furrows in his forehead as he continued to look at me.

He turned around, setting down the bowl he had had me to drink from.

'Is Mexia with you?' I asked.

He turned quickly and looked at me. 'Yes,' he said. Then, 'Yes, you'd know her.'

He brought something else from a bowl that he rubbed on my forehead and neck.

'How did you find me?' I asked.

'My family used to live here until the men from the quilombo, the Palmarista men came and used this for a hiding place. I took my family away then, but when I returned the Portuguese soldiers were here. When I returned again, there were others living here, having found the place abandoned. I returned now thinking that there would be no one and found you here with malaria.'

'Where have you and your family been living?' I asked.

'In a cave nearby.'

I nodded. I got tired again and drifted off to sleep.

'They turn into wolves a night, but Jaboti tricked them,' I thought I heard. 'That's the difference between craft and force.'

I turned. Mexia was sitting in a hammock, holding a child of two or three in her lap. Jaguaribe was sitting beside her touching the child's head. The child was looking up at him laughing.

I was sitting in the dark room, my shoulders covered by a shawl.

Then the little turtle Jaboti came inside. He was looking at me with suspicion.

'Are you Almeyda?' he asked.

'Yes,' I said.

'They sent me to be your companion and protector on the journey.'

'What journey?'

He was silent, then he said, 'Well, you certainly fit the description I was given. They said that you were a solitary and morbid woman, and very timid. They said that you were like the Mimosa Pudica.'

'What's that?'

'It's a very sensitive plant. Her leaves close whenever you touch them, but she's a special friend of mine. She only seems morbid and sensitive; underneath she's as playful and mischievous as I am. On the surface I'm quiet and shy too. They said that I'd find you alone, and that you'd behave coldly but that I shouldn't mind that ... They also said that if you weren't ready, I should wait. They said that you weren't very spiritually adventuresome and might have to be coaxed,

but if anyone should be able to do it, it's me. They think I'm a "smart
fellow,"' he said with a laugh. 'That's because I'm not an ordinary war-
rior, I'm an explorer of the soul.'

I watched them for a long time before Mexia saw me and handing the
child to his father, she got up and came over to my hammock.

'How are you, Almeyda?' she asked.

'All right,' I said.

She was wearing a dress made of bark cloth and a shawl of anteater's
hair draped about her shoulders.

She looked at me pensively for a long time, but did not speak. After a moment, she touched my forehead, then the side of my neck.
She lay her hand on my shoulder, and then went to sit back beside her
husband.

'Was one called Anninho among them?' I asked.

'What?'

'Did a man called Anninho ever come here?'

'I did not know that one,' said Jaguaribe. 'I did not know their
names, only the name of their king, Zumbi. The others I did not know.
Only Zumbi and the one they call Garrostazu.'

'Was Garrostazu with the others?'

'No, he came apart from the others. He came before them.' I looked
at Mexia and then back at Jaguaribe.

'He told us that they would be coming,' he said. 'He told us about
King Zumbi and the place called Palmares and the forthcoming battle.
That was when I took my family away. He offered cures and protection
for them, the Palmaristas, while I protected my family.'

I felt stronger. I wondered what medicine he had given me. There
was the smell of ginger.

'Who is Anninho?' Mexia asked.

'My husband,' I said, looking at her.

'You believe he was with the quilombo men the Portuguese captured?'

'No. I thought perhaps he came afterwards. I don't know. He didn't
escape with King Zumbi. We were together. In the forest. A riverbank.

'There were Portuguese soldiers. I don't remember. They . . .'

'Yes, I saw their cruelty,' said Jaguaribe.

He looked at me strangely. He had set the child in his wife's lap, and
stood up – a tall, well-built man with a narrow, handsome face and very

black eyes. He stood near the door. Mexia watched him. He looked at Mexia and then went out.

She was silent, holding the child, who kept twisting in her lap, looking at her and then at me.

'Were you one of those they captured and took to the quilombo?' she asked.

'Yes,' I said. 'That was where I met my husband.'

'We stayed in the forests near the plantation. We lived in the bushes like Aimores for a while. And then when Jaboti was expected, we came here and Jaguaribe built the cabin here.'

'Jaboti?'

'Yes, you know the Indian stories about the mystical Jaboti?' I nodded.

'This is Jaboti,' she said, touching the child's head.

The child kept rubbing his round face against the anteater's hair. He twisted suddenly and stared at me with huge, brown eyes.

'I didn't see any of the men from the quilombo,' she said. The child quieted down suddenly, and sat motionless, looking at me. 'Jaguaribe told me that there would be Africans coming here, and so he took us to one of the caves. He had already stored things there. I don't know how he knew when they would be coming. I didn't see any of them. The name of the man you spoke of – Anninho – sounds familiar to me, but I don't know where I've heard it. But we left before the Africans came, and then there were Portuguese soldiers all over the mountain.'

When Jaguaribe returned he had fish, pineapple, Brazil nuts, manioc flour, and sugar. Mexia lay the child in the hammock and she prepared a meal. Jaguaribe gave me more of the malarial medicine to drink, and as I felt stronger I sat up in the hammock. We sat on mats and ate dinner.

Everyone was silent, except the child who would occasionally say something to his father in Tupi-Guarani. His father would nod, say one or two words, and sometimes say his name, Jaboti. I did not know the language. For dessert we had sugarcakes. We drank juice from the sweet cassava.

'You're the one who got into Father Tollinare's bookroom? Isn't she the one?' Jaguaribe asked.

Mexia nodded. She had spoken to him of me? I felt very glad and pleased. She had impressed me during the years when she was the housekeeper – and dare I say slave? – of Father Tollinare, but I did not think that I had been remembered by her. I thought of the silent Mexia of those days, and wondered at how different she seemed now.

'I found my way there,' Jaguaribe said, touching his jaw. 'But he never discovered me. I would take a book and return it before he discovered it was missing. I suppose he is somewhere still experimenting with the "intelligence" of blacks and Indians.'

'He sent you to Europe to study,' I said.

'Yes,' he said. He frowned.

'You must have learned many things there,' I said.

'He's indifferent to it,' said Mexia. 'When we were living like the Aimores he would go to his grandfather and he took as seriously what he would learn from him – the preparation of herbs and medicines. All the time they would spend preparing herbs and medicines together. He took that as seriously as he did the teachings of Father Tollinare and then the European schooling.'

Jaguaribe said something in Tupi-Guarani and Mexia was silent. 'One learns from every place,' he said, looking at me. 'The exact truth is always unknown.'

I said, 'May I stay here tonight? I'll go on my way in the morning.'

'You're welcome to stay here,' said Mexia.

Jaguaribe was silent.

'Which way will you go?' asked Mexia. 'It is still dangerous here. There are bushwhacking captains everywhere.'

'I want to find a woman by the name of Luiza Cosme.'

Jaguaribe stood up and paced again. 'What do you want with her?' he asked.

'Perhaps she can help me to find Anninho.'

Jaguaribe went to the table, and picking up some of the paper that Barcala had left, began making broad and rapid strokes.

'You will need this,' he said, handing the paper to me. 'It will get you through the territory. Some of the bushwhacking captains can't even read, but even they recognize the words for freedom.'

I did not tell him that I could have forged my own free papers. I thanked him.

He looked at me kindly. He said something to his wife in Tupi-Guarani. She looked at me and nodded.

In the morning, Mexia prepared mungaza or munguza, a gruel made from corn and coconut milk and spices. I said goodbye to them and set out in search of Luiza Cosme, whom I felt might lead me to the man who had disappeared.

When I went to the door Mexia said she would walk with me a while. 'You seem different,' I said.

She was silent. She smiled a bit.

'I think he knows him,' she said after a moment.

'What?'

'I think Jaguaribe knows the Anninho you were talking about ... Once before the Palmaristas came, I saw him go outside to meet a man. It seemed as if he called that name. That's where I think I heard it. A handsome, dark-skinned, bearded man.'

'That could be anyone,' I said. 'Did you really hear him call his name?'

'I think so. They talked for a while, and then they clasped hands and the man left. Jaguaribe came in frowning. Then he said he had to go to Bahia. He hid us in a hollow tree for nine days.' She looked at me. 'He gave us something he learned from his grandfather that we ate each morning, and we didn't get hungry or thirsty or tired.'

I looked at her, incredulous. When we got to the place where the path went down the mountain, I embraced her. Then I followed the trail that the others had gone on their way to the New Palmares. But I would not go there. I would go first to find Luiza Cosme. If I could not find her, or if she claimed to know nothing then I would go to Bahia.

Why Don't They Go
to the Interior

I WAS HALFWAY DOWN THE SIDE of the mountain when there were hoofbeats behind me. I prepared to take out the free papers, thinking it was one of those bushwhacking captains searching for runaway slaves, when I turned and there was Jaguaribe on horseback – a black, sleek horse. Jaguaribe jumped down and held the reins.

'You will need this for your journey,' he said.

'Where did he come from?' I asked, looking up at the man, who seemed as tall and thin and young as when I'd first seen him at the mission school.

'You will need him,' he said, passing the reins to my hands.

'Thank you,' I said. I wanted to ask him about Anninho, but he had told me nothing before. If he had known Anninho, why did he not tell me before? Nor did I want to betray Mexia's confidence. I was grateful for the horse, who had moved to stand next to me as soon as I took the reins, but I looked at Jaguaribe with anger, for what he had not told me. He held my elbow and I got upon the horse.

'After you find Luiza, will you go to Bahia?' he asked.

I looked at him. He still seemed as intriguing as he had that first time I had seen him with Father Tollinare, sitting by his desk observing his new pupils. Was he telling me to go there, to Bahia, or asking if I would go?

Did he know that Mexia had spoken to me? Perhaps he knew. I patted the horse on the side of the neck, but said nothing.

'Until we meet again,' Jaguaribe said, lifting his hand.

I nodded to him and turning the horse, went down the narrow path.

I journeyed down the mountain and back through the forest of gameleira trees to the place where Anninho had hidden us. The mat of grass and leaves was still covering it. Could Anninho have made his way back here, could he have escaped and come back? Had he tried to find me, and not having found me, come back here to wait? I tied the horse to the gameleira tree and pushed the mat aside. The sunlight hit the face of a bearded white man lying in the hammock eating a mandacaru. He sat up with his eyes wide when he saw me. He was dressed in dirty white trousers and a ragged gray shirt. I was ready to pull out my free papers when he put his hand up. Three of his fingers were missing. He held the mandacaru in the other hand. Why had he showed me his mutilated hand?

'Is this your place?' he asked.

He was Portuguese. I nodded yes. I stood looking at him, but ready to climb on the horse again.

He threw down the mandacaru, licking the fingers of his left hand, which were intact. His eyes were blue and piercing. Suddenly I recognized him as the same one who had come to the Entralgo plantation to work with Father Tollinare on the Brazilian dictionary. There were lines all around his eyes but they were the same steel blue.

'You're the one.'

'What are you talking about?' he asked as he climbed out of the hole, with difficulty. He stood in front of me.

'The one who worked with Father Tollinare on the dictionary.'

'Who are you?' he asked.

I didn't answer, then I said simply that I had seen him there. I was still ready to take out my papers if there was any problem.

'What happened to your hand?' I asked. He was leaning against the gameleira tree.

'Some people call this the suicide tree,' he said. He looked at his hand with the missing fingers. 'What happened to my fingers?' he asked. 'I cut them off.' He looked at me to see how I would react. 'I have no attraction for Mars. I took our dictionary manuscript to Portugal to try to get it printed, and they tried to conscript me, for the military service to go and fight in Angola. I've seen others mutilate themselves worse than this to avoid military service. Some became priests so they wouldn't have to go, others pretended they were mad or had caught some contagious disease. The recruiting sergeants have gotten wise to the other ploys by now, so that the only thing that still works is mutilation. At least I thought it was the only thing. They're wise to all the lunatics. But there was one young man whom I met on the street afterwards, and I said, "You look like a whole man. What did you do to get out of it?" He was going into a tavern and I went along. "What did I do?" he said. "Have you ever known an instance where a Christian became a Jew?" Do you know what he did? He feigned Jewishness. He said that he was a pure Jew, on his mother's and his father's side, and they let him go! Ha ha. Now Jewishness is the new madness, the new contagious disease. Well, they'll get wise to that in another year, and take the New Jews along with the others. But he stayed a whole man on account of it, and he had to flee the country . . .'

He started laughing again and looking at his hand. 'Mutilation is the only sure thing, and they'll do anything to avoid the garrison. They're drafting convicts to serve there now, because there's hardly anyone else willing, except the real madmen. If they want to get rich they ought to send people into the interior of *this* country. That's what they ought to do. Instead of military service in Angola they ought to send them into the interior, instead of staying like crabs along the coast. That's what the English would do. They'd have the interior explored by now and foreignized, and they'd be wealthy men. But the Portuguese have no imagination. All they know is amours, church, and music ... Instead of filling the garrison at Angola and fighting the Palmaristas ...' He started laughing again, without finishing what he would say. 'Well, I'll let you have your hole back and go find my own ... Did you escape from Entralgo's?'

I explained that I had been sold to another master, but that now I had free papers.

He did not ask to see them.

'I'll bet you're an escaped Palmarista woman,' he said, looking at me.

I took out my papers.

'I don't want to see them,' he said. 'I don't believe in Mars or Venus. Goodbye.'

He started away.

'What happened to your foot?' I asked.

He turned. 'It's the Achilles tendon,' he said. 'I severed it.'

'I'm not coming back,' I said.

'What?'

'I was looking for someone. I'm not coming back, if you want to stay here,' I said, pointing to the underground hut.

He said nothing. I untied the reins of the horse and mounted. 'What would you have done to avoid conscription?' he asked.

I said I did not know about such matters. I heard him laugh as I rode off, turning the horse to the path we had taken to where the Tapuyan women had been.

A Handful of Maize

I STARTED TO RETURN TO THE OLD PALMARES, but I knew what I would find there – the fields burned, and the buildings and huts burned to the ground. Some things had been destroyed before the Portuguese had overridden us, the rest had been destroyed by them.

I turned in the direction that the Tapuyan woman had taken us.

When I came to the clearing, I dismounted, tied the horse to a tree, and going up to the long building, I called, 'Maite.' There was no answer.

333

I did not know the other woman's name. I entered and walked among the rows of hammocks. There was no one. Under two of the hammocks there was the scattered wood of a fire that must have been lit during the night. The Tupis who lived near Entralgo's plantation used to sleep that way. I used to wonder why they were not afraid to sleep with fires under them at night.

My grandmother suggested that they treated their hammocks with something to make them fire resistant. What it was she didn't know or didn't tell me. Entralgo used to tell stories to guests who came nearby from Portugal or other European countries or who lived in towns where there were no Amerindians that the Tupis would be lost without fire, because their ancestors used fire instead of clothes. And that once they had gone into a hut of one of the Tupis and had found some smoked meat – the leg of something. No one knew what it was. Entralgo had hinted that it was the leg of one of their enemies. Then he told them the story of how cannibalism had started in Brazil, that he had read about it in Magalhaes' history of the country. That one day the son of an old woman had been murdered, and when they captured the murderer and brought him to the old woman, in her anger and grief, she had snapped at the murderer and bit him. Somehow the murderer escaped and went back to his people claiming that the other tribe had tried to eat him alive, and showed them the old woman's tooth marks. It was then that the murderer's tribe began to eat their enemies, and the murdered man's tribe began to eat their enemies in earnest. It all started with an old woman's anger and a false story.

It was then that I saw the smoked leg of a tapir hanging against the wall. On the ground below it was a plate of cold manioc cakes. I left the long building, and untying the horse, rode in the direction of the river. I dismounted and tied the horse to a tree before I reached the clearing, and seeing the two women I hid behind a bush, watching them. The 'woman' stood on the bank with gold powder all over her face and body. It was some kind of ritual I had heard about where they made 'gilded' men and women (when I had first heard it I had thought my grandmother had said 'guilty' men and women), but I did not know its meaning nor had I seen the ritual before.

'Gold means nothing to them,' I remembered hearing. Was it Entralgo talking to the foreigners? The 'woman' stood on the edge until her whole body was powdered, and then she walked into the river, ducking her head down, until all of the gold was washed away, then she emerged. Maite stood beside her talking to her cruelly, saying things about her ancestors, as if the woman's ancestor were not her own.

' ... They would kill each other for a handful of maize,' she was saying.

Then she said, looking at the woman, 'You're very beautiful, but very primitive. You powder yourself with gold and dive into the water, and don't even know why you do it.'

The woman was looking at her, embarrassed and uneasy.

'You only care about what you can see and feel. You're very childish and foolish. Here, here are your clothes,' she said, picking up a white dress and handing it to the woman. 'See how you embarrass me,' she said, as the woman picked her garment up. 'In front of the Jesuit. Those people across the ocean, they study everything, they are knowledgeable of everything. They came here looking for the Christian King Prester John. A man of morality and purpose. Do you think a rebellion against them will ever be successful? And your ancestors, the whole world to them was nothing but fighting, ritual, and divination. Why did you embarrass me in front of the Jesuit?'

The 'woman' was silent.

'Those people across the ocean. Ideas are more important to them than gold,' said Maite.

'They came here for gold,' the 'woman' said meekly. She brushed her wet hair back.

'Because they knew what to do with it,' said Maite. 'I can always tell what you're going to say. Always. You're so predictable. You think you're a perplexing and mysterious woman but you're not. I can always tell. It's not the eternal truth you're after, but the eternal lie. They took the gold, but what would you have done with it but toss it into the lake. You're proud of your geometric designs, but you don't even know what they mean. You don't understand the age we're living in, or what is required of you. You don't understand the intellectual, moral, and spiritual demands of the age. Why did you shame me in front of the Jesuit? Place yourself against one of them any day, and see what happens! I have to explain everything to you.

'Ah, if only my ancestors! Why do you behave so? Sure, they made slaves out of the Caete, but didn't the Caete kill the bishop? But some of them sold themselves into slavery too. For what? For a handful of maize!'

The 'woman' picked up a machete and began to dance in a very aggressive and hostile manner around Maite. Then she stood very still as if she were in a trance, reminding me of some African ritual – as if she were being possessed by some god. I stood waiting, as it seemed Maite was waiting for some god to speak through the 'woman' but one never spoke. Then the 'woman' was kneeling making geometric designs on the ground.

'Look at you,' said Maite. 'I'll bet you don't even know what the symbols mean. Something one of the old ones taught you. What good is passing something down if you don't pass the meaning down with it? Look at how seriously and with what dignity you do that.'

'Perhaps I know the meaning and won't *say*,' said the 'woman.' 'You think *he's* a holy man.' She looked at Maite in a strange way. Was she speaking or was some god speaking through her? 'But he's a very immoral man. I've seen him, and after he has molested the women, people gather around her and think something holy has been done to her and that she is sacred. They have the people fooled.'

She continued making the geometric designs.

'Look at you,' scolded Maite. 'Those signs are meaningless to you, no matter what you say. You learn nothing from them. What good are they?'

The 'woman' stood up, looking very confused.

'What good is your mysticism if no knowledge comes from it?'

Then the 'woman' began running and rushing about, as if she were trying to escape from something.

'I'll bet you don't even know what you're trying to escape from,' said Maite.

The 'woman' dropped the machete but continued to move around in a circle trying to escape.

'You don't understand me,' said Maite. 'You don't know what I'm trying to say. It's some kind of little drama, but it's all meaningless, and what do you learn from it? Nothing. Nothing that is useful in the world today. Nothing that's any use in the modern world. And you will never handle their world.'

The 'woman' stood still and silent.

'And handful of maize, and they'd kill a man,' said Maite with disgust then she walked rapidly away.

I ducked down, but kept watching. The 'woman' stood very still and silent, and then she walked away, her long wet hair hanging, with flecks of gold.

A Sword and a Rosary
and a Warrior's Tale

AFTER VIEWING THE STRANGE CEREMONY, I started to go on my way, but perhaps the woman Maite had seen Anninho? Why had she spoken to her 'woman' so? I walked with the horse and tied him to a tree at the edge of the clearing. From where I stood I saw the 'woman' sitting out in front of the longhouse, combing her jet black wet hair and making two braids along the sides. I watched her until she finished, and simply sat there, staring about her. Had it been only a ritual scolding and not a real one?

I approached the woman. She looked surprised and frightened at first and then she rubbed her hands in her hair until it was disheveled and then she began making lamentations. Maite, hearing the lamentations, came out and stood watching me, while the 'woman' continued the lamentations. Then I began to realize that it was the same ritual I had seen when Anninho had been there, and then Maite began to ask me all the places I had been and what hardships had I traveled through since she last saw me?

Not knowing whether I was to answer in the same manner that Anninho had done, saying that I had been luckier than most I told her the truth – of how Portuguese (I did not add 'Tapuya' or the black one I had seen) soldiers had found us, and how one of them without motivation had amputated my breasts, and how I 'woke up' to discover Anninho gone, and myself being transported to a place in the mountains where friends had taken care of me and brought me back to health. I said I did not know what had happened to Anninho, whether they had captured him and taken him prisoner, made him a slave? Had he been killed in some act of defiance?

She looked at me for a long time. Had I been wrong to give her an account of what had happened since I last saw her? Should I have said simply as Anninho had done, that I had been luckier than most? She kept looking at me, while the 'woman' wrung her hands and lamented, her long hair falling about her face.

'Come in,' said Maite, finally. She was wearing a cloth about her loins and the bow strapped across her shoulders. She said something to the woman in Tapuyan, and the woman quickly stopped lamenting and brushed her hair back and went into the house. Then Maite and I entered and sat down on mats. The woman brought us something to drink, in the shells of some large nut, and then she returned to her corner, to prepare something else. I glanced back and saw her in the corner, slicing pieces of the tapir's leg. Thinking of what Entralgo had told the foreigners, I grimaced, and drank some of the manioc juice.

The woman served the slices of tapir, which was cooked very well and tasted like beef and she served manioc cakes and pineapple.

'I have not seen your husband, Anninho, since I last saw you,' Maite said, looking at me carefully. 'What will you do?'

'Continue my search for him,' I said.

I wanted to ask her where she had first met Anninho, and how they had come to know each other. Instead I asked her what Jesuit priest did she know. Instantly I realized that in order to know that, I would have had to have been eavesdropping on them at the river. And she would know it! I stared at my food.

'Ah, there was an old Jesuit traveling through the woods, trying to convert everything he saw,' she said with casualness. 'From a Jesuit college somewhere in Bahia. My wife does not know how to act around strangers. But me,' she said proudly, 'I have had a Jesuit education in a Jesuit mission village.'

Did she mean her 'wife' or did she not know the Portuguese word for her companion?

'Oh, you do not understand,' she said, catching my look. 'It is a custom among my people for certain women who have taken vows ...'

I told her that Anninho had explained to me that she had taken vows of chastity.

'Our "serving women,"' she explained, 'we call our "wives."'

'Oh,' I said.

She laughed. I wondered if she knew what I was thinking. I did not ask her the same question I had asked Anninho.

We sat in silence.

'I was one of their lookouts,' said Maite.

'What?' I asked, chewing a bit of tapir meat.

She was strapping her quiver of arrows across her shoulder.

'I was one of the spies for Palmares. That's how I came to know your husband.'

I nodded. She kept looking at me.

'Such women as myself vow to have nothing to do with a man. I used to see such women when I was a child, hunting and going to war along with the men. Being active in the way the women were not. That's the kind of life I wanted. Not to be a serving woman like that one. If it meant to take such a vow, I would take it. Except now, in this district, there are no more such wars, and the Portuguese recruit the young Tapuyas to fight on their behalf. But me, I hunt and fish for the woman and spy for the Palmaristas, when they were *there*.'

She motioned toward the forest in the direction of the Old Palmares.

'Do you have any idea where Anninho might have gone?' I asked.

'I don't know,' she said. 'I have heard that some have gone to a new place in Parahyba.'

On the ground she drew a map for me of how I could get there. But still I resolved to go there only after I had hunted for him in other places.

I studied the map and then she erased it.

'That's what I wanted,' she said. 'To be a warrior for the Palmaristas, but Anninho said that I would be more useful as a spy for them.'

Why did she keep looking at me so? I looked away from her and stared around the long hut. On one wall was a sword, on another a rosary. When I looked back at her, she was still staring at me, the same intense look. I chewed on a piece of tapir and bit the inside of my cheek.

'What is it?' she asked.

'Nothing,' I said, touching my jaw.

'You shouldn't wander about the country looking like that.'

'What do you mean?'

'I think you should travel as an old woman and not as a young one. It would be easier. To disguise as an old woman and travel as one of those itinerant Negro storytellers I've seen. Otherwise there are many cruelties and dangers and bushwhackers everywhere. Be a curious old woman.'

I remembered one such itinerant storyteller who had come to the Entralgo plantation when I was quite small. I also remembered something that my grandmother had said about an itinerant storyteller. Too naughty for a child to hear and for me to repeat.

'How can I make myself look like an old woman?' I asked.

'I'll fix you,' she said.

She went outside and came back with a handful of leaves that she burned in a basin. She made a paste out of the white ash which she rubbed into my hair. She rubbed charcoal into the corners of my eyes. I stared into a mirror at a woman who looked twenty years older. She explained to me the plants that could be used for dyes.

'That will be better,' she said, looking at me.

She touched the edges of my hair again. I wore my hair long and standing tall all about my head, as my mother wore hers.

'Now you can travel everywhere,' she said. 'Anywhere. I used to dream of it. Afterwards. I'd go about telling my warrior's tales, but there are no more wars, as I have said, in this district, and that one would be lost without me.'

She looked back at the woman, who was in the corner, brushing her clean hair, and who did not look up.

Sword and Sorcery and the Man Who Disappears and Is Thought Immortal

I BID MAITE GOODBYE, while the woman lamented and kissed my hands again.

'I have not seen Anninho but I have seen the Muslim,' said Maite. I did not know whom she meant.

'Anninho's father, the one they call the Mohammed of Bahia,' said the woman.

Why had she not told me this before? 'Where is he?' I asked.

'Perhaps in Bahia again. He is looking for his son as well. He's had no luck with his holy war.'

Yes, I would go to Bahia after I had seen Luiza. 'Good luck to you,' she said.

I said goodbye to her and thanked her for her kindness. I untied the horse and waving to them, rode in the direction of the river, and crossing a wide flat valley, I tried to find the place where the 'castle' had been and the strange man Anninho had met with and whom he called 'Mualim' or teacher. I rode all along the base of the low hills but could not locate it.

'Sword and sorcery,' I was thinking. Where had I heard that phrase?

She had claimed it was a dream, but I had seen her conversing with a man – a man who had scars on his forehead in a certain design that looked familiar, but that I don't remember seeing before.

'Sword and sorcery,' she had said.

She had been standing in the hut conversing with him, a tall, slender but broad-shouldered man with thick black hair.

'That was over forty years ago,' he had said.

She said something about knowing when they met again, there would be no power that could stop them.

He said something about her beauty and mystery being still the same as then.

'It's our last hope,' she said. Then she complained of his cynicism, why did he always ridicule their efforts.

'They still celebrate you,' she said. 'Some think you died and others that you simply disappeared, but they all think you are immortal.'

He said something about a place they could enter but not possess.

I remember it this way because I did not know what they were talking about.

'Then I was at the slave market on Madagascar Island,' my grandmother had said.

Sometimes they would touch each other's shoulders as they talked.

He had a look of piercing intelligence. Sometimes I felt he saw me standing there, hiding, observing them.

The man said that my grandmother did not know what was possible in the world.

'I know everything that was possible in that world,' she said. 'But it's the new one.'

He said something about 'force' and 'guile.'

She complained again of his cynicism. She said that something had possessed her and made her desire to fight with them, using every stratagem, sword, and sorcery.

'But what can I do alone?' she asked. 'Where will the strength come from? What is possible in this new world? I don't know when to intervene in such matters and when to stand back in silence.'

They were drinking rum and sugarcane brandy. When I asked her about the man she had denied him and said that I was a victim of my dreams again or of my own delusions. She was angry, but I had heard him say it, 'Well, your intervention will be as meaningless as your silence.'

She said it would be better to at least try to offer cures and protection than to simply grow old in the New World, to grow old and disappear.

'Grandmother, who was that man?'

'What man, child?'

'The man who disappeared and they thought he was immortal. I saw you talking to such a man.'

'You were dreaming. It was your dreams again. Your imaginings.'

'What shall we do?' I said aloud to the horse and almost as if he'd understood my question, he neighed and shook his mane fiercely. I rubbed his neck and we galloped through the valley and into a forest of cassia trees, and into the road that led to Porto Calvo and the store of Luiza Cosme.

I saw the two Franciscan monks on the road, walking ahead. I jumped down from the horse and moved into the forest. I tied the horse to a tree and walked along the edge of the road, hidden in the brush and the heavy smell of cinnamon from the cassia trees until I was close to where the monks were standing.

'I won't repeat the man's visions. The ignorant people think he's a saint. But they will attach themselves to anyone who they think will give them some power over their crude lives.'

'He's a heretic and a Muslim. They are calling him the Mohammed of Bahia,' said the other. 'He is prophesying to the slaves that the only successful uprising will be a Muslim uprising.'

'Well, when they capture him they'll imprison him or take him to the Negro asylum in Recife.'

'He should be burned, as they do in the old country.'

'He's harmless,' said the other.

'He was harmless while he was preaching a holy war, when he didn't care who the Christians were. But now that he *cares*!'

'They say it's his son who converted *him*.'

I wanted to step out and ask the holy men who they meant. Was it Anninho's father they were conversing about? Had Anninho escaped and joined his father in some plan? Had his father given up his dreams of a holy war and joined his son in his mysterious plans?

'At least we must protect the souls of the Indians from these devils.'

'It's our duty to undo what he's done.'

'They are interrogating the fortune-teller. She was the last to see him.'

'And *that one*. That sullen, unsociable woman who withdraws from everyone. Ah, if it was the old country. She should be in chains. She believes in reincarnation, you know. Though she professes to be a good Catholic. Some of the ignorant ones believe that she can make herself invisible, that she has powers of transformation, that she's enchanted. If I could trick her up. They think they will have their glory days again. But these are the signs of the times! You can't tell who the devils are. You can't tell the New Christians from the old ones. And all the criminals and perverse characters in Europe are directed here, criminals, vagrants, gypsies, all banished to Brazil. But I *know* that one. Did you see the way she looked at the rosary? And when I handed it to her, she wouldn't touch the cross or the body of the Savior, and placed it upside down. That was my spiritual interrogation. I wish it was the old country, or that there was some new bull issued to take care of this place. All the witches from Europe and Africa end up here!'

'That makes our task harder. That's why the Lord has placed us here. It's our test.'

'I'd rather work in a land of devils than a land of angels.'

'What do you mean?'

'Why in that way I know the Lord trusts me a hundred percent. To be sent among heathens and savages is the great gift.'

'Yes, to be sent into a land of heathens and heretics!'

'That's the true test of one's faith.'

'Have you heard the rumor about Sister Catarina?'

'Yes,' he said glumly. 'But she's so fat who can tell. She could have had a dozen of them and who would know.'

'Someone said they saw her speaking with that one!'

'Who knows? Who'd know unless you punched the nun's belly.'

'She makes them better than anyone.'

'B...?'

'No, no. Nun's bellies. Very tasty. The pastries, you know. They call them "nun's bellies." '

'Did you see her speaking with the devil?'

'No. Some confessor. Confessing everyone's sins but her own.'

'Only in the New World.'

'She swears Sister Catarina took a lover and had an angel made.'

'Swears! You let her swear!'

'Well, she said so.'

'You don't know where the devils are.'

'My ear itches every time one's around, that's how I recognize them.'

A minute later he scratched his ear, but did not seem to connect it with what he had just said. I wondered if the other Father noticed. If he did he did not mention it. They began walking slowly. I started to follow them, but one turned at the cracking of a twig. I ducked down. The other said, 'A possum or a rabbit.' I followed them with my eyes, until they disappeared around the bend in the road. I stood there thinking of what I had overheard. If Anninho's father was the man, who was the woman they had meant? If I could unravel that puzzle, would I be closer to *him*? I waited for some moments and then walked back to where the horse was. I untied him, and we entered the road again. I walked him, but did not ride as I did not wish to overtake the holy fathers and I did not want to be questioned or show my papers until it was absolutely necessary. An itinerant storyteller was what I would claim to be, and what if I were asked to tell some story?

Should I tell of a fat nun who was suspected of having numerous pregnancies, and making angels, or of a land full of devils? I walked slowly, pausing now and then, so I would not overtake them.

'Prester John? Who knows if it's myth or reality? A black Christian king, they say. When I was a young man I thought I would be the one to find him and his kingdom. I would travel the world in search of Prester John. There was no poverty, no crime, no strife. All nationalities lived in harmony...no, not an African...A converted Moor...I heard all kinds of stories about him. I don't think they tell Prester John stories anymore. The world is smaller than it was then and there are better communications...He was a priest-king, not simply a king, a spiritual leader, not simply a political one...He was a great book collector, all handwritten and in all the world's languages. A generous and gentle man ... Who are you? What are you doing here?'

I had advanced upon them before I realized it, when I heard them speaking about the legendary black Christian king – and now one of them was staring at me with angry curiosity. The other one was Father Tollinare.

Father Tollinare Does Not Recognize Her But Believes Her Story

FATHER TOLLINARE DID NOT RECOGNIZE ME, or if he did, he did not speak my name. But wasn't I as old as he was now?

'Who are you, old woman?' asked the other priest. Father Tollinare stood looking at me with indifference.

'These are my papers,' I said, taking them out and handing them to him.

He looked at them and handed them back to me. 'Where are you off to?'

'I'm just an old storyteller, taking my wares where they'll most please.'

'An old liar you mean. Well, be off with you.'

I glanced at Father Tollinare, but he was not looking at me. He was looking impatiently up the road.

'God be with you,' I said.

'The Lord in the mouth of devils,' I heard him say behind me as I galloped off.

I wondered if he scratched his ear again.

Gold Smuggling

I TRAVELED TO THE EDGE OF THE TOWN and meeting no one else on the road, went around to the back of the store and tied my horse to a post. I knocked at the back door where the X was carved in the wood. There was no answer. I knocked again. Just as I was turning to go the door opened slightly. The woman saw me but did not recognize me.

'Luiza Cosme?' I asked.

'Yes, what do you want?' Her voice was harsh.

'I'm Martim Anninho's wife.'

She laughed and said sharply, 'I know his wife. I know the young woman. Tell me who you are or go.'

I held my wrist in front of her, so that she could see the leather bracelet she had given me for luck.

She looked at it and then looked at me with penetrating eyes. She opened the door wider and rubbed her fingers in my hair.

'Come in, Almeyda,' she said.

I entered the small back room where the sacks of 'grain' were, and the whale oil lamp.

There was a man sitting on one of the sacks – a slender Sudanese with bushy hair, wearing white cotton trousers and a shirt, holding a wide-brimmed hat on his knee.

He said nothing to me, and so I did not speak. Luiza pointed to one of the sacks, which I sat down on.

Luiza went over to the man and began moving her fingers in his hair as if she were searching for lice. I watched them with curiosity. The man ignored me. Luiza had her side to me. But each time she would locate what she wanted she would put it in a string-tied sack – the long string hung diagonally across her back and chest and the pouch rested on her hip.

'There,' said Luiza, picking the last mysterious item from his hair. The man stood up and bowing slightly to Luiza, without even glancing at me, left.

'He can wash the rest out and spend that on food and a woman.'

'What are you talking about, Luiza?' I asked.

She explained to me that the man was a gold smuggler who worked in the mines near Minas Gerais, and that he would hide gold in his hair.

346

'Some of them have no idea of business. They smuggle the gold in. But they have no idea what can be done with it. They spend all of it on food, drink, and a woman. But that one has been of much use to us.'

'To us?'

She looked at me but did not say more.

'Luiza, I don't know what has become of Anninho. That's why I'm here.'

I told her about the destruction of Palmares, our hiding place, our capture. I did not mention Anninho's plans of leaving Palmares, or the other strange plans I had overheard. I did not tell her more.

'I have not seen him since I last saw you,' she said. 'I knew of the destruction of the old place. I was confident that you and your husband had escaped and had gone to the New Palmares. The Aprigios are there.'

Was this the same Luiza, who had spoken in broken Portuguese before?

'No. I did not go with the others. Perhaps I would have gone if we were together, and he had not made such a decision ... You know no one who might know his whereabouts?'

'If he is alive,' she said with casualness, but did not continue.

'What?'

'I have seen the old one but not the young one.'

'His father?' I asked.

'Yes, but I have not seen Anninho.' She looked at me.

'Where is the old man?'

'He is where I will be leaving to go soon. I am going to take up residence in Bahia.'

'I was intending to go there next,' I said.

She looked at me, but said nothing.

'Perhaps we can travel together,' she said, after a moment. 'You have the needed documents?'

'Yes,' I said, showing her the papers.

She laughed and I heard her say, 'Jaguaribe.'

'You know him?'

She nodded, but did not explain.

She was wearing trousers and a man's vest that I had seen her wearing that last night we had seen her. What were the strange connections of these people?

'Do you think I'll find him there?' I asked, looking at her intently.

347

She was moving about the room as if she were searching for something under the sacks of grain but which she didn't find.

'I don't know,' she said. 'Perhaps if we find the old man.'

'What will you do with your store?' I asked. 'If you take up residence there?'

'It is not necessary for me to be here. Another will take my place.'

Nautch Girls

UIZA AND I LOADED THE CART with tobacco, sugar, rum, candlesticks, and carvings. She tied my horse to the back of it, while hers would pull the cart along.

'How did you come to wear such a disguise?' she inquired.

'A woman, a Tapuyan woman named Maite suggested it to me.'

'Ah, that one, that strange one, where did you meet?'

'The same as I met you. Anninho took me to her. She says she was a spy for Palmares.'

'Yes, I know,' said Luiza. She spoke as if she did not like the woman.

We climbed onto the seats of the cart and she turned into the road. 'We'll arrive near there when it's dark,' she said. 'But it will be best to camp outside the city. It's not good to travel the streets of Bahia after dark. All kinds of crimes and perversity.'

I looked at her but said nothing, feeling uncomfortable on the hard board, as the cart bucked up and down on the road. I longed to be riding the horse again, traveling alone. But she would know the city, and the old man they called the 'Mohammed of Bahia.' Some said he was a pure, full-blooded African; others said he had Arabic blood. Still others said he was born in Morocco. Others on the island of Madagascar. No one seemed to know for sure.

'This isn't the first time he's disappeared.'

'What?'

'This isn't the first time Anninho's disappeared. He disappeared after the destruction of the other Palmares and we thought he was captured or killed, but he was found. He'll be found again. Don't worry.'

She flicked the reins and we rode in silence.

'He's the one who made the contacts with the men in the gold mines,' she said after a while.

'Anninho?' I asked.

'Yes. He has much ingenuity, that one. All kinds of ideas come from him.'

She flicked the reins again and we turned into a familiar road, and there was the inn I remembered. Had she lied to me? Was she taking me to Anninho after all?

'Luiza,' the man exclaimed, as we entered.

He remained sitting, but extended his hand to her. He was smiling a broad smile. He was the same 'white' man that Anninho had visited and the one I had seen in my vision. He did not recognize me for my disguise or he did not recognize me anyway. Luiza sat down across from him, but I remained standing.

'Come and sit down, Almeda,' she said, placing a chair for me. She had left out the 'y.' Did she not want the man to know my true name?

The man looked at me with curiosity, and then turned to Luiza. 'So you are on your way to the Bay of All the Saints,' he said.

'Yes,' she said.

'I'll miss you.'

'But you never see me.'

'They tell me you are there. That's good enough.'

'This is Martim Anninho's wife.'

'This isn't the same woman.'

'She dyed her hair and stained her face with wrinkles. But look at the eyes, they're the same.'

He looked at me carefully. 'How is Martinho?'

'She doesn't know. I thought you might have seen him.'

'No, not in a long time.'

'Before or after the Velho expedition?'

'A long time before. She was here then.'

I was wondering how she could talk to this man with such ease and friendliness? Had my visions of him been true or false?

'I have not seen your husband since that time,' he said, looking at me.

I stared down at my hands.

'It's in Parahyba, I'm told,' he said to Luiza.

The New Palmares was in Parahyba. What was this man talking about? Why did he know so much?

'Well, it will be a long time before I get there. I've got business in Bahia. I don't know what the old man is up to, but the authorities are looking for him. He came to see me, and since that time I've been under suspicion. They're looking for some excuse to put me in jail or into slavery again.'

He said nothing. She said she would be going and stood. I stood. 'Wait,' he said. He got up and walked across the floor on his wooden leg. I listened to the sound. He reached behind the counter and got a flask. He came back slowly, and handed it to Luiza.

'Balso?' she asked.

He nodded and smiled a bit. She shook hands with him. I nodded goodbye and we left.

'I don't understand it,' I said.

'What do you mean?' she asked.

'Anninho was there too. Why do you visit that white man? Why do you confide in him?'

'He's no white man,' she said. 'And even if he were, they're not all devils.'

'Isn't he a Frenchman or a German? I heard him speaking some estrangeirado to Anninho. And Anninho treated him like an old friend.'

'He's of mixed descendance. African, French, German, who knows? 'Maybe he's got everybody's blood in him. He's one of Anninho's whaling contacts. He used to be a whaling man until he lost his leg. He's been useful as a spy for us. They don't know what he is; no one can tell. The Portuguese soldiers and Bandeirantes come here at night to see the Nautch girls and to play the hurdy-gurdy. They don't pester him the way they do me.'

'What are Nautch girls?'

'Oh, you're an innocent.'

She put the flask in the cart under a bag of sugar.

'What's balso?' I asked.

She laughed, then she said, 'Whale's sperm.'

'Why would he give you whale's sperm?' I asked with my eyes wide.

'All kinds of purposes,' she said. 'Some say it can change a person's personality. But me, I use it as a balsam for wounds, and to keep away headaches and constipation. It's as good as honey. For some things it's better. For a man it takes away impotence, cures or protects a woman from infertility. Or so they say. It's good for taciturnity. Someone who is indifferent and cannot express emotion.'

'Why are you looking at me so?' I asked, with a laugh.

She flicked the reins of the horse and we bumped along. I thought of where I would need that balso when we reached Bahia.

'If you make a pomade out of it, it will make the hair grow ... Ronciere says, "Balso, and luck, and good judgment, and everything's taken care of."'

She smiled at me, as we passed one of the mountain trails that I had recently descended. There was the heavy smell of clove and cinnamon. I thought about Mexia and Jaguaribe and wondered if I would still be in the mountain hut if they had not arrived, or would I have affected a cure of my own will and gone in search of Anninho? My grandmother used to say that the will was the deed. 'The will is the deed,' she'd say. I don't know if it was her own notion, or if she were quoting someone. Perhaps for such a woman as her the will was the deed. But I could not discover Anninho by sheer will, by willing him to be beside me now. Ah, if I had such power!

' ... and there are other secret remedies.'

'What?' I asked.

'The balso,' she said, with her eyes on the road.

'I wish it would help me find Anninho,' I said. 'For that you'll need the other two.'

'What?'

'Luck and judgment.'

Broken Bricks and Unripe Fruit

WE TRAVELED ALONG THE COAST, through forests, and spent the nights on deserted beaches. Even when we encountered strangers they would ride up to us as if to question us, but with one look at Luiza they would steer around – as if they had not recognized her from a distance but up close had recognized her, and as she was a free woman of their district, they let her and her 'old companion' pass freely. Finally, we entered the road that led to the city of Salvador da Bahia. I was exhausted but Luiza seemed as fresh as when we had started.

Strewn across the road just before we reached the city were broken bricks and unripe fruit. It looked as if someone had been attacked. Luiza steered the horse to the edge of the road. She left the cart and everything in it, but took the flask of balso, and untying our horses, we went into the woods.

'What do you think happened?' I asked.

'I don't know,' she said.

We tied the horses to a tree and sat down on a fallen log that lay near the edge of a low embankment, overgrown with weeds and bushes.

'Perhaps they chased someone out of town. It is a very suspicious and jealous town. We will ride in tomorrow. You are a stranger. You will be safer with me.'

'You have been here before?'

'I was born here.'

'I think I was born here. Here or in Recife. I don't know my birthplace for sure.'

She was silent, then she said again that perhaps they had chased someone from the city. She said it as if it were a natural thing.

She got up and took a roll that lay across the back of her horse, and unfolding it, produced a hammock which she tied to two trees.

We had a meal of coconut meat and red berries which she picked from a nearby bush.

'Aren't these poison?' I had asked.

'Only if you eat a bunch of them. It's funny,' she said, knowingly, handing me three of the small red berries. 'If you eat two or three of them they're good for your health, but if you eat a whole handful they're fatal.'

I ate mine after she had done so. I told her the story about the poisonous fish, and she laughed heartily, wiping her hands on her vest.

When it was dark, she made a fire under the hammock and climbed into it.

'Come on,' she said. 'There's room for two.'

I got into the hammock and lay down beside her. I rested comfortably at first and then climbed out in a rush. Several times during the night I had to climb out because of the little red berries that were good for the health!

Shellfish, Coconut Oil, and Cold Water

WHEN I AWOKE there were two women kneeling by the fire. One was Luiza, the other was an Aimore woman, her straight black hair hitting her shoulders. I saw only her bare back and the flap of her loincloth hitting against her buttocks as she squatted. Luiza saw me and motioned for me to come over. I rose from the hammock, but feeling the same 'evidence' of the effectiveness of the berries of the night before, I ran into the bushes. I came out shyly and sat down near the fire where the Indian woman was preparing shellfish. She had a small flat nose and very beautiful large almond eyes but her skin had dark splotches on it, not the smooth brown of most of the Indian women I had seen. The rest of her complexion was a pale brown. She looked at me steadily and smiled, but said nothing. She had a white round birthmark on her right arm, shaped like a berry. Neither she nor Luiza was talking. When the woman finished, she put portions on banana leaves and passed them to us. We ate in silence. Luiza did not introduce me to the woman and I did not ask her name – though they began to talk of 'the old man.'

'Yes, I saw him,' the woman said. 'I prepared some mungaza for him and he went into Bahia at night. He said he would wait for you there.'

Luiza said nothing.

'There were heavy rains for nine days like he said there would be. And my hands started bleeding the way he said they would do.'

She showed red spots in the centers of her hands like bruises. 'But he's no longer crazy the way he once was. He no longer talks about "the holy war." I asked him, "Marinheiro, would you kill me too because I'm not a Muslim?" He kept looking into the water, and told me about the rain and that one there coming with you. He said she'd want to learn your science. Do you have any remedies for my complexion? He said you'd have something.'

Luiza gave her the flask of balso and told her to rub it on her face morning and night and to wash it with coconut oil and cold water. The woman thanked her and took the flask, holding it against her bare bosom.

'What did he say of Bahia?'

'He said it was a place of murderers and comedians, but that they all have a taste for the supernatural.'

Luiza began to laugh softly, but for what reason I did not know.

A New Name and a New Place

HERE, I AM KNOWN AS MORAZE,' she said, as we entered the town. 'That is my professional name.'

I did not ask her what she meant. She entered the town as if it could mean no harm to her. We were not riding the horses but leading them behind us, as we walked down a flat very wide street. There was no one on the street we entered, though it seemed to be a commercial district – all the buildings were white, box-shaped, one and two story warehouses.

I looked at her and it seemed as if she had grown an inch taller, and her shoulders which had seemed narrow were now broad and square as if they were padded with small cushions. I stared at the side of her handsome face as she gazed ahead, yet seemed at the same time to be watching me out of the corner of her eye.

'In Minas Gerais they know me as Zibatra,' she said without blinking, 'but here I am Moraze.'

I stared at her. We came to the end of the street, to a long warehouse. We tied the horses to the post outside and I entered after her.

When we were inside, she remained the tall, strange woman. 'What shall I call you?'

'I am Luiza Cosme to you,' she said. 'But I tell you the other names so that you'll recognize me anywhere.'

Inside, in the first room, were wooden benches and shelves filled with bottles and wooden statues of saints.

'Are you a witch?' I asked.

She looked at me with fierceness.

'No, I am not a witch. A witch is a very evil thing. It's a very evil thing. I'm a curer of witches. I'm a curer. I offer medicines, spiritual protection, and supernatural visions.'

She turned away from me and went into the next room, leaving me standing there. She came out again and stood looking at me in silence.

'If you have any power,' I said. 'You can tell me where to find Anninho, and what became of him. You can tell me my future.'

'Ah, you're not afraid of the future? You're no longer afraid of it?' I looked at her and then I turned away.

'Where are you going, Almeyda?' she asked.

'I don't know,' I said, without turning.

'Stay here with me, if you intend to search the city for him,' she said. 'This is a place of murderers and thieves. They'll kill you for a handful of maize.'

I turned.

'Show me what I should do.'

'What?'

'Help me to find him. Give me a vision.'

She didn't answer. She indicated for me to follow her into the next room.

This back room was much like her 'store' in Porto Calvo. There were grain sacks and leathern bags all along the walls. Two hammocks hung on opposite sides and Oriental tapestries and silks hung on the walls. There was the portrait of a dark-skinned, high-cheekboned, longhaired woman with large hoop earrings on the wall. There was a resemblance to Luiza but it was not her. Did she really change appearance with each change of name? Under one of the hammocks was a long trunk. A red candle sat on top of it, and a clay mold in the shape of a pyramid. That was her hammock she said, and the other one, with nothing underneath it was mine.

'I do not wish to show you anything of the future yet,' she said, looking at me. 'I don't know about you, but I like to avoid deceits.'

What did she mean? How could I deceive her? Wasn't it the greater possibility that she could deceive me with some false precognition?

I looked at her, and then looked at a closed door that led to yet another room.

'That's my library,' she said. 'I call it my "inner chamber." It's locked. I won't allow you in there. Not yet. You want to learn from me, but I do not know what is possible yet.'

There was a knock on the door and she left me and went back to the first room. I did not follow. But I heard her.

'I can't wash the gold out of your head until tomorrow,' she told the visitor. 'What is it?'

'It's mal de bicho.'

'Ah, those gold mines. They're horrible. Every kind of disease comes from them. What do I recommend? A daily bath, and a dose of brandy every morning. I know it's uncomfortable, but it will go away. I've said so, haven't I? If it doesn't, come back to me. This is such a time and place.

'The will isn't always the deed. Some say the will is the deed, but it isn't always. Anyway, come back tomorrow afternoon, and I'll wash the gold out. No, perhaps it's best if I do it now.'

An Angolan followed her into the room where I was sitting in the hammock. He was barefoot and walked with some difficulty as he followed Luiza. His eyes looked red from sleeplessness. His hair and shirt and trousers were dusty. Luiza took a basin from the corner and he sat on the floor near it. She washed his hair first and started to wash his beard.

'There. I'll leave that for you,' she said.

He said that there was no woman he wanted in that city and that he could get quail or cotia in the forest. He said it was more important to help with someone's freedom.

Luiza rinsed his beard and stood up. He looked at me and tilted his chin toward me but said nothing.

'Good day, Madam Zibatra,' he said to her and went out the back door.

'Is it some secret society?' I asked.

'What are you talking about?' she asked. She slid the basin beside the trunk under her hammock but did not filter the gold out.

'I have heard of such societies, secret societies where they make contributions to purchase the freedom of others and build churches,' I said.

'Then they are not so secret,' she said. 'Perhaps we purchase freedom, but we don't build churches.'

She climbed into her hammock looking at me with wide black eyes. 'Do you build ships?' I asked.

She still looked at me, but didn't answer.

'Don't you think that would cost a vast sum?' she asked after a moment, but she did not intend the question to be answered.

I was silent.

'Tomorrow or perhaps the next day I will decide about you.'

'What? To let me into your confidence?'

'Do you think I am already in *yours*?' she asked.

'What do you mean?'

'You want to be my apprentice. But it's not your choice; it must be mine.'

'Why do I want that?' I asked.

'You want to find Anninho, don't you? You want to prevent another destruction of the New Palmares. You want to take what I know and learn what I do not know. I don't know whether I will accept you.'

She lay down on her hammock and turned over on her side, away from me, and went to sleep. As I was also very tired from the journey, I lay down and slept as well.

The Dream of the Good Man

I CLIMBED ONTO THE HORSE, traveling along the mountain road. I had gone back in time, and Aguaribe had just given me the horse, and now I had climbed on. Aguaribe became Anninho, walking along beside me holding the reins and then Aguaribe-Anninho disappeared. But before he disappeared, he said, 'Beware of the first evil.'

'What is the first evil?' I asked.

'What is the first good?' asked another man, who appeared at the side of the mountain road, as Anninho disappeared. It was the dictionary maker who had mutilated his hand and foot to avoid military service.

'I don't believe it was the first evil,' he said, as he walked along beside me. 'Do you think that's what he meant?'

'What?' I asked.

'The shortage of white women and the necessity of the mulatto?'

357

The horse began to trot, but even with the increased speed the dictionary maker continued to keep up in spite of his severed Achilles tendon. His black hair was longer than the last time I'd seen him and it flapped behind him.

'I don't believe in Mars or Venus, but will you go to Minas Gerais with me? I believe that Negroes are lucky. They have special powers.'

'I don't know what you're talking about.'

The horse made sharp turns; the man followed. At some turns he was wedged between the horse and rock, but he continued alongside.

'Why, powers for finding gold. They tell me that every gold miner lives with a Negress. Don't you agree that wealth is more important than color?' he asked earnestly.

I was silent.

'As long as I have to be silent and exiled in Brazil why not strike it rich!'

I said nothing.

'Don't you think I'm a good man?' he asked. 'I put years of work on that dictionary and they still wouldn't print it. But I know you have powers for discovering gold. Come along.'

I still said nothing.

'The Brazilians are beasts. The Portuguese are beasts. Do you think there's one good man or woman? A fool on horseback.'

It was there that the horse quickened his pace and I got away from him, but yet wasn't that him again, standing at the base of the mountain, waiting?

When I got there it was not him, but a black man – a Cabo Verde? A Crioulo do Rio? A Mina? My grandmother had taught me how to recognize the different Africans, but I couldn't recognize this one. He had an 'F' on his shoulder for 'fugitivo,' and one of his ears was cut off, meaning that he had escaped twice and the third time if he was captured his Achilles tendon might be severed, or something worse.

I stopped the horse, and he climbed on – not behind me but in front of me.

'Are you a slave or a free woman?' he asked. I started to answer but discovered that I could not.

'My name is Amur Yefik,' he said with a laugh. 'I won't cost you anything but distance and time.'

He turned the horse away from the road I had intended to take. 'We'd better head for the interior,' he said. 'Perhaps we can escape from the bushwhacking captains.'

He turned from the road into a path that looked as if it had not been traveled by men.

'You're right!' he said. 'It's a tapir trail. I used to use them to smuggle gold. Hide it in my hair and in bags of sugar. For good purposes. And especially for freedom buying. I'm a man of no drink and no gambling. Let's go here. A tapir's been through here.'

We camped underneath a tree I had never seen in Brazil. It seemed to be several trees connected, as if a branch of one tree had gone down to the ground, replanted itself, and become the trunk of another tree, so that there was a whole line of such connected trees.

He tied the horse to one of them and we sat down under it.

He took a sheaf of papers out of his shirt. 'Here's a poem that's circulating. It's not mine. But someone who couldn't get it printed is just circulating the manuscript.'

I read:

The Brazilians are beasts who work all their lives
To maintain the rascals of Portugal.

I handed it back to him. He placed it under the other papers. 'By Gregorio de Mattos,' he said. 'Some traveler gave it to me.

'There are poetasters everywhere in Brazil, but no printers. I'm a bit of a bard myself. I'm writing my own national episodes.'

'What's it about?' I asked.

'A man's travels,' he said. 'Travels. It's a satire on the whole society ... But such books must always have one good man, one "el Bueno," one idealist, one searcher for Truth. Don't you think that's so?'

I started to answer. Luiza was laughing. I opened my eyes and she was sitting in her hammock, staring at me.

I closed my eyes to hear what else the man would say, but he was not there, only the strange interconnected trees, the leaves moving softly, as if they had joined Luiza in her mirth.

'It's a banyan tree, árvore de banyan,' she said, letting me know that she could see my vision too. 'It's a sacred tree in the East.'

I opened my eyes and looked at her.

'I am the granddaughter of an Azande woman,' she said. 'When she was back in the other country, a woman was not admitted into the inner circle. All of the witch doctors were men. Women and only old ones were allowed to do anything – and this was only the very lowly position of being a leech. They said she was not old enough even to be a leech, but she persisted, and they allowed her that. They said they liked a woman who stood on her own feet and fought for what she believed in, and worked at the difficulties, and showed some dignity. They praised her, but kept her in that position. But she refused to keep to that position because she wanted to cure spiritual ailments as the men did. It was then that they accused her of witchcraft. Only because she wanted to be a curer of witches as they were. But she was not a witch. A witch is a very evil thing. She wanted to be a curer of witches.'

'What became of her?'

'There was a certain man who "cured" her of witchcraft, even though he did not believe the others' suspicions. When she was cured, she paid him her fees to learn from him and learned from him all she could, and then she came here.'

'Did she come here on her own?'

'She said so.'

I was silent.

'My mother, under the influence of Benedictine priests, would have nothing to do with her magic, but I wanted it.'

'How can you tell a witch from a curer of witches?' I asked.

'Do they cause harm or good?' she asked.

'Suppose good for one is harm for another?'

She did not reply. She got up and went into the back room, locking the door.

I started to get up and go into the front room and examine the various bottles and wooden figurines that were on the shelves, but was afraid to, not knowing what magic they contained and because my grandmother had said that the same things that can cause good can cause harm if in ignorant hands. I would wait to see whether she would decide to teach me. I lay down in the hammock, restless.

I remembered a conversation my mother and grandmother had had. I had been four or five, so it had meant little to me then.

'How do you know whether it's revelation or illusion?' my mother had asked. 'How do you know you're not simply a madwoman?'

My grandmother had replied that in some societies mad people were considered mystics, that they were considered to be divine.

'And their hallucinations taken as realities,' said my mother.

'Do you think I'm a liar?'

'I think you believe what you tell me.'

'Then you think I believe lies?' persisted my grandmother. My mother said nothing.

'Maybe it's best not to argue it,' said my grandmother. She touched my forehead. 'Here's one who will leave one world to explore another and multiply the possibilities of choice.'

My mother looked frightened and put her hand on my grandmother's arm and drew it away. Then she lifted me and put me in the hammock with her.

'They say he's cold to the touch and gives no pleasure. Do you think I would want such a one?' asked my grandmother.

Three masked witch doctors stood in front of her. They were wearing leopard skins and gourds and whistles hung from their waists.

'You were seen rubbing yourself with devil's grease and changing into a goat.'

'I don't want to be simply a leech. I want some knowledge of the spirits' forces.'

'You were seen changing into a weasel, a mole, a bat, and a horse, and a big, white, bearded man came and kissed you on the lips, and you were seen giving him turnips to eat.'

'Do you think I would want such a one?'

'Tell us how you affected the transformations. Tell us about your rendezvous with the devil.'

'It's a tiresome story. We met at the Harz Mountains in Germany and at Blakulla in Sweden and at La Hendaze in France. Long, difficult travels.'

'She admits! Tell us how the devil equips himself?'

'There are a multiplicity of possibilities. But how should I know which ones are real and which illusions?'

'Banish her to Brazil, the filthy woman.'

One man stepped forward, 'No, I'll cure her.'

'With what, roots and wild honey?' asked one.

'No,' said the man. 'Experience and intuition.'

361

He came towards her. 'I like a woman who stands on her own feet, and works against difficulties, and shows dignity.'

I awoke to the smell of onion soup, coconut, and wild honey.

The Apprentice

I DON'T EAT MEAT OF ANY KIND,' she said, as we sat on mats on the floor, eating supper. The mats were not square but triangular. 'It weakens the spirit.'

She explained to me that it was her belief that the characteristics of the thing eaten would come into one.

I said nothing as I ate the onion soup and manioc cakes, the coconut meat, and drank coconut milk mixed with wild honey.

'That will keep you healthy and keep you from going insane,' she said. 'I will teach you some of what I know, the rest you will have to add onto. Perhaps you will never be admitted into the inner circle. Who knows? Have you anything of value?'

'No,' I said.

'Give me that necklace.'

She pointed to the necklace of seeds and shells I was wearing.

'I can't part with it,' I said. 'It's a gift from Anninho. Anyway, it has no value in money.'

'Did I say value in money? Then return the bracelet I gave you.'

I took off the bracelet and handed it to her. She put it back on her own wrist.

'A pupil must always pay fees,' she said. 'I am the older woman. Do you think you can lie your way into eternity in the same manner?'

I was silent.

She rose and went into the front room. When she came back she had a small bowl, which she gave to me to drink from.

'Drink this,' she said. 'It will strengthen your soul.' I drank the liquid and handed the bowl back to her.

'I'll teach you how to prepare it along with other magical and medicinal potions,' she said. 'You're not my only apprentice, but I'll teach you in private. Your soul is very weak, so how can you meet in the company of others? Perhaps when your soul is stronger ... or perhaps you will never be in the inner circle.'

I looked at her. How was I to know if she were speaking the truth or lying? Was she a woman speaking lies? Should I believe her?

'Intuition and experience,' she said suddenly. Then she laughed. 'I am everywhere. Those who do not know me as Zibatra or Moraze believe that this is "The Library and Philosophical Society for the Moral and Intellectual Advancement of Free Coloured Women." It's that too.' She went to the door of the back room, unlocked it and swung it open and let me see all the books it contained, but would not let me enter. 'It's a good collection,' she said. 'Very good. It reminds you of *his*, doesn't it? Of Father Tollinare's library of forbidden books. Do you think it's something of value? A good library is the architecture of opportunity. I just acquired *A Manual of Tropical Medicine*. Some things I've corrected. I should write my own. I know as much about the medicine of the tropics as anyone. I won't deny my own knowledge.'

She kept looking at me as if she were laughing at me, or as if there were some private joke. She came back and sat down beside me.

'After you learn what I tell you, you will learn what's in that room.' I looked at her.

'You poor soul,' she said. 'O inocente. Do you think it will take till the end of the world?! Would you rather that I showed you Pindamonhangaba Road and you accompanied some stranger to the gold mines at Minas Gerais?'

'No,' I said with a laugh.

Secret Remedies

I CANNOT BE SPECIFIC IN THIS PART of the history, as the knowledge that I learned is secret and to reveal anything secret is to lose the power that it has. I will say that I was given more medicines to strengthen my soul, because Luiza said that my soul was very weak and that even after I had completed my apprenticeship, that I would not be able to challenge the spiritual powers of others such as herself, and that the cures I had affected could only be done in private, and that no one would come to me as they came to her, for they would instantly see the weakness of my position, and would have little faith in my cures. I would have no effect on strangers, as she had, but only on those who knew me well and whom I could protect in secret. And she continued to call me O inocente.

'You begin from a position of weakness and not one of strength,' she had said. 'But you will progress in knowledge. Now you are a novice. But don't believe, however, that you can ever challenge the powers of such a woman as myself and certainly not the paje's daughter, Maite, who controls spiritual forces that are even unknown to me. It is hard to conceive of you as a medicine woman, O inocente, but perhaps through silence and fasting and chastity we can purify your soul. But of course your magic will never be active but always passive.'

She drew symbols on my skin, some geometric, others strange animals and symbolic creatures that looked like serpents and birds but were neither. She gave me an amulet, a painted eye, that I must wear in some secret place and that must never be seen by anyone.

'No one?'

'Perhaps Anninho, when the time comes. But no one else. And I've seen it – as one's nakedness is seen at birth – but even I must not see it again, or it will lose its power.'

'To protect or harm?'

'Is it not an object of protection?' she asked.

I was shown the mystical serpent Iararaca and the magic plant Ipecacuanha, and another plant that shriveled up when she touched it, but that remained whole when I placed my hand on it, and so she said it would become my 'power plant' as the Ipecacuanha was hers.

I was shown many trees and plants and told of the medicines they contained, to do both harm and good. I learned about those that everyone knows: the copaiba tree and how to get sap from it when the moon was full, how one cures wounds and bruises without leaving a scar; she tapped the plant and rubbed it on my bosom, removing the scars that were there, praying and chanting along with its application.

'This is the female copaiba. It does not work with the male tree. This is how you tell the difference. You see the holes and scratches here?

'Some animals, wounded, have sought it as a cure. God puts things like this about for all his creatures. Some are wiser even than we humans in knowledge of the healing power of plants. This is better than all the magic salves in Europe.'

I learned about the caborahiba, another tree that produces balsam. I learned of its ordinary uses and uses that were not commonly known. I learned of the obira paramacaci that could be either a purge or a fatal poison.

I found my 'magic plant' the 'herva viva' growing in many places. Whenever Luiza or anyone else touched it, it would recoil. But when I touched it, it would remain whole, and even become stronger and greener. Sometimes it would flower.

'It has special powers for you to discover,' she said.

I learned of other plants not commonly known, and of the magic powers of ordinary plants – not only medicinal powers, but also powers to affect the spirit, the emotions, the intellect, the will. But these I cannot name particularly here, as such information must be given only to one's apprentices, or those other doctors who sell and buy medicines among themselves, and exchange secrets.

'There will be some knowledge that you yourself will discover, that will be yours alone, that you will not wish to exchange with anyone.'

I learned to generate a certain phlegm that was beneficial to the soul and body. I learned how to prepare many things, how to cook and stir them, what incantations or prayers to pray over them.

My body was rubbed with oil and ashes. I was taken all about the district to learn rare medicines – from both plants and animals – and I learned many medical secrets. 'As I said, some of these you will learn more from than I have taught you, as everyone must make her own discoveries. But remember, your power will not work against mine. O inocente, you cannot challenge me.'

I was taught dances and songs.

'These dances and songs anyone can learn and fool the people with. They are not the true magic.'

I was told to observe chastity, even though I had been observing it for some time now. I fasted. I was given more medicines to strengthen my soul.

'I cannot give you the gift of prophecy,' she said. 'That cannot come from me. Though in the other country my grandmother said that the old man gave her medicines to eat and drink which not only made her soul strong, but gave her the ability to prophesy. But I cannot grant you such a power. But you will know it if it comes. Then you will hear what others cannot hear, and see what is invisible to others. All I can teach you are rites of healing magic, and actions necessary to the future, but not how to perceive it. I will give you the rudiments. But most of your progression in knowledge will be on your own. That is the way for all students. You are given the rudiments, and then you add to the knowledge. You make discoveries on your own. And maybe that will be to the end of the world!'

She told me about her belief in reincarnation.

Finally, I was given more medicines to eat and drink, and then I was covered by a triangular mat, and earth was heaped on top of me. I don't know how many days I remained that way – perhaps three days, perhaps a week – but I felt neither tiredness nor hunger. When this ritual was complete, she told me to rise. I got to my feet, and she rubbed medicines into my body, and I was given a new name.

'What of Almeyda?' I asked.

'That's your name. But a new name must be given for the new person.'

She decorated me with feathers and bracelets and anklets of seeds and shells. She tied calabashes and a magic whistle around my waist, and a horn filled with herbal medicines.

'Jaguara,' she said, kissing my forehead.

Armadillo

WE MIXED THE THICK GUMMY JUICE with the oil from the iguaragua, the emus. We squeezed the testicles of a certain lizard. A nauseating odor. We gathered the feathers of eagles, falcons, hawks, forest hens, partridges, pigeons, doves, wild ducks, parrots, macaws, tuyns, seabirds, the red ibis. She made a dish of bananas, pineapple, Brazil nuts, mixing it inside the shell of an armadillo.

I was taught to recognize many poisons, and was made to be immune to those poisons and to be immune against the venom of the sucuryuba and the tapukara.

A liniment of a red color was prepared for my face and then Luiza sent me into the library and locked the door behind me. I would stay in there several days at a time, eating nothing but the meat from a coconut, and drinking liquid from the armadillo shell. There was something else she gave me. Was it the shredded bark from a supernatural tree?

The books in the library I will not list, though they were mostly medical and religious and natural histories. The medical books spoke of Egyptian, European, Algerian, Chinese medicines, among others. Many of them she had scratched and written in, making corrections. In some of the pages were scattered grains of gold like ordinary dust.

Acts of Cruelty and Sadism

DURING THE DAYS I was not in the library studying, Luiza and I would travel together, searching for rare medicinal plants, and new uses for old plants; we would visit doctors in other territories and exchange ideas, buy and sell medicines, observe new remedies. We would visit certain plantations. We visited only those on which the slaves received cruel and sadistic abuse. We would visit them only during the night. Before we would enter, Luiza would rub a special oil and ashes from a special plant on our skin. Then we were 'safe' and we could enter and give instructions to the 'nurses' – old women who directed the plantation 'hospitals' – the huts of those women who were too old to work any longer in the field.

Luiza would supply these women with salves and medicines besides the salts and emetics that the plantation owners would give them to cure all manner of ailments, from mal de bicho to epileptic fits. Then we would remain with the nurses and visit those of her patients who had special difficulties. We treated women who had induced miscarriages and who had aborted themselves so that their children would not be born into the horror that they themselves had been born into. But because of her belief in reincarnation, Luiza claimed that she herself did not perform abortions. 'Perhaps they will pay more dearly in another life,' she would say, and then she would speak mysteriously of how she had lived through her horror in this one and saw in the future her 'glory days.'

She told me: 'There's a contraceptive plant that I've been trying to find, so that these women can prevent conception before it occurs. Maite knows it, but she won't exchange the secret with me, though it is not her last mystery.' What she meant by 'last mystery' is that each doctor kept some final secret, some final 'trick' – that was usually self-discovered or inherited – that was revealed to no one. However, it usually involved some spiritual maneuver or stratagem, rather than a physical or material one, as the former were more difficult to come by.

'Cozinheiros have their "last mystery" – their most secret recipe – and we have ours.'

We put salve on the back of a man who had been beaten with braided straps of leather rolled in sand. Then he had been cut with a razor and lemon juice, salt and urine had been rubbed into the wounds. We cleansed him with cold water and then applied the sap from the copaiba tree. Luiza claimed that his wounds would be healed by the morning, though he would have some trouble sleeping during the night.

We gave potions to many who were exhausted from overwork and eating only mush, cane syrup, and rotten dried meat. Coconut milk was the base of it, but I will not give the other ingredients. When it was mixed, however, it took on the color of deep rust. She took out fruit and fish from a basket, leaving it for the old woman, while we ate the mush, salt pork, and pumpkin the woman served us. I watched with surprise when she ate the salt pork, for hadn't she claimed to eat no meat? Perhaps it was for mere purposes of conviviality with this old escrava.

At another plantation we visited, a dreadful thing was done. The owner, who had been some kind of magistrate in Rio or Olinda – a man of title – kept a pool of piranha, and whenever one of his slaves was disobedient, or if for some reason he took dislike to what the slave said or did or refused to say or do he would plunge a hand or an arm of that slave into the pool. The slaves who came to us, therefore had different lengths of arms – on some the fingers were missing, others the whole hand, the arm up to the elbow, the whole arm. It was both physical and psychological cures that were administered. One slave had been affected so that her whole system had stopped working, and she was given a purge of Malagueta pepper. It was this woman who Luiza told how she might poison the piranha with an ordinary weed that could be found about the plantation.

'We've poisoned them before, and he simply gets others,' said the distressed woman, whose hand was gone. 'And he gets them in greater abundance.'

'Well, this will prevent him from getting others,' said Luiza.

The woman did as Luiza instructed her, and we heard of no more trouble there with piranhas. Several months later, however, we saw the woman on the streets of Bahia selling papaya preserves and coconut candy.

'Aren't you Iguarita from the Mascarenho plantation?' Luiza had asked the woman.

'Yes, Madam Zibatra. I'm the same woman.'

'Why are you here in town selling preserves and candy?'

'You know why,' said the woman. 'It was not the fish that were poisoned but Mascarenho.'

'Did I not tell you to poison the fish?' asked Luiza-Zibatra.

'And I poisoned the fish, but it was not the fish the poison took effect on but the master.'

She was shy of her stub and kept it in the pocket of a full skirt. The basket of preserves and candy was tied by a strap around her neck so that she could work freely with one hand.

'Well, who has you selling preserves and candy?'

'His wife, Madam. You know it. After her husband died, she sold all of the men and kept the women – laundresses and cake makers and candy makers and seamstresses, to hire us out and send us into town to sell the sweets we make.'

'Is that all?' asked Luiza.

'No, Madam. There's another thing she has us do that I dare not speak of.'

'What thing?'

'You know it. I dare not say its name.'

'Those who were not mutilated by her husband?' asked Luiza.

'Yes, Madam, and an even crueler thing it is. She takes the women's money for doing it and then she laughs at them.'

'Go back home and watch her stop laughing,' said Luiza.

The woman obeyed and some days later it was heard that the mistress of the Mascarenho plantation died from a spoiled batch of preserves that she liked to eat in the mornings with manioc toast and butter. The remaining women were purchased by a 'foreign' buyer and given their freedom, and could be seen selling their own wares about the streets of

Bahia and pocketing their own money. There was one of the unmutilated women, however, who continued in the 'profession' that the mistress Mascarenho had started her in. Luiza frowned on her and complained about her. One morning she was found lying in the streets of Bahia, a victim of some thief.

The Virtue of Plants and a Lecture on the Intellect and Morality; Strange Sounds

I WAS INSIDE MAKING MASKS and perfumes when Luiza entered from outside. I still wore my 'old woman's' disguise even though it appeared that I was safe in this city with Luiza, and I still had my papers.

I was making an assortment of perfumes to correspond to different emotions, and arranging colors on the masks to produce a variety of emotions and affections. Each day I would practice increasing the range of feelings my products were capable of producing – moving through love, passion, anger, uncertainty, etc. Luiza had lectured me on the importance of odor, music, color in magic, and medicinal rituals, and I was completing my first assignment – using oils and secretions from plants and animals, and plant and animal dyes. 'The more you learn you will see that there is very little magic in magic and at the same time very much,' she said, looking at me with her intense eyes.

She came and examined the work that I was doing, and nodded approvingly at the first one, frowned disapprovingly at the second.

'No, no, no,' she said. 'This could make some dangerous and immoral feelings. So you know how to make it? But why should you cause people to abuse themselves? Raise them up. Make them fearless, ambitious, proud, strong, intelligent. Create heroic feelings to produce heroic deeds, victories of the spirit. Are you a witch or a doctor of witches?'

Instead of destroying the bottle, she mixed it with something from another bottle, changing the 'wrong' mixture to a right one.

'I like to work with the range of "high" feelings, not the "lowest" ones,' Luiza said.

'Shouldn't we try to reproduce the *range* of affections? And aren't those others true affections?' I asked.

She said nothing. She examined the other perfumes, frowned on them.

'I have a very high reputation,' said the woman. 'People don't fear me for the harm I've done to them. People don't have to expect miracles to reach the states these concoctions could put them in. I've never done anything I can't respect. Get rid of this, and come, let me teach you how to work with sound.'

Before she started creating the sounds, she explained to me that music/sound like verbal and visual images could affect the body's rhythms. She explained to me more about the biological aspects of sound – how it could alter the body's functions and change the affections, and even the intellectual level – one's understanding and alertness. I was made to listen and tell her what I 'felt' – what new energies or what new thoughts. Then the final time she asked me to listen I heard nothing, yet I felt a strange relaxation and inner peace, and then just as suddenly I felt nervous, giddy, restless. She gave me some figures and asked me to calculate them. I confused the figures. She said something to me, asked me to respond and I could not, as her words seemed scrambled. Then I felt the strange calm again.

'Those are the ranges of inaudible sounds – inaudible to you, but not to me, and not to many of the animals in the forests, though I hear at greater depth than even they – and yet what changes these sounds make. Sounds you can't even hear, and look at what they've done to you. Ah, there's a lot that can be done with silent sound. Imagine what things?'

I said nothing. I wondered if such a stratagem could be used against one's enemies. I looked at her immediately, but she said nothing. She simply replaced the instruments in the trunk.

'You will practice all of this tomorrow,' she said. 'You will practice it until you know it perfectly, and you must be very careful. Imagine what such knowledge could do in corrupt hands?'

Then she showed me a new medicine she had learned from the Indians – what might be done with the dried and triturated tail of an opossum.

I waited nearly the whole of the next day for her to tell me about the 'silent sounds' but she did not.

Finally in the evening I said, 'Luiza, you promised to tell me about the sounds. I want to know most about the sounds one cannot hear.'

'Always,' she said with a smile. 'Always you want to know first what's hidden. First we will begin with the drum playing and then the hand piano. I'll teach you how to play with skill and energy. We'll talk first about the effects on the body and then those on the mind and the spirit.'

It was only after several months that she talked to me about the sounds one could not hear.

'You've been making them all along and didn't know it,' she said. 'In the spaces between what the others call the real sounds. But we both know it's all real.' She looked at me carefully. 'Why are you thinking of the nerve destroying sounds first? Why do you always think immediately of destruction?'

I was silent.

'Let's go outdoors. We'll start first with the invisible sounds in nature and then we'll make our own. Invisible did I say? And are sounds ever visible?' She winked at me. 'Come along, Jaguara, let's examine the strange sounds in the air.'

CURANDEIRA

The Bushwhacking
Captain's Wife

THE WOMAN SEEMED ONE OF THOSE QUIET and reserved kinds, as she stood in the 'shop.' She was wearing a clean, plain cut tan dress, and a thin cotton shawl was wrapped about her shoulders.

'This will be for the perfumes,' said Luiza, before the woman even entered.

'Are you from the Marcgraf plantation?' asked Luiza when the woman entered. Why she asked such a question I don't know, because this was obviously a free woman with a little property.

'No, I'm a free woman,' said the woman.

She had not closed the door and looked as if she did not know whether to enter or go back out.

'Close the door and come in if you want my help in that matter,' said Luiza.

The woman closed the door, but still stood with her hands twisted in the shawl. She was a thin, handsome but not pretty woman, though she might have been pretty if she carried herself differently. Her eyes wandered about the shop and came to rest on me, then jumped back to Luiza-Zibatra.

'You're Madam Zibatra?' she asked her.

'Yes. Sit down and let's talk. I can't do anything until you tell me your problem.'

'You spoke as if you already knew,' said the woman. 'My apprentice doesn't know your trouble,' said Zibatra.

The woman sat down on a bench. Zibatra sat across from her. I remained standing, but drew nearer.

'My husband's a bushwhacking captain,' said the woman. 'Do you know what I mean by that?'

'Explain what you mean.'

The woman, who had fine dark eyes, looked down at her hands, which were still twisting themselves in the ends of the shawl. I had never seen such a 'private' woman.

'Would you like a glass of water?' asked Zibatra.

'No thank you,' said the woman. She looked up suddenly. 'You're behaving as if this is an inquisition, or the follow-up of one.'

'I'm no inquisitor,' said Zibatra. 'You came here freely, didn't you? You must have some confidence in me.'

'Oh, I have confidence in you,' said the woman, with a sudden aliveness. She twisted on the bench. Suddenly the combination of Scottish whisky and coconut milk came into my head. Why, I didn't know.

'Tell me your story,' said Zibatra gently, coaxing the woman. 'My grandmother was a fearsome woman, but I'm not. I'm kind and tolerant.'

'People fear you.'

'Do you think I'm a devil fixed up like a human woman?' asked Zibatra.

'No,' said the woman with fine dark eyes. Zibatra looked at her but said nothing.

'Well, you wanted me to explain what a bushwhacking captain is,' said the woman. 'You see, he's a soldier of a kind.'

'Is he independent or does he work in a small band?'

'Independent. Is that important? He's not an evil man. I know he doesn't do what some of the others do.'

'Why do you insist that you know it?'

'He did keep a man once, beyond the time he was supposed to turn him in to his master. He made him work for him, and then when he returned him, he pretended he had just caught him, and took the full reward. But he doesn't mistreat or torture anyone.'

'How do you know it?'

'He would tell me if he did so.'

'What kinds of things have the others done?'

'Oh, they've abused the men they've captured. They've abused them as much as the English or the Portuguese. A woman doesn't understand.

'Or rather, I don't understand it. He himself was captured by a bushwhacking captain, and brought back to slavery, and now he becomes one himself.'

'In exchange for his freedom?' I asked, thinking of Pedro who had gained his freedom in a similar manner except he had been a soldier, and had even fought against the Palmaristas. I thought of the first time I met him when we were both slaves of the Polish shoemaker, our capture by the Palmaristas. I thought of the whole story of Pedro while I looked at the woman. I thought of my mixed feelings, of harshness and compassion. Or was it tenderness I felt. Was tenderness the same as compassion?

The woman nodded, but looked at me as if it were an obvious and therefore foolish thing to ask.

'He himself was captured and abused horribly.'

'You say he captures but does not abuse?' asked Zibatra.

'No, he captures the runaway slaves and returns them, that's all. There was only one man he kept and made work for him. It wasn't for a very long time. And there is no cruelty.'

'How is he paid for this, besides his freedom?'

'They pay him in gold depending on how much time it takes him and how much distance he has to travel.'

'What else does he do besides capture runaways?'

'He ... well, he helps them sometimes to find and destroy quilombos.'

'Palmares,' I asked. 'Did he help them to destroy Palmares?'

'Keep your feelings,' said Zibatra, looking at me and raising her hand and frowning. I started to say something. 'Keep them,' she repeated.

'He wasn't the only one,' said the woman in defense of him. 'There were other black soldiers along.'

Zibatra was still looking at me with her hand raised.

'There were quilombos everywhere,' said the woman. 'They say they are all in the mountains. Smaller ones than Palmares.'

'Yes,' said Zibatra. 'You said he does his job and only necessary cruelty.'

'He doesn't mistreat anyone.'

'What do you want from me?' asked Zibatra.

'That he stop being a bushwhacking captain. He has his freedom now but he keeps working for them.'

'Have you spoken to him?'

'Yes, but he continues.'

'What does he say?'

'He won't say anything. He just continues to do it.'

'Perhaps he feels ...'

'What?'

Zibatra was silent. She looked as if she were in a trance.

The woman continued talking. 'He thinks he's damned whether he turns back or goes on.'

'I thought he didn't speak to you about it,' I said, when Zibatra had said nothing.

The woman looked at me as one looks at an intruder. I was silent. 'I heard him once at night talking in a dream. A nightmare. He said that and then he said they were all looking for him to kill. I didn't know if it meant for *him* to kill someone. Or if he were the object of it. Do you know? It was a nightmare. I brought him Scotch whiskey and coconut milk. It always calms him when he's like that.'

My eyes lit up.

Zibatra was silent for a long time, then she said, 'Is his name Queiroz?'

'Yes,' said the woman, looking at her with amazement.

It might as well be Pedro, I was thinking, but I didn't say it.

'Go home,' said Zibatra. 'Queiroz is incapable of metamorphosis. I understand him because I can see history. I can see his whole story. Go home.'

The woman stood up, but kept looking at her.

'But I . . . I thought you could help me.'

'Go home,' said Zibatra. 'I try to avoid deceits. There is nothing I can do.'

'But I've told you the *truth*,' said the woman, deeply distressed.

'I know it,' said Zibatra. 'Now go. Go home and stay his wife!'

The woman hurried out. I felt as if I could see her, from that time, even more 'private,' and sober and silent, waiting for her husband to return from his bushwhacking expeditions.

I started to say something to Zibatra, reminding her that she had spoken to the woman of her 'kindness and tolerance,' and hadn't she caused harm that time?

As if she'd heard me, Zibatra said, 'I can see history and you can't. Do you think I can change the number of the Beast, just because I want to?' Then she looked at me fiercely. 'Could you have saved Pedro?'

I stood there, looking bewildered.

'Don't you have work to do?' she asked. 'She's the bushwhacker's beloved wife, and you, go look closely and you'll see more of them.'

She was speaking of the 'experiment' she had taught me, of staring

into a glass of water, with several drops of a special oil on top – to in-
duce supernatural visions. Thus far it had not 'worked' for me. I had my
thoughts and dreams, but no supernatural visions.

'You can't get sick just because it's the fashion of epidemics,' she said
lightly and went out, wrapping her own shawl about her shoulders. I
went into the next room and stared into the glass of oil and water.

Visions in a Glass of Water

I SAW THREE OR FOUR HUNDRED, long, narrow canoes
moving down a river; in them were Portuguese, Africans, Indians. Some were sitting, others standing.

Luiza came and sat across from me on one of the cushions. The glass
of water with three drops of oil was on a low table.

'Do you know the name of the guide?'

'Guide?' I asked. I didn't know the meaning of the vision and so
answered, 'No.'

Next there was a large room. If it is possible to see a large room in a
small glass of water I saw it. But it was as if the 'smallness' of that space
had changed, or my relationship to it, and it was as if both Luiza and I
were sitting there in the saloon, with the crowd of people.

'Look at that table over there,' said Luiza.

'Where?'

'In the corner. It's Barcala, isn't it?'

'Yes,' I said.

Her eyes were in front of me, and yet I saw behind them or through
them to the table where Barcala was sitting with a glass of wine and a
book. He did not notice me, even though he looked up on occasion.

'Did you think he was in Holland? What's he doing on Madagascar
Island?'

'Madagascar?' I asked.

'Yes, where the pirates go. It's a pirate stronghold.'

I looked around at the crowd of men and women, who looked like an
assortment of renegades from different nations.

'Is that Alsace?' asked Luiza.

'Alsace?'

'Is she a witch or an enchantress?'

She turned my head in the direction where the woman was standing, apart from the tables, in preparation to sing, as she was holding a mandolin. Her eyes and hair were very black, her hair very long and thick, and she was wearing gold rings in her ears. She was dressed in a long skirt with red and black and gold 'oriental' designs around the hem; her blouse was white and loose. She was looking down at the mandolin.

When she looked up her eyes were the hugest, brightest I'd ever seen. 'What is she?' I asked.

'Morisco,' said Luiza. 'She's a Moroccan woman.'

The woman strummed the mandolin. Most of those in the saloon continued their conversations. I glanced at Barcala, who was looking up.

'Barcala, surrounded by pirates,' said Luiza. 'Is this his solitude and freedom? Is this his contemplative life of writing and study? Do you think he's a pirate too?'

'No,' I said.

Was this some illusion she'd conjured for me to see, somewhere in my imagination she was taking me. Was it reality? Was it the present, the past, the future?

Barcala was looking at the woman with admiration. I turned back to her. She began to sing, but in a language I did not understand. She moved through many emotions and seemed to hold many different emotions simultaneously – love, jealousy, anger, pity, remorse. And there were other emotions which I knew no names for.

When she finished, I glanced at Barcala, who lifted his glass to her. 'A Toast To You, Moriana,' said Luiza, though she was still looking at me.

'Is she Moriana?' I asked.

'That's the song,' said Luiza.

'What language was she singing in?'

'Arabic. A Moorish ballad.'

'Do you know the words?' I asked her.

She lifted her chin a bit and then began to recite. I heard the woman reciting and Luiza translating at the same time, translating the ballad for me; she said it was a ballad that she had heard many times; it was also part of the repertoire of the Spanish balladeers, many of whose ballads were of Moorish origin:

Don Alonso got up early a little after sunrise.

He went to invite friends and kinfolk to his wedding.
He stopped his horse

At Moriana's door.

'Good morning, Moriana.'

'Don Alonso, welcome.'

'I come to drink a toast to you, Moriana, for my wedding
Sunday.'

'That wedding, Don Alonso, ought to be with me.

But since it's not,

I accept the invitation just as well, and to prove we're still
friends, drink this fresh wine,

The kind you used to drink

In my room filled with flowers.' Moriana went quickly

Into her room.

Three ounces of soliman with ground-up steel, and the eyes
of a viper,

And the blood of a live scorpion.

'Drink, Don Alonso. Drink this fresh wine.'

'You drink first, Moriana. That is the custom.'

Moriana raised the wineglass to her lips. She kept her teeth
together. Not a drop went inside.

But when Don Alonso drank, not a drop was lost.

'What did you give me, Moriana, What did you give
me in this wine? I've the reins in my hands and I can't
see my horse!'

'Go home, Don Alonso. The day is already passing, and your
wife will be jealous if you stay here with me.'

'What did you give me, Moriana, that I lose all my senses?
Cure me of this poison, and I'll marry you!'

'It can't be, Don Alonso, Because your heart is gone.'

'My wretched mother, who will never see me alive again.'

'More wretched mine, since I've known you.'

When she concluded, she raised the glass on the table and drank some. She put it down. I was silent, then I heard shouts. I stared into the glass.

'Alsace! The spy! The imposter! Hang her!'

They rushed toward the woman. She was held. Barcala stood up, but did not move forward with the others.

'I'm no traitor,' said the woman.

'Zairagia will know,' said one of the women from the crowd, a blonde, full-figured, dressed in trousers and a vest, a jealous look on her face. 'If she's telling the truth Zairagia will find out. She's never wrong. The only time she's been wrong has been when there've been air devils, but ordinary devils of our own world never fool her. Once she discovered such devils had entered me and she lay with me three whole nights before the devils dispersed.'

'The filthy witch,' said one of the pirates. 'She only claimed that for her own lusts. Let the woman go. What harm can she do?'

An old woman came forward with a glass of water, chalk, and a black tablecloth. She spread the cloth on one of the tables, put the glass and the chalk down and took a vial of oil from her pocket. She set the vial beside the glass and took up her chalk.

There was the smell of a very strong perfume. She began to draw four large circles on the tablecloth. In the first circle she drew a cross. The second one she divided into four parts, the third into seven parts, the fourth into twelve parts. Then she began to draw a number of vertical and horizontal lines all along the table, placing numbers beside them.

'Zairagia demands a resolution to the question,' she kept saying. 'Zairagia demands a resolution to the question. A resolution is demanded. Zairagia demands it.'

She began to make little Arabic letters beside the numbers. Then she said again, 'A resolution is demanded.'

She did not seem to get any resolution and so she began to make geometric figures on the palms and backs of the Moroccan woman's hands and then made designs on the woman's forehead.

'Travel backwards in time,' she said. 'Tell me the place and position where the devils entered. A resolution is demanded, an answer to the question.'

She placed several drops of oil into the glass.

'Look in it,' she told the woman. 'Do you see devils dancing?'

'I see nothing but oil in water,' said the Moroccan.

'No devils dancing or speaking to you, no devil saying anything?'

'She's the Black Devil,' said the blonde woman.

'No,' said the Moor.

There was still the smell of the strange perfume.

'Tell me, devils,' said Zairagia. 'Are you devils of the earth or of the air?'

She waited, and though no one else heard the reply, she told them the devils claimed they were of the earth. And she informed them further that in that case she had power over the said devils.

'At what time and place did you enter the woman and who commanded you to?'

She waited, then said, 'They are very closed-mouthed devils and won't say anything. I can't get anything from them, but I'll discharge them. Get out of the woman,' she commanded.

She smiled and clapped her hands at first and then she looked distressed.

'They tricked me. I'm very sorry, Francesca,' she said to the blonde. 'But when the devils left this one, they ran into you, and they will be harder to remove now. It will take the old remedy.'

'Oh, no,' exclaimed the woman. 'Why do they always come into me?'

'What do we do with the itinerant singer?' asked a pirate. 'Let her go,' said Zairagia. 'She can't harm anyone now.'

'I say toss her into the sea,' said Francesca.

'We've got to get the devils out of you,' said Zairagia.

The Moorish woman broke away from the crowd who were now gathered around Zairagia and the woman. Zairagia took Francesca's arm and was leading her away.

'Don't go with her,' said one of the pirates. 'She's a liar. I've seen the world, and I know she's lying. It's all for her own lusts. I'll take care of your devils!'

There was loud laughter. Before I could glance back at Barcala and the Moorish woman the 'scene' dissolved.

I had once been told that some of my ancestors were Moroccan and wondered if this was the reason for the scene. But I was no enchanted Mooress.

There was a new picture. A windmill, a man standing on a country road.

'Is that Barcala?' asked Luiza.

'Yes, where is he?'

'Amsterdam.'

'Is this the present?' I asked. She was silent.

'Did Alsace go with him?'

'Do you see her?'

Yes, I saw a woman now, coming out of a house. A small house, smoke coming from the chimney, behind and to the left of the windmill. A black-haired woman. A Dutch woman? She was wearing an apron and a blue dress. She was smiling.

I grew angry. 'It's not Barcala I want to see. Where's Anninho? Is he there too? He's the one I want to find. I came to you to help me find Anninho.'

'Did I bring this vision?' asked Luiza, shrugging. 'Am I to blame?' She shrugged again and stood up.

I watched Barcala standing with the woman talking and smiling, then they walked back to the house together. I could see through the open door a table piled with books and papers.

'Would you rather he'd stayed on the island with the Moroccan woman?'

I was silent.

'Or stayed here with *you*?' she asked.

'It's not Barcala I wished to see, but Anninho,' I insisted. 'I don't want games or riddles.'

'Did I bring him?' she asked, then said, 'Perhaps you've seen him and don't know it. This is no diviner's game. These are your own visions.'

I poured the water out on the floor. She tossed a rag at me to clean it up. When I finished, she was still looking at me. One of her eyes was green and the other was brown. Why hadn't I noticed before that her eyes were of different colors? Her whole face seemed radiant.

'Why don't you take a rest,' she said.

Her hands on her hips, she turned and walked into the front room. I put the glass upright and placed the towel on the table, and climbed into my hammock.

I saw a circle of tents in a desert.

Parasitic Organisms and Malaria

I COULD NOT RAISE UP from the hammock. I felt chills and fever. I was sweating. Luiza kept a cool cloth on my forehead. Why did she keep pricking my skin? What was she doing with my blood? Had she caused this with some 'silent sound'? And was she now pretending to relieve it? She raised my head and tried to give me something to drink. I heard her say 'Ata' something. What words was she mumbling over me? Her face got closer. She pulled my eyelids up. She admonished me for something.

Was she putting the blame on me for my illness? She was talking about something. She was standing in front of me and behind me talking. How was that possible?

'You must be intrepid. You can't get sick just because it's a fashion of epidemics.'

She mixed blood and milk. What was she doing?

'It's a difficult task, but not impossible.'

'How many blacks do you think there are on whaling ships?'

'Don't think of the past but the future.'

'This one has a fascination with the impossible.'

'Its main virtue is that it gives one more power.'

'All of the books are on the Index.'

'The whole thing is coming to the surface.'

'Who do you think is the source of all power, knowledge, and will?'

'Will?'

'He is the principle of the best.'

'That book is too technical for you. Experiments and calculations?'

'What is the relationship between apples, tides, and planets?'

I told them the prophecy, but it wasn't believed. I was there. I don't behave this way out of fear, but decorum. Ah, that one. He has illusions. What do you think was the real conquest of Palmares? There has always been a conflict between what one can imagine and what one can do in the world. Do you think the will is the deed? Do you want to know my vision? Unity of the power of both of us. But we have a different conception of time, you and I. Of the past and future. A different conception of heroic action. But we're both intruders in the New World.'

'I'm no intruder.'

'Different degrees of responsibility and irresponsibility. And Barcala.'

'All of my complaints are with myself.'

'Not others? He thinks irresponsibility is freedom.'

'No, no. He's a fatalist about the state of the world.'

'And himself? I can see history. Yet don't I take chances?'

'What's your goal?'

'Goal?'

'Why, I take every new existence as it comes. Here's the chart of my personal development. Here's the chart of the world's. Don't you see my position? I've got my work and you've got yours to do. Goal? I have my tasks, and all the armies of Brazil can't keep me from performing them. Ah, that's the difference between the visible and the invisible world.'

'Barcala's illusions of honor and social standing ... and your ...'

'Hallucinations of a melancholy woman?' she laughed.

'What?'

She rubbed my forehead and neck and body with some kind of oil.

'Is this the little prison you've made?' she asked. 'Don't you think the times aren't crucial enough? What little evil have you done? Are you responsible for some wickedness?'

She drew blood from me again and examined it. I saw her with the bark of a plant, leaves, a cluster of small flowers. She shaved the bark and powdered it and mixed the powder in water, leaving the stalk-like leaves and flowers on the table with the mortar and pestle.

'Do you think I'm wasting your blood? Those parasites should be out of your body by now, or be making some sure plans of escape. It's been two weeks. Drink this down and they'll all be fugitives tomorrow.'

She raised my head and I drank the tasteless liquid. In the morning, I got to my feet and went about the day's tasks.

A Cure for Taciturnity

SHE DOESN'T TALK TO ANYONE. I don't know if she can't or won't,' said the woman.

I looked at the girl closely. Her face looked familiar, but she was no one I remembered knowing.

'No, she doesn't say anything,' the woman repeated. 'The people around here think she's an idiota. But I don't think so. See how pretty she is? She's so pretty and has such a beautiful smile. And she behaves like an angel. How can such a child be an idiota?'

Luiza went over to the child and had taken her hands and was holding them.

'Is she your daughter?' asked Luiza.

'No, she's not my daughter. Well, in my soul she is, but it's impossible for me to bear children. Eu não posso ter filhos. I found her. I found her wandering alone. I still don't know anything about her. She is very strange. She doesn't say anything. I don't know where she comes from. I just have a pass for today. I'm a housekeeper from the Carvalho plantation. She's such a sweet child, but she's making everyone in the Carvalho household nervous. They say she's a little witch and are going to put her in the field. But look at her. She's an angel.'

I looked at her, a very pretty child, with a shiny brown face and huge brown eyes. Why did she seem so familiar? She was looking at Luiza.

'She has an overfondness for paper,' said the woman. 'She collects every scrap of paper.'

'What do you mean?'

'She writes things down on them.'

'What kind of things?'

'She won't show me, but I think it's things that happen in the household, and on the plantation.'

The girl kept looking at Luiza with a radiant smile. Her whole face seemed to be glowing with friendliness and some secret.

'She has such mystery,' said the woman. 'She's very sweet. I feel as if it's some blessing that's been given me. To have found her. That it's my blessing. At first I thought she didn't like me or that she thought I was foolish and I tried to make conversations with her. But now I realize that she cares for me, and that she's my blessing.'

'Does it bother you that she doesn't talk?' asked Luiza.

'No, but it's the master and mistress. I'm afraid they'll put her in the field or sell her. And I couldn't bear it if they separated us. I can't have children. She's a blessing. Ah, look at her. Look at her eyes. They say the eyes are the revelation of the soul. Sometimes I just sit and look at her. They say she's a devil or an evil spirit, but she's an angel.'

'Has she harmed them in any way?'

'No. She's just silent. And anytime anything happens, they blame her.'

'What things?'

'Little illnesses their children have. Such things.'

'Do they mistreat her?'

'No.'

Luiza was silent. She was still holding the child's hands. 'I don't know if I can cure her taciturnity,' said Luiza.

'I'm just so afraid they'll send her out of the house. She's like sunshine.'

'What's her name?'

'Jaguara. She didn't tell me. She wrote it down on a piece of paper. I'd been calling her "my blessing" when I didn't know her true name.' My eyes widened.

'She doesn't trouble you with her silence so why should you change her?'

'But I understand. *They* don't. They don't believe she's human.'

Luiza stooped down so that she was the same size of the girl. She still held her hands.

'Take her back home,' said Luiza, standing.

'But if I take her back they'll send her away, or put her in the field,' cried the woman. 'She's the joy of my life!'

'They won't send her away or put her in the field either,' said Luiza with a slight smile.

'You've made her so she'll talk?' asked the woman, brightening, and touching the child's head.

'No, she won't talk,' said Luiza. 'She won't talk, but they won't send her away either and there's no field work for this one.'

The woman looked confused. She went out, holding the back of the girl's head.

Luiza learned some weeks later that the little girl had committed suicide.

'How?'

'By eating earth.'

'Couldn't you have done something? Didn't you say you had a cure for taciturnity?'

'Come on,' said Luiza. 'Let's go and hear Mass. You can light a candle for the girl's soul.'

The Shore of the New World
or Manioc and Couscous

THAT'S CALLED MOURARIA,' said Luiza, pointing to a certain quarter of the city, as we walked on the wide cobble-stoned street. Between the townhouses and commerce buildings one could see down the hill to the sea and the docked ships, Spanish, Portuguese, and Dutch merchantmen. Only black slaves could be seen on the street, carrying loads on their heads from warehouses down to the ships, and businessmen's messengers and apprentices. Men and women 'of quality' occasionally rode by in covered carriages and hammocks.

'It's set aside for Gypsies,' Luiza said of the quarter. 'Oh, maybe it isn't now.'

'What are you talking about?' I asked, as I stepped aside for something that had been emptied into the street.

'Oh, sometimes I'm not sure. He hasn't banished the Gypsies to Brazil yet, so maybe they aren't there.'

'Who?'

'Why, the king of Portugal. He doesn't want them to use their own language. It's always the language. I hope the Gypsies don't steal colored children. The horses and mules I don't care about.'

I looked at her curiously, but did not ask her again what she was talking about. Imagine being with someone who knows what's going to happen tomorrow, and begins talking about it, as if it were an ordinary thing. Someone who knows the future as well as the past and present.

We climbed another hill to the cathedral.

Inside the church I lit a candle for the little girl. Luiza called St George Ogun and said something to him in a strange language.

She touched my shoulder. 'Ayida, come,' she said. 'Let's go sit in the gallery.'

Why had she mispronounced my name? Or was this another new one?

We sat in the gallery and listened to a peculiar sermon. The priest began speaking, not in Latin but in Portuguese, and talking familiarly. He began talking about the Church's place in preserving the Indians and defending them, his concern for their 'human dignity,' that the church should continue its battle on behalf of the Indians. Then he also started talking about the 'kingdom of Angola' 'by whose sad blood, and black but unfortunate souls, Brazil is nurtured, animated, sustained, served, and preserved.' Then he started talking about unhappy souls and happy souls. He spoke some about the Society of Jesus, and about their library in Bahia that he had visited and felt very proud of, and of the importance of the 'learned man.' Then he talked again about the slaves. He said that he was glad that at least the colored people in Bahia were allowed to hear Mass.

When we left, Luiza said, 'He's a very famous priest. Very celebrated. He's written all kinds of books. I suppose he'll spend a couple more years here on the shores of the New World. We're fortunate that he's in Bahia to preach.'

She said nothing about the subject of his sermon.

'I've never heard a priest talk so much and in such a manner about the Indians and the treatment of slaves here, even Father Tollinare didn't, though he taught us all ... Who is he?'

'Father Antonio Viera.'

When we got back we ate manioc cakes and couscous for lunch.

Jequitinhonho

SHE WRAPPED TOBACCO in the leaf of a palm tree. It was the first time I'd seen her smoke.

'I don't smoke very often,' she said. 'Just when I'm fasting. It keeps hunger and thirst away for a time. Otherwise it's not very wholesome.'

She sat on the triangular cushion in the center of the floor. She listened while I reproduced the sounds she had taught me.

'Let your superior soul rule there,' she said. 'Let go of your inferior soul and let the superior soul rule. Now go through the transformations that I taught you.'

I made a small mistake, but it angered her.

'How do you expect to know the past and future history of anyone?' she asked. 'How do you ever expect to learn anything about people and events, whether past, present, or future?'

I was silent. I redid the sound. When I finished, she said, 'Now go study the magic in the written word.'

I got up and went into the study.

About an hour later she opened the door of the study. Behind her walked a tall, brown-skinned, shorthaired Tapuya Indian, dressed in a striped suit, and carrying books. A very handsome man – yet to me all the Tapuyas were handsome people. Perhaps to another Tapuya he was an ordinary-looking man.

Luiza took the books from him and placed them on the table. 'Here's some theology,' she said. 'From the Jesuit College Library. What I want is some mathematics. There are some good ones but they're all on the Index of Forbidden Books. Jequitinhonho, this is Almeyda,' said Luiza to the man. 'If I'm not here, give the books to her.'

'I've already been there,' he said. 'Indians are barred from the School of Military Engineering.'

'Ah,' said Luiza, slapping her forehead. 'Negroes are barred from the Jesuit College Library, but the Indian can go. I suppose you have to have papers to prove you have no mulatta or native grandmother before you can get into the military engineering school.'

The man said nothing.

'Not even Froger's wife could find these books from her French husband's store. Eh, these churchmen. It's wasteful and primitive.'

'I should get back,' said the man.

'Who is he?' I asked, when he had left.

'He works in the Jesuit College Library. The Jesuits brought him up,' she said. 'They're saving his soul. You see, he brings me all the books he's told to destroy. Everything that comes in is checked, examined, rechecked, and re-examined. It's very entertaining, I'm sure, for the examiners. But most of the great works, I'm sure, are destroyed before they even get in the country, probably before they leave the continent. If the biblical prophets had written in these days! And any books on mathematical principles are lost unless they calculate the Ten Commandments or the dimensions of the holy cross. But the Law, it doesn't change with the new enthusiasms of an age!'

'What Law?'

She looked at me with pity and clicked her teeth. 'There's only One Knowledge, One Power, One Will,' she said. 'How do you ever hope to perform miracles, to prophesy, to receive revelations? You might as well spend your days fishing in the river. But come, I'll teach you the one thousand pressure points and how to read the turtle's back. You're laughing, but everything in the world is part science and part magic and part foolishness. But one must have some dignity in one's own surroundings.'

Science, Magic, and Foolishness

TWO WOMEN ENTERED – one was Portuguese, her dark hair tied in a knot on the top of her head – the other woman was fair-haired, with rosy cheeks, and plump, middle-aged – an English woman? A Dutch? The Portuguese woman looked at Luiza with a familiar expression, the other woman with friendly curiosity. The Portuguese woman looked to be in her late twenties.

'Is this the Brazilian mystic?' asked the other woman, speaking with an English accent and in a tone I did not recognize. But I recognized the woman as someone, a person of note, I'd seen during my slavery days, although we'd both grown older, and she, of course, did not recognize me. She'd been to stay at one of the plantations, because there were no inns or public houses like the ones in England.

'Yes, this is Moraze,' said the Portuguese woman. She stepped forward at first boldly. She was wearing a brown cotton dress and a red shawl and brown mantilla. The English woman was wearing a violet satin that buttoned down the front and had lace around the collar, no shawl, but a feathered hat that matched the dress. When the young Portuguese woman saw Moraze's expression – which I could not see, for I was in the corner in back of her, grinding some new leaves we had obtained – she stood silent.

'My name is Mrs Florence Pepperell,' said the woman. 'I'm a writer from London, England. I'm presently writing a book on the natural history of Brazil. Right now I'm working on the flora and fauna, a section of native medicines that make use of plants and animals. This is not my first time to Brazil. I traveled here quite frequently as a young woman. I have already completed my study of the Indian medicine men and women, and I am beginning my work with the Negroes. I'm not new to this country, as I said, but it never stops fascinating me. Everything's here. You're fortunate to be the first that I'll be talking to among the Negroes. I'd like you to teach me what you know. Madam Froger was kind enough to tell me all about you. She's said very good things about you.'

She paused finally. Luiza was silent. I wanted to see her expression, but there was no way. She stayed silent.

The English woman was smiling at first, her teeth very white, her cheeks very rosy, then the smile and the rosiness left. She looked confused and then angry.

'Why won't you talk to me?' she asked. Moraze was silent.

'Why won't she talk to me?' she asked Madam Froger.

The Portuguese woman looked embarrassed, and somewhat apprehensive.

'I'm a very reputable woman,' said the English woman, whose blonde hair had a reddish tint. 'My works are very well known in England and throughout Europe – the Europe that matters – England and France. I say "my works," because I write under the pen name of a man. Otherwise they wouldn't be taken seriously, perhaps not even printed. I've traveled throughout Africa and India collecting material. I have letters to recommend me, but I didn't think I had to show them to you. My works are very well known, my dear. Why won't you say something to me? Why won't you say something? You're probably a quack anyway. You're probably not a "dear" at all. Well, you're not the only black witch in Brazil! I'm sure one of them will speak to me.'

The Portuguese woman's face was 'white.' The English woman turned around and walked out. Madam Froger glanced timidly at Luiza-Moraze and then followed the other one. Luiza closed the door. But still she did not turn around. When she turned, I still could not see her expression, because of the way the sunlight fell on the back of her; it showed over the top of her head and hit my eyes, so that it seemed as if her whole face and body were in shadow.

'I must speak to Madam Froger,' she said. 'She probably thinks she was doing something wonderful for me, to have her friend put me in her *Flora and Fauna of Brazil*. She's a very good person, bringing me books and all, but she doesn't really know me. Should I have let that woman talk to you?'

I shook my head. She was standing very straight and her shoulders were very square.

'Does she think I'd want the people in Europe to laugh at me over their tea? Even their own medicine is a mixture of science and magic and foolishness. Why should they laugh at mine? No, Madam Froger does not know me well.'

'You could have had fun with her, tricked her and told her lies,' I said before I realized it. It was as if I were speaking someone else's thoughts.

'Do you think I'd do that? It's best to tell her nothing. And even that's no guarantee.'

'Of what?'

'She's angry. Who knows what she'll put in her book and blame and discredit me with?'

'So one is doomed either way, isn't one?' said I. 'Whether one does or one doesn't.' I started to tell her that I'd seen that woman years ago and that she indeed did write books and had approval letters, whatever such letters were called that were presented to the plantation owners – yes, 'letters of introduction' – but for some reason didn't want to admit knowing her, or rather, having seen her before. She did not recognize me, and for some reason I didn't want to admit how easily I recognized her. I felt bewildered.

'No, not either way,' she said, then she was silent. I kept grinding leaves.

'Russian furs and vodka,' she said after a moment. She was still standing in the door, looking at me.

'That's what they're unloading down at the dock. There'll be ladies of fashion tomorrow going to Mass, wearing their Russian furs. So silly. And how hot do you think the sun is here?'

The Philosophic Society
for the Advancement of
Free Colored Women

FREE WOMEN FROM THE TOWN OF BAHIA and outlying areas came. They were all well dressed, wearing clean cotton dresses and cotton scarves, or straightened hair, about ten of them. Several of the women, however, wore silk dresses and silk sun hats. Most of the women were medium brown to dark. There were two mulattoes and a yellow freckled woman with red squirrel hair. They sat in the benches in the front room. Luiza had moved a long table into the room and covered the shelves with tapestry. The table was full of books and pamphlets. It almost looked like a sitting room. I served the women tea and cakes. (The only one who said thank you was the one I'll call 'Esquila.') Luiza sat on a bench apart from the others as if she were the leader. Another woman sat beside her with a pen and paper – the club's secretary? When I finished serving the women I set the remaining tea and cakes down on the table beside the books. I stood against the back wall. Luiza looked at me disapprovingly, and so I sat down at one of the benches in the back. I was not used to the company of such women. They all seemed very strange to me and again I felt a sense of bewilderment. There had been 'free' women in Palmares, but these women were 'free' in the Portuguese world and possibly anywhere in the wide world.

Luiza asked if any of the women wished to make any comments before they started.

One of the women began talking. She was an attractive dark brown skinned woman with her hair tied in a bun in the back. I only saw the bun, and the side of her animated face. She began by saying that she was new in Bahia, and that she felt fortunate to be here among intelligent, sensitive, and gifted black women, that she had not expected such fortune, of finding such women to converse and communicate with in this region. There were murmurs of approval and appreciation as she spoke. She went on to say that there were many Portuguese who did not believe that there were blacks of high cultural standards. She said that it made her proud to be a Negro in the company of women of such obvious moral and intellectual achievements and distinction, women who knew and understood the moral worth and refinement of other women, other freeborn women of good character and worthiness.

One of the women said that she had not been born free, but that she had earned her freedom, and that for her too it had been very uplifting to be a part of such a society, that even while she was a slave she had cared about moral and literary and philosophical pursuits, and that she agreed with the woman who had just spoken, that she knew had regained her freedom after much effort, and that not all slaves were hewers of wood or meant to be, that her mother had been a 'tutor' to even her master's children and had tutored her and some of the other slaves in secret. She said that she was grateful for the mental and moral discipline that had been a part of her upbringing and going to Mass every day, even though she had to sit in the gallery, and she was grateful to be continuing that kind of discipline in such a society.

I glanced at Luiza while both the women were talking. She sat silently and seemed to be looking on with a kind of amusement, though not a 'smug' amusement. The woman who sat beside her, wearing a yellow silk sun hat and acting as secretary to the group took notes.

Other women started talking and said much of what these women had said. It was almost as if I were hearing the same woman talk. Each of them flattered the others on their intelligence, sensitivity, their worth and worthiness, and their 'gifts.' What these 'gifts' were I did not know, except for Luiza's, for having worked with her closely for so many months.

However, I had never heard her brag about her accomplishments.

When I listened again another woman was talking about her commitment to the struggles of these women, and that they should each re-commit themselves to each other's struggles, re-affirm their loyalty to each other, so that they might be victorious over the insanities and oppression of their country, the hardships and cruelties, the desperation.

She spoke of her love and admiration and respect for all the women present. All courageous and yet tenderhearted women. She admitted that her accomplishments were more modest than theirs, and thus she was grateful to have been invited be among them. Then she commented on the name of the society. She said that it should be called 'The Society of the Forgotten Women.'

There was a hush, and someone said it was not what they *were* but what they would be!

Luiza had a strange expression on her face. What was she thinking, and why had she made no comments? I had made none, but this was my first such meeting, and I did not feel at home with such women.

'Yes, I think we should keep the name we first chose,' said the woman with red squirrel hair. 'Because our advancement is what the society is about. The contributions that we have made and can make. Perhaps among the Portuguese we are the forgotten ...' She paused as if she was uncertain how to express her next thought. 'However, we should be *mindful* of ourselves.'

One of the mulatto women laughed and then covered her mouth. '... but the society represents our future. Perhaps Maria's mother was not so forgotten.'

Maria started to say something, but didn't. Her cheeks were red.

Then more women spoke of their own intelligence and morality and refinement, and it still seemed as if they were all the same woman speaking. I wondered what these women were really like, what distinguished one from the other, which one I would have developed a fondness for, or deep feeling, and furthermore what were their deepest feelings, the emotions, what was each of them imagining now, what were their daydreams, what memories did each individual woman have, what were their real personalities, what was not being spoken? Then I thought of something. If Luiza could hear the inaudible, then wouldn't she *know*? Wouldn't she know them for their true selves? Didn't her amusement go beyond what the women were *saying*, but what they were *thinking*? I looked at her and she was looking right at me. Did she know? I looked away from her and thought of Scottish whiskey and coconut milk. I got up and served more tea and cakes. Again, the squirrel-haired woman was the only one who said 'Obrigado.' When I served Luiza, she winked at me. I almost spilled the tea.

I sat back down in the back of the room.

One of the women was standing now. She had a sheet of paper and was reciting something.

When sugar was gold men killed for sugar
But now that gold is gold men kill for gold.

She sat down. Some asked if gold meant more than gold. How can gold be more than gold? asked another. I mean as a symbol of something, said the first one. The inability to distinguish between the divine and the ... gold is a thing of the earth. Someone laughed and said it wasn't a poem; it was a thought. But a complete thought, another said. But it wasn't a poem, insisted another. Someone else commented that it did not rhyme, and all good poetry should rhyme. Another said she should have written an essay.

Another woman stood and read the following:

'What Shall Be the Destiny of Truth?'
What shall be the destiny of Truth, while falsehood sweeps
    the land?
Will she be caressed by gentle zephyrs sweet, or buffered
    to a universe of darkness?
I see her! Standing, always in a clear blue sky, touching every hand.

Why is Truth a *her*? Asked someone. Someone else commented that only two words rhymed, hand and land. Another asked to see the poem and told her that she had misspelled destiny and written 'density' and so the poem was really 'What Shall Be the Density of Truth?' although in reciting it she had spoken correctly, pronouncing 'destiny.' Then she informed the others that the woman had signed the poem 'A Free Lady of Color.'

'Why didn't you use your name?' she asked.

'Because I didn't think my name mattered,' replied the woman. 'It's what I *believe*. And I think it can stand for what every colored woman believes.'

The woman with red squirrel hair asked if they were all ready to perform the play that Moraze had written. My ears opened and I sat up straight.

One of the women complained that she did not understand it, though she was quite ready to do it. She knew all her lines.

Another woman said that she understood it quite well. That it was about how one always sees one's enemies as devils, but never oneself. 'Isn't that so, Moraze? Nao e assim?'

Luiza-Moraze had smiled, but made no comment.

'No, it isn't,' said another. 'Nao, nao e assim. It's about the lunatic they call the Mohammed of Bahia.'

Luiza spoke, asking the woman if she'd seen the man.

'No, I haven't seen him. But he tried to organize a Male rebellion and they got him and put him in jail.'

'In jail!' declared Moraze.

'Well, he's not in jail now,' said the woman. 'They transformed him ... I mean to say they transferred him from the jail to the Negro asylum.'

Luiza started to say something else, but did not. She must not have wanted anyone to know her interest in the man. Or had she herself planned to be a part of the Male conspiracy?

'Why are you so interested in the lunatic?' asked the woman.

'She wrote a play about him, silly,' said another. 'All authors have an interest in those people who spark their creative imaginations. It's only natural. That's why she wrote "O Maome da Bahia."'

Luiza nodded, but said nothing.

'Well I think it's an ambiguous play,' said another. 'And Moraze won't comment on it. She never comments on anything. How can we progress in knowledge of the Truth? My poem, for instance, is about a new criterion for superiority, not based on color, but on truthful qualities, and truthful actions. It's important to make comments, assert what one's position and viewpoint are on every subject. Well, every subject that one knows. Viewpoint is very important.'

The woman in the silk sun hat said, 'Ladies, we'd better get started. We have to get back to our respective homes before dark. You know how dangerous the streets are at night. They found another poor soul last night.'

'Who?' everyone asked.

'Some army captain. So you know how dangerous ...'

'Let's not talk about it,' said the mulatto, Maria.

'Does everyone have her part of the play?'

'Yes,' everyone said.

They arranged two of the benches on opposite sides of the table, and the woman in the silk hat stood at the head of the table.

They were all silent and then the woman in the silk sun hat said, 'Some are calling me the Mohammed of Bahia, others are calling me the fool of Bahia. What's your viewpoint on the subject?'

Alguns esta chamando o 'Maome da Bahia,' outros 'o tolo da Bahia' – Qual e a sua opiniao?

Everyone was silent, as the play began.

'No viewpoint?' asked the woman. 'Except for the promulgation of my faith, I am a silent man.' She laughed and said, 'I feel silly saying that, but it's in the play.' She went on. 'To the Africans I say it will preserve their languages and mythologies. They will be able to read and write in a language unknown to the planters.' She added an aside that she herself was a good Catholic. She continued, 'And in that way huge bodies of knowledge will remain open to them, in science, astronomy, medicine, philosophy, many bodies of knowledge ... What can I do? I am surrounded by nothing but Christians and New Christians. In the old days, I would have killed all of you. The only God is Allah. The only victory is victory over the infidels.' Then she exchanged places with one of the mulatto women, who stood at the head of the table. She stared at one of the women and said, 'Look how she's looking with such eyes. Look. Don't you know that silence is against God?'

The woman sat silently. Then there was the following exchange of dialogue that I did not understand, nor whom the characters represented who were speaking the lines, though it in places seemed to be some kind of inquisition.

'It's reckless talk that God disapproves of.'

'And the government. I told them to bring that African and they made a mistake and brought this Portuguese Jew.'

'I thought he was a New Christian.'

'He might have told them he was. But wasn't it that government that showed its disapproval of your reckless talk? Ha ... But why didn't they bring me that little African, either the sculptor or the poet. I'm not particular ... To them it's all the same, they don't care. It's all the same to them.'

'May Allah make you grow in sweetness. The only God is Allah.'

'The only God is God.'

'Do you know what I'd do to you if I was my old self? When I was in the asylum they kept hitting me in my head and I'm not my old self anymore. But you don't know when to expect the expected one.'

'Are you the enchanted Moor?'

'No.'

'What do you have to say, Zerifina?'

'Her name's not Zerifina, it's Zeferina. I have a great deal of respect for this woman. Don't call her by the wrong name.'

'I don't believe her name's either one of them.'

'Well how's one to know anything if she doesn't talk. I remember her face but I don't know her name. How do you know she's even a woman? I don't even know if she's a woman.'

'I thought you'd be as ignorant and brutal as the others.'

'What ignorance, what brutality? It's not my brutality, it's the woman's.'

Then she corrected the line.

'It's not my brutality, it's the world's.'

Then Luiza told her that the original line was correct.

'He thinks because he wrote those forty volumes on the Koran that he's not as ignorant and brutal as you are. I don't trust anyone who mixes religion and blood, and besides that, I've read the work, studied it thoroughly. It's the work of a crazed man, and besides that it's not correct Arabic at all. Most of the final letters and even whole syllables are missing. And there's no order whatsoever to the ideas, if they are ideas – they're irrational, incoherent, and if you permit me to judge, it's the work of a poor, ignorant, fanatic, miserable, insane devil. I'm not sure it's human.'

'God is enough for me.'

'See how incapable he is of argument. If he has any thoughts let's hear them. As for the work, he attempts to combine religion and science in some ridiculous attempt at a mystical vocabulary. Forty volumes?'

'Yes, forty.'

'These are your spiritual ancestors. That's why I've gotten them together.'

'You've gotten us together! Ha!'

'Not me. You said yourself they brought the wrong one. Do you want me to go look for the Africans?'

'I'm an African. I'm enough, and I have the true religion. My religion is the complete revelation of the will of God.'

'He believes his is the only true religion, though he claims he's a convert. Me? I came here and built everything without any Negroes. I worked like a Negro myself. No, I worked like a Moor. Ha. I did everything ... But tell me. Why were your hands amputated by the government? What reckless talk?'

'Not talk really. You see I'm a playwright, a very popular playwright I might add – with everyone but the government and the Catholic Church.

'Social, political, religious satires I wrote. The people adored me, but you see what the attitude of the officials was. I defied them and continued to write, tying quills to my wrists. But this last time they were going to execute me.'

'I thought you were executed.'

'No, I escaped and came here to Brazil.'

'And do you intend to import your satires here? Well, if you do we don't have any theaters or any printing presses, so the joke's on you. Ha.'

'Maybe I'll go to North America.'

'It's up to you, ha. But they're worse on freaks than we are! Ha!

'They're worse on freaks than we are!'

The woman began turning the pages of a large book that was on the table.

'What are you doing?'

'This is the Index of Condemned Books. Don't you recognize it?'

'Well, what are you doing with it?'

'I'm going to continue my playwriting here. And I'm going to put all the subject matter into my plays that is forbidden.'

'Go ahead. You'll be hanged for that. You'll be hanged for sure.'

'I bet he doesn't put subject matter that goes against his religion.'

'You'll be hanged for sure. Tell me, New Christian, when they hang you, will you laugh at them or tell them dirty stories?'

'Not dirty. Satirical.'

'What's the difference between comedy and satire? Did you import comedy or satire?'

'Do you think it's Mohammed I worship and not "The God"?'

'Which one of you wrote The Book of Healing of the Soul?' No one answered.

'You all deny it?'

'It must be no one here.'

'And yes, we've caught you too. We've caught you this time! Yes, we caught you. Who do you think you are, the enchanted Mooress, disappearing like that? Savage! Speak. Why were you brought here? Is it sorcery? Did anyone else see her disappear?'

I do not include the full play here, but when they finished and I laughed everyone stared at me. Then one of the women said, 'I don't understand it either. I read my part but I didn't understand it. Yet I don't laugh at it. It's unwise to laugh at it.'

'Why are you so surprised that he's in the asylum if in the play you have him in there?' asked another.

'I'd forgotten where I put him in the play,' said Moraze. 'I'd forgotten that I placed him in an asylum.'

There was silence.

'Well, we'd better go for today,' said the woman in the silk hat.

'I don't like it because there wasn't any humor in it,' said someone. 'A good play has to have some humor.'

'Yes, there was humor in some places,' said another.

'Anyway, we'd better go,' said yet another. 'You all know what the streets are like at night. Moraze, thank you, my dear, may you grow in sweetness.'

The women put the sheets of paper they had brought with them in a basket in the corner of the room.

All of the women hugged and kissed each other and told Moraze and myself goodbye. They looked at me strangely, though as if they didn't know whether I was also a free woman or Moraze's slave.

One of the women looked at me so strangely that Moraze introduced us, explaining that I was her apprentice, and that at the next meeting I would give a lecture on certain natural things that one could use to maintain health and beauty. The woman looked at me with delight and we shook hands, and then the woman left, telling the others who I was.

'I saw you back there looking smug,' said Luiza when the women had left.

'Me?'

'Yes you,' said Luiza.

She looked at me and winked.

'What is it?' I asked.

She said nothing, and took out the green corn and began preparing dinner.

'I want to go visit him tomorrow,' she said.

'Who?' I asked.

'The Mohammed of Bahia.'

'May I come along?' I asked.

She didn't answer. I continued to look at her.

'Was there something you wanted to tell me?' she asked.

'No.'

'Bring me the cinnamon and coconut.' I brought it to her.

'Do you think all that flattering is necessary?' I asked. 'Why were those women flattering themselves?'

She would not say. But when we were eating supper, the dish she had made, and fruit, and drinking manioc juice she said, 'Don't you think I'd like to finish my work, then play, eat fruit, and exchange tales, like any free woman?'

I did not know how to answer. I just looked at her.

May Allah make you grow in sweetness.

The Negro Asylum in Bahia

THE CITY BUILT THIS ASYLUM in connection with the Church,' said Luiza as we were going there. We turned down a steep, wide, dirt street with many holes in it. 'It would be an easy thing for them to fix good roads here,' said Luiza. 'But they don't care, since they don't have to walk on the street. And God forbid it if any of their daughters did.'

The building looked like a huge gray-brown warehouse with barred windows.

'There's all kinds of sadistic abuse going on here,' she said. 'But we won't see it. They're unchaining him now and leading him to one of the visiting rooms. What of those whom no one is ever permitted to see?'

I pictured a low-ceilinged, dark, dank basement with straw on the ground, and men and women chained by the ankles and the wrists to the wall. The rooms above them were bleak, used by the staff during the day, and used as visiting rooms, and perhaps by the more 'tractable' lunatics. In the 'hole' water was thrown on them when they 'stank' too much, they were kicked when they misbehaved, they were given salts and emetics when they complained of any ailments. And some of them who were perhaps not as recognizably insane as others, or those who had been 'cured' were smuggled out and sold as slaves to tobacco and sugarcane plantations outside Bahia, and in Recife and Olinda and Porto Seguro, and perhaps to the mines at Minas Gerais.

'How does one get to Minas Gerais?' I asked.

'Perhaps one could follow the Sao Francisco River and then go across land to the West when it branches into the Rio do Velhos. Perhaps one could do that. But are you thinking of leaving me already? Are you thinking of going to Minas Gerais? Do you think you've learned everything?'

I said, 'No.' Then I asked her how she had obtained permission to come to the asylum.

'One of the holy fathers,' she said.

'Father Viera?'

'One of them.'

She was silent as we stood at the face of the building. There was no gallery or veranda, but a huge door. The building went up like the huge wall of a mountain.

Luiza knocked. The door was opened by an old Portuguese. Luiza handed him the papers. He squinted his eyes and looked at them, then he led us down one of the dark, narrow corridors. 'Por aqui. Por aqui. Rapidamente.' He unlocked the door to one of the rooms, and we entered. He locked the door behind us. Inside the bare room there was a man lying in a hammock.

'Do you think I need special custody?' asked the man.

He was a dark man with a white turban wrapped around his head.

He looked to be in his fifties. There were strands of gray in his short beard and mustache. He had a huge mole on his left cheek, jutting out at the edge of where the beard began. There were deep furrows in his broad forehead. He was wearing a white shirt and trousers. When he looked at me, I looked away in embarrassment. His eyes were the same as Anninho's – piercing and dark.

'You haven't told me the name of the woman,' he said.

'She is called Almeyda.'

'Call me the fool of Bahia,' he said. I looked at Luiza. She was silent.

'Are you the wife of anyone?' he asked me.

'She's Martinho's wife,' said Luiza, 'and she's looking for him. She's disguised that way, for safety.'

'I haven't seen him,' said the man. 'The world is a savage and brutal place. But Allah is here all the time, to bless me. He doesn't keep them from hitting me in the head. Eles me batiam na cabeca o tempo todo. They hit me in the head all the time. But look at me. I'm still whole. I still look good.'

'When did you last see him?' asked Luiza.

'I haven't seen him in a very long time. He's very unfaithful. Do you think that if I had led the others in a holy war, my son would have joined me?'

'I thought you had made peace with him that you had joined *him*.'

'Do you think I would have killed him in the holy war? No, I would have locked him up with the Indians until the war was over, and then made him serve his God. But he won't come to his senses. I haven't seen him. I haven't seen him since he took up with the Palmaristas.'

'Palmares was destroyed,' said Luiza.

'I know that,' said the man. 'I knew it would be. Didn't I say so? The only true rebellion is a Male rebellion. Allah is against them. Didn't I say he would be?' He looked at me. 'Why isn't she saying anything? She must be a shy woman. Você é tímido? Você é uma mulher tímida?'

'Do you want me to help you escape from here?' asked Luiza.

He was still looking at me. 'How old are you? You must be about thirty.'

'Yes,' I said. 'I'm almost thirty.'

'*He's* thirty. This world is a savage place. Savage and brutal. The only God is Allah.'

He looked at me with large fierce eyes. 'Are you a Christian woman?'

I said yes that I was Catholic.

'Católica? Ah, if I had not made my peace, I would have killed all of you.'

'How long have you been here?' Luiza asked.

'I don't know. And these others. What can I do? This is how they've made their peace with the world. How can I gather forces when I'm surrounded by lunatics and New Christians? How can I make warriors out of them?'

He stared at Luiza fiercely and then at me fiercely. 'None of them know the sacred language. I try to teach them the Koran and they close their ears. So what do I do? I don't know how long I've been here. I'm writing about the Koran. Forty volumes. And translating it into Portuguese, but they're so stingy, they won't give me any paper!'

He started to say something else but the guard came and unlocked the door and motioned for us to leave.

'Venha comigo. The Mohammedan should rest now.'

'I'm not a Mohammedan. Do you think I worship Mohammed? It's not Mohammed I worship, but Allah. I'm a Muslim. I'm of the tribe of Mecca. There's only one God. The God who feeds me with his spirit and protects me from the likes of *you*!'

I stared at Luiza as we were leaving, but she wouldn't look or say anything.

'You should have known him before,' she said solemnly when we were outside. 'You should have known him when he was waging his holy war. But he would have killed us both then. But still he was a very wise and thoughtful man.'

'I don't understand,' I said.

She said something about belief and not color being the significant thing.

'No, that's not what I'm talking about,' I said. 'I thought that once I found him I'd know where Anninho was. Whether he's wise or thoughtful or a fool, I thought he'd point me toward Anninho. I don't know what I'm going to do now. None of what you've taught *works* – not for me. Oh, I'm capable of healing. I can make medicines, but I don't have any real power. I can't command the supernatural. None of my visions have told me where *he* is. I can't predict where he'll be tomorrow. I want to leave. I want to search for him in the real world, in the visible world.'

She was silent.

'How much of the real world is invisible?' she asked. I was silent.

'You are very ignorant,' she said, when we had returned home. 'You are too ignorant to leave now. What do you *know*? The time must be right. Haven't I taught you the importance of time in everything one accomplishes? O tempo é mais importante do que qualquer outra coisa.'

'I must go, Luiza. I'm very grateful. I'll always be grateful for what you've taught to me. The world is not as fearsome a place.'

'The world is always a fearsome place!' she said, turning away from me. 'You have learned nothing. Você é uma mulher tola.'

'Tomorrow, early in the morning I'll leave,' I said. 'And I have learned much and am grateful to you. Perhaps I am a fool, but I'm a more knowledgeable fool.'

I don't know if she heard me or not, for she had gone into the study and locked the door.

The paje's daughter leads me to the Indian woman and the old man who still sits in the shadows of his long hut. The same barbaric ritual. I touch the women. Their skins become smooth and supple. They are middle-aged and still very beautiful.

'We are saved,' one of them says.

But they continue to sit in front of the hut, as if that is the only place they know.

'More is needed,' says the paje's daughter. 'You have cured their bodies but that is not sufficient. Their wills must be cured.'

'I only have the power of bodily healing,' I reply. 'I am not yet able to heal the spirit.'

'Curandeira, and your will?' she asks.

I touch their forehead and eyes and the women rise and leave.

'Now they are whole women again,' says the paje's daughter, laughing.

'But I'll never *know*,' I said. 'I should have followed my first plan, to pretend to be a traveling storyteller, to go about the country looking.'

'You are so ignorant,' she said, her eyes blazing. She made furrows along her nose and forehead. She frowned and squinted at me. 'You are too ignorant to leave me. You know nothing. I'm more than an ordinary woman.'

'You taught me how to heal myself with medicines found everywhere. I know the tapir's trails. I know how to follow rivers. I have a horse and a good disguise. Now I also know how to observe nature and make good use of it. Perhaps I am still an ordinary woman, and an ignorant one according to your knowledge, but to those who don't know the power of plants, perhaps I too am a master of magic. Those who don't know that there are sounds in the air, that the untrained ear cannot hear, will think that I can hear inaudible sounds. Those who fear their dreams will think that I have some power over them. Those who observe in bad light, will think that I'm a magician, because I watch in *good* light.'

'You want to be a fraud as well as a fool.'

'No, no, you don't understand. I *am* an ordinary woman, but you have taught me things that will be useful in my journey to find him. And perhaps this is better than being a contador de histórias.'

'You're a poor, ignorant woman to leave me now. With me, there is still so much to learn. Ah, you foolish woman. I'd bring him back to you with such ease.'

'All these months I've asked you to give me some vision, and you haven't, or you couldn't.'

The old man, hearing them go, comes out screaming. He has not relinquished his embrace of the straw woman.

'What can be done?' I ask.

'Nothing,' she says.

I leave them, afraid to look back.

Have You Always Been a Woman Alone?

THROUGHOUT THE REST OF THE EVENING, Luiza would not speak to me.

After a few hours she came out of the study, but she would neither look at me nor speak to me. She triturated dried parts of certain animals and plants and filled empty bottles. I offered to help her, but she waved me away, so I went into the study and got one of the books and brought it out and sat on my hammock to read. She passed by me, seeing me with the book. She looked at me fiercely. I thought she would grab the book away from me, but she didn't. She went into the study, got her own book, and sat across from me but said nothing. Once we looked at each other at the same time. I smiled, but she sulked.

'Luiza,' I said after a while. She did not look up. 'I've enjoyed staying here. I've learned more from you than anyone. What you've taught me, and from the books, even the forbidden books. I've really felt at home here. I really have. You've been very kind to me. Perhaps after I find him ...'

'No you won't.'

'What?'

'No you won't,' she repeated.

'Does that mean I won't find him or I won't see you again?' I asked, after a minute.

She still did not look at me.

'It means what you say it means. You're the wise one,' she said. 'A mulher sábia, that's what I should call you. Or you think you are.' She looked up at me. 'You're the woman of *will*.'

'I can't accept your *will*. You're not being fair.' She laughed a bit, then was silent.

'If I stayed here any longer, it wouldn't be a home, it would be a prison. I'd feel like those lunatics chained in the dungeon. Or it would be like being your slave.'

She twisted her mouth to the side.

'Have you ever ...' I began. 'Have you always been a woman alone? Have you ever been in love with anyone? Have you ever loved anyone?'

She looked up at me, but was silent. She looked back down at her book.

'Azamor,' she said quietly.

'What did you say?'

She was silent.

Was he the one who taught her?

The Explorer

SHE LOOKED AT ME, though she kept her hand inside the book.

She said, 'He wanted to be an explorer and discoverer. I shouldn't say he wanted to be – that's what he was, what he became. Ele era um explorador. A city of the Indians in the interior of the country. He was the slave to a Portuguese explorer. There were Spanish and Portuguese on the expedition. He was more than a slave really, though he was owned by that one. He was a guide and an interpreter for them among the Indians. He knew all kinds of Indian languages and dialects. He could pick it up just like that. Even the Aimores who have always been the enemies of the Portuguese and every other tribe, would talk to him. He knew their language, and he had healed many of their people. In fact, he was the one who got the expedition as far as they went. He was more than their equal. *I'll* say it, though history won't say so. Their storytellers won't tell that tale.

'Do you know why I liked Anninho from the beginning? Because he reminded me of that one. Don't look at me so. There was nothing that you imagine in our relationship. Azamor was all.

'In the wilderness, in the bush there is no distinction between slaves and freemen. They are all slaves, all freemen – and any claim to superiority was in their work, their actions, their faith.' She looked at me carefully. Their *will*.

'Azamor was a medicine man as well as a guide and interpreter. He was useful in aiding them and the Indians. The Indians began to look on him, however, with the greatest distinction and began to follow him, because of his cures. The white men, because of the hardships of the land, finally turned back. But since he had such "luck," his master told him to go on, to send reports, while he returned to the coast, and finally back to Portugal. So Broadilla returned. Broadilla was his master's name.

'So Azamor went on exploring the interior, getting further and further and further into the "lost cities of gold" of the interior. As cidades de ouro that they built legends of.

'Why did he not accept my prophecy? He was neither my teacher nor me his. But he was esteemed by the Indians and he felt he would be esteemed and honored by the Portuguese as well – indeed, by the whole world.

'He continually sent messages, reports, maps, drawings, plus details regarding the characteristics of the Indians, and how to establish friendship with them and be assured of a good reception. As he traveled, he cured many of them and made many medical discoveries as well. And they exchanged knowledge. He taught them many things and they taught him. Many things that I know are because he knew. I was the one who was sent his medical notes and not *them*, although they got all the maps and drawings and other detailed reports. But how would they have received those medical notes? They were not concerned with the native knowledge, ours or those of the Indians, only the gold. Eles foram hipnotizados por ouro. Ouro. Ouro. Ouro.

'After he discovered the golden city that everyone had been looking for, he was betrayed. They claimed that the Indians killed him, but the Indians were very civil to him. You see how civil they are to me? But he picked up an Indian dialect just like that!' She snapped her finger. 'Even the Aimores!

'This is what happened. You're an old storyteller. Listen. After he discovered the territory, the master who had never seen the place claimed discovery, and published and disseminated all the information he had received from Azamor. Everything. Except, of course, the medical notes which came to me. But he probably wouldn't have known what to do with those. He might have even destroyed them as worthless knowledge or forbidden knowledge.'

She was silent for a long time, then she said, 'All the districts the master claimed to have discovered, Almeyda, he never even saw! He never laid eyes on that interior land. All the maps, the reports, and the documents were Azamor's. He discovered the place everyone was looking for. The golden city. When Broadilla presented his report to the crown, there was no mention of Azamor. Even as a guide and interpreter. No. Everything went to Broadilla's credit and honor. Everyone thought he had explored the territory.

'What did they fear? I'll tell you. An alliance with the Indians? That's all the story I want to tell you. It's the same tale in the end. Betrayal, capture, execution. It's the same tale from the beginning to the end. É a mesma história.'

She would not tell me the whole story. But why was she looking at me as if I were somehow to blame? I could not take my eyes off her strange, fierce ones.

'Why was he called Azamor?' I asked.

She kept looking at me, then she said, 'I don't know his true name. Some called him "do Broadilla," naming him after his master, as they do with slaves, but he refused that name. He called himself after a place that he was born in Africa, a town in Morocco called Azamor.'

'Then he too was a Mohammedan like Anninho?' I asked.

'Don't call them Mohammedan, that's depreciativo. Muslim or Catholic, it's not his faith that matters, it's his *deeds*. I have no proof of his accomplishments, which are the property of the master, the same as the slave, only notes on medicinal plants and herbs and other wonders.'

The Departure

I STILL BELIEVE YOU'RE IGNORANT and foolish,' said Luiza, as she walked with me to the door at sunrise the next morning.

When we were at the door, she kissed my forehead and said, 'Take shelter from bad weather ... Travel *as if* you had such powers.'

She kissed my forehead again and we embraced, and then I went outside and untying the horse, rode off.

I turned down the hill leading to the docks. Even though it was so early, there were slaves on the road, walking down the hill, carrying grain, textiles, Brazil wood, and manufactured products to the foreign ships and those that only traveled along Brazil's own coast. If not the Bay of All Saints, I was thinking, what bay? What coastal town? If he had not been captured, if he escaped and the maritime plans had continued, should I travel along the coast, or go into the interior? *Had Luiza pointed me toward the interior by telling me the unfinished story about the explorer? Should I go to Minas Gerais or travel along the coast to Porto Seguro?*

Ahead, a gang of newly arrived slaves, chained together, were walking toward me. I spurred the horse around and rode back up the hill, and through the commercial district to the edge of the city. Was it not a crime in this territory for an African to be on horseback? I left the city, and dismounting, led the horse into the forest, following the trail of a tapir, going westward, into the interior.

The Russian

I CAME TO A CLEARING AND A SMALL STREAM. I did not see the man until I was upon him – a black-haired man sitting on a rock. He was wearing a loose white blouse and black trousers and high boots. When he looked up he remained silent, but looked at me with some interest. He had one of his hands in his tuft of black curls. I stopped the horse, ready to turn around or present free papers. But there were those who stole solitary freemen and returned them to slavery.

Then he asked me in Portuguese but in a foreign accent whether *I* spoke Portuguese.

I told him yes.

'Are you a Brazilian?'

No one had ever asked me that before. I answered, 'Yes.'

'I'm from the Russian ship that unloaded furs and vodka. Well, it's not a Russian ship. Dutchmen built it. They imported Dutch shipbuilders from Holland. It cost nine thousand rubles. Absolutely no one is supposed to be where I am, but I don't think they'll search for me. Maybe they'll get a vagabond seaman from the dock or a nigger and take him back. They're making some repairs now, and then they'll go on. It may not be a year before I'm back in Moscow. It's a hard life for Kalita to be a seaman's wife. I should write her a letter, and then she'll fall in love with another one, instead of waiting for my return. An extraordinary woman, though she thinks she's an ordinary one. She could have a chance to marry a Moscow doctor. I'll ask her to forgive me. Maybe she won't be able to, but then she'll love someone else and I'll stay in this strange city, or go to the gold field. Everyone will call me a scoundrel but things will be more hopeful.

'Sometimes new circumstances demand a new code of conduct. If I were working in a factory in Moscow making cannons and bells, things wouldn't be so. I'd have the old demands and the same tasks and I could be faithful to the woman. Sometimes I dream she's in someone else's arms anyway. But Kalita's not. She's not like that. I have to think hard about it, before they miss me. But I knew she would be better off with a new love, who could spend regular time with her and someone who has some authority over his own life and doesn't have so many people telling him what to do. I know things would be different and better. She'll call me a scoundrel at first, my whole family will call me a scoundrel, but then she'll find some new love – someone who'll protect her from dangers and difficulties because he'll be living with her in the same city. A doctor or a professor or an engineer. Do you think that's possible? She doesn't look like a peasant. Sometimes I think they made a mistake and gave her parents the wrong child. And she reads a lot, everything she can get her hands on, and she knows the real meanings behind the words, so it's in my opinion that she'll make a good wife for any worthy man. She reads Russian poetry and Russian history.

'She's a kind and melancholy woman and a dreamer and she needs someone to take care of her all the time. At first when I was going away to sea she pictured it in her mind that I was going on some great romantic adventure and then when I returned to her ... but I disappointed her. I was different, but not in the way she imagined. It's a brutal life aboard a ship, full of confusion and uncertainty. I returned a more complex man, but she couldn't see it. Her dreams of my adventures and heroism. I didn't fit her "idea." I'm a man of humble beginnings, and they made some mistake with her and gave her the wrong people. I'm not a mean-spirited man. I'm very kindhearted, but I have memories and fears like any other man. They'll all call me a scoundrel – my friends and relatives, my brothers and sisters and nephews.

'Some professor who has any common sense will take notice of her, or some influential people will spot her melancholy and thoughtful looks.

'That's the expression that all the ladies of high birth and quality have.

'Someone will see her and see her inner nature because it shines in her eyes so. She's very intelligent, but very truthful and sometimes lets her feelings get ahead of her, and she doesn't have any judgment.

'I don't know what to do. If I go back I won't be free to choose my own life. Maybe I'll stay here and become a rich man and not lift a finger. They say that all the rich men here never lifted a finger. There I'm nobody, but here I've seen common men give a wink and have work done.

They say all you have to do here is get seven niggers and the government will give you a sugar plantation, and it's not held on lease from the king but a man's free and clear. Seven niggers aren't too many, do you think? They say it goes all right at first but then all the niggers want to be freemen and run away, and so you have to buy more, every twelve years.

'I can do that and then write to her and tell her that I *am* in a new situation in a new country, and that nobody tells me what to do. I will send her the money and if she loves me she will come. I'm suspicious and timid because it's the kind of life I've had to lead, but this is a new country with new ideas and new opportunities for a common man. I'll stay here and wink and get rich. I'll have slaves, and honor and feel like a human being again, and smoke tobacco, and drink imported vodka from Russia, and shave my chin like the tsar does. Have you ever seen such a free man?!' he asked.

He jumped up and ran into the stream and began scooping up water and tossing it onto his head. Then he looked despondent suddenly.

'But maybe she won't want to come here. She's a woman of tradition and believes in her links to the past. Maybe she won't leave her relatives and come to a new country,' he said standing in the stream. 'They make it hard for a man to think what to do, because they tell him when to get up and when to sleep. It's only the upper classes who can think for themselves and the high nobility. For everyone else it's "take counsel, take counsel." Running a sugar plantation must be a complicated business. You wink, but you have to know what to wink for. You have to have knowledge behind the wink. The only thing I know how to do is on a ship. And I don't like smoking tobacco. They say it's not what goes into a man, but what comes out of him that befouls him.' He looked at me sharply. 'They say this country's full of Jews and Jesuits.'

I said yes, there were a lot of Jesuits, but that Jews were not allowed, unless they were converted Jews, 'New Christians,' but it was widely felt that they still practiced Jewry, but not in public – covertly and in secret. That is, I added, there must be plenty of secret Jews in the country.

'I don't want to cut my beard or change my faith,' he said.

He paused and looked at me, but not so sharply this time. Was he admitting that he was a Jew? And did he know what I was the way he spoke so freely about getting seven of us and the vocabulary he used?

'No, I won't cut my beard and I won't change my faith,' he repeated. 'Having nothing to do bores me. I can't sit around being patient. I can't wink and get others to work. I need excitement and trouble, and not knowing when there'll be calm weather or a storm, or when some captain will hit me in the head and fuss about nothing.'

He looked suddenly happy. He ran his hand through his curly hair and fingered his beard, and then coming out of the water, and with the expression as if he were off to perform some brave deed in the world, though he did not know whether it was bad or good, he left in the direction that I had come. He walked as if he were slightly off balance, then he straightened himself and headed into the woods. I walked the horse into the stream and let him drink.

An Honest Woman

WHEN THE HORSE HAD FINISHED drinking, I crossed the stream and continued. I remembered that one of the plantations we had visited, Luiza and I, was not very far, so I headed in that direction. I saw an old woman coming toward me with a basket of clothes on her head. I did not recognize her at first, but then I realized that she was one of the 'nurses' that Luiza and I had visited. She set the small basket down on the side of the path and held up her hands. I stopped the horse and got down. She did not call me by name, but spoke of me as Luiza's friend. She asked me where I was going. I told her that I was on my way to – Minas Gerais, I said with surprise.

'Why isn't Madam Moraze along?'

'I'm going on my own,' I said.

'You must come and stay with me awhile,' she said. 'I like your company. They won't notice a new face. Tie your horse up in the woods and let him eat grass, and come along with me. I've got to wash these clothes first. No, they won't notice a new face. And there's a strange fellow there and the mistress has given us all a holiday so we can hear him.

'Some traveling preaching man. The Father doesn't want him there and thinks he's misguiding everyone, but the mistress does. Want him there, I mean. Last night him and the Jesuit got into a row. He calls the man a wizard and a fortune-teller – maybe even a fortune-hunter – but the mistress wants him to stay.'

'If it's a holiday, why are you washing clothes?' I asked.

'These are my own and my niece's,' she said.

I went with her to the stream and helped her wash and rinse the clothes, then we walked back together over a path covered with thick vines. I checked the horse again who was content eating sape grass. I walked with the woman back to her hut, which was on the edge of the plantation, near the forest. There was a crowd around the porch of the big house. We left the clothes in her cabin.

'Are you sure it's all right?' I asked.

'Yes, today they won't notice a new face, the mistress is so taken with this new visitor.'

'Does the mistress run the plantation?' I asked.

'Well, she might as well,' said the woman, as we stood at the back of the crowd, looking up at the veranda. 'She's married to a Frenchman and he lets her have her way ... He's not as charmed by this visitor as she is, folks say, because he's from Europe and is used to every kind of new idea. But me? I don't know. I don't trust anyone, but I'll listen. The priest is the only one who detests him, so he stays in the chapel whenever that one's talking, and won't even let him go in there to pray, in spite of the woman.

'He's a French Jesuit. They're supposed to be the strictest kind. He calls this man a wizard and a fortune-teller or a fortune-hunter, a voyante and a chasseur de fortune he called him; I've learned a few of the Frenchman's words myself with him as the master – and not a holy man. I don't know, because I don't trust anyone.'

She stopped talking and I stared at the woman sitting on the veranda, her black hair piled up on top of her head in an elaborate hairdo. She was wearing a blue sundress, and there was a sunbonnet in her lap. She was the same young woman who had come into the shop – Madam Froger.

I watched her as she sat slightly forward, looking engrossed, almost as if she were mesmerized.

I finally looked at the man who was wearing a long robe like a monk's robe; his hair and eyes were very dark, like a Turk's. He was very handsome. He talked very smoothly, and looked about the crowd as well as at Madam Froger. He had that kind of expression and the kind of voice that made it seem as if he were talking to each person particularly. I heard him say something about 'Quietism' and his field of vision being larger.

'You're not a part of history,' I heard him say. 'But do you want to be a part of history? What is history, but the story of devils and demons? It is only devils and demons that play the leading roles in the Devil's plays.

'Me? I do not want to be on the stage of the world. It is the sinners who are permitted. You should feel grateful that you have not been given any roles, that you are outside history, as another man shall reveal someday, and that you don't have to swim in the sea of blood.'

He paused for a moment, looking at everyone gently, caressing them with his gaze.

'You are fortunate souls and should be happy souls. Now let's everyone quietly experience the love of God and the love of love, the love of each other. Friends, listen. Do good deeds today and tomorrow. Don't contemplate the good deeds, but let them take hold of your soul joyfully unpremeditated and by surprise.'

He asked if there were any Tupi among the crowd and then he tried to say the words 'Friends, listen' in the Tupi language.

He looked at everyone with supreme kindness, and then turned to the woman, went over, and kissed her hands.

'Since he's been here, every morning has been a holiday,' said the woman, as we walked back to her hut.

I wanted to glance back to see what the man was doing, but dared not, as I did not want to be noticed now that the crowd was dispersing.

'Me?' she was saying, as we got back to her hut. 'I don't trust anybody. No, I don't let anybody take my soul by surprise.'

She laughed. We went inside and she sat in her hammock, while I sat on one of the mats on the floor. She had taken a long pipe from out of the corner, the kind my mother and grandmother smoked, and was smoking it. She offered smoke to me, but I said that I didn't.

'Are you on your own now?' she asked.

'What?'

'Have you won your independence? Sua liberdade?' I looked at her not knowing what she meant.

'Are you ready to cure by yourself?' she asked.

'Oh,' I said. Then I said, 'Yes,' not telling her that I had left prematurely.

'Then when they come tonight, you can tell me what to do,' she said. 'There is one poor child I want you to see. I don't know how to help. It's not the body. It's a thing in her head that's all wrong. I think she'll go mad.'

I told her that I couldn't stay till that night, that I had to be going before midday.

'They won't know that you're here,' she said. 'Nobody bothers me.' I was silent.

'Madam Moraze will have to help you, I'm not allowed to,' I said. She looked at me with surprise, then curiosity, then anger.

'I have never known a cure doctor to refuse to cure anyone. I'm an honest woman. I don't understand all the mysteries of this new world, but I think you lie. I think you are a menteuse. I don't want you to stay with me. Go on.'

'But I . . .'

'Go on away. Allez-y,' she said with anger. 'That's why you're leaving, because Madam Moraze discovered some falsehood and sent you away. I'll send for her and have her get rid of the evil that you've brought. I don't trust you. Menteuse. I don't want you to stay here.'

I got up. I turned back and started to explain that I had left prematurely on my own, that I was not sure of my powers and that I might do more harm than good, especially if it was not a physical healing. I did not know how to drive devils away. I knew the rituals, but for me they were empty. I did not know what they meant or how they worked.

I started to explain but she started calling me horrible names in both Portuguese and French and some African language I didn't understand.

'Menteuse. Menteuse. Allez-y. Allez-y. Mwongo wa kike. Mentirosa. Get on with you!'

It seemed like she was calling me names in every language. As she started up from the hammock, I ran out the door and into the forest.

Herbs and Long Nails

I UNTIED THE HORSE AND MOUNTED. Keeping the sun at my back when I was in the clearings and examining on which side of the trees the moss grew when I was in the forest, I continued westward, though I had no idea how far or how long I would have to go to reach the Sao Francisco River. I ate herbs, berries, and oils. I slept on the hammock that Luiza had rolled up and thrown across the back of the horse, tying it to the trees the way Luiza had done, scraping the grass away, and lighting a small fire underneath.

There were special herbs that Luiza had taught me to burn in these fires to keep strange animals away during the night. One night I found a spider crawling on my belly. The next night I rubbed my body with a certain oil which I had forgotten about – an oil that was odorless to me, but that Luiza said was unbearable to all kinds of insects. I rubbed it on my body and into my hair. I rubbed it on my face and eyelids. I noticed that my fingernails had grown very long since the time I had been living with Luiza. I smiled, because when I was a girl, I remembered my mother would cut my nails whenever they got too long. I would complain because the mistress and her daughters' nails were long and I wanted mine so. She explained that it was a fashion with them, how they displayed their social standing. I laughed, and tying the hammock securely, and the horse nearby, I climbed into it and went to sleep. I did not know how many leagues I had traveled in the several days. I did not know why I had made up my mind to go to Minas Gerais, rather than traveling along the coast, or going to Parahyba, to the New Palmares. But hadn't someone said – hadn't Luiza said – that Anninho had made contacts with the Africans who worked in the mines? I vaguely remembered her saying that.

Turiri

I TIED UP THE HAMMOCK and lay it across the back of my horse and was about to continue my journey, when a young Indian of about eight or nine confronted me, asking partly in Portuguese and partly in Tupi and partly in Spanish what I was doing there. He stood across the path I was about to travel. He was wearing only a white cloth about his loins and holding a spear he had shaped from the branch of a tree.

I told him that I was on my way to Minas Gerais, to the mines there. 'You're going the wrong way,' he said. 'You're on the road to my village.'

I noticed that he was not holding the spear as if to challenge me, but that it pointed to the ground. He kept his arms folded and his legs spread across the path. From a distance it looked as if his eyes were swollen and they slanted downward, but as I drew nearer, the liquid that I took to be sweat or recent tears, was a kind of pus coming for the eyes. He had an eye infection.

I asked him if I could come closer.

'You don't need to come closer. All you need to do is to turn around and leave my town.'

I too spoke in part Tupi and part Portuguese telling him that I wanted to come closer because there was something wrong with his eyes and I wanted to examine them.

'My eyes are good,' he said. 'I can see you are Anhanguera.'

He was telling me that I was an 'evil spirit' or an 'old devil' and that I would trick him.

'Will you take me to your mother or your father and let me explain to them why you can't see as well as you should, and that perhaps I have the medicine that will cure your eyes.'

'You'll make them worse,' he said. 'Turn back. I'll tell them that I saw Anhanguera and forced him back.'

'I'm not a man, I'm a woman,' I said.

'Evil can come in the form of a man or a woman,' said he.

I was silent. Then I asked, 'If I let you lead the horse into your village, may I follow you?'

'You have a horse,' he exclaimed. 'Only gods ride horses!'

'Hold your hand out and I'll give you the reins.'

He held his hand out and as I placed the reins in his hands, I stooped down and looked at his eyes. They were badly inflamed, as if someone had thrown Malagueta pepper into them. Pus was running from the corners of them. When I was close to him he started to rub his eyes, but I took his hand away.

'You'll make them worse,' I said. He led the horse in and I followed.

When we entered the village, there were several longhouses like the one that Maite lived in. Sitting in the doors of them were women, weaving something.

'What are they making?' I asked the boy.

'Coxonilhos,' he said.

Horse blankets.

'Why are they making horse blankets if they have no horses?'

'They are making them for Zune. Zune has told them to.'

'Is he the chief?'

The boy laughed and said, 'No.'

'Where are the men?'

'They're hunting.'

'For Zune?' I asked.

'Yes, and for the rest of us.'

'Where's your mother?' I was asking when one of the women saw us and got up and ran to the boy, took his shoulder, and pulled him away. She stared at the horse and then at me.

'Mother, she has a horse,' said the boy. 'She wants to cure my eyes.'

She told him to go bring his grandmother. He walked toward one of the long huts. The woman was very young, not yet twenty. Her breasts were bare, and she too was wearing only a cloth about her loins.

'Who are you?'

'My name is Almeyda. I was troubled by your son's eye infection. I have seen that before, and I have cured it. I wanted to offer my help.'

'If my mother has not been able to help him, you cannot,' she said. 'But I'll wait for her to come.'

She was a very beautiful woman, but she did not look at me directly now. She stood with her shoulders hunched and rounded, and narrowed her eyes and stared at the ground. She stayed standing that way and remained silent until the boy came back with his grandmother.

The older Tupi woman looked at me straight in the eyes. I had expected a very old woman, but this one was in her late thirties, her hair was long and black as the girl's, her face as smooth, but tighter and firmer. She kept her steady gaze, then her eyes fell to my waist. She touched the whistle and the gourd that was tied there. She looked at them with surprise and recognition. When she finished examining them, she looked up at me.

I told her in Tupi that I was a friend, and that I only wanted to be of help to the boy. I saw him rubbing his eyes again, but I did not move his hands away. I looked at the woman waiting for her to speak. For a long time she said nothing, then she said, 'You're wearing the same thing *he* wore. Come on, let's see what you do.'

Tying the horse to a nearby tree, I followed her into the long hut. The boy and his mother came behind us. The grandmother and I placed mats on the floor for the boy to lie on. I asked the grandmother if she would go into the forest with me. She said yes.

'Do you have a moringa?'

'Moringa?' asked the woman.

'A water pot,' said the boy in Tupi.

'Yes,' said the woman, getting it from the corner.

She was silent, but she watched me carefully as I gathered the herbs I would need – some herbs to make tea, others to bathe his eyes in. Every time I got something she would ask me what it was for and what it was called. 'That one I don't know,' she would say of some things. Others she would have her own names for and tell me which ailments she would procure them for.

'Copaiba. I have known copaiba for a long long time.'

'Oh, for that I give strong tea and oak bark, and keep the limbs warm. A very dangerous plant ... Oh, that plant, just touching it can be fatal.' She showed me a plant that ate insects and some small animals.

'I've heard of such carnivorous plants,' I said.

'There are some that eat men,' she said. 'But each time we see one we cut it down.'

When we finished gathering the herbs, we went to a nearby stream and filled the pot with clear, cold water.

When we returned the boy was still lying on the mats. His mother was kneeling beside him. She smiled when we entered, and moved aside, but remained sitting and kept her head lowered.

The grandmother made tea from the roots I gave her. She gathered the materials that I would need, another jug and a basin, and a mortar and pestle. I washed my hands with water, cacao pod ash, and carap oil. I put a mat under the child's head to lift it more. I cleansed the area around his eyes with a damp cloth. I tilted his head to the side and held the empty jug under his head. Then I raised the eyelids and slowly put drops of the solution I had made into his eyes. The excess water ran into the jug. I told him to close his eyes while I dried them. For several days I cleansed his eyes and his grandmother gave him the strong tea to drink. After the first few days I placed a certain oil on the linings of his eyelids so that he would coat his eyes with it.

During the nights, I slept in the hut with his mother and grand-mother.

After a week his eyes cleared and were very bright. I scrubbed his hands with the solution I had scrubbed my own with and explained to him that he should not rub his eyes. If they itched or bothered him I showed him how to close them and touch the eyelids in certain places to avoid infecting them. I showed him eye exercises and pressure points around the eyes.

After the boy was cured, another woman brought a child to me, one who was having fits of convulsion. She explained that the child was always restless and unable to sit still. That whenever she was asked to perform any simple task, to pick up something or carry water or even to feed herself, that she would start making jerky movements, she would be silent at times, other times laugh or cry about nothing. The only time that she would stop behaving so was when she was asleep. But even then sometimes she would wake up, squinting her eyes, and twitching.

I went into the child's hut. She was quiet, but behaved as if she didn't see or hear me and kept her hands clenched tightly together. Whenever she would begin to cry I would place a cool cloth on her head. I asked the mother what kind of food the child had been eating. She told me, and I told her from now on only to feed the child a certain list of items which I named for her. I gave the child a special emetic. I waited with the girl until the fever was gone. Suddenly she recognized my presence, looked at me with bewilderment and fell immediately to sleep. All I could tell the mother was to give the child the foods I had prescribed, to boil the root of a certain plant, to cool the 'tea,' and whenever the convulsions occurred to rub the child's body with the cool solution and to keep a cloth soaked in it on her forehead. After a few days, whenever she would do this, the convulsions would stop immediately and the child would sleep. After a week, the convulsions did not recur.

Her mother was very grateful to me and others began to come, bringing their children and themselves.

I had been there for a month when I met the one they called Zune.

When the women had finished making the horse blankets, they gathered them together and took them somewhere. Each time they finished the blankets were gathered and taken away. At first I did not notice it, but then I noticed the gold strands that were interwoven with some sort of bark or plant fiber.

'Where are they taking the blankets?' I asked the mother of Turiri, the young boy I had first cured.

'To Zune,' she said.

'Who is Zune?'

'The white one who came and gave us our religion.'

I asked the woman to explain to me but she would not say more than that to me.

'May I go along with them?' I asked. 'The next time they visit Zune.'

She was silent. Whenever she spoke with me she still kept her head lowered, and there seemed to be a perpetual melancholy look in her eyes.

'I don't know,' she said finally. 'They'll have to ask *him*. My mother will have to ask *him*.'

The next time the grandmother told me that I could come along, that perhaps I would not be able to see him, only if he chose to reveal himself to me.

All of the women entered the cave taking the coxonilhos.

I remained outside, standing with the grandmother, whose name was Itacolomi. (Her daughter's name was Itambe.)

I could not see inside the cave, but there was someone or something there in the darkness.

When the women delivered the blankets, they came out and stood beside Itacolomi. She went inside, stayed a moment and came out. She came up to me and said that I might enter.

I could not make out his features in the darkness of the cave, only the paleness of his skin and hair.

'Who are you?' I asked. 'They call you Zune.'

'I'm the founder of their religion,' he said.

'I've heard of their myth of Zune.'

'Then I'm their myth made flesh.'

'I don't believe so.'

'You're the one who's been healing them.'

'Or they've been healing themselves,' I said.

'How long do you plan to remain here?'

'Where do you send the blankets?' I asked.

'I don't send them anywhere.'

'Do you send them to the coast, where someone takes the gold threads out?'

'They're my blankets. Why should I send them anywhere?'

'Because you're not Zune.'

'If I tell them to send you away, they'll do it. If I tell them to destroy you, they'll do it. If I tell them to take your certificates and sell you back into slavery when the next bush captain comes, they'll do that. They follow my commands as they would Zune's. So am I not Zune?'

426

'You're some vagabond who's decided it's easier to rob these people than to go to Minas Gerais and get your own gold.'

'I've been to Minas Gerais. There's nothing but quarrels and fights and murders ... Is it true that you can live on herbs and oils?'

'Yes,' I said.

'Any word from me that you're Anhanguera, the evil one, and you won't escape alive,' he said.

'I've cured many of them,' I said. 'What have you done?'

'I'm their spiritual ancestor. They have faith in me. No matter what you were to tell them about me, they wouldn't believe you. They'd continue making their horse blankets and their esteiros and bring them to me.'

'Do they make their esteiros with straw and gold?' I asked. He said nothing.

'You're nothing but a pirate,' I said.

He began to laugh. 'That's what I was, before. Well, first I was in the Spanish fleet, and we were captured and I was forced to work in the galley of a Turkish ship. A pirate ship defeated them and I managed to convince them to let me join them. So you see I know all about robbery and abduction, and I'll bet you do too. But I was at Minas. I found a gold mine. I turned in the dust and collected certificates for it. And then when I went to claim my gold, they refused to give it to me, pretending that the certificates were forgeries. So you see, I know everything about robbery. You know. But tell them, and what do you think they'll do if you tell evil lies against their Zune?' He laughed. 'Or even have the slightest suspicion that you disapprove of me? Anyway, gold means nothing to these people. It has no meaning for them. They don't know what to do with it.'

'They're good human beings, who think you're really Zune,' I said. 'Gold has no meaning for them. They don't know what to do with it.'

'Why shouldn't they bring it to their Zune, who gives them his blessings and protection? You'd better go, and don't let them even slightly suspect your heresy!'

I left the cave. When I came out all of the women gathered about with many exclamations, telling me of the honor that I had just had having come into the presence of Zune, that I was the only 'stranger' that he had allowed in his presence, and that from that moment, they would trust me completely with any ailment that they might have.

When I got back to the grandmother's hut, I asked her in what way might I go to Minas Gerais – what was the best direction.

'Are you going to leave us?' she asked.

'Yes.'

'You're the only stranger Zune has allowed to stay here.' I was silent.

'I don't know the way to Minas,' she said. 'But I will ask Itambe's husband when he returns.'

I was silent.

'What's wrong with you?' she asked.

'Nothing,' I said. 'How long will it be before he returns?'

'I don't know.'

I laughed. 'So you would keep me here till a time you don't know?' She said yes.

'I'll stay till tomorrow,' I said.

She tossed her head to the side, but was silent. I sat down on the mat and watched her grandson Turiri carving a miniature fishing boat.

'Does your father make large ones?' I asked.

'Yes, he makes very big ones,' said the boy, looking at me with his large bright eyes. 'Sometimes he ties two or three of them together.'

'Is there a river near here?'

'Yes, that way,' he said pointing. 'I've walked there with my father.'

I said nothing. I had been near the Sao Francisco for nearly a month and had not known it. I looked at the grandmother, but she did not speak. I wondered what would happen if I told her about the imposter in their sacred cave.

'Are there any here who do not believe in Zune?' I asked the woman.

'No,' she said.

'What would happen to such a one?'

'I don't know. We would ask Zune and Zune would decide.'

I watched Turiri carve onto the side of the little boat – Almeyda, my friend. He fixed it so that I could tie it around my waist with the medicine gourd and the magic whistle.

ALMEYDA CONTINUES HER JOURNEY, OR THE NEW PALMARES

The Stranger

WHEN I CAME TO MY SENSES I was sitting in a clearing in the forest. I remembered saying goodbye to Turiri and his mother and grandmother, and the others in the Tupi village. The horse was some distance from me, untied, eating sape grass. I was sitting on the ground, but on a mat of sape grass. In the near distance, though I could not see it, I could hear the violent rushing of a river. I looked around me in bewilderment, reminding myself of one of the children I had cured. Who had I not seen or heard? I remembered Moraze, the medicine woman, had told me of a certain plant that enabled one to change one's location suddenly. She had never shown the plant to me, nor did I ever see her making use of it anywhere in my presence. What had happened and why was I sitting here now? Had I fallen from the horse and struck my head?

'You mustn't eat very much of it,' he said suddenly, from behind me. 'It's like poison if you eat too much at one time.'

He had a basketful of a long yellow fruit. He was a black man, dressed in a dark shirt and trousers, a quiver of arrows and a bow strapped across his chest. He knelt down in front of me and offered me the fruit. He looked to be about my age or a few years older. His forehead was very high and he wore his hair brushed back. I smiled at him and then realized that he saw not the young woman I was, but the 'old one' I had disguised myself as. I took the fruit and thanked him, but looked at him cautiously.

No, if he were a bushwhacking captain hunting fugitives, I was thinking he would not reckon an old woman to bring much profit.

I was going to bite into the whole fruit, but he showed me how to peel the skin away. I took a bite. It was very delicious.

'What happened to me?' I asked.

'You don't remember?'

'No. It's as if I just woke up a few seconds ago.'

'I don't know. When I found you, you were here. I thought perhaps you had fallen, but there were no bruises. Your eyes were open, but I don't think you saw or heard me.'

I ate the fruit and looked at him. 'That's a fine horse,' he said.

Would he steal my horse, I wondered. I kept watching him. 'Where are you on your way to?' he asked.

'Minas Gerais,' I said. He laughed.

'What?'

He didn't reply.

'The gold fever,' he said with another laugh. 'Are you a newly emancipated slave gone to seek your fortune?' he asked.

'No,' I said, but did not tell him my purpose for going there.

'Why else does one go to a mining town?' I said nothing.

'This is very good but very harmful if you eat too much of it,' he said.

'What does it do?' I asked, thinking about the fruit Luiza had given me and not wanting to repeat its effects.

'Sometimes it causes fever, if you eat a lot. Though one is very good for the health.'

I ate it cautiously.

'You'll have to eat very fast in Minas Gerais,' he said.

'What do you mean?'

'Everyone eats fast in Minas. They eat fast and they don't talk. I suppose it's because the food is so expensive and so scarce.'

I ate slowly.

'How do you plan to go there?' he asked. I told him.

'As simply as that?' he asked. I told him how far I'd come.

'How do you expect to cross the river?'

I said I did not know. He said that there were barges going across at certain points, that charged heavily, but besides that it was not the best way for an African, as many of them were also man-sellers.

'How do you suggest I cross?' I asked.

He smiled. He got up and disappeared in the woods. Should I get away from him now? I did not. I waited. He came back leading a chestnut-colored horse.

'I've got my own pony, why should I steal yours?' he said, as if he'd read my thoughts.

I was silent. I stood up.

'Are you okay? Are you dizzy or anything?' he asked, touching my forehead.

'No,' I said, backing slightly away from him. But wasn't it an old woman he saw?

'I'll take you to a place where you can cross the river,' he said, 'if it's true Minas Gerais is where you want to go. After you get across, things should be easier. Now that gold has been discovered there, there are many trails leading that way. It's not like it was in the days when I first came to this country.'

I asked him who he was.

'I haven't asked you who you are, now have I?' he said, as he helped me to mount my horse, then he mounted his.

'In some of the Spanish territories, it's a crime for a black man to be riding a horse, unless he's traveling on some expedition with a master.'

I said nothing.

'We're strangers,' he said as he started off and indicated for me to follow. 'We're strangers who perform the rites of kindness of strangers. There's nothing about me that you need to know.'

He guided me to the place where the water was shallow enough to cross. He rode across with me and pointed me in the right direction and indicated one of the trails I might follow. He touched my elbow and nodded goodbye. When I turned I saw him galloping back across the river. I wondered if things might have been different if I had not been disguised so, then I turned into the trail.

An Anaconda Keeps Her from Taking That Trail

I TIGHTENED THE MUSCLES IN MY LEGS against the sides of the horse and pulled back on the reins. I saw it before the horse could be startled and throw me. It was lying across the branch, hanging down in front of the path – olive green with black blotches. Some anacondas got to be as long as thirty feet or more, but this one was 'small,' about twenty feet. I turned and galloped back toward the river. It was not a poisonous snake, it was a constrictor – it killed its prey by constricting it to death. I stood on the bank of the river breathing heavily. When I had been with Luiza, the medicine woman, I had not feared them, because she would always take control. I started to re-cross the river but pictured a huge anaconda, lying along the bottom, waiting. First entangling the legs of my horse, then me. I rode along the bank, and I took a trail that led into the mountains.

Mauritia

PATCHES OF FOREST covered the mountain. As I rode through the thickets, I kept looking from branch to branch expecting to see an anaconda coiled along one of the branches. I rode through a rocky stretch of mountain. Below were grassy plains, forest, the river. I rode through a thicket of Araucaria pine, and gathered some of the kernels for food. I met no one on the trail. I heard the water of a mountain stream and headed toward it.

Standing in the stream with her skirt tied up about her thighs was a woman, rotating a bateia, a kind of basin. Her hair was longish and wild, and she was about the shape and size and complexion of my mother, so that when I first saw her I thought it was her, or a vision of her, except she was in her middle thirties and my mother, by that time, would have been much older.

I was upon her before she looked up. Her eyes were widely spaced and shaped like almonds. She had a high forehead and cheekbones, and a solid chin. Her mouth was slightly open and what I took to be a gap in her teeth was gold. The front of her dress she had pulled between her legs and had it tied in the back, so it looked as if she were wearing a strange kind of pantaloon.

She looked up, but I did not startle her. She kept looking at me but continued rotating the bateia.

'Where are you off to, old woman?' she asked me.

'To the mines,' I said.

As the water ran off the side of the bateia, particles of gold dust settled at the bottom.

'What will you do there?' she asked. 'You're too old to lie with a Mineiro.'

I looked at her.

'Do I offend you?' she asked. 'Don't look at me so. What are you going to do there?'

I told her that I was an itinerant storyteller.

'And I'm an itinerant prospector,' she said with a laugh, her gold tooth sparkling in the sunlight. 'I search for gold in the streams around here. All of the best gold washings are claimed by the Paulistas and the Portuguese, but I make enough for a day's meal.'

'And do you lie with the Mineiros as well?' I asked.

She raised an eyebrow but was silent. She circled the bateia again. 'This way I make enough for a day's meal,' she said coldly. She stopped rotating and looked at me. 'But I was owned by one of them. He thought I had luck for finding gold. Luck for him, but not for me, eh? No luck for him either. But why should I tell you the story. You're the story-teller, tell me one.'

I was silent.

'Well, that's the worse one I've heard,' she said with good humor. 'It's not very good. Is that the way you always tell them?'

I said nothing, then I laughed finally.

'I'm Mauritia,' she said, coming out of the stream, holding the basin carefully, though the gold was barely visible.

'I'm Almeyda,' I said, jumping down from the horse.

She looked at me with curiosity, then said, 'Come home with me. I can't offer you anything but toucinho and beans.'

'I can eat the beans, but I can't eat fat bacon.'

'That's all I have. Tomorrow I'll go buy beef from Father Guilherme.'

I apologized, saying that I had not meant to offend her – that I was grateful for her hospitality – that I had simply meant that I had made a vow not to eat meat of any kind.

'Me? I can't live without meat,' she said. 'In Minas it costs twelve drams for a chicken! Father Guilherme sells cattle to them at prices you can't believe. That's why he's so rich, with that and lending money at high interest.'

'He's a priest?' I asked.

'A secular priest. A Paulista,' she said.

'Is that who you buy meat from?'

'Yes, there's no one else around. He has a cattle ranch on the banks of the Sao Francisco. Over that way. Tame and wild cattle too. He's got a dairy and a place where they salt-cure hides. His house looks like a palace and everything is well-built and very sturdy. A lot of fences. I buy meat there and Mina cheese, when I have the money. The rest of the time I live on fish – which I hate – and what I can get from the woods. Miners send their slaves all over the woods looking for food.'

I was expecting a hut made of sticks and mud, but this was a small house made of timber from the Araucaria pines I had seen.

Inside was furniture made from the same wood.

'I thought you were "itinerant," ' I said. 'This looks as if you've settled here.'

'This is my home, but when there's no gold washing here, I go all about,' she said.

She set the basin down on a table, and untied her dress, and let the hem fall to her ankles. She put her bare feet into a pair of leather sandals.

She went to the fireplace, and stirring the pot, brought me back a bowl of the beans, and herself the beans mixed with toucinho.

I ate and took out the Araucaria kernels. 'What's that?' she asked.

I said that they are edible.

'I see those all around everywhere.'

I handed one of them to her. She tasted it. She nodded. I gave her another kernel.

'So you never told me why you are going to Minas,' she asked, looking at me carefully.

'I'm looking for someone,' I said. 'But I can't tell you about that.'

'Slave or freeman?'

'I don't know.'

'They're not supposed to sell anyone slaves here from the coast, but they do anyway, and they work them very hard. A man of my age looks yours. A man of your age wouldn't last very long, not unless he belonged to a tavern keeper or a gambler.'

'I didn't say I was looking for an old man.'

'A son, or daughter?'

I was silent.

'The men they send to the mines, and the women they take to live with them. They believe that African women are lucky, that they have

436

some intuition about where new gold deposits are. There are hardly any white women in Minas.'

'You said that you lived with a miner.'

'Yes. A cowboy, a Spaniard from Paraguay. But the Paulistas, they detest foreigners coming here. Even the Portuguese to them are foreigners, and Brazilians from the coast. There is always some little war over gold deposits and washings. Who knows that it won't grow into a big one? It's all jealousy and suspicion. It keeps getting worse for strangers, but they keep coming. It gets very wild. So the vaqueiro from Paraguay was disliked and was murdered. His murderers are still there, mining.'

'They haven't been punished?'

'No, it happens all the time. Once a very prominent man from the coast was murdered. And *his* murderers are still here. They'll be free as long as they stay away from civilization.'

'How do I get to the town?'

'Follow the trail in the direction you were going. You'll probably find some little mining camps before you get there, but that's where the churches and public buildings are. Some of the gold miners have houses that look like palaces, but others live in huts made of mud and sticks, spending in food whatever they get from the mines, and buying slaves on credit.'

I asked her how did one buy a slave on credit.

She was silent, then she said, 'That's Father Guilherme's other business. He sells slaves to the miners on credit, eighty-five percent interest. They're still paying for the slaves, even when they don't have them anymore.

'Some of them would have been better off if they'd stayed on their sugar farms, but others are very rich and ride around in carriages ... But if you're looking for an old man in Minas, he's been worked to death by now.'

I looked at her. How could she talk so easily about such matters, as if they were everyday stories? Perhaps these stories and worse, were everyday stories in Minas.

'How can you trade with that Guilherme if he's such a bad man?'

She was silent, then she said, 'Ah, I could refuse to trade with the devil, I could refuse to do that.'

I waited, thinking she would offer me some excuse, but she did not. Why did I feel myself being drawn to her?

'You're the storyteller and here I am doing all the talking. Tell me a story,' she said. She had finished her beans and fat bacon and set the bowl down on the table. She was watching me.

'Is it all right to bathe in that stream?' I asked. 'I haven't had a bath in a very long time.'

She said yes, that there was a part of the stream that ran behind the house that it would be safe for me to bathe in.

When I came back, she laughed at me. 'I thought a young woman would return.'

'How did you know?'

'When you got down from the horse,' she said. 'Though I have seen spry old women, I thought I did not know the whole story. You'd be luckier to keep your disguise if you go to Minas.'

I said that I would replace it before I left there.

'If you had not jumped down so, you would have fooled this one. Yes, replace it or someone will steal you surely ... Who is it you are searching for?'

I felt afraid even to say his name out loud, as if that would make my finding him more difficult.

'Is it all right, Mauritia, if I don't say?'

'Do you *know* he's there?'

'No. Not for sure. Perhaps he might be. How long have you been in this territory?'

'Twelve years.'

'Maybe I'll tell you his name, but not right now.'

'How do you expect to fool anyone, being so taciturn, so close-mouthed?'

'What?'

'You're a storyteller.'

'So far you're the only one who's asked me to tell a story.' She was silent. I told her the story about Zune.

'That's a very bad story.'

'It's true.'

'I don't like it.'

It was very hot inside with the heat from the cooking fire. She finally doused it.

'Did their men ever return?'

'What?'

'The husbands of the Indian women.'

438

'No, not while I was there.'

'I wonder what else he commands of them?'

'I suppose that's so.'

'Yes,' she said. I was silent.

'Is it a lover you're looking for?'

'My husband. We were married in a place called Palmares.'

She showed an instant of recognition, but did not comment on the name of the place.

'It's a very good business here to be a speculator in food supplies,' she said suddenly. 'It's better than owning a mine. You're assured of success.'

'You haven't had a new master after that one?' I asked.

'Yes, I've had several since that cowboy. They all got in fights over gold deposits. Now everyone knows Mauritia. But they don't think I'm for luck for anyone. There're stories about me all around Minas. Now no one will take me even on credit. So in that way I am free.'

I looked at her with fascination.

A Quiet and Conservative Man

IT WAS A LARGE RANCH, with many buildings, fenced in grassy plains with cattle grazing about a thousand head.

'He's a very quiet and conservative man,' she said, as we walked up the long road. 'If you didn't know about his business, you'd think he had some quiet "flock" somewhere. There's a rumor that he's got Aimore blood in his veins, but who knows?'

He was sitting on the porch of the mansion wearing a large, flat, black hat and a cassock. He had very thick black straight hair worn in bangs sticking out of his hat. There were dark shadows around his eyes, his nose was blunt, his lips full, his chin broad and wide.

Mauritia handed him the basin. He emptied the dust into his palm, and seemed to be weighing it, then he put it in a bag he carried around his waist.

'This will only buy chaque,' he said.

Mauritia frowned and complained of the 'dried meat.' He said the Minieros had already cleared out the 'smoked' and that he had not yet had any more slaughtered.

The priest kept staring at me, but didn't say anything. He spoke rapidly to an Indian woman who was standing in the doorway. She disappeared and came back with a small bundle, which she gave to Mauritia. The chaque was wrapped in cured hide.

The priest kept staring at me. Suddenly I wondered if she'd brought me to 'trade.'

'A lot can be done with that one,' he said. 'We're very low in that product.'

'She's one of Tamarutaca's women,' she said.

He looked away from me and folded his hands in his lap. Mauritia bid him good day.

'Who's Tamarutaca?' I asked when we were back on the trail.

'Someone he fears. A man whom he fears.'

'Who is he?'

'He's very courageous. Guilherme believes he's the one who steals the slaves and frees them, and that he raids the cattle. Perhaps I should not have used his name. But if he thinks you're Tamarutaca's woman he'll let you come and go as you please.'

'Have you seen this man?'

'No, no one has. But every time a slave or cattle is missing he thinks it's Tamarutaca. Perhaps he thinks I'm Tamarutaca's woman too.'

'I thought you said they thought you weren't luck for anyone.'

'For one of *them*.' She laughed. 'But I've not seen this Tamarutaca. How could I be his woman?'

Mauritia's Search
for Tamarutaca

MAURITIA ATE THE CHAQUE FOR DINNER, while I ate greens and a small fish I'd caught. I knew the good fish now from the poisonous ones. We sat in wooden chairs at a wooden table.

'Did one of your murdered masters build this little house?' I asked. She nodded, but was silent.

'That Tamarutaca,' she said. 'Perhaps Father Guilherme made him up. Who knows? Perhaps hostile Indians in the territory raid his cattle and let the slaves go, and he's made up this man. But if there is such a man I'd like to find him and know him. I'd like to search for him in the same way that you're searching for your mystery.'

I said nothing, then I said, 'But I know of *his* existence. I knew of it.'

'Tomorrow I'm going to search for more streams. The streams I wash aren't very lucrative but there's no trouble, no danger – no quarrels over them.'

'I need to talk to some miners whom he might have contacted.'

'Slaves or masters?'

'Slaves,' I said.

'Sometimes I meet with those who are hunting for game with their masters. Tell me his name.'

I still would not.

'You'll have to trust someone to know it, if you're hunting for him.' I said nothing.

'Well, it's good to be cautious,' she said. 'One should be cautious of strangers. How do you know I'm not Father Guilherme's woman, waiting to entrap you?'

'Because he would have given you more than chaque,' I said with a laugh.

She was silent.

'I know a woman in Minas, who works for a tavern keeper,' she said suddenly. 'She knows everyone. She would know who to talk to. We'll work our way there and go see Mariana.'

'Mariana?' I asked.

'What? Do you know her?'

'No, no,' I said. 'I've never been to Minas.' She took a bite of the tough, dried meat.

'We'll leave tomorrow,' she said. 'I don't have a horse, but I suppose we can double up on that one.'

I nodded.

'And you should disguise yourself again. I'm known in this territory, but I can't protect a handsome woman everywhere with the name of Tamarutaca ... Let's catch and salt some fish before we go.' I thought she would say for our meal on the way there, but she said, 'It sells for seven or eight drams of gold in the city. We'll take beans and maize and salt too. The last time I was there someone traded a slave for maize and gave a pound of gold for a flask of salt.'

'It seems as if one gets gold easier being a street vendor in Minas than a prospector.'

'But it's dangerous, too. Imagine being murdered over a flask of salt?'

'Or a handful of maize?'

'None of it makes any sense. Sometimes miners will hear of a better hole and desert one mining camp for another. I go to the streams that have been deserted.'

We fished and salted the fish and prepared bundles of maize, salt, beans. Then we slept, and in the morning bathed in the stream, and I put on my 'old storyteller's' disguise. Mauritia wrapped the bundles in hide, and we tied them along the back of the horse. Mauritia went back inside and came out with a bow and arrow strapped across her chest and carrying a musket. She was wearing trousers. She handed me the musket, which also had a leather strap.

Mauritia climbed on first as she knew the way to Minas. Slinging the musket over my shoulder, I rode behind her.

After we had traveled a league, she explained that we would have to make a detour because the streams in the forests there were full of piranha, meat-eating fish, and electric eels. I pictured us riding up to the piranha-infested streams and myself jumping off the horse and gathering obira paramacaci, feeding it to the piranha, so that they dropped dead from the poison. I pictured Mauritia looking at me with wonderment. But I did not suggest that we continue on the piranha-infested trail. Mauritia steered the horse in another direction.

'A lot of people, who don't know the trails, perish even before they reach Minas. If it's not from poison fish and insects or wild beasts and snakes, or attacks from hostile Indians, it's from starvation. It's three weeks from the coast to Minas, and some hear of the mines and start off without anything and don't know the trails. I don't know how you've managed to come this far without incident.'

'Neither do I,' I said.

Aldeia de Visita

Y*ou shall have no other gods before me.*
*'You shall not make for yourself a graven
image.*
'You shall not take the name of the Lord your God in vain.
'Remember the Sabbath day, to keep it holy.
'Honor your father and your mother.
'You shall not kill.
'You shall not commit adultery.
'You shall not steal.
'You shall not bear false witness against your neighbor.
'You shall not covet anything that is your neighbors.'

We heard the children's voices reciting in unison, but saw no one.

*'Hail, Mary, O favored one, the Lord is with you. Blessed are you
among women, and Blessed is the fruit of your womb, Jesus.'*

'What is the meaning of this?' I whispered to Mauritia, when the voices
had silenced.

'We're nearing an Indian village maintained by the Jesuits,' she said.
'They're going through their daily prayers.'

She stopped the horse as we listened to them recite the Lord's Prayer,
first in Portuguese and then in Tupi.

When they finished, Mauritia dismounted and so I did. We walked
the horse to the edge of the village.

The children sat in rows on the ground, while two Jesuit priests conducted their prayers. She tied the horse to a tree and put one of the hide-
wrapped bundles under her arm.

We walked behind the children to one of the longhouses.

The woman had her back to us, so that I only saw her straight back
and the long gray and black hair. She was kneeling before a portable altar
which had on it an hourglass and a bell. Spread on the floor around her
was devotional literature – a bible, and some Jesuit pamphlets.

Inside the longhouse were rows of hammocks, mats on the floor, pictures of saints on the wall. Some 'official,' others crudely drawn, looking more like painted birds than saints.

We waited silently until the woman finished her prayers. She kept praying and coughing and praying. Then she turned.

I thought she would be startled to see us, but she wasn't. She quietly smiled and sat down on one of the mats to the side of the altar. She coughed.

Mauritia went to her with reverence and handed her the hide-wrapped package. The woman thanked her and, without opening it, set the package down beside her. She indicated with her eyes for both of us to be seated.

'Who have you brought with you this time?' she asked. She coughed again.

'This is Almeyda,' she told the woman. 'And this, Almeyda, is Palmyra.'

The woman nodded to me and I nodded to her, but we did not speak.

Mauritia started talking to her in Tupi. Did she not know that I also knew how to speak it? Though she did not say anything that I could not have heard, or would have been offended by. She told the woman about her last visit to Father Guilherme and how he had had his eyes on me, but that she had told him that I was Tamarutaca's woman and that he had been dissuaded. The old woman laughed, showing a set of perfect teeth. Then she told Mauritia that this Tamarutaca reminded her of a Guiacuru Indian that she knew when she was a young woman. She admitted shyly that he had been her 'lover' though their respective tribes had not been on friendly terms and were still enemies, because the Guiacuru Indians were nomadic horsemen who had never accepted the white man's presence and were always fighting them. The stories she would hear of this Tamarutaca, even though he was an African, reminded her of what the other one would have done as a young man.

'How did you meet him?' asked Mauritia.

'Eh, I found him in the woods, wounded, and I nursed him back to health. I healed him. But he was opposed to everything. The Guiacurus were always fighting white men but they were joined by the Paragua Indians and would attack them.'

'Was he killed?'

'I don't know. If not, he's an old man now somewhere, and I bet he's still fighting.'

I wanted to ask the woman why and how did she 'break' with the man, but I did not want to speak Tupi, letting them know that I also spoke it.

'I'm a medium,' said the woman. 'Even with all these spiritual exercises I'm still a medium.'

Mauritia asked her what she meant.

'The Paragua and the Guiacuru are joined together now fighting against the white men, but when the Guiacuru disappear it won't be the white man's doings. The Paragua and the Guiacuru will become enemies. The Guiacuru will be defeated, not by the white man, but by other Indians.' She coughed. 'Do you see what I mean? He hated me for saying that,' she said, looking at me. 'But I can't help it, it's the truth. And all the Jesuit exercises in the world won't keep me from knowing it.' She looked at me again, then she looked at Mauritia. 'So if he's an old man, he's still fighting, and if he saw me now and recognized me, he'll say, Eh Palmyra, it has happened! Not yet, I'd say, but this is only the first half of a difficult century. Oh, but wasn't he disgusted with my prophecy. So now I flee from prophecy! I flee from it. But all the Jesuit exercises in the world won't tell me it's not so ...' Then she coughed and looked at me and said in careful Portuguese, 'Do you have something for my cough?'

I nodded. Mauritia looked at both of us with wonderment. I handed Palmyra some dried leaves from a pouch I carried and said that she should make tea from it.

She looked at me. 'Did you think I wouldn't recognize you?' Now it was my turn to look at her with bewilderment.

'But I have, haven't I?'

I nodded, though I still looked bewildered, because I did not recognize this woman. Did she recognize me behind the disguise, or with it? Then I wondered. Perhaps it was not me she recognized, but my grandmother? I looked at her.

She began talking in Tupi again, looking from Mauritia to me.

'Those priests are so silly. They never leave each other's sight. It's a law. They're supposed to visit the aldeia regularly, but they're not supposed to leave each other's sight. What do you think they're afraid of?'

Now we heard the children singing a religious song. 'How long are they staying this time?' asked Mauritia.

'I don't know. But the grass never grows under their feet. But what's it to me? It's nothing to me. When they finished the Ave Marias, the Lord's Prayer, the Ten Commandments, the catechism, and the Creed, they send the children out into the woods to gather cacao, cinnamon, vanilla, assia, and sarsaparilla for them to take back to the coast. Why do you think that's so?'

We sat silently listening to the religious music.

'The two priests, they're feeling like peacocks now,' she said.

I looked at her. It seemed strange that she had all their devotional literature, and at the same time continued to make such comments.

'They stopped me from raising young eagles,' said the woman. She coughed. 'They thought I was worshiping them, but I wasn't. I was only using their feathers to decorate myself and the children. Do I say they worship the cacao plant because they always want gatherers for it? Do I say they worship cinnamon? ... Ah, if it had not been such an amarracao, such a tangled-up love affair?'

The woman offered us canjica, a dessert made of grated green corn, sugar, cinnamon, coconut milk, and butter. She made the tea for herself and drank it in my presence.

'Eh, they always come in pairs and are never parted. They don't think anyone saw them, but I did. With tobacco and sugarcane brandy ... If he's an old man he's still a warrior. He thinks that I betrayed him. But what did I do but talk, and tell him what I knew to be so? He's mistaken. I'm as constant as any good woman, even if I don't wear a European petticoat.

'But what is time but a serpent chewing his own tail?'

'Why don't we follow the Sao Francisco?' I asked Mauritia.

'No, no,' she said. 'There are too many estates all along the river. I'd rather travel through the jungle. If the wild beasts attack me for trespassing, I know they'd do the same for anyone. Besides it is a shorter distance to go this way, though one has to know the jungle.'

More Regarding Tamarutaca

THEY SAY THAT TAMARUTACA was raised by Guiacuru Indians. That's why he has that strange name. There was a convoy of canoes coming from Porto Fez, full of gold and provisions and slaves, and when they were attacked by the Paragua Indians and the Guiacuru, everyone was killed, the black slaves and the white masters, and one of the Guiacuru found a little bundle and took the child home to his woman. The Guiacuru woman named him Tamarutaca, which means mantis shrimp. Ha, but he's no mantis shrimp now. Others know him as ...' The horse gave a jolt over the rough ground and she steadied him, and so did not finish.

'As who?' I asked.

'Some know him as Aguiar and others Jaguarete, but in these parts we call him Tamarutaca. Perhaps he's no real man and whenever any slave escapes or any cattle is lost, they say it's Tamarutaca who's responsible.'

'How do you know so much about him?'

'People always know much about legends. I wish I could discover he's a true man.'

I told her about King Zumbi and Palmares.

'Yes, I have heard of that one, but he was executed, wasn't he?'

'Yes, to prove to us he was not immortal. But some feel that he only disappeared and will return again.'

'They always think that.'

'What do you mean?'

'That such men will return and return and return. Eh, it's the old serpent chewing his tail again.'

I frowned.

'And this one you're looking for, is he of the same sort?'

'No,' I replied, but did not make any other remarks.

'What does that woman know of you? She recognized you. Where have you known her before?'

'I don't know,' I said. 'Perhaps she knows someone who looks like me.'

'You're very secretive. I wonder how many secrets you are carrying, but I like you.'

I smiled, but said nothing.

A Cloud of Mosquitoes

MAURITIA DISMOUNTED and gathered huge palm leaves and tied several of them together with vines. She gave one of these to me and kept the other.

'What's this for?' I asked, as she mounted the horse again.

'The mosquitoes are denser here. Sometimes there are clouds of them. This will fan them away. I have some mosquito fans made of thin pieces of wood, but I forgot to bring them.'

Again I did not tell her of the special remedy – an oil one could use for that purpose. I thanked her for the fan made of palm leaves.

We rode on, swishing the mosquitoes. Another time she stopped.

'What is it?' I asked.

'We can't go this way.'

'Why?'

'There's quicksand.'

I was silent. Suppose I had ridden on alone? I wondered how many people had disappeared on that trail.

'How do you know the trails so well?' I asked. 'But I suppose you've traveled it often.'

'Yes,' she said.

After traveling a while, she said, 'Get our mosquito fan ready, there's a cloud of them here.'

We reached a deserted mining camp – cloth tents and huts made of wood and straw.

Mauritia said that we could spend the night in one of the deserted buildings.

'How do you know there's no one here?' I asked her, as we had stopped in front of and entered the first building we'd come to.

'They'd be lined up in the stream washing for gold,' she said.

That was just what she did after she had tied up the horse. She took the basin. I walked down to the steam with her, as she rolled up the legs of her trousers and entered the stream. I stood on the bank while she dipped and rotated the basin. Gold powder settled at the bottom.

'This is a perfectly good stream,' she said. 'But that's how they do. Just a rumor of a better one and they're off. Let's stay here and work this one for a while. I'll teach you how to pan for gold.'

'All right,' I said.

The Mining Camp

WHEN MAURITIA WOULD TIRE I would rotate the basin, watching the gold powder settle to the bottom. We stayed in the camp for several days collecting the dust, which Mauritia divided with me. Perhaps Mauritia would have stayed there longer, but I was impatient to get to Minas, and after the third day she said that we would leave in the morning. We stayed in the first hut that we had found, the one at the edge of the forest.

'You're very nervous and impatient,' said Mauritia.

'Am I?' I asked.

'Yes,' she said as we lay in hammocks on opposite sides of the hut.

In some of the cabins' hammocks, cooking utensils and other items had been left behind, and we had gathered what we needed together in this hut.

In the morning I woke with chills and fever. Mauritia was bending over me.

'What's wrong?'

She fussed at herself for letting me stand in the water so long, thinking that I had a delicate constitution.

'No,' I whispered, it wasn't that. I knew what it was, it was a recurrence of malarial fever that had followed me for so long.

She looked troubled, then she said she would ride into the town and return with some medicines from there, that there was a physician there who had a new drug from Europe that cured malarial fever, as they had had a malarial fever epidemic there not very long ago.

I told her that I knew what to do to cure myself of the fever.

She looked at me with doubt, and said that she would bring enough provisions with me into the hut, so that I would not want for anything – that as she had the horse and knew the trails so well, she would be back very quickly.

I argued with her softly about this matter, explaining to her that I had seen the tree that had the bark I would need for the purpose of curing myself – that it was not very far from the camp, that I had noticed it when we passed it, but had not stopped because I did not expect the fever to plague me anymore, and besides I did not want her to think I was a crazy and foolish woman, any more than she did already.

She placed a horsehair blanket over me.

'I never thought you were crazy or foolish,' she said. 'If I expected to find Tamarutaca in Minas, I would be just as crazy. But this? How do you know it will work? I don't believe in magic or supernatural trees. Should I waste time here bringing you something that we don't know will do you any good, and may possibly do you harm? I know the European medicine will work, as I have seen it.'

'And I have seen this work, and felt it work. And I know it to be so. It's not a supernatural tree, but a very natural one, that has power over this ailment. Surely it's more natural than that medicine you will bring. How do I know *that* won't poison me? This I *know*.'

She looked at me.

'Believe me, Mauritia.'

'Fine,' she said. 'Tell me where I should go for it, and how I should gather it. Should I go when the moon is full?'

'No,' I said, twisting my mouth to the side. 'Go now.' I explained to her how the tree would look and how its leaves would be shaped.

'I know that one,' she said. 'I see that one all the time.'

'Yes,' I said.

I told her how much of the bark to scrape away, and I gave her a sharp flat stone that looked like the head of an arrow.

When she returned with the bark, I was too weak to prepare it, and so spoke to her how she should prepare it for me. She did, giving it to me to drink. By the next morning, I was ready to ride into Minas.

She did not express her amazement at what I had done. In fact, she did not even mention it. She seemed even to be 'against' the measures I had taken to cure myself.

We rode in silence while Mauritia directed us around quicksand, piranha streams, and places that were especially thick with mosquitoes. She was even capable of spotting the tracks and signs of certain wild beasts, that we avoided, though once she had said very quietly, 'Hand me your musket.' I started to question her, but she said, 'Hush.' She had pointed and fired before I had even seen the jaguar. Together, we dragged the white, brown, and black jaguar against the side of the trail, though Mauritia complained that if we'd had some way to transport it, that in town it would go for surely at least a pound of gold – that they were paying as much as ten drams for house cats.

'They eat house cats?' I asked.

'When other meat is scarce,' she said as we continued on the trail.
'Give me Araucaria kernels any day!' said I.
She laughed.
Seeing her good mood, I started to say how we made a good 'team' – my knowledge of medicines and hers of the trails. But I kept silent.

Another Mining Camp

WE ARRIVED AT ANOTHER deserted mining camp at noon that day, a smaller camp than the other, with only two buildings. Mauritia stopped the horse, and grabbing her basin, went to explore the stream. I reluctantly dismounted, tied the horse to a tree and followed her.

She had not been rotating the basin two minutes, when a voice behind us said, 'This is my 'ole.'

Startled and afraid, I turned around to face the grizzly Paulista, who was looking around me at Mauritia.

'I thought this was an abandoned hole,' she said casually and without alarm. The man, who had scratchy gray hair and beard, and a sun-darkened complexion, seemed to ignore my presence and was staring fixedly at her. I also turned to watch her. She emptied the basin of its contents and rinsed it in the stream, then she came onto the bank.

'Well, I still have my claim, but I don't work it anymore.'

He was carrying a musket, though he had not pointed it at us. He seemed ready to level it if it became necessary.

I glanced at Mauritia, who was staring at him calmly, while I felt every kind of apprehension, thinking of her tales of all the murders over claims.

'Why don't you work it?' Mauritia asked. 'It's a very rich claim.' He made a sneering face.

'Eh, I'm giving up mining and turning to agriculture. I'm not suited to gold-mining.'

'What do you mean suited to it? Don't you have any slaves to work your claim?'

I looked at Mauritia with surprise.

'I've got Indian half-breeds,' he said matter-of-factly. 'But I'm setting them to planting manioc.'

'This isn't very good soil for manioc. Not much of this region is any good for planting.'

'Hmph. Well, I've set them to growing manioc. It's enough for a man to subsist on, and it's better for his moral existence.'

Now he was neither looking at Mauritia nor me, though he was still staring in our direction. His blue eyes seemed to be hidden in the face of white hair.

'This is the cause of the moral decline of the people, their decadence and degeneracy. Right here, right where you're standing. Agriculture will put them on a higher level. I've turned it into a manioc plantation. It's a resting place for strangers and muleteers. Do you travelers want any free food or fodder for your horse?'

I started to say no but Mauritia said, 'Yes.' Was she pressing our luck? Couldn't she see that this was some crazy man?

He placed fodder in front of the horse.

We followed the 'manioc farmer' into a crudely built hut that was covered with carnauba palm thatch. Inside there was a rudely built table and bench. Mauritia sat down first and I sat beside her. There was the smell of fermenting manioc root. The man put two dishes of fish, rice, and farinha d'agua on the table. The 'manioc mush' looked awful, so I ate the fish and rice first. Though I saw Mauritia starting on the bowl of mush. I hoped that all the 'poison' juice had fermented out of it, so I took a spoonful of it to 'test' for Mauritia's protection. It was all right, so I went back to the fish and rice, though the rice was hard and the fish was almost raw.

The man fixed his plate and then sat down at the table across from us. I picked a small bone from my teeth and put it on the plate. I almost swallowed another small bone, coughed, turned aside, and found it, deposited it on the plate. When I turned the man was looking at me, though not as someone who really 'sees' another. I wondered why he had not asked to examine our documents. Did he already know Mauritia?

'That's why there's such a shortage of food,' the man said, as if he were continuing a long conversation. 'That's why there's such a shortage of food, and what little food, and what little food there is sells at such high prices. What I say is that they should put their energies into crops and not into this metal. Hunger and high prices always go together.

That's why I'm investing my energies not in metal but in the bread of the land!'

Mauritia finally moved to the plate of fish and rice and ate it carefully while I struggled with the bowl of manioc mush.

The man continued talking about his investment in the 'bread of the land' and not in the 'corrupting' metal.

'That's why there's a shortage of food and hunger. Isn't manioc hearty and wholesome? It's more wholesome than wheat or corn.'

When we finished eating, Mauritia continued to sit and listen to the man, though he continued to say the same thing over and over again.

Then finally he noticed that we had finished eating. 'Do you travelers want anything else?' he asked.

Mauritia said that we were quite full and didn't care for any more but that we were grateful for his hospitality, as we had been traveling for quite some time.

'That's the way it is,' he said, standing. Mauritia stood up, and so did I.

We followed the man outside.

'Well, if you're ever back this way,' he said, 'you have a resting place to come to that doesn't have any brawling and gambling and drunkenness.'

When we were back on the trail, Mauritia said, 'I was afraid of that man.'

'What? I thought you knew him. I was scared. But you seemed to know exactly what to do.'

'No, I just went along with what he suggested. I don't know what he might have done with that musket.'

I breathed deeply. I was more frightened now that I knew she had also been.

'I certainly thought you knew the Paulista,' I said.

'Paulista. He was no Paulista. No Paulista would talk that way. A Paulista would run from agriculture, the same as I would!'

A Freshwater Lake

WE CAME TO A FRESHWATER LAKE and Mauritia wanted to catch more fish to take into the town. We dismounted and tied the horse to an iuca tree. I had also wanted to stop, but it was not fish I wanted to catch but a certain lizard that lived in freshwater lakes. If any incident like the one with the old Paulista, or whoever he had been, occurred again I wanted to be prepared. I moved away from Mauritia to a different part of the lake to fish.

'We should keep together,' she said with concern.

'I won't go far. We can still see each other. We'll catch more.'

As I fished, I looked out for the lizard, and when I saw it, caught it with my hand, and with the small sharp stone, as I had seen Luiza do, I cut off the parts of the lizard that I would need and placed them in the medicine gourd. Then I looked up, seeing the canoes made of long, hollowed-out logs. Some of the Indians were standing, others sitting. I wondered if they were 'friendly' or whether they would attack us. I looked toward Mauritia.

She was also looking up, but without alarm. She held up her hand and said something in an Indian dialect I had not heard before. One of the men responded. The Indians did not come to the shore but continued on their way.

Mauritia raised her hand up to me too indicating that I should stay where I was. When the Indians had disappeared around the curve of the lake, she came to me.

'What tribe was that?' I asked.

'Paragua.'

'They're very hostile. Why didn't they attack us?'

'Palmyra taught me some words in their dialect.'

'Ah, that's luck.'

'I don't believe in luck,' she said. 'But let's go.' We climbed back on the horse and rode off.

'People say they can catch fish with their bare hands,' I said.

'What?'

'The Paragua.'

'I don't know,' she said. 'But I never trust what "people say."' I was silent.

454

'How did you meet Palmyra?' I asked.

'I met her a long time ago,' she said. 'That was when they murdered the Paraguayan. They were going to murder me too, or do worse things, but I escaped. One of them shot me. One of them started after me, but the other said, "Leave her, Engenho." I would have bled to death if Palmyra hadn't come. She stopped the bleeding and took me back with her. She taught me what I know about the trails, and the dialects of certain tribes. I might have stayed with her, but the two Jesuits came and made me leave. They thought I would corrupt her and that it was her soul that they were bound to protect.'

'Why didn't they stop you from seeing her?'

'She convinced them to let me visit her, but I can't stay there for long periods.'

'Where did you go when they made you leave her?'

'I just wandered. Until I was captured by a new master ... you know the rest.'

A Tavern in Vila Rica

Is THAT MINAS?' I asked, when we were in view of the town.

She explained that actually Minas was the territory, the captaincy as a whole, so that we had been in Minas all along – that the towns in it had different names, and that the one we were entering was called Vila Rica.

Before we entered the city, Mauritia wrapped the musket in leather and hid it, together with the bow and arrow, under a tree. She covered the weapons with vines, grass, and leaves. She also tied the horse to the tree, took the leather-wrapped bundles and the pouch of gold, and we walked into the town.

We did not walk down the main street, but through the backstreets of the town. There was a mixture of 'fine' houses, smelting warehouses, churches, public buildings, boarding houses, taverns, stick and mud huts.

We passed many street vendors, got out of the way of muleteers and miners on their way to smelting houses.

Mauritia walked up to one of the vendors. I thought she was going to buy fish from the woman, though we already had fish.

'Capistrana,' she said, kissing the cheek of the woman.

'Eh, Mauritia, it's been a long time.'

'I've brought you some merchandise,' said Mauritia, placing all of her bundles on the woman's table.

The woman, who seemed to be perhaps ten years younger than Mauritia, thanked her. There was a resemblance between them. Were they sisters, cousins? She also placed the pouch – her share or a share of her share of the gold – in the woman's bosom. Would she come back for it when she needed it, or was everything a gift?

'This is my sister, Capistrana,' she said. 'This is Almeyda.'

The woman said hello to me and then looked again at her sister.

Behind her was a square two-story building made of white sandstone. To the left were stairs leading up to a little balcony.

'But why are you here?' asked Capistrana.

'She's looking for someone, though she won't tell me who he is – and I agreed to be her guide. Otherwise I would not have come here, as I said I did not care to see Vila Rica again.'

'Eh, you're the same rascal.'

'Why do you call me a rascal? Because I don't care to live in this city?'

'You could be very prosperous here. Me? I'm owned by the forasteiro. What can I do? But you could be very prosperous and a "free agent."'

'And if they had bad luck, or got in trouble with the authorities for not paying the king his share, or there was an epidemic of smallpox or some such ill, I'd be the first they'd blame. No, I prefer the wilderness.'

'Eh,' said her sister, tossing her head. 'If I didn't know you, I'd think you'd murdered the men yourself!'

Mauritia said nothing though I looked at her and saw her flinch. 'So that now, you can live your life of rascality.'

Mauritia was silent, though she sighed deeply. Then she looked at me, 'Well, do you want to tell Capistrana the name of the fellow you're looking for? She's been in Vila Rica and in the Minas district for a long time.'

'I'd like to talk to Mariana first.'

'I thought you said you didn't know her.'

'I've heard her name before. Perhaps it's not the same Mariana.'

Capistrana was looking at me so intensely that I felt uncomfortable. I wondered why I had come here. How did I expect to find him here?

Now Capistrana was opening the bundles of salted and fresh fish and other items that Mauritia had brought her. Why had she given her the gold? I wondered.

'Well, we're going to see Mariana,' Mauritia said.

Capistrana looked up and said, 'All right ... How long will you stay in Vila Rica?'

'I don't know,' said Mauritia.

'Why does she call you a rascal?' I asked, when we were some distance from the woman.

'Because if she had my "freedom" she would use it differently. But I'm only free here in this district where they had that myth of me.'

She stopped at the back door of one of the taverns.

'There's discipline in freedom that she wouldn't understand,' she said. 'But do I? If I were a man I'd go into the backlands.'

'Why don't you?'

Without answering, she knocked softly on the back door. A handsome young mulatto woman opened it only part way, so that she only saw me.

'Mariana, this is Mauritia. Can my friend and I come in?'

'I'm not Mariana, but come in.'

She opened the door. I stood aside, so that Mauritia was the first to enter.

In the kitchen there was a long table full of different kinds of dishes, and there were several pots cooking in a fireplace. There was another woman, about my age, an Angolan, who stood at the fireplace stirring and cooking the pots. The woman turned.

'Sit down, Mauritia, and your friend too,' said Mariana.

I had expected the longhaired mulatto to be 'Mariana' as she'd been in my dream.

The 'dark' woman was tall, slender, wearing her fuzzy hair brushed back from her forehead. She was wearing a white apron over her blue cotton dress. She reminded me of one of the women I had worked with at the manioc plantation.

'My friend's name is Almeyda,' said Mauritia.

'I'm Mariana and this is Garimpeira,' she said of the mulatto woman.

The mulatta nodded, but did not say anything. She arranged plates on a wooden tray and went out. We could not see into the saloon, but we could hear the conversations. Mariana asked us to sit down. We sat down on a bench placed against the wall, while she stood carving beef.

'Girl, bring me some strong beer for my cough,' said someone. 'It's

457

not for my cough. Come here, girl, and take me to Brazil's paradise on earth.'

'There're plenty on the coast.'

'Eh, Buspar Belaude. What would you take for this one?'

'This one's like the wilderness, that's why I like her. That's why my name's Sertao, because I love the wilderness. I can't exist without the wilderness. I'd like to take this wilderness into my wilderness. I like to keep my distance from the cities to avoid the authorities, I don't like government, but I certainly wouldn't keep my distance from that one.'

The mulatta came back into the room, without showing any expression. She deposited empty plates and fixed another tray.

'Is that why you're Sertao?' asked a voice from inside.

'Yes.'

'Are you a criminal?'

'No, I'm no criminal, I just like to stay free of authorities. I don't like governments.'

'I thought you were a miner.'

'No, I'm a Sertanista and an explorer. I haven't seen the coast in twenty years.'

'What are you doing here?'

'I come back here every few years for a good drink and to see what has developed.'

'And a good woman, eh?'

They continued talking, but Mauritia was telling Mariana that they had come there because I was in search of someone, and that since she saw many of the miners, who came there during their 'holidays' . . .

'Do they allow Negroes in there?' I asked suddenly.

'No, they have their meals and drink in here,' said Mariana, as Garimpeira went back into the saloon. 'Who are you looking for?'

'A Sudanese, a Mohammedan, eh, I mean to say Muslim from the coast. A man.'

She laughed. 'Ah, I know many Sudanese from the coast. What's his name? When was he brought here?'

'She won't give his name.'

'I'm sure he would have gone by another name if he was here.'

'I don't know how you expect us to help you if you can't even trust us with his name,' said Mauritia.

'It's Anninho,' said I.

458

I couldn't tell by her look whether she knew the name or not, but she said, 'No.'

'Are you sure?' asked Mauritia. There was a strange sound in her voice, or my imagination put it there.

'Well, nearly all the miners have been here one holiday or another.'

'How do they get money to buy food?' I asked.

There was laughter from the women, but I didn't ask its meaning.

'Some of them are required to turn into their masters a set amount of gold, and they may keep the rest for their own use. Some have been able to buy their freedom in that manner. But where that is not the case, don't you think it would be easy for me to get gold dust in my hair if I worked in a mine, and transport it with me anywhere?'

'Yes, yes,' I said.

'But this Anninho. No. I would recognize such a name.'

I told her also about Palmares and King Zumbi, and that I had first met Anninho there.

She said she had heard of Palmares, of how they had executed the leader, and the survivors had scattered, but did not recognize the man I was speaking of.

'He's her husband,' said Mauritia.

'I don't know him.'

'He wouldn't have been exactly a miner. He would have been passing through. He was a free man.'

'I still don't know him.'

I did not know what else to say. Should I tell them that he might have spoken to some miners here? That there was some plan ... I could not explain it to them. I did not *know* these women.

'There are other towns in Minas,' said Mauritia, shaking her head.

'Tomorrow's Sunday,' I said. 'Will many miners be here then?'

'Yes,' said Mariana. 'Would you like something to eat?'

Mauritia said yes, but that 'Almeyda' only ate fish, grain, and vegetables. Mariana looked at me oddly, then prepared our plates.

'I thought there was a food shortage here,' said Mauritia, holding a plate of pork and green vegetables. Mariana had given me fish and manioc cakes.

'If *he* comes in I'll say you paid me for it,' she said quickly.

I started to offer her gold from my pouch, but she said, 'No, No,' then she answered Mauritia's question. 'There *is* a food shortage, but you wouldn't know it by him. He has ways of getting it. When he can't get beef he buys whale. When it's cooked with cabbage or beans you think it's beef.'

'This is pork, isn't it?' Mauritia asked, her fork pausing in the air.

'Yes, yes,' said Mariana, 'and very good pork. This is real beef. I'd serve it to you, but I'm afraid he'll come in. But I'll give you some to take with you.'

Mariana looked at me. 'Yes, there are a lot of Mohammedan Negroes ...'

I quickly interrupted and explained that 'Mohammedan' was considered a pejorative term for Muslims, and perhaps even an insult because they don't worship 'Mohammed' but 'Allah,' their word for 'God.' I thought of the Mohammed of Bahia.

'Allah is *their* "Almighty God." '

'Well, Muslim then,' she went on. 'There are a lot of Negroes of that faith from the coast. Is that why you won't eat pork?'

'What?'

'They don't eat pork. Is that why you don't eat pork?'

'No, I'm a Christian, a Catholic to be more precise,' I said.

'Well, all of the *Muslim* Negroes I know stay together and don't like to mix. Did your husband try to make you change your faith?'

'No.'

'You're asking too many questions,' said Mauritia. 'Don't you see she's shy of answering them.'

'Oh, am I asking too many questions? I'm sorry.'

'That's all right,' I said. I told them how when we were married we had both a Muslim and a Christian ceremony.

'That's a luxury,' said Mauritia.

'To get married in both faiths?' I asked.

'To have the luxury of a marriage to a man you love,' she said.

'Ah, that was when we were in Palmares,' I said. 'If Palmares hadn't happened, I don't know!'

'You're such a loner, Mauritia,' said Mariana. 'Why should it matter to *you*?'

'It's not impossible for me to imagine another world,' said Mauritia. 'Or myself in different circumstances in this one,' she added.

No one spoke. The mulatta, Garimpeira, had left the kitchen and returned several times since we were talking. She did not say anything to us, but once when she came into the kitchen I caught her eye. Her look was friendly, though 'restrained.'

'Bring me some more.'

'Throw him some more. All of those foreigners in from the coast, trying to take over.'

'Foreigners? This is my country as much as yours.'

'You're all crabs, fit to crawl along the coast. No more.'

'Leather breeches.'

'Sure, I wear leather breeches to protect me in the wilderness. But I'm no bird with feathered legs!'

'You're more cowardly.'

'Cowardly, eh? These foreigners think they have a right to everything. If it wasn't for me and men like me, you bird legs wouldn't even know there was gold here. You wouldn't even know the country had an interior.'

'That's why I stay out of cities,' said another voice. 'I prefer exploring to *this*.'

'Eh, we'd know it was here. We knew it was here before y'all did, we just ain't seen it with our own eyes. But I knew there was lakes of gold here.'

'Superstition. All those tales of shiny mountains and golden lakes mean nothing unless a man sees them with his own eyes. All you "birds" wait until other men sees them and then you want to make claims to things you ain't never seen.'

'If it wasn't for us this country wouldn't have any development. It would be all wilderness if it was up to you irresponsible men. Maybe you did find it, but we came in and developed it. And now it's ...'

'Armchairs and plumed hats.'

'That's better than ambushes and assaults.'

'I don't assault nobody. Y'all birds come here last and then you want the best 'oles. Ain't that so, man?'

'I'm a stranger here.'

'You're a Paulista, ain't you?'

'Yeah. But I'm a trapper, not a miner.'

'If it wasn't for us this town would still be mud and sticks.'

'Belaude, have the woman dance and sing for us, or I'll start a war here me own self. If you fellows is so panting after development why don't you go off to the African colonies? We're our own men here.' He clapped his hands. 'Have her dance or I'll start me own war with these Emboabas and gold-thieves!'

There was some commotion, as if some of the men were exchanging fists. Then there was the plaintive sound of a mandolin, and the commotion was hushed. There was a very warm, private sound in the music.

'Put some spark in it, girl,' someone said when the first song was done. 'Be more venturesome.'

'Tuck up your skirt.'

'Play a sultry air.'

'Bring the black one out and turn her loose.'

'Give me a big embrace. That will bring you to life.'

'See how her eyes take everything in. I've seen cut diamonds that ain't no brighter.'

'Stand there too long you'll grow mouldy.'

'Sweetheart, play us a air you can dance to. It ain't against your religion is it? No, it can't be. What are you doing, standing there contemplating God?'

'It takes her a while to get started,' said another, more authoritative and measured voice. Belaude, the owner? 'She'll play a dancing tune in a moment, and kick up her heels, and tuck up her skirt to the pumpkins, or she'll get forty lashes.'

Then there was livelier music and the sound of heels clicking. 'Shake your head more.'

'Show some fire.'

'Yes, that's what gets me.'

'That puts a twinkle in the eye.'

'Aye, and in more than the eye.'

The music got more intense. One of the men began to roar and bellow.

'Sit down, Urano, you're acting like a simpleton.'

'Consider the beam in your own eye.'

'Yes, Mister, I'm given up to vice. But if you don't sow you don't reap.'

'What's wrong with her?'

'She gone into hysterics.'

'And a swoon!'

'She's playacting.'

'In ecstasy.'

'No, I think the woman's ill.'

'It's just exhaustion. I'll take her in the kitchen.'

He came in, a tall muscular Paulista, carrying Garimpeira. 'Get up, girls,' he said, 'and let me put her on the bench.' He lay her on the hard bench.

'Take care of her, Mariana. Give her some salt or something.'

He went back into the other room. Mariana came over and put something under Garimpeira's nose. She moved her head to the side but that didn't revive her. She touched her forehead.

'She's got a fever. Those simpletons making her dance about so.'

'They may be simpletons, but they're dangerous,' said Mauritia.

We had placed our empty plates on the table, and stood by watching.

'I think we should take her to Dr Rosa,' said Mariana. 'I don't think it's just exhaustion.'

'Could I see her?' I said.

'Do you think it's malarial fever?'

I looked back at her. 'I don't know.'

I knelt down and put my hand to the woman's forehead and under her neck and chin.

'Do you know medicine and healing?' asked Mariana, but I said nothing.

I heard Mauritia mumble, but I could not make out what she said.

I kept touching the woman about the face and neck until she woke up. She complained of chills and a pain in her back and a severe headache.

'Maybe a good night's rest,' said Mariana.

'I don't think so,' I said. 'Will Dr Rosa treat her if we take her to him?'

'Yes, he'll treat her. He treats everyone,' said Mariana.

'Can't you cure her?' asked Mauritia.

'I think we'd better take her to him. Does he have rooms set aside for hospital?'

'Yes, but not for slaves. But he'll see her.'

'What's wrong with her?' asked Mauritia.

'We three can take her there,' I said. 'We've already breathed the same air as she has anyway. All he can really do is relieve the headache and backache, but the rest we'll have to wait for.'

'What are you talking about?' asked Mauritia.

463

We carried the woman to Dr Rosa, who was an 'Emboaba' – a Portuguese from the coast. A younger man than I had expected to see, he looked to be about thirty-five and wore a black coat and black trousers cut in the European manner.

We were told to carry her to a room and she was placed on another table – while he went to see other patients. It was nearly two hours before he came to us. There were other slave women lying in hammocks in the long room. I suggested to Mariana and Mauritia that they wait outside, but they wouldn't.

'What about you?'

'I'm protected against it.'

'Against what?'

'I'm waiting for Dr Rosa to say what it is,' said Mauritia. When the doctor came in he told us all to leave.

I stepped forward to ask him if I might stay while he examined her. 'Certainly not,' he said.

'But I . . . I'm protected against it.'

'Against what? Go on with you.'

When he was done with examining her, he sent for us and told us to take her home – that it was merely exhaustion, and in the morning she would be well again. He would give her an emetic to be administered to her before she went to bed.

'But you can't send her back,' I said. 'Aren't you going to keep her here and observe her, aren't you going to have us destroy the things that she's touched, and wash the things that can't be replaced?'

'Destroy the things she's touched!' exclaimed Mariana. Mauritia also laughed.

'Yes,' I said.

'It's just some light tropical ailment,' said Dr Rosa, as he handed Mariana the emetic, and started preparing to 'bleed' another patient. 'My medicines wouldn't do her any good, anyway, because she doesn't have the right constitution for them. All she needs is plenty of rest and a room full of sunshine. That's the best cure in the tropics.'

I wanted to call him a quack, a curandeiro, but the other two women were preparing to help Garimpeira off the table and back to the tavern, where she and Mariana had rooms in the back.

'But aren't you going to observe her for at least three days?'

'Come on, Almeyda, and don't make a fool of yourself,' said Mauritia. 'She fancies herself a medicine woman,' she said to the doctor, who smiled with tolerance.

'I don't fancy myself,' said I. 'Perhaps you know what it is and don't want to leave her here.'

'Of course, I know what it is,' he said. 'Exhaustion. Now I have other people to see. Excuse me.'

'We brought her here for nothing,' said Mariana. 'Just a good night's sleep and taking care of.'

'Yes, for nothing,' I said, as I helped them carry Garimpeira back to the tavern, and we put her in a hammock in the back room, and as she complained of chills, covered her with a cloak of anteater's hair. Mariana brought her hot teas to drink, but she could barely get them down without feeling as if she would vomit. Then she slept.

'What did you fancy she had?' asked Mauritia.

'I won't know for several days. But I have something that you and Mariana should take for your protection – if what I believe is right.'

'Eh, I don't believe in witchcraft and magic.'

'Eh, I've seen you picking up every disgusting thing. Every time we'd stop you'd pick up some disgusting thing. Well, not disgusting ... but, foolishness.'

'May I stay with her?' I asked.

'If you promise not to give her anything,' said Mariana. 'I'm following the doctor's orders. Mauritia, she can sleep in the room with me.'

'Yes, and I'll help you cook and serve tomorrow.'

'Where have you been?' asked Belaude from outside.

'To Dr Rosa's.'

'What did the witch say?'

'Eh, that it's mere exhaustion and she must rest,' said Mariana.

'That's what I said. Oh, I know as much as the witch.'

I wondered at how he spoke of Dr Rosa in the same way that *they* spoke of me.

In several days, the small red bumps began to form on her forehead and then on her wrists and feet. After six days there were blisters. On the eighth day, the blisters ran with pus. But by then the smallpox epidemic had begun. Everyone who had been in the Belaude tavern immediately came down with it. Garimpeira was the only one who let me look after her. I kept her skin clean and applied a solution to it. I wouldn't let her scratch herself but stopped the itching with an ointment that I mixed. I kept her drinking liquids and eating fish and fruit and vegetables. When the others were being ravaged by the ailment, she was already convalescing with only a few dried scales on her skin and very few pockmarks on her neck and hairline.

'Are you a witch as they say?' she asked.

'No I'm not. A witch is a very terrible thing to be,' I said, when she was sitting up in the hammock. 'I know a little about healing, but for me to know such things – it's witchcraft or superstition.'

'Let me see my face,' she said. 'I've been afraid to ask.'

She was sitting up in the hammock. I brought her a small mirror. 'Eh, I thought I'd have holes all over my face.'

Mariana and Mauritia, when they recovered, did have pockmarks all over their faces. They looked at Garimpeira with amazement, but still Mauritia would not give me credit for the feat – claiming that it was something in Garimpeira's blood mixture that kept her pretty.

'And me?' I asked. 'Don't you think my blood has some ingredient in it that protects me from that ailment?'

But Mauritia would not answer. 'Why am I wrong?' I asked Mauritia.

'What do you mean?'

'Whenever I do something it's wrong. Dr Rosa misjudged her illness, and he's still *right*.'

'How should I know what's right!' she said, turning on me with anger. 'Do you think the secrets of the world have been revealed to me that I should know what's *right*!?' she said, and stomped out.

'Sometimes I think she's crazy,' said Garimpeira. 'She can see with her own eyes that you're right.'

'Mauritia doesn't believe anything,' said Mariana. 'I don't even think she believes what she can see with her own eyes. She complains about everything.'

'I don't understand her,' I said.

'Nobody does,' said Mariana.

I told them the story she had told me about her three masters who had been murdered.

'Yes, that's true,' said Mariana. 'That's a true story. She didn't lie about that. Why isn't she glad that they leave her alone, that she's not passed from hand to hand?'

'Does anyone suspect that she murdered them herself?'

'No, of course. Because the Paulistas and Emboabas are always war-

466

ring. You heard them in there. They're always warring. Do you know what I think?'

'What?' I asked.

'I think she's afraid of "magic." I think she believes that story that she's "bad luck." And so she's afraid of magic because she's afraid of her own. If it's true that you have powers to heal – then it might be true that she's got powers to destroy.'

I said that that was possible, that it was a very good explanation. 'Do you think she dislikes me?' I asked.

'No, she doesn't. Because when we were coming here she was telling me how kindly you treated her. In fact, you're the only one I know she's ever even mentioned liking. We've known each other a long time, but she doesn't really like me. And she always complains about everything, all the time. At least that's the Mauritia that *I* know.'

I was silent, watching the pockmarks on her chin and neck.

A Shy, Silent, and Confused Woman

HAVE ANY OF THOSE MEN ever bothered you?' I asked Garimpeira once.

'That's no question,' she said. 'But to answer it, Belaude keeps them away from me. But not himself.'

'I could make it so he'd stay away.'

'Eh, how could you do that?'

'I can't explain, but I can do it.'

'Eh, I can't exist without someone,' she said.

'You could make it your choice,' said I. 'Isn't there another man here that you'd choose if you had that power?'

She looked confused and was silent.

'Think about it,' I said. 'And let me know what you decide.'

She said, 'Of course,' but she did not give me her answer, or decide anything, and whenever I would look at her directly she would look away, shy, silent, and confused.

A Prosperous Man
and the Incarceration

THE TOWN WAS GETTING BACK TO NORMAL after the epidemic. Mauritia and I continued to help out in the kitchen of the tavern. Whenever a miner would come in on Sundays, I would ask if he knew of an Anninho from the coast. At first they would invariably think that I meant newly arrived from the coast of Africa, but I would explain the Brazilian coast – the Porto Calvo-Olinda-Recife area. No one had heard of or seen such a man, though they would always add that there were many 'Mohammedan Negroes' there. I did not always correct their nomenclature.

There continued to be brawling between the Paulistas and the Emboabas and there was confusion over claims, and a number of arrests of those who did not or could not make payment to the king his royal fifths. Several of these men had been arrested since I had come, and then incarcerated. Some had their gold mines confiscated by the government or they were deported to a prison in Lisbon or to one of Portugal's African colonies to serve in the garrison there. This as well as the 'foreigners' was cause of much violence and bloodshed, though a number of quarrels were also settled over strong beer, and many new quarrels were made at gambling tables. I also discovered that not all of the blacks in the town were slaves and that some had come here to make their fortunes in mines the same as the white men. Some of these men also had slaves, others were independent prospectors, or worked in groups of freemen. I had spoken with some of these men who were eager to elevate themselves through 'wealth' and the 'possibility of commerce' if they couldn't through the 'prestige of blood' or 'their civilization.'

There were still others who felt that they already had 'prestige of blood' and 'civilization' and that the wealth would only enhance their possibilities. One such man was a prosperous black trader, who owned a fleet of canoes and transported things on the Parana and Paranapanema Rivers. When I had first seen him hollowing out tree trunks, making pitch and tar from the sap of certain trees, and thinning wood for sails – working along with the other workmen, I had thought that he was a

468

slave. He seemed very intelligent and 'quick' and I had singled him out to converse with still not knowing that he was the owner of everything that I saw and that the others were his workmen. He had said that he had not heard of such a man, but that he had never worked with the miners, but only transported merchandise to and from Minas and also Porto Fez. Still I did not feel he had meant *he* himself had done this. Even when he began to speak about the 'possibilities of commerce' and 'the spirit of enterprise and self-reliance' that the mining industry created for free men of vision, I did not feel that this was to be taken personally.

It was only when he came to 'court' me and I refused to go out with him, explaining that I was a married woman, that I learned who he was.

'Don't you know who that was?' asked Mariana.

'Who?'

'Jaime Carvalho.'

'Who's Jaime Carvalho?'

'A very prosperous man. Do you know what they say of him? That he used to be a Negro but now he's so rich that he's not anymore.'

'Is that good?' I asked.

'They treat him like a white man,' she said. I said nothing.

'No one has ever refused him. He'll give you riches and buy your freedom.'

'He's too old for me, and besides, I'm married.'

'What do you mean too old?'

I'd forgotten that I was an old woman she was seeing, and that Carvalho was in his late forties, must appear a few years younger than my 'fifty years.'

'Eh, nothing, but I'm a married woman, looking for her husband. Anyway, most such men want younger women.'

'You might be old, but you're handsome. Ah, what an opportunity.'

'Then I give it to you.'

'Oh, he wouldn't want me.'

But what was funny was that he had seen her, and the next time he came there, it was not me but her that he came to see, but still she was disturbed.

'Why does he like me?' she asked when she returned.

'Because you're a very intelligent and kind woman.'

'But wait till he sees Garimpeira. Just let him see Garimpeira and I won't be anything.'

'I don't think he's like that,' I said. 'He wanted to court me, didn't he? And besides, there are mulattas everywhere. If he wanted a mulatta ...'

'But my face.'

'You have a very pretty face. And the pockmarks don't look as bad as you imagine they do. Half the city has them.'

She seemed more cheerful, but still met Carvalho with uncertainty.

I do not know how things turned out for them, whether he purchased her freedom and married her, or whether, as she said, he had seen Garimpeira and had taken her to wife. I don't know. What I remember of that day is stopping to talk with Mauritia's sister, Capistrana, who fascinated me with her ability for 'trading.' If she had not had to turn the money over to her owner she would have made a good sum as a businesswoman, and she was also very 'ambitious.' She had the opposite personality of Mauritia who was a private, secretive, sometimes morose and taciturn woman. At least Capistrana's 'public performance' was noisome and gregarious as she solicited town folk and strangers to buy the fish and corn and manioc cakes and chaque that she was selling.

Sometimes after a purchaser would leave, she would joke and call out under her breath something awful that they had just purchased, pretending that she had sold them 'electric eels and piranha cakes' and we would laugh.

'How much is it?'

'Eight drams.'

'Hello, Almeyda.'

'How many piranha cakes have you sold today?'

'I'd say several dozen.'

After seeing her I went to take care of and feed the horse, whom we had constructed a crude shelter for, and I had surrounded with plants to ward off beasts and poisonous insects. Then I had gone back into the town. There was a crowd standing by a public pillory. A Negro woman was being lashed. I asked someone who was the slave.

'She's a free Negro. Someone sold some gold to her,' said a woman, who had a bundle on her head. 'They're to give her four hundred lashes.'

'What did they do to the one who sold it?'

'Nothing.'

I started to ask more questions but I couldn't watch any longer and so departed. But before I could get back to the tavern, two men grabbed my arms. They were constables.

'What is this? What's the matter?'

But they would not reply. They took me roughly to the jail, and put me in the 'dungeon.' There was straw on the floor, a dirty hammock, a small window on the level of the street. As horses galloped by or mules passed, the dust flew in.

'What am I here for?' But I was not told.

The Interrogation

I SAT ON THE HAMMOCK, still not knowing why they had brought me here. Had Dr Rosa, hearing of my more effective cure of Garimpeira, accused me of magic or witchcraft? Was this a witch's inquisition? They had already kept me here overnight without telling me anything. I had not slept, wondering why I had been brought here. Had they mistaken me for someone else? Did they think I was the one who had sold the gold to the free Negro woman? I wondered when or if they would come and let me know what their charges were against me.

'Almeyda.'

I turned and went to the small window. Mauritia was stooping down, looking in.

'How did you know I was here?' I whispered.

She also whispered. 'Capistrana saw them bring you here. She was afraid, and came and warned me. She thought they would arrest me next. But they haven't, though I've been in plain sight. Why are you here?'

'I don't know,' I said. 'They simply brought me here. They didn't tell me why.'

She looked puzzled. 'Well, have you done anything that you feel they might have arrested you for?'

'No. I don't know,' I said, shaking my head.

'Is there anything that you want? Is there anything that I can bring you?'

'No,' I said. 'Anyway I don't want you to get into any trouble.'

'Do you have your free papers with you?'

'Yes.'

She looked at me for a long time without saying anything.

'You'd better go. I think I hear someone,' I said hurriedly. She left and I rushed back to the hammock.

Two men came. Paulistas, wearing black trousers, loose white shirts, high jackboots, and broad round-brimmed hats. Their faces were thick with beard and mustache, but one could see the pockmarks on the upper part of their faces. One had brown, hard eyes. The other had blue eyes, squinting, one eye larger than the other.

'I'll stick to that, I'll take my stand on it,' the blue-eyed man was saying to the other one, as they entered. About what I didn't know. Then they both stood silently, looking at me. The blue-eyed one looked as if he could very easily lose his head about little matters, that he could go mad quickly. The other seemed to be habitually steady, serious. Neither one was there to get me out of my difficulties.

'Where is he?' asked the brown eyes. I looked at him.

'Tell us where he is and we'll let you go,' said the blue eyes.

'I don't know who you mean,' I said finally. 'Where is who?'

'You're Tamarutaca's woman. Tell us where he and his renegades are hiding. Where is their quilombo?'

My mouth was open when they said 'Tamarutaca's woman.'

A woman came in with a bucket and washed my face and wet the 'gray' on my hair, so that it ran.

'Now tell us you're not his woman. Why else would you have come into town disguised this way?'

'Who told you I was his woman?'

'That's neither here nor there,' said the brown eyes. 'But you admit that you are?'

'No, I do not admit it. I am not.'

'Tell us where he is hidden.'

'Truth and oil are always on top,' said the woman with the bucket.

'You have nothing to do with this, Verao,' said the brown eyes. 'Be gone.'

'Tell us where the viper is before he bites again.' Blue.

'You'll be obliged to tell us,' said Brown.

'I don't know.'

472

'Eh, his woman does not know his whereabouts. I don't believe that.'
Blue.

'I'm not his woman and I don't know anything.'

'What mission did he send you on?' Brown. 'I'd like to flog the cow.'

'Have patience. Let's leave her alone for now.'

'Put her to the sword piece by piece.'

'Let's leave her alone and let her ponder *that*,' said brown eyes. They left, locking the door.

It was difficult to believe. Who had told them that I was Tamarutaca's woman? Had Mauritia's lie followed me from Guilherme's, and did someone here dislike me and spread that story? I lay down in the hammock, breathing heavily. Then I sat up suddenly and reached into my medicine gourd.

'I'm not Tamarutaca's woman,' I whispered as I was working. 'It's not necessary to keep me here. You have enough to do to keep the disturbances from breaking out, the riots, and demonstrations.'

There was the sound of a great deal of excitement on the street, of rushing, and scurrying off.

'Almeyda,' Mauritia whispered.

I went to the window. 'What's going on out there?'

'The government confiscated the property – slaves and gold of some men who refused to pay the royal fifths. There's a big protest. The officials are imprisoning a lot of people, running others out of town. The street vendors they're even after, so Capistrana has gone home. Have they harmed you in any way?'

'No,' I said. 'But I suppose they're too busy to. I haven't seen them since this morning.'

'Did you find out what they imprisoned you for?'

'It's crazy. They think I'm Tamarutaca's woman.'

'Ah!' She twisted her hands in her hair. 'I didn't think Father Guilherme would go to those extremes. He's obsessed with him. He must have had someone follow us.'

'But it's been a long time since ...'

'The smallpox may have kept them all away. Ah, it's my fault.'

'No, don't blame yourself.'

'What's that smell?'

'I don't know.'

'It's nauseating.'

'Yes.'

'Look, I'll come back.'

'I don't want to put you in danger.'

'There's no danger. It's all wild now.' She rushed away from the window.

They came back into the cell.

'We didn't forget you,' said the blue-eyed one. 'There's been trouble in the city. It's over. It's nothing. But Tamarutaca and his band of rascals are perpetual trouble. A wart on the face of the country. Tell us where the bandit is.'

'I know no more today than I did yesterday.'

'I thought by today you would have grown in wisdom,' said brown eyes.

I was silent.

'Aren't you hungry? Is there something you want in exchange for telling us?' He came near me. 'What's that sweet smell?' he asked.

'I don't know.'

'It's a very sweet smell.'

Blue eyes had his hand on his stomach. 'It's nauseating,' he said. He stood farthest away from me. 'I don't like perfume.'

'It's a very sweet smell,' said brown eyes. 'And you're obviously a very sweet woman.' He touched my shoulder. 'Don't you want to stay sweet and tell me the rogue's hiding place? What part of the mountains or the jungle is he hidden?' He squeezed my shoulder digging his nails in.

His nails were long and hard and tough and brown. The blood ran onto his fingers.

'You're stubborn as a donkey,' he said. 'It's nauseating.'

Brown eyes patted my shoulder and then wiped my blood on the side of my face and in my hair.

'I'm going to vomit,' said the other, rushing out.

Brown eyes patted my shoulder again and said, 'Maybe you'll be wiser tomorrow.'

He wiped the rest of the blood on my blouse and skirt.

When they left, I put more of the perfume on, made from the testi-

cles and musk glands of a certain lizard found in freshwater lakes. It has a
very sweet smell, but then it becomes nauseating and takes away appetite.

The next day blue eyes came and read me a story about what was done
to someone in a certain history. He didn't tell me what it was. First the
man's nose was cut off then his ears, then his fingers, his hands, his arms.
He kept reading, looking up at me each time, then he held his stomach
and ran out. I heard him vomiting.

'Did you go to the doctor?'

'Yes, but I still can't put anything on my stomach.'

'Engoda,' he called me, staring at me with his hard brown eyes.

He dug his nails into my scalp and then held his claw in front of my
face as if to claw my eyes out, and then as if to claw the sides of my face.

'Those are some of the possibilities,' he said.

'Why do you call me "engoda"?' I asked, as my scalp stung. The
word meant 'allurement.'

'Ah, do you think if the highwayman knows you are here, he will try
to rescue you?'

'Since I'm not his woman that won't happen,' I said.

'Won't he?'

He tore my blouse away, then stood stunned at my flat, bare bosom.
He threw the torn blouse at me and walked out.

Some while later a man came with keys and released me. The woman,
Verao, who was standing outside the door, handed me a cotton shawl.

'Truth and oil rise to the top,' she said with a laugh.

'Almeyda,' said Mauritia, when she opened the back door of the tavern.
'You're free, but why did they release you?'

'I don't know. I couldn't tell them anything since I'm not Tamarutaca's woman. But I can't look for *him* here. If I find him, maybe they'll
think *he's* Tamarutaca.'

'What are you going to do?'

'I'm going back to the coast.'

Preparations for a Return

WHERE WILL YOU GO?' asked Mauritia after we had bid Garimpeira and Mariana goodbye. We left before dawn. Capistrana was setting her wares out for the early miners and men on their way to the smelting houses.

'When will you come back here?' Capistrana asked her sister.

'I don't know. Maybe I won't.'

'I'm sorry about your difficulties,' Capistrana said to me. 'There's always some trouble here.'

'Or you bring it, Manganaa.'

Why did she call her 'rascal,' again?

Mauritia was silent, then she hugged Capistrana and I said goodbye to her.

We got our weapons from the hiding place. The musket had gotten damp so would not have fired that day if it had become necessary. We took the horse out of the shed and walked him onto the road.

'So you'll go back to Bahia?' asked Mauritia.

'Yes, and then probably on to the New Palmares, which they say is in Parahyba. If he's not there, I'll wait for him there. At least that's one place we both *know*.'

She was silent, then she said, 'I suppose that's the practical thing to do.'

'But you don't think it's a good idea?'

'I think it's a good idea. But don't go by me. I hate cities. If I were a man I'd be a Sertanista not a Palmarista. I'd call myself Sertao too, like that man we heard talk, and go to the wildest wilderness, and avoid everyone.'

I said nothing. I thought of the 'explorer' that Luiza had told me about. I wondered why she had never finished his story.

'He had such plans as the man, Carvalho, the one with the sailing canoes,' I said.

'Who?'

'Anninho. But I don't know the whole story. Maritime trade. But I shouldn't talk about it. I should have stayed on the coast.'

'What are you rambling about?' she asked with irritation.

'Nothing.'

'How large is the New Palmares?'

'I don't know. It's made of the few that escaped from the Old Palmares. I don't know how many people have come there or have been captured.'

'Captured?'

I explained that some of the new recruits, who refused to come, were captured and taken there. I did not say there had been slaves in Palmares.

'They rescued me from slavery,' I said.

'Ah. I thought you had always been a free woman.'

'Me? No. Why did you think so?'

'You seem so adventuresome.'

'No, I'm not really.'

We rode along the edge of forest that sloped down like a precipice, but was covered with trees and grass so thick that one could not tell how far.

'They tossed one of them over a place like that,' she said, looking down.

'Eh, that's awful.'

'Yes.'

She steadied the horse as we rounded the corner and came back to even ground.

'It's because I'm unattached and independent that she calls me a rascal,' she said. 'Or because I'm indifferent to the things she finds necessary. But I wouldn't be unfettered if chance hadn't brought it about.

'Well, unfettered here in Minas. I couldn't go to Bahia with you because I don't have the certificates.'

'I could forge such documents,' I said. 'I know how to write, and I've done that before.'

'Ah, I'll think about it. I like you, but I get muddled in the city. I get confused. There's so much tumult. The least thing disturbs me. I like to be free from oppression. Even when I had those owners, they were independent prospectors, like myself, very despegado, very despegado. If I were cattle, I'd always stray from the herd ... When she called me "rascal," she didn't mean any misconduct. I don't want you to think she did. It's just her way. She doesn't know the difference between being "unbridled" and independent.'

'You don't have to explain.'

'I'll go with you as far as I can and show you the best way, but maybe I won't go into the city.'

'As I said, I'd like you to accompany me as far as you care to, and as I said, I can provide the proper certificates.'

'I still wonder at how you healed her without any scars.'

'There were some.'

'But so unnoticed. My face is chiseled. But I'm no whimperer. Agora é que di em cheio. Now I've had the devil's own luck, but who needs to squeak about it? Maybe if I keep good company,' she said with a laugh, 'maybe I'll be of that number. I'm not annoying you, am I, with my chatter?'

'No, no.'

'I'm usually very taciturn, and I don't want to make a nuisance of myself.'

'No, you're not.'

She noticed wild boar bristle around the trunk of a tree and we took another trail because she didn't want to 'waste our powder.' I, however, had noticed something that she hadn't. That the wild boar had been scratching at the base of the tree to get the copaiba sap to cure a wound. I did not mention this as we rode on in the new trail.

'If I go with you on your adventure,' she said, 'Who knows, but perhaps I really will meet Tamarutaca.'

The Heroes of Turiri's Village

MAURITIA OBSERVED ONE MORE FEAT of my 'magic.' Infection had set in from the 'scratchings' the Paulista had given me in the prison cell. It was not until we reached the freshwater lake that I saw another copaiba tree. I persuaded Mauritia that we camp there until midnight, at which time I drew the sap from the tree. In the morning the swelling and fever were gone.

Again she did not 'make over' my performance, and seemed to resent it. Was it jealousy or envy? Still what I was doing was elementary compared to Luiza's feats and the things I might have learned had I remained with her. I did not tell any of this to Mauritia. Once when I saw the 'herva viva' I wanted to 'show off' again with 'my plant.' I would have told her to touch it, and it would have shriveled up and shrunk away from her. Then when I touched it, it would have remained whole and blossomed. But I decided against this, for if she did feel herself to be 'evil luck,' then she would have felt it even more and her resentment might have been deeper. So when I spotted the 'herva viva' I merely smiled without indicating it and we continued our journey.

'We will not go back to my house,' said Mauritia. 'I am afraid that if Father Guilherme is responsible for those men arresting you, then he will harass you there.'

'All right,' I said. I had not told her about the man tearing my blouse and discovering my 'empty' bosom, which may or may not have been responsible for my release.

'Do you leave your house "solitary" often?' I asked. 'But you said you did.'

'Yes.'

'But you never found any strangers living there?'

'No.'

When we crossed the Sao Francisco I kept expecting to see the 'stranger' that I had met on my way to Minas. Somehow in my mind I thought we would see him again, that he would be the Tamarutaca that everyone had spoken of, that he and Mauritia would develop a deep affection for each other, and that Mauritia would remain with him while I continued on my journey to Bahia. But that did not happen. We passed the place where I had 'awoken' to discover him. I looked around oddly, so that Mauritia asked, 'What is it?'

'Nothing,' I said.

'I want to go this way,' I said, as Mauritia was about to turn in another direction.

'Why this way?'

'There's an Indian village here that I want to visit.'

'Tupi?' she asked.

I said yes.

We exchanged places and I rode in front so that the first person they saw would not be a stranger but a familiar face.

Before we got there however I saw the boy Turiri, sitting in a gameleira tree.

'Greetings, Almeyda,' he said, as I pulled back on the reins.

'I was just going to see you,' I said. 'How are you?'

'I'm fine,' he said. 'And my eyes haven't hurt me anymore.'

'That's good,' I said. 'This is my friend, Mauritia. This is Turiri.'
They exchanged greetings.

'My father and the other men returned,' he said. 'They told the
women a story that the women would not believe.'

'What story?'

'That the man Zune was a false one and a liar. That really he was
not Zune but an imposter, that they had seen him talking to other white
men, loading the gold blankets on canoes. But my mother and grandmother and the other women wouldn't believe my father or the other
men. So the women stayed on Zune's side. Though the men told him
to go to thunder! The women continued to make the gold blankets for
him.'

'Why didn't they kill Zune?'

'Because the women would have nothing to do with them then. My
grandmother swore she would give them a certain plant that would prevent the women from having children anymore. My grandmother swore
she would do this, and all the women swore they would accept this plant
if any harm was brought to Zune. He had become like a god to them,
even though in the history he was no god, but only an ordinary man who
had brought them in the past a religion. But the women continued to feel
he was some god, some miracle from the past, so the men would take no
action against him, for fear that the foolish women would destroy their
whole race for the imposter. So they did not dare even to flog the devil.

'But all is not gold that glitters,' he said with a laugh.

'What do you mean?' I asked.

'I mean just that,' he said, straddling a limb. 'He thought the new
blankets were gold because they glittered like gold. Then when he gave
the others the new blankets, they thought he had fooled them, and murdered Zune themselves. So that kept the women from taking the secret
contraceptive plant. But still they're not the same.'

'How have they changed?'

'They still go to the cave where Zune used to be, taking him gold
treasures.'

'How can they take him gold treasures if he's not there?'

'They think he only disappeared, like he did centuries ago, and that
he will return. No, they won't take that plant, because they believe he'll
return, and they want there to be other generations. They feel some other

lucky generation will have the good fortune they've had. But the men know that that was not Zune, and so do I!'

'Can't the men convince the women that he was false?'

'No, no matter what we tell them. That's why I'm here waiting for you. Every day I wait for you to come back.'

'Why?' I asked. 'I might not have come this way, or I might have stayed in Minas.'

'I thought you'd come and I don't want anything to happen to you, because you cured me. I saw you all the way back there. I've got eyes like a hawk.'

'What would happen to me?' I asked.

'If you come back to the village the women will kill you. They think you're Anhanguera. They think you're the Old Devil who chased Zune away!'

I was silent. I thought perhaps I could take off my disguise and go through the village as myself, but suppose they recognized me?

'Then we'll go back,' I said. 'But I wish there was something I could do.'

'No, no,' he said.

I thanked him and we bid him goodbye. I turned the horse around and when we got to the path that Mauritia had originally wanted to go, we exchanged places.

'Did you believe the boy?' she asked.

'Yes,' I said, wondering why she had asked that.

Rapadura, the Glass Beads, and a Promise of a Hidden Paradise

WHEN I SAW THE OLD WOMAN, I halted, as I thought she would chase me out of the vicinity again. But she did not. She held up her hand in greeting. I rode up to the stream and Mauritia and I dismounted. The laundry was spread out on rocks and branches drying, the woman sat smoking a long pipe. There was the smell of fermenting manioc in the air, from the nearby plantation.

'I thought you'd chase me away again,' I said, after greeting her.

'Oh, Madam Moraze explained to me that you had left on your own accord. She doesn't hold any rancor toward you so why should I?'

At first I had thought of coming to Bahia without visiting Moraze, but now I took courage.

'This is my friend, Mauritia,' I said. The two women greeted each other.

'Sit and talk to me. I have to stay here and wait for the clothes to dry.'

I wanted to continue, but I did not want to offend the woman. And what if Luiza-Moraze rejected me? I would need some friend in Bahia. She offered us rapadura, small raw brown sugar cakes.

'That's my name,' she said, 'if you want to know.'

'What?'

'Rapadura,' she said with a laugh.

Had she given me her name before? I could not remember.

'Is the preacher still here?' I asked, not knowing what else to say.

'Eh, he and the woman have gone,' she said waving her hand in the air. 'There's no one there now except the Holy Father and the Frenchman.'

'What happened?' I asked.

'He convinced her to go with him to some paradise. He promised her a paradise – unlimited. But such men always come in the shape of promises. I don't trust him, but she went off with him. But he'll fall short of her expectations. I've never met a man who didn't disillusion me, whether bound or free. It's like that man who came around here selling glass beads or showing them and telling folks they was diamonds. If they wouldn't buy the glass beads, he'd sell them maps of the diamond mines in Mato Grosso and Goias. Those who didn't buy the diamonds bought the maps.'

'Did any go in search of the diamond mines?'

'Yeah, and when they got there they found that the mines was always mined by the crown, that none of the diamond districts had been opened up, not to regular folk, and so their trips was for nothing. Those regions that were opened didn't contain very much, and when they tried to sell the diamonds the authorities wouldn't pay them their true value.'

'Why didn't her husband keep her from going, wherever it was they went?'

482

'He's like that. He's always refraining from comment on the things that she does, the things that get into her head. But he's always a step ahead of her. She thinks she's a free woman. But he knows what will happen. When she purchased the glass beads from that other stranger and found out they weren't diamonds, he made her keep them. He's like that. And this time. He knows she'll come back, needing someone to protect and defend her. But me, I'll have no sympathy and no respect for her ... I've never met a man who wasn't a disappointment, master or slave. I don't trust anyone, whole or part-time.'

She began gathering up the clothes from the rocks and branches.

Mauritia and I helped her, and then we bid her goodbye.

'I used to feel that way,' said Mauritia, and we entered the road, leading into Bahia. 'But she hasn't lost any spirit!'

'No. Do you still feel that way?'

'No.'

We had ridden for some time before she said, 'It was more destructive to me, more of a hazard ... But who's completely independent?'

Luiza-Moraze

WHO IS MORAZE?' she asked.
'A woman who lives here in Bahia. I want to visit her, but I don't think we'll stay here in this city. I think it will be useless to search for him here.'

'Already Tamarutaca is a legend,' she said, under her breath.

We had reached the back door of the 'warehouse,' but before I could even knock, Luiza said from inside, 'Let your friend enter, for I'd like to meet her, but you, Almeyda, I don't wish to see.'

Mauritia looked at me with wonderment, but she entered, and the door closed. I stood in the yard looking bewildered and despondent.

'Brazil and Angola,' I thought I heard, but there were no clear voices from inside, and it was as the sounds one hears on the wind.

I wondered if Luiza-Moraze had refused to let me enter, only to keep her 'prediction' true. It was nearly three hours before Mauritia emerged.

She had a strange expression on her face. Don't ask me to describe it. But it was not the same Mauritia who had entered. What trick had Luiza played?

'I can't continue with you to Parahyba,' she said. 'I *must* stay here.'

'What do you mean you must stay? I need your company. Haven't we been luck for each other?'

'Did I say the secrets of the world had not been revealed to me? What should I do if they have a chance of being?'

'Don't trust her,' I said. 'She's like the seller of glass beads for diamonds and false maps in the place of true ones.'

'She told me you would say as much, because you were jealous of her and her powers.'

'Haven't you seen my powers?'

'Yes, but they're nothing compared to what I saw in there. And you could not help me to find my lost spirit or to find *him*.'

'Is it Tamarutaca?' I asked. 'She did not help me to find Anninho.'

'But you did not stay with her long enough, you did not trust her. So that is why you've had to wander for nothing. But she'll help me to find him and she'll also cure me of my bad luck, so that when I find him, I can protect him, and he can protect me, and we can protect each other.'

I looked at her in despair.

'She's not what she pretends to be.'

'She said you'd say as much and that *you're* not.'

'I must have you with me,' I said. 'She's mesmerized you, tricked you into staying.'

'She said you'd say as much. And she says I mustn't talk with you too long, or you'll trick me into following you nowhere.'

'Nowhere?'

'She has books on everything, literature, art, music, science. And she knew about my gold-mining before I even opened my mouth.'

'She knew I was going *there*. That's why. It's no supernatural power.'

'She said you'd disparage her.'

'I'm not. She's a good woman. But she'll want everything. She'll want to control everything. Your intellect, your affections, your will.'

'I'm not rejecting *you*,' she said. 'I'm not choosing her over you. But if I go with you I see destruction.'

'Do you see it or did she see it? Did she *make* you see it?'

'In that direction I see destruction. But if I stay here, I see development, of all my capacities, and then I'll find *him*!'

'Nothing I say will have any effect on you. She's made up your mind. If she had any real power, she'd come to the New Palmares with me, and we'd work together to prevent its destruction.'

'Her strength is in different things. If she spent her time fighting for ordinary things that others take for granted, she'd never make any progress. How could she accomplish anything, or contribute anything? I want to learn to observe and question and perceive what she does. You don't know what she's developing, you have no idea. She can't spend her time on the same thing, every generation. But you don't understand. You wouldn't take advantage of what she offers and now you're jealous that I *do*!'

'Come with me,' I asked again.

'No. I can't stay out here too long,' she said. 'You don't understand what this will mean to me. You don't know what my life has been.'

She kissed me quickly and went into the 'warehouse.'

I slowly untied the horse, and leaving Bahia, rode off in the direction of Parahyba.

The New Palmares

HALT,' SAID THE MAN ON THE PARAPET. 'Who are you?'

I looked up at a stranger. I realized that most of the people in this new place would not know me, even though I had removed my disguise before entering the trail.

'My name is Almeyda. I am the wife of a certain Martim Anninho. I used to live in the Palmares that was destroyed before this one was built,' I said. I felt a dizziness suddenly and held onto the horse's neck.

He seemed to show some recognition, but continued to stare at me with suspicion.

'Enter, but stay just inside the gate,' he said.

I entered, but did not ride into the city. I dismounted and tied the horse to a tree. I sat down on the ground as I was told to do the day that I had first arrived at the Old Palmares.

He came, finally, and took my hand, and lifted me up, and we embraced. I tried to tell him hurriedly about the places I had been seeking him. If I had known that he had been here all along . . .

'I have not been here all along.'

'What?'

'Hush, let's be quiet now. We'll go to my home and you'll rest and then we'll tell our stories.'

Anninho's Story

REST, AND THEN WE'LL TALK,' he said, as he helped me into the hammock. I felt the dizziness again as I held his arm. He kissed me and I lay back. I watched him standing with his back to me. His shoulders seemed broader, his arms more muscular, as if he'd been rowing. I went to sleep and woke and saw him again, sitting at a table, drawing figures, designs. What had become of his plans? Why was he here in the New Palmares? I thought again of the thing that Mauritia had said, or that Luiza-Moraze had had her say to me. What would he be accomplishing if he had not chosen to come back here and fight for what other men took for granted, and what he himself could claim any time? What might I be doing if I had stayed with Moraze, or if I could change my circumstances in this world? The smell of butter and chocolate. What would I like to do? It gets dark and he lights a candle. Yes, the way he's sitting, as if he's spent days in the galley of a ship. What would I wish to be doing? I'd be like Barcala, writing histories of the country. I'd write a history of this place, this Palmares – but how can one write such a history and live through it at the same time? And many herbals. Books and books about the medical properties of all the plants in the country, roaming about, observing and questioning and finding new cures.

When we were coming here they were returning another deserter and condemning him. I wondered what his story was. There was a woman watching.

'Who's that woman?'

'Cere.'

'What's she to the man?'

'They were going to be married.'

'So the same laws here as before?'

'Yes. He'll be whipped and then executed.'

Sound of rain, wind, thunder. He covers me with a blanket. Joanna comes to the door, carefully wrapped up, wearing boots. 'Is it true Almeyda's come? Oh, yes.'

'Yes, and she's very tired and has been sleeping. She's asked about you and we'll visit you tomorrow, or will invite you here to have dinner with us.'

'I've given her my prayers.'

The smell of cabbage and potatoes and black beans. Cere comes in, her arms and legs bleeding.

'What happened?' he asked. He gets a wet towel and starts rubbing her arms and legs down.

'He hung himself before they got a chance to. I tried to stop him but they flogged me.'

I got up and took the towel from Anninho, who was holding it clumsily. I wiped the blood from the woman, and washed the blood off, then I rubbed her with an ointment from the medicine gourd. Anninho looked at me strangely, though he continued to console the woman.

'Think of what his choices were, Cere.'

'I wanted to climb into the halter with him, but they flogged me and kept me away.'

He asked her if she wanted to sit down, but she refused to, and when I had finished coating her wounds, she ran out into the night.

I looked up at Anninho, but he said nothing. I looked at the drawings and documents, an assortment of maps and manuscripts on his desk, and then back at him.

'Nobrega prepared a nice dinner for us,' he said.

'Nobrega is here?'

'Yes.'

'And my grandmother, did my grandmother escape too?' I asked eagerly.

'No, she's not here.'

I looked down. He touched my shoulders.

'I suspect she's all right. She's a cunning old woman.'

I wondered again if the Indian woman who had mistaken me for someone she knew, might not have met my grandmother instead. Then a thought hit me. Suppose *she* were to venture into Turiri's village. Would they not also mistake her for me? Would they not think she was the Old Devil?

'What is it?' he asked.

'Nothing.'

'Let's sit down to the meal.'

He took my hand and we sat down. He kept looking at me. I felt as nervous as the first time.

'You've changed,' he said.

'I look awful,' I said.

'No, you look very good, maybe better than before.'

We ate for a while in silence. I stared at the writing desk, and the candle, papers, glass bottle of ink.

'So you've had adventures,' he said. 'What have you learned from them?'

I looked up at him in alarm. What alarm I don't know. Was it that I felt after leaving Moraze's I had received nothing? Had my adventures taught me no lesson? Had not Moraze said that adventures were worthless unless one learned something?

'I can tell you what's happened,' I said, looking down. 'But I'm not sure of what's come of it. I learned a great many things when I stayed in Bahia with Luiza. Do you know she's a medicine woman?'

He nodded.

'Yes, and she taught me many things. But I left her prematurely. Did you see how I fixed the woman? The wounds will be gone in the morning. But I can't do anything for her soul. I wish I could have cured her spirit too. But I'll tell you what's happened from the beginning to this day I've found you. A lot of wandering about and maybe I've learned nothing.'

I told him everything, except about Luiza-Moraze's prediction of the destruction of the New Palmares. Why I could not tell him that I don't know. He listened carefully. When I told him Luiza's story about Azamor the explorer, his eyes lit up and a strange expression took hold of him when I mentioned her feelings that the Angolans and Sudanese were too busy fighting each other to accomplish anything and that it was all the same circle – betrayal, capture, and execution. Indeed, she had even left the story unfinished.

'I have never heard her talk that way,' he said. 'But I have not seen her in a very long time, and perhaps she is not so hopeful as she was in the old days. It surprises me that she did not try to dissuade you from coming here then.'

It was just then that Joanna rushed in and told us what had just happened to Cere, that she had walked barefooted over the caltrops, spikes in the ground used for defense against our enemies, and that she in that way had caused her own death. I started to go along, but Anninho made me remain while he went to see about the woman, though there was nothing that could be done now.

When he returned I looked at him, but he sat down quietly.

'You see if I could have repaired what really needed to be repaired,' I said.

He said nothing, then he said, 'Why isn't the woman Mauritia with you? I thought you had made such a friendship.'

'She decided to stay in Bahia.'

'I thought cities muddled her.'

'I don't know. When we got there, she decided to stay. The devil knows why.'

'No one has bothered you in all this time? It's strange that a woman alone . . .'

'But don't you see, I disguised myself.'

'Ah, yes, but I bet you were still handsome.' I was silent.

'And . . .' I started to touch my bosom. 'Yes,' he said, with a short nod.

I was silent.

'You still have my necklace.'

'What?'

'The necklace I gave you.'

'Yes.'

I thought again of the woman's horrible suicide and looked melancholy.

'Who was the discontented old woman?'

'What?'

'The one you mentioned. The one who was discontented with every fellow she met.'

'Ah, Rapadura.'

'Like the sugar cakes.'

'Yes.'

He smiled. 'Did you have any amusements?'

'What?'

'On your journey. Were there no amusements?'

'No. Well, maybe some things are funny now. Like that crazy miner, the one so fond of agriculture. I thought he was going to keep us there and make us work for him on his manioc plantation, but he was content to talk our ears off. It's funny now, but I was scared to death then.'

He had his hand on his forehead and was rubbing his temples. I felt as if I had said something foolish and so looked away.

'Ah, tell me your story now,' I said, looking back at him. He was looking at me with his intense dark eyes and I thought of the Mohammed of Bahia again. 'Mine is full of neither real amusements nor real misfortunes. Ah, the great fortune was finding you again! Ah, I've been luckier than most!'

He said nothing, but he smiled.

He said he could not give his story in as much detail as mine, though many things had happened to him. Most of his adventures were not controlled by himself, but by others, his capture and his being sold to a maritime trader, was ironical, but it was true.

'A fleet of canoes, he had, like the man you told me about, except he was a Portuguese. There were perhaps three hundred or four hundred canoes in his convoy, that went through very difficult regions, full of ambushes and assaults from Indians – the very ones you spoke of – the Paraguas would attack us from their canoes, while the others, the Guiacuru would attack from the shore, riding on horseback. I knew no words of friendship for them. I fought to stay alive. Since I was one of the boldest fighters, after some time, I got to be one of the guides. There was no real stratagem for these attacks. How could there be any stratagem, when one never knew when to expect them. One had to stay open, and use one's judgment at the time. In the final war, the Paraguas and Guiacuru had joined each other, and it seemed impossible. We knew we were doomed, but nevertheless, two of us escaped, myself and another African, an Angolan, who were the bravest fighters. I think the Indians had respect for us even though we were enemies, and we respected them as well. But we escaped, and taking one of the best canoes, took to the sea. Lucky for us we were captured again, or I don't know what misfortune would have befallen us.'

My mouth was open when he said that, but I was silent and kept listening until he eventually explained what he meant.

'Cosme was delirious from hunger or some disease and once he even tried to leap overboard but I restrained him, though he kept saying how he wanted to end with dignity and honor ... A flying fish jumped into the boat and we ate it raw. Surely Allah had sent it. He took spirit again and so did I, even though I had caught some fever as well. But we were captured, I should explain,' he said with a slight smile and a fierce twinkle in his eyes, 'by African pirates who took us aboard. I thought at first that they were slaves of European pirates, but they were their own men.

'Different tribes, some from slave ships that had been captured, others had always been free. They stayed at sea most of the time, because the only place they were welcome was Madagascar Island. Privateers as well as navies were after them, so they were in perpetual warfare, and each of them expected some day to be hanged at Execution Dock. For some reason I was not well liked; perhaps the leader felt that I wanted to be a prince. Not only were the tribes fighting others, but they were also fighting among themselves; each tribe wanted to have its ruler to rule the others.

'The Sudanese wanted to put me up though I did not want to play the role. The Angolans put Cosme up. But I refused to play such a game, and there was much resentment, and many disparaging accounts of my conduct, even though I was as bold as any of them in our encounters, but I refused to do any unnecessary cruelty. Finally, I was set ashore on the African coast, but not my homeland – but North Africa, where they knew the Arabs would take me and make me a slave again, as I had no ransom, and what gold I had accumulated had been taken from me. It began as they thought it would, with my enslavement, but my knowledge of the scriptures and of the Muslim ships that my master owned, won me respect, and I was put into one of the Arab military units, riding about the land on raids, sailing in their ships, learning their stratagems, fighting with them in their wars against the Spaniards. My service bought my freedom from them. But I had to go to Morocco before I could get a ship that would bring me back here without my fearing I'd be tricked into slavery again. I searched the Barriaga mountains for you, and finally came here. Perhaps you were the reason I came back at first, but there were things I learned on the raids that would be useful here when we prepare to fight the Portuguese again.'

I was silent. I looked at him.

'It's a longer story than it comes out as being in my telling it,' Anninho said, 'and there are atrocities that I have not told you, and amusements that I haven't told you either and I have learned things in a day of that adventure, that I might not have learned in two days without it. There is a secondary story about the maritime plans I made that involves betrayal, but I will not tell you about that one today – but there will be other days to tell you the details of that story, and to fill in the gaps in the other one.'

1701